INDEPENDENCE

★★★★★★★★★★★★★

Kate Kasserman

Center 61

Center 61, Chicago Illinois USA
Copyright © 2009 by Kate Kasserman
All rights reserved.

ISBN 978-0-9843639-0-2

Cover art "Portrait of Margaret Kemble Gage" by John Singleton Copley and "An Appeal to Heaven flag" from Wikimedia Commons (http://commons.wikimedia.org).

For news and updates about *Independence*, its upcoming sequel *The Line*, and other books, or to contact the author:

www.katekasserman.com

for SGP

Chapter 1

Kolkhorst farm, South Carolina Colony, 1767

Rachel had finished her lessons for the evening, but no one would tell her if she had finished them correctly. The house was quiet. Christoph sat at the table with his legs propped up on Rachel's chair, reading one of father's books with a scowl of intense focus. Christoph was three years older, eleven to her eight, and Rachel was jealous that he knew Greek and she did not.

"Christoph?" she said. His scowl deepened, and he didn't look at her.

"What?" he muttered. If father had been inside, Rachel wouldn't have dared interrupt Christoph's reading. But then if father had been inside, Christoph wouldn't have dared put his feet on a chair, either. She did not know what father could be doing outdoors every night in the dark. It was as though he simply could not bear their company any more.

"I memorized a poem."

Christoph didn't look up. "And it goes like this: *bok bok begaa bok bok begaa bok bok –*"

He would never let her forget that she'd once reported in a lather of excitement that she'd heard the chickens clucking in iambs. But that had been two years ago! Rachel wanted to hit him, but she wanted him to check her work more. "Could you just –" she swallowed the words "shut up" and continued, "– see whether I'm missing any words?"

Christoph sighed and held out his hand for the poem, swinging his feet to the ground. Rachel brightened and gave him the folio before he could change his mind. She folded her hands in front of her skirt and began.

"The curfew tolls the knell of parting day,

"The lowing herd wind slowly o'er the lea..."

Christoph nodded slightly to himself, eyes ticking down the page as Rachel continued her recitation, and she slowly gained confidence. The beginning of a poem was always the hardest for her to remember properly.

The door thumped open and shut behind her, and Rachel heard her father's heavy tread. Her heart quickened. He had always taken pains with his children's education, before, and she thought how pleased he would be to hear her now. Her voice grew slightly louder and she raised her chin.

"Perhaps in this neglected spot is laid

"Some heart once pregnant with celestial fire;

"Hands, that the rod of empire might have sway'd,

"Or wak'd to ecstasy the living lyre."

Two quick steps. The door opened and shut again. Father was gone.

Rachel fell silent.

Christoph, his face closed, merely said, "Yes, I think you've got it," even though the poem wasn't even half complete, and he put the folio on the table.

As she lay in bed that night, while Christoph twisted and sighed beneath his blanket across the room – he never had trouble slipping into his dreams – Rachel wondered if father would re-marry. The farm sat miles upon miles from its nearest neighbor, and they almost never saw anyone. But perhaps someone will come anyway, she told herself. Perhaps someone will come, somehow. And she wished that it would be so. She was not sure whether it would be right to pray to God for such a thing, though, so she did not do that.

Her father and Christoph went out to work at first light in the morning, leaving Rachel to her chores. She worked quickly, the way mother had taught her. Wasting time was not just wrong but wicked. "Your family is a gift from God that you must spend the rest of your life earning," Rachel's mother had said many times when Rachel had wanted her to leave the chickens and the breakfast table and the dishes and the floor and the water and the bedding so that they could play. "When you have children, Rachel, perhaps you'll bring them here, to your old parents in their old home."

"And then we'll play?"

Her mother would laugh. "And then you'll do all the chores yourself without my help, and your children and I will play."

That would not happen now, with mother dead. But in Heaven they would all play together, if only Rachel could earn her place there.

It was one of the first truly fine days of spring, and Rachel had thrown open the doors and windows for the sweet air to flush out the musty smells of bodies and old cooking. Now the honeyed sunlight enticed her as it danced on the fresh green leaves and sparkled in the clouds. She glanced through an open window with longing. She did not feel like reading or lessons today.

I could get some flowers for the table, Rachel decided. She loved to wander through the trees and grasses. Perhaps the flowers weren't terribly important. But they were pretty, and surely someone would notice them, and perhaps even thank Rachel for her thoughtfulness, or remark how cheerful the little house seemed that day. So she tied on a bonnet and slipped a shallow basket over her arm, her mind made up to go. It occurred to her as she left that the weather might turn or the wind grow fierce while she was out, so she shut the windows and closed the door behind her. She always tried to be careful, when she remembered.

Rachel could see the distant forms of her father and brother in the yellow grass of the valley to the east. It looked like they were mending a low fence near the heavy brown shapes of browsing cattle. She darted around quickly to the other side of the house, hoping they wouldn't see her. They might think she wasn't working, though she was. The flowers were sure to be more abundant towards the west anyway, on the uneven ground by the edge of the woods where the cows never grazed.

A sweet breeze carried the scent of the fields and the clucking of the chickens. Rachel walked with a light step, swinging the basket at her side. She was pleased with herself, having memorized two poems last night and finished her chores early this afternoon, and the brightness of the sky and the warmth of the earth made it seem as though the world shared her opinion.

The tiny family cemetery lay on a small patch of land set off by a simple wooden fence about a hundred yards from the house. It contained her mother's grave and four little graves beside it. An old oak stood above them, its budding leaves casting little shadow. Rachel lowered her eyes and walked more slowly, at a respectful pace, as she drew close. The graves were neat but bare, marked by gray and brown stones that her father had polished and carved himself. Rachel knew the scant details by heart.

Tobias Kolkhorst, 1755, aged three months; Renata Kolkhorst, 1758, aged one year; Angela Kolkhorst, 1762, aged one year. Then the most recent, the stones still clean and raw. Mary Donnelly Kolkhorst, 1766, aged thirty-two years, beloved wife and mother; and Infant Boy Kolkhorst, 1766, aged four days. Her father had not named that last child. A pang of guilt struck Rachel.

"I'll bring flowers for you first," she whispered, and she felt a little better.

She plucked a few black-eyed Susans she passed as she wandered towards the trees, because there were so many and their yellow petals were so cheerful, but they were a common sort of flower and she didn't want to fill the whole basket with them, and she continued to the edge of the woods, where the delicate spiked lobelias liked to grow. After a determined search, she found one at last, its tall stalk thick with little wrinkled blooms, but its tough stem proved too hardy for her fingernails, and all her pinching and twisting accomplished was to mangle the poor plant. She'd forgotten to bring a knife.

"I've ruined it anyway," she mused, and she plucked the pale blue blossoms from the crushed stalk. She couldn't use them on the table without the stem, but she thought a pile of blooms would look pretty on the baby's grave.

Then Rachel found some daisies, some goldenrod, and happily even a little mistflower whose powder-puff blooms would supply the blue she'd lost by her failure with the spiked lobelia. Time passed, and before she knew it, she'd filled the basket to overflowing. She examined her work and frowned. She didn't have enough. Even a slender bouquet for each of the graves would leave nothing for the house. She sat herself down cross-legged in a sunny spot and spread her bounty on the ground, pinching the leaves from the stems with her fingernails to make more room.

The task absorbed her until a patch of cold damp touched her thigh. "Oh!" she exclaimed in annoyance, springing to her feet and twisting around to look at the back of her dress. It was soaked through with gritty mud. "Thoughtless, careless, stupid!" Of course she'd known it had rained yesterday. But today was so sunny, she'd forgotten. Her better dress was dirty too, so now she'd have to wash them both and go around all evening in wet clothes. She brushed at the mud without much hope that it would help.

A shiver vibrated through her legs as the ground beneath her trembled with a low note of distant thunder. Rachel looked up in surprise. She hadn't noticed any clouds earlier; and yet yesterday's rain might not yet be spent. But the sky remained a serene robin's-egg blue. Perhaps she'd imagined it. But no; there it was again, a rumble in the air and a faint vibration beneath her feet. Rachel snatched up her basket, stuffing a few quick handfuls of flowers back into place, and glanced back at the house, wondering whether she should run for it. Perhaps she could save herself a soaking; but it also occurred to her that getting caught in the rain would give her an excuse for the state of her clothes. She looked at the sky again, hesitating. Nothing but the sun.

And yet the thunder grew louder, until Rachel realized it was not a storm, but horses.

But they never had visitors here.

When she brought her eyes down from the heavens, she saw them at once, nine or ten riders racing at a full gallop. The horses were pretty brown-and-white piebald creatures with long legs that stretched out almost to their full reach, seizing the ground greedily with every step. The riders' black hair streamed behind them like ribbons of silk, and at first Rachel thought in blank amazement that a crowd of women was descending upon them as if in answer to her prayer for a wife to come for her father. But such terrible women - riding their horses astride and bodies tensed with purpose. And then just as Rachel realized that the riders' course would take them close by her, an icy terror stabbed her through the heart. Not women. Indians.

She threw herself down into the sweet grasses and curled into a ball, squeezing her eyes shut. She'd seen them plainly. It was impossible they hadn't seen her. But she was too frightened to run. And she couldn't run far enough anyway.

"Idiot," she mouthed soundlessly. Of course she should have run. Even an Indian couldn't gallop through the trees, and she was so close to the woods. But now it was too late. The pounding of the hooves shook her body and filled her ears. Her shoulders clenched against the blow that would come any moment now. An arrow through her ribs, or a tomahawk cracking her skull, or a hoof shattering her spine. The pain would be terrible, but that wasn't the worst thing, the worst thing was that she knew she wouldn't get to Heaven, she just wouldn't, because she hadn't tried her best, she'd been lazy and stupid all afternoon, and you were supposed to love God with all your heart, and Rachel was always angry about so many things, and now...

The galloping faded.

Rachel opened her eyes. She was still in the same place, with the tangled grass in front of her and the discarded leaves she'd pinched from the flowers. There was her basket, just where she'd dropped it. Rachel felt over her scalp and body for blood or arrows. She was whole and unharmed. Nothing had happened. The Indians had passed her by.

She pushed herself with weak and shaking arms to a seated position and watched the Indians ride for the house. She had not known her father to have any dealings with the Indians. They lived in a separate world. She did not know what they could want with her family now.

The answer came in a wild, high scream and the tinkling of glass as the Indians shattered the windows with their tomahawks and veered away, twisting around on their horses' backs to pour a volley of arrows into the house.

Rachel felt a strange, blank void open inside her – something was happening that she could not understand. They had no quarrel with the Indians. They had no quarrel with anyone. And yet her home was being turned into a ruin.

Her heart was loud in her ears. She felt nothing at all, only a strange frozen inability to move or think or feel.

She watched.

One of the Indians swung his leg over the side of his horse and jumped to the ground. He walked to the front door with a confident, dominant stride.

Good, Rachel thought, surprising herself. *Let them destroy the house. Let them destroy it and go away. I'm safe in the grass, and father and Christoph are safe in the field. Maybe the house is cursed. They can wreck it, and then they can go.*

The Indian banged the door once, then seemed to think better of it, and pressed the handle. The door swung open. He turned back to the others a moment. Rachel imagined he was grinning. She felt a surge of rage.

The house contained nothing – nothing but father's library that he did not love any more. Let them take it all and go away. Surely the Indians could see that the house was empty. Let them take what they pleased and just go away, go away, go away...

"Rachel! My Gott!"

Even at this distance, she could hear her father's anguished cry, and the Prussian accent that he never quite lost.

"You filthy barbarians – sons of whores – get avay from her!"

Rachel leapt to her feet. In the distance, she could see the tiny brown-and-white shapes of her father and Christoph running back to the house.

They were trying to protect Rachel, but Rachel was safe, if only she'd told them where she was going that afternoon, if only she hadn't ducked out of sight, if only –

Her father brandished the axe he'd been using in his work. Christoph had nothing but his hands. He tried to sprint ahead of father, but the older man shoved him back roughly.

"Murdering dogs! She is a child!"

The Indians turned.

The one who had dismounted jumped back onto his horse.

They rode to meet her father and brother.

"Father!" Rachel tried to scream. "Father, it's me, I'm safe!" Her lungs held no air, her voice barely more than a gasp. She waved her hands frantically over her head. It didn't matter any more if the Indians saw her, if only her father did too. But no one heard her, and no one saw.

The Indians closed in on the two men. Rachel tried to scream again, but all she could hear was the rush of her blood, pounding, beating against her skin.

The knot of men and horses tightened into a flurry of quick activity and then abruptly relaxed. She held her breath. There was no trouble now, no fighting – of course her father must have explained to them that he was not their enemy, that everything was fine, that – The Indians turned around and trotted back to the house. Rachel searched the field feverishly with her eyes for her father and brother, but she did not find them. A few Indians dismounted and entered the house.

"Father?" Rachel whispered. But she knew where he and Christoph were. She was not stupid. They were lying in the grass, as she had been, only they would not rise.

The world stopped. Rachel went blank. There was nothing in her mind. Nothing in her heart. She sank down in the grass again and did not feel it when it brushed against her skin.

She smelled smoke in the air, but she did not look up to see her home burn.

Time must have passed, because she saw dimly that the horses stood around her, sweating and whickering with excitement. Their shadows covered her, blocking out the sky, and their massive hooves cut into the earth as they shifted. Nine Indians stared down at her with unreadable expressions. Smoke and dirt streaked their skin. One of them shrugged and remarked something in their own language to one of the others, who shrugged in return.

The Indian swung himself down from the horse and walked to Rachel. He stood in front of her and waited a moment, as if expecting her to say something. Two fresh scalps hung from his tomahawk.

The world started again, a slow, creaking start choked with confusion and pain. She could speak now, if she chose. But she would not. He wanted her to, so she would not.

She waited for death.

"Girl, you alone now," the Indian said at last in halting but understandable English. "You come with us." He reached down to take her arm.

Rachel shoved him away and struck at his face, her fingers curled into claws. The Indian slapped her. It wasn't a hard blow, but it startled her. Before she could regain her senses, he slapped her again, and then his arm was around her waist, and she was hauled up onto the horse. He mounted ahead of her. The smell of untanned leather and smoke was strong enough to make her gag.

The Indian grabbed her arms and pulled them around his waist. He clicked at his horse, and it wheeled around obediently.

"You hold onto me," he said. "We ride fast. You fall off horse, you die."

Chapter 2

The Indians were Wolf clan Cherokee, and in the evening Rachel was informed by the man who spoke English that she was now one of them, and her name was Koga Adisgahluvsga. The others laughed at this name, and Rachel hated them.

She wanted to fight them, but she was afraid. She wanted to tell them how much she contemned them, hated them, and the man who spoke English she knew would understand her words, but somehow she did not speak them. The terror kept her silent as the Indians laughed and whooped and chatted with each other all evening long, and she hoped that they would comprehend her silence for abhorrence and not the humiliating cowardice that she knew it must be. She did not eat the food they offered her, but when an old woman with a lined, coppery face took Rachel by the arm and led her into a stinking Indian tent, Rachel did not strike her or scratch her face. Her failure shamed her. She followed the old woman dully and lay down on the rough bedding that had been put out for her.

But she had not given into them. Nor would she. Some of the numbness had left her now, enough that a single thought could pierce through the fog.

Perhaps she was too weak to fight, but she could *run.* Run before the Indians corrected their oversight and killed Rachel too – run before they could skin her and boil her and eat her flesh, as Christoph had told her they did to white people. Run before they ripped the hair from her head and decorated a spear with it. Run before they decided which torture to inflict first. And at least, if she could not avenge her duty to her family, she would spare the enemy its final victory.

Rachel peered through lowered eyelids, feigning sleep, her heart beating wildly.

The old woman lay down upon her own blankets with a sigh. Her breathing grew regular. In a few minutes, her mouth dropped open and she began to snore softly.

Rachel pushed back her blankets carefully, soundlessly, and crept on hands and knees to the flap of the tent. She could not risk the time to gather her shoes. Nor did she deserve shoes anyway. She lifted a trembling hand and pushed back the fabric, peeking outside.

She heard shouting and movement, and the red light of the bonfire flickered on some of the nearby tents, but no one was in sight. She wished everyone were asleep, as proper people should be at this hour, but these were savages, and she might never have a better chance. With a last glance at the old woman, who remained snoring peacefully, Rachel crawled outside. She stood.

And then she ran.

"Ey!" A startled man shouted with a voice as harsh as a dog's bark, leaping up from where he had been crouching beside his tent. Rachel's legs pounded furiously, but he was faster and stronger and caught her in an instant.

"No!" Rachel shrieked, thrashing, biting at his hands, scratching at his face. The Indian grunted angrily, and wrapped his arms around her so tightly she could not move anything but her legs, so she kicked him, driving her heels into his shins. She had to escape; but she did not believe she would. And so she wanted to hurt him. She wanted to make him bruise and bleed.

The Indian flung her to the ground. The impact shocked her motionless, just for a moment, but long enough for him to wrap himself around her again, this time with his legs pinning her own to the ground so that she could not move at all. Rachel opened her mouth wide and screamed, but he clapped his hand over her mouth. It smelled of sweat and musk and something strange, she hated it, she was gagging, she could not breathe. Now he would cut her, she knew. Perhaps her death would be swift; perhaps she had earned that much.

But the Indian merely remained still until exhaustion stilled Rachel's fruitless writhing. He lifted his hand cautiously from her mouth, and Rachel sucked in a ragged lungful of air, her body shuddering. She did not scream. She did not have the strength.

The Indian grunted again and unhooked his legs from hers. He stood, dragging her to her feet by the back of her dress, and then he shoved her roughly back to the tent she had escaped.

The man called out, waking the old woman, and said something to her that made the old woman nod and yammer. And then he pushed Rachel's head down and forced her inside the tent. The old woman followed.

She pointed at Rachel's blankets and said something in her ugly tongue. But Rachel knew what she meant. And she had no choice. So Rachel lay down on her mat again and pulled the blankets over her. She would try again later. She would try again and again until they killed her or she got away.

A shuffling behind her. Rachel tensed and opened her eyes.

The old woman smiled and nodded and said something incomprehensible. Then she lay down beside Rachel, in Rachel's bed, and wrapped her arms around the girl.

Rachel turned her back. The old woman held her gently, her warm, soft body pressed against Rachel's back.

And God forgive her if it were possible, Rachel closed her eyes, and the warmth drained the tension from her muscles, and in moments, she was asleep.

When morning came, the tent was empty. Rachel lay still for a long time, and no one troubled her. She could hear footfalls outside, and the bang and scrape of work, and the barking words of the savages, and occasional bursts of laughter. Dull light filtered in through a small hole at the top of the tepee, where the nine stout poles that made its conical frame met. The door-flap had been dyed bright red. A cheerful color. She hated it.

She started to wonder if her life had been spared not just temporarily because the Indians had time to do with her as they pleased, but indefinitely because the Indians held her in too much contempt to offer her death. They had laughed at her new name, which was not her name and she would never say it. Probably it meant slave. She was going to be a slave now, because she was too harmless to be a threat. A slave to murderers. She would make them kill her first.

Rachel remained in her bed all day and did not leave the tent, nor did she eat when food was put out for her. She knew better than to try to escape again so soon; they would be expecting that, and she was going to be too clever for them, and deny their hospitality as well. But in the evening, her mouth was so dry and her head hurt so badly that she sipped from a clay bowl of water, eyeing with hatred the woman who had left it. Rachel knew she was a coward for drinking, and she knew the woman would laugh and mock her again for her weakness.

She would show them later, when she escaped. Or if she could not escape, when she fought them again.

The woman smiled and nodded, her dark eyes shining with triumph at Rachel's concession. "Kamama," she said, pointing to herself. Then she pointed at Rachel. "Koga." As if Rachel hadn't understood that well enough yesterday. She expected Kamama to laugh again, but the old woman did not. Kamama shuffled forward on her knees with a hand raised as if to pat Rachel, and Rachel flinched backwards, spilling the bowl. Kamama stopped and nodded again. She picked up the empty bowl of water and the untouched bowl of food and went outside, returning with fresh water that she left at a safe distance from Rachel, and then she left the tent, and Rachel was alone, knowing she had failed. If Kamama was a murderer like the others, Rachel had not shown her enough scorn. And if Kamama was only being kind, Rachel had not returned the consideration.

No one came inside the tent but Kamama, and on the third day of her imprisonment, Rachel finally ate. She could not escape or fight very well when she was almost too dizzy to hold herself upright, after all. And if it were a crime to accept hospitality with hatred in her heart, what of it, a greater crime had been committed first. The thick stew made her sleepy, and she lay down again as Kamama watched thoughtfully. Later, when Rachel woke, she saw Kamama sitting quietly on her own bedding-pile and stitching away with a bone needle at a pile of mending. The scene was both familiar and strange, as if Rachel were looking through a distorted window at her own past, watching her mother sew, but everything made rougher and darker. Kamama must have noticed the shift in Rachel's body, because she looked over with a smile and waved Rachel over.

Rachel pushed herself up and smoothed a hand down her tangled hair. Kamama nodded, her smile broadening. She grunted and waved again, pulling out a pair of torn leggings and patting them. She wanted help.

"Koga," Kamama said. Rachel stiffened, and her brows contracted. Kamama looked confused a moment, and then she tried again, "Koga?"

Rachel shook her head, clenching her jaws. "Uwetsi." Rachel did not know what that meant either. Another word for slave, perhaps; a trick.

Rachel did not want to be a slave. But she did not think it was right of her to refuse to work this time, because it was Kamama who asked, and she knew now that Kamama was kind and surely could be no murderer. She brushed the blankets from her legs and, holding her skirts, walked over on her knees.

"Ah," Kamama said, nodding with satisfaction. She placed the leggings on Rachel's lap.

Rachel was not accustomed to working with leather, and it hurt her hands to push the needle through the thick skin. But Kamama showed her, patiently, how it was to be done.

The work was a relief. Rachel's thoughts left her when she was busy, and she was pleased when she improved, and Kamama murmured praise.

On the morning of the fourth day, Kamama gestured to Rachel that they should go outside. Rachel hesitated; but it was Kamama who was asking. She did not think it had been long enough since her last break that the Indians would allow her an opening to run again, but she did want to breathe fresh air. The air did not belong to the Indians. It was God's, and Rachel had a right to it. So she rose, her muscles aching, and slipped her feet into her shoes, and followed Kamama into the bright day.

The Indians glanced at Rachel curiously, but no one approached her as they went about their business. It all seemed so normal, cooking and talking and chores. A strange light feeling fluttered in Rachel's stomach. She could not help thinking that it should be as simple as tearing away a veil, and the tents would become houses, and the leggings and fringed coats would turn into breeches and jackets, and the glossy black hair would turn red and brown and blonde, and the strange noises would reveal themselves as proper English, and she would find herself in the town where father went to trade a few times a year, and she would see her father soon, hurrying outside from wherever he had done his shopping – And yet the veil remained.

Kamama tugged at her arm gently. Rachel noticed that the old woman was carrying a large pot painted with simple geometric patterns, and she reached for it automatically. An old woman should not have to carry anything while a young person was able. Kamama smiled. Rachel wrapped her arms slowly around the rough pottery and held it against her chest.

Kamama made soft noises, leading Rachel on. She supposed they were going to get water.

A man emerged from a tent nearby, his shirt open and his neck bare to the cold. He scanned the area, frowning. "Uwetsi!" he called. Rachel stopped, her eyes widening, but the man paid her no mind, even though *uwetsi* was the word that Kamama had used for Rachel. A little girl hardly bigger than a cat scrambled around the side of the tent, her hands and face covered in dirt. "Doda?" she said. The man huffed and pulled her back inside.

Rachel turned to Kamama curiously. "Uwetsi?" she said hesitantly. The man had called his daughter that. And Kamama had called Rachel that.

Kamama beamed and nodded. "Koga. Uwetsi," she said, taking Rachel's arm again. Then she pointed to herself. "Kamama. Unitsi."

"Unitsi?"

Kamama grinned and said very slowly, "Utsi."

"Utsi," Rachel repeated, wondering if she had just called this strange creature mother.

She soon learned that she had.

Rachel did her chores, which were hard and strange but not so strange that she could not learn them. And eventually, as the weeks passed, it dawned upon her that she had nowhere to run to if she ran. And so she did not.

Summer stretched into autumn. The Indians' language was strange and seemed to have nothing in common with either English or German, but she picked up words and phrases over time. The man who spoke English kept his distance from her, and she was glad of that. She did not much want to speak to anyone anyway.

There was a boy, Walosi, a few years younger than Rachel, who took a particular delight in her pale hair and skin and eyes and followed her constantly whenever someone did not shoo him off to do some work. Walosi was always trying to teach her new words, and although Rachel did not like to acknowledge him, she was secretly grateful for the lessons. She hated the feeling that things were being spoken above her and around her and she did not know what they were. Walosi either could tell that she appreciated his efforts or else was far too thick-skinned to mind her sullen silence, because he kept up his good-natured instruction even without any signs of encouragement. Perhaps he simply liked to talk.

One day when Rachel was filling a pot with water at the stream, Walosi touched her arm excitedly and pointed at the far bank. Rachel looked up, frowning. A crow stood with a cocked head and open beak. Occasionally it would shift between its feet and utter a rasping caw.

"Koga," Walosi said excitedly. "Koga."

"Yes, I see it," Rachel said in irritation, and then she realized what he was trying to tell her. He was not saying the name she hated, and he knew that she hated. He was showing her what a *koga* was – a crow.

Suddenly she was crying, the pot forgotten on the ground. Walosi took her arm and shook her slightly, his face twisted with worry.

"Koga? What is the matter? Koga?"

"You named me for an animal that eats the dead," she choked.

Walosi must have reported this to the others, because that night, Kamama told Rachel about how the crow was the cleverest of all the animals. "But crow was proud, remember that," Kamama said. "That is why the Creator did not make him beautiful. But you see he gets along all right anyway."

Rachel listened quietly. "What is Adisgahluvsga?" she asked.

"Ah! Like this." Kamama pulled a blanket over her head. "You cannot see me! Adisgahluvsga!"

"Hiding," Rachel said.

Kamama dropped the blanket into her lap and grinned. She possessed only a few teeth, all quite brown. "It is a very long name that you have," she said. "But, eh, nothing else will do sometimes."

The village moved. No one said why, and there was plenty of game and water where they had been before, but they pulled down the tents and loaded the horses. There seemed to be no haste about it, but Rachel could not understand why they were leaving. She asked Kamama, who grinned. "Don't be lazy. No one likes a lazy girl. Sometimes it is good to move, to see new places. It keeps your brain from being lazy."

Rachel paused a moment. "Is that the reason we're going?"

"Every fact has so many reasons only the Creator understands them all."

That seemed to be the end of the answer. Rachel wondered whether talking about whatever these many reasons were, even if they were too numerous to comprehend fully, also might not keep her brain from being lazy. Her father would have loved a question like that, or would have before Rachel's mother had died. So Rachel asked.

Kamama did not laugh or pat her head or tell Rachel she was clever. She looked irritated and did not raise her eyes from the task of folding the stiff hide of the tepee. "You're like a man in a canoe who decides to save time by paddling on one side twice as hard. Hold that piece. You're too slow." So Rachel did not ask again. Eventually, the preparations were complete, and after a few days' easy travel they came to a new place that the people seemed to have known from before. Or Rachel thought so, from what she overheard. She did not want to make a fool of herself by asking anything again.

Except with Walosi, who seemed to have no greater pleasure on earth than the delight of instructing someone who was older than him. Rachel was not sure if she could ever think of Kamama as her mother, although she had come to love her. But Walosi was like God returning one of the younger brothers that had been snatched away before Rachel had properly known them – despite Walosi's insistence that he would marry her when they were grown.

There was less to do in the winter, and everyone, even the children, had more time. Rachel decided that she would ask Walosi to help her learn how to ride better. She was so terribly far behind everyone else, and she was afraid that one day they would move again and leave her behind if she could not keep up. So she would learn now, while they were at liberty. Even though he was so young, when Walosi rode, even though he was so young, he seemed to become part of his horse, and Rachel knew that he would be able to teach her well.

"That's exactly it," Walosi explained in a superior voice as Rachel clutched the mane of Walosi's obviously frustrated horse and tried to remember not to squeeze her knees into its side, or it would start going fast again. "You keep thinking the horse is separate from you."

"Yes, that's because it is," Rachel answered in a tight voice. Her hands were slick with sweat, and the horse kept twitching its skin in a way that made her nervous.

Walosi snorted in frustration. "Yes, but pretend it isn't – you be the brain and let the horse be the body. Horses are stupid, but even they follow their brains. So relax! Koga! No, not like that – hey, hold on," he said anxiously and ran in front of the horse, stopping it and petting its long nose. Rachel wiped her damp hands against her legs, grateful for the pause. The horse settled. Rachel leaned forward, shifting her weight to dismount. She much preferred to execute that maneuver when Walosi was nearby to help.

But he put his hand on her leg. "What're you doing?"

"That's enough for today."

His eyes widened in outrage. "You've hardly ridden at all, and you're not even trying to listen to me!"

"I have, I am, and I will think about it," Rachel retorted. Her body hurt, and she wanted to go home. But Walosi held his hand in place.

"Prove it."

"You'll see next time. I'll be better."

"Not if you always give up, lazy girl. I bet you can't make it to that tree and back. Not even if you walk her. Because you're not listening to me, no matter what you say. I'll give you my turkey feather if you come back in one piece." Walosi had found a turkey feather the other day and was unreasonably pleased with it. "Well, you'll come back in one piece all right – your head's like a rock, nothing can break it," he corrected himself. "If you come back without falling off is what I mean. And without making me come get you."

That seemed a little unkind. Rachel had managed to stay on a walking horse for days – she'd gotten sore, it was true, but she hadn't fallen off. Suddenly she wanted that stupid feather very much. "Fine," she said, straightening.

"It's not just your head right now. Your whole body is like a rock. Imagine what would happen to a rock on my horse's back once my horse started to move. It'll be funny. Good luck," Walosi sniffed.

Rachel looked at the tree, an unassuming chestnut oak of middling size. She leaned her body slightly to point herself towards it. *All right, horse – read my mind,* Rachel thought without much hope. She squeezed her legs slightly.

The long-suffering horse turned its head and ambled towards the tree. "Good boy!" Rachel exclaimed in surprise and stroked its neck. Then she remembered to pay attention again and focused on the tree. She wanted to tense up, to cling to the horse – but she willed her body to relax, because Walosi was completely wrong about everything, she had been listening, and she would prove it right now.

And suddenly everything became easy. The horse wasn't annoyed and Rachel wasn't clinging for dear life. They were just walking.

The horse paused a few times along the way, but Rachel squeezed her legs again and petted the beast and reminded him that the tree was almost there now, and the horse obligingly continued until the objective was reached at last. She managed to turn the creature, the dear, wonderful, best horse ever, back to Walosi, and when it had walked a few yards, Rachel decided that she would deprive her friend of any opportunity to gloat. She gave a little nudge with her knees. "We can go faster, boy," she whispered, her heart thumping in her chest. Her body tensed.

The horse began to trot. It rattled her, and Rachel seized up in fright, but she remembered that she was the brain, and a terrified brain was useless. A sack of flour. She remembered the way a sack of flour had sat on the back of her father's horse, perfectly safe even without being tied when he came back from one of his trips for supplies. Heavy and firm – but soft. She loosened her muscles. And she stayed on.

"There," she said, her eyes flashing with triumph as they reached Walosi.

Her victory didn't stop him from being smug, because after all she'd only done at long last what he'd been telling her all along, but he did have to give her the feather, and Rachel stuck it in her hair. Kamama complimented her on it that evening. The feather was a little worn and dirty after all Walosi's handling of it, but Rachel did not hear any sarcasm in Kamama's voice. And Rachel could not help smiling broadly. She was proud of her feather, and she kept reaching up to touch it.

It was too late for visiting hours, almost time for sleep, when a gnarled hand shoved back the door flap and Walosi's mother Guhgwe entered, her black eyes hard with anger. Kamama smiled and offered her a drink, but Guhgwe had no time for that.

She pointed a finger directly in Rachel's face. "She took my son's feather," Guhgwe said.

Kamama blinked and turned to Rachel. "Is this true, daughter?"

"It isn't," Rachel protested, "I would never do such a thing! I am not a thief, and certainly not from Walosi," and then she explained about the bet that Walosi had made and that she had won. But Guhgwe only seemed to get angrier. Rachel couldn't understand it. Surely Guhgwe should be pleased that Walosi knew how to ride so well that he could teach others.

"I have heard all of this from Walosi already. You think I don't know your tricks?" she spat.

"The tricks of women, Guhgwe?" Kamama asked, unflustered.

"The tricks of the English," Guhgwe snapped. "Thieves, all of them. Like the crow," she added with a malicious glare at Rachel.

"It wasn't a trick - I didn't ask him to -" But when Rachel heard her own voice, it sounded thin and defensive, like a lie. So she gave the feather back to Guhgwe, who snatched it and left with a farewell to Kamama but not to Rachel. The tent was silent a moment.

"I promise I didn't think it was a trick," Rachel said at last.

"I know it wasn't," Kamama replied. "You are a good girl, Koga. And besides, you are not English."

Walosi was not happy to have his feather returned to him. The next day he stuck it in the ground by its shaft, and he and Rachel practiced throwing rocks at it until it was crushed. They placed no stakes on the contest, and since Walosi had far better aim, he won it easily.

Rachel did not see another white face for years. Her birthday was coming soon - her real birthday - but she had been given a new birthday by the Wolves and so no one but Rachel knew that she was going to turn thirteen in a few days.

It was a small secret that tied her to her first home, and so perhaps she should not have been surprised to dream of it that night when she slept, an old dream that had come to her often at first but less so as the years went by. She did not see her father or brother, although she longed to. The dream was filled with smoke and fire. But she knew the flames would not touch her in her sleep, because it had not touched her in life, and because it was a familiar dream that always ended the same way, without a conclusion - raging blindly and then fading into something else. She could not save anyone here. So even as she slept, she merely let the fire burn around her and said, "I pray for you, Christoph, father. It is all I can do. And I pray that you forgive me if you ever see me again."

But along with the smoke and fire there were screams and shots, and this confused her, because her fire-dreams had never had screaming before, and it frightened her.

The dream shattered and Rachel opened her eyes to the dark.

It was neither dark nor day. She still smelled smoke, heard screams. The heavy sound of horses' hooves and the animals' nervous snorting. There was a shot, sudden, loud, quickly followed by another. Chilling her, the deep laughter of men - voices she did not recognize. Fierce red light shone around the entrance flap of the tepee and flickered in Kamama's wide eyes.

"Run, Koga," Kamama said, pulling the blankets off her daughter. "Run."

Rachel did not understand. "What is - where?"

"Just run! I will find you! I will go first, and they will follow me. Then run!" And then Kamama, for all her age, rushed outside the tent.

Rachel did not run. The strange peace of hopelessness settled upon her, as if she had been waiting for nothing but this event for a long time without knowing it. So the fire had come for her again, only this time she was not safe in a field, but in her home, where she could be caught. She thought she had cheated the fire long ago; now she knew she had not. It would wash over her and take her. Rachel lay back on her side, her eyes empty, and pulled the blankets over her body again. A spark thumped against the tepee and flames began to crawl around the edges of the hide. She could smell it but not feel its heat. That would be soon. She hoped it would be brief. Her body trembled.

A hand ripped open the entrance flap. "Kamama?" Rachel said, suddenly terrified that she had forced the woman to return for her.

But it was a man, a white man, sweaty and flushed and pistol at the ready. He grinned with savage glee. And then his eyes found Rachel, and his face went blank with astonishment.

"Jesus Christ, you're white," he said. She had not heard English in so long the accent sounded strange and harsh to her ears. And then he said, "The bastards," and his face twisted with rage again, but there was no smile in it any more.

The man yanked her to her knees, his rough, wild beard scraping against her face, and then dragged her out of the burning tepee and into a charnel pit that was a village no longer. She saw Kamama. Or she saw Kamama's back, pressed into the dirt, a dark, wet stain on her back gleaming in the firelight. Bodies lay everywhere, broken and useless. The world was on fire. And a score of white men in soiled clothes on horseback, destroying everything, destroying –

She did not know when they questioned her, nor remembered afterwards precisely what she told them, but one of the white raiders supposed he could use an extra maid, if she were a hard worker and not turned into a worthless savage bitch.

He repeated this often enough that it sank into Rachel's numbed mind.

When the raider first brought her to his home, his wife was not pleased about it.

"What do we need with another maid?"

"Anne don't seem able to keep up with things, does she?" the raider replied. They spoke right in front of Rachel as if she weren't there, or couldn't understand.

The raider's wife, a thin woman with a sharp nose and round, bulbous eyes flicked a glance at Rachel. "You can't make a servant out of a savage. They break things and run off."

"She ain't a savage, look at her – her eyes are blue, so she ain't even a half-breed..."

"Lookit the way she's dressed."

"She can't help that, can she? She's smaller than Sarah. We'll put her in one of the girl's old dresses. She can earn the rest," the raider said. "If she ain't no good, we'll find someone else to take her, all right?"

"Just make sure she don't steal nothing," his wife sniffed. "If you can promise me that."

"I don't steal, ma'am," Rachel said, the first words she had spoken since leaving the destroyed village. The raider and his wife looked at her in surprise. Rachel swallowed. The English words came slowly to her, but they came. "I don't steal, and – I am, I am better than an indifferent housekeeper, I hope. I lived on a farm. I would be, be eager to –" She could not say "repay your kindness" although she knew she should. "To demonstrate my usefulness and earn my way. I am very – very, sensible of my – unfortunate condition and would be grateful for an, an opportunity to improve it."

The raider and his wife were silent for a moment, and then he said, "Tell me she's not white – even the Reverend don't speak half so pretty."

"We'll give it a week," his wife said grudgingly.

Rachel curtsied and went to work at once, without a word. She found what she needed. The house was organized logically enough. She knew the washing, and the sewing, and the cleaning. She had done all of them before, and she knew that she must prove she was more white than Indian and not stumble once. She did not think the raider and his wife would be as patient with her as the Cherokee had been. And she would not lie to herself this time that there was anything cunning or glorious or noble about what she was doing. She knew she simply would not let herself starve, and so she could not let herself be cast out. She could not forgive herself for it, but she did not want to die. And she was so afraid that she would be thrown away to starve in the woods.

A week passed, and no one mentioned anything at the end of it. Rachel did everything right and nothing wrong, and that made it easy to forget her, although the senior maid Anne resented the new occupant in her bed. It seemed that the raider's family took Rachel for granted and somehow felt that she had always been there, washing clothes and scrubbing floors and cooking simple meals when Anne did not feel like it, which was usually. She had a place.

And so she stayed there.

Rachel grew unnoticed from a somber, diligent girl into a somber, diligent young woman, and she might have grown old that way too, creeping around the edges of the rooms and working, working, always in silence. When she was free, she did not chat with Anne or make friends with the other girls in the village. She slipped books from the master's library, an unwanted inheritance from his father, and read them in her room. And she did her lessons once more, though with no one to check her work or her understanding, and the family was content to let her do so, because it was quiet at least and made the books look like they'd been read, which impressed the neighbors.

She wondered when the raider's family would die.

Because death dogged Rachel's heels. She could not escape it. She knew that now. A small skirmish had destroyed her farm; a larger fight had destroyed the Cherokee village. Only a battle could threaten the town where she lived now, and so of course a war had appeared.

The colonies were in revolt and had declared war on the greatest nation on the Earth, England. And what a fool's errand it was. The rebels facing England's might were untrained, inexperienced, and poorly equipped. If that weren't bad enough, their only truly fine general, Charles Lee of Virginia, unaccountably remained second in command, leaving the Continental Army in the hands of a planter and occasional former soldier named Washington – a man who had lost not only every fight in which he'd engaged, but also more than three-quarters of his troops to capture or desertion. Everyone knew this. Even Rachel had heard all about it from the gossip and the weekly newspaper that came by post.

And so the war was a disaster that promised not honest battles but blind slaughters. And it was coming for her. Rachel knew it even before she heard the rumors that the regulars were headed to the area in force. She couldn't imagine what the army could want from this tiny backwater. The rebels had some sympathizers among the people, this was true, but there were no troops here, no stockpiles, nothing of any use. And yet the news kept coming in, reports of long columns of frightening blood-red coats that covered the ground as far as the eye could see, and angry Loyalist and Patriot militia sacking homes and killing indiscriminately in the name of the Crown or of Liberty but in the pursuit of personal gain – too many reports for even the most optimistic to cling to any doubt. But it was the regulars who were most feared, and their godless Hessian mercenaries, who had no soul. They would be here soon, and then they would do whatever they pleased. Rebels would receive no pity, people said, and Loyalists might not either. The Continentals were nowhere to be seen, but no one expected them to be any help anyway.

Rumor took on the force of certainty and seized almost everyone. Anyone who could fled.

The countryside degenerated into a frenzy of packing, and the roads filled with refugees gambling to preserve a small part of their possessions rather than risk losing them all. The family that had taken Rachel also decided to run, and, surprised, she exulted in her heart. For once, Death had shown its dark form before being at the door, quite. Perhaps flight provided only a temporary grace. But perhaps, too, one could keep running forever. Finally Rachel would run, the way she should have every time before.

Or so she thought until she discovered that rather than a prize to be captured, she had suddenly become an expense too dear to bear.

Rachel was walking down the second-floor hallway to put a fresh candle in Miss Sarah's room. The old one was half burned down, which always made Miss Sarah, who was afraid of the dark, nervous. Anne never tended to these things, and Rachel always remembered.

She walked quietly. The Cherokee had taught her how to do this in the forest, and it was a lesson she'd had little difficulty in applying to the irregularities of a wooden floor. Rachel passed the closed door of the master's bedroom, twirling the candle in her fingers and thinking of very little, when she heard his hushed tones and the sharp note beneath them that caught her attention.

"We've done enough for that girl as it is. Let her stand on her own two feet. We've got trouble enough taking care of ourselves now."

Rachel froze.

She stopped mid-step and strained to hear the mistress's reply, but her high-pitched tones were too quiet for clear words to come through the door. And yet there was no mistaking that spiteful, self-congratulatory tone in her voice.

Rachel knew precisely who they were talking about and exactly what they meant, as much as she would have liked not to. The family would leave the house, as she had known; but Rachel was part of the house, not of the family. She lowered her head and continued on her way to Miss Sarah's room, the candle a dead weight in her hand, her mind seething.

By "done enough," Rachel supposed bitterly the master meant when he had killed her adoptive family and brought her away from the Cherokee. And perhaps it was so, perhaps he had done her a service, because after all her adoptive family had helped kill her real father and brother, so on reflection Rachel did not know what she thought or felt about the man's claim, whether it was just or cruel, and her heart grew smooth and cool as a stone.

She did not care any more.

When he told Rachel late in the afternoon that they could not afford to keep her any longer, given the circumstances, and she was to be left behind, she merely nodded as if he'd made a casual remark about the weather. The man waited a moment. Rachel said nothing. She went on with her polishing. If the silverware was going to be packed, it still needed to be clean.

At length the man shook his head and sighed. "We'll give you a dollar and a letter, child. It's all we can spare." He thought a moment. "And that book you're always reading. You can take it with you, if you like." Then he walked away, his footsteps clattering heavily on the floor.

Nor did she grieve two days later when the house was shuttered and the cart with the family's belongings lumbered across the dirt track that led south, its timbers groaning beneath their burden. Rachel stood on the porch, the locked door behind her, and watched the cart go, Miss Sarah holding onto her bonnet with her small hand. The family did not watch their house as they rode away from it. She supposed they did not want to see her standing there. She would have waved if they had looked; she had never brought them discredit or shame, and she would not do so now. But they did not look.

Soon the cart dwindled to an unrecognizable speck in the distance. Then it merged with the horizon and vanished forever.

Perhaps Rachel was not as cold as she now believed. Perhaps there was grief at this new separation after all, only anger obscured it, if not shame. The family had kept Anne, the other maid, even though she was sloppy in her work and a gossip, while Rachel did the work of three people and never raised her voice or lied or wasted time or caused mischief. And yet it was Rachel the family did not want. Would they regret their choice later, when the clothes were dirty and supper late and the poorly made candles sputtered with more smoke than flame, frightening Miss Sarah into one of her fits? But no. She had to give up that spiteful hope. There was some curse, some black sign marking her, and Rachel feared sometimes that no diligence, no sweetness of temper, no modesty or accomplishment would ever wipe that mark clean.

"I would have preferred to have a destiny," she murmured. "But it seems I must settle for a fate." A smile touched the corner of her mouth. No matter what she said, she was not quite certain, not yet, that she must resign herself to endless separation and loss. It was as though everyone else in the world was a key that opened the door to a happy home, while Rachel was a strange little key whose purpose was forgotten. And so it was right and proper that everyone else should be valued, and Rachel, the odd one, merely endured when there was mercy to spare. But perhaps, she could not help thinking, perhaps the strange little key did fit a lock somewhere. What that lock opened, she wasn't sure. But it might be wanted some day.

Rachel was seventeen years old. She owned four and a half dollars, a well-used copy of Alexander Pope's *An Essay on Man*, and two sets of clothes, one for church and one for work. She had not made or wanted a friend since she had seen her second family lie slaughtered on the cold earth, and without friends, there was no one to help her, no one to do more than shrug at the thought of yet another orphaned serving-girl without a job. Her helplessness might have meant little to the world. It meant something to Rachel. She had to eat and to have a place to lay her head at night, and the empty porch where she stood would serve neither purpose.

So she tucked her money inside the clothes she wore and clutched the spare set tightly under her arm, and Rachel set off on her own. She descended from the porch and struck out across the open field with a fine golden light in the sky and a cool wind that foreshadowed the coming autumn reddening her cheeks. She headed north. The choice of direction was no accident. The fighting was that way. There is opportunity in war for those who survive, even the friendless and poor, and it was opportunity that Rachel required.

Chapter 3

"I can pay for my board tonight," Rachel explained, showing the coins she held in her palm. "But if I could work for it instead, that would suit me better."

The manageress of the Brass Bull was a thin, dry woman with a prematurely lined face. She wiped her hands on her skirt, even though they weren't wet or dirty as far as Rachel could tell.

"Well, it's getting colder, and that puts men in a drinking mood, so we might do with an extra serving maid." She eyed Rachel. "But you never know what kind of crowd we'll have at night. Do you mind it much if the men talk a little freely?"

"On what topic?" Rachel asked. It had not occurred to her that she should have an opinion herself about the opinions of others.

The manageress sighed. "Well, I suppose you won't steal from me at least."

Rachel's face grew hot. "Of course not! I would never – madam, you don't know me, but I showed you my money..."

"My dear, you've shown me your money once and your innocence at least three times. Don't look that way, or I'll think you won't be able to handle the rough talk after all." Rachel blinked and tried to look as eager as she could at the prospect. She did appreciate the kindness.

And that was how she found herself in a roar of masculine voices, weaving through a perilous course of tipped chairs, outstretched boots, tobacco spit, and the occasional grabbing hand, all while trying to balance a tray of ale and cider and every now and then a bowl of stew. At least no one complained when she spilled a little. It seemed to be expected. The talk and laughter thundered at a deafening pitch, and Rachel wondered how the tavern-room ever could have seemed spare, even barren to her when she'd first seen it early in the morning, a plain room with rough and well-worn furniture. Rachel didn't mind the impolite and even profane speech. She'd heard plenty of it in the raider's home. It had nothing to do with her personally, and everyone seemed good-natured enough, so long as they were drunk.

"Mother of God, Bellew, stop waving at Peg! She might see you!"

"I thought you wanted another drink."

"We've had four rounds from that old cab horse. I want the pretty one. Hey. Hey, hey, hey!" Rachel felt a sharp tug on her skirt from behind. She turned and discovered to her astonishment that the pink-faced man who had grabbed her dress still held onto it, grinning oafishly and feeling the fabric between his fingers. He sat with two other men, both of whom looked almost as surprised as Rachel was by his fondling of her dress. All three wore the dark blue coats of Continental officers. She had not noticed them come in earlier, or she would have looked at them more closely. So these were the rebels, the ones who were causing all the trouble. So far, she failed to find it very surprising. If this was how the officers acted, she shuddered to imagine the enlisted men. Rachel placed her tray on their table, shoving aside a clutter of mostly empty mugs, and yanked her skirt free.

"Excuse me, sir," she said. She kept her voice even, but the humiliation burned. This wasn't a sly comment or a thinly veiled suggestion; the man had touched her. She'd seen a few men treat Peg, the manageress, that way, even circling her waist sometimes, and Peg didn't seem to make anything of it. But Rachel didn't like being touched. She picked up her tray again, careful to face the drunk man and keep her distance as she did so.

"No trouble at all," he replied with a leer. He was a young man with baby fat still in his cheeks. It would have been easier to forgive him if he'd just stayed quiet, but Rachel nodded shortly, hoping to escape as quickly as possible.

One of the man's companions shot to his feet. Rachel froze in surprise, and fear. Her thoughts must have been too plain on her face, despite her silence. She had not meant to start an argument – she hoped she had not offended anyone. Peg would not forgive her for insulting a customer or starting a fight. And it was too cold to sleep outside. If only she'd still had a blanket!

The man pressed the knuckles of both hands hard against the table. His dark blue eyes were steady and grave, and his brows contracted slightly. His brown hair, unpowdered, hung in a short, simple pigtail, but there was something formal and even almost elegant about his demeanor. "Miss," he said, "I apologize for my friend's manners. It's been a long day, and he's not himself. Please accept my sincere regrets on his behalf for his importunity. In the morning, he will regret it deeply; and so I offer now the apology he will most assuredly desire to offer then."

Rachel looked at him, expecting some sort of beery mockery. But he had too open and serious a face, Rachel decided, to be making fun of her.

"It's all right," she murmured, unable to muster more in her surprise and relief.

"Why does everything have to be a full-on battle with you, Bellew? She's a barmaid. She's used to it," the drunk man complained.

"You can tell she isn't," Bellew answered, his eyes snapping to his friend.

The drunk man sniffed. He crossed his arms and gave Rachel a long look, though he answered Bellew. "You're silly about women. But as you like, I'll leave this one alone. I'm sure it's much rougher than the poor thing's accustomed to in the *ton*," he added with a faint curl to his lip, as if she could have missed the sarcasm.

Rachel dropped her eyes. The fight was coming after all, unless she made herself very humble very fast. Bellew looked brittle enough to start one, and the other man drunk enough to answer it. "I'm sorry, sir," she said in a low voice to Bellew. "Your friend is quite correct, please don't concern yourself over the matter. I don't even know what a *ton* is."

"The *ton* is what results when rich people get inbred, and bless you for a dear creature for not having heard of it," the third man interjected. He was older than the other two, with a heavy-built body turning to fat. "Your family excepted, Bellew, I'm sure. Masterson, you'll tell the girl yourself you're sorry," he said in a clear, polite voice that brooked no refusal. He turned back to Rachel and smiled. "Did you grow up on a farm?"

"Yes, sir," Rachel added after a moment's hesitation. The immediate danger seemed to have passed, but she still wished heartily to be free of this company.

"Decided to see a bit of the world?"

"I'm an orphan, sir. I had nowhere else to go but the world."

The third man cast a glance at Masterson, whose face fell. "I am sorry," Masterson said in a changed voice. "I let myself get carried away."

"It's really – it's quite all right," Rachel whispered, fidgeting, and Masterson's face took on an even more doleful cast.

Bellew, to her infinite relief, seemed to find this satisfactory. The tension drained from his shoulders, and he removed his hands from the table and sat down. Rachel hesitated. The men seemed to be waiting for her to do or say something, but as so often happened to her, she did not know what this could be.

"Oh!" she exclaimed. "I forgot! You said you wanted another drink." From their expressions, this wasn't what they'd expected from her, but they each asked for another strong ale, and when Rachel brought them their order, Bellew insisted on paying her double.

"It's Masterson's money anyway. I won it off him at cards," he said with a grin. Masterson sighed and behaved himself. So Rachel thanked him and thought that the matter was at an end, rather hoping that Peg would bring the rebels their next round. She tucked her empty tray beneath her arm and threaded her way to the back of the room, where Peg was taking a breather and sipping a cider of her own by her husband. She handed her the six pennies from the Continentals. The manageress nodded and passed the coins to her husband, who was as broad as Peg was thin and did not present an easy mark for robbery.

"Miss, I beg your pardon!" A familiar voice startled her.

Rachel looked up to see Mr. Bellew standing in front of her, a pained expression on his face. Or Lieutenant Bellew, or Major Bellew, or whatever he might be. She couldn't read the military etiquette of uniforms, and she wasn't sure it applied much in the rebel forces anyway.

"I'm sorry, sir, is something wrong?" she asked hesitantly.

Bellew gestured at the manageress and swallowed. "I beg your pardon. But it seemed to me that you gave your employer all the money I just gave you." He must have been watching her. It was a strange sensation, and not entirely unpleasant, except that apparently he had expected her to pocket the money he had given her.

"Of course," she said, trying to stifle her indignation. Apparently there was so much thievery in the world these days that everyone expected it.

A small sigh escaped Bellew. "Miss, the extra was a tip for your trouble. You were supposed to keep that."

Peg rolled her eyes and tilted back her head, as if applying to the heavens for aid. "You've been giving me your tips all night, haven't you," she said. "I thought it seemed we were doing a pretty brisk business for the number of men." Her husband grinned to himself and took a swallow from his wife's mug.

"I didn't think I was supposed to get tips," Rachel said.

"It's how servers make their living, miss," Bellew replied patiently. He still looked vaguely worried.

"I know that, sir, thank you, I understand the concept, it's just that I didn't think it applied to me."

"And why on Earth wouldn't it?" His eyebrows knotted, but he smiled.

"Because I don't work here, not precisely. I offered to trade a day's work for a night's keep, and Peg was good enough to accept this bargain."

"Did she?" Bellew asked, glancing at Peg as if he were pleasantly surprised.

"The world's bad enough on its own without me making it worse," Peg answered shortly. She turned to Rachel. "I don't suppose you have any idea how much of your own money you've turned over to me tonight?"

Rachel shook her head. "I'm sorry if I've caused a difficulty." She couldn't help thinking of all those pennies she'd let slip through her fingers and how useful they might have been. But far better to lose the pennies and keep Peg on her side. She needed the room tonight, and the meal.

Peg sighed too, a bit louder than Bellew's. "All right then, I suppose there's nothing to be done about it. Just mind that you keep the rest of it. And for what's already done and can't be fixed, I'll see that you eat and sleep like royalty tonight." Peg gave a sharp nod, concluding the matter.

"Thank you." Rachel curled her toes in embarrassment. She'd meant only to make a fair trade and then go on her unobtrusive way. But perhaps it would be all right if she said what she wanted – perhaps Peg wouldn't mind. "Ma'am, Peg, if it wouldn't be too much trouble, it would do me more aid, and might be easier for you to offer, if instead of a feast tonight I could have some plain bread for my journey when I leave tomorrow."

Peg's eyes softened. "As you like, my dear, of course."

"Are you not staying longer than the night?" Bellew asked. Rachel wondered why he was still here.

"No, I'm going north."

"You do have some relatives living, then?"

"No, sir. I merely hoped...that I might be of some aid where there was fighting." She decided it would be impolitic to mention that she had no particular feelings about the war itself, other than that it was simply the way the world was.

Bellew's face brightened instantly. "O'Malley was righter than he knew, you are a dear creature indeed!" he exclaimed. "If a tenth of the women in America had your spirit, let alone the men, we'd already have won!"

Rachel blushed as much for the injustice of the remark as its warmth. "I don't know about any of that," she muttered vaguely, hating herself for dropping her gaze. She would have liked very much to meet his eyes again, and see his face shining with approval. No one had ever looked at her that way before, as if he'd discovered something wonderful. But she lacked the courage to face it directly.

"There's people thirsty, dear," Peg interrupted with a gentle nudge. "And I'd like to finish my cider."

Rachel's head shot up, her blush intensifying. She'd been thinking about her pay and her foolishness and not about her work. To suffer a rebuke, however mild, was terrible enough; but to have earned it was agonizing.

"Actually, sweetheart, your cider's almost done for," Peg's husband remarked cheerfully, his lips wet.

"Oh Lord, am I cursed, that trouble must follow me like a shadow?" Peg burst out, which seemed a bit strong for a half-pilfered cider, but then Rachel saw what her benefactress meant.

Four men had just come through the tavern door. One of them pointed at an empty table, and they made their way towards it, grabbing empty chairs as they went. It wasn't two yards from the Continentals, whom they seemed not to have noticed. All four new men wore the scarlet coats of the English regular army.

Chapter 4

Bellew's face hardened into a mask, and he returned to his friends without another word, leaving Peg and Rachel with a curt nod. He did not have to pass by the redcoats, fortunately. Rachel glanced at him as he sat at his table, her heart beating a little faster. She was being silly. He had certainly forgotten her already.

Peg finished her cider in a quick swallow and shoved the empty mug at her husband. "I'll see to the others. You go take the new gentlemen's order. A pretty face may distract 'em," she whispered. "And for God's sake, take the long way around so they don't look in the wrong direction."

Rachel nodded and circled around the room, picking up a few used dishes to give herself an excuse. When she came to the redcoats' table, they smiled at her. Their uniforms weren't so bright up close, she noticed. One of them showed the unmistakable hand of a man's inexpert darning, and all of them were travel-stained. They smelled strongly of horse.

"Thank heavens, at last. All right, miss, what have you got in the way of food here?"

Rachel answered promptly. "There's fish stew, sirs, that seems to be what most people are eating. Or there's cold beef and bread, if you'd like. And some apples."

"All right. Bring some of all of it, and strong ale. Except spare us the apples, for the love of the heavens."

"You have an aversion to apples?"

"I like 'em well enough in Yorkshire, but there must be something about the climate here that makes them grow poorly. I find the apples here rather mealy, and I'd rather no apple than a mealy one," the redcoat said cheerfully.

"I will have to ask you to repeat that, sir!" Bellew's voice rang out sharp and clear.

Rachel winced. Bellew was on his feet again, glaring at the regulars. Masterson had pushed his chair around so he could watch, and even the peace-making O'Malley had a hard look in his eye. The regulars turned in mild surprise, followed by a flash of recognition at the Continentals' coats.

"Ah," the redcoat said, holding up his hands. "I meant no disrespect to the colonies, sir. Merely a remark on the climate, which I'm sure you'll admit is blessed changeable here." Rachel could not escape from the table without passing between the redcoat and Bellew. She did not dare move.

"I find the climate quite steady, sir. Both clear and consistent." Bellew enunciated each word with care.

"I meant the weather," the redcoat answered in a tired voice. He still did not rise. "You'll forgive me, sir. It hardly takes a philosopher to describe our difference of opinion on certain matters, but I beg you to understand that my friends and I are on leave, and it is our hope that it will continue to be a peaceful one. We've just been visiting my cousins here, and I assure you that they took no exception to my opinion of their apples or their weather, and rather shared it than otherwise. I did not realize I would give offense by my comments, and I apologize for it."

"I thought this place was the Brass Bull, not the Brass Balls," a second redcoat muttered to one of his friends. Rachel prayed it was too low for Bellew to hear.

O'Malley quirked an eyebrow at Bellew. Bellew apparently saw the gesture and tightened his jaw. "I accept your apology, sir," he snapped. He gave a curt nod and sat down again.

Conversation slowly returned to the room. Bellew fiddled with his mug and kept staring at the redcoats, despite the regulars' immediate and rather pointed resumption of their own conversation. Masterson didn't turn his chair around again. As Rachel went past, she tried to smile at Bellew, but he wasn't looking at her.

"Let it go, lad," she heard O'Malley say. "The war won't be won in duels."

Perhaps the trouble was merely simmering rather than put out.

Rachel hurried into the kitchen and prepared the food, making sure to pile on generous portions. Full men liked to sleep more than they liked to fight. She wished they hadn't ordered the strong ale.

But when she returned, the détente still held. Bellew hadn't made any progress on his ale, and the redcoats greeted their food with a hearty politeness that Rachel found a little forced. That might have been the end of the matter, if one of the tradesmen between the two groups hadn't leaned behind Masterson and rapped the table in front of Bellew.

"You heard what he said?" the tradesman murmured. Bellew looked at him sharply. "He wasn't rude about it," the tradesman said quickly, "but they was talking. He says the redcoats are in Philadelphia. They've got the capital."

Rachel stared at Bellew's face, waiting for his reaction. She was surprised to find that her heart sank at the news of the occupation of Philadelphia; the matter held no real importance to her. And it was hardly unexpected. But she remembered how happy Bellew had looked a moment ago when he'd thought she meant to help the rebels fight, and her heart sank deeper. It meant so much to him.

Masterson twisted around, scowling, and Bellew's face turned pale. The tradesman shrugged and grimaced in sympathy. Bellew rose to his feet again, his bearing cautious this time. He walked over to the redcoats and offered a short bow. The regulars regarded him without much sign of welcome. They placed their spoons beside their cooling stew.

"I beg your pardon," Bellew started hesitantly. "I do not like to impose my presence, nor interrupt your meal, and I should like to say that I do not mean to have words with you again. But this is a matter that I believe concerns us both, and I ask your...help. I've heard that the regulars have taken our capital city. Do you know whether this is true?"

"We hold Philadelphia now, yes," the redcoat answered evenly.

"I see," Bellew said, a terrible stillness in his voice. He rubbed the thumb of one hand. "If I may impose a moment longer – were many lost?"

"It's a soldier's lot," the redcoat shrugged. He was at least ten years older than Bellew. Rachel wondered how many battles he had seen. "But no. If there are friends about whom you are concerned, let me put your mind at ease. There was no fight at all. Your General Washington had retreated well in advance." That sounded consistent with what little Rachel had heard of General Washington.

"Thank you for the information. I am much obliged for your kindness, and I will not interrupt you further," Bellew said with another short bow. He rubbed the knuckle of his right forefinger and bit his lip as he returned to his table with a vacant, lost air.

The Continentals left soon afterwards. They'd already paid, so Rachel had no reason to speak to them. Bellew held open the door to let a new man come inside. Then he walked out into the night, his body awkward and uncertain as if he could barely bring himself to move, and the door sagged shut behind him. As Rachel cleared away their abandoned mugs, all but O'Malley's still full of liquor, the regulars were talking about the departed men in low voices.

"Back to their homes, I would imagine. I don't imagine there'll be another campaign this year, and the insurgents have got no decent place for winter quarters. Come spring, our friends here will find reasons to delay going back, and it'll all be over by the time they make up their minds. A fancy of youth, soon passing."

"Damned deadly fancy."

"Aren't they all?" The redcoat grinned and took a drink of his ale. "Still, it ends eventually, and one gets back to the business of living."

"But that Bellew..."

"Who?"

"The touchy one. His friend called him Bellew. I half expected him to blow his brains out on the spot when you told him about Philadelphia."

"Bellew. Irish name," the redcoat mused. He shrugged. "He'll be fine. The Irish like to live with broken hearts."

Chapter 5

Rachel did not leave the next day. The war by which she had hoped to improve her prospects seemed to have died a natural death, which left her without an immediate plan. Still, it came as a relief to know that there would be less fighting. Peg had assured Rachel she'd be glad to keep her on at the Brass Bull, which took care of Rachel's immediate concerns about a place to stay, but when a week had gone by Rachel was certain that she could not remain much longer. The crowds and boozy laughter wore her down, and she found herself daydreaming too often of wandering through the woods, both as a small girl on the farm and later when she'd lived with the Wolves. Even her stay with the raider's family had been easier in some ways than this. The family's barely veiled distaste for her had given Rachel time for the solitude she desired.

She might have liked a place in a home again. She'd been a good maid and could prove it again quickly enough, if she could get someone to take her. But then other days she thought if she could just endure the work at the Brass Bull for a few years, with luck she would put together enough money to open a little shop of her own where she could pass the rest of her days in peace undisturbed by the whims and demands of a master. That prospect had far more appeal. And she'd endured a week here, after all. A week could turn into a month soon enough, and a month a year, and one year five. But it was difficult to take pleasure in the thought.

Of all the many people who returned to the tavern night after night, the Continentals did not. Rachel supposed that the redcoat must have been correct. They'd returned to their homes, wherever those might be. She tried to imagine where Bellew lived. She assumed it must have been Charlestown, from his manner and the way his friends spoke of his family, but his accent was wrong for the city, and his friends were both clearly from the country. But he never came back, and so she resigned herself that she would never know. Still, she thought of him often.

It turned out to be not a war that took her from the Brass Bull, but a storm.

The sky had dawned a sickly livid color and slowly turned black as the day wore on. Rachel checked the windows nervously at short intervals as she hurried between her cleaning tasks and serving the few men who came in early. She hated thunder. The storm held off through noon and a few hours past, but she could tell it would not be denied indefinitely; the clouds were too dense, the air too pregnant. Late in the afternoon, the sky growled at last and the first fat raindrops pattered to the ground.

"Looks like we'd better put down roots," one of their sparse customers laughed, and the rum drinkers switched to ale. Sure enough, it wasn't long before the cautious sprinkling turned into relentless sheets of water lashing mud into the air and beating the inn like a drum.

Rachel didn't mind the water, even though it was loud and the roof leaked in several spots, which obliged her to use all the buckets and empty them frequently. But she wished the thunder would stop. Each roll of it made her heart trip faster than the rain, and she jumped at each rifle-crack of lightning that followed.

"You poor sweet creature, you're shaking like a leaf! Look at those little hands," exclaimed her regular customer Mr. Darling, who emphasized the point by pressing her cold hands in his warm and rather sweaty ones.

Rachel pulled herself free. "It's only a storm," she murmured, turning away.

"Oh, tut, the buckets aren't overflowing right now. Why don't you sit down a moment, child. It'll do you good. I'll tell you an amusing story, and you'll have forgotten the weather before you know it."

Rachel felt certain she would find Mr. Darling's stories as little amusing as she found the man himself. He had spied Rachel for the first time on her third night at the Brass Bull and had become a daily visitor since, leaving his prosperous chandlery in the care of three apprentices who were doubtless grateful for his absence. Mr. Darling did not keep to himself when he came. He complimented Rachel and asked her to sit with him and complimented her again, loudly, to the other patrons, worse and worse as he got deeper into his cups, and she had difficulty finding his interest in her as avuncular as he claimed. He had brought his wife for supper one evening, a heavy, sour woman, and had winked at Rachel the whole time behind his wife's back as if he and Rachel shared some private secret. Rachel very much doubted this was the case, as Mrs. Darling could hardly be unaware that her husband was a boor.

"I'm sorry, sir, but my duties –"

Mr. Darling shook his head and raised a finger to silence her. "You're trying to make Peg fat by letting her spend all day sitting and drinking cider. Now enough of that silliness. Such a beautiful creature as you hardly need be jealous of the more modest endowments of other women."

"I'm sorry, sir, I beg your pardon." Rachel couldn't think of another excuse. She prayed for an interruption. Didn't anyone need a new ale?

The door burst open, bringing in a flood that filled the room with a sweet, earthy mist. Rachel wheeled around. At first she thought the wind had done it, but no, someone had arrived even in this weather. A man and a woman sheathed in sodden capes stood on the threshold looking rattled and out of place. The man struggled to close the door again, muttering something under his breath.

"Oh la, Robert, this is just awful, don't make it worse," the woman sighed in a high, musical voice, lifting her skirts with a faint grimace of distaste as she stepped into the room. Her lovely gray eyes flicked over the tavern, and she sighed again. "Please, could someone just take this for me?" She loosened her cape at the neck, revealing a pale green gown of shining silk. "Oh, and my shoes!" she cried in fresh distress, looking down at the slippers on her feet, whose yellow could only barely be discerned peeping through the mud.

"Take them off, madam, and I'll clean those for you at once," Rachel said, rushing forward and leaving Mr. Darling behind.

"Bare feet!" The woman shot an accusatory glare at her companion, who remained unmoved at whatever personal disagreement was being referred to. "Oh, but I can't walk on this – *floor* in my stockings!"

Rachel had seen rich people before, but never such fine ones. She glanced at the floor as if seeing its warped dirtiness for the first time. Heat rose in her cheeks. Rachel stepped out of her clogs and placed them in front of the lady. "These will protect your stockings at least, ma'am," she said, curling her toes so that the woman would not see the hole in Rachel's own stocking that she had felt too tired to darn last night.

The woman hesitated a moment, and then lifted her feet from the slippers and placed them gingerly in the clogs, which gaped around her narrow heels. "Well. Please inform the proprietor that Mr. and Mrs. Robert Addison require two rooms at *once.*"

"And try to clean off a table for the lady. We'll need supper as quick as you can bring it," Mr. Addison grumbled, having won his battle with the door. He was at least ten years older than his beautiful wife, and about twice as wide. He removed his hat and knocked it against his leg to shake off some of the rain. His hair had powder in it.

"Oh, Robert, wouldn't the private rooms be better?"

"I'll have it all set up in the wink of an eye, madam," Peg said, emerging from her cider and hurrying up. She curtsied awkwardly. "Rachel, get their cloaks and get a table set up properly."

"No, I don't think I could stomach to eat," Mrs. Addison said.

"Well, my dear, I could. The horses are eating in the stable, the boys are doubtless gorging themselves in the kitchen by now, and I don't see why we should fare worse than slaves and animals. Besides, the good people here need time to prepare the rooms."

"I told you I couldn't bear it. Perhaps when I'm dry and have my privacy again, Robert," Mrs. Addison said, the edge in her voice growing sharper. This settled the matter. Peg went for fresh linens, leaving Rachel to try to figure out whether to take the slippers or the cloaks first, and what to do about the table, because even if they weren't eating, these weren't the sort of people who would be content to stand while they waited. She decided the cloaks were the most pressing, so she draped both over her arm and hurried across the room to hang them. The feet of her stockings were wet through in a few steps, and the floor felt wincingly cold through the thumbnail-sized hole at the ball of her foot. She found a clean-looking rag and wiped at the nicest table, although its wood bore a few knife-marks left absently by some long-vanished patron and there were some rings from old mugs that simply would not come out. But at last she got the Addisons settled, Mrs. Addison moving awkwardly in the borrowed clogs. Rachel bent to pick up the slippers, but Mr. Addison stopped her.

"Bring us some warm cider at least. Warm," he repeated.

Rachel nodded and turned back towards the kitchen.

"Do you think the mud has set in already?" Mrs. Addison interrupted, and then Rachel decided she'd better get the slippers first after all. So she plucked the muddy shoes from the floor, not liking her prospects of getting them clean much when she saw the miserable ribbons drooping from the toes, and turned again for the kitchen only to find Mr. Darling standing in her way, a satisfied grin on his face.

"My dear girl," he said. "Allow me to be of some assistance." She hoped he meant to do something useful like tell the kitchen to heat some cider, but then she noticed he was a little shorter than she remembered. His eyes flicked downward, and hers followed. His empty shoes lay before him, clean but worn to the shape of his feet.

Rachel shook her head. "I can't..." She paused, realizing it would be cruel to make a mockery of him by leaving him barefoot. She took a breath. "Thank you, sir. You're always very kind to me," she said, sliding her feet into his shoes almost as unwillingly as Mrs. Addison had accepted the clogs.

Mr. Darling beamed and sat again, wiggling his toes. "Just bring them back when you can, dear. I won't be going anywhere."

The rooms were ready as fast as Peg promised, much faster than the cider would warm. Mrs. Addison didn't want to wait, so Rachel followed them upstairs with the cider and rushed back downstairs at once to put together the dinner.

"Don't forget the apples, they're very nice," Peg said, ladling stew into two bowls miraculously free of chips in the rim. "And cut them into little pieces first. Mrs. Addison doesn't look like much of a chewer."

Rachel felt fairly certain that Mr. Addison was English, and she mistrusted how well he'd take to the apples. But it was Mrs. Addison who seemed more prone to complain, and her accent was colonial – a northerner, curiously – so Rachel reasoned that perhaps the apples wouldn't cause these good people too much additional distress.

"The stew is simple, sir, madam, but Isaac is an excellent cook," Rachel murmured as she laid out the table in their biggest room. The window rattled with the force of the rain, which continued unabated. Mrs. Addison stared outside with an irritated expression, while Mr. Addison read a newspaper that one of his slaves had produced from the luggage. "But if it's not to your liking, there are a few other dishes we might make. Peg can steam a fish that's light as air." Rachel had put the apples out first because she knew how quickly they'd turn brown. She was gratified to see Mrs. Addison take a nibble. The woman seemed calmer now.

"I feel too much like a fish myself after today, thank you," Mr. Addison remarked absently. "Stew will serve nicely."

"We don't want to be any more trouble to you good people. We do appreciate that you're doing the best you can," Mrs. Addison said, clearly in a much improved mood. She twisted a little golden ring on her finger. Even in the dim light, it sparkled.

"It's no trouble, madam. I'm sorry that the weather turned so foul."

"We would have had to stop somewhere anyway," Mrs. Addison continued, growing expansive. "We've got a fair bit of travel ahead of us." She waved a hand. "But forgive me. I'm just bored, and I'm being thoughtless. I know you have your duties to return to. And of course that beau of yours."

Rachel blinked. "My beau?"

"Yes, the fellow with the shoes. Very gallant." She slid her feet from Rachel's clogs and pushed them gently away with her toes. "You can return them to him now and give him his reward. A kiss, I think, is customary?"

Rachel looked down at the man's shoes on her feet. Her skin crawled, and not from the damp. "Mr. Darling is a customer, madam, but he is no particular friend of mine, and certainly not...not that."

Mrs. Addison looked up in surprise, a faint smile curling her lips. "Really? He's obviously smitten. You ought at least to talk to the man." Rachel was not sure what she had done to gain this fine lady's attention, but she wished to the marrow of her bones that it had been for anything other than some supposed romance with the lecherous Mr. Darling.

"I leave that to his wife, madam."

"Oh!" Mrs. Addison's eyebrows shot up in delight. "I do enjoy the *complicated* love stories."

"But it isn't one, he was merely being kind..."

"Is he well-off?"

Rachel hesitated. "I understand so, yes."

"Well, then, it isn't so complicated after all, is it? You should most certainly talk to him. We all have to make our way in the world, and you're only young for so long." She smiled at her husband, but he ignored it.

Rachel flushed again. She cleared her throat. "I could not think of entering into an arrangement like that, madam."

"Leave off, Margaret. She's a good girl. They do exist," Mr. Addison said, folding the paper under his arm and walking to the supper-table.

Mrs. Addison, however, was not so easily discouraged. She leaned towards Rachel so eagerly that a shoulder slipped free of her shawl. Her husband spread the paper on the table next to his bowl and tucked into the meal as if the two women did not exist.

"But my dear!" Mrs. Addison said, her eyes sparkling. "You have to understand that even if you feel no passion for that worthy fellow now, that might change over time. Certainly in the interim you should show some respect of his passion for you."

Is this what everyone thought? That Rachel would surely end up in Mr. Darling's arms? Now her humiliation was complete, and before she realized what she was doing, Rachel retorted, "He is motivated by no passion, madam, other than a heavy wife and a light character."

Mrs. Addison froze and blinked. Rachel swallowed, horrified at herself. How could she have gone so far? She should have remained silent, should have dipped her head and taken her clogs and retreated. Decent people acted that way. What had made her open her mouth like that?

And then Mrs. Addison laughed, flashing small, even teeth as bright as pearls. "Did you hear that, Robert? That's exactly what I should have said about that Titchener friend of yours who was always hanging about. That's exactly what it was, only you wouldn't believe me. He had a heavy wife and a light character." She clapped her hands in delight. "A heavy wife and a light character. That's Titchener to a T."

Mr. Addison grunted in response.

"I'm sorry to hear that, madam," Rachel said, immediately wishing again that she'd kept silent. But she had felt sorry to hear that even someone like Mrs. Addison still had to deal with the Mr. Darlings of the world, and it had simply fallen out of her mouth. Mrs. Addison turned her fine eyes, alive with curiosity, back to Rachel.

"Oh, Titchener and his like aren't so bad. Anyway, we all have our crosses to bear," she shrugged. "Tell me, dear, you haven't worked here long, have you? Or else tavern-maids have become very different from when I was a child."

"A little over two weeks."

"Are you as amusing with the customers as you are with me? You must be popular."

"No one seems very interested in my conversation, madam. I had not thought to offer it."

"Oh, Robert, see?" Mrs. Addison wheedled.

"See what?" he grunted around a mouthful of stew.

Mrs. Addison shook her head in annoyance and turned back to Rachel. "Say something else droll."

Rachel blinked. "On what topic?" Her mind raced helplessly. She did not think of herself as clever, and the request seemed strange.

"I don't know. On, on people doing stupid things. Why do people do stupid things? Tell me something about that. Because it happens all the time, you know. People should have something to say about it."

Rachel fingered her skirt nervously. What could she possibly say about stupidity? Stupidity was coarse, ugly, foolish. What of that? Everyone knew that about stupidity, it was merely a definition of the word, and that hardly seemed like a witticism. What else? Well, stupidity was wrong-headed; or sometimes it was merely empty of content...

And then she had it.

"I would say it proves only that inanition, like any vacuum, possesses a type of motive power." Rachel bounced on her toes slightly, childish in her glee. The observation struck her as amusing, but she watched Mrs. Addison closely for her reaction. Was this what she wanted? It was the sort of thing that Rachel said to herself, but she hardly dared expect that anyone else would be particularly interested in her private notions. But Mrs. Addison had, after all, asked.

Mrs. Addison cocked her head to the side as if listening hard for something in the distance. A single fine line appeared between her eyebrows. Rachel swallowed. Her heart sank. She should have known that anything she would say would strike other people as merely odd. And that might be entertaining once, but it wore thin fast.

"Inanition means foolishness, dear," Mr. Addison remarked between bites.

"I *know* what it means, Robert," Mrs. Addison said in a sharp tone that suggested she knew only because he'd just told her. "Well. It is rather clever, isn't it? Because a vacuum – beyond being empty, like stupidity, it's a sort of sucking thing, so it promotes movement... All right. I do get the notion, although it's a bit dry and overly scientific. Still, I didn't give you much time. No, it's entertaining," she decided. "Here, now let me explain, because this is something that Mr. Addison and you don't seem to understand. Mr. Addison doesn't like talking much, and I can't endure to listen to the slaves' gabble a moment longer, only we've so many days left on our trip. What was your name? Someone said it, I think, but I wasn't paying attention."

"It's Rachel Kolkhorst, madam."

"Rachel. So, Rachel, do you like being a tavern-maid, or could I interest you in a new position as my companion? It would be such a burden lifted from my shoulders, to have someone amusing to talk to during this horrible long ride."

"You mean...for me to go with you? It is a generous offer," Rachel said hesitantly. Her heart beat faster in her breast. Here, quite suddenly, was the chance she hadn't dared hope for. The Addisons would take her to some new place and give her a little money, and then she could start anew, if only Rachel could find something permanent before her small store of funds ran out. She paused to calculate how much she'd saved in the past two weeks. She'd added a little over a dollar to her original four and a half, far more money than she'd held ever in her life before. But no matter how optimistically she looked at the sum, it wouldn't be enough to live on for long.

A shadow of pique crossed Mrs. Addison's face, as if she'd gone to a great deal of trouble and expense to buy a child a present, and the child had proved more interested in the wrapping. Before Mrs. Addison retracted her proposal, Rachel added hastily, "And appealing also, of course, I hardly need say, I hope. It is far more flattering than I merit. It's just...I have a place that does not fit me well here, but my employers are kind, and it is a place nevertheless. Might I ask where you are traveling, and if you might know the prospects for my finding work as a maid when we arrive? I do have experience, and also a letter of recommendation from my former employer –"

"Oh, for heaven's sake!" Mrs. Addison exclaimed. Relief spread across her features, and she looked pleased with herself again. It suited her. "Of course I'm offering you a real place, a place with me. Did you really think I'd discard you after a week's travel?"

Rachel smiled nervously. She had thought this, but it seemed the wrong thing to say.

"No no no." Mrs. Addison fluttered a hand in the air. A trace scent of powder tickled Rachel's nose. "I'll need a maid terribly, desperately when we get to Philadelphia. Help is very hard to find there now, I hear, just impossible. Half the population fled when the rebels moved out. And when our friends moved in, they hired what few servants remained. The slaves are fine for most things, but I'll need a maid of my own, well, at least until we get home again. When is that...let's see, we'll be in Philadelphia for perhaps two months, depending, and then maybe visit my family for a month or two more, before we decide what to do next. It depends on so many things –"

"We're going to New-York, and then back to London," Mr. Addison remarked shortly without looking up.

"Well, a few months then, maybe a year."

"Not a year," Mr. Addison said.

Mrs. Addison went on as if he hadn't spoken. "And of course after that long I'll be terribly attached to you, and you'll simply have to stay with us when we return to London. You'll like London. Everyone does. You don't want to be the sort of person who's never seen it. And Robert pays his people very well. So you'll come, then? It's settled?"

Everything about it dazzled Rachel.

She didn't need more than five minutes to explain to Peg, and another five to pack her things.

Chapter 6

Rachel had never ridden inside a coach before. It did not take her long to discover that it made her ill, and every nauseating jostle and bump redoubled her envy of the slaves Abraham and Jacob for their perch above in the cold, clean air. Outside the coach's travel-dirtied windows, sharp wind shredded the few remaining wisps of cloud. Yesterday's storm had vanished, leaving behind only dirty puddles in the road and splintered tree-branches lying everywhere, as if some angry god had kicked over his kindling-pile.

"Who owns that land? There, those hills. To the right," Mrs. Addison demanded. She looked slightly unwell too. Her behavior had been increasingly fretful all morning, ever since the three of them had climbed into the narrow confines of the coach and settled themselves on the hard rectangular cushions.

"I don't know, madam, I'm new to the area here," Rachel said. She swallowed a mouthful of sour bile back down into her stomach. It went unwillingly. The coach gave a precipitous lurch and then righted itself again as its wheels crossed a deep rut. Rachel closed her eyes.

This nearly identical "I don't know" with which Rachel had responded to the last five queries addressed her way was unlikely to endear her much to her new employer. Rachel knew this with painful clarity. She swallowed again and curled her fingers around the edge of her bench, steadying herself. It didn't help much. She looked up and offered a weak smile, but, to her despair, Mrs. Addison wore a peevish expression and would not make eye contact. No doubt she was regretting her hastily struck bargain to take on some stupid bar-maid. Inanition indeed. Rachel had not been much of a conversationalist in the tavern. What had made her think she'd do better here, with these far grander people?

Mr. Addison stared absently through the open window. It was far too bumpy a ride for reading, and his heavy jowls shook with the coach's movement. His skin glowed pink from his shave that morning. A curled wig sat beneath his cocked hat. Mrs. Addison wore her own hair, piled high and fresh with liberal doses of powder. The fresh smell of lilacs that wafted from her skin was the only thing that kept Rachel's gorge even barely under control. The scent had come from a tiny crystal bottle covered in a net of golden thread that Mrs. Addison had dabbed behind each ear as a final touch before leaving the Brass Bull. Rachel had never seen such a pretty little bottle before, and Mrs. Addison had laughed at her for admiring it. "You're like a savage coveting a bead," she had said, and Rachel had quickly turned away from the bottle.

Rachel wore her second-best dress and the clogs that Mrs. Addison had despised. She felt so shabby that she could not endure to see even a glimpse of the rough gray wool resting against her lap. She did not belong here, except that Mrs. Addison had wanted her, which now Mrs. Addison might very well not. She almost wished she could run away, so that she would not have to endure the constant oppression of her inadequacy.

But such thoughts were foolish. She could not leap from the coach, she could not return to the Brass Bull, and she could not disappoint her benefactors. The hills; Mrs. Addison expressed an interest in the hills. So Rachel's mind thrashed for something interesting to say about the landscape, unexceptional low hummocks covered with a tangle of wild scrub. A good hunting ground for small game like rabbits and grouse. And for larger game too, Rachel realized, her face clearing.

"Although I must say it does surprise me that the road runs past them," she burst out. Mrs. Addison turned around with an arch look, and Mr. Addison seemed startled to hear her voice. Rachel cleared her throat and continued. "The hills, I mean, I'm sorry, madam. I'm surprised the road runs past them."

"Why? I thought you didn't know these hills."

"I don't, but they make a perfect spot for an ambush. I suppose the hills must go on for quite a while, if this was the best path through them."

"An ambush?" Mrs. Addison paled and brought a slender hand to her neck. Her pulse throbbed in the soft dip where her throat curved into her chest. A pearl dangling from a cream silk ribbon trembled with every heartbeat.

"Yes." Rachel pointed, eager to prove that she knew something a bit out of the ordinary. "You see, there are plenty of good look-out points at the tops of the hills, and the brush is thick enough that you would have perfect cover. Then your troops would be hiding there, behind that hill, you see, or that one. When your reconnaissance gives the word from the top of the hill, your troops come out and surround your quarry in a twinkling."

Mr. Addison snorted. "Girl has a point," he said. "Thinks like an Indian, though." He flicked a glance at her. A quick look would have more than sufficed to remind him how pale she was, if that was what he was checking. His eyes slid away again.

"Do you think we're going to be *ambushed*?" Mrs. Addison said in a weak voice. She glared at the rough brown hills as if she could shame them into behaving properly.

"Oh no, madam, I didn't mean...I'm so sorry," Rachel stammered. She scrambled to correct her error. "I'm sure any ambush would have happened already by now, so we're quite all right."

"Is that a witticism?" Mrs. Addison sat rigidly upright.

"No, I mean it sincerely, and I very much regret bringing up the topic. I simply hoped to say something of interest so that you wouldn't be bored..."

Mr. Addison covered a snort of laughter with an unconvincing cough. Mrs. Addison produced a handkerchief and pressed it against her nose, as if Rachel had suddenly developed an unpleasant smell.

"Anyway, I don't think the Indians themselves would think we were in any danger there," Rachel blurted. She wished she could think of something more genteel to say, but nothing else came to mind, and she had to say something.

"And why on earth not? You've explained admirably the precariousness of the terrain."

"Perhaps they know my line of business, dear," Mr. Addison said with a smile.

"Savages don't care about *anything*, Robert."

"No, look." Rachel pointed out the window again. "You see those bare spots around the hills?" A few bald patches of red dirt lay on the ground. Rachel couldn't be sure of the size from this distance, but they would suffice for her to tell her story. She regretted bringing up the Cherokee, and she hoped the Addisons would not inquire too closely how she knew their legends. But she had to do something to correct her error and calm Mrs. Addison's fears.

"You mean that not every inch is ripe for savages to take cover in. Well, yes, some of it is a bit rocky."

"No, but the parts that are swept clean of rock also. The Indians say that places like that are the homes for the Nvnehi."

"The nuh-neigh – what? Now I am entirely at ease."

"The Nvnehi are a type of spirit-people who live in homes we cannot see. But sometimes you can tell where they live anyway, because they clear the ground there. The Nvnehi are peaceful and prefer to keep to themselves –"

Mr. Addison snorted again. "Yes, a good explanation for why we don't see them."

"But they hate unkindness or injustice. So if they see an attack against the defenseless, they appear by hundreds like smoke from the air and fight. When they have destroyed the wicked or driven them off, they vanish again and return to their homes. The Nvnehi would not allow an ambush here."

"So I am to feel reassured by this fairy tale," Mrs. Addison replied, but her face showed interest.

"The Indians believe it, at least," Rachel said, blushing. "They would not attack anyone near the homes of the Nvnehi."

"Hm." Mrs. Addison was silent a moment, gazing at the landscape. "You do encounter some curiosities on the frontier. Do you know any other Indian stories?"

"A few."

"Tell me those, perhaps. I might prefer them to your personal observations at the moment."

So Rachel wracked her brain for any stories she could remember from the long days of cooking and sewing and the long nights sitting around the fire. The tales of sad lovers and talking animals and spirits who walked in the forest and sky had less magic somehow in the closeness of the coach, with Mr. Addison's indifference and Mrs. Addison's occasional grunts as her only response. It came as a relief when Mr. Addison remarked that unless the slaves had communicated their laziness to the nags pulling the coach, they should reach that evening's accommodation soon.

"Do you know the inn?" Rachel inquired. She half-suspected she would be left there, and she hoped that it would be a homely enough place she might be able to find some work.

"Good heavens, not another inn. No, we're staying with our friends the Churches. They were expecting us yesterday."

Rachel looked out the window. Friends of the Addisons must have a plantation, not a small farm like her father's, and she was curious to see the fields, though the harvest would have all long since been brought in. A light dusting of snow sprinkled the ground here over an icy crust. It was colder here. She hoped that hadn't meant sleet when the storm had blown through.

"Oh!" Rachel exclaimed and slammed herself back into her seat. She pressed her fingernails into the palms of her hands.

"What? What is it?" Mrs. Addison cried. "Are they coming?"

"No, ma'am, no one's coming – just please don't look."

Mr. Addison felt no such compunction. He glanced outside. "My word. Someone's just lying there." He leaned out of the window and called out, "Hey there! Jacob, Abraham! Stop the damned horses, will you? Are you blind? There's a man on the ground." He sat down again and exhaled hard.

"Do you think he's all right?" Mrs. Addison asked with a tremulous note in her voice. She didn't seem to mind her husband's swearing, and she didn't look out the window.

Mr. Addison shrugged. Rachel dropped her eyes. She did not see how a man could lie face-down on the ice that way and not be dead. But Mr. Addison seemed to think there was some hope.

The coach bounced to a halt and then lurched heavily to the side as the slaves sprang to the ground and Mr. Addison stepped out the door. He closed it firmly behind him. The horses whickered, and their harnesses clanked as they shifted nervously. They didn't like this place.

"He is all right, isn't he?" Mrs. Addison repeated, staring at the seat her husband had vacated. She twisted her handkerchief into a spindle. Rachel peered out the window, but she could see nothing other than the bent backs of the men in a huddle. They didn't seem to be doing anything with great haste.

"I think it might be too late," Rachel whispered. Sure enough, the coach lurched again as the slaves climbed up onto their perch and Mr. Addison stepped inside with a sigh, unaccompanied.

"Oh," Mrs. Addison said, her expression both angry and sad.

"Well. If he was an honest man, he's a poor devil," Mr. Addison grunted. "Not five minutes from the plantation. They'd have given him a bit of bread."

"Why wouldn't he have been an honest man? You think he was a thief, Robert? Was he carrying something?" If Mrs. Addison was so curious for information, Rachel wondered why she didn't look out the window herself.

"He was an Indian. We didn't search him." He shrugged again. "Didn't seem to have a wound. Must have starved, or been sick perhaps. Storm did him in, most likely. Didn't think to pack shovels. We'll let the Churches know."

The coach started off with a jerk and rumbled across the hard ground. They rode in silence. The path, it could hardly be called a road, that they followed took a curve around a copse of trees, and when they rounded it, the stubble of wide fields recently shorn stretched around them for acres to all sides. The house where they would stay the night was a bright speck in the distance, shining like a beacon in the low rays of late afternoon across the rough, sharp shadows of the fields. It broke Rachel's heart to discover that Mr. Addison's estimation had been correct. The dead man had fallen less than a mile from help. Mrs. Addison must have been thinking the same thing. "Oh la," she whispered, tapping her leg and turning her face to the side.

"Rachel," she said abruptly, "do these Nvnehi of yours ever give food or shelter to Indians who are lost, or are they a purely military function?"

"They do," Rachel said.

"Then he might have expected them to come to his aid."

"I don't know, madam. Perhaps."

"I think he most certainly did," Mrs. Addison said. "I think he fell into a comfortable sleep with the full expectation that he would be cared for, and that's every bit as good as if it were true." She seemed to feel better.

As they got closer, the Church home proved less grand than Rachel had imagined, wood rather than stone; but it was still a very large house, two stories high and painted white. A plump middle-aged woman in a blue polonaise dress and a white shawl came running out when the coach rumbled up the curving drive. Mrs. Church beamed and waved at them. "Oh, you made it, we were so worried about you!" Rachel liked her immediately.

"Betsy, you can't imagine, you just can't," Mrs. Addison said as her husband helped her from the coach. Mr. Addison shot his wife a warning glance, but Mrs. Addison had already retreated to a wordless shaking of her head.

"Margaret, you poor thing, you aren't meant for travel. But we are grateful to Robert for bring you to visit," Mrs. Church replied, evidently thinking it was the carriage-ride that had upset her friend.

The cold cut through Rachel's thin wool dress when she stepped outside. She shivered involuntarily.

"Oh, and you've found a new maid," Mrs. Church continued, turning her attention to Rachel and smiling brightly. "She suits you perfectly, I can just tell."

Rachel looked up in surprise and bobbed a curtsy.

Mrs. Church smiled. "Such a pretty little thing. Like you've charmed a fairy into serving you, and if anyone could, Margaret, it's you. Now you must come inside at once. Henry is pretending not to care that you're late, but he's been a bear since yesterday afternoon."

Rachel found herself without any immediate duties, since the Addisons' slaves took charge of the luggage and the Churches' slaves took care of the Addisons, installing them in a snug parlor rendered almost too warm by a lively fire. Rachel stood nervously in the background, unsure whether she should remain or try to make herself useful with the slaves. She had never been in a private home when she did not have a task to perform, and it made her uneasy.

"Miss? Are you coming out or in?" A pleasant voice broke into her thoughts, and Rachel wheeled around in embarrassment. A long-faced man in the red-and-blue uniform of a provincial officer waited patiently behind her. She'd been so careful to stay out of the way of anyone in the room that she'd managed to place herself in the middle of the doorway.

"I don't know where I'm wanted," she murmured, blushing and moving to the side, and the man replied with a chuckle that perhaps she'd better sit by the fire then, because that was what he usually did in such cases.

"Ah, Henry – I mean, *Colonel* Church," Mr. Addison exclaimed, rising with more animation than Rachel had seen out of him before. She had been offered a seat by the fire, but she did not feel quite that she could take it. Mrs. Church and Mrs. Addison were sitting. And if Rachel took a chair, even a small, uncomfortable chair, it might look as though she were claiming equality of sorts. She remained by the door. No one noticed, so she reasoned she had chosen correctly.

Col. Church grinned and tugged at his jacket. "I wasn't sure it would still fit. But I thought I'd try it for old times' sake." He pressed Mr. Addison's hand between both of his own. "It's good to see you again, Robert. I haven't played cards in ages. And Margaret, you're more beautiful than ever. It's a good thing Betsy's such an amiable soul she doesn't mind my noticing."

"Oh, I imagine I still have some surprises to offer you."

"Well, it's a good thing she has a poor throwing arm, then. The storm didn't give you much trouble?"

Mr. Addison's face darkened, and he jerked his chin to suggest a private word as Mrs. Church burst out, "Margaret was white as a sheet when they first got in. It's so cold you can't imagine. Where *can* Ezekiel be, I told him to bring some toddies."

Because Rachel had remained near the edge of the room, she could hear Mr. Addison plainly as he took Col. Church's shoulder and said in a low voice, "There was a dead Indian about a mile back lying on the ground, gave Margaret a fright."

Col. Church's heavy eyebrows flicked upward in surprise. Mr. Addison shook his head. "No funny business," he went on. "Looks like the storm keeled him over. But you might want to bury him before he troubles Betsy."

Col. Church frowned. "I'll send a man in the morning. It's late now, and every hand I've got is busy repairing the damage. I was a little worried the storm might have caught you. We had sleet here that punched a hole in the barn roof and knocked a couple fences down. Killed some cows too. I hope it doesn't mean a bad winter."

"I hate to leave the poor fellow lying there like a dog," Mr. Addison said. "I'll send Jacob and Abraham to take care of it, if you'll lend them a couple shovels. I imagine they can get it done before dark, if they don't pretend they've lost the way, as they usually do when I try to send 'em on an errand."

"They'll be in a hurry to get back by the fire, I'm sure."

"Excuse me, sirs," Rachel put in hesitantly, curtsying again. "I remember very plainly where it, where, where he was. I could show them the way, if you think that would help." She also did not like the thought of a body lying unburied.

"Bless your heart, child, I forgot you were there," Col. Church exclaimed, reddening slightly as he turned around to face her. Mr. Addison glanced at Rachel with that curious flick of the eyes again.

"Margaret's new maid. An odd one," he muttered, and then shrugged, which Rachel took for assent.

The cold didn't cut as deep when she went outside again, leaving the Churches and the Addisons to a happy reunion of which she had no part. The fire had warmed her, and it helped too that Jacob and Abraham wanted to keep a lively pace down the slick path of frozen mud. The shovels clanked rhythmically against Abraham's leg. Jacob kept casting an anxious face towards the heavens.

"Gettin' dark," he muttered. "Don't like to be round no dead man in the dark." Abraham merely shrugged, though he looked no happier about the situation.

In about fifteen minutes, they rounded the edge of the trees. The body lay prostrate on the ground, a smudge of darkness against the snow. Rachel lowered her eyes. The body seemed smaller this time. It might have been a wad of dirty rags discarded on the ground.

"Don't like to do this without no preacher," Jacob said.

"He probably wasn't a Christian," Rachel said. Jacob looked at her.

"Well, he should of been. How else he gonna get to heaven?"

"The Indians have a heaven of their own." The three of them stood over the body now. The dead man's flesh had paled, rendering the black of his hair as dark as a spill of ink. The cold had shrunk his skin tight around his bones. A small round shield lay under his hand. Abraham handed a shovel to Jacob and pointed to a spot on the ground where he meant for them to dig.

Rachel crouched and turned the shield over carefully. Snow and dirt had ruined the feathers. "He was a Cherokee," she said. The men turned around in surprise.

"It make a difference?"

"Dig the grave so he can face the west," Rachel said, ignoring the question. "You need to point his body so that his soul knows the way to go to get to heaven. Indian heaven."

Jacob glanced at the sky to get his bearings. "He ain't facing west," he said with a shudder. "Where you think his soul heading now?"

"He'll straighten it out once his body is interred," Rachel answered with more certainty than she felt. She stood and wiped the cold of the dead man's shield from her fingers. The men did not ask her how she knew the Indian was a Cherokee, and they did not question her order about how to position the body. She was grateful for their lack of curiosity.

The shovels struck the icy earth with a series of metal clangs. The work went slowly, and Rachel found herself with little to do other than look at the dead man and watch the sun sink into the forested horizon like some great fire-bird coming to roost. A crescent of dry and yellowed eye showed between the Indian's lids, giving the unpleasant impression that he was returning her stare when she glanced at him. Rachel tied and untied her shawl in a knot. She hoped Mrs. Addison wasn't angry at her absence. She had not expected to be gone so long. But of course Mrs. Addison wanted only entertainment, and the Churches would supply that in abundance.

The men did not speak as they worked, and she did not notice for a moment that the shovels had fallen silent too. Rachel looked up to see that Abraham and Jacob were staring at her. Abraham rested against his shovel.

"Is there something?" she asked.

"It's getting dark, and the ground's pretty hard," Abraham said. "What do you think, Miss Rachel? This good enough?"

Rachel walked to the hole and looked inside. It stretched under six feet long – the Indian wasn't tall, so that would do – but it was hardly two feet deep. Rachel could see the hard edges of the half-frozen ground where the shovels had cut it. She tapped her foot against the bottom of the hole. Solid as rock. And although a little light remained in the sky, shadow covered almost everything on earth.

"It's not very deep, but we can cover the grave with stones."

Abraham nodded. "That'll keep the animals out. And it'll be a lot quicker."

It occurred to her then that Abraham hadn't asked for her opinion, but rather her approval. They must have thought that she'd been sent to supervise their work.

"I only asked to come because I didn't know my place in the Churches' and I thought I might be of some help here," Rachel blurted. She knew Abraham and Jacob were slaves, but she hated to think they imagined she held herself over them. They had a place in the world they were sure of. She did not.

"You know that Indian stuff," Jacob said, unfazed by her outburst.

Abraham eyed her expressionlessly. "You come to tell us to do Indian stuff for him?"

"I suppose I did," Rachel said. She realized it was true. She'd wanted to make sure not just that the man was buried, but that he was buried correctly. "But other than make sure he's covered decently and facing west, I suppose there's nothing else that can be done for a proper burial."

"What else is supposed to happen, for a real Indian burial?" Jacob asked, his eyes wide.

"Almost everything else is really for the survivors, not for the person who died, and we don't know who they are. His widow, if he, if he was married..." Her breath caught in her throat at the idea that this man might have a family somewhere, worrying about him, praying for his safe return. She shook her head slightly and continued. "His widow would make herself ugly so that no one would want her and she wouldn't get married again too soon. And all his relatives would be considered unclean until the priests decided enough time had passed. And all the dead man's possessions would be burned or buried with him, because they were unclean too."

"They act like they hate the dead man." Jacob looked at the corpse with pity.

Rachel shook her head. "No, not at all, it isn't that. Perhaps I shouldn't have said *unclean.*"

"*Unclean* is the right word," Abraham put in, his face expressionless. "You don't fool around with the dead. That don't mix with the living."

"I think that's more what they mean," Rachel agreed.

"You think he got people?"

Rachel shrugged.

"Course he's got people, everybody's got people," Abraham growled. "Now quit asking fool questions and help me get that man into the ground, or we gonna be walking back in the dark with a cold, angry spirit on the night wind blowing all round us."

"I won't listen if it come calling," Jacob said, trembling.

"You don't have to. Spirit can blow right up your nose, or in your mouth, or even get in your eyes, and once it's inside you, it can eat up your soul. Now you gonna get moving or not?"

Jacob moved quickly.

The body sagged when the men lifted it, and a faint sweet odor rose from him. The side of the dead man's face that had lain against the ground was swollen and bruised almost black. It reminded Rachel of the way syrup sank to the bottom of a sponge-cake, and her stomach clenched with nausea. She turned her face to the side. She heard the men's feet scrape across the ground. When it stopped, she looked up again. Jacob wiped his hands against his pants. The body lay in its hole, turned towards the setting sun. Abraham had already picked up his shovel and scattered a pile of loose earth over the corpse. The dirt and pebbles rattled against the man's body.

"Wait a moment," Rachel said. She picked up the forgotten shield from the ground and ran over to the grave. She placed it carefully against the dead man's chest. Then the slaves finished filling the hole with dirt, and Rachel helped them gather stones to cover the sad little mound.

While searching for a final few rocks, Jacob had found a tiny deerskin bundle that contained a light jacket, a pair of trousers, a bone necklace, and a knife whose handle was wrapped in frayed and worn leather. They did not want to open the man's grave again. Rachel wanted to leave the pack there, but Jacob insisted she take charge of it, so she accepted the burden and carried it pressed against her side. The hide warmed as she held it, feeling almost like a living thing. Rachel found herself rather wishing it had remained undiscovered.

Only a faint haze of medium blue showed over the horizon of trees by the time they finished and turned back towards the house, but Abraham assured Jacob that even a little light would probably be enough to keep the spirit at bay. Rachel did not get the impression that Abraham believed in superstition much, and she thought it a little unkind of him to play on Jacob's fears.

They rounded the trees, and the house came into view again. Even from a distance, it glowed with friendly light peeping through the curtains of the downstairs windows. Rachel quickened her step unconsciously, as did the men.

"Hope there's something in the kitchen. I'm hungry enough to eat a mule," Abraham said. Rachel was too, though it seemed disrespectful of the sad burial and so she didn't like to admit it. She'd been indisposed when they'd stopped for a brief luncheon early in the afternoon and so had taken only a piece of plain bread and a small-beer.

"All I can think about is that poor man's babies wondering where he is and what's become of their daddy," Jacob said, shaking his head.

"We don't know a thing about that dead man, and now you giving him babies to cry over?"

Abraham looked cross again, a state that seemed to require little provocation, and so Rachel stepped in. "There is something the Cherokee do when a man dies. To know how his sons will fare without their father," she said, suddenly remembering the ritual she had seen only twice.

"You mean we can know if his babies is all right?"

"Well – yes. You catch a bird and cut a piece of meat from its breast. The mourners gather around a fire, and you throw the meat into the flames. If it burns without popping, the dead man's sons are safe. But if the meat spits in the direction of the sons, it means they're to die also."

"What kind of bird?" Jacob was painfully eager.

"I don't remem – I don't know," Rachel said.

Abraham snorted. "A real skinny, lean one that don't got no fat in it."

"Would that work, Miss Rachel? If I found me a real skinny bird, you think it would work?"

"I'm sure it would," she said. This pleased him, and they walked in silence for a few moments. The house seemed small and far. The wind carried the smell of ice, and the dead leaves on the trees whispered when the air touched them. Their footsteps sounded loud. Rachel looked down, a strange sad feeling hanging in her chest. "When I die, Jacob, I hope it's someone as kind as you who buries me," she remarked after a while.

"Now, Miss Rachel, don't go on that way," Abraham said. He took a considerably gentler tone with Rachel than he did with his friend Jacob. "You ain't dying, and anyway, when the day comes, you'll have your children and grandchildren and all that around you to take care of things."

"Perhaps," Rachel said uncertainly.

"A pretty girl like you? You're bound to have all sorts of beaus. That's how Mrs. Addison keeps losing her maids. She only likes the pretty ones around her, only that's what the gentlemen like too, and it's always the gentlemen that wins out in the end."

An unpleasant image of Mr. Darling rose unbidden in Rachel's mind, mixed in confusion with the young officer Bellew who had risen to her defense. She remembered the strength of Bellew's hands pressed against the table and the pleading intensity of his stare in that one moment when he'd first spoken to her. She felt an odd ache inside her body. She put it out of her mind. Mr. Darling was married as well as repellant, and Bellew nothing but a passing stranger who had disappeared.

"I don't," she replied.

"Well, give it time."

Rachel shrugged and shook her head.

She slept that night with one of the Churches' maids who informed her cheerfully that she normally had a bed to herself because no one else could get a decent rest at her side. It proved to be true. Colleen muttered to herself and thrashed about in her sleep as if she were wrestling all the dogs of hell, so Rachel rose early and weary. She slipped into her clothes and, since she did not seem to have any duties until Mrs. Addison woke, she took her Alexander Pope down to the parlor, where a fire had already been laid.

She had been reading only a few minutes when Col. Church, wearing a fine green hunting jacket and riding boots, entered the room. "Ah! Good morning." He seemed surprised to find her there. She did not know why it was so difficult for her to do what was expected.

Rachel rose hurriedly and curtsied. "Good morning, sir."

"Bright and early. Good to see. Mrs. Addison is a bit of a night owl, though, you'll find." He glanced at her reading curiously. "May I?"

Rachel handed it to him. He turned the volume over in his hand and chuckled. "*An Essay on Man.* Has Mrs. A asked you to spare her the trouble of reading it herself?"

Rachel wasn't sure what he meant. "No, sir. It's my own book."

"Would you recommend it?"

"Have you read it, sir?" Rachel asked, her interest roused. The idea that she might speak to someone about something she had read was a novelty to her.

"Alexander Pope? Of course, dear child. 'Whatever is, is right.' A fine sentiment. Things are the way they are for a reason. Are you enjoying it?"

Rachel looked at him uncertainly. His face was open and candid, and it did not seem as though he was teasing her. "It depends, I think, on how you define 'right' and 'reason'," she said carefully. "And probably 'is' and 'are' as well. Mr. Pope certainly writes like an angel. But when he says 'whatever is, is right', I am not convinced that he means it is right for us to resign ourselves to it. To accept it, perhaps. But not blindly. And perhaps we can only accept it once we see how it is wrong."

Col. Church blinked in astonishment. "How do I define 'is' and 'are'?" His face was blank for a moment. Then he laughed. Rachel offered a hesitant smile. "Good Lord, Robert was right, you are an odd one. Hm. Do you read French?"

"No, sir," Rachel answered, lowering her eyes. "Although I have some German."

"That's a pity. A friend just sent over a novel from Paris that might be more in line with your thinking about this 'best of all possible worlds'. You'd have plenty of time to read it in the mornings before Mrs. Addison wakes. If you knew French, of course. German but no French. Hm."

"I am very fond of this world, sir, but I am not sure it is the best of all possible ones."

"Yes, yes, that's Monsieur Voltaire's contention, except I'm not sure he'd concur with your fondness. Where did Mrs. Addison find you, pray?"

Heat rose in Rachel's face. "In...I was working in a tavern."

"I suppose a free thinker might as well," Col. Church shrugged. "Well, I must see to the dogs. Hm." He strode from the room.

Rachel did not have time to take up her book again. Almost no sooner had Col. Church left than Jacob hurried inside, his face shiny from exercise and the cold wind. He clutched his right hand in a fist and brought a disgruntled Abraham in tow. "You see?" he told Abraham. "I told you Miss Rachel would be here."

Rachel looked to Abraham for explanation, but his face betrayed nothing other than his annoyance.

"I got the bird, and I cut out its breast," Jacob explained, opening his fist to reveal a bloody strip of meat. "Now, the three of us is the only mourners that man got, so we all got to be here. You understand, Abraham?" Abraham breathed out hard. "We got to know that man's babies is safe. Right, Miss Rachel?"

"Of course," Rachel said. Guilt stung her. She'd been wishing she'd known French and wondering if she really was a free thinker who belonged in a tavern or prison or anywhere other than a church, and she had forgotten all about the dead man. The fact that she'd never known him in life didn't matter. As Jacob said, the three of them were all the mourners that poor soul would ever have.

Abraham pulled his sleeves over his hands to protect them and dragged the fire-screen to the side. They knelt on the hearth. Jacob held the mangled bit of meat in his upturned palm. Fine lines of blood stained the creases of his hand.

"Is there anything I's supposed to say or do," he whispered to Rachel. She shook her head. "All right then." He closed his eyes and then in a sudden quick movement that made Rachel startle, he flung the meat into the heart of the fire. Rachel's breath caught in her throat. Even Abraham wore an expression of hopeful suspense.

The meat trembled in the flames. It burst with a pop, a fine grapeshot of fat spitting out in all directions. Then the fire took hold of the flesh, twisting it and turning it slowly black.

The three of them were silent, staring. Rachel wiped a bit of grease from her face. Jacob bowed his head and wrapped his arms around his legs. His face was turned to Rachel, but his eyes didn't register her presence.

Mr. Addison burst into the room. "There you are. For heaven's sake, what are you doing crouched on the floor like that?"

Rachel leapt to her feet and spun around. "I'm so sorry, sir, does Mrs. Addison –"

"Not you," he muttered irritably. "Jacob. We're ready for the hunt, and I'm wandering around like a fool looking for my damned boy. Will you quit malingering and put on your damned boots?"

"I'll go with you, Master," Abraham said, rising. "Jacob's feeling poorly. He wouldn't be no good anyway." Rachel glanced at Jacob. He did not seem to hear Mr. Addison. Tears leaked down his face, leaving dark trails down his coffee-colored skin.

Mr. Addison glanced at Jacob. "Better not be sick. We've still got a long way to go."

"He'll be fine later, Master. Just needs a bit of rest. I'll be changed in an instant," Abraham replied, leaving the room quickly. Mr. Addison remained a moment longer, regarding his motionless slave.

"Bit early for a nap, some might say," Mr. Addison muttered before turning to go.

Chapter 7

Three days later, they were back in the carriage and jolting along the rough road once again. Rachel did not like the coach any better upon her return to it, but she was glad that she would not be sleeping by the snoring, thrashing Colleen any more. Her thoughts strayed to Philadelphia. Rachel felt far from certain she would not be replaced shortly after their arrival, no matter what her mistress claimed. She had already proved incompetent at fixing Mrs. Addison's hair. What else of her new duties didn't Rachel know? She couldn't guess. Her ignorance and her slips didn't matter so much by the frontier, but Philadelphia was a grand city. She wished she could learn French, but she did not know how to go about it or who to ask for help. She had tried asking Mrs. Addison a few words of that language as they rode, but Mrs. Addison promptly dubbed the exercise remarkably tedious, and Rachel had to let it drop.

A long trip remained ahead of them. Rachel had plenty of time to worry.

Near the border of South Carolina, they stopped to rest and have a bite to eat in a small town a passer-by informed them was called Griffin's Ford. The inn contained almost no customers. It might have been a slow town, or a slow day, but the serving-maid kept peeping out the window until Mrs. Addison felt compelled to ask if there were some sort of festival keeping the local population entertained. They hadn't noticed anything on the way in.

"Better than that, ma'am," the serving-maid answered with shining eyes. "There's rebels in town come recruiting."

"Is the population here so much involved in independency?" Mrs. Addison inquired, lifting her eyebrows in doubt.

"Oh, I don't know about that, ma'am, and I suppose most of the men don't neither. But the rebels do put on a fine show."

"Isn't it tedious? Army recruitment, good heavens."

"No, ma'am, never," the serving-maid insisted. "At least, not from what I've heard from other folks," she added a little sadly, her eyes drawn to the uninformative window again.

Mrs. Addison decided that she had to see it for herself, so when they finished their meal, they gathered Jacob and Abraham from the stable and walked to the far side of town. It wasn't hard to find the rebels. A crowd of almost a hundred people had gathered, more people than Rachel had ever seen in one place before, and three men in fine blue coats stood on display. One of them was in the midst of what sounded like a pretty heated harangue, but Rachel couldn't make out the words over the muttering and the chuckling in the crowd. Four other rebels, not in uniform, stood behind the officers looking ill at ease. Their horses were tied loosely to the trees. Two of the beasts were heavy creatures clearly unaccustomed to the burden of a saddle. To the side, a camp desk bore papers weighted down with a rock. Rachel supposed they were enlistment contracts. The Addisons moved around the edge of the throng to find a spot close enough to hear without actually entering the crowd itself. Mrs. Addison declared she would not be jostled.

The speaker paused for a moment, and the crowd took up the slack.

"All this talk. Ain't you gonna try and get us drunk?" a skinny youth called, prompting laughter.

The apparent leader of the rebels was a stout middle-aged man with a booming voice. He seemed unfazed the heckling and called cheerfully, "You get a five-dollar enlistment bonus, boys, and it's yours to spend as you will. There's worse uses for it than rum. But once you're in the army, all your rum is free."

"Oh!" Rachel exclaimed and stopped in her tracks. Although she was not close enough to see his face, she found she remembered the way he stood and moved too exactly to be mistaken. The man standing to the right of the leader was unquestionably Bellew. He hadn't gone home after all, and he hadn't lost his spirit, whether Philadelphia fell or no. She should have known he was too fine a gentleman for that. She wanted to wave to him. And then she wanted, suddenly, to turn around and run back to the coach. Her step faltered.

Jacob reached out a hand, assuming she needed help. "You turned all pale, Miss Rachel." Rachel flushed at his words. "Now you all red," Jacob corrected himself helpfully.

"I was just surprised. I know one of them," she explained. She realized then that of course she knew all three; the other two must be O'Malley and Masterson. Yes – that was O'Malley, speaking to the crowd.

"A friend of yours, Rachel?"

"No, I mean – I don't really know him. I just recognized him from the Brass Bull. Those three men, the officers, stopped by a week or two before your arrival."

"Tavern's about the place where you'll find people like that," Mr. Addison said.

"Mr. Bellew is a gentleman, sir. I heard his friends remark that he was from the, the *ton*," Rachel said with an obscure pride.

Mrs. Addison's eyebrows arched at that. "Which one is Bellew?" Rachel pointed him out with a self-conscious lowering of her head. She did not want Bellew to see her pointing at him. She need not have concerned herself; his attention was fixed on the men in the crowd, scanning their faces, his expression a mixture of confidence and apprehension. It did not appear that anyone had enlisted yet.

"Never seen him before. But he's handsome enough," Mrs. Addison concluded with a shrug.

O'Malley bent to the side and cupped his ear to listen to some comment from the crowd, making a great show of paying close attention. Rachel could not make out the words. O'Malley nodded several times and straightened quickly. He placed his hands on his hips and addressed the crowd again. "I have been asked an excellent question that doubtless has occurred to every honest man, like my good friend here, who has given the matter a candid examination. And that is, are these taxes of Parliament's so onerous, a mean little fifteen pence on a pound of tea here or there, that we should salt the earth of our fields with the blood of our veins rather than pay? And you are expecting me to cry yes, yes we must. But in fact I answer you: No." He widened his eyes, smiling a little. He knew that would have an effect. And it did.

Rachel's curiosity was aroused, despite a pretty fair indifference to the matter of taxation rates. And he certainly had the crowd's attention, far more than when he'd been asking for enlistments. The little gathering fell entirely silent for the first time. Rachel could hear birds twittering in the trees. Even Mrs. Addison looked interested. Bellew's mouth quirked in a smile, quickly suppressed. Rachel smiled too, although she didn't know quite why. So the rebels were claiming there was no cause for the rebellion? What then? Sport?

O'Malley held a hand in the air and paused, clearly enjoying the moment.

"No, my friends," he said, "The amount of these taxes, most of 'em, is not unreasonable. You won't hear everyone say that, but you'll hear it from me. The truth. No, the amount of these taxes is not an undue burden, although it falls pretty heavy on some. No, the amount of these taxes is not disproportionate to the expense of defending our land. So, why, you ask, do I wear this uniform? Why do I tell you that it is time to put down your hammers and plows and drop the hands of your children to take up your muskets in the cause of independence?"

He took a step towards the crowd, his eyes burning with a sudden intensity. Rachel blinked. The genial mask was gone. O'Malley was angry, and he let it show. "Gentlemen, it is because we *are* independent now in all but name. We have ceased to be Englishmen, whether anyone wills it or no. We are a new people, a new race, and a new nation. Great Britain knows it. It is a long time since she treated us as her own. We are to her not Englishmen, but a fund of worker-slaves fit to serve, but not to speak. She does not give us a place in Parliament to express our views. She demands that her soldiers be permitted to search our homes without even the pretext of a pretended cause. She wags an imperious finger and tells us what we are allowed to buy and sell, and where we are allowed to do it. She forces us into her wars and then charges us for the burial of our own sons and daughters. Gentlemen, my throat chokes on the words, but they must be said: she holds us in contempt. And so I tell you it is not the cost of the taxes that we resent and resist. It is that there is any tax, any imposition, any act of control whatsoever from that cold and distant potentate. Shall we send taxes, whether reasonable or no, to the Czar of Russia? Or to King of Spain? Shall we ask Frederick the Great to tell us how much wheat to plant or when to kiss our wives? And if not – why should we accord Parliament the honor – what reason other than that its soldiers demand it with musket-ball and bayonet?

"Yes, Great Britain knows that we are a different people from her own – when she speaks of loyalty, my friends, she does not speak of the loyalty of a brother for a brother, but of a dog for its master. And I am no dog, my friends, and neither are you. Now the mortal hour has come to prove it. It is here. It is now. England has shown her fangs and raised her bloody claw. We can rise to meet it, risking our throats, or we can turn away and bear the wounds of slavery across our backs. So I ask each of you: what kind of men are we? Do we fight for our God-given freedom? Or do we prefer to fall, a conquered race for all time, without even once lifting our knees from the mud? Because there is no third alternative."

With that he fell silent. He had asked a question. Now everyone waited for the response. No one seemed inclined to offer one. The crowd murmured among itself, and some feet shuffled uncomfortably. A light breeze stirred the leaves. O'Malley wheeled around and yanked the top sheet from the pile of enlistment papers and banged it against the camp desk with the flat of his hand. His eyes held a challenge. He said nothing, and neither did the crowd.

Rachel watched Bellew. There was no sign of that brief smile on his lips now, and he looked at the ground. She did not realize how tightly she had balled her fists until the pain of her nails cutting into her skin forced her to relax her hands. She knew it would take only one volunteer to bring forward the hesitant and uncertain. If only she were a man, she could force her way through the press of bodies and sign her name, and she would, too. Wouldn't he be proud of her then! Her mind flicked back to the dead Indian's clothes packed with her belongings in the coach. Why, she almost could dress as a man, couldn't she. The enlistment wouldn't hold, of course, but it would break the spell of silence that gripped the crowd.

Only it was impossible. It would take too long, and Rachel could hardly afford to throw her position with the Addisons, and she knew she lacked the nerve for the gesture anyway. Like so much of what filled her mind, it was nothing but an empty fantasy.

"Stirring speech, wasn't it, Robert?" Mrs. Addison whispered to her husband with a sly smile. "Why don't you make father happy and sign up?"

"Don't think he'd care much for an enlisted man as a son," Mr. Addison replied blandly.

The whispered exchange was enough to draw the attention of all three Continentals. Rachel flushed when Bellew lifted his eyes. Evidently he decided quickly enough that Mr. Addison was not a good prospect, because his attention settled on Mrs. Addison in her blue watered silk. And that was perfectly natural. Rachel glanced at her mistress. Mrs. Addison was both graceful and beautiful, more beautiful the longer you looked at her, with the perfect oval of her face and her long, gray eyes, and all the fragile little bits of jewelry dangling from her ears and neck and wrists. Rachel wondered what it would be like to be so pretty and know that no matter where you went or what you did, people would see you first. But that was only an empty fantasy too, because Rachel knew very well that she was not, and nothing would make her so.

But while Bellew might have been ready to dismiss Mr. Addison, O'Malley was not. "You, sir!" O'Malley cried out. "Don't be shy. It looks like your affairs have prospered – surely your business could spare you six months while you serve your country and your cause!"

Mr. Addison shook his head irritably, waving a hand in the air, but O'Malley persisted. "Do not fear that you could not make a valuable contribution – as long as you're hale enough to hold a gun, age is no impediment."

"So I have heard," Mr. Addison replied. "It is my understanding that the Continental Army consists primarily, in fact, of boys too young to shave and men too old to hold their water."

The crowd laughed at this. Rachel's heart sank. But O'Malley took it in good humor, patting the front of his jacket. "Don't be fooled by this belly of mine, sir, I'm thirty-four, and you can see my Lieutenants and our new recruits are young men in their prime. But perhaps you'd like a demonstration of the caliber of our troops before you cast your judgment upon them." The crowd murmured its approval of this, a sense of excitement in the general straightening of bodies and craning of necks, and Rachel realized that this, at last, was the show for which they had interrupted their day's work. O'Malley grinned, back in control. "Well then. Has anyone here got something they don't mind losing? Bring up any object you like, and we'll call it Parliament." A woman remarked that they could have her husband, and O'Malley replied that he'd be glad to take him off her hands, but not by shooting him.

Rachel realized with a start that she had a handkerchief in her pocket, and she reached inside her skirt with trembling hands to bring it out. She could always make another from a scrap. But before she could close her fingers on her prize, a crooked-faced boy pushed his way through the crowd, holding a large green apple aloft. "Parliament the apple, Parliament the apple," the boy chuckled as he went. He had an ungainly way of walking and seemed not quite right in the head.

"He'd fit in nicely," Mr. Addison muttered.

The boy reached O'Malley and handed over his gift. O'Malley offered a slight bow in return and answered gravely, "Thank you, my lad, for Parliament the apple. Ladies and gentlemen, Parliament the apple." O'Malley held it aloft for everyone to see. The boy gawped, overcome at the popular interest in his snack. "Pretty small for a target, isn't it?" O'Malley said.

The crowd eventually decided it could agree that yes, the apple was large for an apple, but small for a target.

"Any of you think a man could hit it with a musket at twenty yards?" Murmurs, some laughter. A wit remarked that he was not in the habit of hunting apples. "Well. So I take it that some of you could, and maybe some are not such practiced shots. No, you're right, twenty yards is no test. Now, you. You, sir. May I ask you to pace out –" O'Malley leaned forward with a smile. "Two hundred yards? And put this apple on the ground. Yes, sir, you. I don't want any question that I shorted the distance if I did it myself." He kicked a line in the dirt with his boot.

The chosen man stepped forward self-consciously and measured out his steps carefully from the starting-line. The crowd rearranged itself for a better view. It was hard enough to hit a mark at thirty yards with a musket. Two hundred was preposterous.

Bellew rolled his shoulders a few times and picked up his musket from where it leaned against a tree. His jacket tightened against his back when he moved, revealing the lines of muscle beneath. He flipped open the powder-horn on his belt and poured a trickle of black dust from its narrow end into the musket's barrel.

"Do you want me to find a stump or something to put it on?" the man with the apple shouted back when he had made about a quarter the distance.

"The ground will do fine. Lieutenant Bellew could pick out a black cat's shadow at midnight," O'Malley cried back. Bellew quirked his mouth at this but said nothing. The man shrugged, finished his pace, put the apple on the ground, and ran back to the crowd. Rachel thought he might have just moved a bit to the side and gotten a better view, but perhaps he felt it more prudent to keep his distance from a shot that was bound to go wild.

Bellew walked slowly to the scuffed line and half-cocked the firing-pan. Masterson grinned at him, and Bellew nodded back with a quick smile. He brought his gun to his shoulder and sighted into the distance. Rachel stood on tiptoe, but there were too many people in the way who were too much taller than her to make out much beyond Bellew's form.

Silence, except for the birds.

A single shot.

The horses whickered and shifted on their hooves. A puff of dirt exploded from the ground in the distance. A cloud of smoke from the musket obscured Bellew's head for a moment. When it cleared, he stood expressionless, staring at his mark. The birds fell silent. The crowd muttered uncertainly, neighbor asking neighbor if anything could be made out.

"Did he hit it?" Rachel asked Abraham. "Can you see? Did he get it?" Her mouth was dry. She so wanted him to have done well.

"Don't know," Abraham mused. No one seemed to.

Bellew shouldered his gun again and nodded at the man who'd placed the apple. "You may see what's left of it," he said in an even, polite tone. The man blinked and then jogged towards the spot where he'd left the apple. A few others went with him, including the half-wit boy.

When the man reached the spot he remembered, he looked around in confusion. It wasn't until the boy scooped something off the ground and ran back crowing at the top of his lungs, "Parliament got smooshed!" that the crowd erupted into applause. The boy rushed towards his neighbors in his shambling lope, and people pressed around him to see the torn bit of green-skinned flesh in his hand, all that remained of the atomized apple.

Rachel glowed with almost as much pride as if she'd made the shot herself, and she clapped happily with the others. Mrs. Addison glanced at her with an ironic smile, and Mr. Addison slapped a few fingers against his palm in polite boredom. One of the men who'd gone to fetch the apple shrugged and, with a half-grin at his friends in the crowd, veered to the camp desk to sign up. O'Malley winked cheerfully at Bellew, who was reloading his gun.

"Man has a rifled musket," Mr. Addison remarked with an admiring note in his voice. "Fine shooting, even so." A rifle was a hunting gun; both her father and the raider had owned one. The barrel was narrower than a regular musket and grooved with a spiral inside; loading took a long time, but the modifications improved the accuracy and length of the shot enormously. Still, Rachel had never heard of anyone who could hit an apple at two hundred yards before. She could not imagine how steady his hands and his eyes must be.

"Your friend is very talented," Mrs. Addison said, smiling.

"I always knew he was a gentleman, even before his friends said anything," Rachel replied. She could not take her eyes off him. Bellew had bent his head and was saying something in a low voice to the new conscript.

Mr. Addison snorted. "If only he were as honest as he's as good a shot."

Rachel whipped her head around in sudden outrage. "I beg your pardon, Mr. Addison?" Abraham flashed her a worried look.

Mr. Addison quirked his mouth, unworried by her anger but apparently amused by it. "You'll find about as many *gentlemen* from the *ton* with rifled muskets as you'll see tucking into boiled squirrel," he said, and then laughed at his own joke. "Boiled squirrel," he repeated.

"Don't be disgusting, Robert. I was finding Lieutenant Bellew perfectly decorative, and now you've gone and spoiled the image with your squirrel."

"Why wouldn't a gentleman have a rifled musket, sir?" Rachel asked. She doubted Mr. Addison would be able to present a good reason for his assertion, which was, after all, obviously incorrect.

"Because a gentleman is not a sniper or an assassin, my dear girl. He may be a soldier, but soldiery relies upon discipline and uniformity, and that level of accuracy is not only unnecessary, it is deleterious insofar as it obliges the shooter to take too long over his aim." He turned to his wife.

"Would you like to stay and watch your decorative Lieutenant Bellew a little longer? It looks like he's going to take another shot."

Rachel's heart jumped. She clutched her handkerchief. She wouldn't be slow this time. She could tack it to a tree, and he could shoot it clean through, and she could keep it afterwards.

But Mrs. Addison wrinkled her nose. "No," she decided. "That would be repetitive, and we've dawdled long enough as it is."

Rachel twisted the handkerchief around her fingers. She replaced it in her pocket.

"Go on then, what're you waiting for?" Mr. Addison snapped to the slaves, who turned and hurried ahead of the rest of them back to the tavern where the horses were kept.

Rachel took one final glance at Bellew as they left. His teeth flashed white as he laughed with a new conscript, and one hand waved expansively in the air to illustrate what he was saying. He was happy now, enjoying himself. The sun was in his face, forcing him to squint slightly. She remembered from the tavern that his eyes were dark blue. Strands of golden red shone in the brown of his hair. She hadn't noticed the red before. How dear he was, everything about him. She wished she could have said hello. But he had his path, and she had hers, and so there wasn't much more to say than hello itself, and there wasn't much point in that. And yet even with everyone admiring his successful shot, Rachel wondered if anyone thought of him quite as she did. And she was sure that they did not.

She knew it was foolish of her to think so much of him. But she was not in the habit of controlling her thoughts and now she found herself unable to.

* * *

Bellew demolished two more apples, a piece of paper tacked to a tree, and an oddly shaped rock that was declared a success by default when it could not be located afterwards. He let Masterson hit a few targets, even though that entailed a little risk since Bellew was aware, he hoped without arrogance, that he was by far the better shot. But Masterson came through all right and then displayed some of his knife-throwing, which Bellew didn't think would be much use in a battle but seemed to please the crowd anyway. The day was fine, and the sun not too low in the sky yet. Perhaps they should follow that earlier fellow's advice and see if there was any rum to be found. That would keep the crowd longer.

He hated recruiting. He felt like a trained animal on display for bored ladies and children who wanted something to watch while they sucked sweets. Like a sword-swallower or some oddly colored animal with an extra limb. But they'd picked up a second conscript today, and with the one from Springfield and the three from Mapleton, they were starting to make a respectable looking group. Still, Bellew supposed that he'd have to resign himself to weeks more of these embarrassing shows. O'Malley's commission, and Bellew's by extension, depended upon their bringing a company of forty men.

"When are we leaving?" one of the new men, John Cowles, asked. "Sir," he added hastily, remembering that he was a soldier now.

"It's getting late. I imagine we'll stay the night, if there are accommodations to be had," Bellew replied.

"There's an inn, sir, but it isn't much. I can put up a couple myself, and I'm sure Jamie can do the same. Make it easier to meet up in the morning as well."

"It is more convenient if we travel together, but if your affairs require some time to settle, you can always join us in a few days. We won't be going far, not at this rate."

Cowles shook his head. "No, sir. They know my feelings at the shop and won't be surprised to see me off. My family as well. I only need time to put together a few belongings, but I suppose I can do that in the morning."

Their work here was done. A few men, perhaps a little sympathy for the cause. Bellew would have to take satisfaction from it. The crowd began to break up.

A mocking voice brought the stragglers back, and jolted Bellew's thoughts from the food and bed waiting for him with Cowles.

"So when you face His Majesty's troops, you gonna throw knives at 'em? I can belch for a good half-minute, and it's pretty amazing, but I don't expect it to win me any wars," called out a lean man in a brown cloak, echoing Bellew's thoughts a little more closely than he liked from an evident Tory. The crowd chuckled. O'Malley sighed, softly enough that only Bellew and perhaps Cowles could hear. Masterson, insulted, shoved his knife back into his belt.

"Merely a demonstration of skill," O'Malley replied, smiling and stepping forward again. Nothing flustered him for long, which Bellew admired, although he did not quite aspire to emulate it. Still, placating the locals was likelier to win people to their cause than brawling with them, no matter how offensive they seemed determined to make themselves sometimes. "If you find the shooting more convincing, we will be happy to oblige with more of that. Although I can't imagine anyone doubts the marksmanship at our disposal." Bellew had leaned his rifle against a tree. He picked it up and walked slowly to O'Malley's side.

"The regulars don't come at you one at a time for you to pick 'em off like that anyway," the lean man said. "You want to impress me, why don't you prove you can shoot all together, same as they do?"

O'Malley glanced at Bellew and shrugged. Bellew nodded his resigned agreement. It would make a loud noise; presumably that would be entertaining. "If you like," O'Malley answered the man. "I'm not as good a shot as my lieutenants, I must admit, but I'm pretty fair. And understand that our new soldiers are a bit untested, and today's recruits aren't exactly prepared."

"Should I run for my musket, sir?" Cowles asked in an undertone. Bellew considered the matter and then shook his head.

"They'll lose interest if we make them wait too long," he decided. "Just stand back for now." A thought occurred to him. "You know how to use that musket?" he asked.

"Pretty well – I'd say yes," Cowles replied with a grin, to Bellew's relief. Too many of their conscripts were raw amateurs who barely knew how to load their guns, let alone fire them. Bellew had given them a little training – Masterson didn't have the patience for it – but he still half-suspected that at least one of the new men was going to blow himself up before he ever saw a battlefield.

At O'Malley's nod, the seven men with muskets or rifles at hand loaded them. Bellew performed the familiar actions automatically, glancing down to make sure he tipped the right amount of powder into the firing-lock and the barrel. One of the Mapleton men, the one Bellew worried about, sat cross-legged on the ground and stuck out his tongue as he worked, as if struggling to remember the proper order of powder, ball, and wadding. It was almost impossible to get a proper angle on the barrel from that position, and the man was making a mess of it. Bellew sighed inwardly. He supposed it probably wasn't the time to correct the fellow's form. He'd give another lesson in the evening, when he'd be greasing more rifle-shot for himself anyway. At least he'd made sure that everyone had cleaned his musket last night. The gun would probably fire, and that was the main thing.

It took at least five minutes for all the men to get themselves ready, when it ought to take less than one. Then they had to discuss whether it was better to fire into the trees or over the open ground.

"I recommend the open ground, sir," Bellew said at last, stifling his frustration. O'Malley had a kind heart and didn't like to rule the men with too firm a hand, but the idea about the trees was simply preposterous. "For this exercise, we'd like to be certain we're *not* hitting anything."

So the open ground it was, and the men lined up at the scuffed mark, facing into the emptiness. The two new recruits without muskets decided in the spirit of camaraderie that they would line up too and go through the motions.

"Present arms," O'Malley cried. They raised their guns. Some of them hadn't remembered to half-cock their firelocks, and they hurried to correct the oversight. This took longer than it should too. "Aim – fire!"

Seven shots in ragged unison split the air. Smoke burned Bellew's eyes, and his ears rang. He knew it was an impressive spectacle, though he couldn't see much through the smoke, and the crowd broke into scattered applause even though the shots hadn't hit anything.

"In the name of His Majesty King George, you're all under arrest!" the lean man's voice rang out. Bellew wheeled around, blinking the sting from his eyes. Six men in the crowd threw off their cloaks, revealing the scarlet jackets beneath.

"Regulars," Bellew cursed, his heart racing.

All the redcoats held their pistols at the ready. Bellew's hand twitched for his powder horn, but he knew he didn't have time to reload. None of them did. That had been the point.

The crowd, nervous and excited, parted to make way for the regulars. Bellew and the other Continentals were surrounded in an instant.

"Hand over your guns, you damned rebels," one of them snarled in Bellew's face, eyeing him. "Like to pick us off, do you, rifleman?" His cheeks were raw from a dry shave. The redcoats must have been sleeping rough.

Bellew leveled a stare at the man. He said nothing. Nor did he move. The redcoat seemed happy to wait. Bellew could see the rage ticking upwards in tiny pulses behind the man's moist brown eyes. Bellew gritted his teeth. He had been fairly caught, and he must take the consequences of it. He steeled himself and thrust his rifle at the man. The redcoat yanked it away with a savage twist and turned to the next man. Bellew felt naked as well as shamed. His hand was cold where sweat from his grip dried in the autumn air.

"Picked a fine time to join up, didn't you, boys," the redcoat sneered at Cowles and jerked his chin further down the line at Jamie, the other new man. "I bet your mothers always told you you were smart and lucky, and now you know it's true." Cowles merely stared, trembling.

"What's going to happen," he said, blinking in confusion.

"What's happened is we're prisoners of war," Bellew said, but he only half-believed it. He felt like a fraud. If he'd enlisted as a regular soldier, he might have been in a battle by now, might actually have served the cause, might even have earned some of the glory he craved. But he'd been too proud not to be an officer, with the result that he'd spent his entire brief service parading around the countryside like a carnival performer and succeeded in nothing but getting himself and his comrades arrested without having fired a single shot at anything more significant than an apple.

"My name is Colonel August Anders," a middle-aged redcoat announced, stepping forward, though there was no mistaking his air of authority. He eyed them coolly and then approached O'Malley. "I believe you are the commanding officer here?"

"I am, sir," O'Malley replied stiffly. "Captain Samuel O'Malley."

Colonel Anders held out his hand. "Your commission, please?"

O'Malley hesitated briefly. He opened his jacket and pulled out a folded piece of parchment with slow movements. Bellew's mind flashed to Masterson and his knife. But that was stupid – there was no way even superb knife-throwing could buy them enough time to seize back their guns and reload them. And anyway, he now saw with regret, the knife had been confiscated too.

But perhaps the crowd – but no. Bellew flicked a glance at the people watching and saw they would find no help there. The women were hiding behind the men, and the men merely looked stunned. A few of them chuckled at a better show than they'd anticipated. A bitter taste filled Bellew's mouth. This, he decided, was what made soldiers hard. Not the battles so much. The cruel indifference of the people. He had offered his life and his name to this war. And in return – this. Failure and mockery.

Colonel Anders perused the commission down the length of his nose. He returned it to O'Malley, who tucked it back into his jacket pocket. Colonel Anders said, "It claims, Captain O'Malley, that you are a captain of infantry in the South Carolina militia upon raising a company of forty men. That was the purpose, ostensibly, of your actions here?"

"That was our general purpose, sir, yes."

"But it was not achieved, I take it?"

"No, sir." O'Malley took in a breath as if to say something else but evidently thought better of it.

Bellew felt a faint stirring of unexpected hope. Perhaps the technicality of not having raised their company would prevent their being classified as soldiers. It wasn't impossible that this cold-eyed Col. Anders would see matters with that rigid British sense of what was proper and what was not.

"Then you're all to be considered enlisted men," Col. Anders stated coolly. "Corporal Waxman, kindly bring these men's horses over here. We're to set off immediately."

"Excuse me, Colonel Anders," Cowles said in a shaking voice. "My horse ain't here. I can go and get her..."

"Those of you without horses can ride behind your...friends," Col. Anders replied. "The proximity may give you the opportunity to better consider your choice of acquaintance in the future." He turned away.

"Colonel Anders, sir!" O'Malley cried. Col. Anders twisted his head with one eyebrow arched in irritation. "May I ask where you're taking us?"

Col. Anders considered the question. Evidently he decided there was no harm in answering. "We're returning to headquarters in Philadelphia," he said. "Your former so-called capital, I understand. Although the population seemed precious glad to see us when we came, by my lights."

Chapter 8

Cowles sat behind Bellew, and O'Malley took Jamie on his horse. It made for awkward riding, but Bellew knew that O'Malley too felt painfully responsible for the new men.

The weather remained mild, as Col. Anders insisted they sleep in the open most nights. This dashed Bellew's hopes that some sympathetic town might help them effect an escape, but that the redcoats were suffering almost as much privation as the prisoners was some consolation.

It was two weeks' hard travel before they reached Philadelphia. Bellew smelled water on the wind before he saw the city, and it stirred his blood with vague thoughts of adventure that made his present captivity all the more bitter. Birds cried and wheeled in the air. He glanced into the sky. Gulls and ravens; specks of black and white against the icy blue.

The city was beautiful from a distance and only gained loveliness as they approached. It was far larger than town he had known. His mother had told him a few times about Charlestown, when she was younger and happier and then in the later, wandering months of her life, but Bellew had been only an infant when the ship had carried them here from Ireland and did not remember it himself. And Philadelphia was far more splendid than Charlestown, anyway. He was sure of it. He found himself staring at the tall buildings made of dark stone and the high white steeples of churches, crowned with crosses and weather-vanes, and even the narrow cobbled streets crowded with wooden shops and homes struck him as inexpressibly charming. Winter-bare trees stood everywhere, their dry branches clouds of brown bristle whispering in the breeze. He imagined how fine the streets would look in spring, long arcades of cool green, Nature's splendor nestling side-by-side with the grand stone creations of Man. It lacerated his heart to think of it in the hands of the English. If only some decent citizens would raze the place to the ground, as they had done in New-York.

Bellew found himself no less an object of interest to the passers-by than they were to himself. He did not recognize the fashions the women wore, round little hats perched atop their heads and skirts so full he wondered how they managed to sit. The men nodded and touched their hats respectfully as the redcoats went past. Their eyes flicked over the prisoners. Sympathy was rare, and Bellew learned quickly to keep his gaze to himself.

"All right, men, there's soft beds for you tonight, so let's move sharp," Col. Anders barked, and the redcoats needed no encouragement. But it seemed they did not know the way precisely, because Col. Anders spotted a corporal walking briskly in the other direction and bent down for a word. The corporal turned and pointed.

"The old sugar house is the closest prison, sir. You're almost there. Two streets over and a couple hundred yards farther along."

Bellew shared a glance with Masterson, who rode next to him. A sugar house was not an appealing prospect, but at least there would be a blanket and a meal, even if of poor stuff. Bellew's legs and back ached from too long on horseback, and the redcoats had been pretty stingy with sharing their food, claiming they hadn't been expecting to take a prize on their journey and were unprepared to feed them. Masterson had offered to trap some wild hares for all of them, but the redcoats had laughed and said they'd be blessed if they'd put a knife in his hands. Bellew knew the offer had been honest.

They turned their horses onto the next side-street, which took an unexpected twist but in the correct direction so that at the next intersection they found the sugar house almost directly before them. It was a large rectangular building with a peaked roof. All its windows save one had been covered with blacking. A guard of four bored soldiers stood outside the locked door, chatting with each other. They straightened when they saw Col. Anders and presented a salute, which Col. Anders returned with a nod.

"Do you have room for nine more?" he inquired.

The guards looked at each other uncertainly. "Well, sir, we took out two dead last night...but I'm not sure how much tighter we can pack 'em."

"We'd rather be done with this," Col. Anders snapped. "Do you have room for these prisoners or not?"

One guard shrugged and pulled a heavy ring with the key to the lock from his waist. The others stepped back and held their muskets with fixed bayonets at the ready.

The first guard pulled back one of the double doors. The hinges moved smoothly. It was too dark inside for Bellew to make out much past a row of thin, dirty men with beards standing surprisingly close to the entrance, as if they'd been waiting there. The prisoners blinked in the dim twilight.

"Sir, Colfax is dead," one of prisoners said in a soft voice before the guards could make a survey of the room. Perhaps that was why they'd been waiting at the door, to give the news about Colfax, the poor bastard.

"Right. Pass him out then." The guard gave an encouraging nod and lifted his eyebrows at Col. Anders, holding up three fingers. Col. Anders showed no sign of pleasure.

Shadowy movement rippled through the depths of the black room. It seemed the prisoners were moving the body along from man to man as in a fire-brigade rather than simply carrying him outside, which Bellew found odd. Perhaps it was a sign of respect somehow; every hand would touch the departed fellow at least once.

At last three prisoners in the front got hold of the departed Colfax, still covered in the filth of his final sickness, and stepped outside just far enough to lay the body down. They glanced up at the guards as if making sure they had not offended them.

"Lord God have mercy on us all," Bellew murmured. Colfax could not have been more than fifteen years old.

"All right, we've got him, back inside, hurry up now," the guard ordered. His face wore an expression of distaste. Bellew realized that it wasn't just the body that stank. It was the prisoners too. Not just the sharp musk of unbathed men, but a sweet, nauseating odor that clung to them and made Bellew's stomach twist.

Two of the prisoners complied meekly, but one clutched his hands together and bit his lip, holding his ground. "Get inside," the guard repeated with a warning note in his voice. The other guards firmed their grips on their muskets.

The prisoner spoke, his eyes low. "Sir – I beg your pardon, sir – it's just – I'd like to enlist with the regulars, sir. If the offer's still open, sir."

The first guard nodded. "Seen the error of your ways, have you?"

"Yes, sir," the prisoner said meekly.

"How dare you!" Bellew exploded in sudden rage, every muscle so tense it felt it might snap inside him. "How dare you, sir!"

All eyes turned to him. The prisoner hung his head low and turned slightly away. Bellew's face blazed. He could feel every hard, fast beat of his heart. That this miserable wretch should mock the cause, should mock the country, should mock the men who had give up their families and homes only to be imprisoned along with Bellew – if he had had one of the redcoat's bayonets, he would have run the traitor through like the dog he was.

"You had your chance with him," grinned the redcoat who'd taken Bellew's rifle. O'Malley flashed him a warning look, and Bellew clenched his jaw shut. He balled his hands into fists and focused on the pressure of his nails against his flesh. The traitor hunched his shoulders. He said nothing in his own defense.

"Well, that makes four we can take, then, sir," the guard said.

"What do you propose I do with the remainder?"

"Try the ships. At least one of them's sure to have space."

Col. Anders sighed, defeated. "All right. You four. Get off." He waved at Bellew, O'Malley, and their riders.

The guard blinked in surprise. "Officers, sir?"

"They're not officers, they just like to dress like them. And I'd like to save their horses if I could. They've borne up well under the burden. A few days' rest, and I think they'll be fit for service."

"They are good-looking animals, sir," the guard replied.

So Bellew waited for Cowles to slide from the back of the horse, and then he dismounted himself. He made sure not to show how wearied he was from the ride. The lobster-backs would see that the real Continental Army had plenty of spirit and vigor. They were welcome to their traitor recruit, and he hoped they would take satisfaction in his inestimable services.

"In you go, then," said the guard.

Bellew and the three others murmured quick good-byes to their companions, and he stroked his horse's neck a final time. He strode forward, shoulders straight, through the redcoats and towards the crowd of prisoners. The cloying reek that had been bad enough when he'd caught only a whiff of it surrounded him. Bellew's throat spasmed, and he swallowed quickly to cover it.

The prisoners watched with tired faces. But they would not move to let the new men past. Bellew and the others were forced to stop on the very threshold. "Excuse us, please," O'Malley said politely after a moment, but the men remained where they stood, as if they were cattle.

"If you'll just let us get a little farther in, you can have your place by the door," Bellew said. Perhaps they had been offended by his outrage somehow, though he imagined they more would have shared it than otherwise. But perhaps the traitor had been a friend of theirs.

"Move in," the guard said. "Move in. Come on there, look sharp."

The crowd did not give them any room. At last the guard grunted in annoyance, and the door slammed shut, bumping Bellew forward a step that put him directly in a prisoner's face. The lock clanked shut, and the heavy chain thudded against the door.

"Again, sir, if you'll just step aside, I will be happy to cede you your place," Bellew repeated, trying to keep the edge out of his voice. Was the man deaf?

"Yes sir, only there's nowhere for me to go," the prisoner murmured, speaking softly and turning his head to the side so that he did not breathe directly in Bellew's face. "Wait till your eyes get used to the light. You'll see."

And as Bellew's eyes adjusted to the thin illumination from the one clear window in the back, he slowly made out the contents of the room. The great vats used for sugar-refinery had been removed. Everything had been removed. Everything except the men. All Bellew could see was a sea of heads, packed tight like goods in a crate, from wall to wall. There were hundreds of them, in a space where fifty would have made an awkward crowd. Each prisoner stood quietly in his place. Nothing else was possible here. Bellew's mouth opened, but he found he had no words.

"Jesus, Mary, and Joseph," O'Malley breathed.

"We take turns sitting," the prisoner said. "You're just in, so you won't be up for a while."

"Is there a container of sorts, for...for necessaries?" Cowles asked. Bellew could feel him tremble, pressed against Bellew's arm.

A few of the prisoners snorted mirthlessly. "Go on and do it on the door. Maybe the guards'll take it for the fine salute it is."

"I don't want to offend them unnecessarily..." Cowles began, but the prisoner interrupted him.

"The door's the best you're going to be able to do," he said, flat with resignation. "It doesn't matter. Anywhere's as bad as anywhere else. Sometimes they wash the place out when they let us walk in the yard, but in general it's best not to think too much about the floor. We've got at least twenty men with the bloody flux."

"Colfax was one of them," Bellew murmured, remembering the boy's stained form.

"Aye."

The smell alone was close to making Bellew sick, let alone the risk of contagion. He would simply have to trust in God and the strength of his constitution, having no other options.

He noticed to his surprise that a prisoner near him had his hands cupped to his face and seemed to be chewing on something. The prisoner whimpered as he ate. Bellew supposed he would whimper whenever he had to eat in here too.

"It seems we've missed supper, but that's just as well," he said bitterly. "I've no appetite."

Several men shook their heads grimly. "Don't get supper here. Only a bit of spoiled raw pork or wormy biscuit ever' now and then, but not today."

"You can't mean they don't even feed us!" Bellew cried. He no longer fully believed he was awake. A hell like this could be the product only of a fevered dream – reality was cruel sometimes, and base often, but never, never so utterly vicious. And nothing he had seen of the English had given him cause to expect such treatment. His mind raced for an explanation. Found none. "Hasn't someone anyone contacted the Commissary of Prisoners?"

The man in Bellew's face snorted. "It's possible that the redcoats are stealing from Commissioner Loring," he said. "But in general we think it's more likely that they're in it together."

"Not an American," Cowles said in a hesitant voice.

"Oh, he's one of ours all right," the prisoner replied dully.

"That man must have saved his food, then," Bellew said, lifting his chin towards the chewing prisoner. "Laudable foresight. Though if rations are as tight as you say, I'm not sure I'll be able to show the same forbearance."

The prisoner glanced over in the direction of Bellew's gaze. He flattened his mouth. "Well, Jaspers has got will enough for ten men and more nerve than I, I'll give him that." A grim note gave the compliment a half-hearted air at best. Bellew frowned. The prisoner lowered his voice further. "He's been in here longer than me. He's eating his finger."

For a moment, Bellew did not understand, so the prisoner explained further. "He's eating his finger. Right off his hand."

The whimpering.

Blind rage rose in Bellew. He closed his eyes, waiting for the hot waters to recede. He knew his fury had no home here. If he beat the door, the guards would ignore it or laugh. And if he shouted or cursed, he would punish no one other than the people around him, who had enough suffering to bear. But at least the rage covered the horror and the fear. The powerlessness.

Which brought him back to rage again.

He kept himself still. Breathed slowly. Like focusing before a shot.

"How can you do that?" Cowles wailed. He made no effort to keep his voice low. "How can you just...how can you eat the flesh off your own bone?"

"He'd a cut it off if he could a had a knife," another prisoner put in.

"Man gets hungry, you'll be surprised what he'll eat. That's not the worst I've seen," the prisoner in front of Bellew said.

Jaspers's eyes flicked over to the conversation. He knew he was being talked about, and he didn't like it. He bent his head below the level of his shoulder and continued gnawing.

"He'll bleed to death!"

"He wraps the stump in a rag when he's done. It's worked so far."

"The same one over and over?"

"It's as clean as anything else in here. And I swear to you, sir – I have always thought myself a proud man, but if Jaspers throws away that bloody rag of his, I will snatch it up from the floor and suck it dry, and God help any man who stands in my way."

Chapter 9

Rachel loved Philadelphia, and she loved the beautiful house the Addisons took there. A three-story town home made of gray stone, it had pride of place on an elm-lined street with other houses Rachel would have thought were inexpressibly fine if she had not had the honor of living in something better. She was starting to realize how very rich the Addisons were. At each crisp new dawn in the finest city in any of the colonies when Rachel woke with the softness of a plump featherbed molded around her body in the bed she had to herself, she marveled anew at her good fortune.

She wasted no time in proving herself indispensable as a maid. She took delight in washing the windows until they sparkled, even the tight corners around the leading. She thought the parquet floors were far too delicate to scrub with a holystone, so she wiped them with rags to a golden shine. Because she did not know how to clean the silk that covered the chairs and divans, she waited early one morning behind one of the neighboring houses and humbly asked the maid there for advice when she emerged. Rachel did not want to disappoint the Addisons. But also, she hated to think that she might spoil even a tiny corner of the beauty of the wonderful mansion and its furnishings by an ignorant mistake. The owners had even left their library behind; but while Rachel dusted the long rows of leather spines twice a week without fail, she did not have time to read books now with the size of the house and the variety of her duties within it.

"What a diligent little thing it is," Mrs. Addison remarked and announced to her husband that with the slaves to take care of the heavy work, all they lacked was a decent permanent cook. Rachel's skill at this art was sadly limited – what had sufficed for the raider's family most assuredly did not go over well here – but the Addisons did not seem to hold it against her, particularly as they dined out most evenings. Rachel had learned by now how to do Mrs. Addison's hair properly, teasing it and powdering it to a silvery cloud surrounding the oval of face, and Mrs. Addison found the results acceptable.

But what made Rachel's heart almost burst with joy was the continued friendship shown to her by her employer, even with boredom of the long journey behind them. She was not a failure as a companion after all. Mrs. Addison frequently asked Rachel to sit in the room when company visited, and even took her along when Mrs. Addison went calling on her numerous friends. Rachel had two new dresses of imported fabric, one rose and one blue, to wear for these occasions, and a good woolen cloak. If anyone considered it odd that Mrs. Addison should have her maid as a companion, they did not mention it; but neither did they speak to Rachel much. This was more a relief than otherwise. She usually did not know the people and events of which they spoke. She was much happier just watching and listening to the others and having them forget she was there, which never took long.

After they bundled themselves back into the carriage and started away, Mrs. Addison would turn to Rachel conspiratorially and ask her, "Well, and what do you think of Caroline Haughton?" or whatever other person or event had struck Mrs. Addison's fancy, and then Rachel had her chance to speak.

"I believe Mrs. Haughton is trying to compensate for getting long in tooth by pretending she's still in short curls."

Mrs. Addison would laugh and clasped her hands in amusement, and Rachel would glow with pride. "Yes, she does act a little girl, doesn't she – I hadn't thought of that. Yes, that's Caroline to a T."

It did not take Rachel long to learn that her more cutting remarks were better received. When they gossiped in the carriage heading home, the horses' hooves clattering smartly against the street and the sights of the city flashing by the window while they sat snug and safe inside, Rachel pretended sometimes that she really belonged here, that she was no servant but that Mrs. Addison was a dear older sister of hers who had married well. But when the carriage arrived at their own door at last and the conversation had to end, Rachel hurried inside without waiting for Abraham to hand her out, and she worked twice as hard at the cleaning the rest of the day to make up for her presumptuous fantasies. Mr. Addison seemed to take advantage of his wife's absences to smoke heavily, and Mrs. Addison didn't like the smell of it in the upholstery, so Rachel had more than ample opportunity to expiate her guilt.

Rachel's wages were as generous as Mrs. Addison had promised, and she might have saved up enough for a little shop in a year or two, except that she no longer had any such desire. She could not imagine anything more splendid than living with the Addisons forever in their glittering world. It was a shame that Mrs. Addison did not have any children. But she was not so much older than Rachel, only six years. Perhaps there would be children yet. And even if not, it was not unreasonable to hope that the position might last the rest of Rachel's life, as Rachel did indeed hope with all her heart. At night, when she said her prayers, she would always add, "And please let Mrs. Addison have everything she desires, and to live longer than me. I know You know my heart and see the selfishness there, but I love her so much more than she loves me, so I am not asking her to bear more than a little discomfort at my passing, while my desolation would be complete."

Rachel did not know how Mr. Addison spent most of his days, but his nights were devoted to card-playing, a pastime his wife did not seem to find particularly agreeable. "I am long past telling him that it's boring," Mrs. Addison confided one day in Mr. Addison's earshot.

"Nothing that involves money can be entirely dull, my dear," Mr. Addison replied absently.

"Well, try to get in early enough that you can wake at a decent hour tomorrow." A decent hour to Mrs. Addison did not mean before eleven o'clock in the morning, unless special considerations intervened.

"I assume you have a purpose in this request," Mr. Addison remarked, curious enough to look up from the overdone meat at which he had been scraping with limited success. Rachel could cook breakfast-foods, which Mrs. Addison disdained and Mr. Addison rarely woke for, and she could boil a good stew, but that was heavy food for laborers and not deemed acceptable.

"Mrs. Loring has invited us to visit after luncheon." When this did not appear to impress Mr. Addison much, his wife continued, "She is receiving her guests at General Howe's."

Mr. Addison's eyebrows ticked upward in surprise. "Ah! I see. Well, very good, then. Will it run late?"

"No, there's nothing official about it. Just a gathering of friends," Mrs. Addison said. "Still, I thought you might like to get a little business in."

"Could speed things up considerably. General Howe's a good sort. Thank you, my dear," Mr. Addison replied.

Mrs. Addison turned her head. "Oh, good, Rachel, you're still hovering. Wear your rose dress tomorrow. It's more the English style."

"Yes, ma'am," Rachel said, and hurried into the kitchen to finish her errand. Her mind buzzed with excitement. General Howe was not only the commander of all the army in the colonies, he was the younger brother to an actual lord. Her thoughts tangled with confused images of being seen in such illustrious company and impressing General Howe and finding out some tidbit of information that would prove indispensable to Lieutenant Bellew, to his undying gratitude. She knew it was all silly, if for no other reason than that she knew she would not see Lieutenant Bellew again. The Continentals had built their winter quarters in the wilderness outside Philadelphia and would hardly risk coming into town. And Rachel knew that she would not learn anything from Mrs. Loring's salon other than who was most in favor in society, and that she could not willingly pass on information that would get anyone hurt or killed anyway. But she took pleasure in the thought nevertheless. Because she knew it was nothing but a fantasy, she could indulge herself. She would be a triumph with General Howe and Lieutenant Bellew alike – the details remained pleasantly foggy.

The new day could not come soon enough. Rachel stayed up late to clean her shoes and woke before the sun to make sure her chores were in order.

Mrs. Addison wore her yellow silk with the three-quarter length sleeves. Rachel hurried to get her ready before changing into her rose dress and tying up her own hair in a knot with one strand dangling down the side, which Mrs. Addison had told her was appropriate for a respectable-looking background person.

It was only a brief carriage-ride, and walking would have been a good deal less inconvenient, but Rachel was glad they were not taking any chances with a stray splash of mud or gust of wind to disorder their careful attire. Mr. Addison, who very rarely troubled about such things, wore his best day-suit and a tidy wig Rachel had not seen before.

General Howe's home was no less excellent than the Addisons' but busier, with a smart guard of two men standing in attendance at the door. Rachel remembered how gentlemanly the regulars had been at the Brass Bull, and she hazarded a shy smile at the guard as she passed them. One man smiled back, his blue eyes crinkling slightly at the corners. But he kept his eyes straight ahead so as not to spoil the fineness of his appearance.

Another uniformed soldier ushered them through a cool entrance hall into the warmth of a broad, comfortable parlor where eight people in splendid dress sat chatting.

"Margaret! I was afraid you'd forgotten me!" a delicate blonde cried in a high-pitched voice, rising to her feet and extending her hands. If anyone could have rivaled Mrs. Addison's beauty, it was this exquisite creature shining in blue silk and gold trinkets. Rachel was glad that Mrs. Addison had told her to wear the rose dress, which suited her better, but she still felt acutely what a shabby thing she was in comparison. She slid backward half a step so that she would be more completely eclipsed.

"Oh, there was some trouble with the carriage, I'm so sorry," Mrs. Addison replied, accepting Mrs. Loring's hands and smiling. Rachel knew very well that Mrs. Addison did not like to arrive anywhere too early, and since she recognized a few faces in the room, she supposed that pretty well everyone else knew it too.

Rachel curtsied politely and kept her eyes low as Mrs. Addison made an off-handed introduction to her companion. But she peeked through her lashes to examine the main object of her curiosity, the famous General Howe.

He proved rather a disappointment at first glance. He had the heavy build of a professional soldier, but it was the coarseness of his face that surprised her most. His eyes had a slight bulge, and his broad nose and thick lips gave him the appearance of a potato-farmer more than the son of a lord. He smiled kindly enough at their entrance, though, and after he rose and bowed to Mrs. Addison, he said, "Addison. Good to see you again. Just the man I need," which Rachel took well on Mr. Addison's part.

Once the Addisons settled themselves, the conversation resumed. Rachel did not find much of interest in it, platitudes and pleasantries as bright and insubstantial as tinsel about a world that was not Rachel's own. It was the ladies who carried most of it forward while the men sipped their drinks. Of more interest than what they said was watching the people themselves. Rachel had not paid much attention at first when Mrs. Addison had said that Mrs. Loring would be holding her salon at General

Howe's house, but a niggling doubt began to creep into her thoughts. Mr. Loring was present, as ill-looking a person as General Howe but in a small, mean way that Rachel found herself disliking, to her chagrin. He laughed too quickly and too loud at General Howe's remarks, most of which Rachel did not think were intended as jokes, and he seemed quite content that his wife sat next to the General and leaned towards her neighbor fondly while Mr. Loring himself was consigned to a solitary chair by the door.

"Sherry, miss?" Rachel startled and realized a soldier stood politely to the side holding a small crystal glass of amber liquid.

"Thank you," she murmured, blushing slightly as she accepted the unfamiliar drink. She took a quick sip to cover her confusion. Sweetness with a pleasing aftertaste of burnt wood spread through her mouth, and her nervousness began to dissipate. No one paid the slightest attention to her, after all, so she was perfectly safe. She doubted they even remembered her name, and that was even better.

"Mr. Loring. I'm so pleased you were able to take time away from your duties today," Mrs. Haughton remarked in a sugary voice. She wore more powder on her face than her hair, and Rachel supposed she was trying to get attention from the only man in the room who might be inclined to give it to her. "I imagine the winter hiatus is an unimaginable relief to you."

Mr. Loring shrugged. "We still get new prisoners. Not as many in this season, but it's no small matter, I assure you, to keep track of them all. I am much pressed, much pressed." He took a sip of sherry.

"Still new prisoners?" Mrs. Haughton exclaimed. "For heaven's sake. I can't imagine what's possessing people."

"There are a few odd lots in any parcel, madam."

"Yes, but *honestly*," Mrs. Haughton persisted. She turned to Mrs. Addison, and Rachel could tell by the spiteful quirk at the corner of her mouth that she was preparing some sort of dig. "Margaret, we all imagine you must have some *particular* insight into the thought processes of these people in the insurgency. What on earth possesses them to take on such a ridiculous and harmful course of action, even when it's clear it's already all over?"

Rachel was not sure what Mrs. Haughton meant by this, though it seemed from the general stiffening that others in the room did. Rachel grew cold, though a small coal of anger burned in her stomach. Her Mrs. Addison was being slapped. Rachel had recognized the spite lurking beneath Mrs. Haughton's saccharine manner long before, and she longed to leap up and say so at once. But it was not her place, and would have been highly improper even if it were, unless she and Mrs. Haughton were both suddenly transformed into men.

Mrs. Addison, however, did not seem to feel the need for rescue. She smiled faintly and dropped the lids of her eyes a fraction, tilting back her head. "I would say," she answered coolly, "it proves only that inanition, like any vacuum, possesses a type of motive power."

"Oh! Well said!" Mrs. Loring exclaimed happily and clapped. The men lifted from their apathy in surprise. The rest of the room followed Mrs. Loring's example and applauded lightly, even General Howe, who had to put down his sherry to do so. Mrs. Haughton had to endure it, and she clapped silently along with the others.

"Margaret, you are always infinitely surprising. I did not realize you were a wit as well as a beauty. You could terrify the French by beating them at their own game!"

"No doubt it's what's holding them at bay."

"I had no idea your wife had such a scientific turn of mind. We have our own Dr. Franklin, and ours is prettier." Mr. Addison smiled and shrugged at the praise of his wife.

Rachel pressed her hands together around the stem of her glass. She was not sure whether it would be proper for her to clap or not. She felt a flush creeping up her cheeks and over her ears, and she hoped it wasn't noticeable. She could not believe that her comment, something she had thought of herself, could be so well-received by such fine people. She turned to Mrs. Addison and smiled, feeling a gratitude she knew she could never repay. But Mrs. Addison merely sipped her sherry, accepting her triumph with composure, and did not look to the side.

The subject of the rebellion having been dealt with, the conversation turned to hats. Mr. Loring was alone of the men in making a game effort to engage the topic.

General Howe leaned over the intervening Mrs. Loring and murmured to Mr. Addison, "Can you spare a moment?"

Mr. Addison nodded, and Rachel knew him well enough to read the muted pleasure on his face.

General Howe stood. "Ladies, if you will excuse Mr. Addison and myself a few minutes, we need to handle a bit of business."

"Oh, business! In the afternoon, yet!"

General Howe bowed. "Madam, we are not only sensible of the great care you take with these sartorial matters but more appreciative than you know of their fine results. However, our own less gentle matters exact their due, and we must attend to them at times." Rachel found herself, rather to her surprise, impressed by the civility of his manner. He didn't seem ugly any more, and she felt sorry for her initial impression.

Mrs. Loring looked anxiously at her friend but apparently was satisfied that he meant no rebuke by his absence, upon which she seemed to forget about the General entirely. Mr. Loring rose slightly when General Howe left as if he meant to move beside his wife, but he must have thought better of it, because he sat down again quickly enough. Rachel considered it wise of him, if he meant to maintain any appearance of self-respect.

She took a second sherry when it was offered and had grown quite comfortable on her chair when Mrs. Haughton struck again, seeking a weaker target this time.

"You know, Margaret, practically every time I've seen you, you've had that girl with you, and I don't think I've heard her utter a peep. What was your name again, dear?"

All eyes turned to her. Rachel felt her glass slip in her hand, and she clutched it tighter. "My name is Rachel Kolkhorst, ma'am," she managed to say. She barely recognized her own voice.

"What a peculiar thing to be called. Are you married to one of our Hessians? It seems to me I heard one of them called by that name. A horrible, hulking brute with braided mustaches down to here." She gestured to the middle of her plump body and uttered a brittle laugh. "Although I'm sure he seems otherwise to you. Eyes of love and all that."

Rachel blinked. "I'm afraid I don't know the person in question, ma'am. My father was Prussian."

"Oh," Mrs. Haughton said. "Well, what are you doing in this country precisely, then?"

Rachel frowned, confused. The soldiers had a purpose in being in this country, she supposed, but what was hers? She had simply been born here, and there was nothing more to it than that. "Whatever God wills of me, ma'am," she said blankly.

There was a brief uncomfortable pause. "Ye-es, a most salutary attitude, and I'm sure the Lord will give it all the attention it deserves," Mrs. Haughton purred in satisfaction.

"I never think of the deity as being particularly detail-oriented," Mr. Loring put in, earning a grateful glance from Mrs. Haughton that gave him the heart to continue, "As an administrator myself –"

"Good heavens, we aren't going to discuss religion, please," Mrs. Loring said, and Mr. Loring fell quiet.

After a second miserable silence, the group's attention turned thankfully to other matters as Rachel stared at her lap in humiliation. She dared not meet Mrs. Addison's eyes after having proved herself publicly sententious and vapid. It was all the worse that Rachel had come here under Mrs. Addison's protection and therefore reflected upon her, in some small way. But the older woman slipped her hand over Rachel's and gave it a brief squeeze.

No one spoke to Rachel again, and she did not want to drink more sherry, since her head was quite light enough. Her brief and unsatisfactory encounter with Mrs. Haughton had given her a distaste for this company, and the time passed slowly.

Mrs. Addison seemed restless too. A clock chimed, and she glanced up with an expression of surprise that Rachel knew was feigned. "Good heavens, is it four o'clock? Betsey, I should be very angry at you for making the hours go so quickly. Robert and I should have left half an hour ago."

"Oh, my word, I need to get ready for supper myself," Mrs. Loring replied. "What on earth is the General doing with your husband?"

"Probably smoking cigars and playing cards. When men talk about needing to do business, I find that's what's usually involved."

"General Howe does retain some of the less fortunate habits of a military career," Mrs. Loring sighed.

"I doubt he's got much to teach Robert." Mrs. Addison twisted around. "I don't see your man. Rachel, could you go upstairs and pull Robert out of his terribly important business? We're late as it is."

Rachel nodded and rose quickly, curtsying to the room. The blood drained from her head, and for a moment she was not sure she would be able to keep her feet under her. She was not sure precisely how much sherry she had drunk. It had given her something to do with her hands, and so the answer was probably far too much. But she managed to keep her balance and get out of the room somehow, brushing past Mr. Loring. Even he didn't bother to acknowledge her. The conversation continued without Rachel and did not seem to miss her much.

She did not know her way around this house, but she could not imagine it would be difficult to find the men. She returned to the entrance hall and started up the broad stairs. Footsteps clattered above her, and Rachel froze. A soldier's long legs appeared, trotting rapidly. Rachel pressed herself against the wall and opened her dry mouth to explain that she was on an errand, but the soldier merely brought himself up short when he saw her and smiled.

"Pardon me, miss." He bobbed his head and continued at a more proper pace.

Once her heart wasn't beating so fast, Rachel thought she might ask the soldier where the study was, but he was already whisked through the front door, off on his own business.

She climbed the rest of the stairs and looked both ways down the dark corridor. A small knot of soldiers spoke in low tones at the far end to the right, so deeply involved in their conversation that they did not notice Rachel's gaze. She lowered her eyes anyway, and walked to the left.

The air bore a faint, cloying whiff of sweet cigar-smoke, and Rachel, encouraged, followed it until she recognized Mr. Addison's voice from behind a door that hung slightly ajar, as if its bolt had failed to catch.

"I'll confess to you, General, I don't like the image of bayonets in the hands of those Godless Hessians."

"Neither do the locals," General Howe's slightly fainter voice replied. "That's what gives it particular importance."

The door to the study stood before her. Rachel raised her hand to knock. And yet she hesitated. She found herself suddenly quite intensely interested in the conversation and did not want to end it prematurely. She glanced nervously at the soldiers. One of them gestured roughly with his hand, and her heart stuttered, but she realized they still had not noticed her and were only deeply involved with their own discussion.

"Well. I can get you a thousand by next month easily," Mr. Addison replied.

"Remarkable."

"I have men in St. Croix."

"Ah. I was supposing that you had some magic to make horses ride over the waters of the Atlantic and blow away the storms with a puff from their nostrils." Rachel had not realized that General Howe had such an imaginative turn of mind, and she found herself warming to him further.

"Would that I did, sir. I'd have them puff away the extremists for you first, and I imagine that would simplify your life considerably."

There was a pause before General Howe replied. "It's a damned tricky business, Robert, but I suppose it will be good for yours. I've got fools and rascals teetering on one side of the beam at home and rascals and fools bouncing on the other side of the beam here. If I could dash both extremes to bits at once, the matter could be over in weeks. But there's only one I can destroy, and I'm afraid doing so would be an incalculable disaster. That army of theirs, that mob, is no impediment, for the love of Christ. But if I swat it out of the way, what are we left? The true maniacs, of which there are far too many, clogging up the legislatures and performing rifle assassinations from behind trees. And that, Robert, is a truly endless prospect, whose view terminates only with the annihilation of the colonies, like burning a house down for a single rotted shingle. It's a fine land here, and fine people, mostly. A loyal people. And I must, must treat them accordingly. It is my duty to protect, not obliterate them. No one wants to destroy them, except the mad. And the mad are held in check only as long as they believe we are fighting a proper army that will yield to a proper battle - which is simply not the case."

"Most people are not so intransigent, I am sure," Mr. Addison said politely.

"They are not; but too many are. They feel badly used and bloody unappreciated by the colonies. And the few that want to punish our sons and daughters here rather than bring them back into the fold speak loudly and carry their weight hard."

"Reasonable men tend to speak at a reasonable volume, and unreasonable men et cetera. An unfortunate fact of life."

Rachel blinked in astonishment. She had not known Mr. Addison's views, other than that they were vaguely Tory, but to hear General Howe speak as bitterly of the English who surely supported his efforts more than anyone as he did of the rebellion itself was an amazement to her.

General Howe continued in a voice low with repressed passion, "But I would give my eyeteeth to wipe out this insurgency before the poison spreads further. If only in conscience I could."

"Perhaps it would be better," Mr. Addison suggested. "You would have no specter of armed rebels with which to frighten the extremists, but you might find that the absence of organized resistance would soften everyone's high tone."

"It did not previously."

"No," Mr. Addison said after a pause. "It did not."

The discussion farther down the hall ended, and the soldiers separated. Rachel raised her trembling hand to knock once more. But two of the men went down the stairs without paying her any mind, and the other two entered a room at their own end of the hall. The door shut behind them with a soft thump.

Rachel held her damp hand still.

"And what did that high tone bring them? It brought them the dead bodies of my men at Breed's Hill, Robert. No. The only path through this swamp is through the middle, because the opposing boundaries have grown too wide and too far to skirt. But it'll be a damned slow slog. I aim to tire them out. All of them. And I'll do it, too. My men are the finest in the world. They'll stay the course if it's a month or a year or a century. These bloody-minded screaming idiots shrieking *independency* or *destroy the Americas* aren't likely to be able to say the same. I'll let 'em shout at each other until they're hoarse, and that'll keep 'em occupied, and then we'll bring matters back into more reasonable line."

Rachel had never given the matter much thought, but she had always imagined that generalship involved little more than a minute knowledge of artillery-fire and the speed at which horses could run over grass or hill or roads and the rate at which muskets could be loaded. New ideas whizzed through her brain like a flock of birds trapped in a room.

"I hear they're starving themselves out at Valley Forge."

"Pretty quickly, too. Typical of their planning. Typical of the planning of all these radical sorts. And typical in the way it gets men killed. General Washington was a tolerable surveyor, I hear, but far from the finest officer we've had from the colonials, although certainly one of the touchier ones. The man started the Seven Years' War through his imprudence, for God's sake. I'll waste no tears when he's hanged." There was a pause, and General Howe continued in a gentler voice, "Of course, there will be less stern accommodation made for less symbolic participants in this foolishness. This...inanition. It's a pity that your wife's good sense does not seem to have come from her father. In fact, it's a pity that your wife's good sense can't be transmitted to all the colonials."

"By far the vast majority here..."

"Are reasonable men. Yes, they are. They're loyal subjects, and it is my duty and honor to protect them."

Rachel did knock then, and when Mr. Addison opened the door with a thin, brown cigar in his hand a visible fog of smoke drifted out with him. General Howe's eyes flicked over Rachel briefly, showing no interest. She transmitted Mrs. Addison's message, and General Howe nodded his dismissal.

On the brief carriage ride home, Mr. Addison was silent and thoughtful while Mrs. Addison tried to console Rachel for Mrs. Haughton's attack. "It really says something about her character, doesn't it, Rachel? I mean, you're obviously not society. She might as well insult Jacob's intelligence as yours."

"It's all right," Rachel said. "I have said some unkind things about her, after all."

"Well, you're taking it in awfully good part," Mrs. Addison replied in surprise. "In fact, you look quite happy. I didn't think you'd brush it off so well."

Rachel would not have brushed it off at all, except that she held a glowing secret so deliciously warm in her heart that it drove all other thoughts from her mind. In a way, her every unreasonable hope for the salon had been achieved, except that she herself should be admired, which had been a wholly unworthy aspiration that shamed her to remember anyway. Her aphorism had been a success, and she had found out a bit of intelligence that could help or even, she dared to hope, save Lieutenant Bellew. And it would do so without costing any lives or causing new pain and difficulty to General Howe, whose character Rachel esteemed more and more upon reflection.

At last there was something she could do, and Rachel meant to do it.

Chapter 10

"Miss Rachel? Miss Rachel?" Rachel looked up from her tiny desk by the window. Only a faint twilight filtered through its panes, and it took her eyes a moment to focus on Jacob standing hesitantly at her door in the grainy shadow of evening. She had not lit a candle.

"Miss Rachel, you want me to set out the master and the missus's bedrooms? You ain't done it yet."

"Oh!" Rachel placed the inky quill carefully to the side of the foolscap and flexed her cramped hand. She hadn't realized how late it had gotten, and she was behind.

Jacob shook his head and took a step forward. "I only mean I'd be glad to help and do it myself, since you's so involved in something." He took another step and craned his neck, unwilling to come any closer. He was already inside her room. "What is it?"

"I'm writing something for the newspaper," Rachel said proudly and pushed back her chair. The floor squeaked. "You can look at it if you like."

Jacob advanced in hesitant steps, which gave Rachel more than enough time to strike a spark and light a candle so that he could see in the dim light. He peered over her shoulder.

"Here," Rachel said, shuffling through papers. She plucked out a sheet with inky fingers. "This is where the final copy starts."

Jacob pinched it gingerly by the edges and held it up to his face. He looked at her with wide eyes. "The papers like Mr. Addison reads?"

"Exactly like the papers Mr. Addison reads. I'm going to give this to the *Sentinel-Observer.*"

"That one's his favorite." Jacob peered at the sheet a few moments and then handed it back as if it were a piece of spun glass he was afraid he might crush.

"Do you want to see the next page?" Rachel asked.

"You got real pretty handwriting."

"Not really," Rachel laughed. "I was just careful with the copying. But what do you think of what it says?"

Jacob hesitated. "You been talking to Abraham." Rachel looked at him blankly. "He's always getting at me, Jacob, you better learn to read, Jacob, you ain't no good if you can't even tell what the sign says and someday the master's gonna ask to go to the hat shop and you gonna take him to the Red Rooster by mistake. Only that ain't so, cause they always got pictures on the signs, and I ain't never yet seen a picture so bad it made a rooster look like a hat. And anyway, I don't think Abraham reads too good his self, I heard some fellas laugh at him one day when he was soundin' out the words, and I don't think I got no cause to make people laugh at me." He glanced down and fidgeted. "I'm real sorry I can't read this, though."

She had not meant to embarrass him, not Jacob of all people. "I can read it to you, if you like," Rachel said. "It isn't the reading that's the important part. I just wanted to know what you thought."

Jacob's face brightened. "All right," he said.

So Rachel tilted the first sheet nervously towards the window and began to read.

A Maid of Philadelphia Speaks

These are perilous times, dark days that touch every one of us, great and small. And because even the most insignificant of us is affected by them, it gives even the weak the right to speak and be heard candidly on these matters that affect our well-being so intimately down to the most minute matters of our day-to-day existence. Thus I beg your indulgence for a moment as I put down my kettle and take up my pen.

The honest gentlemen who read this paper perhaps do not imagine that the weaker sex is troubled much by the storm that swallowed our land. Politics, you may rightly claim, is the province of men, while ours is the home. And yet I assure you this storm has struck our homes, and not merely the plucked finer chords that sing in the hearts of men. It has struck the food we do not find to place on the table to feed our families, the brothers lost to battles, the fears for our safety from the predations of a transient soldiery as we lie in our beds at night. And thus we rouse ourselves from our hearths to examine the causes of this contest, and with gentle hands to press back the dangerous flame that threatens to consume us before all is lost: our tables, our brothers, our honor, and even our very lives.

England strikes a single note. She asks her colonies to honor their loyalty to the land where their blood first quickened to life. You have a King, she says, and you have a government that is the admiration of the world. These are at your service even unto death, as the too-recent conflict with the Indians and the French has proved. Even good men are only men after all, and not every law is just, nor every ordinance fitting. But the government corrects itself when it has erred; and that is part of the world's admiration for it. Give your government and your King, England says, the right to rule justly, even if not perfectly, and may we share our blessings and our joys with one another for all the time that God allows.

The insurgency, meanwhile, makes so many and so varied demands and claims that we scarce know where to begin. It claims we should not have to pay taxes on paper, because this is an INTERNAL tax. The hated internal tax is rescinded; then the rebels claim that we should not have to pay EXTERNAL taxes either, and even when some of these taxes are rescinded, they dump an entire shipload of tea into the water in an act any mother or sister will recognize as a spiteful tantrum. So our government is to levy neither internal nor external taxes upon us, and yet is to remain obliged to protect us from the incursions of the Indians at our every border, to hold back the pirates and French threatening our shores, to build our roads and buildings, to provide relief to the helpless, to staff our courts with educated men who can settle the disputes that arise naturally between citizens in the course of their affairs. And yet the government is to do all this without a single penny torn from our clenched fists. Perhaps the government is supposed to be a chameleon, that can live upon the air. Again, I tell you, my sisters and I recognize the petulance of a child who eats his dinner without wondering where it came from, and who sulks when he does not get a cake even when he has not seen fit to do his lessons or complete his simple chores.

At first, the uprising held that it wanted only an open ear to its opinions. While this was still in process, the uprising opened their throats wider and demanded furthermore that they receive redress for their grievances, whether real or phantasm, without further discussion of their merits. And when these redresses had begun to be offered, these dissenters, drunk on the sound of their own voices, insisted that no compensation was enough (it might be more accurate to say that no compensation would have been FAIR) and that they would settle for nothing less than their own representation in the Parliament they so maligned. And this matter had barely even begun to be discussed before these noble and judicious creatures, who clamored so loud and so long to be heard themselves, refused to hear what their government would reply and shrieked that nothing would do but a full separation be effected at once, and that the colonies – they spoke for all of us, and I for one was not asked – required complete INDEPENDENCE. What they will ask for next, I fear to guess.

A child who is given treats to stop his screaming learns quickly enough that screaming means candy, but he does not see that a diet of candy will make him sicken and die.

The insurrection claims that the freedom of men is its overarching goal, and my sisters and I applaud the sentiment in the company of the rest of mankind. And yet upon a moment's reflection, the doubts grow louder than the applause. England has a long tradition of liberty, and it is made flesh in the Parliament, which is elected to counterbalance the possible danger of a whimsical or unjust monarch, so that such a King's hand would be stayed before it fell upon the neck of the people. One would think that Parliament would be the rebels' natural ally. And yet what, I must ask, what was the first object of their reproach? Was it a hereditary monarch? No. It was the Parliament that these dissatisfied men attacked with insult and resentment. And to whom did they apply for aid? To the King, whom they begged to overrule the elected servants of Parliament. The hearts of men guide their actions; and the hearts of THESE men clearly inclined towards the lightning-blast intercession of arbitrary fiat, rather than the noble and deliberative process of objective law. They claim freedom as their guiding star, and perhaps they believe it in the boiling heat of their thoughtless passion; but their actions speak the truth, and we are not blind to them. They call themselves revolutionaries; but they behave like reactionaries, and my sisters and I fear they mean to undo centuries of progress in the false name of liberty and freedom in a single bloody stroke.

If you ask a sulking child what he would like to make him feel better, he is likely to reply that nothing will do but a dragon with a jeweled halter or a pair of wings to fly to the moon. Generally what he requires is a nap.

Finally, because my sisters and I grow weary with this endless litany of complaint and must finish somewhere, the rebels assert that the late conflict with the French and Indians was not our war at all, but England's, and that she has no right to ask us to pay for any part of it. It is a remarkable war, I must say, that raids our homes and kills our citizens, without being our war in the slightest. And if the Indians have strong feelings about London or His Majesty, they couch them in the most peculiar manner when they say it is the settlers competing with them for their ancestral lands to which they object. And if the French caused the war by allowing their diplomat to be slaughtered in the woods by then-Colonel Washington and his band of Indian allies, they took a remarkably painful and uncertain path to it, unless we are expected to believe that Colonel Washington was in their pay and poor Monsieur Jumonville a willing sacrifice. This argument that England was the source of that ruinously expensive war is so clearly foolish that I hardly see the need to spend any time upon it.

So when we take the full matter in hand, what do we see? A plea for honor, and peace, and RULE OF LAW; while in opposition, a helter-skelter of confused petulance that would be laughable if it were not so deadly in the hands of grown men who bear muskets and ropes and knives.

The rebels say that a partisan and interested minority should not be permitted to have its way over the lives and happiness of the people in full. And on this, my sisters and I agree with them with all our hearts.

To the gentle readers of this paper, I ask that you listen to these humble thoughts of your wives, sisters, and daughters. They are honest and practical, even if they are not learned and wise. The peace that all good people claim as their dearest wish is within the reach of our hands, if we will only grasp it.

And grasp it we must. A fatal hour has been pressed upon us, and we are in grave danger of losing all. For it is not only the rebels who are children, although I chide them for it; we are all children in the hands of our God, our King, and our country. It is a terrible thing to raise one's hand against one's father. His love and protection have no substitute in all of creation. And his tender embrace once lost may never be regained, and regretted bitterly through all the crippled years that follow.

Rachel's voice fell still. The sudden silence rang in her ears, and she realized that she had grown loud in her reading as she had warmed to her topic. Her essay was so sure of itself, she found herself more than half-convinced by the arguments she had labored over all afternoon with no other object than to come up with something plausible. General Howe must believe that the people here were with him. As long as he believed that, he would not destroy the Continental army – he had said so – and Lieutenant Bellew would remain alive. But for her plan to work, the essay had to. Of course no single essay would turn public sentiment from wherever it lay – Rachel was not sure of what public sentiment was, even, overall. But as long as General Howe heard loud voices, constant voices assuring him that the people here were worth saving for England, he would continue to believe it, and act accordingly. That was all Rachel desired.

Jacob stood motionless, the whites of his eyes shining in the near-dark of the room. When Rachel looked at him, he blinked and said, "Is that all of it?"

Rachel's heart sank. She dropped her eyes and turned back to her desk, shuffling the papers into a pile. "Yes, that's it. Well, maybe it's not good enough to be printed."

"Not good enough for the paper!" Jacob exclaimed. "Miss Rachel, I wish it coulda gone on for hours! I never knew anyone that said anything so fine and, and *pretty* before."

Rachel looked up sharply. "Do you really think so?" She curled her toes in pleasure and plucked a strand of congealed wax from the candle and pressed it flat.

"Do I ever! Why, at first when you was goin' on I thought, oh yes, she's for the rebels all right, and then you turns it around on me and calls 'em punks and you tells it so I can see it just like a snotty little kid that don't know his own mind and won't mind anyone else neither, so I guess that's what they must be. Only thing I don't understand, you keep talking about your sisters, and I thought you said before you was alone in the world."

"Well, I am," Rachel replied slowly. "By my sisters, I meant all womankind. I hoped to imply that this was the way most women felt."

"Oh." Jacob's face fell a fraction. "Well, I wish there was some way of puttin' me in there too, cause I sure wouldn't mind saying Jacob Carter thinks this is a fine way of puttin' things."

"But you are! That's why I read it to you," Rachel said, and Jacob looked at her uncertainly. "The single most important thing isn't so much what I say, but what people think of it. And I'm so grateful that you liked it."

Jacob shrugged one shoulder and rubbed the knuckles of his hand with his thumb, glancing to the side. He seemed uncertain what to say or how to react. "You want me to get them beds turned and all while you run it down to the paper?" he asked at last. *Well, why not tonight – the sooner the better,* Rachel thought, flushed with her success. She accepted his help gratefully.

They left the room together, Rachel clutching her precious copy, and saw Mrs. Addison coming up the stairs. "Oh, there you are," she said, a faint line appearing between her eyebrows.

Rachel swallowed. She was not paid to write newspaper articles, and she knew very well her scribbling could have waited until the night when everyone was in bed. So she nodded and hoped that Mrs. Addison would not notice the black stains on her fingers. She curtsied and moved her hands with the papers in them behind her back.

"Miss Rachel been writing for the paper, ma'am," Jacob said proudly. Rachel cringed.

Mrs. Addison tilted her head to the side and touched an earring as if she did not quite trust what she heard. "I beg your pardon?" she inquired, her eyes flicking from Jacob back to Rachel.

"I'm sorry, ma'am, I didn't realize how long it was taking," Rachel whispered. "I'm sure they won't care about it anyway." Her elegant plan seemed more foolish and futile and hollow every second longer that Mrs. Addison's curious gaze held her.

She must have seen something in Rachel's face, because Mrs. Addison's eyes suddenly widened and acquired an interested glitter. She took the last few stairs with a rapid rustling of skirts. "You don't mean it's true, then? It's true? How utterly delicious! A servant-woman writing for the papers – Rachel, I think you've lied to me, you must be French. Where is this article of yours? Is it finished? Is it in your room?" Rachel produced her copy reluctantly, and Mrs. Addison seized it, bringing it close to her face to read in the poor light.

She slipped the first page to the bottom of the pile, her face expressionless. When she reached the end at last, a small smile curled the corners of her mouth. She handed the pages back to Rachel with a low chuckle. "I had no idea you were such a dyed in the wool Tory," she said in an even tone, but her eyes gleamed with mischief, and for a moment Rachel could see the little girl that Mrs. Addison had once been – petted, spoiled, charming, easily bored, just as easily amused. The years would not have changed her, and perhaps they never would.

"My own views..." Rachel fell silent. She could not quite say that she did not entirely feel what she had written, not after Jacob's enthusiasm, but Mrs. Addison's sharp eyes pried out that Rachel was holding something back, even if she did not correctly guess it.

"Oh, I see. Yes, I thought you seemed particularly impressed by General Howe earlier. Some people take him that way. I don't see it myself, but." She shrugged. "There it is. There are worse things to say about a man than that women like him."

"Mrs. Howe might not agree," Rachel said, slipping easily and with relief into the familiar routine of their gossiping.

"But there is no Mrs. Howe, my dear."

"In name, or in fact? It seemed to me the position was functionally filled," Rachel said.

"O-o-oh, you're in rare form today," Mrs. Addison breathed. Rachel realized that perhaps she had gone too far. No, of course she had, and while what she said was true, to say it openly that way was unkind both to General Howe and the woman who had offered them hospitality. It did not make her feel much better to see by Mrs. Addison's good humor that she had caused no offense in this quarter. "You don't mind taking on either side, do you. Perhaps Mrs. Haughton did needle you a bit after all. Well. I'll need your help with my hair, but after that, I can take care of everything myself, so you'll be free. You were running off to the newspaper with that, weren't you?"

Rachel curtsied again. "I'm sure they won't take it."

"Which paper did you have in mind?"

"The *Sentinel-Observer.*"

"Oh, they'll take it all right," Mrs. Addison chuckled. "Though you may need to say you've brought it for your master. Or your husband, or whatever you like. Only be so good as not to bring Mr. Addison into it."

Chapter 11

Even though Rachel had to scrub her hands first to get rid of the black stains that marked them, Mrs. Addison's hair didn't take much time, and her employer encouraged her to hurry. Mrs. Addison seemed almost as excited at Rachel's project as she herself. Still, the sun had long set by the time Rachel stepped out onto the dark street clutching her folded essay in her hand inside the pocket of her cloak. A silver mist lit by the moon softened the edges of the houses and rendered the street shining and slick. Rachel wore her old clogs, and the hard soles clapped against the stones like rifle-shot.

By the time she got close to the center of town, the fog had grown so much heavier it seemed like the dead of night, and the horses and people that passed her like wraiths haunting it. The watery light of the street-lamps cast a bilious glow. Although the night was not too cold, the dampness had crept into the fabric of her clothes, and her skin prickled. Rachel was sure she would not find the newspaper office in time, and regretted the warm house she had left behind. She asked a passer-by where to find the *Sentinel-Observer* but did not have the heart to ask whether they might be open so late.

She need not have worried. She heard the newspaper office halfway down the block, a low, heavy thumping that battered the air rhythmically, like the anvil of Hell.

Rachel came to the fifth door on the left, as she had been instructed, and knocked. It seemed impossible that her gentle tap could have been heard over the pounding inside, so she raised her hand to strike the door again and almost put her knuckles in the face of the harried man in shirtsleeves who yanked the door open. He looked like a professional man and was not young, so she took him for the editor.

The editor flinched, raising a hand to protect himself, and Rachel froze in horror.

"Oh, I'm so sorry, I'm *so* sorry," she stammered.

The editor straightened and grinned, tugging his waistcoat back into position. "The apology is mine to offer, miss," he said. "I thought you were a man."

"Not even men come to your door to punch you in the face without a single word, I hope," Rachel said.

"You'd be surprised, then. Well, what can I do for you? We're fresh out of today's paper, if that's what you're looking for." His eyes softened at something in her face, and he said in a gentler voice, "Well, I always keep a couple copies for myself, and I might let you have one for ten cents if you really need it."

"May I step inside a moment?" The editor stood back to let her enter, and Rachel walked into the front office. The rhythmic thumping shook her teeth, and the smell of black ink hung heavy in the air. Two messy desks marked with repeated old ink-spills sat haphazardly in a small room lit by several hung lanterns dirty with inattention. A ruddy-cheeked young man sat at one of the desks, writing furiously. He glanced up briefly at Rachel's entrance and then returned to his work.

The editor who had opened the door waited, his impatience barely concealed beneath a polite smile. Rachel pressed her lips together. She did not know quite how to begin. She cleared her throat. "I admire the remarkable and consistent quality of your paper all the more seeing how much activity goes into it," she began slowly.

"Thank you very much, miss. Always appreciated. Sorry about the noise. We're doing a pamphlet. No sense in letting the press go idle," the editor said, making a small movement back to the door.

"I have a small contribution," Rachel blurted and reached into her pocket. The editor nodded, his face showing comprehension.

"Marvelous, marvelous," he said and walked to the empty desk. He lifted up a quill and went to dip it in the ink but frowned. He pressed the point of the quill against his thumb to test it and then took up a small knife, scraping it against the hollow shaft. "Where shall we send your subscription?"

"It, ah, isn't a subscription," Rachel said in a small voice. She pulled out her folded manuscript, its edges softened by damp. It looked such a poor thing that she wished heartily once more she were home again and not trying to be clever. "It's, I, I wrote an article for you." She realized too late that she had forgotten Mrs. Addison's advice, making matters worse.

The editor froze, and the young man with ruddy cheeks looked up again with a small smile. "That you wrote, miss?"

"You've published letters by women before," Rachel said defensively. She still held out her papers. The editor took them gently but did not unfold them.

"Not that I know of," the editor said, scratching his jawbone with the hand holding her essay. "People pretend they are, sometimes, dear, but that's for rhetorical effect, you understand. No one writes under his own name anyway."

Rachel's cheeks burned. She had not known even that simple fact. If the editor had not held her papers, she might have left in shame that moment. But the thought of reporting failure to Mrs. Addison, after her long and anxious walk and the generous release from her duties, made her stand her ground just a moment longer. "I do apologize, sir, but I have written it even if only in ignorance, and if you would just take a brief look, perhaps you could tell me whether or not you find it acceptable irrespective of its source."

The editor gave a slight sigh, apparently deciding that the quickest way to be done with the matter would be to do as she asked. So he pulled a pair of spectacles from his pocket and hung them over his ears and sat, unfolding the papers and straightening them with a sharp knock against the desk, and then he settled down to read for a few minutes. Rachel watched him, but she could tell nothing from his face. He simply finished one page and turned to the next. When he finished, he pressed his lips together.

"Huh," he said. "Have a look at this, Tom." He leaned over and handed the manuscript to his assistant. Then Tom put down his quill and read her letter while Rachel stood in an agony of uncertainty. Perhaps the editor liked it. Or more likely, he thought it was so foolish that he wanted to be able to share the joke with his assistant once he'd sent Rachel on her way.

Tom showed no expression as he read either, until he came to the end of it. He glanced at the editor and smiled. "It sounds exactly like a woman," he said, raising his sandy eyebrows. "Except it's spelled properly, and it's readable."

"Does Billy already have that rotten 'Honest Chandler' piece laid out for tomorrow?" Tom nodded. "Well, go in the back and tell him to earn his keep. This is about the same length, and I'll be happy not to have to embarrass myself with the 'Honest Chandler' for a few more days, or ever, God willing."

"You'll take it, then?" Rachel exclaimed, clutching her hands together. "You'll take it?"

"With pleasure, miss. It's got a little bite, and we like that here. I suppose you've got a boyfriend in the regulars, have you? Well, you can let him know to look for it bright and early tomorrow. I'll send you a copy, free and gratis, if he doesn't subscribe. Where would you like it delivered?"

Rachel swallowed. "I...I would rather not say, sir."

"Ah, it's like that, then," the editor replied with interest. "What do you think of that, Tom?"

"Father doesn't like the lover much. What I think is we know who's going to win that battle," Tom replied cheerfully.

Rachel considered correcting them, but she was not sure they would believe her, and the important thing anyway was that she not bring Mr. Addison's name into it, as Mrs. Addison had asked. So she let them believe what they will, and accepted her small pay, and took her leave. The essay would be printed – and people seemed to like it – and General Howe would see it for certain! Rachel discovered that she had not really believed her mission would be a success, because she felt utterly unprepared and astounded by the fact of it.

The night did not seem dark or damp or cold any more when she stepped back into it. Rachel's heart glowed with triumph, and she smiled at the people she passed on the street. She wondered over and over again that she had dared such a bold venture, and it seemed nothing short of a miracle that she had begun it, let alone brought it to a successful conclusion. A saying from her childhood floated into her brain, that when a person seemed out of his head that it only meant the Great Spirit had chosen to use him for His own purposes, and it struck her as good an explanation as any.

She skipped a little when she crossed the street and turned a corner. It was only after several minutes when the new road took a curious and unfamiliar bend that she realized she had missed her way. She stopped and looked back. The fog obscured the path behind her.

"Well, it doesn't matter," she told herself. She was not far from the main roads, so she turned around and retraced her steps.

It was late enough now that traffic had thinned considerably. Rachel came to a main thoroughfare with relief, until she noticed that it was unfamiliar too, and not the street she had thought she would find. She could not see the moon, and after all the twists and turns she was not quite certain any more which direction she faced.

But she had a bit of money in her pocket from the editor, and she supposed she could always hire a cab if she happened to see one pass by. Only she had been walking for rather a long time, and the streets were silent, and she did not see a passer-by to ask where she was.

She walked slower every second even though she knew it made more sense to go quicker. But the fear that she might be taking herself farther from her goal prevented her feet from listening to sense. She started to grow afraid. "Don't be a fool," she whispered to herself, and the sound of her voice frightened her anew, hollow in the empty streets. But she knew she hadn't gone too far. It didn't matter if she'd wandered a bit astray. The first person she met could set her right.

The fog shivered with the muted sound of boots. Rachel perked up and tilted her head to hear better. It seemed to be coming from her left rather than ahead, so she quickly took the next corner, praying that this side street would prove straight enough to take her to the next after that directly.

At first she had taken the boots for the tread of soldiers, but as she walked down the cross-street she was able to make out the moan of melancholy voices rising over the foot-falls. "Ah God, take pity upon me for my sins!" "Dearest Lord, forgive me, forgive all of us, I beg of you." "If you could only have a thought for my dear mother, sweet Jesus, it is all I ask." And she recognized the whisper of bare soles on stone mixed in with the tread of boots.

She had not realized there were so many Catholics in Philadelphia that they could form a procession, though it did not surprise her that they had chosen such a gloomy night for it. But she supposed that Catholics could tell her the direction as well as anyone else, so it pleased her that the side street went true, and she emerged onto a broad avenue where a line of about twenty men marched.

"Excuse me," she said to the first shadow figure that passed, but the man did not seem to hear her, engrossed in his lamentations. "Excuse me," she tried again, and suddenly a redcoat appeared out of the mist holding his musket at an angle so that his bayonet was at the ready.

"Hey you, what are you about!" the redcoat cried roughly, and Rachel's voice deserted her in astonishment. "Ah, it's just a girl," another English voice floated through the air. Rachel stepped back into the mist, hoping it would conceal her, but then she saw something that froze her in place and would not let her run away.

The haggard, bearded face of one of the barefoot men in the procession was familiar to her. She looked more closely. There was no mistaking him, but she did not understand. She barely knew how she managed to cry out, "Lieutenant Masterson? Lieutenant Masterson!"

Masterson raised his hollow-cheeked face and looked about wildly into the night. Rachel darted towards him, not caring if anyone would try to stop her, and came to his side. Masterson kept walking as he searched her face, his eyes haunted and confused. "Lieutenant Masterson? From the Brass Bull?"

Recognition slowly dawned, followed by horror. It took Rachel aback. "Ah God, for a handful of pretty skirt, the unkind things I've done," Masterson said. "Will ghosts trouble me even before I'm dead?"

"Oh, what do you mean!" Rachel cried as she walked beside him. "I'm no ghost, Lieutenant Masterson, it's just me, and what in God's name is this?"

"Are you alive, miss, or are you a sign from beyond showing me what waits for me there?"

"Waits for you – beyond? What, what do you mean? I can't understand you, and I need to know, I *need* to know why you're here! Where are the others?" She peered at the other ragged men. She did not think she recognized any of them, but she could not be sure.

"They're taking us to be hanged."

"Hanged!" Rachel cried in despair. "What in the name of Heaven for?"

"Can't say. No trial, no warning, they just pulled the six of us out of prison, didn't even ask our names, just pointed at men. When we were off the ship, they told us what they intended," Masterson replied dully. Rachel was not sure whether he believed she was truly among the living or not, and she seized his damp hand. Hanged? He was to be killed – all these men were to be killed? Simply plucked from prison and murdered by whim in the dead of night? Anonymously, as if they had no souls, as if there were no one who loved them and pined for their safe return, or at least for word of their fate?

"Get off now, that's enough, you've had your word," a redcoat barked, stepping forward with a threatening manner. It might have been the same man, or a different one. Rachel did not know or care.

"Hanged – they can't – you can't – where is Lieutenant Bellew," Rachel begged in agony. She could see nothing in this fog.

"I don't know, miss. They put him and O'Malley in a different prison when we were taken. Perhaps I'll see him soon. Ah God, but we may not be going to the same place. Will you forgive me, miss? Will you pray for me, I beg you," Masterson said with a sudden urgency that terrified her even more than his ruined visage. "Will you pray for my immortal soul?"

"Will you leave off, girl, this is no place for you. Get home now."

"Every day, Lieutenant Masterson," Rachel answered. The wetness on her face was hot, and she realized she was crying helplessly, without sobs, as if her grief were a force outside herself. "Every day, I swear, every day as long as I live, oh God."

The redcoat, his patience exhausted, seized her by the shoulder. Rachel reached into her pocket and thrust her handkerchief into Masterson's hand. "God knows the goodness in your heart, Lieutenant Masterson, He will have pity for..." But then the redcoat thrust her away, and when she regained her feet, she caught a final glimpse of Masterson, holding the handkerchief in his fist and rubbing the softness of its fabric against his skin.

The procession filed away, with its prayers and its relentless tread. The street fell silent again.

She had not known this face of the war. She had not known this face of the army. She was a stupid, worthless thing, and she trembled to think of the heartless, gloating tone her essay had delighted in. This was what she had been defending. This was what she had sworn upon her honor was virtue and duty.

And Lieutenant Bellew was not in the winter quarters where General Howe's lofty political views might save him. If he lived, he was in the hands of these monsters, where Rachel's words could only drive any possible help farther from his side.

Rachel tried to return to the newspaper office, but she was so badly turned around that she could not find it and gave up at last in despair. She did not know afterwards how she found her way home, only that it was so late she heard Abraham in the stables awake already and tending to the horses.

She crept to her room in misery and knelt down beside her bed without taking off her cloak. Rachel closed her eyes and leaned her forehead against the mattress. She tried to pray as she had promised. Her mouth was numb and dry. "Dear God – dear God, please have mercy upon Lieutenant Masterson. Please show him Your forgiveness and love. Please have mercy upon him, please...mercy..." But the words died on her lips. She took no comfort in them. If only Masterson had asked someone good to pray for him, the prayer might be heard. But Rachel knew she was no such person. The knowledge of what she had done was a sickness in her blood, and each new beat of her heart pushed it deeper into the fibers of her body and soul, as if they were a sponge greedy to drink her sin.

Chapter 12

"How do you find the papers this morning, dear?" Mrs. Addison asked with a catlike glance at Rachel.

Mr. Addison flicked his eyes at her curiously over the top of his reading. "Consistent," he replied.

Rachel held the bottom of the coffee-pot with her left hand to keep it from trembling as she poured Mr. Addison a fresh cup. There was nothing less she wanted to hear about than her miserable essay, but she could hardly say so. She did not dare tell Mrs. Addison what she had seen, nor Jacob, nor anyone. Visions of those hopeless skeletal forms marching to their death in the dead of night pressed against her mind and heart. She wondered whether General Howe knew that such things happened under his command. He had seemed an honorable man; but he was a soldier, and every soldier must have some seed of cruelty inside him that he trained and nurtured, or else he would not be able to kill. And Rachel knew that rebels were subject to death. But surely not summary death without a trial, as if they were vermin to be exterminated rather than men. The guards might as well simply fire their muskets into the prison.

Who was to say they did not?

"Here, that's a bit full," Mr. Addison protested. Rachel murmured an apology and jerked back the coffee-pot before Mr. Addison's cup spilled over. The rich smell filled the air. Rachel liked coffee; she did not know why the thought of it turned her stomach now. Mr. Addison took a cautious sip to bring the liquid down to a safe level before resuming his interrupted reading.

"General Howe takes the *Sentinel-Observer,* doesn't he?" Mrs. Addison continued with another sly sideways glance.

"Believe so," Mr. Addison muttered. He put down his paper abruptly. "Margaret, I entirely forgot."

"Which papers the General follows? Oh, and I'll have that when you're through, please." She nodded at the newspaper. Mr. Addison folded it and placed it before her absently.

"He asked me a favor. I said yes, of course, but it slipped my mind."

"I imagine he has plenty need of your services even in the winter lull."

"Not that. He's got an officer under parole he rather hoped we might be able to put up."

Rachel's heart leaped despite herself. There were hundreds of officers other than Lieutenant Bellew; and it was hardly likely that General Howe would take a personal interest in a man so far beneath his rank. And yet she could not help thinking what a dear burden it would be to wash his sheets and brush out his coat and place his eggs in front of him at breakfast-time. She knew she would get better at cooking. And if he were paroled he would be safe, safe.

"Good Heavens, whatever for?"

"Your father, presumably. But mostly I think General Howe wants him to have enough room for his entourage and knows we can bear it without strain."

"An entourage," Mrs. Addison said with distaste. "Do we know him, then?"

"We've met in passing. General Charles Lee."

"Ah," Mrs. Addison replied thoughtfully. "Hm. I suppose you've already said yes, and that we haven't really an option. Well, when can we expect him?"

She hadn't really expected Lieutenant Bellew, but this news was almost as stunning. General Lee, the rebellion's finest leader and only military genius, the great man whose loss had doomed the insurrection to swift failure rather than merely inevitable. And yet General Howe was showing the most painstaking care towards his well-being and comfort, and suddenly Rachel knew with certainty that he could not know of the treatment the other prisoners suffered. It was a slight burden lifted from her heart, but not more than that. Because the treatment remained; and, worse, the moment before she was afforded the opportunity to be near the man who above all others could steer the fortunes and fate of Lieutenant Bellew, whom she had to believe was still alive, she had rendered herself nugatory through that blind and foolish Tory article, which would prevent General Lee from feeling the slenderest hint of sympathy for her opinions.

But perhaps he would not know of it.

"Later today, if we give the word – I did wait for you, my dear, before finalizing anything. Or tomorrow."

"Rachel –" Mrs. Addison began, and then stopped short at the expression on Rachel's face. "I'm sure he won't be that much trouble, dear. You seem to find enough time, I'm sure you'll manage," she went on in a gentler voice.

Rachel tried to compose her expression. It galled her to think that Mrs. Addison might suspect she was unhappy at the prospect of more work. "Even I have heard of General Lee, madam," Rachel said. "It will be an honor to be any small service to him."

Mrs. Addison looked at her quizzically. "Well, just getting everything done will be quite enough, without honor entering into it," she replied at last. "Is there something else then? You have the most worried look. I hope it isn't on General Lee's account. I assure you, from my recollection, he is far from particular."

"Pretty exacting about his dogs," Mr. Addison said.

"We'll let Abraham worry about that, he's good with animals. So, I think the east bedroom on the second floor has the prettiest view. And a nice breeze in the morning. Do we need more than one room for him, Robert?"

"I don't believe so, at this juncture."

"I'll get it ready at once," Rachel said with a curtsy. "And then shall I tell General Howe that you're ready to receive General Lee?"

"You'll be running around plenty, Jacob can go." Rachel glanced down. She had a vague image of somehow communicating the horrors of last night's execution to General Howe, who would surely correct such terrible matters at once, although she did not know how she would find words to broach the subject once she was in his presence. Now it proved she would not be in his presence anyway, and the ghostly hope evaporated before fully taking shape.

The day was clear, if overcast, so Rachel hung the dry sheets in the back yard to make them fresh. Then she unlatched the windows in the east bedroom and propped them open to make sure that the wind, which today was a little more stiff than nice, would not blow them shut. When she hurried back to the kitchen to finish the washing up, she found Jacob dipping a ladle-full of water for a quick drink. Rachel brightened.

"Jacob!" she cried, and he startled, dropping the ladle with a splash. "No, no, I'm just glad I found you before you left," Rachel continued in a rush as Jacob eyed her in alarm.

"Left for where, Miss Rachel?"

"Mr. Addison is going to send you to General Howe. I want you to do me a favor, if you can." Jacob nodded. "Thank you. I'm going to give you a letter – I haven't written it yet – and I want you to tell General Howe that you found it outside his home and don't know where it's from."

"Why's it such a secret for? What if he ask me directly?" Jacob frowned. He rolled up his sleeve and reached into the water to retrieve the lost ladle.

Rachel flushed. She suddenly realized that she was demanding of Jacob that he tell a lie, and that he do so to a very important person.

"I'm sorry," she said. Jacob had asked her for information before, but he had never questioned her, and she wondered if she had gotten above herself. Too high-toned, too heedless. But this was something that needed to be done, even if she was an imperfect tool. "It's...I don't want to upset you, it's some of his troops who have gotten out of line, and I'm sure he can't be aware of it, and he ought to be. But I don't really know General Howe, you see, and so I can't tell him directly. And if I say who I am, then it will come back to our house, and it might reflect poorly on the Addisons somehow. But you can see the letter first – I mean, I'll read it to you," she corrected herself hastily. "I promise you I'll tell you everything it says. Only...only I think you might rather not know."

Jacob nodded. "Then that's all right. Don't read it to me," he said firmly and headed towards the back door.

But before he could make his escape, Mrs. Addison peered into the kitchen. "Oh, there you are, Jacob. Come here, please. I have an errand for you. Your shirt is disordered. And you'll need your jacket."

Jacob flashed an apologetic look at Rachel before murmuring "Yes'm" and walking with bent head to Mrs. Addison's side. And thus vanished Rachel's second plan.

Her face must have shown her defeat, because Mrs. Addison looked at Rachel thoughtfully. "I do think Mr. Addison read your piece and liked it," she said kindly. "If he had thought it was out of place, he would have said something. He's quite uninhibited on such judgments."

Rachel did not want to think about her article. "Is General Lee an acquaintance of your father, ma'am?" she asked. She had been curious about that remark of Mr. Addison's.

Mrs. Addison blinked and was silent a moment. She smiled, but there was something brittle about it. "Well, yes, I suppose they must know each other pretty well." She fiddled with her skirt. "My father is also a general."

"I did not know!" Rachel cried. "Is he here, or in New York?" She had known Mrs. Addison was American by birth, judging by her accent; but that did not mean her family was. Her father might have served in the colonies for a long time.

"It would be quite impossible for him in either location, I'm afraid. General van Dortmund serves in the Continental Army, my dear. He's currently at Valley Forge with the rest of them."

The dish slipped from Rachel's hands. She caught it in time, but only barely, and only because it was still dry. Her face paled. "Your father is a Continental, madam?"

"Yes, he has – these views," Mrs. Addison remarked.

A thousand little details swam into focus and formed a picture at last. The father was a Whig and a rebel – of course there'd been slighting references in Mrs. Loring's drawing-room and polite reassurances in General Howe's study. And Rachel had remained oblivious to all of it, had shown Mrs. Addison that fire-breathing Tory piece and expected not only her endurance of it but her praise. What devil had possessed her to undertake that terrible, idiotic project? When, when would she learn to still her tongue? She squeezed her eyes shut in pain. "I am so sorry, madam, so very, very sorry –"

"Whatever for?"

"I should not have written that bit for the newspapers, I have regretted it every moment since, and I do not even understand how you could be so gentle with me –"

"Why, child! Hush!" Mrs. Addison's composure was fully returned. She even seemed a little amused. "You've done no violence to my views, if that's your concern. Really. I take no personal stand on the current conflict other than that it exists, nor do I think one would be a fit employment. I simply have people I like, and some of them are Tories, and some of them are Whigs, and I leave them to it. Women aren't intellectual creatures, dear. I'm sure you'll come to understand this when you're older."

"I don't suppose men are any more so," Rachel replied. She was a little stung at the dismissal of the labor that had cost her so much anxiety and pain. But it was, she had to admit, a vast and palpable relief nevertheless to be of no consequence. That was surely for the best.

"Perhaps not, but it is a necessary lie in their case, since they're obliged to handle the affairs of the world. Now, don't trouble yourself about that any more, please. We have more than enough to attend to at the moment." Mrs. Addison shook her head at some private reflection.

"Is there something I should know about General Lee's preferences, madam?" Rachel asked meekly, returning to the subject that she knew was her responsibility and that therefore had the right to her full attention.

Mrs. Addison shrugged and grimaced. "He is very much a soldier, as I recall. He certainly made no effort to disguise it on our brief meeting. I expect we will need more liquor. And those infernal dogs. Disgusting creatures. But they will remain outside. Absolutely. Oh, but Rachel, we will need a proper cook. Don't take it as a criticism, dear, your meal preparation is quite - interesting, but General Lee is I believe related to a baronetcy on his mother's side and would probably prefer something a little more elaborate. And I suppose it's high time we started entertaining anyway. Everyone is desperate to see our house. And they ought to be."

"I am sure I will take to the cook immediately, if you've chosen her," Rachel said. "And I will endeavor to learn as much as I can of her art."

"But we haven't got her, Rachel, that's exactly the problem. Once you've got the east bedroom ready, why don't you go out to the market and see if you can find a good woman for hire. I can't get references for one. Everyone's snapped up the regular help, of course, and left nothing for me. That's why we've been making do with your corn-cakes."

"What shall I use to judge her by," Rachel asked dubiously. She had not hired someone before, and it would be more than just a humiliation if she chose poorly and made the household seem badly managed in front of their illustrious guest.

"Well, yes, that is a problem, but we can make it fun! See if you can engage a few of them on trial. We'll test them out tonight, each assigned a different course and the best to get the job. We'll pay them all for their trouble, naturally." Mrs. Addison's eyes brightened at the prospect.

Rachel thought that if she had been obliged to compete for her position, she would have been so frightened she would have served the soup with forks and set Mrs. Addison's hair on fire, but she supposed that cooks must be a hardier breed, dealing with chopping and plucking and boiling all day as they did.

"Jacob, are you still here?" Mrs. Addison said crossly, remembering her first task but forgetting she had not told Jacob what it was.

Rachel took a half-step forward. "Mrs. Addison – madam," she began hesitantly. Mrs. Addison waited, her annoyance suspended. Rachel decided she should have confided in her employer from the first. Mrs. Addison knew everyone, knew General Howe, General Lee, everyone who was important on either side. And she was beautiful and charming, and everyone liked her, or men did, at least. She would know what to do. "When I was coming home last night, ma'am, I saw – I saw something, something the regulars were doing that was not right, and I have been turning it over and over ever since in my mind."

Mrs. Addison grew still. "They didn't try to touch you, did they?" She rubbed the fingers of one hand nervously.

Rachel paused a moment before she understood. She blinked. "Oh, no, ma'am, no, nothing like that, surely."

Mrs. Addison looked relieved. "Well, then, whatever it was, it isn't your affair, and perhaps you misunderstood."

Rachel shook her head. "No, ma'am, I couldn't have –"

"Rachel, war is a terrible thing and terrible events occur regularly," Mrs. Addison interrupted her with an air of reciting a school-lesson. "I am sure they are very upsetting – I know they are. But it is best simply to put them out of one's thoughts and return to pleasanter occupations. I must insist upon this. Jacob, come here please, where are you wandering off to?"

And then Mrs. Addison and Jacob were gone, leaving Rachel alone with her thoughts, which were occupied by nothing pleasant at all.

Was it possible that she had mistaken the ordinary cruelty of war for something worse? Lieutenant Masterson, rest his soul, and the others with him had been terrified and broken, and their bodies had shown ill-use; but perhaps that was simply the privations of a soldier's life, and the melancholy properly attendant upon having to make one's accounting before God. Men died in war, and died often. It was the nature of the thing. And had she understood him rightly when he said they had been chosen at whim and given no trial or hearing – perhaps she had not. She did not know Lieutenant Masterson well enough to say she was certain he had done nothing for which an enemy army might rightly hang him.

The more she thought, the less certain Rachel felt not only of her conclusions, but even of her memories of the previous night. And possibly this is what Mrs. Addison had meant, and surely Rachel would do well to take her advice. If Rachel ever meant to improve herself, as she claimed, she could ask for no plainer path to follow than the example of her betters – not to assume their entitlements, as she had been guilty of with Jacob, but to breathe in the air of their knowledge and sentiments until it became part of her being. A shadow had no independent existence. And it had a responsibility not to make a mockery of the finer form that cast it, and to show the lines of that form truly.

Chapter 13

O'Malley took sick on the fifth day. He had been quiet all morning, uttering not a sound until suddenly he had coughed violently and pressed his hand against his mouth, swallowing hard. Then he crouched down, jostling the men next to him, and vomited onto his shoes. Most of what emerged from his throat was clear, sticky liquid. "I apologize," O'Malley said, his face pale, and then he coughed and retched again, bringing up nothing this time but a line of drool.

"Here, give this man room," one of the others cried out, but O'Malley held out his hand.

"I'm all right now, the bad is out, no need." Bellew reached his arm around O'Malley's shoulders and helped him to his feet. His body felt hot even through the fabric of his jacket. O'Malley gave a shaky smile, embarrassed.

But he wasn't all right, and as the days passed, O'Malley spent more and more time leaning against Bellew's shoulder in a half-doze. Occasionally his mind would clear for a brief moment. He murmured once, "Better to keep your distance, lad, Heaven only knows what I've got," and pushed Bellew away weakly.

"It's all the same, in this place," Bellew replied, holding firm to O'Malley's side. And it was true. They were packed so tight that the distance of a few feet one way or the other would make no difference. And even if some small separation would protect Bellew, it would only doom another man.

Bellew could feel himself changing under the force of this strange and terrible existence. Tiny events that before would have flitted past his consciousness without leaving a mark now rose up as vast as an ocean, consuming him. He once watched the light move across the high, narrow window by slow degrees for the better part of a day, without a single other thought interrupting him until Cowles nudged him gently and told him it was his turn to sit by the wall. And Bellew's first reaction to Cowles's prod had been anger that he had been distracted from his absorbing task. Another day, the prisoners received some wormy biscuit for rations. Bellew accepted his bread expressionlessly. He broke the biscuit in two carefully his hand, so as not to let any crumbs fall to the ground. Then he licked the dust from his palm and carefully picked out the squirming maggots exposed by the break, dropping them one by one onto the ground and crushing them beneath his boot. Some men ate them, but Bellew thought it unwise. And when he had cleared out all the maggots he could see, he broke another piece of the biscuit in two and began the process over again.

It was only on the third break, when the biscuit had been reduced to not much more than a handful of powder that still writhed, miraculously, with what seemed like hundreds of worms, that Bellew realized what the guard had said when he'd opened the door to shove in the bread. "Here's more worms to keep you company." The man had called them worms, and Bellew had not even noticed, had not even registered the words, had only taken his biscuit when it was passed to him and enjoyed the fresh, cool scent of the outdoors while it lingered.

The realization burned him with the force of a lightning-bolt. He almost cast the remains of his biscuit on the ground and wept for the pale, contemptible thing that he had become, except that he knew he must preserve what little of his strength remained.

"We must keep up our spirits," he announced grimly, speaking to the room in general and shattering the absorbed stillness of other men picking at other maggots and other crumbs. "Now, more than ever. If any man ever had cause to doubt that Britain despises us, surely that ground has long since fallen from under our feet."

Silence met his words. A few heads lifted. Most men were transfixed by their biscuits, as Bellew had been a moment ago, or by the shadows, or the light, or their breathing, or the beating of their hearts and the trickle of their sweat, or any of the thousand thousand other matters that had taken full possession of their minds and souls.

Perhaps they were too far gone. Perhaps they were lost, all of them.

"What do you recommend, sir?" Cowles asked him at last. Bellew's heart lifted.

"Only that we remember that we are men, no matter how they try to drive it from us." Even as he spoke, Bellew felt the hollowness of his words. Men needed something more solid to cling to if they were to pull themselves from a pit as deep and treacherous as this terrible impotence.

"It is not merely our pride that we cherish," Bellew went on. "It is all the little sweetnesses of life that we hold dear of which we have also been deprived in this place. For God's sake, a cup of coffee in the morning or a pillow at night. Think of these things, and how we will treasure them when we are free again." The memory of coffee came back to him so strong that Bellew almost forgot where he was, and he was silent, feeling the hot bitterness against his tongue as if he were home again on his mother's farm before starting the day's labors.

He blinked. Remembered himself. Felt a moment of despair at the continued silence in the room.

"My wife," a faint voice said somewhere in the shadows, and then the sound of weeping.

They had heard him. Good. If the memories caused pain, at least that was the pain of a living man and not an animal or a shell. And if the memories were no less a narcotic than the light moving across the window or picking maggots out of bread, at least it meant their minds were turned to their liberty rather than accommodating themselves entirely to this hopeless subjugation.

For the next few weeks, occasionally a man would say, "Warm rum," or "A pipe," or "Sally Pembroke - Lord forgive me, but she developed early, and her mother still dresses her as a girl, and it shows a little more than mother may have intended." There was a little laughter at this last one. But more often, the few words would provoke a few grunts followed by silence again. It was a shared silence, though, of a thousand different memories of the same thing. No one ever spoke these thoughts when the guards opened the doors to give them water or rotten pork or to take out the dead or ask the living if they were ready to enlist in a real army. It was their most solemn secret.

Once or twice a week the guards released them into the fenced yard in back for an hour or two. They received no advance warning when the event was going to come, other than the prisoners standing in back would call out that they heard the rear door unlocking.

"Hey!" one of those men cried now, his excitement startling in the dark and gloom. "Hey, they're at the door!"

"Just the wind," his neighbor muttered, but the first man said, "No it ain't, the wind might rattle the chain but it wouldn't squeak the lock that way." The argument resolved itself when the rear door swung open. The slice of sharp winter light was blinding. Bellew's eyes watered, and he squeezed them shut for a moment.

"Exercise. Get out, all of you," a guard shouted. He was in a foul temper. The guards never liked having to slop out the sugar house, as if they blamed the prisoners for having nowhere else to leave their excrement.

Bellew gave O'Malley's dozing form a slight shake. "They're sending us out," he murmured. O'Malley's eyes blinked open and slowly focused.

"Out?" he said through cracked lips. His beard had grown so slowly over the course of his illness that it was still no more than rough stubble across his skin. His breath was foul.

"Just in the yard." O'Malley nodded, and Bellew's heart sank to see the shadow of resignation settle over his friend's features once more.

It was a single door in back, and the men were weak, so it took a long time for them to file out. Even through his coat, Bellew was chilled through by the winter air before he had moved more than ten feet from his original spot, with fifty feet at least yet to go.

"How's the Captain holding up?" a prisoner to Bellew's right asked solicitously. The other men had been appalled when the news had spread that officers were placed among them, and sometimes Bellew thought the men were grieved no less than he himself by his friend's illness. They gave O'Malley more than his share of time lying down or against the wall. At first O'Malley had refused stoutly, even indignantly when Bellew and then Cowles and the other Griffin's Ford man, Jamie Dolittle, tried to soothe him that they were giving up only their turns, and no one else's, which was not true. But as the disease progressed, O'Malley was too often confused or half-asleep to know what was his natural right and what was not.

"Well enough," Bellew answered.

"Well enough to answer for himself, even," O'Malley interrupted with a forced smile. Bellew was sure the effort at good humor had cost O'Malley dearly, and he could feel the older man trembling under the support of his arm. But the men around them cheered up visibly at this modest show of spirit, and Bellew knew why O'Malley had done it.

The yard was a flat stretch of mostly bare land enclosed by the iron bars of a piked fence. No plants grew here. Whatever weeds might have existed once had long since been plucked and eaten, and no passing seed had taken root to replace them. There was room enough for the men to walk around a little, or to sit or lie if they preferred that to exercise. An unofficial agreement had designated the southwest corner, which had a little privacy from the nearness of a neighboring building, as a latrine.

"I think I might stretch out in the sun a bit," O'Malley said, and Bellew helped him gently to the ground. He took off his coat and laid it across the captain as a blanket. "I'm too warm already," O'Malley demurred.

"So am I. Only you've got a fever to sweat out," Bellew replied, and the second part was true. O'Malley smiled and closed his eyes, instantly asleep again.

Bellew watched him a minute or two and then wandered towards the fence, which offered as good a destination as any. His stiff legs protested the unaccustomed movement, and he rolled his shoulders and stretched his back.

He reached the fence and wrapped a hand around one of its bars. Bellew smiled to himself. His knuckles at least were free, if only briefly. He wished he were not so tired all the time now. But he was, and he leaned against the fence. The cold hardness pressed against his face felt good, and he thought he would be content to stand that way a long time.

"Lady! There's a lady coming!" one of the prisoners shouted in alarm. The men in the latrine corner scrambled to pull up their trousers. One of them pitched forward onto his face, his hands tangled in his obstinate clothes and unable to break his fall. Bellew stifled a grin. He was glad to see the men still cared about such things.

"Ah, Lord, Varney, she's lookin' right at your upturned bottom, apologies, Miss, apologies, we didn't know anyone was coming, and it ain't like us, I promise."

Bellew considered that it would be a pretty bold lady, if a lady at all, to stare openly at a naked man that way, and he turned with a faint smile, expecting to see a licentious old washer-woman or something like that, and anything but the vision that confronted him.

She was a lady indeed, and a pretty one at that, a slender creature surely not even twenty years old with fair hair and light blue eyes. She wore a seal-skin jacket that must have been frighteningly expensive, and made the simple brown dress beneath seem all the more fetchingly modest. Her small mouth was parted in astonishment, showing a flash of even, white teeth. It was not, however, Varney's exposed buttocks that had captured her attention. It was Bellew at whom she stared openly, as if surprised. When he turned to meet her gaze, she blinked and flushed slightly, bringing a hand to her pink cheek.

"Lieutenant Bellew?" she asked, so soft he could barely hear it. "Oh, Lieutenant Bellew, it is you, isn't it!"

Bellew could hardly have been more surprised if General Washington had emerged from the clouds with a peal of thunder, swooped down on angel's wings, and lifted him bodily from prison. "I'm afraid you have the advantage of me, Miss," he managed to say.

"Oh, you wouldn't remember, it's just that you were kind to me once," the lady answered, evidently much agitated in mind and wringing her hands. Nervous, like a bird. Judging by the other men, Bellew knew he must present an awful appearance, his face bearded, his body starved, his hair rough, his clothes stained and foul. He could not imagine how this near-stranger could have recognized him through all the terrible changes of the last few weeks, and he searched her face for any hint of where he might have known her from. There were not many people rich enough for a seal-skin jacket near his mother's farm, and none of the daughters of the nearby families had been half so pretty, because that he most assuredly would have remembered very well.

"I'm sorry, Miss," he said, shaking his head in confusion.

"I'm Rachel – I don't think you ever knew my name, it's Rachel Kolkhorst, I was working at the Brass Bull, a tavern you stopped at in South Carolina with Lieutenant Masterson and Captain O'Malley – is Captain O'Malley with you?" she said in a frantic burst that he could hardly follow, but he did pick out her name. Rachel Kolkhorst. It meant nothing to him.

She moved closer to the fence and grasped the bar next to the one that he held. He could feel the warmth of her fingers through the thin membrane of air that separated their hands. The jacket gave off a pleasant musky odor. Bellew was suddenly acutely conscious of how badly he must smell. He took a small step backward.

"The tavern-maid," he realized abruptly. A smile flitted over her face, and he knew he was right. "You didn't know what a tip was and you were going to war." The memory returned slowly, as if it had to slog through a swamp. That explained why she had not asked about Lieutenant Masterson, who had been drunk and behaved pretty callously that night, as he recalled. God above, he hoped Masterson's conditions weren't as grim as his own. Yes, the tavern-maid had been a pretty creature. But he had not remembered her being half as pretty as he saw she was now. What was she doing dressed so well?

"I found more regular employment," Miss Kolkhorst explained without being asked, turning her head to the side as if embarrassed. Bellew wondered briefly what exactly that might be. One hardly gave a seal-skin jacket to a common maid; but one usually gave jewelry and silks to a mistress, and Miss Kolkhorst wore neither. And then he cursed himself for such an unworthy thought. No doubt the jacket was a cast-off from its wealthy owner, who had tired of it already even though it seemed new. If she had been married, surely she would not have used the word *employment*. "Lieutenant Bellew – forgive me for asking, but you seem – all the men here seem – do the guards not see your condition? Are you on hunger strike?"

Bellew smiled bitterly. Some of the men around him were eavesdropping, a forgivable sin given the novelty of a conversation with someone from the outside world. But now they dropped their eyes or mumbled darkly to each other, and Miss Kolkhorst frowned, her eyes dancing from face to face without finding satisfaction. Bellew shook his head, and her sad, almost pleading eyes turned back to him. He said, "It would be difficult for them to tell the difference if we did, Miss Kolkhorst, because they do not feed us enough to keep a rat alive, and what they give us a rat would not touch."

"But what of Mr. Loring? Isn't he the Commissioner of Prisoners? Doesn't he manage your keep so that it will be clean and fair? He is paid for it." A few of the men snorted and crossed their arms. The general feeling was pretty hard against Mr. Loring, but Bellew did not know for certain that the man was responsible for their privations and so would not hold it against him.

"You are remarkably well informed."

"My mistress knows him, or knows his wife -" Ah - so she was a lady's maid, it was confirmed. "- and so I have seen him, and I thought I understood that - why are you not being fed then? And that man is sick! That man is lying on the ground, he is perfectly unwell, and no one is doing a thing about it," she cried, pointing her hand through the bars at O'Malley's form. "Look, there's the guard back there - why is he just standing like that? That man needs a doctor!"

Her voice had become loud with excitement. The guard looked over from the other end of the yard, frowning and apparently weighing whether or not it was worth the trouble to make his way through the crowd.

The guard was neither kind nor gentle, and he could cause trouble. Miss Kolkhorst would have to leave soon. Bellew would protect this innocent girl, at least, even if he had protected no one else thus far. He took her hand gently in his own and pressed it back through the space between the bars. He had expected to have to remonstrate with her to be silent, but she gasped slightly at his touch and stopped talking. In a moment, she remembered herself and pulled free of his grasp, holding her hand against her chest. Bellew was sorry he had offended her, but he could not let her attract any more attention.

"Do not ask the guards to attend. There is no help there. They know very well what they are about. They want us to die, Miss Kolkhorst. They want us to perish in both body and soul, and everything they do here is calculated to that end."

"But this isn't incarceration, it's torture, it's - they haven't hanged Captain O'Malley, have they?" she asked and then bit her lip.

"Hanged him? No - that's him lying on the ground."

"Oh!" She raised her hand to her mouth. "He is so thin!"

"Miss Kolkhorst - I thank you and offer you every blessing for your kindness in coming over, but you need to leave. The guard will be coming over soon, and it'll be hard on all of us if he doesn't like what he sees."

"But all we're doing is talking," she protested. "Oh, aren't you allowed even to talk!"

"You must leave."

"I will see that Commissioner Loring knows all about this place, I promise you, I won't let it -"

"Could you write to General Washington instead?" one of the other men suggested timidly.

"I will, I will write to General Washington, and I will write to General Howe, and everyone, and I will tell General Lee, and –"

"And please *go*, Miss Kolkhorst, *please*," Bellew stressed. The guard had decided to bestir himself after all, and he was less than ten yards distant.

"I ´ –" Miss Kolkhorst's face twisted as if in pain. She took a step backward from the fence but then stopped. Bellew wished he could reach through the fence and push her like an obstinate horse. He knew she wanted to help him, and he blessed her for a tender heart; but couldn't she see that he was doing the only thing left in his power to be a gentleman and a protector, and that was to bid her leave? "Lieutenant Bellew," she said, eyes fixed on her toes, "if I might know your Christian name, and Captain O'Malley's, so that when I write –"

"I am Stephen and he is Samuel," Bellew interrupted her.

"And my name is Charlie Waters of Litchfield, Connecticut, if you could tell my wife I'm still alive!" the man next to Bellew cried. Miss Kolkhorst looked up and nodded sharply.

Before Bellew could remonstrate with her again, she wheeled and hurried down the street. To Bellew's astonishment, she had not gone twenty yards before she broke into a run. It wasn't the running so much that surprised him as how well she did it, a full run that covered the ground quickly and was as far from the mincing shuffle that most women adopted as a leopard is from a mouse. But he remembered now that she'd said in the tavern that she'd grown up on a farm. As he knew well, that was a freer world, and a freer life.

"Do you think she heard me?" Charlie Waters asked.

"I'm sure of it." The girl had spent time picking out shouted orders from the background roar of a drunken crowd, and Charlie had been perfectly clear.

"So what are you about then, here?" the guard demanded, picking his way through the prisoners to Bellew at last.

"It was only a girl," he replied evenly.

The guard glanced out onto the street, but Miss Kolkhorst's form had long since disappeared down the twists and bends. "I'm sure a girl would have plenty to say to the likes of you handsome fellows," the guard said, but there was nothing more to be done, and he did not seem to like the company much, so he wheeled around and returned to his post at the far side of the yard.

Bellew's gaze returned to O'Malley, napping in the cold rays of the sun. Miss Kolkhorst had been correct; he needed a doctor, and care, and he needed it soon, or there would be no restoring his health. Bellew wondered whether her efforts would have any effect. There was something beyond indifference in the contemptuous savagery of their conditions here, and he felt far from certain that calling it to anyone's attention was the cure that was required. But it could not make matters worse. At least it was something. And the pretty Miss Kolkhorst's kindness towards him was something, too, and it did not weigh too inconsiderable in his mind. How he wished he presented a less repellant figure, all filth and starvation and reek. He knew it inspired sympathy, but sympathy was nothing but a nasty spoonful of medicine whose taste was not improved by the sugar with which it was served. Still, he was forced to admit that it was a favor he needed more at the moment than admiration.

The interesting interview left Bellew with a little more energy and even a restlessness that compelled him to leave the fence and stroll through the yard. He did not lose himself in the terrible fugue of captivity but he hardly knew what his thoughts were, and it surprised him that an hour at least must have passed because the guards threw open the door from the inside and called out, "Back to quarters. Come on, now."

Men began filing inside without complaint. The sugar house was miserable, but it was warm and quiet, and standing outside in the cold, even if there was a little more room and breathable air, was pretty uncomfortable too after a while. Bellew walked over to O'Malley and nodded thanks to the men who had stood by him on watch. He slid his arm around O'Malley's shoulders and propped him up, taking his coat and shaking first one arm and then the other back into it. "Time to go back," he murmured. O'Malley's eyes fluttered open at his voice as they had not at his touch. Bellew smiled. "Pleasant dreams?" he asked.

"I was having a marvelous time," O'Malley replied. "Only I'm a little embarrassed to admit it."

"Was there a woman?"

"Worse. I was a king."

From the corner of his eye, Bellew noticed one of the men hanging back from the others. It was the man's nervous shifting from foot to foot that had attracted his attention. Perhaps he wanted to help but was too shy to put himself forward. Bellew smiled at him and waved him over. He was capable of handling O'Malley himself, especially now that the older man had lost so much flesh. But he would not deny a fellow soldier the opportunity to feel useful.

The man clutched his hands together and paled. But Bellew merely waited patiently, and at last the man came. "Yes, sir?" he asked in a voice tight with worry.

"You wanted to give me a hand?" Bellew said.

The man looked aside in agony. He clutched his hands into fists and then pressed one against his thigh. "I can't go back in there," he said in a low voice. "God forgive me, Lieutenant Bellew, and say what you will, and you'll be right in all of it, I swear – and if you'd rather break my neck on the spot, I won't stop you. But I can't go back in there. I can't go back into that hole."

And then Bellew understood. The man had not been waiting to help Bellew; he had been waiting for Bellew to leave, so that he would not see the man speak to the guard. There were only two ways to leave the sugar house prison: dead, or enlistment papers.

Bellew closed his eyes a moment. When he opened them again, he saw tears streaming down the man's face. "I'm so sorry, sir, I'm so sorry, I know my duty, but I can't, I just can't –"

Bellew laid O'Malley down again and stood. He took the man by the shoulder and pulled him close. "I'm your superior officer, soldier, and I'll be the one to tell you your duty," he snapped. The man sobbed and offered no resistance. Bellew continued in a murmur, "And that duty is to enlist with the damned bastards occupying our country and have them spend as much money as they will on training you, feeding you, clothing you, and giving you a good weapon – and then to desert them as quick as you can and bring that fine investment of theirs to General Washington." He stepped back and clapped the man on his shoulder with a sharp nod.

The man stared at him, the tears drying on his face. "Thank you, sir," he whispered, and then he walked quickly to the guard at the rear of the enclosure.

O'Malley had sat up again on his own, Bellew saw with surprise when he turned back to his friend. He slipped his arm under O'Malley's arms and helped him to his feet. "You're stronger," he noted cautiously.

"Ah, lad, I'm sure I am," O'Malley replied. "To hear you talk that way to that poor soul was worth a hundred doctors to me."

Chapter 14

Rachel was so overcome by her unexpected meeting with Lieutenant Bellew – alive, surely, but in such a terrible state – that she scarcely knew what she did or said when she got to the market, only that she managed to secure three women who seemed glad at the chance of work and were more than willing to accompany her home for Mrs. Addison's contest. She placed an order with the grocer, the butcher, and the dry-goods man for everything the potential cooks said they wanted, and the eagerness of these tradesmen to extend the Addisons credit did more than any argument or description Rachel could have mustered to convince the women of the value of this position.

"You mustn't fret so, Miss Kolkhorst," said the youngest of the three women, a dark creature with remarkably long, fine fingers whose last name was something that Rachel found vaguely Italian, Rimini or some such, and whose Christian name was Maria. She carried a paper parcel of lamb's meat under her arm. She had claimed that it did not matter if the lambs were so old they were better called sheep; she would turn their flesh as soft as butter, and would be able to do the same trick even if they were monkeys. The idea of monkey meat unsettled the other two women, who scowled at the same time – a rare moment of unity because, as Rachel had realized to her despair only after engaging them, the two older women detested each other heartily. "Your mistress's dinner will go beautifully, I promise you. I do not speak only for myself; I know a little of Mrs. Abernethy and Mrs. Carroll, and I assure you their dishes would fill even a Duke to bursting." Neither Mrs. Abernethy nor Mrs. Carroll seemed willing to accept a compliment that involved the other, and so they maintained a frosty silence. And Rachel wasn't sure that much of a compliment was meant, either; a Duke could be filled with sand as well as a roast.

"It isn't that, Mrs. – Mrs. Rimini," Rachel said, hoping she'd gotten the name right. She swallowed hard, and then she confided a little of what she'd seen earlier at the prison, the frighteningly rapid loss of weight, the squalor, the illnesses permitted to bloom and left to fester. These women from the working classes had no more power over affairs than Rachel did; but it was a relief to unburden her mind a little.

"Ah." Mrs. Rimini tilted her head back as if the information meant something particular to her.

"War is a terrible –" Mrs. Carroll began.

"Yes, I know war is a terrible thing," Rachel interrupted almost rudely. She did not want to hear another school-lesson. "You've heard of this, Mrs. Rimini?"

"Yes – I believe so," Mrs. Rimini answered slowly. "I lived in New-York before and stayed there a few months after the regulars took it. I heard stories like this there."

"Then it's everywhere?" Rachel cried in despair. "This is simply how they treat their prisoners, and there's no appeal to be made?"

"I don't know. Perhaps. But what they said in New-York was that the worst of it was at the pleasure of the Provost-Marshall, Captain Cunningham. And it wasn't only that he treated the prisoners like bottle-flies, making 'em gasp out their lives packed cheek to jowl in ships filled with corpses and waste –"

"Here, now," Mrs. Abernethy protested sturdily.

"– but that knowing men died at his command was not enough for him, he needed to see, it, smell it, feel it with his own hands." Here Mrs. Rimini cupped her palms in front of her expressively, with her elegant fingers curled into claws. "So in the middle of the night, he would send out his men to one of the ships. He would tell his soldiers, bring me six – which six, they would say – it don't matter, he would say, just six – and the soldiers would choose six men from the stinking hold, and as soon as the prisoners were outside, that was when they would tell them – you, sirs, are all traitors, murderers, and scoundrels, and you are to be hanged at once, the world is well rid of you – and then the poor souls would be forced to march down the street weeping and praying for their souls until they reached the scaffold, where Captain Cunningham sat waiting."

"And then they were hanged," Rachel said in a dull voice.

"Aye." Mrs. Rimini nodded. "And then they were hanged, right before his bloody eyes. Sometimes when the need got too fierce on him, he'd do it every night. Only the path the men took from the ships to the scaffold had a lot of houses along the way, and some of the women up and complained that all that crying and praying in the dead of night was disturbing their slumber, which I bet it was, and they got it to stop somehow. At least, that's what my friends in New-York tell me. The prison ships are still there, but the hangings are stopped. What's replaced 'em, I can't say. But I do know that this Captain Cunningham – well, he ain't in New-York any more. He was transferred. Transferred – here," Mrs. Rimini concluded with dramatic relish. "And they still give the prisoners to his tender care."

"I don't care for ghost stories," Mrs. Carroll said, holding her eggs so tightly Rachel was sure they'd pop open all over her dress.

"Well, it ain't one." Mrs. Rimini frowned. She had clearly enjoyed telling her story and didn't like to hear exception taken to its quality.

"I know it isn't," Rachel said quickly. "Would Heaven that it were."

"Oh, I think the Lord will have a thing or two to say to Captain Cunningham when He gets His hands on him, and that's a show I'd pay more'n a penny to see," Mrs. Rimini concluded enthusiastically.

"His will is just," Mrs. Abernethy added, probably to irritate Mrs. Carroll.

"But this guest of your Mrs. Addison," Mrs. Rimini went on. "Now, he's a prisoner that seems to be getting the sort of punishment most of us would give our eye-teeth for." Mrs. Rimini grinned, and Rachel noticed that she was missing one of her eye-teeth already.

"General Lee is very high-ranking, and he's on parole," Rachel said. "It's General *Charles* Lee." This information had a less stupendous effect than she'd hoped. "Anyway, I'm not even sure he's coming for dinner tonight. Probably he won't, and it will be just the family. It's pretty short notice."

They walked down Broad Street, the cooks expressing their admiration for the grand mansions and yards and particular satisfaction when Rachel pointed to the Addisons' home. "I'll take you in to meet Mrs. Addison, and then I'll show you what you need to get to work," Rachel said. "What time is it?" Mrs. Carroll informed her that the bells had rung two o'clock not too long ago, while Mrs. Abernethy insisted that it had been only one. "Well, dinner's at four. You'll have enough time anyway." She turned the handle of the front door. An odd scrabbling noise came from inside, but before Rachel had time to wonder what it might be, the door was open and a terrible inhuman form leaped upon her with a devilish cough, its eyes blazing with madness. Hard claws sank through her clothes, pressing into her flesh, and Rachel fell back, a scream choked in her throat.

Abraham appeared, his eyes bright with a lively alarm Rachel had never seen in him before. "Down!" he shouted in a peremptory voice. "Down!" He grabbed the dog by the scruff of its neck and flung it off Rachel. The dog, a sleek greyhound, was not much deterred by this initial setback, and it whuffled and yapped behind the obstacle of Abraham's body, trying to get at Rachel again to greet her or devour her or whatever it was. She could still feel the wetness of its breath on her face. Abraham braced himself bodily across the doorway and kicked at the dog to keep it back.

"What by all the angels –" Mrs. Abernethy demanded. Abraham ignored her and addressed Rachel hurriedly.

"General Lee's got four of 'em, Miss Rachel, and it's all I can do to keep 'em off Mrs. Addison, so go by the kitchen door, if you please, if these is the cooks!"

Rachel nodded understanding and shut the door – Abraham's hands were too full for that task. The dog yelped in defeat, and Rachel could hear it throw itself against the door. More of the strange scrabbling sounds, and more strange, short barks. Perhaps all four dogs were planning to make a united thrust at the offensive door. At least it would keep them away from Mrs. Addison.

Rachel cleared her throat. "I am sorry," she said. "Apparently General Lee has arrived, and he, I knew he had dogs, but I didn't realize –"

"What are they doing inside the house?" Mrs. Abernethy said in horror.

"He must have just come now. I'm sure the condition won't last – Mrs. Addison was very clear on her feelings about General Lee's dogs, and now I understand, I'm afraid. We'll just go around the back."

The kitchen was mercifully free of dogs. Rachel showed the women where everything was and left them busy with their plans and preparations. She had foolishly opened her new jacket after getting too hot running from the prison, and the greyhound's claws had ripped a small tear in the neck of her dress. Now she needed to repair it. But no sooner had she placed her foot on the first stair than she heard Mrs. Addison's voice calling from the drawing room. "Rachel, is that you? If you could come here a moment, please."

Rachel quickly fastened the jacket to cover her disorder. She entered the drawing room and bobbed a curtsy, her head lowered modestly. "I found three cooks, madam, and they're in the kitchen now."

Mrs. Addison was pale and tense, rather than pleased at the news. One of the dogs was wandering behind her chair, and it clearly distracted her attention. A grim-faced Abraham herded a second dog back into the room from wherever its most recent whim had taken it. The remaining greyhounds sat alert at the feet of what could only be General Charles Lee himself. One of them licked at something from his hand, and the other bounced on its hindquarters, demanding its own treat.

When Rachel thought of a General, or a baronet's bloodline, she certainly never imagined anything like the disheveled form slouching on the blue silk chair she had taken so long over a cleaning she would need to repeat, and soon. His face was ordinary and might have passed for reasonably handsome if animated by a pleasant expression, which Rachel did not find. His eyes were lively but cold, reminding Rachel a little of the dog that Abraham had just pulled off her. The shadow of a stain discolored the stomach of his coat, as if he had spilled something on himself at breakfast and simply forgotten about it.

Almost as surprising was Mr. Addison, who was animated to the point of being almost energetic by this interesting company. A cheerful flush covered the slabs of his cheeks, and his dark eyes were alert.

General Lee glanced up. "Three cooks?" he said with a short laugh. "I can see my appetites were anticipated." He took a small cake and ate it absently with the same hand that his dog had been licking. The neglected dog stood and yelped. He patted it on its head with his free hand, and it snapped at him, angry about the food.

"We're only keeping one of them, General," Mrs. Addison said with a brittle smile. Then she explained her idea for the contest in lieu of having been able to find a cook with references in Philadelphia's current state.

"Hm," General Lee said. "Sounds like a lot of damned complication over a simple matter, like most women's affairs." He grinned at Mr. Addison, and the two shared a moment of sympathy.

Rachel froze in astonishment. Had the man actually uttered a profanity in a polite drawing room? She must have misheard somehow; but she could not imagine what else the word might have reasonably been. Mrs. Addison was glancing down at her lap, fiddling with a ring. How General Lee could be so unkind not only to a lady, but his hostess, was impossible to understand.

"I hope you haven't gone to all that trouble on my account," General Lee went on smoothly, as if he neither knew nor cared that his manner had been abominable. He took another corn-cake and held it in the air. "I find these quite delightful, wherever it is that you've come by them. I haven't tasted authentic corn-cakes since I lived with the Mohawk, and I find I rather miss them." He suddenly clucked his tongue against the roof of his mouth. All four of the dogs pricked up their ears, the neglected one with particular avidity. The creature was not disappointed. General Lee tossed the much-praised corn-cake onto the floor, and the dog pounced on it immediately. Its brothers gathered around, pushing for their share of the treat, but the first greyhound knew its rights and made plain it meant to defend them to the last extremity. The noise of the growling and snapping was not easily ignored. General Lee managed to do so nevertheless.

"Yes, that was Rachel," Mrs. Addison said loudly and leaning forward to make herself heard over the din. "She knows all sorts of Indian things, having grown up on the frontier. Are those Mohawk cakes, dear?"

Rachel shook her head. "The Mohawk inhabit more the New-York area, I believe," she said. "Although of course they will travel substantial distances on their various affairs. In South Carolina, we are more familiar with other tribes – where I grew up, the Cherokee mostly."

"And so these are Cherokee corn-cakes."

"Yes, ma'am."

"Well, that's very informative, and I'm sure Rachel will be more than pleased to produce as many of these delicacies as you like. In the meantime, Rachel, would you show General Lee up to his room? I think Jacob must have finished the unpacking by now, and Abraham – is occupied." Abraham was exceedingly occupied. One of the dogs was trying to climb a spindly étagère filled with enamel boxes and porcelain figurines to get at some imagined threat in the shadows high on the wall, and Abraham had to restrain the beast with one hand while the other hand remained firmly on the étagère. All its little treasures rattled and trembled like drops of water clinging to a leaf in a storm. Rachel could hardly endure to watch.

"Yes, of course. If you'll come with me, sir," she said.

General Lee grunted and rose, crumbs spilling from his jacket in profusion, though a few clung like frightened parasites. Rachel bowed her head in respect and led the way silently. It disturbed her that she liked General Lee so little. She knew that great men were prone to eccentricity. And it was small of her to judge him by his deficiencies, when no doubt these were a mere by-product of his mind being taken up by far more important matters. As Rachel climbed the stairs, and General Lee followed her, she talked herself by degrees out of her initial impressions of the man, and by the time they reached the east bedroom, she was entirely his partisan again, dogs and all.

"This is your room, sir," she said, opening the door gently. "Mrs. Addison thinks highly of the view and hoped you would enjoy it. Of course, she says you're entirely welcome to choose another room if you find one more to your liking." This last was an extemporization on Rachel's part, but she was sure Mrs. Addison would endorse the offer.

General Lee gave a short nod and strode past her into the room. Rachel noted with approval that his sloppy, inattentive manner was replaced by a martial precision now that he was called to make a judgment, and she felt redeemed in her decision to give him the benefit of the doubt. He clasped his hands behind his back and stared out the central window a moment. Whatever his opinion of the view, he concluded it, and then glanced inside the wardrobe to see that his belongings had been unpacked. Next he walked over to the bed and pressed it with his hand, testing its firmness. He eyed the low fire burning in the grate as if measuring it somehow, and then he really did measure it, lining himself up with the foot of the bed and counting the steps till he reached the fire. Six.

General Lee turned to Rachel and looked at her for the first time with a steady, unsmiling gaze. He did not say anything, and she began to grow uncomfortable. "Is it, is it acceptable, sir?"

"Bed's a bit cold," he replied abruptly.

"Oh! I'm sorry. The fire hasn't been going long enough, I'm sure." She thought a moment. "I could heat the foot-warmer and put it on the mattress. That will chase away the chill for now, and I'm sure the fire will have caught up with the rest of the room by bed-time and keep it snug."

"Waste of time," General Lee said.

"I'm sorry, sir, but any other room I prepare now will be even slower to heat, I'm afraid; this fire's been going for three hours now, and any other I start will only have just begun. I assure you the expedient of the foot-warmer will –"

"It just needs the chill taken off, and I'm sure it will be fine," General Lee said in a conciliatory tone. "Why don't you just sit on it a moment? That would be quicker than the foot-warmer, and then we won't have to trouble about it any more."

Rachel frowned. His request did not make sense. The foot-warmer would be much faster. But when she did not move immediately, impatience gathered behind General Lee's eyes as a storm on the horizon. So she decided it was better to humor his odd request than to press her own better idea, and she bobbed her head, spun around, and sat. Air sighed from the feather-bed and tickled the tiny hairs around her face. It was a little cool, she had to admit, if he meant to have a nap any time soon.

"Come on, then, we don't want to be all day about this," General Lee snapped, watching her with a frown.

Rachel looked at him blankly. She could not imagine what else it was he expected her to do. She was already sitting on the bed. There was no furnace inside her body where she could heap fuel to raise her temperature. She pressed her palms against the blankets and, when the heat deserted her skin, she flipped her hands over and pressed down their backs. A bed had never seemed so overwhelmingly, depressingly vast. General Lee was waiting, his annoyance only barely in check. The bed was not warmer in the slightest, as nearly as Rachel could tell, although she had succeeded in making it almost as wrinkled and slovenly as General Lee's clothes. Where were those miserable dogs of his, when they might have been of some use? Rachel doubted that General Lee would object to dog-hair on his blankets, and the one greyhound that had breathed in Rachel's face had had breath hot enough to bake an egg.

Still pushing her hands into the plump softness of the featherbed, Rachel leaned to the side and rested her cheek against the pillow. She realized too late that General Lee might reasonably want his pillow to remain cool.

"Hey, Robert! Now this is a fine bed," General Lee called to the hallway in a sudden excellent humor, evidently having established an intimacy with Mr. Addison quickly enough to entitle the use of his first name, unless it was simply another one of General Lee's unreflective arrogations.

Mr. Addison glanced in the room curiously. His eyes flashed amusement, quickly damped down to a polite level.

"Afraid there's no fish in those waters, Charles," Mr. Addison replied dryly.

"The innocent ones can be the easiest," General Lee opined.

Rachel abruptly realized her position, lying down on a strange man's bed. A hot flush covered her body, and her pulse hammered rapidly in her ears. Her eyes swelled with a flood of unshed tears. It was not that her blood merely rose; it felt as though she were drowning in a sea of it.

"Sir!" Rachel choked out, trembling. She scrambled to her feet. The blush reached even her hands, turning them a healthy rose. She could only imagine the blazing red of her cheeks. Rachel was putting out more than enough heat, now, to have turned the bed behind her into ash; and no occurrence could have pleased her better. It was all she could do not to burst out crying.

"It's all right, dear," Mr. Addison said easily. "Off you go."

"No, do that business with the foot-warmer first," General Lee said brusquely, forgetting her already. Rachel had to brush past his detestable form to get to the fire. She kept her eyes low, not from modesty or embarrassment, but so that he would not see the raw anger that burned hotter than any coal. Rachel had been treated as a burden many times before, and even as a trifle; but not until now with such dehumanizing contempt. Even poor Lieutenant Masterson's fondling of her skirt had not been designed to humiliate her, although it had been performed without much regard for her intrinsic dignity. The skirt itself had been a valued and desired object at least. But with General Lee, Rachel did not think he'd had any intention of seducing her. All he'd wanted to do was make her look cheap and mean. She could not imagine Lieutenant Bellew suffering this man's orders for long.

But perhaps it was only captivity, no matter how gilded, that showed General Lee in a poor light. Although a truly great man – a truly worthy one – bore even the most caustic gall without letting it eat away at the bedrock of his soul, no doubt a man who was only in the process of becoming great had his moments of petulance en route.

General Lee and Mr. Addison strolled from the room chatting amiably, leaving Rachel to her work. The foot-warmer was a tin box ventilated with punched holes that sketched out the outlines of intertwined hearts. She slid up the front panel and pulled out the drawer. As she plucked embers from the fire with the tongs and nestled them in the drawer, Rachel reconciled herself to General Lee yet again, for the second time in less than fifteen minutes. After all, he had no actual obligation to treat equally with Rachel, even if polite condescension was a gentlemanly quality. Insofar as he was a creature of prodigious talents that he had pledged to the service of a greater cause, this was the sum and entirety of his duty.

And she prayed that he might rise again to fill it. For fill it he must. The Continental Army was in obvious tatters, with neither center nor direction to hold it together. It was not merely partisans who said so; everyone did, whether they were happy about it or not. If it hadn't been for General Howe's political views and generous feelings towards the people here, Rachel was sure the remaining American forces would have been mopped up in an instant. She did not wish this to happen. Lieutenant Bellew's condition, and his hopes, loomed large in her thoughts but formed only part of her developing opinion on the rebellion. If she were honest with herself – and if she ignored Mrs. Addison's doubtless practical advice to avoid subjects that required analysis – she felt that both sides had valid insights and valid arguments based upon them; and yet their conclusions were wholly at odds. The question was not, therefore, which side possessed truth. It was a question that could not, therefore, be answered by discussion. It could not be dissected by scrutiny. It could not be resolved in principle. It could be resolved only in fact.

If it were resolved in England's favor, so be it. But Britain would have to earn her victory, not assume it as the God-given right that it was not.

Rachel pressed the rectangular base of the foot-warmer against every square inch of the bed in turn, until she was satisfied that General Lee could have no cause for complaint. She let the faint impressions in the covers remain. She wanted General Lee to rest assured that she had followed his instructions in every particular; and she also was very eager to speak with Mrs. Addison as quickly as possible and did not want to waste time shaking out the blankets.

Rachel hurried downstairs and found Mrs. Addison still in the drawing room, alone and to all appearances grateful for it. Mrs. Addison bent over the blue silk chair where General Lee had sat. Her face turned up to Rachel's in anguish.

"There's a hole poked all the way through," she said, sticking a finger at a gouge-mark in the fabric. "Look, Rachel. Wolves are better-behaved."

"Perhaps the dogs are part feral."

"I meant better-behaved than General Lee," Mrs. Addison said in an undertone, straightening. "This is awful, just awful." Her eyes searched the shadows past Rachel to be sure no one was coming who might hear.

"I'm sure he's merely fatigued."

"From his harrowing fifteen-minute carriage ride. Yes, I'm sure also. At the same time as I cannot imagine why on earth his former hosts would have found themselves unable to oblige his delightful presence any longer."

A dry skittering sounded in the darkness behind Rachel. She wheeled around in a cold terror, her hands already raised to protect herself. But the source of the frightening noise proved to be nothing worse than the graceful teardrop shape of a dead elm-leaf dried to the color of honey hopping along the stone floor. Rachel bent down and plucked it up with relief. "Where are the dogs?" she asked with a lightness she did not feel.

"I had Abraham take them outside after you left the room. No matter what General Lee claims about the creatures' delicacy, I am *sure* they will profit from the exercise," Mrs. Addison said in a strained voice.

"And if the excitement and the weather prove too much for them, then the profit will be to the rest of us," Rachel replied.

Mrs. Addison smiled and sat down on the ruined chair. "Rachel, I am so grateful to have you," she said warmly. "You don't know what a relief you are to me, in so many ways." Some of the tension seemed to leave her narrow frame, and the billows of her flocked green polonaise swelled up around her form as if to cushion her in a flowery cloud.

"You know that I owe you everything, and I hope you know that I am aware of it too," Rachel said. "Any service that I might be for you will never repay my debt."

"Why, how you talk. I assure you, Rachel, sometimes you make me feel as if I am living in 'The Song of Roland' or 'Beowulf' or something like that. Everything always so portentous."

"I mention it because I feel obliged to ask a further favor of you, and I know I do not merit it." Then she explained the condition in which she had found Lieutenant Bellew earlier that day. Mrs. Addison's face fell serious, and she looked aside. Rachel pressed on, describing Captain O'Malley, whom she was sure Mrs. Addison would remember from his fine speech, lying sick and untended beneath the cold winter sky, with nothing but a coat to cover him.

"I don't know why you're telling me these things," Mrs. Addison said at last. Her voice was sharp, and the line between her eyebrows pronounced. "To acknowledge life's crueler face may be necessary at times, but this seems - Rachel, it's like you're wallowing in it, and if you simply want someone to share your intense disapproval of its existence, very well, rest assured that I do so quite implicitly and would rather not be obliged to demonstrate it over and over again." She breathed out heavily.

"I don't mean - I'm sorry - it's because of your father, ma'am! Surely General van Dortmund could explain matters to General Washington! And he would know what to do."

Mrs. Addison blinked. She looked surprised, and a little relieved. "Ah - my father," she said. "Well, yes, of course he must see General Washington regularly at the moment - yes, all right, I'll send him a note," Mrs. Addison decided. "Putting officers in with enlisted men is just unfathomably strange."

"Oh, thank you, ma'am!" Rachel cried, delighted at her sudden conquest. "I'll go get some paper at once -"

"I can't do it right now," Mrs. Addison said with a scowl, swatting irritably at the folds of her dress. "Not at the moment, I'm sure you understand, we are a little pressed personally without involving ourselves in additional concerns, and dinner so soon. And I would be quite surprised if the intelligence is going to prove novel to General

Washington. But it will make you feel better, dear, and father will be pleased to see me demonstrate an interest."

Rachel curtsied, and Mrs. Addison sighed, steeling herself, and rising to her feet. "I'll need you in thirty minutes for my dress," she said, leaving the room, and Rachel curtsied again.

A small, hopeful excitement burned in her breast. The victory was total, and the defeat small. A few hours one way or the other were unlikely to make a difference when Mrs. Addison's note would still have to find a messenger, and that messenger would have to wait either until he had official clearance or some lightning-bolt of bravery or whiskey fueled his courage to take a chance without, and even then there remained one or two days' travel to reach Valley Forge. Rachel returned to her duties with a heart that was heavier by far than it had been two days ago, but so much lighter than it had seemed for the past few hours that she felt she must almost fly to the ceiling for sheer joy.

The étagère was in terrible disarray. That was a small thing, but it needed attention, and Rachel busied herself among the bric-a-brac. She knew precisely the position and angle at which every piece belonged – the swan with a bent neck, the three Muses in joyful dance, the glass lily – just as she knew every object in this mansion that she loved so dearly.

The smells starting to leak from the kitchen were enticing, and even the noises held promise: the popping of fat and the low bubble of a simmering pot. Rachel was sure that a good meal would put everyone in a better state of mind. Guilt struck her immediately; she remembered Lieutenant Bellew's painful starvation. And poor Captain O'Malley. If he were as sick as he seemed, he probably had no appetite at all; and that was even worse than an unsatisfied one.

"Miss Rachel?" Rachel turned in surprise to see Jacob standing anxiously behind her. "You got that letter? You know – the one you talked about before?"

"Thank you, Jacob, but I don't suppose it would seem natural if you delivered it now," she said.

"Sure, but it might be that Mrs. Addison send me over there on something else, or the master do, and if you give me that letter, I'll keep it with me all the time and be ready."

Rachel blinked. "You're quite right," she said. "Thank you. No, I haven't written it yet, but I'll do it first thing. That was very clever of you, Jacob. Much cleverer than I've been." She began to frame the words in her mind. It did not have to be a long note or an elaborate one, only clear and exacting enough to make plain that the prisoners were subjected not merely to privation but to ungentlemanly abuse.

Her mind held a new question, though, and an unpleasant one. Mrs. Rimini's description of Captain Cunningham's history and career left little doubt that either his methods were countenanced or that the man was, which was just as bad. Whatever General Howe's reasons might be for this, she no longer felt as sure as she had even a few hours earlier that he was unaware of the situation and would hasten to correct it once he knew.

But she had to try everything. If she were trapped in inhuman bondage, there would be no balm for her soul but to hope that someone, somewhere was trying with all his might to free her from it. If she cared for Lieutenant Bellew at all – if she meant to honor the spirit of her promise to Lieutenant Masterson – if she hoped to hold any worth in her own eyes, she could not do less than everything in her power. Jacob was right. And she was grateful to him too that he did not question the contradiction between her new views, even if he did not know the details, and her old. She was not sure she herself would have been so kind.

A less worthy happiness also sent heat and energy through her limbs, one that she hardly dared admit. And this was that it would be her hand, not another's, to lift the pall of despair from Lieutenant Bellew and Captain O'Malley – that Lieutenant Bellew knew her now, and knew she was his friend. Surely he must think of her as the same. He would not forget her again, this time. He might forget a kindness that he had done; he would never forget another's.

It had no bearing on the situation or her duty within it. And yet this was the thought that crept back into her mind repeatedly as she whirled through her chores, helped Mrs. Addison with her elaborate toilette, and finally smartened herself by changing into an untorn dress and smoothing her hair.

The supper-table was perfect. Rachel knew it was, not only because she'd worked so hard at it, but because no one seemed to take notice of it one way or the other, and that meant that nothing was wrong. The cooks in the kitchen were fussing over the last details with enough concern that Mrs. Carroll and Mrs. Abernethy had forgotten to fight. Mrs. Addison took her seat, and then the gentlemen took theirs. General Lee glanced around. "Where's Phaeton?" He tucked his lower lip beneath his front teeth and blew a shrill whistle.

Mrs. Addison leaned forward to say distinctly, "I believe Abraham has them quite contentedly enjoying –" but then a chorus of barks and baying made further conversation impossible, and there was nothing for it but to let the greyhounds back into the house. They galloped to their master's side and panted noisily and made a general nuisance of themselves by not sitting still.

Rachel kept half a wary eye on them. She did not think she would be forgiven a spill, no matter how treacherous the terrain. She brought out the courses in turn, starting with a light rice soup and sliced pears, followed by dishes of spiced nuts and candied blossoms, then beef medallions and roasted potatoes still in their skins. Jacob poured the wine, and Rachel felt even sorrier for him than she did for herself, because she could catch herself if she stepped on a dog – which she did once or twice – but a falling bottle of wine was hard to recover. He had the balance of a cat and managed somehow.

Mrs. Addison seemed to have resigned herself to the dogs, ignoring them politely when they pushed their snouts at her for treats the same way she would ignore a child blowing its nose into its sleeve, and she maintained an appearance of charming interest in the conversation without contributing to it much. Mr. Addison and General Lee, meanwhile, talked animatedly as if they were the best of old friends reunited after too long an absence, laughing and thumping the table and signaling for frequent refills of their wine-glasses.

"Did you see the *Atlantic Gazetteer* this morning?"

"No, I haven't read anything today – I had the most suffocating headache until one, and then it was time to leave."

"I'm surprised the Higbies didn't show you the notice. Don't they take the *A-G*?"

"What was in it?"

"Some pretty favorable reflections upon your abilities. I'll show it to you after dinner, with port." Mr. Addison's mind had already drifted far from the delicate lobster pie that Rachel placed in front of him.

General Lee snorted. "Then I imagine the *A-G* is about to be banned reading in the Continentals," he said.

"Oh, now -" Mrs. Addison began, leaning forward with a sympathetic expression.

Rachel stepped over Phaeton, or Pelias, she couldn't tell the difference and didn't think she'd be able to learn, and retreated to the kitchen to put Mrs. Rimini's lamb-olives into bowls.

"Has anyone said anything yet?" Mrs. Rimini asked her eagerly, helping her with the lamb-olives. Rachel noticed she had a good eye for balance and arranged the tidbits neatly even while seeming to pay little attention to them.

"They seem quite pleased with everything," Rachel murmured. "They're finishing every plate."

"Then they're eating too much and won't have any appetite for my blancmange," Mrs. Abernethy complained. "I'll hardly get a fair trial."

"The pear slices were yours," Mrs. Carroll replied consolingly, with a broad smile.

"I'm sure if they're less hungry, they'll have more attention to spare to your artistry," Rachel said, but Mrs. Abernethy still seemed down in spirits. Still, she must have roused herself for a final effort, because twenty minutes later when Rachel brought out the blancmanges, they had been trimmed into lovely scalloped shapes and decorated with paper-thin slices of almond.

"Oh, how pretty," Mrs. Addison exclaimed. She scooped a tiny bite with the edge of her spoon and tasted it, even though she usually avoided desserts.

The desserts were consumed with yet more wine, and Mr. Addison pushed himself back from the table and declared himself more than ready to start on the port.

"But Robert, what about the contest?"

"Hmm?" he grunted in confusion.

Rachel felt sorry for Mrs. Addison. Her contest idea had certainly been a success in finding good cooks; but it had failed in providing amusement, and Rachel knew which matter her employer set greater store by.

But Mrs. Addison did not take the disappointment hard. "Oh well. The cooks, Robert. We were going to pick one after testing them out. Have you established a preference?"

"Well, who did the, did the, I'm not quite sure which – it was all fine, Margaret, you choose," Mr. Addison concluded. He was more than respectably drunk.

"Why not bring 'em out," General Lee suggested. Rachel could imagine nothing more exquisitely painful than being weighed and judged to one's face, but Mrs. Addison shrugged and asked Rachel to call the three cooks for their final disposition.

"Which one of us is it?" Mrs. Carroll whispered excitedly when Rachel told them they were summoned to the dining room.

"I'm afraid they haven't decided yet." This intelligence satisfied no one, and the cooks kept a wary, competitive distance from each other as they followed Rachel. "Watch out for the dogs," she whispered quickly, and then she went about clearing the dishes from the table. Mrs. Abernethy's eyes lighted on the barely touched blancmange in front of Mrs. Addison, and her expression wilted. Rachel wished she could explain that a half-eaten dessert was a remarkable victory in that quarter.

"Who did those medallions?" General Lee demanded as if he were addressing a line of fresh ensigns. Mrs. Carroll smiled hesitantly and lifted the tips of her fingers in acknowledgment.

"Blessed fine beef," Mr. Addison interposed, and Mrs. Addison nodded her agreement. So it would be Mrs. Carroll.

But General Lee did not look satisfied. "Ah. Thank you," he nodded sharply, his eyes raking over the women and settling upon a close perusal of Mrs. Rimini, who Rachel suddenly realized was quite handsome, even if her lushness was already going to seed a little. But Mrs. Rimini doubtless had a good five years of attractiveness left in her; and twenty years at least before she reached the age or stoutness of either Mrs. Carroll or Mrs. Abernethy. "And you, my good woman," General Lee said. "What was your contribution to our meal today?"

Mrs. Rimini curtsied and took a deep breath. Rachel didn't think she was nervous. But the inhalation certainly did force the fullness of her bosom to swell over her stays. Rachel dropped her head quickly so that her astonishment would not show. Surely she was mistaken – and the suspicion did her no credit, when Mrs. Rimini had been nothing but amiable and kind and devoted to her work.

"The veal-olives were, in my opinion, my best work, sir," Mrs. Rimini replied. "But I leave it to your judgment, of course."

General Lee's eyes did not travel higher than her neck. "Well," he said, thumping his hand against the table. "Well. I myself think we need look no farther than those delightful veal-olives. But I am only a guest here."

"The veal-olives were both inventive and agreeable," Mr. Addison said.

Mrs. Addison glanced between the two men, a thin smile fixed on her lips. "Is that the consensus, then?"

"Veal-olives, my dear!"

"Yes, Robert. Very well. Your name, my good woman?"

Mrs. Rimini curtsied. "Mrs. Maria Rimini, madam." Rachel had gotten the name right, then.

"The job is yours, if you're willing. And my thanks to all of you and your splendid work," she said, graciously inclining her head to the defeated Mrs. Carroll and Mrs. Abernethy.

Mrs. Rimini glowed with palpable delight and seized fistfuls of her skirt in her excitement. She regained control of herself and curtsied her acknowledgment to Mrs. Addison with a modest dip of her head. General Lee, his cheeks mottled with wine, leaned conspiratorially towards her. "Now, don't forget who backed your sally, my dear," he said.

"I never forget my friends, sir," Mrs. Rimini replied. "And I like to have as many as possible."

Chapter 15

Mrs. Rimini found the length of the walk to the Addisons' mansion inconvenient and decided that she must be installed in one of the spare rooms, of which admittedly there was a superabundance.

"Shouldn't you speak with Mr. Rimini first?" Rachel inquired. She placed a stack of four greasy dishes on the counter. "I'm sure he'll concur with your judgment, but he might want a say in a matter that affects him so intimately."

"You're welcome to ask him yourself, if you can find him," Mrs. Rimini answered breezily. "Jacob, go pick up my things at 18 Greenbrier Alley, if you know Greenbrier? Just go down Cayuga towards the river, and someone will show you the way. It's on the top floor. Anyone can show you the room."

Jacob had been helping the two women clean the dinner-plates. He looked up at Mrs. Rimini doubtfully. "I don't know," he said, shaking his head back and forth in the slow rhythm that Rachel had learned meant serious misgivings. "Maybe you should ask Mrs. Addison if you gonna up and –"

"Now, you don't make her come down and deal with every minute detail in the household herself, do you? No wonder she looks so dreadfully tired," Mrs. Rimini exclaimed. Guilt stabbed Rachel's heart. Was Mrs. Addison truly weary, and not merely aggravated by the events of the day? She wiped the plate in her hands hard enough almost to crack it. Jacob also had no response, and so Mrs. Rimini won her point by default.

Rachel suggested that Mrs. Rimini send Jacob with a note authorizing him to remove her belongings, but Mrs. Rimini demurred, saying she did not have a very good hand. Rachel offered to write the note herself, but Mrs. Rimini demurred again, saying that the landlady read about as well as Mrs. Rimini wrote, so probably it was best if Jacob just went and extemporized around any difficulties that arose. Then Mrs. Rimini wiped her damp hands on her skirts and gave all of them a few veal-olives she'd saved, accepting their compliments happily.

Mr. Addison and General Lee had ensconced themselves in Mr. Addison's study with the door shut tight, although the rich, bitter smell of tobacco leaked freely from it and Rachel heard the low roar of masculine laughter when she walked past. She couldn't hear their voices well enough to make out any words, but she supposed she probably didn't want to know the details of their conversation, judging by the effect General Lee seemed to have on Mr. Addison. How she regretted not having been able to unburden herself to General Lee when they had been alone, but his conduct had made that impossible. She would speak with him later. General Lee's position as a fellow-prisoner might make it ticklish for him to raise the subject of ill-treatment; but it might have the opposite effect, too, because General Lee could rightly claim that he knew General Howe had done well by him and therefore obviously intended nothing but the most generous fairness to his captives; and it would be difficult for General Howe to claim otherwise to General Lee's face.

Two of the greyhounds patrolled the hallways, snuffling their noses into Rachel's skirts and begging for attention or favor or she did not know what, but she swallowed her fright well enough to pat them on the head and at least wasn't mauled again for her pains, although she was slobbered on considerably. The beasts meant well, she supposed, only no one had shown them how to act.

She had no time to make friends with them now, anyway. There was Mrs. Rimini's room to prepare. Rachel thought the matter over and decided that it would seem most welcoming if she put Mrs. Rimini next to herself. There was something about the new cook that Rachel found a little off-putting, although she couldn't lay her finger on the source of her unease. The woman was agreeable and amiable in manner, she was proficient at her work and had not shown any of the minute signs that Rachel hated of a malingerer. Rachel hoped she was not merely jealous of a newcomer whose talents would make her indispensable. And certainly, she was grateful for Mrs. Rimini's intelligence about Captain Cunningham.

Oh, and – Lieutenant Bellew. The letter for Jacob on the off chance he might have opportunity to hand it to General Howe. Surely that was more important than anything else, even if Jacob was busy on Mrs. Rimini's errand and Mrs. Addison had taken to her room for a nap. The dogs hadn't caused any new mischief, and the house was reasonably in order. Rachel hurriedly made up the bed in Mrs. Rimini's room and set the fire, and then she went to her own little desk by her own little window and dashed off a note in disguised handwriting. Rachel started to sign it *A Loyal Subject of Britain*, but her hand froze. She could not bring herself to say that, quite, and so she altered it mid-stream to *A Loyal Friend* instead.

Once she began writing, a new thought occurred to her. She had managed to get herself published in the *Sentinel-Observer*. What was the patriot newspaper Mr. Addison had mentioned at dinner? The *Atlantic Gazetteer*. Excitement seized her, and she shoved her hasty note aside. Rachel had not taken much ink from Mr. Addison's study yesterday, because it was expensive and she had not felt sure of her right to it. Now the level in the little glass well was sadly depleted. But if she could just get it in her head first so that she wrote without the need for corrections, and if she didn't make a copy, she thought the ink would stretch far enough.

At last, she began to write.

The Winter of Mankind

Every season has its glory, as God has decreed, and these glories make light the burdens that God has also placed on each time in its turn. Who does not cherish the tender blossoms and sweet zephyrs of Spring more than he deplores the rains that make the roads impassable and the restiveness of the animals? Who does not love the bright light of Summer and the cooling shade of thick foliage enough to forget the heat that dampens every brow and the sickness that sweeps through the crowded cities? Who does not revel in the color of Autumn and the richness of her harvest so much that he does not ignore Death's cold breath on the leaves and in the paling skies?

And then comes Winter, who drops a fairy-cloak of glittering white over all the world and bids it rest from the riot that has gone before. Perhaps no season is more secret, or more fair, despite its plainness, because for all the beauties and treasures the other three seasons offer, it is only Winter that brings peace. Seeds hide in their thick jackets beneath dirt hardened by ice. Animals return to their secret places to sleep. Even the sun shows its weariness at last, and raises its head above the horizon for only a few brief hours before slipping back to its strange dreams. Man has long followed God's law in this, and paused even his bitterest wars as long as Winter, the season of rest, held sway.

But there are always those among men who are not content to follow God's will but must flout it according to their own baser nature – and those who take this challenge onto themselves are often, alas, the basest of us all. In Spring, they see only pretty girls to ruin; in Summer, only lazy indolence; in Autumn, they drink themselves blind. And when Winter comes, these wicked monkeys playing at God think not of the peace that Heaven has bestowed on all of Creation, but see only the slow strangulation of a funeral-shroud, and their claws itch to pull it tighter.

Perhaps our first instinct should be to pity such men, who delight in the imperfection that we share at birth rather than deplore it for its shame. It is our duty to pity them, but to do so with care, because they are always dangerous and, like cowards, attack only the easiest prey – that which is closest to them, and that which, in its innocence, does not think to offer defense.

When such a man comes into power over the lives of other men, all those men he controls are his prey. And then we must tremble. Because that man now enters into his full estate of terror, and we must put our pity aside and cut him off like a gangrened limb. When we discover such a person in such a position, the preeminent duty of every one of us is not to pity but to expose him and root him out, to drag his iniquities from the shadows where they breed and let the full light of day wither their strength. For such men are clever, and they lie and wheedle and play the fool or the friend as long as it gets them their way, while as soon as their masters' backs are turned, they gorge themselves on corpses like demons. We must call upon their masters to look them full in the face and know them for what they are, and to cast them out. Beliefs may differ, and do, and men may disagree, and do – but we join together as one when we see that which is DISHONORABLE and perverts and mocks GOD'S LAW, even as it violates MAN'S.

We ask General Howe, a gracious and manly soldier of unimpeachable conduct and ability, no longer to trust a certain Provost-Marshall under his command named Captain William Cunningham, whose vile abuse of prisoners sickens and astonishes loyal servants of the Crown perhaps even more than it does the most fervent rebel. A high tone such as these words take can be justified only by high crimes – and we will list some that can be easily verified by any inhabitant of this town who cares to make inquiries. We trust General Howe's judiciousness to do so promptly and thoroughly – WE do not ask that any man be punished without a fair examination of the evidence, nor hanged without a fair trial.

HIS CRIMES:

FIRST, that Captain Cunningham crowds his prisoners into unclean accommodations not able to hold a tenth as many men, so that they have no rest, and grow weak, and easy prey to disease, which spreads unfettered through their ranks.

SECOND, that Captain Cunningham allows them so little food an infant would starve upon it.

THIRD, that the sustenance he does allow them is rotten and unfit for consumption.

FOURTH, that he does not permit the sick any relief, nor allow their illnesses to be tended by doctors.

FIFTH, that, at his pleasure, and by the authority of no court or law, he chooses men at random to be immediately hanged without trial or notice, and without any opportunity to purify their souls before meeting their Creator except what their own tearful prayers may bring.

And SIXTH, that in doing these things, he implicates the men under his command in his inhuman conduct, scoring deep wounds upon their souls.

That Captain Cunningham is guilty of more, we suspect, but we do not know, and so we do not claim it here.

The horror of these despicable crimes speaks louder than any words our quill can fashion. It is enough. We will stop here.

And let us all pray God that Captain Cunningham will also.

Rachel's trembling hand fell still. A thin puddle of ink remained at the bottom of the well, but she was exhausted and sick at heart and could say no more. The sun had set while she wrote, and the lengthening darkness invaded her soul.

Rachel watched the final curving line of ink lose its sheen and dry to flatness. She'd forgotten to lay her own fire, and her skin felt stiff and cold, like wax.

A thump in the hallway jolted her back to life with an icy shot of terror. Mrs. Addison was awake – or perhaps Mr. Addison and the general were finished in the study – someone wanted her – she would be unable to get away to the paper tonight, and another whole day wasted while Lieutenant Bellew stood pressed against the stinking bodies of his dying friends, breathed in their sickness, imagined Rachel was a flighty girl who had forgotten him and probably never cared at all. Rachel leapt to her feet and peeked out the door. One of the greyhounds sat there, staring at the wall. It half-rose on its haunches and whined when it saw her. Pity touched her.

"It's not your fault you're so intolerable," she whispered, scratching the creature behind its ears as it panted and bounced, unable to make up its mind whether to remain sitting or run around and break something. The poor thing needed either to be free entirely, or else for its nature to be given some structure or direction. Perhaps Abraham would have a chance to train the dogs after all, if General Lee and Mr. Addison were going to be very much absorbed by each other's company.

Rachel fastened her jacket around her shoulders and gathered her papers. On the way out, she saw Jacob, and handed him the note with a quick nod and smile.

"You goin' out again?" Jacob said.

"I'll be back quicker this time," Rachel promised. "I know the streets a little better now. If someone requires me before then, tell them – tell them, I don't know, that I forgot one of Mrs. Rimini's requirements – if it's Mr. Addison, tell him it's a feminine concern, and he won't want to know any more, and if it's Mrs. Addison, just that – I'll be back soon. I prepared the room next to mine for Mrs. Rimini."

"You better hurry, if you don't want to be missed," Jacob warned. Rachel took his advice.

A few last rays of red sunlight clung to the edges of things but the lamp-lighter, a stolid boy a few years older than Rachel, was already making his rounds when she left the house. She nodded a greeting to him, and he paused in his work to wave. She did not know the exact location of the *Atlantic Gazetteer*'s office, but presumably it would not be far from the *Sentinel-Observer* – usually industries clustered together, although in this case she supposed mutual antipathy might keep a little prudent distance between the two and any other political enemies. She retraced her steps without difficulty, wondering how she could have strayed so far the night before. Night fell, and a nearby church tolled five o'clock, echoed by several others farther away. Supper would not be until nine. Mrs. Addison would need to dress again after rising from her nap, but that couldn't be helped. This would be the last absence. She dared not take any more risks.

A friendly man in a battered slouch hat beamed at her request for directions to the *Atlantic Gazetteer* and insisted on walking her to the door itself. The office was a small building on Fox Street not two blocks away from the *Sentinel-Observer*. "Mr. Beltreau doesn't always open the door to strangers," he explained cheerfully, pulling the bell. "I'll let him know you're all right."

Rachel remembered how the editor of the *Sentinel-Observer* had braced himself for a punch in the face, and she nodded her understanding, though she wasn't quite sure how this kind man had decided that she was "all right," except that she was a woman.

The now familiar sounds of grinding and thumping made a muted din that Rachel could feel in her flesh almost as easily as she could hear. Of course the bell was drowned by it. The man in the slouch hat rang again, and then he knocked hard. At last the door opened.

"Hullo, Randolph," a thin, ginger-colored man in shirt-sleeves said.

"Hullo, Martin," Rachel's new friend replied. "Here's a young lady to see you. I thought you wouldn't want to miss a chance like that." Then he smiled and took his leave.

"Miss," Mr. Beltreau said, turning his pale eyes to Rachel and offering her a short bow. "Your servant." He was well-bred, despite his state of undress, and Rachel dropped a curtsy.

"If I might have a moment of your time, sir," she asked in a low voice, and Mr. Beltreau let her inside quickly, shutting the door behind her.

The room was a bit larger than the *Sentinel-Observer*'s office, and it contained several well-used desks but no other human occupants. "I sent the boys out for beer," Mr. Beltreau explained. He took a chair from one of the other desks and set it facing his own. Rachel sat, twisting her fingers nervously in an unconscious adoption of Mrs. Addison's habit, except that she wore no rings. Mr. Beltreau walked around her and sat in his own chair. He clasped his hands together and smiled gravely. "Perhaps I assume too much, Miss, but I imagine that a girl who comes to a newspaper-man must do so with the object of imparting some piece of intelligence that she's heard. If that is the case, I assure you that we have complete privacy here. The press-men can't hear a word, and the boys won't be back for an hour at least. And you have my complete attention."

Rachel's spirits lifted, and she took a sudden liking for this pale, somber man. "I do have intelligence to offer, something terribly important, something that people must know," she said eagerly. "And I've - I've also written it up for you. For the paper." She pulled the folded sheets of her essay from her skirt pocket and placed them on his desk, smoothing out their creases.

Mr. Beltreau's expression remained unchanged. It was respectful and attentive. But he did not take the pages. "Miss, I thank you for your efforts, and I'm sure they're very fine ones, but we don't print feuilletons here. You might try the *Weekly Advertiser.* I believe they're doing some experiments with the form. The editor there is a Mr. Cato Jones -"

"But it's not a feuilleton!" Rachel said in astonishment.

Lines of resignation appeared around Mr. Beltreau's mouth. "Women write about three things," he said. "Love, Nature, and God. And I concur fully that these are perhaps the matters most greatly deserving of our reverence - but our energies, in a newspaper, are devoted to practical issues of the day." He ticked off points on his fingers. "Love, we'll cover only if it gets someone killed or disgraced. Nature, only if she kicks up her traces and destroys a ship or something along those lines. God, same as Nature."

"But it's not -" Rachel choked on her words. She wished heartily she had chosen some introduction other than God's order of the seasons, but there was nothing to be done about it now. "If you'll just glance at its contents, Mr. Beltreau, it won't take a moment, and people must know, they must understand what's happening right under their noses, terrible crimes... I've been published by the newspapers before."

Mr. Beltreau sighed and balanced a pair of half-spectacles on the bridge of his nose. "What newspapers?" he asked, glancing over their rims.

Rachel hesitated. "The *Sentinel-Observer,*" she admitted.

Mr. Beltreau's sandy eyebrows shot up practically to his hairline, and he bit his lips together to repress a smile. "A bit Tory, are we?"

"Not unless you are," Rachel answered, stung. "I simply felt the *Sentinel-Observer* was the best venue for some particular thoughts, while these –" she pushed her manuscript gently closer to Mr. Beltreau, who watched her with amusement, "belong more properly here. In my opinion, of course. If, upon reading the essay, you honestly think the *Sentinel-Observer* would take it, I would be more than happy to renew my acquaintance there."

"Well, Edwards is a good fellow, despite his politics, but he doesn't publish much that doesn't toe the line pretty close," Mr. Beltreau said with a chuckle. "All right, dear. Let's see what you've got." He straightened the papers with an indulgent air and set them in front of himself. Rachel watched his eyes carefully as they flicked from line to line. An initial light of curiosity dimmed.

"Please read it all," she whispered, mortally ashamed of her Spring blossoms and Winter fairy-cloaks.

Mr. Beltreau smiled kindly. "I have always been partial to Autumn myself," he said. "It reminds me of my first day at college. Finest day of my life." But he spoke absently, still running his eyes over her words.

His pale face suddenly turned perfectly white. His back stiffened, and the chair beneath him squeaked. Then he let out a slight groan and leaned his head in his hand as he read the last page, sighed, removed his spectacles and closed his eyes. He spread a surprisingly large hand over her essay so that only a few isolated words peeked out between his fingers: unclean, rotten, hanged, hanged, souls.

Even with the pounding of the press next door, the room felt suddenly quiet.

"It's true," Rachel said. "I'm attesting only that which I've seen with my own eyes. Or – I didn't see the men being hanged, I only saw them walking to their fate, with no shoes, and their bodies ruined, and –"

Mr. Beltreau held out his hand. "Miss, I can tell you exactly where you should place this essay of yours. Not in the *Gazetteer*, and not in the *Sentinel-Observer* either, but the nearest, hottest fire you can find."

Rachel flushed. "Then do so and write the editorial yourself, Mr. Beltreau! I'll show you what you need to see – there's an old sugar house on Walnut being used as a prison – I'll take you there, and you can satisfy yourself as to the facts –"

"I am wholly satisfied as to the facts," Mr. Beltreau said in a tired voice. "Yes, I could go to your sugar house, or three more besides, or two churches and three meeting-houses, or three ships rotting in the harbor and see exactly what you describe. And if I went to your sugar house on Walnut first, I might even catch a glimpse of Captain Cunningham himself on the way, as his quarters are not far. You misunderstand me. I do not deny a single word you've written – I assert only that you should be very grateful indeed that the God who is so busy balancing sprays of jonquils against irritating rainfalls took the time this evening to be sure that you were not stopped by patrols while this was in your possession. And no, I will certainly not print it."

"But why?" Rachel cried. "What clearer, colder proof could you ask for that Britain holds us in contempt and treats us as less than human, for all her fine words and promises? Have I mistaken your sympathies?"

"Is Miss *Sentinel-Observer* for independency, then?" Mr. Beltreau said with a smile.

"I am – I have not – I wish I had not made a hasty judgment before, and I do not wish to compound my error by doing so again," Rachel said. "But set aside the cause. What of the men, Mr. Beltreau? What of the suffering men? Our brothers and friends, not just killed, but treated in this, in this – fashion."

Mr. Beltreau's face grew serious again. "I have friends among them," he answered shortly. "But getting my newspaper shut down and myself hanged won't help anyone. If you have friends taken prisoner – yes, I see you do – I advise you to take up their cases individually and discreetly rather than blasting your eighteen-pound gun at the whole system."

"But every man in prison is someone's friend or brother – and even those who are all alone in the world have no less right not to be abused," Rachel said, near tears.

Mr. Beltreau grimaced and shook his head. "Yes, they do," he said softly, not looking at her. "And I am sorry."

Rachel squeezed a handful of skirt. She had been so certain that even if her essay were rejected, the information about Captain Cunningham would be met by interest and indignation. She had never imagined such a complete failure with a man who professed himself in full agreement with the facts and her views. Of course she could not ask Mr. Beltreau to get himself hanged. But, oh, couldn't he at least try to be a little braver on his own accord? "Mr. Beltreau, if I could only ask you – perhaps my words are too intemperate or precise to be suitable for publication, but I am sure you can find better - it seems such a small thing, and so desirable for all parties, that this one wicked man be removed from his office, that surely you must be able think of some way we can effect it. Some things may be in my power - a word to General Howe. Or to Mr. Loring, perhaps. For all his complaints about his administrative duties, he must keep pretty far from the scene and rely on others' reports, because -"

"Do you know these people?" Mr. Beltreau asked, looking at her with sudden sharp interest.

"No, not - not well. But well enough to get information to them; and I know people who know them well," Rachel said, blushing at the near-lie.

"Well, for Heaven's sake, don't," Mr. Beltreau cried, leaning forward to press her hands. "Forgive me, but please, Miss - are you listening to me?" He pressed her hands harder and gave them a small shake. "Discuss this with neither of them - Lord, those two of all... There's nothing worse you could do. Dear child, I won't ask your name, but I think if your family were powerful enough to be reckoned with, I would have known your face before now, and I don't. General Howe is unlikely to do more than ignore you, unless pushed hard. But Mr. Loring is more spiteful, not just by temperament but by cuckold -" He bit off his words, faint color rising in his cheeks, and pulled back his hands, embarrassed at having forgotten himself and being far too direct.

"I know about Mrs. Loring and General Howe," Rachel said quietly, slipping her hands from the desk and curling them onto her lap. "They don't seem to make much of a secret about it. But that doesn't make General Howe wicked - it's a common enough failing, and there is no Mrs. Howe to disappoint."

"You don't say anything in Mr. Loring's defense, which proves to me your claim that you've met him." Mr. Beltreau sighed and pressed his lips together, looking to the side for a long moment. He sighed again, apparently coming to a decision. "If you have a few minutes to spare, Miss, let me tell you a brief story. Everything in it is thoroughly hypothetical, you understand. A hypothetical situation involving hypothetical people. But I know how fond women are of made-up tales, and I sadly missed the third member of the triumvirate in your little piece - you gave me God and Nature, but not a single jot of love."

"Of course," Rachel said. She was angry and frustrated, but she liked Mr. Beltreau all the same, even if he had disappointed her. She already knew that he was aware of far more than he was willing to admit in his newspaper.

"All right then. Say that once there was a fine general from a long line of fine generals in the mightiest empire on Earth," Mr. Beltreau began. "And he came to a far country to fight a war. But it wasn't fighting all the time, especially since the general's first efforts had gone so well, and there were plenty of people in the far country who sympathized with the empire and wished it success. This general found their company pleasant – particularly the company of one beautiful woman who had cocked her hat for him from the first, which was flattering to the general, as he was neither handsome nor young."

Rachel swallowed and glanced down. Apparently Mr. Beltreau wanted to be plain far more than he wanted to be discreet. She was so upset about so many things that her head felt muddled and entirely unequal to a hard puzzle, and she was grateful for his frankness.

"It might not be right to call this beautiful woman good or bad, but ambitious, certainly. She'd borne the misfortune of having married a man who had not prospered the way she had expected of him, and her life thus far was a disappointment. But her husband admitted his faults freely to her, and so husband and wife were united rather than at each other's throats over his failures, and it was united that they undertook to improve their fortunes. They held one trump card, although they weren't sure how long it would last. This was the wife's beauty, which really was quite extraordinary.

"So the general, who was both rich and powerful, was a Godsend to them. The general knew the beautiful woman was married, and it troubled him, but some men require a storm to whip the spark of infatuation into a flame of love. As time passed, he could not drive her from his thoughts, and he burned for her more every day. Now, the woman had no other goal in her head than to claim the general for her own – so she kept herself near him until one day he could not stop himself from making a suggestion that she seized upon, and then the trap was sprung.

"Afterwards, the general plagued himself with doubts and recrimination. What would the woman's husband say if he found out –

how could the general explain himself, when his conduct had not been as it should, and he knew he was entirely in the wrong? And so it took all an old soldier's grim strength to face the interview when it came. But the husband did not threaten the general. He said he understood. He said it was the sole purpose of his life to make his beautiful wife happy, and he knew that the general did so as the husband himself did not. The general was astonished, and he also thrilled to know that the beautiful woman he so loved returned his affection. And dared he even to hope that the husband would not merely forgive what had passed – that he would let it continue?

"But the husband went on that of course the proprieties must be observed – that his wife could not leave him, because that would be a scandal that none of them could survive, particularly the general, with his heavy responsibility and lofty position. And yet the wife must be cared for somehow, and of course, as always, made happy. So perhaps an accommodation could be found for the husband – a position that would keep him, and his wife, near the general so the love-affair could flourish, and that would also give a good independent living to husband and wife so that all would be content and everything seemingly proper and in order.

"The husband had friends, and the general had friends, and letters were written, and the husband was put in charge of dispensing supplies to the prisoners that fell into the general's hands. It was not a particularly grand appointment, but it had a steady salary, and it meant that the husband and wife would need to remain by the center of the general's operations, wherever they might be. The general was pleased with this solution, and the affair continued.

"A steady salary, however, was far from luxurious enough to come near the husband's and wife's dreams, and it was pretty disappointing to think that her beauty and reputation had been spent for such a modest return. However, it did not take the husband long to realize that while his salary was small, enormous sums passed through his hands routinely to buy the food, medicine, blankets, and other necessities for the prisoners in his charge. So he began to take a little of this money for himself and his wife to supplement his salary. And having taken a little, he found it easier and easier to take greater sums with increased frequency, until he was taking almost all for himself and leaving but a pittance for the hapless souls dependent upon him.

"Eventually – and after not too long, because he was not a stupid man – the general learned of this thievery and was disgusted by it – but what could he do? Any blow at the husband would fall twice as hard on the wife and end the affair for certain. Besides, the sufferer for this crime was only enemy soldiers who had pledged to kill him and his men in battle if they could. And further, the general reasoned, if his own men were to see how badly prisoners fared, would it not increase their fear of being caught themselves, and whip them to greater strength on the field? And so the general decided to let it pass – a larger crime to cover his original small one.

"Now, the husband was in charge only of provisioning. The man who had direct control over the prisoners was a captain in the general's army. And this man was brutal and cruel by nature, though he had not realized it yet. He was even quicker than the general to see that the husband was stealing money, and, unlike the general, the captain went to the husband directly and demanded an explanation. The husband stammered and turned red in defiance, and then the captain pretended to relent, and offered what he'd had in mind all along: that he should have a cut of this money for himself as well, for which he promised his eternal silence – in fact, his complicity guaranteed it. The husband had no choice but to agree, even though having two pairs of hands scooping out the trough left precious little for the prisoners any more, and these sad creatures began actually to starve and to die where they stood, after eating off their clothes and chips of brick and plaster from the walls.

"More and more prisoners came in all the time, and greater sums were given to the husband only to be divided between himself and the captain. The captain in fact took only a small portion after the initial excitement of larceny wore thin, because he had discovered something new about himself on watching his charges starve: that it pleased him to see the prisoners under his care suffer and perish, while money meant little to him. And so he left the bulk of the money to the husband and began to practice his new sport."

"Torture," Rachel whispered.

"Torture," Mr. Beltreau agreed. "When the general learned of this, again, what could he do? His hands were tied. If he brought down the captain, or even threatened him with discipline, it brought down the husband, and if the husband were brought down, the wife went too. And her he still loved with all his heart. And so the general did nothing, and a terrible crime covered a large one that covered the small one at its center. Well. That's a story, anyway," he said.

Rachel was silent.

At last she said, "How can such a disaster spring from love?"

Mr. Beltreau shrugged. "In my line of work, I'd say it's almost invariable."

Chapter 16

Rachel did not take Mr. Beltreau up on his offer to burn her unfortunate article in his office, and now it sat folded in eighths in her pocket. She rubbed it absently as she walked, her thoughts somber. She had barely escaped a second, possibly far deadlier error by Mr. Beltreau's refusal to take her piece, but this brought her no pleasure. She decided to walk down Walnut, even though the chance of seeing Lieutenant Bellew in the yard was remote. Rachel glanced at the sky. A half-moon hung low on the horizon, igniting a wisp of cloud in shining silver as it hurried past and disappeared again into the black. She'd forgotten the hour. No, the chance of seeing him wasn't remote, it was non-existent. Even kind guards who let their prisoners out every day never did so after the sun went down. But she walked along Walnut anyway. It wasn't too far out of her way, and the interview at the *Atlantic Gazetteer* had not taken long.

Was it true what Mr. Beltreau had suggested - that love bore no fruit but grief and sin? Not many people had loved her in her brief life, Rachel mused, and perhaps that was a fortunate thing. Her father and Christoph had died for loving her. If they hadn't wanted to save her life, they wouldn't have returned to the house, and they wouldn't have been cut down. And if she hadn't loved them, she wouldn't have stood and cried out, but Rachel was puzzled as to whether or not it had been wrong of her to do so. Certainly she might have been killed too, once she sprang from cover - but she had not been, and the Cherokee who had taken her had saved her life by doing so, because she had been far too young to make her way on her own in the wilderness.

She had come to love her new family over time. Had that been a sin? Some of them had been in the party that had killed her father and brother. Had she forgotten her first family's love and sacrifice so easily, to transfer her allegiance to their murderers? But so many of the Indians had been so kind to her, making no difference between her and the others even when she did not speak a word of their language at first and could not so much as skin a rabbit - wouldn't refusing to love them have been just as great a sin?

Rachel did not know.

She had told herself when her Cherokee family died that she would never again allow her personal happiness to depend on another human being, and she had held herself aloof from the raider's family. But it had broken her heart, secretly, no matter how cold and angry she had felt, when they'd left her behind, and she must have loved them too. If she saw Miss Sarah this moment, wouldn't she cry and take her hands and want to know everything that had happened to her, and whether she was well and happy? While Miss Sarah – Miss Sarah would probably wonder who this strange girl was.

And then when the raider's family was gone, and Rachel alone again, she hadn't been able to bear it for more than a few weeks before falling in love with Lieutenant –

Rachel brought herself up short. It was ridiculous, even pathetic to use that word about a man she barely knew. She was certain she liked him and admired him greatly; and she had to admit she had a partiality for him as well, but that was foolish and best kept to herself. And the best way to keep it to herself was not to think of it too often. And surely, even as a slight friend, she owed it to him not to dangle his image in her thoughts like a pretty charm when the real flesh-and-blood man's life was hanging by a thread.

But that she loved Mrs. Addison, she felt sure of, even though Mrs. Addison was so far above her that the idea was almost as presumptuous as her thoughts about Lieutenant Bellew. She knew Mrs. Addison was fond of her too, though Rachel did not trust how deep that water ran. It did not make her love Mrs. Addison any less. And surely it was better that Mrs. Addison not concern herself so much over Rachel – not love her the way her father had, and died, but love her the way the raider had not, who had likely forgotten Rachel's name and was happy and safe somewhere by now.

Say his name, Rachel told herself sternly. *He wasn't just* the raider. *His name was George Crawford, and you know it perfectly well. He gave you a home for years. And if you hadn't gotten that practice as a maid, you'd never have gotten this place with Mrs. Addison.*

She came upon the sugar house almost without realizing it. The building, unlit on the inside, was no more than a shadow in the night. The yard where she had spoken to Lieutenant Bellew only a few hours ago was

171

a desolate inky cipher in the blackness. The regulars didn't even give the prisoners a speck of light. A pool of moon-glow reflected from a high, dark window. The shine blocked any hope of seeing inside, and the angle was all wrong, but Rachel stared anyway. She imagined Lieutenant Bellew standing in the close darkness, supporting his sick friend. What did they do through all the long hours, she wondered. What did they think of – what did they say to each other? And suddenly Rachel felt so near to him she almost felt his breath on her neck, as if she were standing beside him with the others, and she wished that she were, that she were pressed close to his side – she would not feel the burden of captivity then, and maybe he would feel it a little less, too.

Rachel seized a handful of pebbles from the ground, possessed with the idea that she would throw them against the window and he would hear the rattle and understand everything that was in her mind, and know someone cared for him. A moment later, she might have thought better of it – so she didn't give herself time, just threw with all her might.

The pebbles spread in the air and flew wide of the window, bouncing harmlessly off the wall of the sugar house and rattling back to earth. If she had been hoping for some sign from the dark building, Rachel was disappointed. The world remained silent and still.

But she had not struck the window, which gleamed with blankness and seemed a crueler barrier somehow even than the thick stone wall. She needed a heavier object to fly true. Rachel bent to her knees and felt over the ground for larger rocks. The earth left cold, burning traces against her fingers, numbing them, but she hardly noticed. There, in the shallow gutter by the side of the street – this was where the larger stones got kicked by people's feet and horses' hooves. She found four good-sized rocks quickly and would have found more if she hadn't been frightened to see a curious form peer around the side of the building. The moonlight was enough to show a hint of the scarlet of his coat, and his buttons flashed white fire. He squinted into the dark. Rachel froze on her knees, hands stretched into the gutter. She hunched down slightly, hoping for aid from the shadows.

"Hey, you!" the guard called. "You! I see you! What are you about, there?" He paused, waiting for an answer. The prison remained silent, as if it were filled with stone and not merely made of it.

Rachel stood and swept a hand absently down her skirt, her heart pounding fast and light. Whether she faced the guard or ran, she needed her feet beneath her. And should she run? He might not catch her if she went back the way she'd come. She glanced behind herself. The street was empty. No one liked to come this way.

Before she could make up her mind, the guard decided she warranted further attention and walked forward briskly, closing the distance between them fast enough to make flight unlikely, then foolish, then simply impossible. He stood before her with an annoyed expression. He had round cheeks and a heavy jaw, and his eyebrows were springy with coarse hair. "You! What's your name and business?"

"I...I dropped two pennies, sir," Rachel said. She shoved her hands in her pockets to hide the rocks, and she touched the folded packet of her essay. Her throat went dry. She had forgotten the essay. She was always forgetting the most important thing.

"Well, you've lost them, then," the redcoat snapped. "What, is there a hole in your pocket?" He glanced at her hands stuffed in her pockets. Rachel stiffened.

"No, sir, I was only tossing them in the air, because they looked pretty in the moonlight, but then I missed my catch, and...I know it was very stupid, sir. I thought they were right by my feet, but then I couldn't find them."

The guard looked at her more closely. His face softened a little, although not as much as Rachel might have liked. "How old are you, dear?" he asked.

"Seventeen," Rachel said. She rubbed the papers in her pocket furiously, praying that the paper would wear thin or the ink smudge.

"And fidgeting like a girl of five. Are you married?"

"No, sir."

"And you never will be, if you don't get your head on your shoulders better than that," the guard said. "What did you say your name was, dear?"

"Sarah Crawford," Rachel blurted. She was sure Miss Sarah would forgive her – or at least that Miss Sarah would never know about it, which was the only sort of matter Miss Sarah ever forgave.

To Rachel's astonishment, the guard offered her a slight bow. "Well, Miss Crawford, I'll tell the men to keep an eye out for your pennies. And if you come by tomorrow before seven, you'll find me here – Corporal Francis Graham, and I'll let you know. But you'll never find them in the dark, and I can't be mucking around here in the back all night."

"Yes sir," Rachel said meekly. One foot shifted in the dirt beneath her, she was so eager to be off. But she had to restrain her impatience, she knew. She could not look like she was running. "Well – good evening, sir..."

"Graham," Corporal Graham prompted her, a hopeful look in his eye.

"And thank you, sir – Corporal Graham. I didn't mean to be any trouble, and I hope I haven't caused you any." Then Rachel left as quickly as she could without seeming to flee.

Her fright drained from her with every step, replaced by loathing. Corporal Graham's presence had polluted her dream of standing close to Lieutenant Bellew, as if Graham's thick form had suddenly thrust itself between the two of them, and instead of the man she – she esteemed, Rachel had found herself pressing against the body of his persecutor, and feeling his hot breath in her ear. She wiped at the side of her face, but the feeling remained.

A flash of red caught her eye, and Rachel suffered a strange disorienting sense that Graham had somehow managed to get in front of her. But the form was far too short and slender, and she saw that it was some other redcoat, a messenger she supposed, because he walked swiftly and with a purposeful expression, and he did not take notice of her as he passed Rachel on the street. Then she remembered the small outpost of regulars she'd noticed when leaving the prison earlier that afternoon, only her mind had been so pregnant with other thoughts she'd scarcely taken notice at the time. She took notice now. She remembered Mr. Beltreau's words – that if he wanted to see Captain Cunningham, he didn't have to go far from the sugar house prison.

It was the lair of the devil himself, and Rachel knew she could not leave until she had looked on the enemy's face. What purpose could be served by it, she did not know. But she had to see what such a monster looked like; if he bore the marks of Lucifer on his face and body, or if, as she suspected, he seemed only an ordinary man, and all the more hateful because of it.

She slipped to the edge of the street and into the shadows. The house where Cunningham was based was not difficult to identify; two regulars stood outside it chatting. Rachel pretended to fiddle with a stone in her shoe, glancing up through her eyelashes, but no one noticed her or asked her what business she had. It helped that there were a few other passers-by on the street. The hour was still early, and the blighted air that clung to the prison did not stretch this far, so people felt comfortable using their usual routes.

Rachel yearned to peer inside the simple three-story wooden house, but she did not see how she could get close enough to do so. And she was being foolish anyway. It served nothing but idle curiosity to look on the man's face. Most likely there would be nothing extraordinary in his features, and even if there were, what use would it be? He must have looked into eyes more innocent than Rachel's every day and not been ashamed. He would not be immolated by the sheer force of her rage. There was nothing she could do here, and she was wasting time when she was needed at home.

"Sir!" The snap of boot-heels hitting the ground hard. Rachel looked up sharply. The two redcoats had abandoned their conversation mid-sentence and stood at stiff attention at the approach of a smiling, dark-haired man in a captain's uniform.

"Timmons leave yet?" the dark-haired man said in a pleasant tenor.

"No, sir, I haven't seen him go," one of the redcoats answered. The dark-haired man's smile vanished, and a scowl took its place as fast and startling as the yanking away of a veil. Rachel knew in that instant, as sure as she was of the breath in her lungs, that this must be Captain Cunningham. Her hands grew slick with sweat, and she shoved them in her pockets. She felt the papers again, but this time they did not make her afraid. She wanted to stick them in his face to show him that she knew what he was – that everyone knew. He could hang her a thousand times. It would not make him a less contemptible thing.

"No, that was him a moment ago," the other redcoat corrected, and Captain Cunningham's face cleared slightly, although a trace of sourness remained.

"Man's a donkey," Captain Cunningham muttered. The first redcoat hastened to open the door, trying to apologize for his mistake.

A terrible fear suddenly seized Rachel. Timmons must have been the redcoat who had passed her. And she knew that when Cunningham hanged prisoners, he sent a man out to choose them first. And Timmons had been heading in the direction of the sugar house prison. And he couldn't – they couldn't –

Her hand released the papers in her pocket and fidgeted with the heavy rocks she had meant to throw at Lieutenant Bellew's window. They had grown warm in her pocket and were slightly damp from melting ice. There was something comforting about their weight and solidity. But one of these rocks was much too large – she didn't know why she'd picked it up. It would have broken the window for certain, if she'd managed to hit her target.

Before she had time to think, Rachel threw it with all her strength across the street at Captain Cunningham's face and screamed, "NO!" Part of her froze disbelievingly. As if in a dream, she saw Cunningham wheel around, his face blank with incomprehension. His eyes widened and he ducked, throwing his hands over his head. The redcoat who'd gone to open the door took the rock in the shoulder and grunted in surprise, falling back a step. And then Rachel was running, running for her life, the astonished face of a passing man opening his mouth to say something, what, she never knew, because she dashed around the corner and through the streets and kept running until her throat was too raw to suck in the cold air any more. Frightened tears stood in her eyes. She could feel the shadow of a hand that was about to fall upon her neck, and she cringed in anticipation of the blow that would capture her. Stupid, stupid girl. But she could not run any more with her breath gone, so she would face her judgment. Gasping, Rachel stopped and looked behind her.

No one was there, other than a few ordinary people on the street, who eyed her curiously. Rachel frowned, straightening, and scanned the street disbelievingly. Street-lanterns hung on their poles, too heavy to sway in the light wind. Cheerful yellow light shone from the houses. Bare trees thrust their arms into the sky, which held the same half-moon and what looked like the same bit of silken cloud flying past it again. And no soldiers anywhere.

Rachel knew the area well. She was only a few minutes away from home. She had flown instinctively for safety, like an animal going to ground, and that had been stupid too. She had not known while she was running that she was not being followed.

Rachel avoided the stares of passers-by and lowered her head, walking swiftly. She prayed she had not been seen running by anyone who knew her, but she did not dare raise her eyes again to check. How could she have been such a fool? Attacking an officer in public, her face in plain view – and what good could that rock have done unless it had killed him, and had she truly meant to kill a man in cold blood?

Rachel had never felt so grateful for the stately beauty of Broad Street. A flawless mathematical precision of symmetry and line was the skeleton of this loveliness, and the order of it, as much as the familiarity, helped to calm her roiled thoughts. She was not composed by the time she gingerly opened the door of her home, but she was more in control, and she did not torment herself with childish fantasies of redcoats hiding in the bushes or lurking behind the door.

Only, let the family not be angry with me, Rachel pleaded silently as she stepped inside. *Let them not have missed me. If they reproach me even with their eyes, they have every right, but I couldn't bear it now. I just couldn't bear it.*

Rachel peeped into the parlor, her heart in her throat. The room was lit but empty except for two sleeping dogs. Rachel held her breath and tiptoed backwards – she had forgotten the dogs, and she hardly wanted a cacophony of barking to announce her arrival. She crept through the first floor room by room, expecting any moment to meet questions and demands, but everything was deserted until she reached the kitchen and found Jacob and Abraham eating cold beef medallions on thick slices of bread.

She must not have looked as composed as she hoped, because both men jumped to their feet in alarm. Jacob choked down his last bite, and Abraham shoved his forgotten meal onto the counter and demanded, "You just tell me real slow what the matter is." He sounded angry, as he always did when confronted with a problem, and a person who didn't know him well might think he was annoyed to the point of being impertinent at having been disturbed from his meal. But Rachel knew that wasn't the case, and that it was the existence of any disorder, any wrongness in the world that Abraham disapproved of so harshly.

"It's nothing – I was just hoping that I hadn't been missed," Rachel stammered. She could not implicate the slaves in her crime by letting them know what she had done, even though Jacob would be hurt to know she had kept a secret from him, and Abraham would be offended that a fact with such dangerous ramifications had been withheld.

Jacob relaxed visibly, though Abraham's eyes remained sharp upon her. "Naw, Miss Rachel," Jacob said, sitting down again. "Mrs. Addison still asleep, and when Mr. Addison call up for more wine from the cellar, I says I'll do it, like I always does, only that General Lee asked if someone prettier could bring it up instead, so I sends that new cook, and the gentlemens seems real happy with her, and nobody asked me where you was." He looked up at her with sudden anxiety, bread frozen halfway to his mouth. "I don't mean that Mrs. Maria is prettier than you, only just that anyone is prettier than me," he added hurriedly.

Rachel smiled. The warmth of the kitchen and its cozy smells, Jacob's impulsive chatter, even Abraham's frown, everything was so comforting and familiar and dear to her that icy pain stabbed her heart to think how close she had come to seeing all of it never again. How safe she felt here; and yet how fragile this home was too. A single breath could blow it away.

Mrs. Addison's bell tinkled. Rachel jumped practically out of her skin.

"You sure they's nothing wrong?" Abraham said glumly, his shoulders hunched in sullen unhappiness.

Rachel took off her jacket hurriedly and touched her hair. "Do I look too awful?"

"You look like you was out, if that's what you –"

"I went to a newspaper again," Rachel explained hurriedly, hoping the half-truth would satisfy Abraham. "But the editor there told me some upsetting things, and I won't be writing for the newspapers any more, never, never again, no matter what, I promise – Jacob, I don't want you to deliver that note, you might get in trouble, the whole family might, and it certainly wouldn't do any good, so please promise me."

Jacob snatched the note out of his jacket pocket. Abraham's gaze followed it with resentful curiosity as Rachel stuffed the note into her skirt beside her incendiary essay – and, dear God, by three damp rocks still in her pocket.

The bell rang again, more insistently. Rachel didn't have time to get rid of the rocks now – or the essay – or the note. She barely had time to lick her fingers and smooth down the worst of her stray hairs as she ran up the stairs, her tired muscles protesting with every step.

Rachel was so flustered she forgot to knock before entering the room, and Mrs. Addison shot bolt upright behind the muslin canopy of her bed, clutching the neck of her shift tightly closed. "Oh!" She turned her shoulder away.

Rachel closed the door quickly behind her. "I'm so sorry, madam, it's only me –"

Mrs. Addison turned back in surprise and released the soft cotton fabric. A slender pink ribbon wove through the neckline, and she fiddled with its satin tail. "I'm sorry, dear, I must not have heard your knock over the bell. Rachel, I'm dying of boredom in here, just dying, but I can't put it off any longer, I've got to go out, I suppose, but – you didn't see where those dogs were, did you?"

"Two of them are asleep downstairs. The others, I'm not sure," Rachel said. "Perhaps they're in the study with Mr. Addison and the General."

"Playing cards, no doubt. I mean Robert, not the dogs," Mrs. Addison sighed. "Well, if I'd known General Lee was a card-player as well as a drinker and his dogs kept him company, I could have spared myself three hours of tedium with my pretend headache. Honestly, Rachel, the man is such a boor – I admit I had a pretty unworthy thought when the door went bursting open that way – not that he would actually *do* anything, of course, but a man who acts the way he does, you just don't know exactly, do you? He seems to delight in being coarse. Every now and then at dinner he would be reasonably polite for a moment and I would almost be relieved, and then everything all off again and General Lee using such words and making such very plain implications that it was becoming a bit of a strain to pretend not to understand him. He's just – he's just a – I don't know, how would *you* put it?" Mrs. Addison swung her slender legs to the floor, tugging the skirt of her chemise to keep it from tangling, and looked at Rachel with a tiny smile of anticipation.

"I would put it that General Lee seems not only to want to be a dog himself, but to be elected to their Parliament," Rachel replied.

Mrs. Addison chuckled. "I knew you'd say something to make me feel better," she said. She wiggled her toes, her good temper restored. "Where on earth have I put my slippers this time?"

Rachel slid the little leather shoes out from under the bed, where Mrs. Addison usually kicked them, and slipped them onto her mistress's feet. She had realized as soon as she spoke that her words were too close to the truth. She feared General Lee simply didn't like people much, if at all. She would still speak to him about the conditions the prisoners faced, the very first chance she had when she could get a quiet word and he wasn't trying to insult or humiliate her, but she had no real hope that he would care enough to stir himself over the matter. Rachel did not like to think that way. But she could do little about how she felt.

"Oh, don't worry about my wrap, it's warm enough – just get my stays – Rachel, I said not to worry about the wrap – oh, what's wrong? Are you ill?" Mrs. Addison sounded sympathetic, but she drew back a little at the suspicion that Rachel might have caught some kind of sickness.

Rachel brought her hand to her face. The skin was cold and dry as paper, and she supposed she was probably as pale as paper too. "Oh, please, madam," she whispered, "Can't you please, please write that letter to your father?"

"What letter?" Mrs. Addison said with a cross frown, tapping one slipper absently against the leg of the bed.

"About – about the prisoners, about how the regulars aren't feeding them, and the hangings –"

"Oh, that. Well, I can't possibly post anything tonight, and anyway we'll see him soon enough, I can just tell him about it," Mrs. Addison said. Her eyes shot open wide. "Rachel! Are you crying?"

Rachel realized her face was wet, and she looked down quickly in embarrassment. "I'm sorry, Mrs. Addison – if you'd only seen them, I know you'd understand – I just can't explain it properly – how abominable it is – and I don't want you to see them, madam, truly I don't, I just wish I weren't so terrible at saying what I mean –"

"You generally express yourself quite clearly," Mrs. Addison said with a quirk of her mouth. "I'm sorry, it was one of your friends, wasn't it? Of course, Rachel, I'll do it first thing in the morning."

Rachel squeezed her eyes shut. She could not make the hot tears stop. Mrs. Addison meant the best, but she would probably have put the letter out of her mind again by morning, because she never could bear to keep ugly things in view for long. And then Rachel would have to remind her again, because she had no other choice – and Mrs. Addison would be angry with her, maybe angry enough to insist that the matter be shelved, and there was nothing else Rachel could do but pray that General Lee was kinder than Rachel believed him to be.

"Here, Rachel. Now, you know I can't lace it myself, not tight enough anyway – oh, your hands are like ice! You are ill, aren't you?" Mrs. Addison twisted in annoyance and pulled away, the stays hanging loose.

"No, ma'am," Rachel said. "I don't think so, anyway."

"Then what – you know, you have a bit of a breezy smell to you. Have you been outside?"

"Yes," Rachel admitted miserably.

"Have you seen something else, then? Is that what this is all about?"

The tears froze inside Rachel's skull. No one must know that she had been anywhere near any prisoners tonight – least of all Mrs. Addison. Rachel wiped her hands quickly against her skirt. "No, ma'am. No, I was just – I was just taking a walk – to keep away from the dogs."

Mrs. Addison sighed, unsatisfied. "Well, stand by the fire a moment and warm yourself up. You may not worry about catching your death, but I'm afraid I will if those hands touch me again."

Rachel walked obediently to the fire and held her hands out to it. She could not feel its warmth except as a painful stinging. There was dirt under her nails, she realized with a jolt of fear. Had Mrs. Addison noticed? No, Rachel had been behind her – but still –

A wooden chair creaked heavily. Rachel turned her head. Mrs. Addison sat at her desk and tossed the stays onto the bed with a sigh. "Well, suppose I write that letter of yours now," she said.

The warmth from the fire suddenly spread through Rachel's body. "Oh, ma'am – if you could!"

"Of course I could, but I don't want you getting your hopes up too high – it is a war, you know," Mrs. Addison replied tartly. "But I rather think we might be leaving Philadelphia to visit father sooner than we'd planned, unless General Lee starts showing himself well enough that I can even think of having company here, and I should let father know we're coming. So I am writing to him anyway. Don't tell Mr. Addison, dear, we'll let him think that it's father who wants us sooner – not that he won't be able to find card-players in the rebel army as well as here. And I want a promise from you, Rachel."

"Yes, of course, I certainly won't tell Mr. Addison, I promise," Rachel said quickly.

"Not that – no more going out on your own at night like this. It always puts you in the oddest temper, and I have more than enough concerns."

Chapter 17

Rachel had almost forgotten poor Charlie Waters and his concern about his wife. She had a letter of her own that she owed. Of course she'd already wasted all her ink and fretted about it the rest of the evening. She kept finding excuses to go past Mr. Addison's study, but the door remained firmly closed until almost eight-thirty when Mrs. Rimini emerged, pink-cheeked and laughing. The air that came with her was thick with smoke and port. Mrs. Rimini glanced up and saw Rachel, and her smile faded from mirth to amiability, her eyes still crinkling at the corners. "The gentlemen say they'll take only a light snack for supper. They're playing cards," she explained.

"I imagine so. I think Jacob and Abraham finished the medallions," Rachel said.

"That's all right, I suppose I need to make something fresh for Mrs. A anyway. I've got some leftover pastry from the lobster pies, and it don't matter too much what you put inside it, you make these little twists...they're darling."

"Mrs. Addison usually has only a bit of bread for supper, if she's not in company, though I forgot to ask today," Rachel said.

Mrs. Rimini winked. "Well, we'll see if I can't tempt her with something better," she said and swished down the hall swinging her skirts. The unworthy thought occurred to Rachel that Mrs. Rimini acted as though she might have been a little drunk herself.

So the men would be in the study till late. Well, they'd just had the interruption of Mrs. Rimini's departure; surely they wouldn't mind another brief one. Rachel curled her hand into a loose fist and knocked gently. All four dogs were inside the room now. She could tell because they set up an immediate howling.

"God's bleeding eyes!" Mr. Addison roared, and General Lee laughed.

Rachel wasn't sure that was quite an invitation, so she knocked again, pretending politely not to have heard the dogs or the oath. "Mr. Addison?" she said timidly.

"Yes, girl, yes." Rachel opened the door just wide enough to squeeze through. The smoke stung her eyes. The dogs were over her in an instant, panting and sticking their noses into her dress, but she tried to ignore that politely too. Mr. Addison and the general sat at a side-table, the last hand of their card game spread out haphazardly before them, with scattered coins and sticky port-stains and clumps of crumbling cigar-ash completing the picture of perfect disorder. Mr. Addison's face was dark with laughter and drink, and his eyes had a strange, shallow glitter that Rachel had not seen in them before. "The dogs like her, Charlie," Mr. Addison said, a giggle catching in his throat.

"The dogs know she doesn't like them," General Lee replied without looking at Rachel. "They're trying to earn her favor, poor damn things. They never will understand people, and I can't say I blame them."

"I think they're very fine animals, sir," Rachel replied as brightly as she could. "Mr. Addison, I'm sorry to disturb you, but I saw Mrs. Rimini go out and thought – would it be all right if I took a little more ink?"

"Ink?" Mr. Addison said, blinking as if trying to remember the word. "More ink? Do you drink the stuff?"

"I need to write a letter, sir," Rachel said. "I'll buy more tomorrow and replace what I use." She hoped he would not ask her to explain further than that.

"Oh, never mind about that – ink. Yes, go ahead," Mr. Addison muttered, gathering up the cards and seemingly forgetting about her. Rachel curtsied. The dogs had settled down enough to stay on all fours now, which made it easier to make her way to the desk. But she wasn't sure with all their pushing and snuffling that she'd be able to pour straight, and Mr. Addison had lost interest in her existence, so she clutched a whole bottle in her hand. The dogs followed her to the door and made half-hearted gestures to leave with her, and Rachel shoved them back as gently as she could with her leg.

"Here, careful with that foot of yours," General Lee snapped without looking up.

"Sorry, sir," Rachel whispered, pushing the door shut. The last greyhound pulled back its wet nose not an instant too soon.

She returned to her room and wrote a brief letter to Mrs. Waters, assuring her that her husband was living and – and quite well, Rachel decided to say. She did not think the wife of an enlisted man could do much to protest his conditions, and she wanted the poor woman's heart to be soothed, not lacerated deeper.

The evening wore on. No soldiers came to arrest her. As the hour grew later, Rachel started cautiously to trust that maybe she'd gotten away with her rock-throwing stupidity after all. She hadn't seen anyone she'd recognized while she was fleeing. So perhaps it would be all right. She knew she could never go back to the sugar house prison again, because Graham knew her face, and that saddened her, because she might have liked to have a word or two with Lieutenant Bellew to give him hope and see how Captain O'Malley was getting on, and to tell Mr. Waters that his letter was sent and perhaps take any other messages that the men might want - she could have made herself useful in a thousand ways, if only her foolishness hadn't intervened. But she would stay clear of any soldiers, and her identity would remain a mystery, and hopefully the matter would be forgotten as one unpleasantness of many by the time the Addisons left and Rachel never had to worry about Philadelphia again.

"I want you to change into your nice - oh, you wore the rose one last time. Well, the blue is all right. Change into your blue dress after breakfast, Rachel. We're going out," Mrs. Addison said brightly over her coffee the next morning. Mr. Addison and General Lee were both subdued, if not positively somber, so conversation had been light. Mr. Addison winced slightly at the sound of dishes clattering from the kitchen. "Robert. You don't mind entertaining General Lee? Or I should say, of course, you're both quite welcome to come with me -"

"That's all right, dear," Mr. Addison said in a low voice. "I'll just catch up on some work."

Rachel was pleased at the prospect of getting away from the house for a few hours. She felt an admittedly disproportionate anxiety about the dogs and was glad to leave the problem of how to keep them from destroying the furnishings to poor Abraham.

It was not until she was helping Mrs. Addison dress later that she thought to ask whom they were going to visit. "Oh, Elizabeth again, Loring. She's planning a twelfth night dance, only of course she's never done much on a proper scale before, so she's going to try to pretend to be asking for aesthetic guidance when she's really looking for what she's supposed to be doing at all."

"At her own home, then?" Rachel asked with a sinking heart.

"No, she does everything at the General's," Mrs. Addison replied. "There's not much point in being coy about it, so she isn't."

General Howe's mansion - swarming with soldiers. Officers, enlisted men, all sorts of redcoats coming and going on business, any one of whom might have been near Captain Cunningham last night - might be Captain Cunningham himself - or that fellow she hit in his place. Rachel's hands began to shake. She clutched them under her arms.

"Rachel, my hair -"

"I'm sorry, ma'am, I just wanted to make sure my hands weren't too cold."

"Well, I don't see why they would be, you haven't been outside."

Rachel took in a deep breath. She could not look afraid. There were thousands of soldiers in Philadelphia, and only a few of them had seen her last night; what was the chance that someone would recognize her at General Howe's?

But she didn't know. And she couldn't be sure.

"I think I might be coming down with something after all," Rachel said in a small voice.

"Oh, Rachel, not now."

"I'm sorry, ma'am - perhaps if I lie down a few minutes, let me just finish your hair."

"Lie down on my bed - no wait, not if you're sick. Well, go sit on that chair and see if you can't bring yourself around, I'll do my own hair," Mrs. Addison sighed in frustration. "Rachel, everyone's going to be there, I was depending on you to tell me - well, to tell me -"

To tell her what to say to sound witty, Rachel thought tiredly as she sat on the chair. But Mrs. Addison herself would become the subject of pointed gossip quickly enough rather than its author if her pet maid were arrested for having attacked an officer of the Crown. "Who else is going to be present?" she asked.

"I'm not sure."

"Well, do you know who isn't going to be there?"

"I don't see what you're getting at. You, apparently, unless – Rachel, you aren't really ill, are you? Oh, you don't look that well. You shouldn't have gone out last night."

"It was only for a moment," Rachel said hurriedly, a chill squeezing her heart. The last thing she wanted was for Mrs. Addison to be complaining to everyone at General Howe's about Rachel's wanders. "I just want to know who isn't there because they're likely to be the topic of conversation."

"Oh, I see." Mrs. Addison frowned and pulled at her hair. Rachel had never been quite this direct before about Mrs. Addison using Rachel's turns of phrase for her own, and she hoped she hadn't offended her – but if she could only prepare Mrs. Addison with a few remarks to get her through tea, perhaps she could render her absence less objectionable. "Well, Mrs. Nathanson is likely to be absent, I suppose. Apparently she's managed to get herself in an interesting condition."

"Mrs. Nathanson is inoffensive enough," Rachel said, rubbing her temple as if she had a headache. "But her husband is a different kettle of fish. Mr. Nathanson aims only not to offend."

"I don't understand what you're getting at."

"When the rebel Congress was here, he was a dyed-in-the-wool Whig, and now that the regulars have moved in, he's turned arch-Tory. I'm not sure what exactly one should call that. 'Tig' doesn't sound quite right."

Mrs. Addison was silent a moment. She tilted her head to the side and regarded her reflection in the mirror thoughtfully. "Hmm. I don't know if I can imply the word 'whorey' in public. Perhaps if the company isn't mixed."

"Well – well –" Rachel cast her mind about frantically. "There's Mrs. MacDonough."

"Oh, Lord, not that creature," Mrs. Addison sniffed. "I can't imagine what MacDonough was thinking, marrying a thing like that."

Rachel had always felt a little sorry for Mrs. MacDonough, who came from no family whatsoever and had apparently been nothing but a pretty rope-maker's widow until the wealthy Mr. MacDonough had spied her one day arguing with a sea-captain about the quality of one of her cables, which had burst at an extremely inconvenient moment. Mr. MacDonough's position had given his new wife entrance into society, but her temper and manners remained firmly that of the docks. "No one else can either, and you can always point out that dressing a pig in velvet won't keep it out of the mud."

Mrs. Addison brightened. "Yes, I might at that," she said.

"And you must have something to say to please General Howe, if he's there."

"You are fond of him, aren't you? You can tell me - I don't think there's any harm in it. It's rather endearing, actually."

"I don't - I don't know him, ma'am."

"Oh, no one ever knows the person they fall in love with," Mrs. Addison sniffed. "It's all just pretty pictures and idle dreams, and the whole trick of it is never to let reality intrude too far. General Howe does have a sort of dash. A rather somber sort, but dash nevertheless. Are you being shy, Rachel? You didn't seem sick at all until I mentioned where we were going."

"I'm afraid I truly don't feel well, ma'am, and I'd be mortified if I were to faint in the middle of the drawing-room, or if my nose started running," Rachel said, well aware that Mrs. Addison would find either event far more appalling than even Rachel would. She rubbed her nose to emphasize the frightening possibility. "Perhaps if General Howe seems worried or pressed by his work, you can remind him that there is no greater weapon against liberty than freedom."

"I'd be informing him that he should be pleased to be overworked?"

"No, ma'am - if it sounds that way, don't say it. Just that the order he's trying to - the things he does - just that you can't let people run amok and do everything they please, or pretty soon no one can do anything they please at all, if there's anyone even left alive."

"Oh, I see. So I'll be complimenting him on the moral aspect of his professional pursuits. You know, Rachel, I think that's rather a sweet way of putting it. Usually when people praise him, it's all about which battle he won and how or such."

"They think if they flatter him, they won't have to say what they really think about the matter."

"Really, Rachel?" Mrs. Addison said archly. "Now you think everyone is a secret insurgent?"

"No, ma'am. I think probably most people General Howe meets are very glad that he's won and won handily. But as far as they're concerned, they flatter him so they won't have to offer thanks. People hold gratitude so dear that the philosopher who could measure its price would be wise enough to spin the sun on his palm like a top."

"You know," Mrs. Addison mused, "Mrs. Halloran never said 'boo' to me about that Chinese silk I gave her for that hideous fat daughter of hers. She just said that of course Mr. Addison was so successful he could always get the best things, and she praised the fabric to the skies, and I never gave it a second thought until now. But if she's not here today, or if she is, I might just say that about gratitude. I might just."

Mrs. Addison wouldn't let Rachel touch her any more, just in case, but she asked Rachel's opinion about her hair and let her hold a hand-mirror in the back so that Mrs. Addison could judge her own work for herself. She fixed a few curls, and then she covered her face and let Rachel blow powder over the coif, and then Rachel was dismissed to her room for rest while Mrs. Addison left to gather Jacob to drive the carriage.

Rachel crept down the hallway quietly. She didn't want to compound her lie about her illness by repeating it to Mr. Addison's face. He wouldn't object, she was sure, but he was pretty cold-eyed and not as easily distracted as his wife, and she didn't like him to think that she might be malingering. Which of course she was, she told herself spitefully. There was nothing for it now but to lie in bed and stare at the ceiling, just as Mrs. Addison had done yesterday. She could say she was better by the evening, and then she could simply pray that there would be no more visits to General Howe's mansion in the next few weeks. And the ball, the ball – Rachel didn't know how to dance, other than the country dance, of course, and she could plead that excuse. But Mrs. Addison wouldn't want her dancing anyway, she'd want her watching the people and listening and whispering words in Mrs. Addison's ear. What would she do about the ball? It would be far more crowded than any tea Mrs. Loring would hold, and Rachel was sure there'd be plenty of guards on hand to make a good show. Perhaps she could powder her face and even wear a little rouge as a mask. Rachel's spirit recoiled against the thought – face-paint was only for the best ladies and the worst, and she hated to think she would be making herself out to be either in Mrs. Addison's eyes. But what else could she do?

Her bed held neither softness nor comfort for Rachel as the same useless thoughts whirled around in her head like leaves in a storm. At last she made up her mind to confront the calamity mentally, since if it was coming for her, there was no way she could avoid it. Say she was caught. She would lose her position, she would lose the regard of her few friends, and then what? Probably they would not hang her for an act that had caused so little real harm, and surely women prisoners were treated more gently than men. And if she had a trial, she might be able to give her reasons in public, and thus perform at least one final service before she disappeared into the abyss. Lieutenant Bellew rose in her thoughts, and she put him firmly out of them again. So she would lose her place and her belongings. What of it? The time in prison would be hard, but either she would die and not have to worry about anything any longer or be released one day, not much worse off than she had been a handful of weeks ago.

Rachel felt a little calmer on coming to this resolution, although it was a cold sort of peace, like the quiet ruins left behind when a city has been sacked and burnt. She rose silently from bed and walked to her little window. She crossed her arms and leaned her head against the icy glass, staring absently at the yard, filled with dead flower-beds and barren shrubs arranged in the neat English style. How lovely it would be in the springtime, when the tidy rows of dirt burst with blooms as thick and soft as clouds and the empty tree-branches filled with leaves that whispered and rattled and whose edges were as sharp as paper.

A short bark started her from her thoughts, and she looked down, closer to the house. The dogs were outside, pawing the earth and scratching the trees, and Abraham, who had never met a creature his gentle firmness could not sway, ran hopelessly between the greyhounds, whistling and clapping his hands for their attention to no avail. It surprised Rachel; it had taken a mild deceit on Mrs. Addison's part yesterday to get the dogs outside through General Lee's opposition, and she did not see the general in the yard now, although she craned her head to look for him.

Her surprise increased at the faint sound of footsteps followed by mingled voices, loud with high spirits and laughter, coming from the first floor. Surely Mr. Addison hadn't expected company himself, or he would have told his wife, so these must be guests of General Lee – and guests he cared about enough to spare them the presence of his odious pets. But with Abraham in back with the dogs, and then Jacob waiting with the carriage at General Howe's, that left only poor Mrs. Rimini who hardly even knew her way around the house to handle everything.

Rachel knew Mrs. Rimini was a splendid cook, but her manners suggested that she hadn't served in a splendid house before, and it seemed all told a pretty heavy load to drop on Mrs. Rimini's shoulders with no warning. She clutched her hands together, torn by indecision. She could not abandon Mrs. Rimini, nor let the Addisons' hospitality show in a poor light, but if she went downstairs now, her only excuse for her presence at home rather than with Mrs. Addison would be her illness, which wouldn't make her presence any too welcome. She could say it was only a headache, although it might seem suspicious that there was such a rash of them in the household lately. Or she could simply stay in her room – and then emerge in the evening recovered, and have Mrs. Addison ask after her health, and have to admit to Mr. Addison and General Lee that she must have heard their company but had secluded herself lazily in her room without a single thought towards their comfort? What a poor job that would be. And what philosopher could measure her own gratitude, indeed, if this was the best she had to show for it.

Rachel ran a hand over her hair. Her fine tresses were frowzy from the pillow, and she took a few moments to brush them flat and refasten them in a hasty bun. She would just check in and see whether anything was required, and let either the company, or Mrs. Rimini privately, know that she was available for any assistance. She crept down the hallway and down the stairs noiselessly, and she had almost reached the drawing-room when a shriek pierced the air.

It sounded like Mrs. Rimini. Had she tripped? Simply lost her mind? Or had one of the dogs made its way back into the house and startled her? Any possibility Rachel could imagine was simply awful – oh, that General Lee had picked today of all days to entertain! She prayed that the guests were soldiers and no friends of Mrs. Addison's set.

Rachel flew down the rest of the stairs and rapped only perfunctorily on the closed drawing-room door before pulling it open and rushing inside. She stopped so suddenly she almost toppled over. The scene that lay before was not only unexpected, it was beyond anything she ever might have imagined. Nine pairs of eyes no less startled than her own fastened upon her. Rachel felt the blood drain from her face. She couldn't even apologize. She didn't know what to say.

General Lee's guests were two regulars – one of them still had on his jacket, so Rachel could see that he was a captain – and four women who wore enough cologne between them that the stink of sandalwood and bruised rose-petals drowned out the liquor and bitter tobacco smoke hanging in the air from newly poured drinks and freshly lit cigars.

The regular who wore his jacket did not have on his trousers, and one of the women sat on his naked lap. Two women had squeezed themselves on either side of General Lee; one had removed her gown and sported nothing but her stays and her chemise, which was thin and showed her breasts plainly. Everyone in the room seemed to be missing an article of clothing or two. She quickly put it together with the cards, since no coins or tokens lay about. Clothes were the stake. A lost hand meant a lost garment – and that the intention was not merely daring but unchaste, Rachel could hardly doubt. The crowd had been here scarcely ten minutes and was already half-naked. And Rachel knew the smell of whiskey, and the women were already pressed against the men in attitudes that would have gotten them banned from the Brass Bull, let alone polite society.

General Lee looked at her with a bored expression, a ruddy expanse of bare neck showing at his open shirt. A flicker of annoyance crossed his face. But Rachel didn't care how irritated General Lee might be with her interruption, because of what else she saw.

Mr. Addison was in the room too, and he had Mrs. Rimini on his lap with her arm thrown casually around his shoulders. Her skirts were pulled up to the thigh, and Mr. Addison had his hand on the thick blue ribbing at the top of Mrs. Rimini's stocking. His hand twitched as if to hide its action when Rachel burst into the room, but evidently Mr. Addison realized the situation was well beyond concealing, so he left his hand resting on Mrs. Rimini's knee. The cook smiled, unembarrassed and unflustered. She shared a complicitous look with Mr. Addison and pulled her skirts to cover her legs, leaving his hand beneath them.

The room was silent until the woman with the nearly bare breasts smiled kindly and said, "You're pale as a ghost, sweet. Take a little whiskey." She looked around for a fresh glass but, finding none, poured half a finger into her own and held it in the air.

"No, thank you, miss," Rachel whispered. Mr. Addison wouldn't look at her. Rachel felt she couldn't get enough air, and her head grew light. Outrage and shame on Mrs. Addison's behalf warred with fear for her position and a strange, disgusted resignation at the hollowness of things. The woman shrugged and sipped the whiskey herself.

Everyone was staring at Rachel, but neither fear nor embarrassment showed in their eyes. They were simply waiting for her to leave so they could get on with their entertainment. And Rachel wanted to leave, almost as badly as she wished she'd never entered the room in the first place. Yet she felt rooted to the spot.

"Well, dear, are you coming in or going out?" General Lee inquired at last with a cool self-possession Rachel could almost admire.

"She's Margaret's pet," Mr. Addison muttered into Mrs. Rimini's neck. Mrs. Rimini smiled and shrugged a sympathetic shoulder at Rachel as if saying, *well, perhaps Mr. Addison needed a pet too.* He took a deep breath and spoke with a harsher tone than he'd ever used with her before. "What are you doing here, girl?" He still wouldn't meet her eyes.

Rachel's voice sounded thin and light in her ears when she spoke. "I just – I heard the people come in – I mean, I was unwell earlier, so I didn't go with – with –" Rachel couldn't bear to say Mrs. Addison's name in this company, in these circumstances. "So I was in my room, and I thought I might be of assistance, but – I am so very sorry for intruding uninvited, and for all resulting misunderstandings, and I won't – it won't happen again." Rachel stopped abruptly. She was talking too much. No one wanted to hear her speak. They wanted her to go.

Rachel curtsied, her head low. Being forced to speak had broken the spell. Her limbs would move again, so she fled from the room and closed the door firmly behind her. The instant the latch caught, Rachel heard the company inside burst into uproarious laughter. Blood rushed to her cheeks.

She could not bear to hear them, nor did she care much for her own company at the moment, so Rachel went to the back yard to see Abraham, even if it meant braving the dogs. The mild winter air made her shiver, and she clutched her arms across her chest as she hurried across the dry ground. There hadn't been much snow yet this season, and none of it had stuck.

Abraham watched her approach expressionlessly. He'd given up trying to rein in the dogs. The creatures were clearly too scatter-brained to take to any but the most rigorous training, which Abraham was unlikely to have the time to provide. So the greyhounds pursued their destruction of the yard according to their whim, and since it was difficult for any of them to hold a purpose in his head for long, most of the damage remained superficial.

Abraham knew, Rachel realized suddenly. "They let you take the dogs out," she said.

"What they did was let the dogs take me out," Abraham replied. "I didn't know you was home, and I guess they didn't either."

"No."

Abraham nodded, his expression unreadable. "You happen to see anything you didn't particularly feel like seeing?" he said at last.

Relief washed over her at not having to bear the secret alone. "Yes – oh, Abraham, I wish I hadn't –" She smiled at Abraham and took a half-step forward to take his hands in gratitude, but he didn't smile back, and Rachel stopped. She let her hands drop by her side.

"Then maybe you just better decide that you didn't see it after all. I'm talking sense to you because you's sillier than a fly in smoke only half the time, Miss Rachel, so maybe you'll listen up. Mr. Addison will let it lie if you do. And even if you don't. Because they's nothing anyone can do about it, and he knows it, and he ain't doing anything different from a lot of gentlemens."

"I'm sure, no, I know you're right, but Abraham – Mrs. Addison trusts him, and she trusts me, and –"

"And don't think she don't know exactly what he gets up to, even if she don't know exactly how and when, and she don't want to, neither. She don't like it much, but it's not the kind of thing you should worry yourself about, Miss Rachel, because it don't hit her in her heart, only in her pride. Now if you start going on like you feel sorry for her, that's gonna hit her in her pride all over again, and it won't do no good for her, and it sure won't do no good for you."

Abraham was right. Rachel knew it. But the sickness in her stomach wouldn't go away. She shifted her foot, and dry leaves crackled beneath her heel. She glanced at the sky, but dreary gray clouds as thick as mud covered the sun. Cold and gray and dry and dead. Everything in the world came back to that eventually. Cold and gray and dry and dead. Why was her heart so hot and red, then? Why did it beat so hard and pain her so deeply? Why couldn't she be cold and gray and dry and dead too – what cruel hand had formed her in this strange mold, to be forever at odds with the nature of things? "I've been with the Addisons so long now, and Mr. Addison has never said the slightest impropriety to me," she whispered, frowning. "Mrs. Rimini has been here only *one day.*"

"People who's up for it has a look about them," Abraham said. "They know each other right off. Mr. Addison knew you weren't that sort, and he knew that the Missus took a shine to you, too. But that cook you found, she's something else. There ain't nothing particularly mean about the Master, Miss Rachel. He just got what he likes and does what he likes and can't really see nor even figure on anything outside that."

The reminder that Rachel had been the one to bring Mrs. Rimini in the household stung, although it was fair enough and Abraham hadn't said it unkindly. "But isn't it cruel to Mrs. Addison, Abraham? Isn't that mean? Because she's deprived of the full love and devotion of a husband – and especially with no children, Abraham, what is there for her, then? What is her life?"

"Money," Abraham shrugged. "Running around with her parties and gossip."

"But she deserves more than that!" Rachel cried. A thousand little details, chance words here and there over the past few months, clicked into place. No, Mrs. Addison was not happy. Perhaps it was not Mr. Addison's fault. Perhaps they were simply ill-suited to each other; but surely they could become better-suited with some effort, only Mr. Addison was always so disengaged, and – and distracted. "She must want it desperately!"

"She sure don't seem to," Abraham replied with a dubious tilt of his head.

Chapter 18

The front door of the prison creaked, and Bellew's heart sank. More men caught. Bellew never felt his condition so badly as when new eyes saw it for the first time, the dirty skin and the straggling hair and sores and filth.

"Captain O'Malley," the guard called out in a bored and peremptory voice. He was only a shadow against the light. "Lieutenant Bellew. Present yourselves."

Bellew's arm tightened around his friend, who leaned against him heavily. He frowned. What further business did the guards plan with him now – and why couldn't they leave at least the sick man be?

"What's that, then?" O'Malley murmured, his eyes still closed. He probably thought one of the other prisoners was addressing him, or perhaps some figure out of his fever dreams.

"Captain O'Malley and Lieutenant Bellew. Present yourselves," the guard repeated, squinting into the gloom. The crowd in front of Bellew shuffled and pressed against itself to make as much of a corridor as possible. All eyes fixed on his face with signs of wariness and curiosity. Uncertain hands reached out to help Bellew guide O'Malley.

"Give us a moment," Bellew snapped back. "Captain O'Malley is unwell." He recognized the guard's voice, and Corporal Graham knew very well that O'Malley was not fit to stand, let alone to make himself sharp over a summons.

"You've been paroled," Corporal Graham continued in an irritated voice. "You'll not be making yourself fat on the Crown's penny any longer."

Bellew's head shot up in astonishment. Corporal Graham had addressed him as an officer, which was new. But he was to be treated as one, and paroled, even? O'Malley's commission had never been finalized, nor Bellew's. How did the Continentals even know he existed?

"Congratulations, sirs." "Well done, sirs." "Best of luck to you, sirs," the other prisoners said, and a thousand other words too that Bellew scarcely heard. He tried to tamp down his excitement when he looked into their hollow faces. Paroled!

His mind went immediately to the practicalities. He had no money now, of course, the redcoats having confiscated everything he owned, but O'Malley still had people in South Carolina who could send something, enough for a doctor and food. That left the immediate problem of what to do until the money arrived. But surely there was some good-hearted patriot in Philadelphia who would be willing to wait for her rent and give them a little room, just someplace where O'Malley could lie down on a bed, even if a rough one. Or if not – that pretty Miss Kolkhorst – she had clearly done well for herself, and she was here in Philadelphia. It shamed Bellew to think of it, but she might be able to lend them a little, if only he'd had the sense to ask where he might find her. But she had never repeated her chance visit, and he did not trust that she would take kindly to a renewal of their acquaintance. He was indigent, hated, foul in appearance, defeated, entirely pathetic – no, she had shown sympathy, but that was likely a combination of surprise and disgust. He did not blame her, for all that it stung his pride. There was nothing about him to inspire friendship, not from a pretty girl rising in the world. He'd had plenty of time to think about their first meeting in the Brass Bull, what he remembered of it, and even then she had seemed better than her circumstances, so terribly innocent and with a quiet gravity that the roughness of the tavern could not soil. He had been above her then, and had wanted to protect and guide her. Now she was above him, infinitely so. Bellew did not think that he himself seemed better than his circumstances. He looked much as the other men. Weak and defeated.

He had made his way to the door, holding O'Malley tight. Corporal Graham stood impatiently, and two other guards had their muskets at the ready with fixed bayonets. The fresh air was as bracing as pure alcohol, cutting through the musky fug and stinging Bellew's eyes till they watered.

"Godspeed, sir." Bellew turned at the familiar voice. Cowles, what was left of him, gave him a shaky smile.

Bellew stared at Cowles blankly. His heart trembled. Of course he had to consider O'Malley's condition, of course he had to do whatever he could to make sure that his friend was taken care of and safe – but here he was choking on his pride, reveling in his luck, calculating his options and resources like a niggardly shopkeeper, while the rest of these men remained in this stinking hell with no hope, no light, no chance.

197

"Thank you," he said quietly. He released O'Malley and let the other prisoners hand him the rest of the way out. Then Bellew turned around, facing back into the massed dark.

"Come on, then," Corporal Graham snapped behind him. "The damned door's closing, Bellew. Get moving." Bellew could feel the cold air on his back.

"Gentlemen!" Bellew spoke into the prison. "I have had no greater honor in my life than your acquaintance." Murmurs rippled through the crowd. Bony hands touched foreheads in respect.

"Get going, sir," Cowles said nervously at his elbow. "Think of Captain O'Malley. Don't throw away your chance, sir. It won't do us any good."

He knew it wouldn't. But his pride, his damned pride burned him like sulfur fire. He could not have the other prisoners think he was running away. He could not have himself think it. Bellew straightened and raised his voice louder. "And we will all be together again, I swear it before God. And I also swear before God – that it will be as men who are free in fact, as well as spirit!"

The prisoners let out a weak cheer. "That's enough of that," Corporal Graham snapped, shouldering his way far enough inside to yank Bellew outside by the arm. The cheer was abruptly muffled as the guards slammed the doors shut. Graham released Bellew's arm and added matter-of-factly, "Hell's where rebels go, and if you want to rule that, you've got some pretty stiff competition."

The cold cut through Bellew's worn clothes. The guards relaxed visibly when the doors were locked again, reminding Bellew bitterly of what a poor figure he cut, harmless as a kitten. O'Malley had come back to his senses a little and blinked confusedly, but he seemed able to bear his own weight now. That would make things easier. Bellew did not know Philadelphia, and he did not know how far they would have to walk. He looked down the street. A few passers-by on foot or horseback gave him a curious glance and then quickly looked away. A lacquered carriage with four good horses and a somber old black driver in green livery with white facing stood waiting on some errand. He did not want to ask the guards where he could find cheap lodgings, but he thought the driver might be able to tell him. Bellew made eye contact with the man, and, to his surprise, the driver not only nodded but flicked the reins, bringing the carriage closer.

"Your ride," Corporal Graham said, and Bellew flushed in humiliation. He turned back to Graham, his eyes lively with anger. Corporal Graham ignored it. "You know the terms of parole, I hope, but allow me to remind you. You are given your liberty at the grace of His Majesty, whose prisoner you remain – I am not going to quarrel with you about whether or not you feel you are His subject, but I do ask you to remember the word *prisoner*, Lieutenant Bellew – and you are not to take any action in word or deed contrary to the interests of the Crown. You are to remain within the city of Philadelphia. You are not free to rejoin your army nor to engage in any military action whatsoever, upon your honor. You may not carry a pistol or other weapon. You have not been exchanged, only paroled. Do you understand this clearly?"

"I do," Bellew replied through a clenched jaw.

"Then off with you, and let's both pray we never meet again." Corporal Graham jerked his chin at the carriage. Bellew glanced at it again and saw to his surprise that the driver had lighted to the ground and was approaching him.

"I'll help you with the gentleman," the driver said, slipping a large dark hand under O'Malley's arms and guiding him gently towards the carriage before Bellew even realized what was happening.

"I am much obliged," Bellew said in astonishment. He eyed the driver with a frown. "Your assistance is greatly valued and more appreciated than I can properly express – but I don't wish to cause trouble for you by interfering with your errand."

"You is my errand, Lieutenant Bellew," the driver said. "It was my mistress that wrote the letter that got you and Captain O'Malley here paroled, and she told me that Captain O'Malley was taken poorly, so she says you better not walk when you's let out."

"Your mistress – my gratitude only deepens!" Bellew exclaimed. "But may I ask who she is, who has my infinite thanks?"

"Mrs. Robert Addison," the driver replied. The name meant nothing to Bellew. He'd seen no one he knew even slightly in this place other than Miss Kolkhorst – had she gotten married? Of course that was better for her than to be only a maid – of course he wished her all the best. And by the looks of the carriage, she had married well. Women could rise so quickly in the world; they could simply find a successful man to marry, and a girl might change magically from a rag-picker to a princess. He was pleased for her, truly. But his heart sank a little. He should be married by now himself, but what did he have to offer? No money, no prospects, no name of his own, no liberty, and his physical form was a disgrace. What sort of woman would accept a man in this condition? No honest one, he feared.

After they managed to get O'Malley inside, Bellew discovered to his shame that he was too weak himself to climb into the carriage without assistance. The driver handed him up, his face expressionless. The carriage creaked and settled under Bellew's weight as he sat on the thin cushion. He hoped his stained clothes were not polluting the fabric. "Thank you again," Bellew said, breathing hard from the exertion. "I apologize – I have not asked your name."

"Folks call me Abraham," the driver replied.

"I am in your debt as well, Abraham. And also of course to Mr. Addison, whom I do not mean to neglect. I suppose he must have connections that he exerted on our behalf."

Abraham shook his large head. "No, that's Mrs. Addison, sir. Her father's General van Dortmund in the Continental Army, and she wrote to her father, and he put a fly in General Washington's ear, and General Washington done wrote to General Howe and says well, how about this putting my officers in with the enlisted men, and General Howe says it was some kind of mistake and he'll fix it right off, and here we is."

General van Dortmund – Bellew had heard of him, an honorable man and very rich – but surely no relation to the orphaned Miss Kolkhorst. General van Dortmund would not have an illegitimate child? His confusion returned. "But – I don't believe I know the lady," he admitted. He did not know whether or not to be disappointed. Miss Kolkhorst had surely forgotten him, then – but who was this new friend?

"Well, I don't know about that. All I know is she's real sorry she can't take you two gentlemens in at the moment, since she's already got all the guests she can handle, but she made sure you's got a place to stay and a little money so's you can get by until you gets your affairs in order." And with that, Abraham shut the door, and a moment later the carriage jerked into motion. The mystery of his benefactress remained stubbornly unresolved. But perhaps it was ungentlemanly of him to inquire too deeply; surely the lady would reveal as much as she wished, and it hardly showed much gratitude if he demanded more. His curiosity was acute nevertheless.

"I am more accustomed to know my friends," he muttered to himself, pressing a knuckle against his mouth.

Bellew felt his exhaustion in every fiber, but the excitement of being free again made him restless in mind. He pulled back the curtain of the window and stared hungrily at the fine city, with its stone buildings and brightly dressed people and tall old trees with gnarled skin.

"It's a far cry from the country, isn't it?" O'Malley remarked softly. Bellew turned quickly and saw that O'Malley was watching the scenery go past with an air of tired affection. He leaned over to pull back O'Malley's curtain as well so that the captain would not have to crane his neck. O'Malley's energy seemed to be returning, and Bellew took heart from that. He could not gauge O'Malley's illness – it was dangerous, certainly, but perhaps fresh air and good accommodations alone would restore his health. Well, the doctor would be the best judge of that – he must have a doctor straight away.

"We'll have it in our hands again soon," Bellew said of the city.

"Oh, aye." O'Malley uttered a weak laugh. He seemed genuinely amused. "But there's no rush about it. If I have my way, the lobsters will sit tight here a good long while. I can't imagine a more useless place for them to keep their men, and it suits me to perfection."

"It's our capital," Bellew replied with a frown.

"That's the way General Howe sees it, no doubt," O'Malley said. "But Philadelphia is not merely a strategic nonentity, it is a positive liability – don't scowl like that, we'll look at a map when we get settled and you'll see what I mean, it's no fun to have a joke that no one else understands. An insurrection doesn't stand or fall by its capital, lad. It stands and falls by its people. If Billy Howe prefers to hold the city than to go after our men, I'm not sure he and I aren't on the same side after all."

Bellew had not heard O'Malley say that many words in a row ever since they'd been captured, and it cheered him so much he didn't even mind the lecture. "And we're still here," he said.

O'Malley smiled and nodded. "And we're still here," he murmured.

The carriage pulled to a stop before a tidy three-story brick house with a shingled roof. Bellew found to his relief that the rooms Mrs. Addison had taken for them were clean and comfortable but far from grand. He knew that he and O'Malley could not afford anything better than this themselves, and he would have hated to be dependent on charity indefinitely. The landlady Mrs. Merriwether was a plain, shy widow with two young daughters who were even shyer and ran off to the back of the house when Bellew and Abraham brought O'Malley inside.

We must look like the walking dead, Bellew thought grimly. He did not like to think of himself as the sort of apparition that would frighten children. Abraham helped him bring O'Malley up the stairs, Mrs. Merriwether keeping a few steps ahead of them and fluttering her hands uselessly. She seemed to feel much better when they reached the second-floor landing, and she could rush ahead to throw open the door to the nearest room – something useful for her to do at last.

"I'll bring up some clear broth. That's the best thing," Mrs. Merriwether said once they'd gotten O'Malley in bed. She opened the window and then shut it again, evidently finding the air too cold for a sick man. Other than the bed, the room contained a solid wardrobe, a small writing-desk, two wooden chairs, and a small table. The floor had the soft shine of a fresh wash, and a sharp but not unpleasing smell of lye hung in the air.

"Ah," O'Malley sighed as his matted head touched the clean sheets. "Now this is just lovely." His eyelids drifted down, and his mouth fell open slightly. Asleep. His eyes were sunken hollows, dark as bruises.

Bellew had not been hungry in a long time, and the thought of even broth made his stomach clench. He whispered, "Madam, since Captain O'Malley is resting, if I might trouble you for a bath instead."

"The broth is what both of you need, sir," Mrs. Merriwether answered. "The lady who came told me they weren't feeding you, and I can see with my own eyes it's true. Terrible, terrible." She looked away and shook her head before resuming. "You may not want to eat, and it'll probably make you sick at first too. But you've got to do it sometime, and I won't have you sitting in hot water until you've got something solid on the inside."

Bellew was too tired to argue with her, and he supposed she was probably right anyway. The three of them left O'Malley's room and closed the door gently behind them. Bellew put his hand on Abraham's arm to stay him. "Abraham, if it would be acceptable to her, and once my appearance is reasonably civil again, I would like very much to offer my thanks to Mrs. Addison in person, even though I will be eternally unable to express how profound my gratitude nor how deep my debt is to her. Not only on my own account, but –" he glanced back at the closed door. "I believe she has saved Captain O'Malley's life through her kindness."

"I'll tell her as you said so, sir," Abraham replied politely, and he bowed before descending the stairs. Bellew noticed that Abraham had not offered him Mrs. Addison's address, only agreed to pass on his message and his request. Well, this mysterious Mrs. Addison knew where he was; whatever her circumstances or motivations, he would by necessity leave it to her discretion whether there would be any further contact between them.

Still, the mystery tickled at him. He hoped she would come.

Bellew's room was similar to O'Malley's, only the shape of it was long and narrow and the chairs by his table looked like they'd been cannibalized from some other part of the house, because they didn't match. When he sat on one of the mismatched chairs and looked back to his own invitingly soft bed, he noticed marks on the wall where something had been removed – perhaps French doors, because there were screw-holes through the plaster for hinges. This might have been a library and study once, or a music-room and a parlor. But no – neither possibility seemed to fit the anxious, practical, easily flustered Mrs. Merriwether very well. He could not see her playing music for friends or reading a book. Perhaps her late husband had come from a different mold. Sometimes people married natures wildly divergent from their own. Bellew did not think much good ever came of that, but people did it all the same. Well, whatever purpose the rooms had served in the past, this house and this family had clearly adapted hastily to a sudden reduction in circumstances.

Bellew stretched out his legs, first one and then the other. He leaned back in the chair and rolled his shoulders. His elbows came up without hitting anyone in the face. All the empty space around him was delicious but disorienting. He had to fight a constant feeling that he was dropping through an empty void.

A knock on the door. "Yes, thank you," Bellew said, sitting up straight, and Mrs. Merriwether entered in a cloud of steam and bustling skirts, bearing a bowl of golden broth as well as a basket of bread and fruit. "I'll let you get started, and I'll bring up the rest," she said, placing the hot bowl on a small octagonal table.

Bellew stuck the spoon in the broth and twirled it, watching the grease form rounded, voluptuous patterns. At length, he managed to overcome his distaste enough to take a mouthful.

It tasted unbearably rich and was harder to choke down than a bowl of melted butter, but shortly after he forced down the last spoonful, Bellew discovered a ravenous appetite and devoured half a salted bread-roll and three bites of apple before he abruptly felt full to bursting and had to give up, flushed and dizzy from the heady excess.

He leaned back in his chair, breathing hard. Mrs. Merriwether peeked inside and saw that he'd given up. She checked how much he'd consumed and nodded to herself.

"Now you ought to be steady enough that it won't be murder to let you have a razor," she said, and she showed him to a small bathing-room containing a battered old copper tub filled with water that steamed slightly in the cool air. "There's a robe for you, and I'll put an old suit of Mr. Merriwether's in your room." She hurried off to do so.

Bellew peeled off his stiff, foul clothes and stepped naked into the water. He meant to clean himself as quickly as possible, but the heat and gentle touch of the bath against his skin loosened his muscles, and he drifted from dizziness to comfort to sleep in the space of a few moments. He did not know how long he napped, but the water was lukewarm when he woke, and the light coming through the window was tentative and shadowy.

He was starting, to his surprise, to feel a little better, a little more like himself already. It gave him hope.

The doctor had come and gone by the time Bellew emerged at last, freshly shaved and his hair tied back with a clean ribbon. The borrowed clothes were both too large and too small, Mr. Merriwether apparently having been built on a stockier model than Bellew. O'Malley's door was open, so Bellew cleared his throat slightly, and Mrs. Merriwether turned around, smiling at the sight of him and becoming serious again in rapid turn. She gestured him over. O'Malley lay very still in his bed, breathing rapidly in his sleep.

"Dr. Patton says it's dysentery and that Captain O'Malley needs one spoonful of medicine every eight hours, so the next will come at ten o'clock," Mrs. Merriwether said. She hesitated and then offered the dark glass bottle to Bellew. Bellew pressed his lips together at the diagnosis. He'd suspected it, but he'd hoped nevertheless that the doctor might find only exhaustion and poor diet. "If you'll be up then," Mrs. Merriwether continued. "If not, I don't mind, as long as you're recovering yourself –"

"You've done too much for us already, and I just slept by accident, so I will be awake for a while. I'll give him the dose," Bellew said.

"All right, but you'll need to understand... It will make him, forgive me for speaking directly, but I'm a mother and I've seen everything, vomit, so you'll need a bowl handy. I've put one by the bed."

It was difficult to imagine one of the timid Merriwether girls doing anything quite as forceful as vomit. Bellew turned the bottle over in his hand and examined it. The shadow of the liquid inside slithered around the glass. "Yes, it should – that's the purpose of the draught," Bellew said. "To purge the body of its disease."

"God willing. The doctor says he'll bleed the captain daily. If that's not enough to bring back his strength, he says he'll take further steps, but that'll do for now. It's not the best case he's seen, but neither is it the worst, and I find that hopeful."

People recovered from dysentery more often on balance than they died of it. If O'Malley's case fell in the middle, the odds favored a good outcome. Bellew smiled hesitantly and nodded in agreement. It was far from perfect reassurance, but a sizable weight off his mind nevertheless.

"I have a few letters I must write immediately," he said. "May I borrow some paper and ink for my desk – or if you could tell me where I might buy some for myself." Abraham had left four pounds with Bellew, so he could afford to purchase any immediate requirements. Bellew trembled at the thought of taking that long staircase again in his condition, the climb down presenting a torturous aspect and the climb up an impossible one, so it came as a great relief when Mrs. Merriwether promised she would supply him with everything he needed and not to trouble himself about it in the slightest, if only he'd be so good as to get more ink if they ran out at some later date.

Bellew had more than a few letters to write, actually. So many wives and fathers and mothers and brothers and sisters waited in pained misery for any chance news of dear ones who seemed to have vanished like wisps of fog in sunlight. Bellew knew the names and home towns of a few dozen fellow-prisoners, at least, and he meant to set as many hearts at rest as he could – that their beloveds were alive, at least. And he knew the names and home towns of a few men who had died, and he knew he must send those letters as well, even if they would bring no joy; but there was peace in certainty, and he owed that at least to the poor families.

And he must find out where Masterson was kept, and have him released – well, paroled – at once. Or had the miraculous Mrs. Addison managed to free Masterson as well – who was as much a lieutenant as Bellew, after all?

Masterson had been a childhood friend and occasional enemy. Their acquaintance had faded over the years to a polite affection, but when both men had decided to join O'Malley's company in the patriot cause, their former rivalrous brotherhood had resumed as if uninterrupted by the intervening years. His friend, his earnest, hot-blooded, difficult friend – the thought of Masterson still suffering in those hellish, hopeless conditions was all but unendurable. It was not the suffering that troubled Bellew, even though he well knew how overwhelming and poisonous that suffering could be. But Masterson and Bellew had spoken too often of their willingness to die on the field – often enough that O'Malley had accused them once of relishing the prospect – for Bellew to discredit his friend by ascribing any fear of pain or privation to him. It was the callous disregard, the being forgotten by the world, the impotence, that Bellew could not endure on Masterson's behalf, who was many things and not all of them good, but none of which deserved to treated like something scraped off a boot.

He did not, he realized, have any idea how to go about finding Masterson. A ship – it had been implied that Masterson was being sent to a ship. But Bellew did not even know which one.

All his reasonable hopes, then, pinned on Mrs. Addison.

"You mentioned that the lady herself came here to let the rooms," Bellew said after a pause, holding up a hand to stay Mrs. Merriwether from leaving O'Malley's room quite yet. She smiled and nodded. "I don't mean to pry into her affairs, of course, particularly being as indebted as I am, so please don't be concerned that I would ask you to violate any confidence she meant for you to keep – but did she happen to mention any other prisoners who might have been liberated by her good offices?"

Mrs. Merriwether shook her head. "No, she didn't say. But she didn't tell me much – just said that she'd heard from the cook that I had a sympathy for a certain political viewpoint and if my rooms were still to let, which they were, would two parolees be acceptable to me if she paid me two weeks in advance. And I'd have taken you even if she hadn't," Mrs. Merriwether added quickly, a pleading look in her face. Bellew supposed she did not like to think that she needed money as badly as she obviously did; and if times were better, he was sure she would have taken them in for nothing more than kindness's sake. In his heart, he gave her the credit for it. "But she said two, I remember it clearly – and I might have put up three if she wanted, but she never asked."

Bellew had no choice but to content himself with that unsatisfactory intelligence for the time being. He set about writing his letters, starting with a reassuring note and a request for funds to O'Malley's cousin John Woolsey whom O'Malley had left in charge of his fur-trading concern. And then, the letters saying nothing more than that such and such a man remained among the living, and thought of his home with love. Soon the regularity of his task absorbed him, and the rest of the world slipped away. He hardly noticed when Mrs. Merriwether lighted two candles in the room and slipped out again. He startled when she returned in what seemed hardly a minute later, bearing a plate of bread and sour apples and a mug of small-beer. "It's almost ten o'clock," she said with a meaningful glance in the direction of O'Malley's room.

"Has he woken yet?"

"I did peep in a few times, and he hasn't seemed to."

But O'Malley was not difficult to rouse for his medicine, and after he'd gagged out the clear, viscous contents of his stomach, he managed to take a little of Mrs. Merriwether's broth and bread. She reckoned that apples would still be too difficult for him, and O'Malley professed himself entirely servile to her opinions and judgment, implicitly. Mrs. Merriwether giggled slightly and blushed, and Bellew marveled for the thousandth time at O'Malley's way with people whether or great or small, and felt a slight twinge of jealousy. Bellew was made of colder, harder material than his friend, for good or ill – people found it easy to admire him sometimes, but they did not think to love him, while O'Malley they loved reflexively.

O'Malley closed his eyes and slept. Suddenly the weariness washed over Bellew again, and he could barely stand.

"Leave the bottle here," Mrs. Merriwether said gently. "If you're not awake by six, I'm not going to rouse you." Bellew nodded, too tired even to thank her properly, and returned to his room.

Countless times over the past weeks, as he stood aching and swaying on swollen feet, prevented from falling over only by the press of other men, Bellew had imagined the sweet yieldingness of a pillow beneath his head. The vision had helped him snatch a few moments of rest here and there. Now a real pillow lay there, soft and clean, and sleep was nowhere to be found. The space around him still unnerved Bellew, and he watched the shadows a long time and listened to the gentle creaking of the house and the trees outside before rest finally claimed him.

Three days passed. Bellew finished his letters to the various families, and wrote politely to Mr. Loring inquiring of Lieutenant Masterson's whereabouts, and became familiar enough to the Misses Merriwether that they did not hide quite every time they saw him. Dr. Patton proved to be a middle-aged man with a square face and deep lines around his mouth that gave his cheeks the appearance of pulled-back stage curtains; he had a soothing manner and assured Bellew that O'Malley was responding as well as might be expected to the treatment, which Dr. Patton did not feel the need to increase. And it was true that while O'Malley showed no interest in getting out of bed, he slept less now than he used to, and he certainly seemed to be getting no worse. Bellew ordered new civilian clothes made for both himself and O'Malley, since they were not allowed uniforms now. These had just arrived on the afternoon of the fourth day when Abraham reappeared, on horseback this time.

"You looks like you's settled in just fine," Abraham said, assessing Bellew in his new set of clothes. Bellew bowed. He'd gained back some of his weight already, and it pleased him that he no longer looked an inhuman and pitiable thing. And then his pleasure at being presentable redoubled again, because Abraham informed him that Mrs. Addison would not object if he felt he wanted to offer his quite unnecessary thanks in person, and she would be at home at the address on her card Wednesday from four until eight and Thursday from three until ten.

Chapter 19

Mrs. Addison divined the changed nature of the relationship between the cook and her husband immediately; Rachel never knew how. But Mrs. Addison complained about nearly every meal, to Mrs. Rimini's smug indifference, and made a poor show of acceding to the joint protestations of Mr. Addison and General Lee that the food was in their opinion more than acceptable.

"Your sensate abilities are more refined in the visual field, my dear," Mr. Addison said one day at supper. "Mrs. Rimini knows her business where the visceral appetites are concerned. Perhaps you'll learn to appreciate it." The room fell silent. Rachel blushed on her wounded mistress's behalf and looked down at her feet. General Lee repressed a smile. The British officer's wife who was dining with them as General Lee's guest tucked into at her pie without comment, as if trying to prove how well she at least understood the earthier side of life.

"Her presentation is certainly – calculated to entice, if that is all I am competent to judge," Mrs. Addison replied coolly, and she did not criticize the food any more.

Rachel's fears that she might be supplanted in Mrs. Addison's affections thus came to nothing, but the canker on Mrs. Addison's heart was a matter they could not discuss, and so the intimacy between them faded a little, for all that Mrs. Addison made a great show, in fact a redoubled one, of her continued patronage and favoritism. Rachel longed to be free of Philadelphia. Lieutenant Bellew and Captain O'Malley were safe. She had done what she could for them. So Philadelphia meant was redcoats everywhere, and the Mrs. Rimini debacle, and of course the boorish General Lee and a constant stream of dubious women Mrs. Addison was obliged to entertain as guests and to smile blandly at even when they appeared, a little worse for wear, at the breakfast-table.

Rachel found it difficult to think of General Lee as a great soldier any more, no matter what anyone said. He seemed to spend little time thinking about military matters. And a man who refused to train four dogs could hardly be expected to organize an army of thousands. But when she hazarded these thoughts to Mrs. Addison, the older woman merely sighed and said, "I don't pretend to know much about soldiery, Rachel, nor to be interested in it - but my father has said often enough that General Lee possessed the finest military mind he had encountered in the colonies, bar none."

"But his habits are not - they're not orderly," Rachel whispered, feeling suddenly rather petty and mean.

"They are not, and we are left only to assume that he is a different man on the field than he is at his leisure."

Rachel was hanging up the laundry with her sleeves rolled back when Jacob hurried to the back to fetch her. She felt a moment's irritation - she could do only one thing at a time - until something in Jacob's excited face made her curious.

"The master and missus and General Lee has a guest. I got them something to drink, but Abraham said maybe you should go and see if they needs anything else," Jacob said. Rachel couldn't understand whether if Jacob was busy, which he didn't seem to be, Mrs. Rimini couldn't deal with whatever dreadful baggage General Lee had dragged into the parlor - it bothered Mrs. Rimini less, and the dogs even seemed to like her.

"I'll be only a moment," she replied, hastily pinning up the last shirt and rolling down her sleeves. Jacob stood there grinning. She wasn't sure why. He didn't usually delight in her discomfort.

"It ain't what you's thinking," he said. "It's a gentleman. Abraham said to come get you real quick, cause it's that same gentleman that was shooting down at Griffin's Ford. You remember how he got that apple from two hundred yards, Miss Rachel? And he's a real polite gentleman, too."

"Oh!" Rachel froze. And then she ran towards the house, her heart hammering, leaving Jacob by the damp shirts hanging in the cool air. Lieutenant Bellew! Of course he had come to offer his thanks - only that was something of a puzzle, because Rachel had never told Mrs. Merriwether where she lived, because the fewer people who associated her face with her address the better. And Mrs. Addison had told Abraham not to make a fuss about it when Rachel had pleaded with her to let the prisoners use the carriage just for a brief ride upon their liberty because they were so sick, and that being a day Mrs. Addison had not planned to go out until evening. And Rachel had instructed Abraham distinctly not to let Lieutenant Bellew know the source of the money that she pressed into Abraham's hand.

But of course Lieutenant Bellew had found out somehow anyway. And he was here – in the house she loved so well, and the furniture looking so polished and fine, and she wished those dogs would head straight back to Hades, but Lieutenant Bellew would make accommodation for their presence, she was sure! How glad she was that he had come, despite every impediment she had placed in his way! She could admit now she was glad he had outfoxed her– or rather she could not deny it, the way her hands shook and her face felt alternately cold and hot. She had not made it possible for him to find her – and yet he had done so anyway, and she was so happy!

Of course it did not mean anything, she reminded herself sternly once she got inside and slowed to a walk, running her shaking hands over her hair to smooth the stray bits that always came free in the wind. The Addisons would be leaving Philadelphia in a few weeks. But they were going to Valley Forge, to Mrs. Addison's father in the Continental Army, and might not Lieutenant Bellew wind up there also? But that would be only for a few weeks or months, until the winter season was ended or Mrs. Addison grew bored or Mr. Addison decided his business needed closer attention, and he did not sell arms to the rebels, Rachel had divined, only to the English. Even if she maintained her acquaintance with Lieutenant Bellew at Valley Forge, then, they would be separated for certain when winter quarters broke, and Bellew went to war, and Rachel went to London. But how sweet and how eternal those few weeks and months seemed, when they were still ahead of her! How dear even this one brief afternoon.

The parlor was open, and Rachel could see inside. Mr. Addison wore the polite, disengaged aspect habitual to him when he was not particularly interested. General Lee, however, was in a fine humor. He grinned broadly and patted the head of one of his awful beasts, which drooled onto his lap. Mrs. Addison wore an arch, pleased expression and leaned forward slightly on the sofa. She tapped her everyday cream lace fan absently against the side of her skirt. And there was Lieutenant Bellew, clean-shaven and wearing a good civilian suit of black wool, with white lace at the cuffs – how proud Rachel was to think that her money had bought it for him, and how fine he looked in it – sitting on the blue silk side-chair and speaking in a low voice, a faint frown on his fine features to emphasize the seriousness of his words. How splendid he seemed, and how natural in these settings. Rachel could not bear to interrupt, and she stopped in the doorway.

Mr. Addison, attending to the conversation with only half an ear, quirked an eyebrow at her. Lieutenant Bellew turned around quickly to see what his host was looking at and rose to his feet on seeing Rachel there.

"Oh, good heavens, Lieutenant Bellew, it's just the maid, you don't need to stand," Mrs. Addison laughed.

"Jacob asked me to see whether you might need anything," Rachel said. Or rather, her lips moved around the words. She could not hear them past the rushing in her ears, and she was not sure she had actually spoken.

"Why, it's Miss Kolkhorst," Lieutenant Bellew said with a delighted smile. "Of course! Now I understand." He bowed to her slightly. Rachel curtsied.

"Understand what?" Mrs. Addison asked, leaning forward a fraction further.

Lieutenant Bellew's smile widened as he turned to face Mrs. Addison again. "How your kindness knew to find Captain O'Malley and myself as its object," he replied. "I hope it suggests no reduction of my gratitude that I had rather wondered how we had been found. Miss Kolkhorst must have mentioned seeing us at the prison."

"Yes, precisely – Rachel said that she had seen officers put in with enlisted men while out on an errand. Well, of course I wrote immediately."

"And not a moment too soon for Captain O'Malley, madam," Lieutenant Bellew answered gravely, a shadow crossing his face again as he took his seat.

"And how is – how is Captain O'Malley, sir?" Rachel asked in a tiny voice.

He turned to face her. "His deterioration has stopped, and the doctor has good hopes for him," Lieutenant Bellew replied, and then he lowered his eyes. "Miss Kolkhorst, I must ask your forgiveness."

"I cannot imagine why," Rachel said with a shy smile. By force of will, she kept her hands from fidgeting with her skirt. It was hard to stand still, with her heart beating this way. She felt she must either sit down in a total collapse or else run at full tilt beneath the open sky.

"I thought you had forgotten us entirely after that chance meeting. Not unkindly, of course - only that I presented such a terrible aspect that you would have wanted to exorcise it from your mind."

"Oh, no, sir - you did not seem terrible to me at all," Rachel protested.

But this lie did not please him as much as she hoped it might. His face cooled slightly. "Well, the conditions in that prison were genuinely dangerous, although I am glad of course that they did not frighten you," he said. He glanced back at Mrs. Addison and smiled again. "It is only your timely intercession, in my belief, that saved Captain O'Malley's life." Mrs. Addison inclined her head graciously. She twirled the ring on her finger. Lieutenant Bellew noticed it. "But I do not mean to embarrass you by expressing my gratitude too freely. I understand by your family connections, and by General Lee's presence here, that you must take the interests of the glorious cause very much to heart, and perhaps to dwell on any particular act does injustice to the scope of your feelings."

Rachel blinked in confusion. Did Lieutenant Bellew believe somehow that she herself didn't care - that she hadn't even thought his situation was dire? She tried to search his eyes, but they were turned away from her now.

"I'm a mere parolee myself, Lieutenant," General Lee replied with a sigh. "Sidelined, and of no use to anyone."

"Sir!" Lieutenant Bellew exclaimed with some heat. "If I may speak frankly -" He paused, and General Lee shrugged. "The regulars performed us a most peculiar service when they were foolish enough to capture you rather than kill you, sir - we have only one leader who can bring us to victory against these terrible odds, sir, and - my commanding officer has told me, sir, that an insurgency depends on its men more than anything else, any foolish unstrategic gains of pointless territory, and surely it depends upon its leader more than any other man among them!"

"More than its capital, you mean," General Lee replied with a sudden sharp look in his eye.

"Yes, sir – those were his words, actually."

"By God, at least I have some men with brains!" General Lee exclaimed, thumping the arm of his easy-chair and startling the dog. "Who is this fellow – what did you say his name was?"

"Captain Samuel O'Malley, sir. Although our company is not yet formed –"

"Well, damn me, if I hadn't been caught, what I could have done with a few dozen captains like this O'Malley of yours! He's exactly right! You don't fight the British Army on the field – it's the finest field force the world has ever seen! You fight them behind trees – behind rocks – you harry them to pieces, and that's how you win! If a certain so-called 'great man' hadn't been so hot to prove himself in open battle, we'd be halfway to victory by now!" Then General Lee put his hand to his chin, his fires abruptly banked. "Ah, but certain 'great men' are far too great to listen. Far too great, then, to win, I'm afraid. It's a pity, Lieutenant Bellew, because that means they are far too great to prevent us all from being hanged." Rachel had never seen General Lee so excited before. She could not judge the truth of his words – but she could see a raw intelligence, suddenly wakened, seething behind them. And the fighting he described was the only kind she had ever known, the way the Indians fought her family and each other, and the way the raiders had fought the Indians in turn. Perhaps he was right. And perhaps she had been wrong, and General Lee was a better soldier than she had been willing to admit. Lieutenant Bellew admired him, Rachel could tell by the light shining in his eyes.

Oh, it was such a simple thing, if only she could explain to Lieutenant Bellew that she had not disparaged his suffering, and that she had not cast it aside as nothing. But she could not speak. She knew she should not even be standing in the doorway listening, except that everyone had forgotten about her. If only Lieutenant Bellew would turn for a moment, glance at her even briefly, just long enough to see what was in her eyes!

"General Howe is treating fairly by you, sir. You may be traded yet," Lieutenant Bellew replied stoutly.

General Lee laughed bitterly. "Aye, well – the fellow who captured me, Tarleton, was an old friend of mine who hoped I'd be hanged as a deserter, a prospect he found infinitely more appealing even than seeing me shot. No, General Howe isn't cut of that cloth. He's a decent man, as men go. But as for our poorly led forces, I don't hold much hope that we'll catch anyone of high enough rank for me to be traded until everything is over."

"Sir – I am sure it is the fervent wish of the men, and very likely the pressing goal of many of them. If I were free to –"

"You're as hamstrung as I am, Lieutenant Bellew," General Lee interrupted. "We might both of us have dysentery ourselves for all we can do. It's out of our hands, I'm afraid."

"Perhaps General Howe is too good a soldier himself to risk the trade, even if a reasonable one is offered," Lieutenant Bellew mused.

Before she knew what she was doing, Rachel blurted, "I'm sure he'd take it, sirs, and then everything would be all right." All eyes turned to her.

Rachel quailed under General Lee's cold stare. But it was too late now – and anyway, it was true, and she knew it. General Howe did not want the rebel army destroyed, not until the political situation had changed in England. He had said so, and she knew he meant it. He must be in despair to see matters to mishandled by the inexperienced General Washington – it must be all he could do not to destroy the Continentals overnight and be done with it. General Howe would be relieved to have General Lee's competent hands at the helm once more – hadn't Mr. Addison told General Lee so? "I only meant that as an honorable man, I'm sure he'd have no grounds to refuse a fair trade – I'm sorry, I shouldn't have spoken," she added hurriedly in a small voice.

"Rachel is quite fond of General Howe, we have to be careful what we say about him in her hearing," Mrs. Addison laughed, and the rest of the company laughed with her. Rachel seized her hands together, and her face burned with shame. Not only to have said something so stupid out loud – but to have Mrs. Addison bring up her strange notion about Rachel's infatuation with General Howe at this of all times, was simply too awful.

"I tell you what, Lieutenant," General Lee said, leaning back in his chair. Rachel was immediately forgotten again. "Why don't you come fox-hunting with us this Saturday? There's damned little to do in this town for a military man, and we need to take our pleasures where we find them."

"Before the dance?" Mr. Addison inquired with a glance at his wife.

"Oh, Lieutenant Bellew, that would be a wonderful idea. Do you have a horse?" Mrs. Addison exclaimed.

"I used to," Lieutenant Bellew answered, the side of his mouth quirking ironically.

"Yes, how silly of me. Well, you can use one of ours. You must come to the hunt and the dance. There's really nothing else to do, if you don't know anyone – well, you know us, of course. And," Mrs. Addison added with a twinkle in her eye, "Who could resist the opportunity to meet his bête noire."

"Who?"

"General Howe."

"He'll be at the hunt?" Lieutenant Bellew asked in astonishment. Apparently the idea that he should go fox-hunting with the supreme general of the enemy force was not as natural to him as it was to General Lee. His eyes flicked at the others: General Lee, Mrs. Addison, Mr. Addison, as if to gauge their reactions and discover whether this was a trick.

"Of course – it's his hunt. And the dance is at his house. Oh, you have to come. It's the winter season; there's no fighting now anyway."

"And mind you don't praise me too highly to him, Lieutenant," General Lee said with an air of satisfaction.

"I – of course, sir, madam. You honor me," Lieutenant Bellew answered, seeming dazed. And then, as if he had made up his mind about something, he suddenly looked pleased.

"It's perfect weather for a hunt. I hope it holds," Mrs. Addison replied.

"I thought you didn't care for hunting, dear," Mr. Addison said.

"Oh, but in such fine weather, Robert – Rachel, good, you're still there, do you know how to ride, dear?"

Rachel's heart surged. And yet the hunt would doubtless be crawling with soldiers, the dance even more so, and if she were recognized and caught –

"Yes, ma'am, I do," Rachel replied firmly. And she did know how to ride, and well, too – only she realized as soon as the words left her mouth that she would have to ride side-saddle here, not astride as she had done with the Cherokee. And she had never ridden side-saddle before. Well, how hard could it be?

Lieutenant Bellew glanced at her quickly. Rachel smiled, and he gave a polite smile in return before turning back to Mrs. Addison. "I have not had opportunity for much exercise lately. I hope not to make too poor a showing."

"You probably need food and rest more than you need further exertions at the moment," Mr. Addison said. His eyes moved between General Lee and his wife as if uncertain what to make of this strange alliance. But Rachel thought she understood. Mrs. Addison was kind, she was bored, and Lieutenant Bellew was interesting and grateful. General Lee simply liked to preen his feathers in the presence of admiration, and he had found an easy source of it in this young lieutenant.

"Oh, no, Lieutenant Bellew, you need to get out in the air, I'm sure you do," Mrs. Addison insisted over her husband's weak objection. "No sitting around for you, or you'll never regain your full strength. And if Captain O'Malley is well enough, I absolutely demand that you bring him along as well. Oh, and come to the dance afterwards too, if you aren't too fatigued," she added off-handedly. "Everyone else will be there. Although for once, I anticipate there won't be a shortage of men."

Lieutenant Bellew smiled. He stood and bowed. "With the promise of your company, madam, I am sure there never is. I see I am outmaneuvered, and by a far superior force. What can I do but accede, and with my thanks yet again. I hope you do not weary of the repetition of them, but you leave me no choice."

Mrs. Addison smiled and waved a hand at him dismissively.

"I profit too much from your company to risk letting my own grow tiresome to you," Lieutenant Bellew continued, still on his feet. "I should tend to Captain O'Malley's medicine."

"Oh, of course. And I do hope he's improving."

"The doctor is an immeasurable help. I expect Captain O'Malley's man to respond to my letter next week, and it would be my honor if you would allow me to repay the sum you forwarded on our account. I am sure you have forgotten it already, but I do not like to think that I would abuse such kindness - and perhaps you may find use for it in the rescue of some other poor soul."

"I won't forget your friend. Lieutenant Masterson, you said? I'll look into it right away," Mrs. Addison replied.

Rachel went cold. Lieutenant Bellew still didn't know what had happened to Lieutenant Masterson. How could he; Rachel had told no one what she'd seen of Masterson's fate, not by name. Bellew bowed and left the room, and Rachel fell into step beside him. He glanced at her and smiled. "It's all right, Miss Kolkhorst, I know where my cloak is."

She flushed. "Well, I still ought to -" And she took his cloak from its hook, the same worn, old cloak that he'd had in the prison. It felt rough and heavy in her hands, and the scent of his sweat had worked its way too deeply into the wool for cleaning to remove it. She slipped it onto his shoulders. The fabric whispered as it settled. She should tell him about Masterson. He had to know. But she couldn't. The words died on her lips.

"Well, good-bye. And thank you again for mentioning me to your mistress," Bellew said.

"Oh, of course - how could I not!" she exclaimed, but his eyes were distant with other thoughts, and he was halfway out the door before she had even finished speaking. He smiled in acknowledgement and bowed his head, and then he was gone.

Rachel watched him walk down the street as long as she could before shutting the door. His step had the same determined firmness that she remembered. No, hard treatment had not broken him. How she wished she might suffer as he had, so that she could rise above it so well! Her hands still tingled with the roughness of his cloak, and the whisper of heat rising from his back when she had placed it upon him. Her mind heavy with confused thoughts, she walked slowly back to the parlor to take up the used dishes.

Mrs. Addison leaned to the side of the sofa, away from her husband, a fine line of dissatisfaction between her brows. "So you even lent money to your decorative Lieutenant Bellew," Mr. Addison was telling her with a thin smile. General Lee stared at the window, apparently lost in his own thoughts. His greyhound had settled again, briefly, and he scratched its neck absently.

"Honestly, Robert, I have no idea what he was going on about there," Mrs. Addison said, scowling in annoyance. She met his eyes briefly and put force into her gaze as if flashing some communication. Rachel did not think Mr. Addison would have missed it. He missed very little. But he ignored it just the same.

"A man can fancy a lot of things, but if he imagines money and it's not there, someone usually brings him up short." Mr. Addison was all but calling her a liar – and that seemed a step too far, to Rachel. Did he begrudge Mrs. Addison a few friends or a few pounds – even if it were true that Mrs. Addison had acted on Lieutenant Bellew's behalf, which she hadn't, because everything had been Rachel or Rachel's prompting, and Mrs. Addison had merely indulged her. Well, if Mrs. Addison had been a little slow to comply, Rachel understood now – she was seeing a new side of Mr. Addison, and every new side of him she saw made her long all the more for the dull, phlegmatic mask he wore more usually. Some people belonged behind masks.

"Well, I didn't give it to him. He must have some other friends," Mrs. Addison replied, a little color rising in her cheeks. "And I don't see why not. He is a perfect delight."

"I'm a delight too when people give me money for no reason."

"Excuse me, ma'am, sir," Rachel said, her eyes wide. Fear at having been the source of this quarrel drowned her anger at Mr. Addison's injustice. "I'm sorry, I didn't mean to cause trouble –"

"Yes, Rachel, you always say that, we take it as a given now, please, what is it?"

"I left the money for Lieutenant Bellew and Captain O'Malley," she said miserably. "I didn't think it would make any difficulty. Only their conditions in the prison – I didn't think they'd have anything when they got out."

"Oh! Well, there you have it, Robert, and you see I didn't have anything to do with it. How much money are we talking about, dear?" Mr. Addison settled back on the sofa with a shrug.

"Eight pounds," Rachel said.

"Eight pounds! Rachel, are you trying to buy the gentlemen?"

It turned out that General Lee was listening after all, because he glanced at Rachel and chuckled to himself. There was nothing particularly friendly about it.

Rachel shook her head. "I only thought they needed a place to stay, so I found those rooms and took them for two weeks, and a doctor for Captain O'Malley of course, so I paid for him to come, and some money for food and clothes, their clothes were so awful, ma'am, and I thought that would do."

"It certainly would. Well, when Lieutenant Bellew returns the money, you shall have it back. And as of now, we'll never mention it again. And you are a dear, sweet creature, but you really have to stop running off and doing things on your own accord. No one knows what to expect, and it can make life terribly difficult sometimes. So will you promise me that, Rachel? No more surprises. I want you to tell me absolutely everything."

"I promise," Rachel replied, her eyes low. She knew she could not keep her word, and the lie burned her tongue. She could not speak about Mrs. Rimini and Mr. Addison – she could not speak about the rock she had thrown at Captain Cunningham – she could not speak about many things. But she would do her best, she swore to herself fiercely, and she would see that anything she could not tell Mrs. Addison would never, never come to light, and perhaps that would be much the same. But as for Mr. Addison – never. Mrs. Addison had extracted no promise on her husband's behalf, but Rachel gave herself the small pleasure of telling herself: *Not him. I won't tell him anything, not ever.* For all that she knew very well he did not care.

Rachel poured another sherry for General Lee and Mr. Addison while she was there, and then she took Lieutenant Bellew's used glass back to the kitchen for washing. Her footsteps echoed in the empty entrance-hall where Bellew had stood only a few moments before. The room had a lonely feel. She almost wished a dog would run by, so that it would not seem so solitary. The vastness of the house had never bothered her before. She twirled the glass in her hand, and an amber jewel of liquid no broader than a thumbprint trembled in its hollow. On sudden impulse, Rachel lifted the glass to her mouth and tilted it back. The sweet, musky liquid that remained was only enough to wet her lips and the tip of her tongue, but a fire rose in her blood just the same, and the taste remained with her the rest of the day and night.

Chapter 20

Rachel discovered to her surprise, when she put on her new high-heeled shoes to go with the old ball-gown of Mrs. Addison's, that she was not much shorter than her mistress after all, even though her feet were certainly larger. "Will you look at yourself! I never would have guessed it. Let me – no, wait a moment, I want to fix your hair, you've made a mess of it," Mrs. Rimini laughed when Rachel tried on her outfit.

"No, I should change and get back to work –"

"Now be quiet, you, I want this to look right," Mrs. Rimini insisted, and she pinned up Rachel's hair on top of her head before she would let Rachel look in the small hand-mirror that Mrs. Addison had given her. Mrs. Rimini seemed fond of Rachel, and it shamed Rachel that she could not quite find it in her heart to love Mrs. Rimini wholly in return. The cook was not to blame for Mr. Addison's behavior, and Rachel supposed she was merely making the best of her situation, with her husband gone and who knows what other personal difficulties. Mrs. Rimini was not one to complain, and Rachel did admire that. And she would have admired Mrs. Rimini's good nature and high spirits too, if she hadn't been so unhappy about their consequences.

Still, there was something about the cook that Rachel could not quite trust, no matter how much Mrs. Rimini fussed over her and made a show of being her friend and not minding in the slightest that Mrs. Addison showed Rachel so many signs of preferment. A new gold bracelet twinkled on Mrs. Rimini's wrist, Rachel noticed. Well, she herself was not jealous in the slightest of Mr. Addison's signs of preferment, so perhaps in Mrs. Rimini's mind they'd divided up the spoils fairly.

"It's all right, I suppose," Rachel said, examining herself. She thought the champagne color of the gown washed out her complexion, so that while the silk of the dress shone prettily, Rachel looked like a drab thing inside it. Mrs. Addison herself had said that it wasn't the most flattering color for her, but it was the best old gown she had, and it wouldn't need taking in, because Mrs. Addison had worn it when she was a teenaged girl. "But it makes me look pale."

"You'll look like an angel," Mrs. Rimini declared firmly. "What color are the masks?"

It was going to be a masked ball, to Rachel's infinite relief. She had made the suggestion hesitantly, hardly expecting that she could be lucky enough to hide her face during the dance. But Mrs. Addison had liked the idea, gleefully accusing Rachel once more of covert Gallicism. And Mrs. Loring did not trust her own taste in matters of elegance, so she was easily swayed by Mrs. Addison's enthusiasm, and a masked ball it was.

"White. Well, cream."

"And isn't that perfect, and the rest of you will be all pale and white after powdering, and there's nothing draws the eye more than a light color. You'll have every gentleman's eye on you all night." The prospect seemed intrinsically delightful to Mrs. Rimini. Rachel was less sure.

Everyone rose early Monday morning, the world outside still a cold, black void not yet brought to life by the sun. Mrs. Addison did not care for the hour and groaned miserably as Rachel helped her dress. "I'm hardly going to be able to stay on my horse," she said. "Why did I ever agree to this, forgive me, infernal hunt? I might have slept until noon."

"Well, you're up now, ma'am, so you might as well make the best of it," Rachel said, quailing at the thought of losing the chance to be in the hunt with Lieutenant Bellew. He would come, wouldn't he? He'd said he would, and Mrs. Addison had sent him a note reminding him to which he'd responded in the most obliging manner. "I'm sure the events of it will provide ample subject for conversation, and surely it would show well if you could take part in it."

"I suppose that's true," Mrs. Addison replied, mollified. "And we did have that riding suit made for you, and it's silly to waste it. I daresay there won't be too much fox-chasing at Valley Forge, and the season will be pretty much over by the time we get to London. There are better entertainments in London anyway. There's next year, of course, but that's so long off."

Rachel was happy to hear Mrs. Addison speak of taking her to London as if it were a settled thing, although not as happy as she had been in the past. The two pleasures she held in life now were Mrs. Addison's company and the thought of Lieutenant Bellew's. The breadth of the Atlantic Ocean might present an insuperable difficulty to the latter, but that was the future, and many things could happen before then. As was her wont, she had grown an impenetrable thicket of wishful possibilities in her mind. Perhaps the war would end, and Lieutenant Bellew might find employment anywhere - or perhaps he would have to return to his patrimony with the cessation of hostilities, and wasn't Bellew an Irish name? Perhaps Lieutenant Bellew would not be so far from her after all - perhaps the relocation to London was in fact no more than another one of these turns of fate that seemed to bring them together.

Rachel had given up trying to tell herself that she did not have a marked partiality for Lieutenant Bellew beyond mere friendship. Ever since his visit to the Broad Street mansion, she had been unable to sleep until she yielded, every night anew, and imagined a little scene she'd constructed for herself with elaborate care, for all its inconsequentiality. In her fantasy, she was back at Griffin's Ford and had gotten separated from the Addisons somehow and lost in the woods. A noise behind her startled her, but when she turned, it was only Lieutenant Bellew, who'd gone looking for her. He told her that the Addisons were waiting back in town, only it was too far to travel tonight, she'd wandered so far, and they'd have to make camp where they were. So they lay on the ground, smelling the damp leaves beneath her face, until she felt a shadow cross her back. "The ground is too hard," Lieutenant Bellew murmured, and he took her gently in his arms and let her rest his head on his shoulder.

When Rachel imagined leaning herself against his body, she bunched up the pillow beneath her head, and peace descended on her, and she was able to sleep at last.

So she loved him. She could not justify or defend this, but it was true.

She did not have much hope, in her position, that he would think of her with equal favor; but it was a balm of sorts nevertheless to have a name for the pain in her soul. And *something* might happen - she did not know what, but she was restless for some unknown change that would give her a better chance, and this was a strange feeling for her, because change had so often been her enemy that she had come to abhor it. But not now; not any more.

General Lee stated that he would ride his hunting horse to the grounds, and Mr. Addison decided he would do the same, but they declared that Mrs. Addison, and Rachel by extension, should not have to face so much night air and really should take the carriage. It turned out to be less a kindness than Rachel had taken it for, because as it happened General Lee wanted his greyhounds to have the sport of the hunt as well, and he thought the carriage would provide them a suitable mode of transport. That made for a bit of a crowd, and by the time they reached the outskirts of the field, as far as the carriage could go, Mrs. Addison was in a boiling rage and Rachel's skirts were covered in slobber.

The poor beasts – Rachel couldn't help feeling sorry for them – were as enthusiastic to leave the carriage as they had been to ride in it. She leaned over and opened the door without waiting for Abraham's assistance, and the greyhounds scrambled out as wild as grapeshot, yapping at the sky and pawing at the earth. "*Thank* you, Rachel. Good lord," Mrs. Addison fumed.

But Rachel listened with only half an ear. Most of the rest of the company had assembled already, Lieutenant Bellew among them. The hesitant light of a fresh dawn made the sturdy chestnut sport horse he rode look black, but his face was clear and bright, and Rachel could read the happiness there through the hesitation with which he regarded the scarlet coats around him. If he loved the hunt, she would love it too, she was sure.

She did not recognize any of the English soldiers other than General Howe, and she was heartily glad of it. That did not mean that one of them might not have seen her before, but it reassured her a little. The one blighted spot on her anticipation of this day had been that fear; but perhaps it would come to nothing after all. Of course it would, she realized. There were thousands of soldiers, and only three she knew of had seen her face that night; well, and Corporal Graham, but he might never put together the girl of the lost pennies with some wild rock-throwing Medusa a few blocks farther down. And besides, he wasn't here. Not that a corporal would be – any more than a maid.

General Lee's greyhounds wasted no time in irritating the piebald fox dogs, and the commotion distracted the crowd for a moment. But when Abraham handed out Mrs. Addison, Rachel saw Lieutenant Bellew glancing back at the carriage instead of the dogs, and she thrilled at the warm light of recognition on his face. She hurried out after Mrs. Addison, barely giving Abraham a chance to help her down, and smiled happily at

Lieutenant Bellew as he trotted his horse to their side. He swung himself down in an efficient motion. "Madam," he said. "Miss Kolkhorst. I'm glad to see you." He took Mrs. Addison's hand and bowed over it.

"Yes, the ride was – for a while I wasn't sure we were going to be able to make it," Mrs. Addison said with an effort at good humor, smiling as best she could at the greyhounds, who had lost the skirmish but entered into the fray anew each time the master of hounds got his dogs under control.

"It was sporting of you to ride with the dogs. I don't know many ladies who'd have endured it," Bellew laughed. "You must love the hunt a great deal."

"Oh – certainly."

"This should be interesting, with the dogs."

"I think they'll chew each other to pieces, and we'll have to find the fox ourselves."

"No, I mean the scent-hounds and the sight-hounds," Lieutenant Bellew said, pointing to the fox-hounds and the greyhounds in turn. "They hunt differently. It'll be interesting to see which tactic wins the day."

"I am sure the visual sense is far superior," Mrs. Addison remarked with a slight stiffening.

"Well, they're General Lee's dogs. I'd like to think you're right," Lieutenant Bellew answered with a grin, and Rachel decided then and there that they were the most wonderful greyhounds in the world, no matter how much they drooled and scratched and lunged at her and broke things.

"Oh – you think the victory would have some military resonance?" Mrs. Addison said with a twinkle, leaning forward so that she could keep her voice low.

"I am not sure how much faith to place in the purely symbolic," Lieutenant Bellew replied. "But I know I would certainly take pleasure in it." Rachel was beside herself trying to think of something clever to say, but her mind was a blank, and so she merely stood behind her mistress with a friendly smile on her face, hoping it made her look amiable and intelligent. And pretty, maybe – the green of her hunting-dress was a decent color for her, and she knew she'd developed a slight flush in the frustration of the dogs in the carriage-ride, and a little flush could be very flattering. Oh, but it was hardly possible that she could look intelligent with such silly, light thoughts in her head, and her smile faltered.

Fortunately, Lieutenant Bellew did not seem to notice. He offered to help Mrs. Addison onto her mild-tempered yellow horse, Buttercup, since Mr. Addison was busy talking with the men. Rachel admired the gentlemanly grace with which he held a hand back to steady her if she needed it and the strength with which he held his other arm firm to boost her by the elbow.

"Come on, Miss Rachel, let's get you on up. You gonna be slow enough on that horse, you don't want a late start too. Mrs. Addison ain't gonna wait for you, and you don't want to get yourself lost out there."

Rachel startled to find Abraham at her elbow. "Oh – I thought Lieutenant Bellew –" But she saw he was sharing a quiet word with Mrs. Addison that made her laugh, and of course it was proper and good that something cheer her up these days, so Rachel accepted Abraham's help and lifted herself awkwardly onto Snowdrop, a little white horse with a pleasant disposition but an easily distracted mind. Rachel had asked Abraham for help learning to ride sidesaddle, and it was Snowdrop that she had practiced on. She still wasn't very good. "Thank you," she said, sitting awkwardly on her hip in the saddle.

"Not like that. Get yourself flat, like I showed you. You's gonna fall off if you do it like that." Rachel shifted her position obediently. "All right. Now here's your whip."

Rachel winced. She didn't like the whip.

"Don't you look at me that way, you ain't punishing the horse with it, you's just got to have something on that side that don't have a leg on it to tell her which way you wants her to go. I don't think girls should never be let on horseback astride," Abraham went on dolefully. "It give you nothing but bad habits that don't do you no good. I don't know what your father was thinking."

"I was very young," Rachel lied, "And it was a farm. There was no one to see my legs."

"Now don't you go talking fresh about legs. And get going. Everybody's ready." Rachel twisted in the saddle and saw that the dogs were indeed under control, or reasonably so, keeping near General Lee, and the company had formed into a loose group. General Lee, she saw to her surprise, was speaking with General Howe, gesturing broadly with his hands while General Howe pressed his mouth into a firm line and nodded agreement.

She wanted so much to respect General Lee, even if she could not, would not like or trust the man. Lieutenant Bellew obviously did not think the dogs were a mark against him, and she supposed even the unchaste behavior was an unsurprising vice in a soldier. That he had been disrespectful to her personally was hard to swallow; but it had been only a joke, after all, and maybe she'd just taken it in bad part. Not been sporting about it. The way she had been with the greyhounds in the carriage – or now decided that she had been. Oh – she noticed now that there was a long stain on the front of General Lee's coat, down the stomach. And hadn't she just cleaned it? No matter – she must remember to judge him as his talents and services merited, even if she found his habits – idiosyncratic. They neither limited nor defined the man.

Fortunately Snowdrop knew and liked Buttercup, so she ambled over to her stablemate without much prompting from Rachel. Lieutenant Bellew was in front, with the men, keeping a respectful distance from General Lee, just far enough so that he would not accidentally overhear the conversation nor intrude upon it. He did the right thing so naturally.

The rolling hills stretched out for what seemed an eternity. Rachel knew Philadelphia was behind her, but if she turned around, she could pretend it didn't exist, and there was nothing but this vast expanse of green. A silver flash of water sliced through the terrain. Darker forests shaded the ground farther to the west, and low mountains raised their heads to the sky. Why, she realized, that was where Valley Forge lay – under those mountains. She could see the Continental Army from here if her eyes were sharp enough. A faint twinge of guilt that men were suffering and starving both before her and behind her worried the back of her mind, but she pressed it firmly down. There was nothing she could do about that now. And the day was proving to be a truly fine one, with a clear, cloudless sky and the scent of cool, damp earth all around. And the hills were so pretty, and the crowd so brightly dressed and cheerful, and even Lieutenant Bellew seemed infected by the magic of the setting, so surely it was all right to be as happy as she was, even if all was not right in the world.

"Oh, this is thrilling," she murmured.

"If you like to see men act like dogs," Mrs. Addison replied. Rachel looked at her in surprise.

"Whatever do you mean, ma'am?"

"I mean they'll be pushing themselves in each other's way and squabbling over our poor quarry as if it meant something. Oh, look at Robert, what *is* he doing," she sighed. Rachel searched the crowd for Mr. Addison's brown jacket.

"He's just talking with that soldier," Rachel said doubtfully.

"No, he's making a wager. Look at what he's doing with his hands." She set her mouth firmly and shrugged.

"Well, I hope he wins," Rachel answered. She felt it was her duty to be loyal.

"I don't care a fig. I'm going to enjoy myself today, and he's welcome to gamble himself blind if he sees fit, as he usually does." Before Rachel could reply, the clarion call of the hunting-horn drowned out everything else, and the dogs were off. The greyhounds surprised her by suddenly focusing their energies and shooting forward in a straight line, heading down the first hill and towards the woods. The fox-hounds followed them, their earlier disagreements forgotten in the excitement of a common enemy.

Buttercup took off at a slow canter, and Snowdrop matched her pace. The others were pulling ahead fast – even another woman, a dashing middle-aged lady in a cloak who worked her whip enthusiastically on her ride's flank. Mrs. Loring was in the middle of the crowd. Her husband did not seem to be in attendance. Bellew was near the front of the riders, half-standing in his stirrups.

Rachel tensed her legs and almost lost her seat. She'd forgotten again, and had thought she was riding properly rather than – well, properly. She touched the whip gently against Snowdrop's right side, a stroke, not a blow, and wriggled herself back into position, but her foot almost came out of the stirrup from her maneuver, and she had to grab onto the saddle before she made it right again. But she did get herself right. She thought she might just barely be able to survive this ride with most of her dignity intact.

So they rode on through the bracing air, Rachel minding her balance on the saddle, while Snowdrop seemed to be minding nothing more than the breeze and the shadows and her own horsey thoughts. The mare's pace slowed further, and Rachel felt grateful for it. The ride was almost pleasant now, when she wasn't afraid of smashing her brains open on the ground, and she glanced up to see whether she could catch sight of anyone she knew.

She could not. The dogs and riders had rounded a hill, and just as Rachel looked up, she saw the very slowest riders disappear around the bend, leaving her entirely alone.

Snowdrop realized this at the same time.

The mare's muscles bunched, and she surged forward in a panicked gallop. Rachel gasped and seized the horse's mane for dear life. Her body rattled as if Snowdrop meant to shake her to bits.

"No," she said firmly, letting her spine and the reins go slack, and praying that she would not lose her tenuous seat, because her feet were so firmly in the stirrups that she would be dragged for certain. A terrible death, bones crushed, flesh torn, horses' hooves everywhere, thundering – Rachel kept her voice steady somehow. She had to be Snowdrop's brain. "Good girl – clever girl – no, you mustn't be afraid, it's all right –" But Snowdrop would not be calmed. She wasn't even running in the right direction. A line of trees was rushing up on them with terrible swiftness. Rachel turned Snowdrop's head to face nearest pine. If only Snowdrop would look up in time –

She did.

Snowdrop snorted in confusion and shook her head, and she stopped abruptly, a scant few feet from the tree. Rachel lurched forward and landed on Snowdrop's neck. She breathed hard for a moment, and then put herself firmly back in the saddle and straightened out her left stirrup again. "All right, girl. Good girl, clever girl. Now, there's nothing to worry about. We're fine, sweetheart, we're fine." Rachel didn't feel fine. She felt something between humiliation, euphoria at both the raw speed and her having survived it, and despair. She stroked Snowdrop's neck. "Now, we'll go just a little slower this time. We'll catch them," Rachel murmured. "Good girl. Sweet girl. It's all right. Go on. Go." She turned the horse back towards the hill, and Snowdrop eased into a canter again. Rachel followed the path the others had taken at this easy pace. She hoped Mrs. Addison wouldn't be too disappointed. Rachel had promised that she could ride – well, she could ride, just not well.

The horn sounded again. It wasn't too far, and it seemed to be coming from the left. Rachel clucked and tacked Snowdrop's course towards the woods there. The horn sounded again. The dogs were definitely onto something. But the horn was farther now, and Rachel realized that even taking a diagonal through the woods was unlikely to make up enough ground that she would catch the others before it was all over. She fervently wished not to make such a poor showing – she wasn't enough of a child to have youth as an excuse, only low breeding, and that was the sort of excuse it was better to be without.

Now, what to do? She could not really hope to catch the other riders. Should she stop Snowdrop and dismount, scuffing her clothes so that she could pretend to have taken a lucky fall – good horsewomen were thrown sometimes, and wouldn't she seem sympathetic at least, and perhaps it would even be Lieutenant Bellew who found her injured form lying on the ground and lifted her gently, as in her dream, and her head would rest on his shoulder, and all would be right in the world.

"Oh, you're an idiot," she muttered. She'd probably only end up getting herself killed or crippled somehow in a failed dismount that would make Snowdrop panic again, and that was sympathetic only in an off-handed pitying sort of way. She'd lose her position for certain if she were badly injured, that was all that would come of it.

But as horn called again in the distance, it occurred to Rachel that just perhaps she could do a little better than trail in the far wake of the stragglers. After all, she knew the kinds of places that foxes liked for their hiding-places and their burrows. She'd watched them often enough when she'd been a Cherokee. The hunting-party was just that – they were hunters, and they thought like hunters. Rachel would think like prey. And they would just see who found the fox first.

She took her bearings, her blood quickening.

She was certain from the direction of the horn that she was in the correct patch of woods, at least; so there was a reasonable chance that if she found a fox, it would be the correct one. The ground was springy beneath a carpet of fallen leaves. Rachel had seen the glittering line of the creek this way, and she edged Snowdrop in that general direction. If there was running water, that usually meant a red fox rather than a gray one. And that was good, because red foxes were easier to find: they couldn't climb trees, so they were always somewhere on the ground, and they liked to hide food. Rachel scanned the ground for the narrow, pointed droppings that foxes used to mark these sites, and she brought Snowdrop down to a walk. The horse seemed resigned to the slow pace now.

"Oh, Snowdrop - look!" Rachel exclaimed, to Snowdrop's indifference. Three finger-length droppings, one gray with desiccation, lay on the ground. The stream was very close now; Rachel could hear its gentle tinkle. She was probably near a burrow. Her heart surged with excitement. Perhaps it was the wrong fox, but she had almost forgotten the other hunt in the interest of her own. It had been a long time since she had followed an animal in the wild, and it was something she had always loved. Just to sit and watch for hours - but that had been a lifetime ago.

It was too early in the season for kits to have been born, so a fox that felt threatened would surely try to reach its burrow if it could. Rachel pushed Snowdrop to a trot. Red foxes liked to build their burrows on steep inclines for further protection, and stream banks, if they were deep enough, offered perfect terrain. Somewhere along that silver line of water was the fox's goal.

The horn sounded again, to her right, very close. Rachel startled, and Snowdrop pricked up her ears. Before she could decide if the sound had come behind her, a blur of red went whizzing by, its soft paws whispering over the ground. The fox! Snowdrop whickered and pranced backward. Hard after the fox came General Lee's greyhounds. They ran straight and true, and in dead silence.

The right fox, even!

Rachel nudged Snowdrop to go after the dogs. "Come on, girl, they aren't interested in you," she whispered. Her heart pounded. She would be there for the catch itself - for the full glory of it!

A shadow crossed her shoulder, and Rachel turned around barely in time to see Lieutenant Bellew's brown horse take a tremendous leap over a patch of scrub that Snowdrop had picked her way around. Bellew stood high in the saddle, a fierce grin of concentration on his face. Muscles strained at the thighs of his breeches and across the shoulder of his jacket, and mud and bits of leaves stuck to his clothes showed how hard he'd been riding. His face turned blank a moment on seeing someone ahead of him, but then his horse landed and he sprinted ahead of Rachel.

"Go, Snowdrop!" Rachel cried, putting the whip to Snowdrop's side, and again, because Snowdrop didn't believe that Rachel really meant for her to gallop now. But the little white horse took off gamely at last, and Rachel caught up to Bellew quickly. He had stopped at a rocky place before the water; it was too steep even for the vicious, clever fox to climb down here, and the greyhounds had him cornered in the low brush. The fox made darting efforts to take off in one direction or another, but the greyhounds were faster, and they moved with single-minded purpose to close off his ground. Bellew watched with intense interest.

"The sight-hounds won!" Rachel said, clasping her hands in delight.

Bellew blinked, his concentration broken, and glanced over at her. "I didn't see you pass me before," he said, puzzled.

The greyhounds formed a semi-circle, yapping and driving the fox back in terror until at last it had no room to maneuver. It was a lovely creature covered in thick red fur, with large black-tipped ears and a white belly. Such a beautiful thing to have a devil's character. Rachel thought it must be a male, although the females weren't much smaller so it was hard to tell. The fox hunkered down and snarled.

"We've got him – why don't you finish him?" Rachel cried.

Bellew twisted around in his saddle and looked anxiously into the woods. "I can't carry a pistol. But the others –"

Before he could finish, the greyhounds pounced upon the fox, tearing into him savagely. Rachel saw his teeth flash, and his claws came up for a few strikes, but the greyhounds were larger, and there were four of them. Blood spattered the ground. She gasped. It may have been justice – foxes killed with worse savagery themselves. But she did not like to see it.

"Hey there!" Bellew shouted at the dogs. "Hey! No!"

The dogs, crazed by blood, paid as little attention to Bellew as they did to anyone else, and they ripped at the fox's limp form. Bellew jumped down from his horse. "Hey! Get back, you!" Snowdrop shifted nervously.

"Lieutenant Bellew, don't get near them!" Rachel cried.

Then the fox-hounds came racing in, maddened by the scent. They barreled past Bellew's legs so hard he had to hold onto his horse to keep his feet, and they forced themselves into the fray. Bellew, defeated, simply stood by his horse, which stood its ground phlegmatically. "The creature's dead now anyway," he said.

But Rachel couldn't look away, even though there was nothing to see now but the squirming backs of dogs. She didn't even hear General Lee approach until he spoke at her side. "Got it, eh?" His voice held a note of wounded disappointment that he did not bother to conceal. He could ignore Rachel being ahead of him, she supposed; but Lieutenant Bellew was a man. It occurred to her that might have been an error for Bellew to outrace the General, who had probably been riding as best he could, no matter how exciting the chase.

Lieutenant Bellew did not seem to realize this yet, quite. "Yes, sir," he replied, standing straighter. "Your dogs found him first. I had to let them dispose of the creature as they liked."

"My boys probably killed it faster than a bullet anyway," General Lee replied, dismounting. "Damn fine beasts. There's nothing they can't do better than a man but make love to a woman, and probably that as well." He laughed.

Bellew blinked, and his eyes flicked over to Rachel, a slight frown on his face. It vanished quickly. He cleared his throat and looked away.

Rachel wished she could explain that General Lee just talked that way, and it was best ignored. The profanity she'd long since accustomed herself to at the Brass Bull; and as for the carnal suggestion, it was so disgusting that it had no power to make her blush. She knew Bellew was embarrassed on her account, and she wished he wouldn't be. She was sporting about it, really she was.

But part of her was hurt just the same. Hadn't Lieutenant Bellew stood up for her when she'd suffered a far lesser insult in the tavern, and he hadn't even known her then? Was she so diminished in his eyes somehow? What had she done wrong?

No, it wasn't that. It was only that General Lee was so talented, and so important, that Bellew understood that something greater was at stake. And Bellew trusted Rachel to understand all this as well. And she did.

General Lee eyed Bellew. "Your commission wasn't filled yet, was that the story?"

"That is correct, sir," Bellew replied.

"Then you haven't seen any action yet in the war."

"No, sir," Bellew answered. "To my regret, I have not. And all the men Captain - Captain O'Malley and Lieutenant Masterson and I recruited have been captured."

"They fire at the men who arrested them, at least?"

Bellew hesitated. "No, sir. All our guns had already been discharged. We were in the middle of a demonstration."

General Lee grunted. He strode forward into the mass of dogs, shoving one of his own aside roughly, and reached down into the mess. When he came up again, his hand dripped with gore. Rachel gasped, thinking he had been hurt, but it was only the fox's blood. General Lee was unharmed. He held his bloody hand upturned slightly and walked back to Bellew, who watched him cautiously.

General Lee wiped the blood in two streaks across Bellew's cheeks, like war paint. "There you go, Lieutenant Bellew. You've been blooded at last," he said.

Chapter 21

The party reconvened at General Howe's High Street mansion for light refreshments. To Rachel's astonishment, General Lee insisted blandly that his greyhounds attend, and so she and Mrs. Addison had to endure another ride with the creatures, whose breath now stank of gore. Rachel couldn't help wondering if this was intended as punishment for her arriving at the kill before him. But no doubt she was overestimating her importance in his eyes; he was just that fond of his dogs. She tried to make friends with the animals as they rode, petting them cautiously on their heads and complimenting them, until Mrs. Addison begged her sharply please to be silent unless Rachel meant to tell her what she was bursting to know, how Rachel had managed to sneak around the others and see the finale.

"I didn't see you ride past me, Rachel, and I'm sure you didn't. You're being awfully coy."

"Well, I hardly know myself," Rachel replied evasively. "There was a great deal happening all at once, it seemed."

"Honestly, Rachel, I know you didn't pass me, don't be evasive – didn't you promise to tell me everything? How on earth did you pull it off?" Mrs. Addison demanded, giving the dog that Rachel was petting a shove with her foot.

It was true; Rachel had promised not to go off and do things on her own, and she'd promised to tell Mrs. Addison her secrets. "Yes – I'm sorry, ma'am. No, I didn't pass you. I fell behind almost at once. I didn't want to admit that I rode as badly as I did, you understand, I only wished so much that I could have been better, and it was as keen a disappointment to me as it was to – well, no one particularly cared, I'm sure, but it was an embarrassment nevertheless. At any rate, I fell behind so quickly, everyone else being such better riders than I, that I decided I'd better look for the fox rather than try to catch the hunting-party. And it happened to be the correct fox, so I was in luck. That's all."

"You found the fox rather than the party?" Mrs. Addison laughed. "Rachel, dear – I hardly know what to say. The point is supposed to be the ride, really, but – for heaven's sake, how on earth did you find the fox?

That's supposed to be what the dogs are for – my goodness, if we could find the fox ourselves, we could do without the dogs entirely." She glanced at the greyhounds.

Rachel explained a little what she knew of the red fox's taste in habitat and behavior, then, until Mrs. Addison grew bored. "Oh, well, along those lines," she said with a wave of her hand. "To tell you the truth, I don't much like to be present for the kill. It isn't particularly appropriate. But I'm glad that General Lee had the honor of it. It may make him a little less intolerable."

Rachel pressed her lips together. She had not much liked that final scene, neither the kill itself nor General Lee's behavior, and she preferred to put it out of her mind. But she had promised to tell Mrs. Addison everything; and it could do no harm, she supposed, and Mrs. Addison did enjoy knowing secrets.

"It wasn't General Lee who was first, you know," she said in a confidential voice. "Although his dogs did make the kill."

"What!" Mrs. Addison exclaimed, looking Rachel full in the face. "But everyone said –"

"I know, and I couldn't contradict them, of course – but Lieutenant Bellew was first. I am sure he is being very gracious about it," Rachel replied. Bellew had wiped the blood from his face before the others arrived, but he had stood back quietly when General Lee took credit for the win. "General Lee being so sensitive on these matters. Oh, he rode so well, ma'am, I wish you'd seen him – I've never seen better! And – and General Lee wasn't second, either. That was me," she added. Well, it was true, after all.

"Oh!" Mrs. Addison exclaimed, clasping her hands together in delight. "Oh, not first, but third, yet! He's going to be just awful! But I can't tell you how happy I am, Rachel – oh, he was outridden by a mere girl! By my maid! Well, it couldn't have happened to a better man!" She patted one of the dogs in her glee.

Rachel couldn't help remembering that General Howe had been gracious enough when he and the two soldiers with him had found her ahead of him at the kill, and he had even nodded his head in acknowledgment after subduing the flicker of surprise on his face. But she thought she wouldn't mention that now. Mrs. Addison was already far too certain that Rachel held tender feelings for General Howe.

She supposed General Howe's failings were far worse than General Lee's. General Howe was permitting an abomination under his command, and nothing so black could be put to General Lee's shame. But General Howe's sin was born, although in perverted and misshapen form, of true feeling for a woman, while General Lee's petty vices sprang from nothing but self-love.

"If a man is possessed of genius, I suppose it is his first duty not to let it be used as a door-stop," Rachel said, half to herself.

"Oh la, but there's little generalship in a fox-hunt, Rachel – General Lee would like to assign every merit of his talents to himself personally, I am sure, but sometimes the two are distinct."

"I think perhaps he only wants everyone to take him at his worst before he shows his best," Rachel replied thoughtfully.

"I think you have a weakness for generals."

Everyone was tatty and stained from the ride, so Rachel did not feel badly about the dog-marks over Mrs. Addison's dress and her own when they joined the boisterous company in General Howe's drawing-room. There were more guests in the dining room and the parlor. The good furniture had been discreetly removed so that it would not suffer too much from the general dirt and to make more space. Mrs. Addison rushed to Mrs. Loring's side to congratulate her on such a thrilling success to start off the festivities, leaving Rachel to trail quietly in her wake. Mr. Addison was nowhere to be seen.

Lieutenant Bellew hung near General Lee's elbow as General Lee described his triumph in detail, omitting only the few salient facts. Rachel did not think she would be welcome in that crowd, which was all men except for the dashing middle-aged lady. Rachel sipped her cider with only half an ear to Mrs. Addison's chatter and Mrs. Loring's gratified responses, and tried to read Lieutenant Bellew's expression. She saw nothing but polite attention in his manner, and General Lee nodded at him to allow him the privilege of agreeing with Lee's statements. Bellew even laughed once, and General Lee joined him. Perhaps the small indiscretion Bellew had shared with General Lee might result in some preferment for Bellew, rather than ostracization, if he maintained his tact, and she felt a surge of complicitous pleasure that she was in on this confidence too.

She could not catch Bellew's eye, but one of the soldiers standing by General Howe kept looking at her curiously – a regular. Rachel looked away quickly whenever he did. There was nothing untoward in his stare, only a puzzled regard, and she did not recognize him except as one of the men who had arrived shortly after General Howe. She thought she would have remembered his face if she had seen it before, even in her blindness and terror of that one dangerous night. He was a handsome man, with features heavier than Lieutenant Bellew's but softened by a bright, quick eye and refined by a narrow, almost pointed nose. Rachel glanced over her shoulder again. The soldier was already looking at her, and he smiled. Rachel spun around in confusion.

"What is it? Is it one of the dogs?" Mrs. Addison said, flinching and looking around her skirts.

"No, I – well, I was –" Rachel could not explain herself, and a blush tingled her ears. "Do you know who that gentleman is standing by General Howe? I believe – I never get the uniforms right, but I think he's a captain?"

Mrs. Addison, Mrs. Loring, and the two Misses Shippen who were in their little group turned as one to look. "Well, the only Captain there is Captain André. He serves General Grey, that's the General over there by the painting. Is that who you mean?" one of the Misses Shippen said, a dainty, rosy-cheeked brunette with lazy eyes that tilted upward at a fetching angle. She could not have been more than sixteen, but she carried herself with a confidence that Rachel envied.

"You mean the one in red? I don't know, of course," Rachel replied with a little more asperity than she'd intended.

"Well, it ought to be who you mean. Everyone adores Captain André," Miss Shippen pronounced. She dimpled and waved one slender finger at the object of her interest. The soldier smiled and wiggled a single finger back. "So now you know, was that the right one or not?"

"Yes, thank you," Rachel said in a gentler tone that she hoped made up for her previous sharpness.

After a casual brunch where the ferocious appetites brought on by exercise warred against the desire to look well in one's nice clothes later, a few of the ladies who had brought their ball-gowns and masks retired upstairs for a nap. Since the Addisons lived so close by, they returned home. Mr. Addison sat with them in the carriage this time, since General Lee decided to let his dogs frolic around his poor horse's legs on the brief ride. Abraham had brought the Addisons' and Rachel's riding horses back to their stable earlier.

Mrs. Addison took immediately to bed and ordered Rachel to do the same, but Rachel found she couldn't sleep. And the more she wished she could rest so that she would be sprightly far into the night, the more agitated she became and the more relentlessly conscious. At last she gave it up as a bad job and crept from her room quietly. She'd been given a reprieve from chores for the day, but if she did just a few of them, it would take her mind off things and make tomorrow less burdensome. She tiptoed down the stairs and crept into the back room where she kept her rags and holy stones and oil and other requirements. The room was dark and quiet, with only a narrow window letting in the sun, and when Rachel reached up to take a rag from its peg on the wall, a shaft of light as thin as a knife-blade cut across the backs of her hands.

"Oh!" Rachel exclaimed in horror. She had not thought of her hands – they were rough and red, and her short nails were uneven. And her hands were practically all of her that anyone would be able to see! She had imagined, dazzled by Mrs. Rimini's compliments, that she would make some small impression at the ball – but Lieutenant Bellew would think it was some sort of ogre behind the pretty mask.

She forgot her plan to clean and ran out back to find Abraham. He knew how to fix things – maybe there was something he could do about this. She did not dare wake Mrs. Addison, and how would Mrs. Addison know anything about hands ruined by work anyway?

She found him leaning on against the ice-house in back in the company of Mrs. Rimini, who was smoking a pipe. Thick smoke curled from the bowl, which glowed when Mrs. Rimini took a puff. Rachel had never seen a white woman do that before, and she blinked in surprise. Mrs. Rimini understood right away and offered the pipe. "You can try if you like, dear," she said.

"No, I – no, thank you." Rachel had learned a superstitious reverence for tobacco. The last thing she wanted now was spirit visions.

"Has something happened? You look in quite a lather. How did the hunt go today?"

"She managed to keep on her horse," Abraham put in.

"I did, thank you Abraham, without you I never – but look at my hands!" Rachel wailed, holding them out.

Abraham didn't know a thing about smoothing rough hands, but it turned out that Mrs. Rimini possessed a wealth of information on the topic. Given the time constraints, she recommended that they return to the kitchen and soak Rachel's skin in heavy cream. "Now, you'll be regretting this when you start back at work tomorrow," Mrs. Rimini said in a warning tone.

"That's all right – oh, thank you so much. And it feels wonderful."

"It does, and the Queen of France herself don't have anything better. Now, if you find it don't do as well as you'd like, just keep your hand curled around your fan. Your fingers show it the worst. The backs of your hands might just have gotten chapped from the ride, and nobody'll know any different." Mrs. Rimini laughed. "I always wondered. When you go on these visits with Mrs. Addison, do you tell people you're her maid or not?"

"Mrs. Addison addresses me as her companion. But, Mrs. Rimini, I don't have a fan."

"Not even one?"

"No, I always thought I'd drop one, and it's not strictly necessary for casual affairs, and – well, we just didn't think of it."

"Well, Mrs. A has plenty. I'm sure she'll have one that'll suit. And if she's lending you the dress, and that little quartz necklace, she won't begrudge you the fan."

Mrs. Addison was as surprised as anyone to discover that they'd overlooked the detail of the fan, but none of her prettier ones went well with the champagne color of the dress, so Rachel ended up taking the everyday cream-colored one. Her toilette was now complete. The pomade felt sticky in her hair, but that was what kept it so high, and besides, the tackiness helped keep the powder in place. Rachel felt as chalky as a porcelain doll, all except for her hands, which had responded wonderfully to Mrs. Rimini's cream-bath. The nails were still short, but her skin felt smooth and tender, and its color was good.

But as much as Rachel marveled at her own changed appearance, she found Mrs. Addison's full glory simply breathtaking. Mrs. Addison's gown was a striking shade of turquoise accented with ecru lace made bright by little seed pearls worked into the pattern, and she wore pearls on her neck and dangling from her ears. Her hair was padded and piled in so many curls it must have added two feet to her height, and silver combs with more seed-pearls added sparkle. Mrs. Addison had debated at length the effect of a curling white feather with downy fronds and eventually decided that yes, it fit and didn't interfere with the aesthetics of the mask too badly. Rachel helped Mrs. Addison fasten her mask, and then she put on her own. It cut down on her peripheral vision, which had a disorienting effect. She had never noticed how much she liked to look out of the corners of her eyes, but tonight that would be impossible.

"I never imagined anything like this," Rachel breathed, sneaking a glance at herself in the mirror. "I promise I'll watch everything and tell you everything I see. I'm sure it will give me stories to tell you for a month."

"Oh, tut. Well, I don't mind you doing that, but mostly this is your reward for being so sweet. I do hope you enjoy yourself. Everyone deserves a little fun."

Rachel looked down quickly. She shouldn't cry, or her face-powder would run. But she was so excited. Mrs. Addison didn't know quite how much the ball meant to her, with the chance to see Lieutenant Bellew again, and as an equal, but it was still so terribly kind.

"I don't know why you've been so generous to me, ma'am," she whispered. "Truly, I don't."

"Well, there was no harm in it, was there?" Mrs. Addison laughed, taking Rachel's hands. "I like things to be interesting, and I thought you would be, and you have, so that's all there is to it. Here, I'm ready. Let's go down."

When they reached the first floor, the men were waiting restively in the entrance area. Rachel would not have recognized Mr. Addison in his dark red silk suit with the gold-and-topaz buckles at his knees and on his shoes, let alone with the black mask covering half his face. "Sir!" she exclaimed in astonishment. "You look perfectly elegant!" Mr. Addison nodded in acknowledgement after a surprised pause. "And that color suits you so well, General Lee – it is entirely dashing," she added quickly, cursing herself for having forgotten to compliment General Lee first. General Lee wore a black suit beneath his black mask, which might have seemed plain except for the gorgeousness of the silk, and the almost daring touches of onyx buckles and black lace at the cuffs. The downturned cast of his mouth showed more prominently when it was all that could be seen of his face.

"And you play the part of a southern lady with passable competence, my dear," General Lee replied.

Most of the guests had already arrived by the time their carriage – without dogs, for once – reached the High Street mansion. The house was alight with torches outside, and the brilliant glitter of chandeliers shone merrily through the windows. Six smart guards stood in attendance in their dress uniforms but no masks.

The women had entered the carriage from the left so that Mrs. Addison would be the first to alight. Rachel reminded herself sternly to wait for Abraham's assistance this time. His hand moved gently under her elbow, and she put her foot carefully onto the small step beneath. The high-heeled slippers that looked so precious and made her feet look almost dainty felt awkward, and her legs were strangely weak. "Do I look all right, Abraham?" she whispered.

"Pretty as a picture," Abraham replied, and although she knew he wouldn't have hurt her feelings by saying anything else, Rachel suddenly felt all the confidence in the world.

She hardly recognized General Howe's house. The servants must have been working like cab-horses all afternoon. The floors gleamed with a mellow shine, and holly garlands speckled with bright red berries festooned the walls and windows. There must have been a hundred people inside, all in fine dress and masked, except for the servants, all soldiers, the scarlet of whose coats had never looked so festive but seemed almost dull in comparison. Rachel's elaborate gown and necklace felt almost homely. She was a little disappointed, but mostly glad. She felt she was putting on airs enough as it was. It was more than ample to be accepted in this splendid crowd. Outshining it was for Mrs. Addison, and she did it beautifully. Heads turned to look at her, and men murmured quick questions to each other. Probably they were wondering if Mrs.

Addison was equally beautiful beneath her mask, and Rachel smiled to know that her mistress was.

"Oh, there you are!" Mrs. Addison cried, apparently recognizing a woman despite her mask, though Rachel did not. Mrs. Addison stopped herself before rushing over and whispered hurriedly in Rachel's ear, "No one knows who you are tonight, dear. Go and have a good time." And then she went over to her friend, gushing happily and dragging Mr. Addison along by taking his arm and obliging him to look as though he was leading her.

Rachel was left standing with General Lee. She glanced at him with a hesitant smile. "Sir, do you –" but before she could finish her empty pleasantry, the General walked off through the crowd, tugging at his jacket uncomfortably.

Rachel realized now that she'd formed no very clear idea of what she would do at a ball, other than misty imaginings of cloistered whispers with Lieutenant Bellew while music played in the background. But now there was only a crowd of masks, and mixed scents of lavender and musk and rose-petals and powder and apple-pomade, and the low roar of men's voices interspersed with the high tinkle of women's laughter. Rachel found herself at an utter loss. Her confidence vanished. Should she just speak to someone at random? She supposed that was what Mrs. Addison would do, only Mrs. Addison would make it seem charming and natural. Rachel did not have that art.

But standing there like a goose was only going to make her look as awkward as she felt. Rachel cast about the room until she saw a sideboard with a bowl of punch, and she made her way in its direction, smiling and murmuring a hello to anyone who looked at her in the hopes that it might spark a conversation. It did not, although the ladies smiled and the men bowed graciously.

"Punch, Miss?" a kilted soldier at the sideboard asked her in a heavy burr. Rachel nodded and smiled, and he dipped the silver ladle into the red liquid and handed her a crystal cup. When she took it, she saw that her hands were shaking. The soldier did not seem to notice. She rested one hand against the sideboard to steady herself.

"They've done up the house so beautifully," Rachel said to him. "They must have been working all afternoon."

"Aye, well, there's something to be said for the Army," the soldier replied with a grin. "We build things right quick." He was a Scot, clearly, and Rachel meant to ask him about it, but two men hurried over and asked for four cups, and the soldier was busy. Rachel drifted to the side so as not to be in the way.

She would drink her punch slowly, and then she would know what to do. She brought the cup to her mouth and took the tiniest sip. The punch was sweet, with a faint bite of wine beneath the fruit. Well, maybe the wine would make her bold. She took a slightly larger sip.

"And the mistress of the hunt tries her hand at a dance," a pleasant voice said in her ear. Rachel startled in surprise and held her cup tight to keep from spilling it. She turned quickly. A heavily built man, still in his late youth, stood beside her, a faint smile curling his lips. His mask was black. He bowed slightly when she faced him. "My apologies, Miss. I had no idea anything could startle a creature who rides so well."

"Oh, thank you, but I don't -" Rachel began before realizing that someone must have recognized her through her mask, and anyone who thought she rode well must have seen her only at the hunt's conclusion. "Captain André?" she asked, bringing her hand quickly to her mouth. "Oh, I'm sorry, we're all supposed to be incognito."

Captain André's smile grew. "Miss Kolkhorst," he replied. "My apologies. I will not mention your name again."

Rachel's raised hand touched her mask.

"Oh, don't worry about that, your mask is admirable, only I have a habit of recognizing people behind them," Captain André replied. "I see you found out my name. You must have heard that I was asking for yours."

"Oh, I - no, actually I hadn't," Rachel admitted. "And I'm terrible at recognizing people, I can't make out anyone here, although no one else seems to have much trouble, I simply - well, logically there weren't that many conclusions I could draw from your statement. Not too many people noticed me at the hunt -"

"Which you took pains about, burying yourself in the trees in that way when the rest of us finally caught up to you. It was a pretty neat trick, managing to camouflage yourself on that white horse. It practically glowed," Captain André laughed.

Rachel offered a weak smile in response. It embarrassed her to have been caught in her evasive half-attempt to make herself inconspicuous.

"And now, here you are, glowing and white again, and still trying to hide," Captain André said. "Forgive my impertinence, miss, of course we do not know each other, but I find your interesting confusion too endearing to let pass."

"I am glad it serves some purpose, then," Rachel murmured. Her embarrassment faded, although it did not quite disappear. Captain André did not seem to be mocking her, and it was something of a relief not to have to pretend to be more confident than she felt.

"And aren't you even going to ask why I wanted to know your name?" he went on in a teasing voice.

"I hadn't considered it," she replied with a levelness she did not feel, her earlier fears about Cunningham springing to life again. "I suppose I simply regarded it as your business."

"Well, you already told me you couldn't see behind masks. Here's a trick you can use until you learn better. Women often have a favorite piece of jewelry, and men you can occasionally know by their facial hair. Or their buckles, perhaps. The thing is, you need to have made these observations in the past to be able to profit from them now – but I suspect you are an observant person."

Her chest unclenched. No, he wasn't going to accuse her of her crime. And now Rachel understood how Mrs. Addison had known her friend so quickly. She took a deeper drink from her cup, and felt the pleasant warmth release the tension in her muscles. She was beginning to enjoy herself. "And why would that be?" The experience of being an object of interest was new to her, and she found it not unpleasant, if strange.

"That there is something a little feral about you, Miss Kolkhorst, if you'll forgive the word, and wild creatures are all observation but very little judgment. It was a pretty neat trick, at the hunt, taking the lead that way. General Lee was in fine form, and he'd have to be, to outrace General Howe. It never would have occurred to me a woman could match him, to tell you the truth. And that other fellow, the young one, rides like one of those wild southerners who were born in a saddle. And yet you perform this amazing feat, and the first thing you do – you try to pretend you didn't."

"Well, I don't think it's appropriate for a, a woman to be at the kill," Rachel said.

"I disagree, but leave that aside, it was a splendid accomplishment just the same. Here, let's drink to it," Captain André said, lifting his punch and swallowing it in one go. Rachel hesitated and then finished her own cup. She looked around for a place to put the empty crystal.

A new voice spoke.

"If I may be of service." Rachel's heart stopped for a brief, eternal moment. And when it started again, life spread through her body in a tingling rush. Lieutenant Bellew – she would know him anywhere by the set of his shoulders, even in his dark suit and mask – stood before her, an anxious smile curling his lips. He held out both hands to her. One was empty, to take her cup. The other held the fan she suddenly realized she had left at the sideboard when she'd leaned against it.

Chapter 22

Rachel handed him her cup. The side of her hand grazed his palm. His hand was soft too, no doubt from the forced inactivity of the past weeks. She wrapped her fingers gently around her fan, still warm from his skin. "I am much obliged, thank you, Lieutenant Bellew." She kept the tremor from her voice, but she could not raise it above a whisper.

Lieutenant Bellew wore a different suit, dark blue and of a slightly older style but well-made. She wondered how he could have afforded it on the small sum she had lent him. His mouth quirked when she said his name, but he did not seem displeased.

"Oh, miss, no names, not after you've gone to the trouble reminding me that we're supposed to be all very mysterious tonight. I judge by your accent that you were born on these shores," Captain André said cheerfully, adapting to the increase in number with no apparent ill-feeling. He'd already spotted Lieutenant Bellew as a southerner before, so Rachel supposed he was merely trying to be polite. A fleeting thought struck her, that it was curious he had not taken Rachel for a southerner herself; but she supposed her manner and accent had changed in the past few months. Mrs. Addison was a northerner, and Mr. Addison of course English, and those had been the voices in her ears and her thoughts.

Lieutenant Bellew offered a short bow. "I was raised in South Carolina, sir, and do not remember any other home, but I was born in Ireland."

"Well, it's much the same. You may settle a slight matter here. What is your feeling, as a local, of a woman who rides as well as man?"

Lieutenant Bellew smiled again. He glanced at Rachel. "My feeling is that it is twice as difficult to ride side-saddle, and that as a consequence her accomplishment is at least twice as great." Rachel was glad of the mask now, covering her blush of delight. She had not been able to read his expression at the kill as to what he had thought of her being there, and then General Lee's actions had overshadowed everything. But now she knew – he admired it! She would practice her riding, she swore, and she would become at least as good as he thought she was.

"So there you have it, and we'll have no more of these feigned deficiencies, I hope, miss champagne-and-cream. You see that people are quite pleased to take you as you are," Captain André said, turning back to Rachel.

"Your generosity offers me no assurance as to the broader population's view of the matter."

"And why not, pray?" Captain André asked.

"Because both of you are kind enough to take a personal interest in me, and an interested position is by definition not an impartial one." She found it easy to speak now.

"How could we take a personal interest? We don't even know who you are," Captain André said, evidently enjoying himself.

"But surely the opinion of friends must carry more weight," Lieutenant Bellew offered, fiddling with her cup absently. He was probably, Rachel realized, at odd ends in this company as much as she was.

"Oh, it does, very much so – only it means all the more that I must not be an embarrassment to them," Rachel said.

"I understand. It is unfortunate that feminine duty too often obliges the fair sex to adopt a sort of Laodicean mediocrity," Captain André said, his voice gentle.

"It is perhaps more unfortunate what masculine duty impels," Rachel answered.

"No doubt. I imagine less than one percent of the male population is suited to pursue glory, and less than that to earn it, but all of us feel required," Captain André said with a shrug.

Lieutenant Bellew smiled with a surprising bitterness, though he recovered his spirits quickly. "But it is curious that the punishment for failure in the pursuit of moderation should be so dramatic and cruel, while a man who does not achieve the fame he seeks is castigated with nothing worse than being ignored," he said.

"So women live privately and suffer publicly, and for men the opposite applies," Rachel said, pleased with herself. It was a tolerable bon mot, and it was nice to have constructed it from Lieutenant Bellew's observation.

"Quite so," Lieutenant Bellew answered, smiling in surprise.

"Perhaps we should try to learn from one another, then," Captain André said. "There is, after all, one realm where women reign supreme, and where they are permitted and in fact expected to shine in full splendor. That being, of course, the finer emotions." He bowed with a teasing glint in his eye. "If you will permit me:

"A fair Diana hunts my heart with skill

"I have no say, she only knows her will."

"Oh! How pretty!" Rachel exclaimed. Had he really just composed a couplet for her? Delight was quickly swamped by anxiety. What would Lieutenant Bellew think?

Captain André bowed again at the compliment. "And there you have it. What do you say, sir? Shall we allow our friend the only glory she is in decency allowed?"

Bellew pressed a knuckle against his mouth. Warring instincts seemed to battle inside him, and he did not respond immediately. Rachel was about to reply something to cover the silence before it grew uncomfortable when Bellew nodded to himself and took a half-step forward. He said:

"The sky may have captured the sun's golden flame

"I see it and feel its warm breath just the same."

Why, he'd done it – oh, and did he really think of her that way, as a flame? Or did he also notice the heat of her skin when they drew near, just as Rachel had felt on far too few occasions?

"I knew southern gallantry would not fail me," Captain André said in satisfaction. "Well said, sir. But are you captured, miss? I am not entirely sure of the gentleman's meaning there."

"But it's exactly what we were talking about, and I think it's wonderful," Rachel said, earning a pleased bow from Lieutenant Bellew.

"Ah, so it's what we were talking about before I brought up love, you mean," Captain André replied.

"Well – well, wait a moment," Rachel said. She could do this, she knew she could. It was only words, and as long as Lieutenant Bellew was nearby, and the wine in her veins, her tongue was free. The simplest way would be thus: iamb, bacchius, bacchius, iamb, do it twice and make it rhyme. That was all. "Here:

"To love is to dream and pray not to wake

"And idle the hours for idleness' sake."

Rachel straightened slightly. She thought that was rather nice. And perhaps it communicated to Lieutenant Bellew that she did not take Major André's flirtation seriously.

Major André roared with laughter. "Bravo!" he cried. "Well, that's done it - we've both been outmaneuvered, sir, if I read your meaning right and our fair object read it wrong." The soft strains of instruments tuning their strings wafted from the room next door. "Ah - well. If you will excuse me," Major André continued. "There is nothing that could take me from this delightful conversation but a promise, and one has been extracted from me for the first dance. I leave you the field, sir."

"I haven't won it," Lieutenant Bellew replied.

"You stood your ground, and you have it just the same," Captain André answered cheerfully, and he made his way into the crowd again.

Rachel was grateful to Captain André for having taken notice of her, but she was doubly grateful to him for leaving. But she knew she had to think of something to say to Lieutenant Bellew quickly, or else he might leave her too. She would have liked very much to renew the previous topic, only she seemed to have killed it off with her couplet.

Lieutenant Bellew relieved her of her difficulty. "I must apologize to you for not asking you to dance. Please feel free, and take no mind of me," he said. "It is not lack of will; I simply do not know how to do a minuet properly, I am afraid."

Neither did Rachel, although it gratified her to think that Bellew assumed she did.

"They don't dance the minuet in Charlestown?" she said.

"I am sure they do, but they did it without me. My mother and I lived in the country."

"Your mother?" There seemed a curious omission in that. "But your father - where was he?"

Bellew hesitated. "He traveled a great deal, I understand." He grimaced as if wrestling with himself, and then shrugged. "I never knew him. My mother told me that their connection was not, not a happy one, and they separated shortly after my birth."

Rachel felt chagrined. "I apologize, I didn't mean to bring up any unpleasantness -"

"It's quite all right. I prefer not to have secrets hanging over my head."

"But he was high-born, wasn't he? I'm sorry, I was just given to understand – I heard –"

"No, you're quite correct. He is John, the fourth Baron Bellew of Duleek. I suppose you knew the name and associated it with my own?" Bellew asked curiously. "It is not a common one, and Duleek is not large."

"I – no, it was just that Captain O'Malley said your family was in the *ton*."

"They are, my relatives are, that is, but I must admit to you frankly that I know little of that world. Have you been to see Captain O'Malley? He did not mention it, nor did Mrs. Merriwether," Lieutenant Bellew said with a confused frown. "Your kindnesses only redouble."

He had forgotten the conversation at the Brass Bull. Well, Rachel didn't much want to remind him of her presence there – oh, how much less so to the son of a baron – so she let it pass. "I cannot imagine a baron particularly being so careless of – of, well, his male issue, even if his changed feelings towards your mother prevented him from regarding you with paternal care. Oh, perhaps he didn't even know she'd gone to America – was your mother hiding from him?" Rachel asked, suddenly horrified at the thought that the Baron Bellew might have been a frightening man, or a cruel one. Well, he must have been cruel, at least a little, to throw aside a wife and child that way.

"I – do not know," Lieutenant Bellew answered slowly. "My mother gave me to understand that I had an older brother who rendered me supernumerary, as long as my brother lived. I have no knowledge of him, and if she had any communication with her home country or former friends, I do not know of it, nor do I know whether that was by her choice or plan. But I do not mean to bore you with my history – I meant only to explain why I cannot ask for the favor of your company on the minuet. If you wish to find a partner –"

The instruments in the other room finished their prefatory coughs and launched into a full-throated melody, stately and pure. Rachel smiled and shrugged. "Well, it's begun, and we have each other's company after all," she said. If he could not dance, that would keep him at her side – all the better. She understood why he felt awkward about being a baron's son; he not been raised in that estate, nor would not come into it, and second sons generally received no favor from their birth other than expensive habits they would have to learn to provide for on their own which, as she understood, generally they did not. But Rachel wanted him to tell her more about his life and origins, even if he seemed wary of the topic. Surely he must realize she wouldn't think less of him for not having been raised in a castle - he knew very well she hadn't been herself. The few morsels of information Rachel had gleaned about him until now had grown worn and thin from over-use, and she was hungry for something more solid at last. She did not care what it was, as long as it was real. Every detail about him was as precious as one of Mrs. Addison's pearls. Oh, had his father really abandoned his mother, and Bellew himself as a helpless babe? How she wished she could dandle that infant in her arms and kiss his plump cheeks until his tears stopped! How could the Baron have let such a treasure slip from his grasp - and wouldn't he be astonished, Rachel decided with sudden determination, to discover what a fine man his abandoned second son had grown into, handsome and skilled and truly noble, in the proper sense the word was meant to convey rather than mere accident of blood. If only Lieutenant Bellew could be free of this place and earn the distinguishment that would bring him to his father's notice for the first time!

She wanted to say all that, but she could not.

And, darker, she knew she should not have felt the secret glee that fluttered in her heart to learn that Bellew was only a second son. But it brought him a little closer to her, though obviously his prospects and connections were infinitely superior. But a little closer to hers nevertheless. Whether he was close enough to touch - that she did not know. But he seemed to like her; and he even composed a couplet for her, even if that was under challenge. And he was sharing confidences with her - just as she had dreamed, but not expected, not really!

"I don't find your history dull in the slightest, and I'd far rather hear it than dance anyway," Rachel said, pressing on. "I can't imagine what your mother must have endured, cast out with a small child - didn't her people help her, or why did she come so far? Oh, but I don't mean to pry again. Perhaps it is painful to discuss. Oh, I am sorry - only I think it was very brave of your mother, and I can scarcely imagine how she managed it - all the way to the colonies with no one to help her - she must have a wonderful spirit, and I am not surprised."

"She died last year," Bellew replied. "Yes, she was – very spirited. And very clever, I suppose. She was also a commoner, though, and I don't believe she had any relatives living at the time to give her aid; none she admitted to me, at any rate. She did not much encourage a discussion of the past, so while your interest gratifies me more than I can say, I can do little to satisfy it. If you do not find it off-putting that I am somewhat less than people might assume by my name, however, I am more than glad to tell you anything you like," Bellew said in a frank voice. Rachel thought she detected a hint of relief in it. Well, wasn't that how she'd felt a moment ago when Captain André hadn't minded about her performance at the hunt, any part of it, and had accepted it, and had even seemed amused?

"I am sorry for your loss, and I hope her later years compensated for her earlier difficulties," Rachel said. "Both my parents – both my parents were commoners, of course." She had first meant to say that both her parents were dead, but that almost seemed like an ugly competition more than sympathy.

"That is perhaps drawing the point too fine," Bellew said with a smile, speaking more easily now that the topic had shifted off him. "It was described to me that you were descended from Peter Minuit, and surely if there were a nobility established in the Americas, he would have been among its first members."

"Who?" Rachel asked blankly.

"Peter Minuit of Delaware – oh yes, forgive me, I forgot the incognito, are we returning to that now that the subject is you?" Lieutenant Bellew laughed.

Rachel had no relatives in Delaware that she knew of – her father had come from Prussia, and her mother's family had been South Carolinians for three generations at least. Mrs. Addison's people were from Delaware, though, so perhaps she would know who Peter Minuit –

He thinks I'm Mrs. Addison, Rachel realized with a sudden cold force. Of course – the fan. And the high-heeled slippers giving her extra height, and nothing but a mouth and powdered hair to judge her face by. Lieutenant Bellew did not see behind masks like Captain André; he merely used the trick of guessing from the peripherals, as Mrs. Addison had done. She knew she must disabuse him at once – and wondered frantically whether she had said anything that would reflect poorly on Mrs. Addison. She cursed herself. Lieutenant Bellew had thought that he was making himself agreeable to the author of his release, when it was only her maid! How annoyed he would be, and how disappointed. So she must tell him promptly, she must. He would leave her, then, but that was only proper – no, she could stay with him a little while to help him find the real Mrs. Addison in the crowd, the person he really admired.

And yet, a less creditable thought wriggled through her brain like a worm, *wasn't it Rachel whose conversation pleased him now?* It wasn't some ghostly vision of Mrs. Addison to whom Lieutenant Bellew had been speaking; it was Rachel herself. She might pretend not to understand – why, in fact, she didn't really know who this Peter Minuit was, and her thoughts about Delaware were mere speculation. Lieutenant Bellew had never actually addressed her by any name. She did not know who he believed she was. She might have been entirely mistaken.

Ah, but he called you "madam" rather than "miss," a cruel voice in her head reminded her.

"I think – perhaps – I also am somewhat less than people might assume," Rachel began carefully.

The minuet ended, and the instruments played a few quick bars of a quicker dance to let the crowd know what was coming next. Lieutenant Bellew pricked up his ears and smiled. "A country dance," he exclaimed. "Well, that's one I know, at least. Unless you are otherwise engaged, may I have the honor of it? We are attending a dance, after all, not a salon." He bowed and lifted her hand delicately a few inches.

It was the only dance Rachel knew – everyone could country-dance, probably even Jacob. But no, she shouldn't, she had to explain first –

"I would be delighted," she answered, her heart hammering in her ears. Lieutenant Bellew smiled happily and led her to the other room.

A few dozen spectators lined the walls. Six couples had already lined up in the center of the room, men to one side and women on the other. "Excuse us," Lieutenant Bellew murmured, brushing his way past a pair of women. Rachel saw Mrs. Addison's bright turquoise with a shock of recognition. Mrs. Addison looked equally surprised, and then she pursed her lips in a repressed smile.

Rachel and Lieutenant Bellew took their places in line. Three more couples followed after them. The room would scarcely hold a longer queue, so the first violinist nodded to the other musicians, and then the song began.

Rachel watched as the first and second couples reached across each other to make a cross of their right arms, each man taking the hand of his neighbor's partner. They moved in step in a circle until the women were on the men's side, and then they dropped hands, making a cross with their left arms this time and danced back into place. The first couple joined hands and danced down the center aisle to the cheerful music of the tune. It was done in the same style with which Rachel was familiar, to her relief.

The first couple returned to place one position lower, and the dance started over again with the first couple and the third. Rachel smiled at Bellew. He smiled back. The first couple made their way down the line, and then the two couples at the head of the line started the pattern anew, so that two stars of silk-clad arms and lace spun their way down the aisle.

At last it was their turn. Rachel took the hand of the strange man who offered it, not feeling it in the slightest, but conscious only of the closeness of Lieutenant Bellew's hand beneath hers. They danced in the careful half-circle, then switched hands and danced back again. Rachel barely had time to settle her excitement before it was time to step and twirl again, and over and over, until at last she and Bellew were at the head of the line, and after they danced with their neighbors, he took her hand in his own at last and walked her down the line. He held her lightly and did not press her fingers, as of course he would not and should not, thinking as he did that she was a married woman – but how delicious the feel of his warm skin damp with light sweat against hers just the same.

After their rule as first couple was done, they had a few more spins as mere members of the corps, not touching each other but looking into each other's eyes and smiling broadly, and then the dance was over, far too soon. The onlookers applauded politely, and then the musicians struck a few notes. "Oh, it's another minuet – we'd better go," Rachel whispered to Lieutenant Bellew, her eyes sparkling with the delight of sharing a secret as much as the dance, which still tingled in her blood. "We'll pretend I'm thirsty and you have to get me a drink." That would keep him at her side a little longer. It didn't seem quite the right time yet to reveal her name.

Perhaps it would be better, actually, not to say who she was at all, but simply to admit she was not Mrs. Addison and leave him with an intriguing mystery. Yes, she decided, that would be best – he could not be too disappointed if he did not know exactly who she was, and the question of the fan could be explained by its being a lookalike, and Bellew would ponder the issue of who he had laughed and danced with, and when he found out later – she was not quite sure how – it would be a different matter, a teasing puzzle solved at last, and perhaps by then he would even be pleased when he discovered its answer.

"Why, they're setting up a snapdragon," Lieutenant Bellew exclaimed when they returned to the parlor. The punch-bowl had been set aside, and the Scottish soldier who had served Rachel her punch was pouring rum into a shallow bowl filled with raisins. "I haven't seen one of those in years."

"Don't tell our hostess that, she likes to think of herself as a la mode."

"Snapdragons never go out of style, if I see our hostess, I will congratulate her on it particularly. Of course, I won't know her, so perhaps I'll simply congratulate every lady I see," Lieutenant Bellew said. He seemed almost as elevated as Rachel by enjoyment of the dance. A frown crossed his face. "I thought this was General Howe's residence, and he was a bachelor."

She should not have brought up Mrs. Loring – Mrs. Addison had had the discretion not to do so. A man might reasonably break bread with his enemy, but not his torturer. Why did there have to be so many secrets! "So you like snapdragons a great deal," she said hurriedly, pushing him back to his original topic.

His face cleared. "I do, although it's childish, I suppose. Are they too silly for you?"

"I can't call them silly. I've always been afraid of them," Rachel admitted, and it was true. The Crawfords had had one every year, like this, on twelfth night, but while Anne had joined in gleefully, Rachel had not.

Lieutenant Bellew turned to her in surprise, a delighted smile on his face. "You're afraid of them?" he said. She did not know why he should seem so happy about it.

"Well – yes –"

"But there's nothing to it – here, we've got to go over now," he declared firmly, and before Rachel knew what had happened, she was standing in the crowd by the bowl of raisins as the Scottish soldier upended a full bottle of brandy with a flourish.

"But you have to do it in the dark!" a lady cried. The Scottish soldier remained unflustered.

"Then all of ye who dare follow me," he huffed, lifting the bowl overhead and carrying it towards the back of the house.

"Good, we'll have the full effect," Bellew laughed, and twenty or so revelers followed the soldier on a winding path through various rooms and guests curious about the strange procession – a path that was so winding and occasionally repetitive that Rachel realized that the soldier was having a bit of fun with them.

"Now, you have to stop sometime, we want to dance too!" another lady cried. The Scottish soldier did stop, but only to regard her balefully.

"Then ye'd better get back to it and dance then. I cannae find a single spot where I don't think you're as likely to burn down the house as anything else with your wee timid fingers." The crowd protested vigorously, and at last the Scottish soldier allowed himself to be swayed, with a vast appearance of ill-humor and a twinkle in his eye, and they all went outside into the cold night air in the back. Shadows swallowed them, seeming all the deeper for the light of the house behind them, and the masked faces of the revelers looked like ghosts and demons floating through the dark.

The soldier placed the bowl carefully on a porch-table and pushed aside the chairs so that people could come close. Lieutenant Bellew made sure that he and Rachel stood in front. "I'm not going to reach in, you know," she whispered to him. "I know I'll catch fire, just like he said."

"No one ever does. I'm not sure it's even possible. Why, children of four play this game! The flames look fierce, but they're not too hot."

"If it would happen to anyone, it would happen to me, I promise you," Rachel insisted fervently.

"Well, perhaps you'll work up your nerve," Lieutenant Bellew replied with a grin. The Scottish soldier produced a tinder-box and struck a spark. A tiny red glow appeared, and the soldier lowered it to the brandy.

The bowl erupted in high blue flames, bathing the crowd in otherworldly light. A few of the ladies gasped. "Well, then, have at it," the Scottish soldier said, and a dozen blue-bathed hands shot forward, snatching the raisins from the bowl. Their fingers dripped blue fire all the way to their lips, and then the flames abruptly extinguished when mouths snapped shut around the burning raisins.

Lieutenant Bellew joined in enthusiastically, grabbing three raisins in rapid succession and then shaking the heat off his hand with a laugh before plunging in again. "Aren't you going to try even once?" he teased.

Rachel shook her head, but he wasn't looking at her any more, his hand in the bowl again. "No," she said, and he spun around and popped a raisin into her open mouth. Rachel squeaked in surprise. The raisin's skin was smooth, swollen from the brandy and the fire, and hot. She pressed it with her tongue with a vague intention of extinguishing the fire, but of course it was already out. Sweetness filled her mouth. It was delicious.

"Now you see there's nothing to be afraid of. Go on, they're almost gone," Lieutenant Bellew said. She supposed she had to. And it was true, no one else was getting immolated, and some of them were quite sloppy. So Rachel worked up her nerve to pull out a single raisin of her own, and watched her flame-dripping fingers in amazement, hot but not uncomfortably so, and sucked the second raisin from them. Lieutenant Bellew grinned.

The blue fire burnt lower now and the raisins were all gone. The Scottish soldier lifted the bowl, Rachel assumed to let everyone know not to burn their fingers for no cause. But to her surprise, he tilted the bowl to his lips and poured a massive swallow of the flaming brandy into his gaping mouth. He put the bowl back down with a heavy thump and snorted happily, shaking his head from side to side. A few of the men, their pride damaged, jostled forward to get their own chance at the trick.

"A highlander, I think," Lieutenant Bellew whispered to Rachel.

"They might be playing another country dance now," she said, looking at him with hopeful eyes.

But he shook his head. "I've monopolized you far too long," Lieutenant Bellew replied. "And I hoped to check in on Captain O'Malley – I don't like to make Mrs. Merriwether stay up late to give him his medicine in my absence. But I do – well, I wanted to come to express my gratitude for your kindness, and I find I've enjoyed myself so much I've let the time slip away."

Now Rachel could not tell him about his mistake. She bade him good-bye, and he hesitated, then reached for her hand as if to kiss it, but thought better of the gesture and bowed. Then he was gone.

The hours that remained did not matter, but they did not pass slowly, either. In fact, they were a delight. Rachel was too happy, her thoughts too full of too many wonderful memories to mind too badly Lieutenant Bellew's absence, for the moment at least, although she longed for him. She found herself in easy conversation with a gentleman and a lady who had been in the country dance with her, and it seemed hardly a moment before Abraham was calling for them at the door, and Mr. Addison and General Lee had to be dragged out of their card-game, and she was in her dear, safe room and her own familiar bed, staring at the black ceiling with the scent of powder still in her nose and the melancholy notes of the violins still in her ears and the brief brush of Lieutenant Bellew's fingers still against her lips.

In her mind, she rested her cheek against his shoulder, and she slept.

Chapter 23

"And the prodigal son returns," O'Malley said. He was awake and had a candle burning when Bellew, his mask gone but the powder still in his hair, entered the room softly. "So how do you rate General Howe's hospitality now? Improved?" His voice was cheerful, but Bellew knew O'Malley well enough to see through it.

"General Lee was present," Bellew replied, flushing slightly. He had not seen General Lee, nor looked for him at the ball. He was not convinced the general liked him too much, not after the hunt, although Bellew hoped he had smoothed over their difficulties a little by ceding the win.

"He's got his reasons. A general has to be at least half a politician, and maybe more. But neither of us is a general, Bellew."

"Our benefactress asked it of me, and I could hardly refuse," Bellew answered. He lifted the bottle of medicine and opened it. O'Malley propped himself up on his pillows without assistance and swallowed the draught with grim determination. Once its effects had passed, Bellew wiped O'Malley's mouth and helped him lie down again. A little effluvium had spattered the sleeve of Mrs. Merriwether's dead husband's coat, hurriedly altered to fit Bellew. He wiped that too.

"If she's Tory enough to hobnob with General Howe, I wonder what she's about with us. Our benefactress," O'Malley said through a scratchy throat.

"I hardly think General van Dortmund's daughter could be much of a Tory."

"Don't rely too heavily on the political views of women, lad. And especially not their consistency."

"It is not their fault if society obliges them to adopt a - a sort of Laodicean mediocrity."

"*For because thou art lukewarm, and neither hot nor cold, I spit thee from my mouth,*" O'Malley murmured. He rubbed a pale finger over his dry lips.

"Well, you can't do that with women. And Mrs. Addison's accommodations to her circumstances - I feel that her husband is a very different sort from she herself. Very different. How the two of them ever – I cannot understand it, frankly. But she must adapt to his views and his society, of course."

O'Malley turned his head on the pillow and regarded Bellew somberly. "Now what's this about this married woman's husband?"

Bellew scowled, taking the bait but not the warning. "I don't believe he's worthy of her. I admit I have little to base it upon – but I am certain of it just the same. Hardly any man would be. She is not only beautiful but clever – she even extemporized a bit of poetry, O'Malley – and I feel her kindness is given few outlets in the cold household where she is trapped. So she takes creatures under her wing when she can – here we are, of course, but she even let her maid come to the hunt."

"That little thing from the Brass Bull? Ah, she was a sweet girl. I'm glad she found a better place."

"She was terribly overwhelmed there. At the Brass Bull, I mean," Bellew said. He was not quite sure whether Miss Kolkhorst had been overwhelmed at the hunt.

"Well, she didn't like it much, but I don't think she's as whey-faced as you take her for. And if she hadn't thought to mention us, don't forget where we'd still be right now."

"I am grateful to her for it, certainly. And she never asked about Masterson, so I suppose she can hold a grudge. And she can ride," Bellew added thoughtfully.

"A good solid farm-girl. I'd expect her to," O'Malley replied. "Now, I'll ask you to put out that candle, and my thanks. Oh, but stay a moment. What's this bit of poetry you had from your Mrs. Addison?"

"Well, it was only a couplet."

"And what was this couplet? I have few forms of amusement here. Share some of her cleverness with me."

Bellew hesitated. Then he shrugged and said, "To love is to dream and pray not to wake/And idle the hours for idleness' sake."

O'Malley breathed out heavily. "And what prompted this burst of poesy?"

"I – don't quite remember the full context," Bellew said, suddenly uncomfortable.

"Well. And I'll ask another favor, as your friend if you will and as your commanding officer if I must."

"What is it?"

"Stay away from that Mrs. Addison as much as you can in decency. Lad, I don't blame you for it, and Lord knows I might have the same trouble if I were younger and well. But I don't like what you're thinking or about to think, and it won't lead to anything but mischief. It's already made you do things you shouldn't have, and I think you know it. You may tell yourself you have good reason. I'm telling you frankly you don't."

* * *

Rachel mulled it over a long time before concluding how to frame the matter. She decided Lieutenant Bellew would be angry and shamed if he thought he had been taken for ungrateful to Mrs. Addison, due to not only his accidental mistake but Rachel's deliberate silence. So she fixed it, if not quite honestly. "And I am glad Lieutenant Bellew had the chance to thank you again," she added off-handedly in the morning as she helped Mrs. Addison dress, while they were gossiping about the previous night.

"What? No, I thought he didn't come," Mrs. Addison said, twisting around in surprise.

"He didn't speak to you, then?" Rachel asked, her heart hammering. She fastened a gold ear-ring in Mrs. Addison's left lobe.

"No, for heaven's sake, obviously. Rachel, you aren't usually this slow. So you spoke to him there?"

"I did – a little. I'm sorry, ma'am, it's just that he was clearly under the impression that he had seen you and offered his thanks. I'm terribly sorry to learn it must have been some other lady. He told me he appeared really only so that he could show appreciation for your kindness, and he left early."

"Well, isn't that annoying," Mrs. Addison said, her brows drawing together. Then, suddenly, she laughed. "Although I wonder what that other lady must have thought – Lieutenant Bellew's protestations in particular tending to such fervency. It doesn't really matter. The will can serve as the deed. Now, dear, we've talked so much about what you saw, but we're getting to something that interests me no less, which is what you did – I saw you take that dance. Now, that is something I'd like to hear about."

"It's the only dance I know," Rachel said.

"Oh la, I don't need to hear the particulars of how to perform a country dance, the point is that someone asked you and you said yes!"

"I'm afraid that's all there is to it," Rachel answered, hating herself for the lie. "I suppose he simply found me nearby at a convenient juncture."

"Oh, nonsense, the two of you were looking at each other and laughing like old friends. If you acquired yourself a beau last night, Rachel, I hope you maintained your incognito – we're not staying here long anyway."

"I did, ma'am," Rachel replied.

The men remained in bed all morning and did not rise even for the very late breakfast, which Mrs. Addison took alone before retreating to her studio to do a bit of painting for lack of anything better. It was going to be a quiet day in Philadelphia, with everyone important recuperating from Mrs. Loring's ball and everyone less important from their own ruder twelfth night entertainments. Rachel was not tired, not in the slightest, and she launched into her postponed work with enthusiasm. The floors needed attention the most. Rachel got a bucket of water, a bottle of oil, and a few rags, and she knelt in the entrance area and got to work scrubbing. Mrs. Rimini, she quickly learned, had been correct. Her hands felt it badly now that their calluses had softened.

A soft knock sounded at the door, surprising her. No one was going to be out today, but perhaps there was a delivery. Since she was nearest, Rachel rose to her feet and opened the door, her face red with exertion and her sleeves wet.

Captain André stood in the dull gray light, his scarlet jacket as bright as a drop of heart's blood. Rachel's hands flew to her hair. Captain André smiled and bowed, showing no alarm at her condition.

"Oh – I – Mr. Addison isn't up yet," Rachel stammered, trying to make sense of his presence.

"That's all right, Miss Kolkhorst, and don't worry about your hair. I wasn't sure what else they had you doing besides serving as Mrs. Addison's companion, but I'm not afraid of hard work myself, and I'm glad you aren't either. I simply wanted to present my compliments and extend our acquaintance, if that would be agreeable to you. If Mrs. Addison is still in bed, perhaps you have a few moments now," Captain André said. He waited with an amiable expression, bouncing on his heels slightly in the cool air. It was too warm to walk with a coat on but a little too brisk to stand comfortably without one.

"Well, I - of course, since you've come, but -"

"You're busy, I understand. I don't mind talking with you while you work, if it would help pass the time. But I'm not familiar with the intimate details of house-keeping; perhaps it takes more concentration than that. I worked in a counting-house before, and conversation was pretty well impossible if one hoped to get anything done."

"No, it really isn't that taxing," Rachel admitted. "Although people tend to think it is. Please do come in. I'm sorry. I was just so surprised to see you." She stood back and let Captain André step inside. He glanced at the surroundings with appreciation. Rachel had been looking forward to a quiet day with nothing but her own thoughts for company, but she could hardly turn Captain André aside now that he had come. Not only from politeness, but also because he had been so generous to her at the ball, and most of all because she found him to be a pleasant and interesting companion whose feelings she would not like to hurt. And she rather liked talking to him.

Only, she was a little afraid that he had been flirting with her before. Yes, he must have been, she realized - why else would he be here now? This presented a difficulty. She was too worried to feel very flattered.

"I was scrubbing the floors," she said apologetically, half-hoping the image would make her seem less appealing. "But I think I'll dust first instead. It's easier to talk that way." So she took two of the dry rags from the floor and led him into the drawing-room. "You can sit if you like, or - or should I bring you some refreshment?" Rachel didn't feel certain what exactly lay within the boundaries of her duties and her rights when dealing with a visitor of her own. The occurrence was novel.

"I'd feel pretty awkward doing it alone, and I don't suppose you can sit and sip, so I'll just wander, if you don't mind," Captain André replied easily. "Don't mind me, really. If I'm keeping you from things, I'll have to go. That's it. I promise not to say anything shocking when you're handling the crystal. Did you enjoy the entertainment last night, I hope?"

"I thought it came off wonderfully." Rachel stood at an angle by the étagère so that she could see Captain André from the corner of her eye as she worked.

"It did seem to go over. I was going to ask you to dance, you know, but I saw you heading towards the line already by the time I was free. You found your feet after all. I was glad to see it."

Rachel paused and replaced the glass lily carefully. She did not turn to face him fully. She did not know how to be indirect about this, but it had to be said. "I feel obliged to inform you, Captain André, and forgive me if this is awkward or I misunderstand, but my heart – my heart is taken."

He seemed unfazed. More than that, he smiled, his eyes lighting up. "You are afraid then that I am making love to you?"

"I – very much appreciate any interest taken in me, more than I can say, but I feel it would be a pretty ungenerous return if I didn't explain matters clearly."

"My dear Miss Kolkhorst," Captain André said in a softened voice. "This is a very understandable misunderstanding, and I apologize for it, if I've given you pause. It's just that most young ladies seem to prefer that particular misunderstanding to the truth, and I'm afraid I've gotten in the habit of courting it." Rachel looked at him curiously. "I see you're not certain. I assure you, I have had my heart broken once and not only am not inclined to repeat the experience, I find myself unable to. My interest in you, I promise, is purely that of friendship." His face was gentle and a little sad, and there was no raillery in it now. She had to believe him; but that only confused her all the more.

"I would be grateful for your friendship – but I don't know what I've done to inspire it," Rachel said.

Captain André shrugged. "You are strange and rather clever, I think you are well-meaning, given our new understanding I am sure you will not mind my mentioning that you are deuced pretty, and there is something about you that is terribly sad. That is more than enough for me," he said. "I fancy myself a student of people, and you make for pleasant study. But your heart is taken? Then perhaps that sad look will fade. That would be well; I would be pleased."

"I would think it had already," Rachel said, who had not been aware that there was anything melancholic about her previously and was not convinced of it.

"Not to my eye," Captain André said, regarding her thoughtfully. "Perhaps it is simply part of your nature."

"I feel myself at a disadvantage. I don't know how to judge the merit of your opinions, most of them, about me –"

"I suppose you will admit to being strange and nothing else," Captain André laughed.

"– but I know so little about you, and if you think I am clever, I am of course gratified, but I have managed to develop little opinion of you except that you work very hard to make yourself agreeable, and are quite successful at it."

He bowed. "You disparage your observation, but it might encompass a great deal. Well, as for me, there is not too much to know yet. I am, as we discussed last night, seeking glory. I have not found it yet. When I succeed, or fail, then there will be something to be said about me other than that I try to make myself agreeable, though I hope I will always pursue that aim. But as for you, Miss Kolkhorst – despite your protestations last night, it seems our gallant southern friend knew something about this heart of yours, and I admit I am curious."

"No – he was mistaken," Rachel said.

"Mistaken about the identity of your beloved, even if he divined correctly that there was one?"

Rachel pressed her lips together and picked up the three muses while she tried to gather an answer. She poked the rag at the creases and gaps in the figure.

"Ah, something occurs to me," Captain André said. "Perhaps he was mistaken about a different identity altogether."

"I – think so," Rachel admitted in a small voice. She wished he were not so quick to read her thoughts – how did he do it? Could others see her thoughts so plainly? She prayed not. Yet with Captain André, she did not mind so much. He did not seem to judge her. He was only, as he said, curious. And she could not help believing that his offer of friendship was sincere. Now that she was not anxious about his broader goals with her, she realized she simply liked him.

"And he was your partner in the dance, of course. I think I see," Captain André said slowly.

He had put it all together.

"Please don't say anything," Rachel cried in a sudden excitement, thrusting the three muses back upon the shelf. "Oh, Captain André - you don't know the trouble I would have -"

He lifted a finger to his lips. His eyes showed some sympathy, but somewhat more pleasure at having figured out the puzzle. "Not a word. But you need to straighten that out."

"I would like to - I would like nothing more, only - well, there are difficulties."

He shrugged. "Ah. I understand."

"You think I am being timid," Rachel said, "But I swear -"

"No, I genuinely do understand. Of course we all want to be loved for who we really are, Miss Kolkhorst. But that is not always entirely possible, I am afraid. When I offered my fortunes to the girl I mentioned before, she informed me regretfully that they were a little too low, so I slaved away like a madman in that counting-house until I had a bit of money to my name and some tolerable prospects. Then when I presented myself a second time, I was informed that it was in fact not so much my circumstances that were unacceptable as myself," Captain André said lightly. But his mouth had a bitter twist to the corner, and a shadow crossed his eyes as he spoke.

"I find that difficult to believe," Rachel said.

Captain André smiled. "Be that as it may, I discovered then that I would gladly have had the lady believe I was someone else, if only that other man she thought I was possessed her esteem and her love. And that, I am afraid, is my best advice to you; which is no advice at all. But speaking as an impartial observer, and perhaps you will believe me this time, whoever Lieutenant Bellew thought you were in theory, last night he was very taken with you in fact."

A bell upstairs rang. Rachel's head snapped up. "It's Mrs. Addison," she said.

"Then I have become an encumbrance," Captain André replied. "I did mean to stay only a moment - and to offer an invitation, if you like. I am residing on High Street – it is not too far – and I think the house might be of some interest to you, if you would like to see it someday."

"Is it a peculiar house?"

"Not so much on the outside, but it belongs to the famous Dr. Franklin, and it possesses an amazing variety of scientific apparatus. Some of it I can't make heads or tails of, I must confess, but it is possible to recapitulate a few of his experiments – it is very diverting, I assure you. Ah, I can see by your face the prospect does entice. Well, I am at your disposal – here is my card."

Of course Rachel had heard of Dr. Franklin's experiments with electricity – people said that the effect was indistinguishable from magic, with flashing lights and the smell of burning air and objects moving as if under their own power. This was a wonder she had forgotten that Philadelphia possessed, among so many others.

"You are full of marvels," she said, taking the card and looking at it.

"Amusing you will amuse me," Captain André replied.

"Rachel?" Mrs. Addison's voice floated from the entrance hall. A moment later Mrs. Addison herself appeared, her hands flecked with paint. "Rachel, I need to – oh! I beg your pardon," Mrs. Addison said, taken aback on seeing the red-coated stranger.

"Mrs. Addison," Captain André said with a bow. "My apologies for taking the attention of Miss Kolkhorst so long. I merely meant to offer an invitation to see Dr. Franklin's home, where I am staying – if you would find it agreeable, I would be delighted if you would also make yourself free. And please forgive my forwardness – I am Captain John André at your service."

"Captain André – of course I know the name. Well, thank you. Yes, perhaps that would be interesting – and very kind of you to offer. Oh, you don't need to be off, do you? I should offer you better hospitality than being all covered in paint this way. Rachel, you could get the sherry – a glass for you too, dear." Mrs. Addison's eyes flicked over Rachel's state of disrepair and widened slightly.

"I am afraid that I have professional duties to which I must attend presently," Captain André replied. "But any time I am free to offer you is entirely at your disposal and your whim."

Mrs. Addison hardly waited for the door to close behind Captain André before pouncing on Rachel. "So that was him, was it?" she said. It was difficult to tell whether she was angry or amused. "Rachel, you said you kept your incognito!"

"I did!" Rachel protested. "Only there's no hiding things from Captain André."

"Oh, so he managed to get you to tell him your name, and I suppose you made it terribly difficult."

"No, ma'am, I never told him my name at all, he addressed me by it in the first place – and Captain André isn't who I danced with, I'm sure of that," Rachel said. "We spoke for barely a few minutes at the ball."

"Well, you certainly made an impression in them. But remember, Rachel – we're gone in two weeks, and that's hardly enough time to arrange a marriage, and you wouldn't like being married to a soldier in the slightest, I can promise you that." Mrs. Addison's sharp eyes searched Rachel's face.

Rachel shook her head. "Captain André took pains to assure me that his intentions were not romantic, and anyway I told him that I – that anything along those lines would be quite impossible, before he even did."

"Hm." Mrs. Addison allowed herself to be mollified, provisionally at least. Her eyes lost their sharpness. "Well, I would like to see Dr. Franklin's house. And I'm not letting you go alone, just in case. I don't want you running off on me, Rachel. It would be personally inconvenient, and I can assure you that a man is very unlikely to be worth giving up anything for."

"I would never do that, ma'am, you know that! And there really isn't anything between Captain André and me. And I would be so grateful for your company. Captain André said he knew how to do a few of Dr. Franklin's experiments – surely that would be something worth seeing."

Mrs. Addison looked pleased. "Oh, really? It rather would, wouldn't it, and while Dr. Franklin himself may enjoy only a very moderate popularity in either political camp, everyone does like to hear about his experiments, so it makes for a safe topic of conversation. I'll arrange it, dear. Perhaps we'll go Wednesday or Thursday."

"Mr. Addison or General Lee might enjoy the opportunity too – oh, but only if there's some way to keep the dogs at home," Rachel said, her face falling, as she thought of all the delicate tubes and glassware and whatever other scientific apparatus.

"Mr. Addison would doubtless decline the pleasure, and so my only pleasure will be in not offering it to him," Mrs. Addison replied. A dark glitter appeared in her eye, and then, as suddenly as it appeared, it was gone. "But Rachel, I meant to tell you – I've finished painting, and I'd like to change so that Abraham can take me out for a ride. I'd like the air to clear my head of last night's fumes."

Rachel helped Mrs. Addison dress and saw her off, and then she went to the studio to clean up the paint-pots before they dried. The studio was a small room with two large windows that filled it with light in almost any weather. Mrs. Addison's easel faced away from them to catch the full benefit of the sunlight. Rachel paused to look at the work in progress. The canvas depicted a landscape not unlike the one from the vantage of the start of the hunt yesterday – Rachel recognized the curve of the creek, outlined in perfect accuracy in light pencil sketch. The trees remained yet as only vague scratches, and Rachel thought that the extent of the forest had been rather diminished in Mrs. Addison's imagination. The hills were smaller, too. But she had taken great pains with the sky, whose shining blue had been shaded so well with bold strokes that it might have been plucked from the heavens, and her ragged little wisps of clouds gave a fine sense of the light wind that had been blowing, though Rachel did not remember having seen any clouds in the real sky that day. Curiously, there were no figures – no horses, no dogs, no riders – to liven the scene. Perhaps Mrs. Addison would put them in later; but that was difficult to do with watercolors, if not impossible, once the background had been filled in.

A hard clatter from downstairs startled Rachel. General Lee's voice followed shortly after, snarling, "Stupid scatter-brained bitch!" Her bucket – she'd forgotten the bucket downstairs, and General Lee must have tripped on it, or perhaps one of the dogs, which would be roaming freely now that the General had left his room. She felt a spark of hard, bright satisfaction, even as she hoped there wouldn't be any trouble over the matter. There hadn't been much water left in the bucket anyway. The spill wouldn't harm anything. But General Lee was out of his room, and downstairs – that made it a good time for her to straighten up his quarters, as she could be sure not to come across him while doing so.

She put the paint-pots away quickly and left the rest of the studio for later, making sure that she hadn't left anything out that someone might accidentally knock over or trip against, and hurried down the hall to General Lee's door, which was shut. If she hadn't heard him downstairs, she'd never have known that he had risen. She knocked timidly just to be safe and, receiving no response, slipped inside.

The first thing she did was pull the curtains, both for light and so she could open the window to let in air. The smell of dog and sweat was suffocating. She discovered some of the cause just barely in time to avoid stepping in it. One of the greyhounds, cooped up too long, had left its waste on the floor. Rachel lifted it gingerly with her rag, leaving the wad of fabric on the floor to remind her where to wash with particular attention.

A blanket lay crumpled on the floor, and the sheets had been twisted so badly they looked like rope. Clothes had been flung everywhere, and papers scattered across his writing desk, a few sheets either finished or else rejected lying beneath the chair. Rachel straightened the bed first, wiping off as much of the dog hair as possible, and then she picked up the clothes and hung them properly. She would clean them later, but at least they wouldn't get dirtier now that they were off the floor. She did not find any more dog-leavings, to her relief and somewhat to her surprise.

A gust of wind blew in welcome freshness, but it also brought the rattling of papers behind her. Rachel wheeled around just in time to see General Lee's work slide across the desk and more of it slip onto the floor. "Oh no," she whispered, cold anxiety seizing her, and she dropped the stained shirt in her hands and slammed her hands down on the desk, preventing any more sheets from going astray. The wind stopped. She shoved the papers she'd rescued back into place, more or less, and pulled the window shut. Then she bent to her knees beneath the desk and gathered up the loose pages, glancing at them worriedly, hoping they were not too important.

Curiosity overcame her, and she peeked at the top sheet. "With the New-England colonies thus isolated from their potential allies..." She realized with a touch of excitement that they were military plans – then these papers certainly were important, and she hoped she hadn't made too bad a mess of them, although she was sure General Lee could straighten them right out again. Rachel knew she was no judge of military thinking, but she was interested just the same – she'd heard so much about General Lee's ability that she longed to observe it in practice.

She flipped through a few more pages. Officers' names and division numbers that meant nothing to her rolled past – it looked like a plan for the British Army to destroy the resistance. She read further until her original impressions were confirmed. So – here she had been thinking that General Lee was doing nothing but sulk and nurse his grievances, when in fact he had been gathering critical intelligence – how clever he was, making friends with General Howe that way! General Howe probably scarcely realized how much he'd let slip – but General Lee had caught every word of it, every morsel, and written it down for General Washington, even if he did not like or respect the man – and General Howe would find himself outfoxed if he should try to make a move! Perhaps, Rachel realized slowly, she had misjudged General Howe; perhaps he had lied to Mr. Addison. Or perhaps he had changed his mind. This was no a plan to bide time; this was a plan to annihilate the Continentals all at once. But General Lee was one step ahead of him, Rachel noted with satisfaction. She would gladly clean up a mountain of dog waste for him now.

She tried to put the shuffled pages of the precious document back in order. It was a difficult task without taking the time to read every word in detail, but here, she'd found the beginning, at least; she could tell because it started: "My Very Dear General –"

Rachel froze. Some of the papers fell from her hands. But not the one on top; not the one she wished she hadn't seen.

"My Very Dear General Howe:

"It is with some diffidence, given your amply and frequently demonstrated intelligence and ability, that I commit to paper my few thoughts concerning your present difficulties and how best to resolve them. But in the hopes that a fellow-soldier will be able to see the merit in my thinking and perhaps find some small area where it develops an idea or a plan he might have neglected in the press of other business, I nevertheless offer this strategy for the defeat of the Continental Army and the pacification of the rebellious colonies, which, as will be explained, are two distinct matters..."

Chapter 24

One of the little girls knocked at Bellew's door.

"There's a lady downstairs, sir," she piped. "She says her name is Mrs. Addison, and you know her?"

Bellew's first feeling was surprised delight, and his first thought was relief that O'Malley was sleeping. The captain had made his feelings clear; and Bellew understood what his friend had told him, and it was true that he felt more than a twinge of discomfort at the thought of his having attended General Howe's hunt and ball, drinking the man's wine and eating his bread.

But even if O'Malley did not want Bellew visiting her, he could hardly expect Bellew to pretend not to be in when she called. He had not even repaid the money yet. So he had happily put down his pen, released from the burden of telling another wife that her husband was dead and hunting fruitlessly for words that had not grown stale from over-use, and walked down the stairs to the drawing-room, where Mrs. Addison sat waiting, the graceful oval of her face upturned to watch him descend the stairs.

The Misses Merriwether giggled somewhere in the back of the house. They were always laughing about something when there was no one to watch them. He thought it was a pity that they should always put on such somber faces when company was near.

Even up close, Mrs. Addison was as beautiful and fresh as if she had not stayed out late the night before. She wore a dark orange silk and garnets on her throat and ears. A little gold ring twinkled on the smallest finger of her left hand. The rich colors made her eyes seem greener than the clear blue they'd shone with last night, and she glowed like a coal on the faded gray fabric of Mrs. Merriwether's best sofa. She shifted slightly in her seat and flashed him a smile, her eyes dancing away before he could answer it. Bellew smiled anyway. He wore his plain black suit. It probably looked as if he were in mourning. In a way, he supposed, he was – in mourning for his country; but he rather wished he hadn't dressed quite so grimly nevertheless. Perhaps in the future he would not. Mrs. Merriwether had been so pleased with the result when she had tailored her husband's old blue suit for Bellew to wear to the ball that she had offered to alter more clothes for him, pointing out that she had no sons to wear them one day.

They said their polite greetings, and Bellew excused O'Malley.

"I am sorry to have missed him. It is an ordinary part of his recuperation, I hope? I was given to understand that he was coming along nicely."

"It is," Bellew said. "The doctor told us to expect his energy to return only slowly. But he is past the worst of the danger. I will tell him that you inquired after his well-being. Until Captain O'Malley is well enough to receive, I'm afraid that my poor thanks will have to serve for both of us."

"Oh, la, enough about that," Mrs. Addison said with an absent flick of her fingers. Her ring sparkled. "I think I should be measured more on the effort to which I went, which was negligible, than the effect I helped render, which I hope was not. The world may be stingy with appreciation in general, but I do not think you can hope to counterbalance that single-handed, although you seem determined to try."

"I believe your calculations have omitted to factor your intentions, which surely deserve some say." Mrs. Addison shrugged her soft shoulders negligently. "But I do not wish to bore you, and you have warned me that I approach this defile at a perilous clip. Do you find that appreciation is such a rare commodity, then?"

She raised her eyebrows and said, "The way people are unwilling to part with it, I think the philosopher who could measure its price would be wise enough to spin the sun in his hand like a top." Bellew smiled. Of course society ladies were trained to be clever, if they had the brains for it, but he could not help admiring her nevertheless. "But I wanted to tell you, I have begun making some inquiries about your Lieutenant Masterson."

Bellew straightened. He knew she would have put the matter differently if she'd had solid information to offer, but his heart quickened in his breast all the same.

"Is there any word?" He rubbed his thumbnail against the arm of his chair, running its edge around the loop of a carved scroll.

"I haven't had a response. I went to Mr. Loring directly. I do not know whether he will be as responsive to my request as General Howe was to General Washington's, but I hardly knew how else to go about the matter."

"I wrote to Mr. Loring," Bellew said. "I have received no answer."

"We know the date when Lieutenant Masterson was taken, of course, but we do not know the destination, which complicates things. If you have any further information, any little thing you might be able to remember –"

"They said they were taking him to a ship. The guard suggested that, at any rate."

"Do you know which one?"

Bellew shook his head, flattening his mouth. Mrs. Addison shook her head. "Well, la! They must have a record of him somewhere, and as long as we can find enough guards who are able to read, we'll find him. General Howe has no desire to see officers thrown in with enlisted men. You've met him, now. I'm sure you agree with me."

"Of course," Bellew murmured. He did not think that the matter of officers and enlisted men together was too important when held against the treatment that the enlisted men were receiving, but if it worked, he would use it. He had seen so many men die in the sugar house, their bodies removed like sacks of spoiled potatoes. But that could not have happened to Masterson. He put it out of his mind. Masterson had to be all right.

And what about Cowles, and the other men Bellew had convinced to sign on? No – that was something else he had to put out of his mind. Not to forget it. But not to let it weigh him down so that he could not move. He served nothing and no one if he paralyzed himself that way.

"I'm sorry to have brought it up. I should have waited until I knew something sure," Mrs. Addison said, frowning slightly. "I did not mean to make you unhappy by the remembrance. I'm sure it will turn out well at last. Is he a very good friend of yours?"

Bellew took a breath and composed himself. "He and Captain O'Malley are my best friends in the world. I would gladly trade places with Lieutenant Masterson to effect his freedom, although I suppose the regulars have little enough reason to fear my liberty that they should desire to end it at this juncture. I suppose I have nothing to offer for Lieutenant Masterson at all," he added bitterly. "I have nothing but my desire."

"But surely that's the main part of anything worth doing."

Bellew looked up, suddenly quite interested in meeting her eyes, but Mrs. Addison was staring at a stiff portrait of the late Mr. Merriwether that hung on the wall. Her lips were parted in concentration. Bellew's fingers tingled with the sudden memory of the softness of those lips from last night, the faint moistness of her tongue. It had been entirely innocent – he had only been teasing her about her strangely, delightfully girlish hesitation. To be afraid of a snapdragon, of all things! He rubbed his finger to make the sensation stop, but it only moved lower in his body. He shifted in his chair and straightened his jacket with a tug.

The soft noise broke her concentration, and Mrs. Addison glanced down. She smiled and leaned towards him. A shadow fell across her face, and one earring glittered red in the shade, like a dragon's eye. The change in position pressed the swell of her bosom higher. Bellew tried not to notice. Only she was so beautiful. He could never quite put that out of his mind, not when she was near. Her face was so close to his now that he did not dare to meet her eyes.

"What an *awful* painting," Mrs. Addison confided in a low, thrilling tone. She straightened again quickly and continued in her normal voice, "Well, Lieutenant Bellew, as nearly as I can tell, you seemed to make a favorable impression on everyone you met yesterday. Perhaps it might add some weight with General Howe if I mention that Lieutenant Masterson is a particular friend of yours. No, I don't think that could hurt."

Bellew swallowed. A sweet, bracing odor hung in the air. It seemed to come from Mrs. Addison's neck. He imagined the pads of her fingers pressing droplets of cologne on the fragile skin behind her ears. "I am a little leery of accepting favors from him. I would not like the matter to be seen in that light," he said uncomfortably. The space seemed cold and empty where her body had been a moment before. Bellew moved forward to the edge of his chair without realizing it until a moment later, when the hard rim bit into the back of his thighs.

"It wouldn't be a favor. It's just if they know you and like you, it helps them see matters in the proper perspective," Mrs. Addison answered with a sly smile. "Are you telling me you would accept imprisonment for Lieutenant Masterson, but you balk at asking a favor?"

"I – accept your correction," Bellew replied.

"As a personal favor?"

"No, madam, merely because you are in the right."

"So there are no favors involved, and you don't wish to make me beholden to you?"

"It would hardly be possible. But of course if there is any favor you wish, it would be my honor to grant it." As soon as he spoke, Bellew wasn't sure his words had come out properly. Had he just told Mrs. Addison that he wished to place her at a disadvantage? Of course he wanted to. Great God, if only he could learn to silence himself sometimes.

Mrs. Addison leaned back into the sofa cushions and fiddled with her ring, looking to the side and saying nothing. Bellew realized with a sinking heart that he'd come across as badly as he'd feared. "I did not mean that I thought there was any service you would need, let alone one that I would be a fit servant for," he began gently, but she interrupted him with a quick shake of her head.

"Well, you see, there is something, only it might seem odd that I'm asking you. We know each other so little. But I think we're friends, aren't we?"

"Yes, of course. You know more about me, I suppose, than most of my other friends do," Bellew answered. "And I feel I know a little about you. I can't imagine anything you would ask that I would find odd, I'm sure."

"Oh, la, I mean presumptuous, not imaginative," Mrs. Addison said with a flash of irritation that vanished as quickly as smoke. "I meant to offer it as another favor to you, only I must admit, Lieutenant Bellew, you've made me a little ashamed of myself, and I have to admit that it is you who would be performing a valued service to me. I would like to ask the favor of your company, if you can spare it, just for an afternoon or two for these next few weeks while we remain in Philadelphia. I know so few people who, well, who care for me at all and don't just wish to scrutinize me so that they can find something to judge, you understand, and honestly – I find it a little wearing sometimes, and I find it makes me rather sad, which is a perfectly useless emotion. I have Rachel, of course, she is such a dear, loyal thing, but it isn't quite the same as an equal. If she married properly, perhaps one day, she is clever enough to learn, but I couldn't bear to let her do that, so there it is. And here, we're going to see Dr. Franklin's house later this week, and it should be quite fascinating, but Rachel is going to be thoroughly distracted by that beau of hers, no matter what she says, and he by her, and I find I just get a little – desolate in circumstances like that. But if there's someone for me to talk to as well, the whole experience will be as delightful as it should."

"If Mr. Addison is too pressed by business, I would be honored to accompany you to Dr. Franklin's," Bellew said in surprise. He did not know what he had expected Mrs. Addison to ask of him, but surely never something as small and kind and humble as merely a friend to stand by her side. Addison sank in Bellew's estimation as rapidly as a stone dropping into the depths of the sea. To have such a wife as this, and to leave her to feel not only unprotected but unloved! And Miss Kolkhorst – she had a beau already, that pretty girl; somehow he felt forgotten and neglected at the news. He was not in a contest with the girl; it was silly of him. He had his own path to follow. A brief image flashed in his mind of taking Mrs. Addison in his arms and pressing his lips against her neck. How soft she would feel, how –

He swallowed. "And certainly I will accompany you also anywhere else, as you like," he continued. "There are few demands on my time here, as you know. I am bound by the terms of my parole not to engage in my professional capacity, and no matter what you say about General Howe's reception of me, I do not find people here clamoring for my presence too often. I must do what I can for Captain O'Malley's health and, if the heavens so will it, Lieutenant Masterson's, once we find him. But other than that, my time is entirely at your disposal, even if you were to ask something that was not so thoroughly agreeable and gratifying to me as this current request, and every other that you have made." Her arms were so slender; he knew her legs would be the same. Damn his thoughts. He could not afford to offend his only protector. For God's sake, he even owed her money. The humiliation. He curled his fingers around the armrest of his chair.

Mrs. Addison looked relieved. "You see, I knew you'd put it something like that," she laughed. "As if arranging an afternoon's outing were something out of an epic poem. That's why I had to be honest with you about my reasons, even if they are a little embarrassing. For goodness sake, it's the worst sensation, actually to be a little jealous of my maid for this silly passing flirtation of hers."

"I thought you said you couldn't bear for her to marry," Bellew answered with a smile. "Aren't you playing with fire by letting her see her friend?" He wondered who this gentleman of Miss Kolkhorst's could be.

"Oh well, nothing's going to come of it, especially not if she's prudent, we're gone so soon. And from what I've heard of Captain André, he's a regular enough favorite with the ladies that I don't suppose he's going to try anything precipitous with any particular one of them."

"Oh, it's Captain André? But what do you mean, what you've heard of him? I thought you knew Captain André pretty well," Bellew laughed. So that was what the two of them must have been talking about last night when Bellew had interrupted them – Mrs. Addison making sure that Captain André would not run off with Miss Kolkhorst, and Captain André reassuring her. And that was all Mrs. Addison had meant with her couplet on the foolishness of love. O'Malley had been wrong about that, too.

"Oh la, everyone knows Captain André, I am almost to the point of being offended that I met him only recently myself."

"He impressed me favorably – for an Englishman. But I think perhaps he's a bit fast for Miss Kolkhorst," Bellew said, frowning suddenly. "You're quite sure he won't do anything – er, that she might interpret as disrespectful?"

"I am sure that Rachel's woebegone look of wounded misery would be more than ample reproach to stop him dead in his tracks, if you've ever seen it."

"I have," Bellew answered. "It is a curiously effective defense."

Mrs. Addison smiled at him warmly, her eyes soft as if from her own heat.

Chapter 25

Rachel's first response was terror. General Lee took on a frightening, monstrous aspect in her mind, as if he were some sort of demon that might immolate her with a single bloody glare. And she could not think of anything but how to make him believe that she had not seen his secret. There was no hiding that she'd been in his room.

She rushed downstairs with the rag of dog waste in her outstretched hand and pretended to discover General Lee by accident as he sat with a newspaper in the drawing-room. Her face twisted in distress. "Oh, General Lee, one of the dogs – I'm airing out your room right now –"

He glanced up, scowling. His eyes flicked to the dirty rag and away again. "It's not one of the four horsemen, girl, it's a pile of shit. Clean it up and get on with it. That's your job. You left your damn bucket in the foyer." He went back to his reading.

Any other time, Rachel would have been angry, or mortified at the very least, to be spoken to in such a manner, but not now. Relief washed over her like a warm bath. He didn't care what she might have seen, although she supposed he had no reason to suspect that she'd been going through his papers.

But as her fright subsided, inch by inch, a harder, colder dread took its place. General Lee remained a traitor, and a dangerous one. Rachel had seen a steady correspondence between Lee and both Valley Forge and York, where the Congress now sat, so she knew he could not have openly switched sides – and that he remained vested with the full confidence of both the rank and file and the highest echelons of the rebellion. The threat he posed was immense, and the information she had stumbled upon too important and too volatile to keep to herself. But there were so few people she could trust, and so few people who might be able to do anything about it.

Only one, really.

But Mrs. Addison did not believe her. "What? Rachel, were you snooping? No, dear, that's quite impossible – General Lee, whatever his personal deficiencies, has come down too hard and too plain on the side of independency to think of switching back now. He even insulted the

King. Oh, I mean, a lot of people do that, but General Lee insulted the King to his face. I don't think he's going to throw his lot in with his birthplace at this point."

"Perhaps he finds his prospects better with the regulars now that he is captured and has no means of preferment with the Continentals. I do not know. All I know is what I saw," Rachel insisted.

"Not quite, because what one sees and what one knows are two very different matters, dear, the latter requiring interpretation. Perhaps General Lee was engaging in a theoretical exercise. Perhaps he is trying to play a trick on General Howe, a sort of misdirection thing. Perhaps he is merely giving bad advice. Perhaps you even read the salutation incorrectly in your haste."

"I am sure I did not, and it did not look like bad advice. He has always maintained that untrained forces could not hold their own against the regulars in an open, pitched battle - you've heard him say it, ma'am! And so he recommends that this is exactly what General Howe forces the Continentals to face, over and over, battles in open fields, and -"

"Really, Rachel, when did you become a military strategist? Was it while you were mopping the floors, or while you were putting up my hair? Really. Are you honestly trying to tell me that you understand every word you read, so that you can instruct the world about it?"

"Well - no."

"There, you see, dear? I think any one of my explanations makes a great deal more sense, and I offered you three." Mrs. Addison softened visibly. "Now, I don't like General Lee any more than you do, but calling him a traitor is the sort of thing that gets whispered around and heats men's blood up and generally involves duels, and I know the last thing you want is to get someone killed over a few foolish, thoughtless words."

Rachel murmured her concession, but she did not feel sure of it. A great deal more men could die of treachery than could perish in any number of duels, which hardly ever killed anyone anyway. Rachel had hoped the matter might be taken care of quietly - a word to Mrs. Addison's father passed discreetly to General Washington's ear. Nothing would have to be done or said openly, if the rebellion only knew not to put confidence any longer where it was not deserved. It was not as though

General Lee were leaving Philadelphia any time soon or, by Rachel's understanding, ever, until the war was through.

But the path of soft influence was closed to her. She did not know what else she could do, other than pray that Mrs. Addison was correct, or that the matter would have no too harmful effect, due to General Lee's being on parole and not free to rejoin the army he had betrayed in his heart. Rachel placed more faith in the latter. Mrs. Addison's theories seemed too tenuous and at odds with what Rachel knew of General Lee's character – he seemed to have no fixed principle other than a hunger for recognition, and to make other people feel small.

When she stole into his room again later to see whether she might make more sense of the document by a closer perusal, she could not find it. Perhaps he had sent it already; or cast it into the fire, if it were nothing but an exercise of which he had tired. Perhaps it was locked in a drawer for safe-keeping. She could not know. But at last she could stop trying to make herself respect the man. That at least she was sure of. And she would try to warn Lieutenant Bellew not to place his fortunes at General Lee's disposal. He might not believe her any more than Mrs. Addison had, but Rachel would find a way somehow.

She was almost glad, almost, that Lieutenant Bellew did not visit the Broad Street mansion that week, where he might fall deeper under General Lee's sway, although it surprised her a little that he did not try to renew his acquaintance with Mrs. Addison after the charming evening they had spent together. She did not know whether to be more pleased or disappointed that it must have been a mere trifle to him – that he had exerted himself to be amiable only out of duty. It had felt to Rachel that they'd shared more than that, in their conversation and their dance. But that must be only because she was so inexperienced and because – well, because she had wanted so badly for it to mean more. And she had rather hoped that she might be able to make some small impression under her own name, if he would only come again. But he did not.

She found herself looking forward to the promised visit with Captain André, which Mrs. Addison assured her had been finalized for Thursday afternoon. Mrs. Addison had not taken her along when she went out on Wednesday, and Rachel badly wanted to get out of the house. She did not know how she had managed to have tense relations with almost everyone inside – Mr. Addison had never been particularly fond of her and had not grown more so since she'd interrupted his game, General Lee positively despised her and Rachel was now half-terrified of him, Mrs. Rimini was friendly as always but Rachel could not, could not forgive her for the indiscretions with Mr. Addison, the dogs were constantly underfoot and soiling or breaking things. She would have liked to spend more time with Jacob and Abraham, but she knew to her regret that they were never entirely at their ease when she was near. What a terrible mess she'd made of everything. It was difficult even to concentrate on her work, which used to bring her such peace.

"Come along, Rachel. The carriage is ready. Here, dry your hands first."

Rachel looked up in surprise, wiping her damp skin obediently with the rag she held. "It isn't half past one yet – if we take the carriage, we'll be early," she said. She would not have minded showing up early, and she was sure Captain André would not object, but it hardly seemed polite.

"Oh, I thought we'd bring Lieutenant Bellew along, he's got so little to do here," Mrs. Addison remarked off-handedly, and Rachel's blood gave a painful jolt that left her dizzy. "Besides, I've got some news for him." She tapped a folded letter against her hand like a fan.

"What is it?" Rachel asked. Her heart was still beating fast, which made it too easy to turn anticipation into foreboding. She clutched the rag tightly.

Mrs. Addison lowered her eyelids and tilted her head to the side. She looked peculiarly satisfied, not worried in the slightest.

"He and Captain O'Malley are being traded," she said.

"Traded! Already – so soon?"

"Well, he and Captain O'Malley are pretty small fish in the army, as you know, and that makes them a favor painlessly granted. Apparently my father made a special request of it. Twenty-odd assorted lieutenants and captains and I think an occasional colonel here or there are being exchanged this time, it's a routine thing, you know, with the enlisted men and the lower echelons of command. Most often it's catch as catch can, and they're swapped like marbles – but father asked General Washington to name Lieutenant Bellew and Captain O'Malley particularly. So it's all but done, and they'll be free to rejoin the army. Or join it in the first place, I suppose."

"Oh, Mrs. Addison, how wonderful – oh, you don't know what this will mean to him! Oh, you really are his angel," Rachel cried. Freedom, and freedom to fight, would return his entire life to him.

Mrs. Addison smiled and shrugged. "I can't say I had anything to do with it. I haven't had time, as you know. But it seems that father thought there was something in my making a particular inquiry about these two gentlemen – or perhaps he merely thought they were owed some recompense for the injustice of their treatment. Father tends to think that way," she mused.

Rachel could hardly contain herself on the brief ride to Mrs. Merriwether's house, and she was so excited she hardly noticed the sway of the carriage under Bellew's weight as he climbed inside, managing to make a bow as he did so. He appeared a little confused at the raw force of the joy shining on the two faces that greeted him.

"I expect this will be highly diverting," he said hesitantly.

Then Mrs. Addison gave him the news, telling him he'd hear it officially in a day or two, only she couldn't wait. And Lieutenant Bellew looked stunned, and then he offered all the proper thanks and gratitude, and Mrs. Addison seemed even more pleased than she had before. But Rachel saw something else in his eyes beyond happiness and relief. Perhaps because she was not part of the conversation, she had more liberty to observe in peace. A shade hovered over his expression, a certain infinitesimal slowness in his smiles and responses, and she knew something troubled him that he felt unable to say.

"Excuse me," she said timidly. Lieutenant Bellew and Mrs. Addison looked up in surprise, as if they had forgotten she was there. The sound of the wheels and the horses' hooves almost drowned out her voice. She swallowed and spoke louder. "Is Captain O'Malley well enough yet to return to service, I hope?"

A brief smile flickered over Lieutenant Bellew's face. "No, not quite, although I'm sure he can recuperate at the army's winter quarters as well as he can here. He'll be fit well before the spring campaign." He turned back to Mrs. Addison. "I feel somewhat awkward, though, presenting myself as an officer without a company, what little we had of ours being wholly imprisoned."

"I'm sure it's not the first time it's happened. I imagine they'll find a place to reassign you, and gladly. A surplus of soldiers is hardly their main concern."

They arrived at the High Street house, a tall, neat, narrow building of stone, shortly after two. A small manservant opened the door and took their cloaks, and Captain André appeared while the servant was still hanging them. "Delighted, delighted!" he exclaimed, bowing. "And I've just this moment finished setting up the experiment I wish to show you. It took a bit of climbing," he added with a grin. "But perhaps you'd like to see the home first? Or I should offer you some refreshment." He glanced at Lieutenant Bellew and then at Rachel; she read a flash of curious sympathy in his eyes, but he was far too clever a person to let anyone else see it.

Everyone had eaten recently, so they preferred the tour. Rachel found the home well-organized and comfortable, but in the main hardly remarkable except for the occasional strange piece of equipment that attested to the genius of its inventor, glass globes and tubes and sharpened bits of metal and wood whose purpose she could not begin to guess. She understood now why Captain André had affirmed he could make neither heads nor tails of most of it.

Their host looked a bit tired and sated, as if he'd stayed up too late eating and still felt heavy from it. He wore his scarlet uniform. When he first saw Lieutenant Bellew, his hand had moved to his jacket as if he somewhat regretted the sartorial choice; but he recovered himself quickly. Not until Lieutenant Bellew and Mrs. Addison had their attention diverted by a well-executed portrait of Dr. Franklin did Captain André bend his head and venture a few words quiet enough that only Rachel could hear.

"The lady invited our gallant southern friend, I take it?" Rachel nodded. Captain André quirked his mouth and murmured, "My dear Miss Kolkhorst, my wonder only increases at the complexity of your relationships. I feel quite an amateur."

After Captain André had shown them the rest of the premises, he led the party into a broad, cluttered study he had passed over earlier and now presented as the tour's culmination. "Forgive the disarray, please – I do not know well enough what is important and what is not to Dr. Franklin, and so I've ordered it not to be cleaned, except for dusting." He directed their attention to a table at the center of the room. "Here, this is what I was climbing for." A long, fine thread of black silk dangled from the ceiling. At the end of it hung a round little piece of burnt cork with eight short threads dangling from its body. "This, as I'm sure you can discern immediately, is supposed to be a spider," Captain André laughed. A length of wire had been fixed in the table and stood upright a few inches away from the spider. Captain André tapped it. "I had a deuce of a time figuring out what this was supposed to be for, until I read a copy of Dr. Franklin's pamphlet."

"Well, what is it for, then?" Mrs. Addison inquired.

Captain André held up a finger. "I would satisfy your curiosity at once, except that I thought some of the preparations might also be of interest. Before our little spider golem shows us his tricks, we must first gather a quantity of that object of our invisible host's investigations, a jar of electrical fire."

"You can pour it into a jar? Where do you pour it from?" Rachel said, pressed against the table and eyeing the little spider. Mrs. Addison stood at her elbow. Lieutenant Bellew kept his distance a few feet back from the table, his expression still troubled. He had been quite silent throughout the tour.

"Well – I'm not entirely sure. But I know how it's done. Here, this is the Leyden jar." He gestured to a shelf where Rachel saw several half-silvered glass jars with cork lids. A thick wire ran through each stopper and into a mass of dark granules that partly filled each jar. The top of each wire was rounded into a knob.

"Is that what electrical fire looks like when it is still?" Rachel said in amazement.

Captain André grinned. "I'm afraid that's only lead, dear."

"Doesn't it leave less room for the electricity?"

"Now, if you're going to start asking me too many questions, you are going to get bored with my answers, which all run along the lines of 'I haven't the faintest idea'." He took a Leyden jar down from the shelf and handed it to Rachel. "Here. Hold it by the bottom, and remember not to touch the top." Rachel followed his instructions, although she rather wished he'd picked some other assistant. "No, don't worry, it doesn't have any electricity yet. Just hold onto it a bit while I – pump this interesting fluid out of the ether, or whatever it is this contraption is supposed to do."

Captain André turned to a side table that held a strange device made of brass, leather, and a round glass globe. The globe was attached to an axis attached to a crank, and Captain André, smiling in acknowledgment of how strange his actions must seem, turned the crank so that the globe spun and rubbed against a leather pad. A long brass rod protruded from the other side of the globe.

The party watched in silence. The crank squeaked rhythmically. Nothing else seemed to happen. "Is it working?" Mrs. Addison asked at last, fidgeting with her fan.

"I haven't the faintest – well, why don't I say 'unquestionably, all is going according to plan' instead," Captain André answered with a grin. "All right, Miss Kolkhorst. Mind you don't shift your grip on that jar, and touch the top of the wire to the brass rod. That's it. Hold it there a moment, and we'll be sure our jar is good and full."

Rachel held the Leyden jar gingerly, expecting something awful to happen. But nothing happened whatsoever, unless Rachel counted a slight snap in the air she was not really sure she'd heard. The jar did not grow hot. It did not get heavy. It seemed as though Rachel were doing nothing but perform some strange pantomime, and that the existence of this electrical fire was nothing but a shared joke, like children pretending to hold dragon treasure in their hands.

"I think that's gotten it," she muttered when her cheeks started to grow warm with embarrassment.

"Do you? Well, then, it must be so. All right, let's see what our spider golem thinks of all this. Bring the jar over to his table, and set it right about here." Captain André rapped a finger against the wood, and Rachel deposited the Leyden jar gingerly on the precise spot he indicated. She pulled herself back quickly.

The spider golem flew through the air, racing towards her. Rachel squeaked and threw up her hands to protect her face, and Mrs. Addison drew in her breath sharply. Captain André laughed, covering it with a cough and placing the back of his hand over his mouth. Lieutenant Bellew took a worried half-step forward.

But Rachel was not the spider's goal. The little golem landed daintily on the exposed wire of the Leyden jar, bending its tiny thread legs with charming delicacy, and then it sprang back in the direction it had come, lighting with equal grace upon the vertical wire. The spider then sprang for the Leyden jar again and repeated the performance over and over again, bouncing tirelessly between the wire and the jar as if there were no occupation in the world as delightful as this dance.

They watched it in wonder. The spider bounced from jar to wire and wire to jar. It did not do anything else, but Rachel felt she could watch it for a thousand years and not be any less astonished.

"How perfectly exquisite," Rachel breathed at last, when she felt sure enough of the magic that she didn't fear a whisper might dispel it. "How utterly marvelous. It is the most amazing thing I have ever seen." She could not imagine how the electric fire – this fictive substance made by turning empty globes and holding empty jars – could show such a definite will and purpose, but she could not deny the evidence of her eyes.

"I thought you would like it. I don't mind telling you I wracked my brains a bit trying to figure out what would entertain you the most, so I'm personally gratified not to have been a failure." Captain André glanced up and smiled. "But I am afraid my calculations were predicated upon a female audience. I don't seem to have amused Lieutenant Bellew as thoroughly. We can do another experiment, if you like. There are slightly more violent ones perhaps better suited to a masculine sensibility. Although they do involve a modest portion of pain." Rachel glanced up then and saw that Bellew wore a frown, and he seemed as though his thoughts had been far away, because he returned only slowly to acknowledge Captain André's remark.

Bellew smiled and shook his head. "Thank you, sir, but not on my account. I find the spider golem as fascinating as it is inexplicable to me. I apologize if I seem distant, but that is due merely to preoccupation. And your splendid electrical spider has distracted me from as much of it as humanly possible, I assure you."

Mrs. Addison straightened abruptly and tilted her head, widening her eyes and looking directly at Captain André. Rachel frowned, the effect was so contrived. Mrs. Addison took great pains over every detail of her appearance and demeanor; she could hardly be unaware that this expression of hers seemed like a mockery. "Oh, Captain André, the fault is mine," Mrs. Addison cooed. A certain stiffness crept into Captain André's smile, and he flashed a quick, unreadable glance at Rachel. "I learned that Lieutenant Bellew was going to be traded and I could not help telling him so on the way over. I did not think, I am sorry to say, that it might be a bit awkward between the two of you." A silence hung in the room for the barest of instants. The spider bounced merrily along, content to be forgotten. Rachel almost doubted her ears, that Mrs. Addison had brought up the matter directly, and spoken of it in such a light tone. She knew that Mrs. Addison took Lieutenant Bellew's welfare to heart, so if there was hostility of some sort, it must have been with Captain André as its object. And surely there was no reason for that! Lieutenant Bellew blinked and frowned, and suddenly seemed ill at ease, where he had been only troubled before.

Captain André, however, took it in good part. He bowed slightly to Mrs. Addison, unruffled as ever, just as if he thought she were genuine in her apology. "But, madam, there need be no awkwardness. A soldier generally meets his end with a bullet – or he hopes to, at least. If it's shot fairly and by an honorable man, all the better. Lieutenant Bellew and I have no quarrel over the issue of fatality. In my opinion, at least; I will defer to my worthy opponent to express his own opinion of the matter." Mrs. Addison smiled but did not quite look him in the eye.

"You have stated it as fully and exactly as I could possibly wish," Lieutenant Bellew replied somberly. A slight chill passed over Rachel. "I – have come to understand that it is ungentlemanly to prosecute a personal animosity where none exists on its own merits, as none does here. Duty prevents us from engaging in our political and philosophical conflict at the moment, and politeness, I think, prevents us from discussing it. I hope I have not been an ungracious guest."

"Far from it. I merely hoped to be an equally good host."

"Sir, you have not only shown me marvels I could not imagine, you have been amiable in manner and impeccable in conduct. You leave me only to wish that you were a countryman of mine."

"Ah, but in my opinion, I am," Captain André laughed. "Only this is the topic we weren't going to discuss."

Chapter 26

The rest of the afternoon passed without incident. Lieutenant Bellew seemed to have decided he liked Captain André after their exchange about dying by bullet and made more of an effort to be sociable, although he still stuck close to Mrs. Addison's side. Rachel shared barely five words with him. Actually, it was precisely five words. "Excuse me, please," followed two hours later by, "Good day." Nine words if she counted his responses.

Her feelings about his obvious friendship with Mrs. Addison were so mixed that she did not dare examine them, but she could not deny the despondency that crept over her heart, slowing her movements and making her thoughts cold and sluggish. The next day, when Jacob brought her a folded note sealed with a hasty blob of red wax, informing her with wide eyes that the boy who'd left it had asked Jacob to deliver it to Rachel personally and not anyone else in the house, her heart sank further. Whether Captain André was cross with her or sympathetic over Mrs. Addison's behavior, Rachel did not feel she could face it yet. She tucked the letter into the pocket of her skirt.

Jacob eyed her cautiously and took a hesitant breath before he went on, "Miss Rachel? I kind of got the impression they was some hurry about it." So Rachel took out the letter and slid her thumb beneath the wax, turning so that the light of the window would fall on the page.

My Very Dear Miss Kolkhorst,

Please forgive me for the presumption, both for intruding upon you while you doubtless have important responsibilities to discharge and for the request I am about to make. But there are certain matters I do not feel I can entrust to the page, and while I confess they primarily concern me, I suspect they are of some interest to you as well. If I might ask the favor of a brief interview with you; it will require no more than a few minutes, I hope. I am waiting outside now at the corner. Forgive again, please, the informal surroundings I ask, but delicacy prevents me from wishing to be overheard at either your home or mine. If the time is inopportune, as I expect it is, but you find another would be acceptable, any hour you set will find me waiting for you. If you feel you cannot accede to my request, or reply to it, I understand fully, and am well aware that the only fault lies with myself, for asking something so strange, and on the basis of such limited acquaintance.

I remain yr. svt.,

S. Bellew

Bellew.

She read the signature twice and even stroked it with her finger to be sure it was not a trick of her mind. The paper seemed to grow warm, and she could feel the ghostly presence of Lieutenant Bellew's hands where he must have touched it. Rachel's heart soared from the abyss to the clouds in a single dizzying moment that left her breathless. He had written to her – she gloried in it, but why? Did he mean to tell her he had some fonder feelings towards her than he had been able to say before – no, she could hardly expect that. But what else could it be? What other secret might two people share, who knew each other so little?

"Is it trouble?" Jacob asked worriedly.

Rachel turned to face him, her eyes shining. "It isn't inopportune at all – not in the slightest!" she exclaimed, hurrying for the door before realizing that her reply to poor Jacob had made no sense. She checked herself long enough to remember to put on her jacket – perhaps the conversation might take a little more time than Lieutenant Bellew thought! – and rushed outside into the clear light of day.

She did not see him. Rachel stopped upon the threshold and looked around, puzzled. A maid from the house next door walked down the street. Rachel knew her a little, because she had told Rachel how to clean silk, and they greeted each other pleasantly. No one else seemed to be about. It was too early for the fine people who lived on this street to be up. Sparse fragments of clouds scudded across the sky, reminding Rachel of Mrs. Addison's unfinished painting. Had Lieutenant Bellew left already – had she taken too long? But before her mind could turn to darker imaginings, she saw him at the far corner by an unlit street-lamp, a distant form in his plain black suit. He must have been watching her closely, because when she turned in his direction, he lifted his hand slightly, although he did not move towards her. Rachel smiled, although he couldn't see it. He certainly had taken pains not to be overheard, or even seen.

She hurried towards him.

Lieutenant Bellew bowed when she came close. "Thank you for coming. I wasn't sure you would," he admitted. His worn black cloak looked a little rusty under the full light of the sun, and Rachel noticed that his hat showed a band inside by the brow that had been worn shiny and smooth from too much use and too little attention. She knew how to roughen the felt and brush it out so that it would seem almost new again. She wished so badly she could take care of him a little, but it was a sweet pang, not a painful one, and she delighted in these small signs of his imperfection. It was not, she decided, so much that they reduced his elevation and brought him closer to her position, even if she had thought so before. It was that they gave her a reason to touch him - not literally, of course, and she almost blushed at her thought, but rather, a reason to have something to do with him, because there were still these small matters that he required.

"Of course," she murmured, and then, growing bolder, added with a shy smile, "Wouldn't you have come, if it had been I who had written that note?" She watched him carefully.

Bellew's eyebrows flicked upward. "Why - of course. But it's a different question for a woman," he said. "I'll get straight to the matter - it's cold, and I hate to keep you outside." But words seemed to fail him a moment. Rachel did not mind. Only she wished she could communicate to him somehow that nothing he would say would meet an unfavorable response - that he need not worry about it so.

Lieutenant Bellew pressed his lips together, and instead of asking what he wanted, he said, "Would you like to walk a little while? I promise not to take you far, only the exercise might prevent you from taking a chill."

She found his hesitation charming, and she would have walked with him to ends of the earth over splinters of steel if he had asked it. "I think a walk would be very pleasant," Rachel said in a high, light voice she hardly recognized as her own. They set off towards the west. The wind, so fierce in the high reaches of the sky, was gentle near the ground, and it only barely touched their faces.

When they had traveled a few dozen yards in silence, Lieutenant Bellew found his tongue at last. "I hoped, Miss Kolkhorst, that you could advise me on how best to extricate myself from a difficulty," he said, keeping his eyes to the ground. "I am keenly appreciative of Mrs. Addison's many efforts on my behalf - heaven knows I have done little enough to deserve them - why are the Addisons in Philadelphia now, if I may ask?" he asked suddenly, turning to her with a frown. "It seems terribly out of keeping with Mrs. Addison's sensibilities and preferences."

This seemed an odd beginning to an avowal. "They never told me exactly," she replied evasively. "I believe Mr. Addison has some business." That was even more evasive. Mr. Addison had indeed done some business with General Howe, but that had come up unexpectedly, although Rachel supposed it was not entirely a surprise, given Mr. Addison's line of business. But the real reason the Addisons had come to Philadelphia had been simpler than that, merely Mrs. Addison's desire for good accommodation and good company. And perhaps, Rachel admitted to herself ruefully, Mr. Addison's desire for good accommodation and bad company.

"Ah," Lieutenant Bellew replied, nodding to himself as if this answered the matter to his satisfaction. "Well, I suppose it is all the more problematic for Mrs. Addison to exert herself for her country's cause in her current circumstances, which makes my debt, and my difficulty, all the greater. The thing is, although I very much value the honor and the opportunity, I cannot - you see, I cannot accept being traded at this juncture."

His words struck Rachel with the force of an earthquake. She almost forgot her disappointment in her astonishment. No, there was no disappointment, not really; she had known that his affection for her, if any, was nothing more than polite and that she could hardly expect an avowal - of course not. And he was confiding in her, after all - that meant something.

But that he would give up being exchanged - that cut against the grain of everything she knew about him, or felt she knew, and Rachel could not understand it.

"What?" she said, stopping mid-step and turning to face him. "I thought - I beg your pardon, Lieutenant Bellew, but my understanding was that your service and the cause meant everything to you - that your beliefs and your desire for advancement found common ground in your service in the army. And this imprisonment - however gentle it has become – prevents you from – why, it prevents you from everything you hold most dear! How can you not want the trade!"

A knot of muscle appeared at Bellew's jaw as Rachel spoke, and she fell silent. "I cannot accept it, nevertheless," he said in a low voice. "Would the heavens that I could. Captain O'Malley should be well enough to ride within a week, if Mrs. Addison – if she still doesn't object to the loan of the horse. I do not aim to tell him of my decision to stay behind, and I hope you will not let it be known. He might give me a direct order, which I could not refuse, or, worse, he might stay with me, and what needs to be done can be performed by one man as well as two."

"What do you intend – no, Lieutenant Bellew, you must tell me – you must not do anything foolish," Rachel cried, drawing closer to him in alarm. She remembered too well the futility and the fear of her rock-throwing. What had that served, after all, but to put herself in danger? It had helped no one. If she had had a gun, though – and then Rachel remembered what a sharp aim Lieutenant Bellew had. But his rifle was doubtless gone, and a regular musket would not serve as well – did Lieutenant Bellew mean to assassinate Captain Cunningham, or Mr. Loring, or a thousand other worthy objects, out of revenge, or a misguided zeal to help the other prisoners? Rachel felt certain that the removal of one man, or two, would not suffice to clean out the corruption, and how many could Lieutenant Bellew reasonably hope to take before he was captured, and hanged for certain?

He understood her meaning immediately. "What? No, Miss Kolkhorst, I am willing to sacrifice my life, but I promise you I hold it dear enough not to throw it away to no purpose. I am not hazarding my life at all, I think. Only something dearer – but I must." He nodded to himself. "I must. When I was released from prison," he continued more slowly, "I felt a great hesitation at being selected for preferential treatment when so many others remained in that squalid pit. I cannot express the horror of it – the prison, I mean. It was as if we were all dead men forced to remain conscious as our bodies rotted. I – forgive me. I should not speak so bluntly to a woman; only I must explain why it struck me as so terrible simply to walk away from my comrades in that place, leaving them behind while I enjoyed the open skies and clean and ample food, and friendship, and – and even entertainments. I did not realize then all that would be waiting for me, beyond the fresh air and light, but even then, it was hard. And I might not have been able to endure the shame of it if the other men had not desired me so fervently to take my freedom, to take the modest comforts they were denied, and to resume the fight on their account. Some of those men are surely dead by now. A day hardly passed that at least one did not die." He rubbed his thumb against his chin and looked away, as if distracted by unhappy memories.

"But your arguments are all for the opposite conclusion than you have drawn," Rachel said.

Lieutenant Bellew smiled and seemed almost amused, though too tired and too worried to laugh. "I beg your pardon – it is a habit of thought I have. I had not previously considered its rhetorical effect. The point I am trying to approach is that it was all but impossible for me to leave those men behind, even though fully aware that I could not improve their conditions nor effect their release. There will be prisoners on both sides for the length of the conflict; every honorable war has them."

"There is nothing honorable in the abuse of captured men – there isn't!" Rachel said. "When you're fighting, every man has an equal chance – in prison, the power of the guards is absolute in every respect. And the greater the power one holds, the less one is permitted to do."

"I agree, but the regulars are unlikely to consult our moral views in the prosecution of their conduct. However, American prisoners exist in plenty now, and there will be many more besides before it's over." He held up his hand. "I understand, you feel I'm still arguing against my conclusion. I just find it difficult – I am trying to explain that the problem is not that my comrades suffer in prison, no matter how hard I take their condition. I do not like it, but I can bear it, because I must. The problem is my friend. There is a different duty owed there."

"But Captain O'Malley will feel entirely deserted if you do not accompany him, and he should!"

"It isn't Captain O'Malley. It's Lieutenant Masterson. I cannot abandon him."

Rachel fell silent and bit her lip. She could not meet his eyes. Her mind seethed with half-thoughts. She had never wanted to tell him about his friend's fate for fear of hurting him and destroying his hopes – she always prayed that he would find out some other way, and by some other messenger – but now it seemed that Lieutenant Bellew was going to discard every dream and ambition he had for himself on a fruitless hunt for a man who had been dead almost a month. She had to tell him. Only, what would he think of her, for not having spoken out before?

Lieutenant Bellew gave a resigned half-shrug. "I know he did not make himself a favorite with you, but that was not all of the man, or even the greater part – he was just a little drunk, and a little thoughtless."

"You misunderstand me," Rachel said in a small voice. "Lieutenant Masterson is in my prayers, every night. I bear him no grudge. The matter between us was a minor thing – and when he apologized, it became an irrelevant one."

"Well. I cannot leave Philadelphia until I know where he is at least," Lieutenant Bellew replied. "He would not leave me in the same circumstances. If Captain O'Malley and I were found to be officers, despite our incomplete commissions, Lieutenant Masterson must be found the same, and I will see that he is treated accordingly, even if I cannot see that he is freed. Mrs. Addison has been good enough to make inquiries, but nothing has come of them. It is as though he vanished into smoke. I suspect one of these half-literate redcoat guards has made a hash of his name in the records, and it may be a deuce of a time untangling it. I would not – it is a ticklish thing to ask, but perhaps your friend Captain André would know how I might go about my inquiries more effectively." He looked at her hopefully.

"I don't know him very well," Rachel whispered.

"It would be a difficult request. I know that," Lieutenant Bellew said gently. "Never mind it, if you cannot. This concern is mine personally, and I do not mean to lay the burden upon anyone else. The favor I meant to ask of you, and that I hope will be within your power, was merely advice. I will need Mrs. Addison's assistance, or at least that of her father, in order to have my name struck from the trades, and this obliges me to inform her that I am declining the most precious generosity of all she has offered me, which I am deeply afraid will cause offense where I least desire to do so. I have not known her as long as you have, and I hope you might have some insight as to how best I should approach the topic."

"I believe –" Rachel pressed her mouth shut and shook her head once, like a half-trained horse trying to rid itself of its bit. She had started to say that the candid explanation for his motives Lieutenant Bellew had just shared with Rachel would surely suffice with Mrs. Addison, only Rachel was not sure any more that this was true. She had been thinking, since yesterday afternoon, that Mrs. Addison's generosity had proved not to be a bodiless, angelic thing constructed of pure shining morality, but did after all possess both claws and teeth. Not terrible ones; but like a cat's, they could still do harm. And the gratitude that Mrs. Addison expected in return for her efforts would not likely prove satisfactory coming by occasional letter from Philadelphia. Rachel supposed that Mrs. Addison probably was looking forward to having friends at Valley Forge, undemanding and uncritical friends – and if Lieutenant Bellew meant to stay here instead, Mrs. Addison's disappointment might very well be acute.

Rachel did not love her mistress less for the discovery of this flaw. The burden it placed upon Rachel was meaningless, because Rachel desired nothing but to be devoted and useful and near. But she recognized the awkwardness of Lieutenant Bellew's position, with his more substantial responsibilities beyond amusing a demanding woman.

"You might – you might soften the blow a bit if – Lieutenant Bellew, why don't you accept the trade and then resign your commission? You would be free then to stay in Philadelphia as long as you needed, and free to join the army again once you – well, whatever comes of your search."

"I could not do that, upon my life," Lieutenant Bellew replied, shaking his head. "I understand your plan, and it is a sound one, and well reasoned – with the single exception that I cannot turn my back on my country in her hour of greatest need."

"But you wouldn't be – you would only be postponing the matter until you were able to attend to it properly."

"If I take the trade and resign, the Continental Army has given the redcoats one more man than it receives in return, and I could not bear the sight of my own face if I were to allow that to happen, nor would I expect anyone else to."

"Only until you rejoined! But, it's – oh, Lieutenant Bellew. Is Lieutenant Masterson so dear to you?" Rachel said, wringing her hands.

"He is like a younger brother. I assure you nothing less would have me postpone my duties, or disappoint my benefactress. Here, you give me little enough heart by looking that way – how can I expect to smooth the waters with Mrs. Addison when you look so grieved? Is my case so hopeless?"

"Yes," Rachel said. "Forgive me, please. Oh, forgive me if you can, if you can try, I never wanted you to know, but I can't - it isn't Mrs. Addison I'm worried about, it's - I never wanted you to know!"

"Know what?" Lieutenant Bellew asked, frowning.

"That Lieutenant Masterson, bless his soul always, is, has been, he's dead. And I do pray for him every night, Lieutenant Bellew, I know you didn't believe me when I said it, but I do!"

Lieutenant Bellew paled and fell back a half-step, as if she had struck him. Silence hung between them. Rachel felt the cold suddenly, all over her body, and she wished more than anything that she were back inside - not just inside, but in her bed, under the covers, in the thickest blackness of the darkest night. But she was not. And she had to endure Lieutenant Bellew's terrible stare. It seemed almost as though he hated her.

"It is not a matter to be taken lightly, Miss Kolkhorst," he said at last, recovering himself, although his eyes remained hard. He rubbed the knuckle of his forefinger with his thumb, a gesture almost like pulling a rifle's trigger. "If you think Mrs. Addison will not endure my defection, say so directly - I will bear it."

"I am not lying about Lieutenant Masterson - I never lied about him, I only - just omitted to say what I knew," Rachel whispered. Her heart beat so quickly it seemed it would burst, only it drove no strength into her muscles. She felt so tired suddenly that she would gladly have lain down on the spot. Lieutenant Bellew's cold rage would not let her. It held her in her place like bands of iron.

"How could you possibly know this fact? Was Captain André a captain of guards? Or do you have other friends among them?"

"What - no! No, Lieutenant Bellew, you must - oh, God, why did I have to say anything!" Rachel cried in distress, but her agony did not soften him.

"I must know what you have to say," he replied, stiff with anger.

Rachel dropped her head. She could not bear to look in his eyes any longer. "As you wish. I was coming home late one night - oh, Lieutenant Bellew, you don't want to know, I promise you, you don't, only be sure that Lieutenant Masterson is at peace now -"

"If you have anything to say, speak," he said in a harsh voice.

Rachel swallowed. "Yes, I – yes. I was coming home late at night, this was a month ago, before I first saw you in the prison yard. I heard a, a sort of disturbance – men walking barefoot and praying, and I thought they might be able to tell me the way, because I had lost it. But when I found the procession, it was prisoners – and they had, it seemed to me they had suffered hard treatment, and there were, there were English guards driving them on, and I recognized Lieutenant Masterson at once, and I know it was him, because I called out his name and he responded to it, and he remembered who I was, and he begged my forgiveness for that foolish, trivial thing, how could he think I would hold it against him when – of course I told him I had forgiven him entirely and beseeched him to explain what they were doing, and a guard tried to drive me off, but I had to know, and Lieutenant Masterson told me – he told me that the guards had chosen six prisoners to be – to be hanged. And he was one of them. I couldn't do anything – and no one would help me, and no one seemed to understand later when I tried to – I gave him my handkerchief to hold so that he might feel that a friend, when the time came, a friend –" Rachel said, tears streaming down her face though she did not remember when she'd started crying. "It was all I could do. And he asked me to pray for him, and every night, every night, I do."

"They hanged him?"

Rachel looked up through her tears. Lieutenant Bellew did not seem angry any more. His face was blank, stunned.

"Yes," she whispered. "I have heard subsequently that – this is – a practice of theirs."

"Ah, God." Lieutenant Bellew clutched his head. "Masterson – let my punishment fall on my own shoulders, on me!" He struck himself hard on the breast with a closed fist. He seemed to have forgotten Rachel was there, nor even to be able to see her any more.

"I am so sorry," Rachel whispered miserably. Lieutenant Bellew's eyes glittered with unshed tears. For a moment she thought he had not heard her either, until he said, "I apologize, Miss Kolkhorst, I cannot see you home, I cannot, I must –" And then he walked away quickly, leaving Rachel alone.

Chapter 27

"It would only be a loan until we reach father's. I don't know why you're being so difficult, Robert. It seems inexplicably foolish to force Captain O'Malley and Lieutenant Bellew to find horses for themselves, and Captain O'Malley being unwell, when we'll have four merely tagging along and not doing any work."

Matters had been particularly tense between Mr. and Mrs. Addison over the past few days. Rachel was not sure of the immediate cause. Everything seemed to provoke a contest of wills. If Mr. Addison did not want to leave Philadelphia yet, he was certainly free to say so, or even to demand that they stay; but he did not.

Rachel had not seen or spoken to Lieutenant Bellew since their disastrous conversation the past Friday. She assumed that, with nothing in Philadelphia to hold him, Lieutenant Bellew had no remaining objection to the trade, and likely desired it more than ever. Mrs. Addison certainly seemed to think that Lieutenant Bellew was coming, and coming furthermore with their small party. But Rachel was not sure whether he would endure her company, even though the trip would not take more than a day and Rachel would be closeted inside the carriage for its duration.

If I were him, and I knew what Mr. Addison was saying behind my back, I would rather walk, Rachel thought. The distance between Philadelphia and Valley Forge was no more than about twenty miles. Depending on the roads, walking might take only half again as long. *And I would also rather walk than have to be within ten yards of someone I hated so much*, she added unnecessarily, remembering his cold glare and hasty departure. She had been tormenting herself this way often lately.

It had been wrong of her not to tell him about Masterson for so long. He had every right to feel tricked, cruelly so, by her.

"But perhaps we won't bring the spare horses," Mr. Addison replied, glancing across the room at General Lee. General Lee had managed to acquire a new dog, a fox-faced and -colored animal with an upswept curling tail and an amazingly fluffy coat. It looked like Rachel's image of a baby lion. General Lee doted on the creature with all the fervency of new love. This had prompted a jealous reaction from his greyhounds, and they'd turned singularly ill-tempered as well as ungovernable since the triumphal advent of the equally untrained Pomeranian. General Lee let the new dog rest its head on his lap and scratched its narrow head as it panted in pleasure, damp crumbs of cake spattering the fur around its mouth. "Charlie will need a horse when we're gone." General Lee grunted noncommittally.

"He's got that one from General Howe, perhaps you've forgotten, dear, since of course he hasn't needed it lately. But even if he did require a horse, he'd hardly require four –"

"Borrowing a horse is less certain than owning it, for one, and he has friends, dear, and not all of them have horses of their own, so yes, he might very well require four horses. He might not really be able to do without them. And he's not in a position to get them for himself." Mr. Addison's cheeks were flushed, Rachel was unsure whether from anger, or embarrassment at the emptiness of the position he seemed determined to hold, or both. Rachel had never heard him be so ridiculously impractical before – to give four horses to a man who didn't need them to spare himself the obligation of loaning two of those horses for a brief ride. She knew he didn't mean it. He was only, just as Mrs. Addison said, being difficult.

"Robert – you aren't thinking," Mrs. Addison said, a sharper edge creeping into her voice even as her smile sweetened. "Now, it goes without saying that I desire nothing less than to discommode General Lee, but I am sure his many friends will rise to the occasion to see that he does not want for whatever transportation he lacks. Of course we don't need the change of horses for Valley Forge, but we will desperately so when we leave for New-York. Coming up from the Carolinas was just so agonizing with only the one set that had to be rested all the time. Now, Robert, I'm sure you remember, it wasn't that long ago, and we talked about it, and decided to buy four horses here, since they would be available, and we simply won't leave them behind."

"You don't mean to give our horses to your pets, then?"

"Oh, don't be ridiculous. They're much too expensive, and we need them ourselves. Oh, Rachel – I forgot. Lieutenant Bellew returned the money. I have it in my room, on the dresser. Go and take it before I forget again, sweet. As soon as you've cleared away the tea things, I mean."

"Hope he didn't pay you in Continental dollars," General Lee remarked without looking up.

"I don't mind however it is denominated, sir," Rachel murmured. "I had intended the money as a gift, anyway."

"It is, if you've gotten Continentals in return," General Lee laughed. "The only dollar that's ever going to be worth a fig is a Spanish one."

"He paid in pound notes, General Lee," Mrs. Addison said. "Robert? We haven't quite settled this strangely intractable question of the one-day ride."

Rachel was glad, mostly, that Lieutenant Bellew's situation must have improved, if he was able to repay the eight pounds. But the money had been a slender thread joining them, even if Bellew had been unaware of its source. That thread was now gone. After so many fateful meetings and curious opportunities to be near and to know each other, it seemed that all that remained as a link between Rachel and Lieutenant Bellew was Mrs. Addison. Everything else had vanished. He had not likely sent the money by messenger, or else Rachel almost certainly would have known of it. Mrs. Addison must have seen him personally, and not mentioned it until now.

"Ah, so our charming young lieutenant returns these many gifts that women shower upon him."

"Well, if that was your concern, it's settled."

"Please don't put words into my mouth," Mr. Addison replied. "I don't want our horses being tired unnecessarily. I don't see why we should put them out."

"Animals are honest, Robert. It makes them easy prey for man, or woman," General Lee interposed in lugubrious tones, lifting his chin slightly. A smear of breakfast-egg lay across the stubble. The Pomeranian noticed this at the same time as Rachel did and licked his master's face enthusiastically. Rachel looked away to hide the expression in her eyes. General Lee was a scoundrel, and a fine one to sulk and whine about honesty. She was glad to leave him behind, and gladder that Lieutenant Bellew would soon be miles away and safe from the threat of his influence, and if his precious dogs swallowed him up, bones and all, the world would be a better place for it.

"Mr. Addison, sir, Captain O'Malley is recovering from dysentery, and the horses are not," Mrs. Addison said.

"Yes, dear, and Lieutenant Bellew has terribly sensitive feet or some such, I suppose. Only, you see, you have your pets and I have mine. And I've grown rather attached to my horse, in a way, and I'd rather not see a man I don't particularly like ride it."

"Robert, he rode the brown at the hunt, I don't think you've ridden Acorn even once – but very well, if that's all that concerns you, he'll ride my Buttercup instead."

General Lee grinned wolfishly to himself.

Rachel did not hear the rest, because Mrs. Addison had thankfully given her the excuse of going upstairs to retrieve the pound notes. She found them on the dresser, as promised, a sheaf of parchment folded into neat quarters. She smoothed them open carefully. The creases were light, and the notes showed no sign of repair, so they were fairly new. Lieutenant Bellew must have chosen the best-looking ones. She flipped through them absently, not admitting to herself that she wanted to touch where his hands had been. A five-pound note and three one-pound notes beneath it. The salutary reminder that *COUNTERFEITING IS DEATH* glared up at her from each of them.

She doubted the total sum she'd given had been exactly eight pounds, with the hodgepodge of currencies that she'd used to pay the landlady and the doctor and leave cash on hand, so maybe a few pennies' worth of her gift remained in Lieutenant Bellew's hands. She liked to think so. But she supposed it was good she had the money back. It represented almost all the ready money she owned, except only two Spanish milled dollar coins, a bent farthing, and a few pennies. Although of course she also had her *Essay on Man*, and all the clothes and things that Mrs. Addison had bought or given to her – so many of them now. Her jacket alone must have cost a great deal more than Rachel could have bought with her own supply of cash, and could probably be traded for a nice sum if necessary. Rachel folded the notes again and placed them slowly in her pocket.

General Lee and his dogs left the Broad Street mansion for a new apartment of his own two days before the Addisons' planned departure.

Mrs. Rimini stayed behind, for the moment. Rachel knew that Mrs. Addison had made it very plain that they would not require a cook in Valley Forge, since they would be staying with her father, who already had one, nor in New-York, where they planned to stop so briefly they would not take a house of their own, which rendered Mrs. Rimini an entirely superfluous expense. Mr. Addison had acceded and on this one point had not put up a fight. Rachel felt relieved, and guilty that she felt relieved, that the cook would no longer be part of their household, but Mrs. Rimini lifted the burden quickly enough, informing Rachel cheerfully not to worry about her because General Lee had taken her on now that he was going to have a place of his own. "I've spent enough time around soldiers to know that I prefer 'em in small doses," Mrs. Rimini laughed. "One general can be a good deal of trouble, but never so much as seven thousand enlisted men. Anyway, we plain folks go where the work is – that's our real home, ain't it?" And Rachel had to agree, even if she found Mrs. Rimini more direct than plain.

Rachel was not sure until Thursday morning arrived whether some final agreement had been worked out regarding Lieutenant Bellew and Captain O'Malley. She did not dare to ask, not only for fear of provoking another slow-burning argument but also because she was not sure what answer she hoped to receive.

But a compromise had indeed been reached, and Rachel discovered later to her astonishment that it had been General Lee who brokered it. Rachel had just finished a last quick survey of the mansion to make sure nothing had been forgotten in the packing, as of course it had not, and when she hurried outside at last to climb into the carriage where everyone was waiting for her, she saw Lieutenant Bellew in his black cloak sitting upon Snowdrop, and Captain O'Malley, his round face much thinned out, upon Buttercup. Thunder and Acorn had been tied to the rear of the carriage to follow along. Rachel came to an abrupt halt on the threshold.

"Oh! I –" She wanted to say something to Lieutenant Bellew, but although he bowed his head to her, he did not meet her eyes. Rachel curtsied. "Captain O'Malley, you look so much better than the last time I saw you, I cannot tell you how much good it does my heart." Both men wore their cloaks drawn tightly around their clothes, but Rachel could see by the buff-colored fabric of their trousers that they must have been wearing their uniforms again.

"I thought I was the soberest among us that night, and here you go disabusing me of my fond self-image," Captain O'Malley said with a grin. Lieutenant Bellew leaned over and spoke a low word into O'Malley's ear. His eyes grew softer. "Ah - well, if you saw me in that condition, never mind, and I do thank you, Miss Kolkhorst. Yes, I'm perfectly fit now, and thank the heavens thinner, although I suppose that won't last long." He patted his stomach.

"Miss Rachel, folks is ready to go," Abraham said dourly from the driver's box. Jacob sat beside him, still sweating from the effort of lashing four heavy trunks to the carriage. The coach door hung open, waiting. Rachel climbed inside, tucking her skirts beneath her leg, and bent down to pull up the folding step.

Lieutenant Bellew was faster. He dismounted from Snowdrop quickly and pushed the step into place for her. She drew back her hand. "Thank you," Rachel murmured. He nodded but did not reply as he shut the door.

Perhaps he did not want to talk to her much, but she thought at least that Lieutenant Bellew had signaled that he meant there to be no rancor between the two of them. Rachel did not take heart from this, quite, but a small weight lifted from her chest, and she breathed easier.

The day was blustery, gray, and cold, and a thick layer of frost made the horses' way difficult as they picked their way down the treacherous street. Dawn had peeped over the horizon less than an hour earlier, and the only people who were about had business driving them and seemed to want to get it done quickly to escape the sharpness of the air. The carriage swayed gently, and its suspension creaked. Rachel kept her face close to the window; she remembered too well how sick prolonged carriage-travel had made her before, and she had learned that the fresh air that leaked around the glass and light helped a little.

"Draw the curtain, Rachel, I'm going to try to take a nap," Mrs. Addison said. So Rachel obediently dropped the curtain into place, and the inside of the carriage almost immediately grew as stuffy and close as a witch's oven. Mr. Addison no longer had light to read, but apparently he decided not to make an issue of the matter, folding his newspaper quietly and placing it on the seat beside him. Mrs. Addison leaned back against the leather cushion and closed her eyes. In a few minutes, her breathing grew heavy and her mouth dropped open. Rachel was sure she must be asleep – Mrs. Addison would never adopt such an undignified pose while conscious – so she worked up the nerve to part a thin sliver between the curtains and peer outside.

Familiar stone and brick buildings moved slowly past. She probably would not see them again, Rachel realized, or if so, not for a very long time. Why, who knows if she would ever even return to the colonies at all, once the Addisons reached London? She felt a surprisingly sharp pang and almost envied the stately bare trees that passed, their trunks still but their snow-dusted branches bobbing rhythmically in the wind. They remained in one place all their lives. She had not realized how attached she had grown to Philadelphia in such a short time. So much had happened here during her brief stay – events and people that were not merely paintings on a backdrop, but in which she had had a hand, even if an imperfect one. In a way, she felt it marked the beginning of her life as herself, rather than a helpless object tossed about by fortune, and yet she was leaving.

But she was not much better than helpless even now, she supposed, despite her hesitant efforts. She had no choice about her destination, or at least no real choice. If she had food and shelter and safety, that was due to Mrs. Addison. If she had prospects, that was due to Mrs. Addison. If Lieutenant Bellew was near, that was due to Mrs. Addison as well, and Mrs. Addison had come to her only by chance. Her own hand was weak and uncertain, and fortune, if capricious, still served her more reliably than she served herself. All Rachel seemed able to create on her own was confusion. She could not even know if other people understood that she meant well – almost always, truly she did, even if the results of her judgment were – inconsistent. She could pick out the cadence of Snowdrop's hooves on the road through the surrounding clatter, each hollow tock sending a tiny shiver through her stomach.

She wondered what the other people she had known in her life would think if they saw her now. The Crawfords, she supposed, would be polite to her face but secretly annoyed that the object of their charity should now wear finer clothes than their own. The Cherokee would be perplexed and take the matter with a shrug. Her family there had regarded white men's habits and customs with a blank incomprehension far too vast for judgment or even opinion to cross. Her father – but what would her father think? Or her mother? Rachel tried and tried, but she could not guess. She did not know them well enough and did not remember enough about them. She let the curtain drop and leaned her head against the corner of the seat, suddenly very tired.

The sound of the leading horses' hooves grew softer, and a moment later the carriage lurched as it left the paved road and entered onto a dirt one. Philadelphia was gone. Rachel looked between the curtains again, hoping to catch a last glimpse, but it was already too late. She could see nothing but rolling fields of ice and snow, a farmhouse in the distance, and a sprinkling of trees. Rachel sat back again. She glanced at Mr. Addison. He had fallen asleep too, his head lolling from side to side with the movements of the carriage. Rachel supposed a nap was a good idea. There would be much to be done once they reached General van Dortmund's home in Valley Forge – all the unpacking and meeting so many new people and trying to keep their names straight and not doing anything to offend them. It would be exhausting, and Rachel would need all her strength. And it would be a blessing not to have to endure consciously six full hours of the carriage swaying and jolting like a drunk. But Rachel did not think she could doze. She leaned back and closed her eyes. As she had expected, thoughts swarmed over her rather than peace.

Until she woke with a start, disoriented in the dark. Rachel did not know when sleep had taken her or for how long, but the carriage had stopped. Outside, a bird chirped. All else was silence. She turned to Mrs. Addison, who looked as befuddled as Rachel felt and patted at her skewed hair. Mr. Addison snored gently. Rachel did not want to wake him, so she did not speak.

Rachel pulled the curtain a few inches, letting the full light of day wash over her face. Outside, she saw nothing but more fields and trees. No soldiers, no encampment. No trace of humanity at all, other than the road, which Rachel saw was deeply scarred by ruts made sharp as knives by the ice. Her confusion deepened, and she opened the door, kicking down the step, Mrs. Addison peering after her curiously with a frown. The cold hit her in the face, and her eyes watered. The ground crunched beneath her feet.

Abraham looked down at her from his high seat. "They still asleep in there?"

"Mr. Addison is," Rachel answered as loudly as she dared.

Abraham nodded to himself. "Ain't no goin' over the road in this condition. Lieutenant Bellew and Captain O'Malley run up on they horses a little bit and say the rough patch only gets worse. Now they goin' farther to see if they can find someone as can give us another way to get through, because I tell you we ain't gettin' this coach over this mess, and if we go any farther, we'll start poppin' off wheels like boys pop the heads off daisies."

Rachel glanced inside the carriage. Mrs. Addison frowned and shook her head. She'd heard. So Rachel folded the step and shut the door gently.

"I see 'em now," Jacob said, looking down the road. Rachel lifted her head. Lieutenant Bellew and Captain O'Malley approached slowly by the side of the useless road, retracing the dark imprints of their horses' hooves in the snow. If only there hadn't been so many trees, the carriage might have traveled off the road, too; but Rachel could not find any clear path through them, and she did not have as good a view as Abraham did.

When he reached the carriage, Lieutenant Bellew shook his head, his expression serious, and shrugged his shoulders in defeat.

"They didn't tell you nothing, sir?"

"We found a farmer," Bellew answered. "He didn't seem to like the looks of us much, but he was willing enough to talk when he saw we meant him no harm. The trouble is, he didn't speak English, and neither of us knows Dutch, so I don't believe I managed to communicate our difficulty, let alone interpret his response to it."

"I think it was German," Captain O'Malley said, "For all the difference it makes."

Rachel blinked. "But I think it might make a difference at that, Captain O'Malley," she said, her heart beating faster. "I speak German, a little – I'm sure I could manage to explain our situation. Is it far?"

"When all this time I took you for a fine Irish girl from clan MacKolkhorst," Captain O'Malley said with a grin. "Well, bless me for a fool. I should have thought of that."

"It's about a mile," Lieutenant Bellew answered.

"Well, that's not bad. I'm sure I'll be back in forty-five minutes," Rachel said, happy to be useful again, and she started walking along the horses' path. The temperature hovered right around the freezing point, so snow melted on her hem faster than she could shake it off. She supposed she would be a sodden fright by the time she returned, but she could always sit up top if the Addisons found her too damp.

"Miss Kolkhorst!" Snowdrop trotted ahead of her quickly and stopped, her breath steaming in the cold air. Lieutenant Bellew looked down at her with a worried expression. "I can't have you go alone. We don't know this man, for all he seems honest enough. I must insist upon accompanying you." Rachel smiled. She hoped he could read the thankfulness in her face. Maybe he understood why she'd been silent about Lieutenant Masterson, or maybe he'd simply forgiven her. But he did not despise her, and that meant a great deal.

"Thank you," Rachel murmured. She smiled and dropped her eyes and turned to walk around Snowdrop, when Lieutenant Bellew moved the horse to block her again.

"Miss Kolkhorst," he insisted in a strained voice, frowning, "I cannot possibly ride while you walk." But the side saddles were packed deep in the trunks, and what remained of the brief winter daylight hours was precious, so Captain O'Malley handed Rachel up to sit behind Bellew on Snowdrop's plump back. Snowdrop snorted in polite annoyance and took a vexed half-step, but Bellew murmured soothing noises and patted her neck, and she was still again.

Rachel had to wrap her arms around his body to keep her place. She could feel Bellew's muscles tightening as he shifted to keep his balance. The smell of wool and sweat hung heavy as musk in her nostrils. Her face was very close to his cloak, but she could not press her cheek against it, no matter how badly she wanted to, and how much easier it would make her insecure perch on Snowdrop's rump.

Once O'Malley remounted, the little procession took off again, this time at a slower pace, as Rachel had no saddle to hold her steady. The last time she had ridden behind a man, she had been eight years old. She had clung to that Indian for dear life, for all that she had wanted to chop him in the neck with the tomahawk tucked into his belt. Rachel held

Lieutenant Bellew as loosely as she dared. Only weaklings and women without honor held men tightly, and Rachel did not want to be taken for either, even if she felt a little jealous at the moment of their prerogatives. A changeable breeze tickled her face occasionally with strands of his reddish-brown hair that flew loose from his pigtail. They tromped through the snowy landscape, accompanied by nothing but bare trees sticking their black arms into the sky.

Conversation would have been difficult. Lieutenant Bellew would have had to twist in the saddle to speak to her, or Rachel would have had to lean dangerously far to the side, so they rode in silence, their bodies swaying in tandem to the gentle rhythm of Snowdrop's trot. O'Malley seemed content with the silence himself and, strangely, there was nothing uncomfortable about it. Even if the company had not been precious to Rachel, the quiet comradeship of their shared journey would have been. Her back and thighs ached from the awkward position, but she felt disappointment nevertheless when she spied the little wooden farmhouse over the edge of a small hill.

The farmer was outside, chopping wood. He straightened at the sound of horses and frowned when he saw them. He looked nothing like her father, although Rachel did not know why she had expected he would. The farmer had coarse blonde hair that hung in a braid down his back, and his skin was so ruddy it was almost pink. More blonde hair grew in such profusion all over him that it was almost as thick as an animal's coat, covering his bare forearms and sprouting from the collar of his shirt. His moustaches were long enough that Rachel imagined they must be terribly inconvenient. Watery blue eyes peered suspiciously from a thick face.

"*Guten tag!*" Rachel cried as they approached, lifting her hand in greeting.

The farmer's eyes widened and suddenly twinkled with the brightness of a summer sky. "*Guten tag, guten tag, fräulein!*" he boomed in a delighted voice, thudding his axe into the scarred stump that served as a chopping-block and striding forward while rolling down his homespun sleeves.

Lieutenant Bellew swung his right leg over Snowdrop's neck lightly and jumped to the ground, helping Rachel dismount. He gripped her by the elbows briefly as her weight descended on him, and then he stepped aside. The German farmer touched his forehead in lieu of a hat. "I see these gentlemen were good enough to bring a pretty translator," he said, or she was fairly sure, at least. She did not know "*übersetzer*", but she thought it must mean "translator".

Rachel curtsied. "Thank you, sir – we don't mean to interrupt you, your, your work," she said slowly. She had to reach into an unfamiliar part of her mind to grasp the old words, stiff from long disuse. "Our – carriage is – about a mile south – the road is bad. The carriage cannot go upon it. We're looking for another way. We're trying to go to Valley Forge. Can you help with advice?"

"Ah – Valley Forge. I thought these two were soldiers, by the look of them," the German farmer said, enunciating carefully and speaking more slowly, apparently having taken accurate measure of Rachel's fluency. "And by their breeches." He tugged at the knee of his own trousers to illustrate. "I thought they were looking for food, to take more than I can give and pay with worthless money. I was glad when they left."

"We aren't trying – to force you – to join the war," Rachel began, when the German farmer burst into such uproarious laughter she was sure she'd said something horrible by mistake and stammered, "Excuse me – excuse me – my German is so bad –" Lieutenant Bellew looked at Rachel for an explanation. She shook her head, blushing.

"No, Miss, I beg your pardon – your German was very correct," the farmer said, still smiling broadly. "I was laughing about something else."

"If you – do not like our side – I understand – we just want advice about a road," Rachel began, but the farmer interrupted her again.

"Ah, I have no opinion about your war, and I bear no grudge. I'm not a soldier any more."

"You were a soldier? Did you –" Rachel knew that some foreigners had come to fight for the colonists – but those foreigners were aristocrats and adventurers, and she could tell this man was neither.

The redcoats, however, had hired Hessian mercenaries by the boatload.

"Oh," she said, paling slightly. The farmer saw her understanding and held up his hand.

"Ach, it doesn't matter, I hold them no ill-will, although why these fellows would choose a soldier's life, I cannot guess. I have become a colonist myself," he said, spreading his arms wide to encompass his little farm. "Ha, and right here! I did not know, when I first came, that the land was so beautiful - just like home, except home a thousand years ago, before all the best of it was taken. When my captors said I was free -"

"You were captured? Held prisoner?" Rachel exclaimed, a dark foreboding gnawing at her. Even if the Continentals treated their prisoners twice as well as the regulars did, this man would have an injury to avenge. She furrowed her brow.

The farmer nodded. "Oh yes, certainly, I was taken at Trenton last year, with more than a thousand of my brothers. That was a sad Christmas at first, I don't mind telling you. But then it was not too bad. The Americans gave us a Christmas celebration nevertheless, to make up for the one they had interrupted, ha! And I thought, these are good people, like the men I have known at home. Some of their soldiers, you know, they are from good Hessian stock - although they have become farmers now and do not know how to fight - well, except sometimes, I have to admit! But they spoke German, like you do, Miss - no, we had a pretty good time in their company. Well, although I wanted my freedom I was not very happy a few months later when they told me they were releasing me to return to my miserable life of blood and dirt and orders and death, because they had traded us for some soldiers of their own. And I thought, bah, I won't do it. So I ran away, and here I am - as I said, a colonist now myself! Ha! And I have my own farm!"

"They treated you well - when you were a prisoner, they treated you well?" Rachel twisted the fabric of her cloak in her hands.

"Yes, of course! Our officers were like their brothers, and the common men such as myself were like their sons - Miss, why are you crying? No, no, dear, don't do that," the farmer said in sudden concern. "What's the matter?" Bellew, unable to follow the course of the conversation but seeing only Rachel's distress, stiffened, and O'Malley frowned.

"No, I'm not, I'm not - it's just the air is so cold," Rachel said, wiping her shoulder against the corner of her eye to annihilate the tear that lay there. "I'm very glad - very glad - you were not hurt. And I am glad that people were - kind to you."

"Ah," the farmer replied. He did not seem convinced. "Well, I am not being so good to you, huh, keeping you out on this winter day. Yes, there is a cart-road that goes most of the way to Valley Forge. A carriage could take it. Yes, certainly, although it will be bumpy. You'll have to rejoin the main road for the last few miles, and I do not know the conditions there. But I am sure the army must keep it clear. Now, how far did you get before you had to stop?"

"About a mile from here. South."

"Then you turn around and go back another mile. Do you remember the mill you passed?"

"I slept," Rachel admitted.

"Well, you'll see it clearly enough. The cart road meets the main road there. It's a longer path, because it goes past the farms, you see, but it is usable. A simple road for simple people," the farmer said with satisfaction.

"Simple people – take a road with many – turns?" Rachel said, not sure whether she got her meaning across, but the farmer laughed again.

"Exactly! Exactly so," he said. He blinked, considering something. "And now – but wait a moment longer, if you don't mind, please, it will be only a minute." He hurried back to his house.

Bellew turned to her quickly. "Did he say something unkind?" he asked.

"Oh, no, not at all – there's a cart road we passed about a mile earlier. If we go back, we'll see it at the mill. It should take us most of the way, and he thinks the main road will be navigable for the rest."

"That's fine, then, Miss," O'Malley said. "Well done."

"Oh, I don't – well, I'm glad that my German was useful, it never has been before. I mean not since – well, not since I was very small."

"Your parents' language?"

"My father's."

"I suppose it's a long time since you heard it," O'Malley said gently, and Rachel was glad to have that as an excuse for her tears, so she merely lowered her eyes and said nothing in reply.

Bellew nodded and cleared his throat as if uncomfortable. "I – now that you've successfully obtained our directions for us, we should get back to the others." He put his left foot in the stirrup.

"Oh! I forgot to say – we have to wait a moment. The farmer had something he wanted to give us."

Bellew and O'Malley exchanged glances. O'Malley shrugged. "Maybe he has a map."

But when the farmer emerged again, he bore a heavy burlap sack on his shoulders and not a map at all. He grinned with puckish delight at the confusion that confronted him and, with Captain O'Malley's aid, got the lumpy burden positioned on Buttercup and balanced well enough to stay put for a short ride.

"Thank you very much," Rachel said cautiously. "But – you can tell me – what it is?"

"Potatoes!" the farmer said, wiping his hands against his legs.

"Thank you," Rachel said again, perplexed.

"Ah, don't mention it. It won't go far, but it's all I have to spare. I've only been a farmer for a year, after all. You made me remember, Miss, how good your soldiers were to me – even though perhaps that was when their fortunes were not so – well, enough about that. I think they can find a use for my sack of potatoes, so I won't begrudge them, and I wish them all the joy of it. Well, I won't keep you any longer. Good-bye, Miss, and Godspeed."

Chapter 28

"*Kartoffeln!*" O'Malley exploded in what Rachel had to admit was a pretty good imitation. Bellew grinned. Because Rachel had her arms around him, she could feel his body shake slightly with a suppressed chuckle. "Tell me again, Bellew, how you ended up riding with the girl, and I ended up riding with the sack of potatoes?"

They returned to the carriage and explained matters, and Abraham followed the farmer's instructions and found both the mill and the cart road without difficulty. Just as the farmer had promised, the narrower path had been kept reasonably smooth by the people who required it to be clear if they did not mean to starve, just as they had neglected the main road that bore little these past months but soldiers, who could never be trusted.

The anxiety of being stranded for an hour had made Mrs. Addison quite alert and unable to nap, so she wanted Rachel to tell her stories to pass the time. Mrs. Addison permitted the curtains to be opened now, so Mr. Addison could read as Rachel related the adventure with the farmer.

"But it requires Captain O'Malley to do justice to the way he sounded," Rachel said. "I hope he never does an impersonation of me. I'm sure it would be devastating."

"Well, it seems I missed a charming escapade. It's always good to have a travel story to tell when one arrives. They'll ask us how things went, and I'll trot out our farmer for service. I'm sure it will please father. He's always trying to tell his men not to be so afraid of the Hessians, no matter how fierce they look or sound – what was it this one shouted with eyes of flame?"

"Potatoes. *Kartoffeln.*"

"*Kartoffeln.* Yes, I think he might like to tell his men that story."

The conversation paused. After a moment, Mrs. Addison puffed a small sigh of frustration and glanced out the window. Rachel thought it might be an opportune time to ask something that had been worrying her. "Ma'am – is there anything in particular I should do or not do, or say or not say, in order to accommodate your family? I would like to make myself useful, if I could, but I don't want to intrude where I'm not wanted, or where I would be in the way."

Mrs. Addison waved a hand. "Oh la, Rachel, they have maids of their own for the household matters, you'll just tend to me, and that will be enough. You won't have any trouble getting along. My sister Clarissa is mild as milk, I've hardly ever heard her object to anything. Mother is rather – she thinks of things in her own way, and as long as no one corrects her, she's perfectly content. Oh, but the witticisms – perhaps you should keep those to yourself around father, actually, he's a bit like Lieutenant Bellew. Half the time he has a wonderful sense of humor. Mind that – half. Wouldn't you say, Robert?"

Mr. Addison grunted and shrugged.

Rachel tried to interest Mrs. Addison in speaking more about her family but received little more than "Oh, I'm sure they're all quite unchanged," and the topic did not seem to engage her mistress, so eventually she stopped. Rachel returned to rehashing the characters of Mrs. Addison's circle of Philadelphia acquaintance, but she did not need to do so long. A tinge of gray light remained in the sky when Rachel heard a man's rough voice call ahead of them at last, "Hi, there, state your name and business!"

"Oh, I think we're here!" Rachel said excitedly, interrupting herself, and peered out the window. She turned her head so that her breath would not mist the glass. The carriage bounced to a halt.

Two armed sentries in ragged, mismatched clothes gripped their muskets but did not hold them at the ready. Rachel supposed a carriage did not present a threatening aspect. The sentries ignored it, directing their attention to the men on horseback.

"I'm Captain Samuel O'Malley, and this is my first Lieutenant, Stephen Bellew," O'Malley said in a hoarse but pleased voice, opening his cloak a little to show his uniform. "And very glad to see you. Can you tell us where to find the South Carolina men, so we can report to duty at last?" Buttercup tried to snatch a mouthful of weeds from the ground, but O'Malley pulled her head up sharply. "Hi there, horse, let's make a better impression than that," he muttered. Snowdrop, Rachel was somehow gratified to see, did not misbehave.

The sentries frowned and supplied no ready answer to what seemed to be a simple enough question. They looked at each other as if for confirmation. "*South* Carolina?" one of them said at last, perplexed. He asked his friend, "We got any *South* Carolina men here?" The friend shook his head, frowning, and shifted his musket for handier access, falling back a step.

"We've been in prison," Lieutenant Bellew explained quickly. "And are just released."

"Well, what company were you in?"

"We were forming our own, but were interrupted," Captain O'Malley answered. "Here." He withdrew two letters from his pocket and presented them. Rachel supposed they must be the commission and the letter confirming the trade.

The sentries puzzled over them, sharing baffled expressions.

"What's the difficulty?" Mrs. Addison said, leaning over and trying to see outside over Rachel. Her breath whispered against Rachel's cheek.

"There's no South Carolina contingent here," Rachel murmured. "If the sentries are correct."

"Well, what are they going to do then?"

Mr. Addison snorted, slapping down his paper. "A lot of blasted nuisance, quibbling over which colony whose name they'll be shot over." He opened his door and leaned out, calling up, "Hi, Abraham! This isn't our concern. Ask the guards for directions to General van Dortmund's and be done with it. They're waiting for us."

The first sentry glanced at the carriage. "You with General van Dortmund?"

"This his daughter and her husband," Abraham's low voice replied. "They ought to have told you we was coming," he added with a touch of dull resentment.

The sentry walked forward and glanced inside the carriage. Rachel smiled at him, but he didn't seem to notice particularly, although he touched his hat in respect. He walked back towards the horses, where he could speak to Abraham better. "Aye, it's ladies in there. All right. Quickest way to get to General van Dortmund's is to go around the camp – circle round to the northeast on this road here and then take the first big branch heading to the east you see – it's a good-sized stone house, I don't know how else to describe it, how would you describe it, Frank?"

"It's a good-sized stone house," the other sentry answered with a shrug.

"Aye, well, ask anyone and they'll tell you when you get closer. The locals call it Briarwood, that might help you."

"Should the gentlemens come with us till all this is straightened out bout where they supposed to go?" Inside the carriage, Rachel smiled to herself, blessing Abraham. She looked out at the sentries hopefully.

"Ah." The first sentry's forehead puckered as he remembered the knotty problem of O'Malley and Bellew. "No, I don't think General van Dortmund would have anything to do with this, only...well, sirs, you ain't got a company, and I don't know rightly where it is you're supposed to belong, only General Washington seems to think you belong somewhere, except he hasn't troubled himself to say where exactly that is." He flapped the letters in the air.

"They got to go back to South Carolina," Frank opined. "That's where the South Carolina men are. South Carolina or Georgia."

"I don't even know if they're properly South Carolina men or not, this commission is for a company that don't exist," the first sentry said in annoyance. He looked up at O'Malley, handing back the papers. "I tell you what, Captain. You two go see General McIntosh."

"General McIntosh is *North* Carolina," Frank pointed out.

"General McIntosh knows the South Carolina crowd, so he'll know what to do or who to ask. And it won't be our problem no more. Besides, it'll be our hides if an officer finds out we had two willing men show up and sent 'em away," the first sentry answered reasonably.

"Excuse me," Lieutenant Bellew said, and Snowdrop, picking up his mood, took two short steps forward. "Being of service is our primary concern. If that requires a return to South Carolina, of course we shall do so at once, if that is where we are required. My understanding, with the caveat that my captain and I have been deprived of solid intelligence for a long time, was that men were needed most urgently here. Since there seems to be some question about where we are supposed to go, I ask that the answer depend on where we could do the most good."

Frank grinned, eyeing Bellew. "Itching for a fight, are you, sir? Well, where was it you were held prisoner?"

"Philadelphia."

Frank grinned more broadly. "Maybe that makes you Pennsylvania men, and you could go see General Wayne. You'll see action with General Wayne, and plenty of it."

"You let General McIntosh figure that out," the first sentry said with a scowl. "General McIntosh makes the most sense for these two."

"Good Lord, this is interminable, like everything the bloody colonists do," Mr. Addison muttered. He opened the door again and shouted to Abraham, "You've got your directions, Abraham, now use 'em! Captain O'Malley – you know where to return the horses?"

"Aye, sir," Captain O'Malley answered, twisting around in his saddle. "And thank you again –"

"Yes, yes, I'm sure we'll be seeing plenty more of you for all that, so good-day, and, Abraham, kindly get moving!" He slammed the door shut and sat heavily. Rachel lifted a hand quickly in farewell, but the carriage started with a jerk and left the scene with the sentries behind so swiftly she doubted he had seen it.

And now they were truly separated.

It felt as though a bubble swelled up inside Rachel's heart and then popped, leaving emptiness. She put it from her mind. She had more than concerns enough. Still, the ache of a vacuum remained.

Briarwood was indeed as promised, a good-sized stone house, its walls weathered soft gray with age. It stood high upon a hill, with a broad view of the surroundings below. The woods were deep and the hills gentle, and the water of the fat Schuylkill and the narrow Valley Creek glittered like silver in the distance not too far. Rachel caught her first glimpse of the Continentals' encampment from here, and that was the only stain interrupting the beauty – rough and squalid, with low wooden huts spreading like some blighted fungus and neither constructed nor laid out to any plan she could discern. The landscape around the camp had been torn up badly, and the snow blackened with mud and filth. She supposed the chaotic nature of the place was due to the haste with which it had been built, and that aesthetic concerns had taken a very reasonable secondary importance in the scheme. But she did not like to think of Lieutenant

Bellew having to live there – or Captain O'Malley, who she did not think had recovered as fully as he presented himself.

But Briarwood was very fine, and Rachel noticed with approval that the grounds had been kept neat, and the windows sparkled brightly from a recent washing. The door flew open even before the carriage stopped, and a girl no more than Rachel's age flew outside, beaming with pleasure. She wore a pale silk sprigged with pink and green flowers, and she had neglected to put a cloak over her lace shawl in her excitement.

"Maggie!" the girl cried. "Maggie, you're here!"

"Clarissa, darling!" Mrs. Addison said. She rapped on the window and waved her fingers.

Clarissa van Dortmund had chestnut hair the same shade and luster as her sister's, and Rachel supposed she could see a resemblance, but clearly all the beauty in the family had been spent upon Mrs. Addison. Clarissa was not even really pretty, although Rachel could not help liking her open, pleasant face. Mrs. Addison's sister waited impatiently for the carriage to halt and stepped from one side to the other, trying to position herself properly. At last Jacob sprang down and opened the door, and Clarissa rushed into Mrs. Addison's arms. Mr. Addison followed more slowly, sighing, and Rachel snuck out behind him as unobtrusively as she could.

"Oh, Maggie, it's been much too long, you're more beautiful than ever – here, do your fellows need any help with the trunks? No? We've got your rooms ready, of course, Hattie or Martha can show them where everything goes – oh, and Robert, you look so well, I hope my sister is taking good care of you?"

"Quite, quite," Mr. Addison mumbled.

Clarissa turned her shining face to Rachel. "And you must be Rachel?" Rachel curtsied. To her surprise, Clarissa seized her hands. "Oh, I'm so very happy to meet you, my sister's told me all about you and what a blessing you've been. I hope you'll find your stay pleasant."

"Miss, I cannot imagine how I could not, in such a kind household."

Clarissa turned back to her sister. "Oh, Maggie, she is wonderful, isn't she? Now, you have to come upstairs. Father uses the first floor for work, and it's just teeming right now – it always is during the day, and half the night too. But mother is waiting in the second-floor parlor – she's been on tenterhooks all day. And there's coffee and things – you must be horribly depleted, such a long day, oh, do your fellows – what are their names? – require anything? Truly, we could get some of father's soldiers to do the lifting, there are so many of them about and they're always happy to be of service."

"Abraham and Jacob have been doing nothing more strenuous than sitting on their backsides for the past eight hours. I'm sure they welcome the exertion," Mr. Addison said.

The foyer was empty, but the air hummed with the sound of footsteps and the low rumble of men's voices. Rachel tried to walk quietly on the wooden floors, terrified of disturbing such serious business. Clarissa noticed. She smiled and whispered conspiratorially, "Rachel – they wouldn't notice if you set off a cannon in here," and then she laughed merrily and led them upstairs. A buxom maid with tight stays and a sly face loitered on the landing, and Clarissa said, "Oh, Martha, honey, don't be shy – the fellows need to know where to put the trunks, they'll be mighty relieved if you show them." Martha didn't look shy in the slightest to Rachel, who recognized a malingerer from her days with Anne. Martha bobbed a curtsy at Clarissa's prompting and slouched down the stairs, trailing her hand along the banister. Rachel watched Mr. Addison's eyes track her lazily. But surely he wouldn't try anything so stupid here – not in Mrs. Addison's father's home.

"Oh, Margaret – oh, my heart," a small, round, and rather overdressed lady said when they entered the bright, neat parlor, pressing a tiny hand against a large bosom covered by a plain cotton scarf. "Oh, I've drunk too much coffee waiting, and I'm all a-flutter." But Mrs. van Dortmund managed to get to her feet and kiss her daughter and son-in-law. "Are you well? You look tired. They're late, aren't they, Clarissa?"

"You can't expect people to start at the crack of dawn, mama," Clarissa murmured, pouring coffee for everyone. Rachel startled and took a half-step forward, but Clarissa shook her head and waved at her to sit down.

"Well, actually there was a delay. We had a bit of an adventure," Mrs. Addison said, settling onto a sofa and leaning back languorously. Mr. Addison sat beside her, stiff and apparently unmoved by his wife's soft, open pose.

Mrs. van Dortmund brightened. She patted her lap with her little hands. "Oh, you have a story for us? What is it?"

"I had wanted to wait for father," Mrs. Addison drawled.

"Bosh, if it's any good you can tell it twice. Why wait for him at all?"

"Because it involves a Hessian."

Mrs. van Dortmund sat bolt upright. "A Hessian! A Hessian! No, Margaret – no one was hurt, were they? A Hessian! You must tell me at once." Then Mrs. Addison related the story of the farmer, although she made it sound as though she had been present and seen it herself to simplify matters.

"Oh my – right by here. Oh my, how terrible, how terrible," Mrs. van Dortmund said at the conclusion, fanning herself. "Oh, what a trial you had."

Rachel blinked in confusion. She had thought the farmer very nice. He hadn't done anything other than give them directions and potatoes, neither of which seemed terribly objectionable. She wondered if Mrs. van Dortmund had really been listening. Mr. Addison clearly wasn't. He stared out the window and sipped his coffee.

"Now, mama, wouldn't it be a fine thing if we could give all the enemy soldiers their little plot of land, and the war be over, and everyone live in peace?" Clarissa said soothingly. She smiled at her sister for support. Mrs. Addison nodded absently.

"Now, Clarissa," Mrs. van Dortmund replied, mocking her daughter's tone, "don't be impractical. Didn't we try that with the Indians already, and where has it gotten us with them, I ask you? And I tell you, these Hessians are not one jot more civilized than an Indian, for all their white skin. There. I'd like to see you answer that."

Rachel's confusion deepened. She glanced at Mrs. Addison for interpretation of this strange remark. Mrs. Addison did not return Rachel's look, but she lifted her fingers in a slight, swift movement that Rachel had no trouble interpreting as *remember – don't contradict her.*

"Oh, mama," Clarissa said.

"That doesn't count as an answer," Mrs. van Dortmund crowed in triumph. Mrs. Addison wore a curious smile, half-comfortable and half-annoyed. She played with her ring, as she did when she was nervous or bored.

Before the conversation could flag, a deep man's voice came from the doorway, interrupting them. "Margaret – Robert. I have only a moment, but I wanted to greet you without delay." Rachel's head shot up, and she replaced her coffee cup on the table hurriedly. A nervous chill gripped her. She felt a specter of judgment enter the room and hang over it like a sword, and Rachel felt very petty and very foolish for sitting drinking coffee when – well, when what? She did not know what else it was she was supposed to have been doing. She stood and curtsied, blushing, hoping that she was not making too much of a display of herself.

General van Dortmund was a slender man of below average height, but he added a few inches by holding his spine as straight as if it were an iron rod. He wore a uniform with red lapels, unlike the blue-and-buff that Lieutenant Bellew and Captain O'Malley had chosen. His narrow chin was clean-shaven, and only a few strands of gray speckled the blackness of his unpowdered hair. He had a dour presence, as if he nursed a wound beneath his coat.

"How good of you, father," Mrs. Addison said coolly, rising to her feet and curtsying. Mr. Addison bowed. Then Mrs. van Dortmund insisted that Mrs. Addison tell the "blood-curdling" story of the Hessian farmer, declaring that surely her husband could make time to hear about his daughter's brush with fatality.

Mrs. Addison's eyes flicked between her mother and father, apparently weighing her mother's whim against her father's expressed lack of time. When General van Dortmund did not immediately move to go, Mrs. Addison made up her mind. She related a hasty version, slowing down for effect only to describe an elaborate and wholly fabricated image of the farmer's ferocious aspect before he exploded with the frightening "*Kartoffeln.*"

"Which means potatoes. So now you can tell your men just what it is these demonic Hessians are shouting about," Mrs. Addison concluded with a degage flick of her fingers.

General van Dortmund's eyes crinkled at the corners. He looked almost warm for a moment. "Potatoes," he repeated. "Very good." His face grew serious again, and he turned his gaze to Rachel, who had to remind herself not to press herself deeper into her chair. She did not know why the general frightened her so much. "I suppose it's you who speaks German, Miss Kolkhorst? I know my daughter and her husband don't."

Rachel blinked. "Yes, sir," she said, wilting under his direct stare.

"Did you get the impression that he meant anything by this odd gift?" His eyes fixed her in place like a pin impaling some insect specimen on a corkboard.

"I - he didn't say, sir." She opened her mouth to say more but then shut it again.

"But he gave you an idea?" General van Dortmund prompted her politely.

Rachel could not collect her thoughts, the man's stare was so intimidating. She took a breath and blurted, "It was - he had told me, us, that he had been captured, and I was so worried that - I know nothing like that would happen under your command, sir, but in Philadelphia, the soldiers the regulars imprisoned were not, were not kept well - so when he said that he'd been treated so decently, like a son, I was so terribly relieved, and I think he noticed, and that was when - he gave us the potatoes as we were leaving, even though we hadn't asked, and he said that I, we had made him remember how the Continentals had treated him, sir, and that this was all he could spare."

General van Dortmund absorbed the information without expression. "Thank you," he said gravely after a moment. He turned back to Mrs. Addison. "Where are these potatoes now?"

"I don't know," Mrs. Addison replied blankly. "Presumably Abraham had the sense to put them in the kitchen."

"See that they aren't. Those potatoes are for the men," General van Dortmund said, his eyes and his voice taking on a hard edge, and Mrs. Addison nodded hurriedly, her face averted. Rachel had never seen Mrs. Addison cowed by anyone.

"But, Thomas - you're so fascinated by these potatoes, and don't you even care about the danger Margaret was in?" Mrs. van Dortmund interrupted, annoyed at the change in direction.

"There were two soldiers accompanying you, I believe."

"Of course - Lieutenant Bellew and Captain O'Malley. Really, mother, we were entirely safe. Father - I would like to ask you about them, by the way," Mrs. Addison went on. "There seems to be some difficulty about placing them in the army here, since they're from South Carolina. Now, surely you can work out –"

General van Dortmund held up his hand. "Speak to me about it later. I am too pressed at the moment." Mrs. Addison fell immediately silent and lowered her eyes again, nodding.

"Oh, it's just endless, isn't it," Mrs. van Dortmund chirped. "You start doing favors, and they just go on and on and on, and you're never free of them. That's why I say never do favors for anyone. I say that, don't I, Clarissa?"

"Yes, mama, but –"

"But nothing!"

General van Dortmund bowed and left, taking his iron chill with him. Mrs. van Dortmund sighed and poured herself another cup of coffee. "Oh la," she trilled. "My, what a day. Now, Robert!"

Mr. Addison stiffened in surprise and tore his attention away from the window to face her, his eyes wide with barely concealed apprehension.

"My poor Robert, you're sitting here entirely neglected. You always liked cards, wasn't that it? Margaret keeps mentioning this game of cards and that game of cards – let's have a game of cards!"

"That's hardly necessary on my account, Mrs. van Dortmund, I am quite content to enjoy you ladies' delightful conversation –"

"Nonsense! You're not just my guest, you're my son, and you have to let me spoil you, so don't put up a fuss. We'll play 'Laugh and Lie Down'. Does everyone know how to play it? It's so much fun, and it doesn't take a second to learn. Now, we each get eight cards, and the rest go face-up in the middle. Then everyone takes a turn, and if you can match a pair with one of the cards in the middle, aces with aces and so forth, you get to capture it and lay down your pair. Now, if you can't match," Mrs. van Dortmund said, lifting her eyebrows and waggling a finger, "You have to lay all your cards in the middle, and you are out, and everyone laughs at you. You see? Laugh and lie down! I could play it for hours and hours, and it's perfectly wonderful to have someone in the house who shares my passion for once. We won't let them say no, Robert, will we?" she said delightedly, patting his hand.

Chapter 29

At first, Bellew thought the soldiers he passed were also recently released from prison, as he knew many had been – but surely not this many? – and he nodded to them with a somber smile of commiseration as Snowdrop and Buttercup picked their way over the muddy snow. He recognized the hollow eyes and cheeks of starvation too well. Although the men did not work quickly, they did work – building huts, digging privy pits and entrenchments – and Bellew felt a grim pride that he too had a bitter new cause to fight all the harder. He almost wished his physical recuperation were less complete, so that he could prove his reliance on nothing but spirit.

But he thought it was rather hard, for all that he admired it, for men who had not regained a tenth of their strength to be permitted to labor. They should be given food and rest; that was the only way they would be ready to fight when the winter ended. Were the men here so few that no quarter could be given to the ill? He saw men without jackets, threadbare blankets thrown over their shoulders Indian-style for warmth. Two lines of pink-stained footprints trailed behind a pair of men who Bellew saw to his shock had no boots, their bare feet showing black patches of frostbite split by raw red cracks. The smell of filth hung everywhere. Bellew cringed to think of the unclean air and water and earth seeping into those open wounds. And as he and O'Malley rode deeper into the camp, Bellew saw more of the same, and worse, but little better – boys hardly fatter than skeletons shivering with fever as they chopped trees for barricades, gloomy men with pale, stockingless legs emerging from tattered trousers, or God help them, from beneath shirt-tails alone. Bellew glanced at his captain. O'Malley's face was thoughtful, but he did not look up to meet Bellew's gaze.

Bellew nudged Snowdrop to a trot, approaching a man sitting cross-legged on the cold ground with a pile of branches beside him. The man whittled their ends to sharp points with a large hunting knife that was not designed for such work. "Excuse me," Bellew said, and the man looked up dully. Registering Bellew's uniform, the man stood with a sigh, brushing wood chips from his bare legs, and saluted. Bellew winced and shook his head quickly. He did not mean to make the fellow's life harder. "Where is your commanding officer?"

"Don't know, sir. Haven't seen him since this morning," the man replied cautiously.

"Does he know you're sharpening sticks?"

"He told me to himself," the man answered, a defensive note creeping into his voice.

"No, I mean – isn't he aware that you haven't any – that you aren't properly fitted out?" Bellew exclaimed. "I commend your zeal, but surely a trip to the commissary would not delay your duties so much."

"The commissary, sir?" the man answered with a sour chuckle. "You just got here, I reckon?"

"Yes, my captain and I have, like you, it seems, lately been imprisoned –" The man snorted, and Bellew stopped in confusion. "I fail to understand what was amusing," he continued after a pause.

"Sorry, sir. Just I never heard of an officer talk about enlistment that way before," the man replied. "Though I guess it's accurate enough, since I'll be shot if I try to leave. Which I wouldn't do, sir," he added hastily.

"If you haven't been in prison – what is the meaning of your condition?" Bellew said, his heart sinking.

The man blinked, thinking. He shrugged. "The meaning of it is I suppose that the clothes I brought with me run out, the food I brought with me run out, there ain't no more of neither round here and they don't give us our pay so's we can buy it for ourselves. Sir," he added hastily, as if to soften his words. "What I got is some sticks, and my knife. It's a good knife, and it won't run out for a long time, so they sets me to sharpening."

Bellew dismounted and opened the small pack of his possessions, giving the man the trousers to both his black suit and the blue one that Mrs. Merriwether had altered for him, and also his spare boots. The man thanked him and promised to pass them on if they did not fit. Bellew nodded shortly, and he and O'Malley rode on.

"You'll bankrupt yourself that way," O'Malley said quietly, as they passed more gaunt, half-naked soldiers moving with the painful slowness of the weak and wounded.

"It is far more desperate than I knew," Bellew muttered. "These men are not an anomaly. These are simply the men we have – good God, how can we – what are we going to do?"

"The best we can," O'Malley replied in an even tone. "You won't help things by making yourself as naked as they are."

"I'll buy more clothes. I have money coming," Bellew said, and it was true. He had not told O'Malley, and would not, the last letter he had written before leaving Philadelphia, to Lewis, the tenant he had taken for his mother's farm. His farm. Or rather, Lewis's farm now, because Bellew had finally accepted Lewis's offer to buy it. It still gave Bellew a twinge to think of that hard-earned land, what little there was of it, passing from his hands, with nothing to show for it but a uniform and hope. But the English had taken his horse, his gun, his ready money – he had nothing left but his debt to O'Malley, and the horse and gun he would have to replace himself, and he could not do it on a lieutenant's salary. He knew O'Malley suspected that Bellew's father had made some kind of provision for him, and he preferred not to disturb the misconception. He would not make himself an object of pity. His father, as he had admitted to Mrs. Addison at the ball, was no more real or tangible to him than a name on his mother's lips. He did not even know for certain whether the Baron Bellew realized that he had a second son. But he did know that he would not go begging to that man, or any other.

If I can help it, he told himself grimly, remembering too clearly the horse that he rode temporarily and the clothes on his back, indeed his very freedom, were the products of the generosity of others. If he had not asked for that generosity, it made no difference; it merely compounded his debt. What could be repaid with money, he would gratefully discharge as soon as he heard back from Lewis. But the kindness itself – that could be repaid only by justifying the trust that had been placed in him.

The sentry had been only partly correct. Bellew had embarked on his adventures as a Continental itching for a fight. Now, he hungered for one the way a drowning man hungers for air. A clean, simple fight – no more tense bows or strained smiles with his oppressors, no more riding the horse of a man whose wife Bellew had to admit he would rather have had for his own. No more tied hands and gritted teeth. No obligation but to prove his worth at last.

Snowdrop, picking up his mood, shook her head and snorted.

General McIntosh proved to be a good-natured middle-aged man with the soft trace of a burr beneath his southern drawl. What he did not have, however, was a good idea of what to do with Bellew and O'Malley, nor much time to devote to the issue.

"I hate to send two fighting men away," he said, shaking his head. "But South Carolina is keeping her own busy down south."

"Then if that's where we're called up, that's where we'll go, sir," Captain O'Malley answered, and that seemed to settle the matter. Bellew had mixed feelings at the prospect of leaving Valley Forge so soon after arriving. The men here were so dispirited and forlorn that he felt almost as though he were leaving a baby beneath the open jaws of a tiger, with the tens of thousands of sleek, well-trained, well-armed redcoats only twenty miles away. His fellow prisoners, even though there were hundreds of them in that hell-pit, could never have overpowered the guard of four to six men that watched over them, and it had not occurred to them to try. It would have been suicide. How was it less so here, with the men in no better condition, and facing far worse numbers? Perhaps in the south, conditions were not so bad – perhaps there he might even be able to do some good. But would it be enough, if the north collapsed? This was by far, Bellew knew, the bulk of the rebellion's army. If it fell, what hope could the few remaining regiments in the south muster? The redcoats could pick them apart by pieces.

And he had mixed feelings about leaving Mrs. Addison, too. Relief formed no small portion. He thought of her too often not to realize that O'Malley's advice was sounder than he'd first admitted. There was no future in desiring a woman who belonged to someone else. The worst part, the damnably worst part, was how tender she had been with him at that accursed dance – he had almost been able to forget that useless husband then, and the memory of it shamed him. Of course she had not meant to be so free; she was lonely, as she had admitted before the visit to Captain André, and it grieved him that someone he cared for should suffer that pain – and he could not help wanting to lighten her burden, but he did not trust himself any more. Nor, if he were honest with himself, did he trust her entirely not to permit something that could cause nothing but grief, if it did not destroy them both. So, for that concern – it was best if he were far away.

But they could hardly take borrowed horses to Charlestown. General McIntosh offered them the hospitality of his home for a few days, until Bellew's money arrived and they could buy horses and provisions. "Mind you get your money in pounds or dollars. Spanish dollars," General McIntosh said. "You'll have no trouble finding what you need in the countryside then, once you get some distance from here – the redcoats cleaned 'em out here pretty well before we settled in. It was a good harvest and it's a mild winter. The farmers have enough to spare."

Bellew was silent a moment. "But they don't offer it freely, sir."

General McIntosh smiled thinly. "A man's first instinct is to look after his own, however he defines it," he said.

Resting before dinner in their small room, crowded with an extra chair that did not really fit, Bellew shared some of his concerns, the ones he could admit, keeping his voice low. "I don't know what's happening in South Carolina, but good God – I don't know how these men here can stand up, let alone hold together."

"We go where we're needed."

"We do, sir," Bellew replied after a pause. It was not his place, as a lieutenant, to make strategic assignments of men. He knew that.

O'Malley fingered the brim of his hat, turning it around on his lap. "Only it seems to me," he said slowly, "that the only real need that's taking us back to Charlestown is an excessive delicacy on the part of everyone around us not to tread on a propriety that I'm not sure has a place in wartime." He glanced up at Bellew. "Do you remember what you said when we heard about Boston?"

"When we took the Heights? Of course. I wanted to go at once – I wanted to go before we took the Heights, actually, I wanted to go when Boston was under martial law – I wanted to look the redcoats in the face and let them see we were not broken. Only mother – I could not leave her," Bellew finished in a low voice.

O'Malley tilted his head, examining Bellew thoughtfully. "She was a fine woman, if a hard one, and she loved you more than you knew, lad. She hated that you knew she was sick, even when she tried to hide it. My Lord, that galled her, and I'm sure it didn't sweeten her temper much. If you'd told her you wanted to go, she would have let you, even if she had to sell that farm of hers, and she'd have put a smile on her face to see you off."

"She never would have sold her land," Bellew said, pressing down the guilt as hard as he could.

"For you, she would have. But let that lie. It wasn't South Carolina you were thinking of when you wanted to throw over your plow and head off to Boston."

"It was the yoke that worried me more than the plow," Bellew replied. "And if it lay heavier on Boston at the moment, that was no more than a sign of what was to come for the rest of us."

"The rest of *us*. Precisely," O'Malley said. "It's all of us that's fighting now, and the regulars I don't think are going to be too particular about which of us they're shooting at, South Carolina men or Massachusetts men or Georgia men. You see – I'm trying to explain myself in advance, because I'm not sure you're going to like what I have to say."

"I have never known you not to be worth listening to."

"Aye, and I have never known you to be too shy of expressing your opinion of it, either. Well, Bellew, here it is – I have more than half a mind to throw over this speculative commission of mine that hasn't been anything but trouble and enlist right here as a regular soldier with whatever regiment will have me."

Bellew blinked in astonishment. "But, sir –" he exclaimed, leaping to his feet.

O'Malley held out his hand. "None of that, please. I may be older than you, and Heaven knows what reason you've had for always looking up to me the way you do, but I am just a common man, and there's plenty older and more experienced than me sharpening sticks and digging ditches in this army here, and I don't see why I should hold myself more precious than them just because I was fortunate enough to be far enough from the fighting to have time to ask for a commission first. I don't need glory, Bellew," he said, fumbling at his jacket. "I've been blessed enough in life, a hundred times over. My situation isn't the same as yours, you see." He pulled out the letter of commission and held it in front of him. Bellew frowned, staring at it. "Take it. Raise the men yourself - you'll make a fine captain, probably a better captain than a lieutenant, to speak frankly.

There's nothing in the letter to stop you – it names myself, and Masterson, rest his soul, and you, but what it doesn't do is say who's got to be what – we just always knew how we wanted it between the three of us. Only Masterson is gone, and the situation has changed."

O'Malley looked at him, waiting.

"I won't take it, sir," Bellew said, keeping his hands stubbornly at his side.

"You don't need me to look after you," O'Malley replied, still holding the letter out. "I'm sure there's plenty of good needs doing in South Carolina, and I can't think of a finer man to see it done. I just have my own path to follow."

"You misunderstand me," Bellew replied. "Please – I am not going to remonstrate with you, but please take back the commission – or throw it in the fire, if you prefer. After what I have seen today, there was only one force that could have prevented me from doing precisely what you have described, and that was, sir – I mean, O'Malley – that neither my heart nor my duty would permit me to leave your side. Only now I see that you have independently reached the same conclusion as I did – and it only shames me that I did not willingly offer to resign my commission first, for the greater cause. It is here that we are needed most. This is where our greatest strength lies – but it lies in ruins. We cannot turn our backs upon it now, if we pretend to serve it."

O'Malley raised his eyebrows. "Well," he said, replacing the commission slowly in his jacket. "Well, Bellew, you have surprised me."

"I hope not unfavorably."

"There's not much glory in being a foot soldier," O'Malley said. "It's a dirty business, and no one much notices whether you live or die, let alone how."

"I know. I thought about it a great deal when we were captured, and while we were in prison, and particularly after the details of our release. If I had gone to Boston when I wanted, I would not have been an officer. It was only later that I began to think that I might – well, I was eager to prove myself, as you know, and I remain so, but I believe I can do so better by getting to the work of it rather than pawing and grasping after honors that I have not yet earned. If I live, I will earn them," Bellew replied, clenching one hand into a fist. "That I swear. I may not receive them, but I will earn them."

As a regular enlisted man, there would be no question of Mrs. Addison. His position would simply be too low to visit her regularly; a lieutenant was closer in rank to an enlisted man than a general, but there was a meaningful difference of kind that eclipsed any difference in scale. He hoped she would not find his decision too sharp a disappointment. Perhaps, she might even understand. And they could talk about it, someday – someday when he had improved his fortunes. And she would forgive him – he was sure of that. Once he had worked his way to a better station, she would forgive him.

When dinner came, and O'Malley informed General McIntosh of their decision, the general frowned and looked at them quizzically. The table fell silent, men staring at them as if they were mad and holding their forgotten forks poised in mid-air. *Well*, Bellew thought dryly, *this is glory of a kind. I suppose I should try to enjoy it.*

"Enlist?" General McIntosh said. He remembered himself and finished chewing before he went on. "You want to enlist – as North Carolina men? Regular soldiers?"

"North Carolina is a fine country, and I promise we will not discredit her," O'Malley replied.

"But you're telling me you want to be regular soldiers? I've got all the lieutenants and captains I can swallow," General McIntosh repeated, gesturing vaguely at the table. "And it's all I can do to keep my majors and colonels from being wholly supplanted by foreigners. The only thing that keeps 'em at bay, the foreigners I mean, is that they all figure they should be generals at least, if not commander-in-chief."

"It seems to Bellew and me, General, that regular soldiers are mainly what is required," O'Malley answered with a wry smile. "And regular soldiers who can afford to feed and clothe themselves through the winter, particularly so."

General McIntosh was silent a moment, thinking. "Gentlemen, I thank you," he replied simply at last, returning to his beef.

O'Malley smiled. Bellew relaxed slightly. It was done. The decision made. If he felt some regret at what he had lost – well, best to put that aside, and let it melt away on its own accord. "We'll gather our things after dinner, sir," O'Malley said.

The general shook his head. "No, stay the night. You can't join the army yet anyway. You'll be out of service for a good couple weeks."

"What do you mean, sir?" Bellew inquired, frowning.

"You have to be inoculated for smallpox before you join the camp permanently. Orders from General Washington himself. No exceptions."

Chapter 30

"Inoculation?" Mrs. Addison cried at the breakfast table. Mrs. van Dortmund still lay in bed, but the rest of the family was up and dipping toast corners into soft-boiled eggs. "But father – Rachel is perfectly healthy. Look at her!"

Rachel straightened in her chair and tried to look as healthy as she could.

"You and Mr. Addison were inoculated in New-York during the earlier outbreak, along with your slaves," General van Dortmund replied, unmoved. "You are consequently exempt. Your maid, however, says she has not been –"

"I'm sure Rachel just forgot," Mrs. Addison said.

"One does not forget the experience of an inoculation, Margaret," General van Dortmund said, his voice dropping a perceptible degree in warmth. "I asked her, and she answered me, and now she must be inoculated before she can rejoin us. Or if she prefers, she can leave the camp and not be inoculated. She cannot, however, remain here until she undergoes the procedure. I'll have Colonel Rawls see to the arrangements."

"How long will I be out of service, sir," Rachel said in a soft voice. Mrs. Addison had shown little interest in her since they arrived, fully absorbed by laughing and catching up on gossip with her sister, and Rachel had been hard pressed to find much use for herself. She wondered if she would be entirely forgotten if she were absent more than a few days.

"A few weeks, perhaps six or seven at the worst," General van Dortmund answered, depressing her further. "It is, however, your decision, Rachel. You must understand there is a slight but not negligible chance that you will develop full smallpox, in which case the length of your recuperation cannot be predicted, nor its outcome."

Rachel turned to Mrs. Addison. "I'd be better well before the trip to New-York, then, ma'am," she said, trying to keep the question out of her voice. "And that's mostly when I believe I will be required. You are so well taken care of here. And we, we aren't leaving Briarwood for a few months, are we?"

"Martha can help you dress until Rachel gets back. She does wonderfully with mama, and you know how picky she is," Clarissa said, stroking her sister's arm. "Oh, Rachel, you're being very brave. You didn't even ask if it would hurt. That's the first thing I asked." Rachel had not considered the details of the inoculation in the slightest, and she blinked in surprise to be reminded of them. No, the inoculation itself didn't matter – it was the absence that she feared, and she feared it enough to put the lie to Clarissa's words.

Mrs. Addison exhaled heavily. "Well, all right, since it seems there's nothing to be done about this foolishness – you'd better get on with it as soon as possible, so that it's over with."

So she was still wanted, Rachel noted with relief. She had half-believed, for a moment, that it had been not an oversight that her inoculation had been forgotten – and she still more than half-believed that Mr. Addison, who showed a fine grasp of details that interested him and who remained studiously focused on his egg during the interchange, would as soon be rid of her as not.

Snowdrop and Buttercup had returned early in the morning, brought by a North Carolina sergeant who also bore a note from Captain O'Malley with his thanks and the astonishing intelligence that Bellew and O'Malley had decided to become North Carolina men. "Whichever way the wind blows," Mr. Addison had sniffed, but there was a second note in Bellew's hand addressed to Mrs. Addison explaining their reasons, and she had read it aloud at the breakfast table, her face drawn.

"But what about South Carolina?" Rachel had said in a small voice, and Clarissa had asked why Rachel was so concerned about South Carolina, and Mrs. Addison explained that it was her home.

"Oh, how foolish of me. I had thought you were from Delaware too, by your accent – you sound just like my sister. But that wouldn't make any sense, they didn't find you in Delaware," Clarissa had laughed.

"South Carolina has less need at the moment. This is an honorable decision. And honorably communicated," General van Dortmund had pronounced, strangling the possibility of anyone venturing any other opinion, and then he had launched into Rachel about inoculation. She had been so distracted by the thrill that General van Dortmund, who was so hard to please, thought highly of Lieutenant Bellew that she had barely noticed what she answered, and then there it was – she had to leave.

Directly after breakfast, Rachel went up to the room she shared with Martha and began the solitary task of putting together her things. She supposed she did not need more than a change of clothes and a little money, but it was difficult to fight the urge to keep everything she owned by her side, just in case. Her little bag looked so small. Was that all she had to show for herself in the world? And so she did pack everything, or would have, except that a shadow crossed the door, and Rachel looked up to see Mrs. Addison standing there, a serious look on her face.

Rachel clutched the dress in her hands nervously. "I'm just packing," she said.

Mrs. Addison nodded somberly and stepped inside the room, taking the dress gently from Rachel's grasp. She examined it absently. "You won't be dressing like this on your sick-bed," she said, putting the gown aside.

Rachel flushed, almost as if she had been caught stealing. "No, I suppose not – I'm sorry, I'm just scattered."

Mrs. Addison sat on the bed next to the empty dress and looked up at Rachel. "You weren't thinking of leaving us entirely, were you, dear?"

Her words struck Rachel like a thunderclap. "Me leave you – but ma'am – but for you, I might be a, a bar-maid, thinking of nothing better than to own my own shop one day –"

"Oh, it was a shop you had in mind back then?" Mrs. Addison said, a faint smile touching her face. "So you were planning to marry that fellow, that rather coarse creature –"

"Mr. Darling! Never!" Rachel said, aghast. "No, I meant to be – alone, I suppose. I thought that was the best I could do," she added quickly.

"Hm. I would have thought you more ambitious. Well," Mrs. Addison said, standing again. She shook out the dress and smoothed her hand down its length. "You won't be going to any dances for the next few weeks, that's for certain. You can leave this here. I'll make sure Martha isn't free with your possessions. She seems a pretty pert creature, and I don't trust her too far. Perhaps you'll have a salutary effect on her when you return."

Mrs. Addison left her alone again. Rachel had a terrible foreboding about not keeping all her possessions under her direct control, but she also knew now that if she packed everything, it would seem like a suggestion that she meant to bolt. Good Heavens, back to Mr. Darling, yet, whose memory Rachel did not much relish the re-acquaintance of. On sudden inspiration, she took the leather bag that had belonged to the poor dead Cherokee and stuffed it into her duffel. If no one wanted her – if everyone disappeared – she would still have clothes and tools to live in the wild.

"You are a perfect goose, and it's a good thing no one knows, or they'd never talk to you even for a second," she told herself, feeling better nevertheless. She wondered what Lieutenant Bellew had seen in the camp that had made him so set upon remaining there, even at the cost of his commission. His letter had seemed clear without really explaining much – that he and Captain O'Malley felt they could be of more service here than they could in the south. She liked the feeling that he was nearby. The air with which she filled her lungs might have touched his lips.

She wondered if he would think the same as Clarissa had, that it was brave of her not to fear the shallow cut in her arm or the fever of an inoculation. Oh, but of course, everyone here had had the inoculation – even Mrs. van Dortmund – so there was nothing that would impress him, she realized. She would just have to get it done, and it would be unpleasant, but it would be brief. She didn't know why she couldn't shake the terrible cloud of apprehension that hung over her.

Rachel would have been happy to walk to her destination, but Colonel Rawls was riding, and he was in a hurry, so she took Snowdrop. The mare seemed glad to see her again, whickering softly and pressing her damp nose into Rachel's hand. "I'm sorry, girl, I didn't bring anything for you," Rachel said, but Snowdrop nuzzled her just the same. They skirted the camp and rode through a path in the woods, dry leaves and needles whispering all around them, until they came to a small town of about forty wooden houses loosely gathered in a clearing beneath the shadow of a hill. Col. Rawls left her in the care of a phlegmatic widow named Hendricks who already had six men recovering in her home but promised she would move two of them so that Rachel could have a room of her own, and then he took Snowdrop and headed back to camp.

"Aren't there any other women?" Rachel asked almost plaintively once Col. Rawls was gone.

Mrs. Hendricks shrugged. "Oh, every now and then – don't worry, dear, the fever really isn't too bad most of the time, but I promise you that you won't feel like company much, nor mind who's with you or not."

Rachel spent the rest of the morning helping Mrs. Hendricks move the two men whose Rachel's arrival had discommoded and then tending to the sick, sitting beside them and placing damp cloths on their flushed skin to ease the fever. They were weak as kittens, and one had a frightful rash that covered his face, but they did not, as everyone had reassured Rachel, seem in any near danger from their illness. When Doctor Rhoades came at last, one of Rachel's charges sat up and insisted that his arm be cut first, to show her that it was no great matter.

"It isn't the cut that's the main thing," the doctor complained, seemingly irritated by the illogic of the request.

"But she's a girl," the recovering soldier said. "It's the cut that will worry her."

"Getting marks on her face, more likely," the doctor responded before Rachel could say that she didn't mind the cut at all. The prospect of having her face scarred stopped the words in her throat, and she blinked foolishly.

"That won't happen, will it?" she asked, touching her cheek. Mrs. Addison had no scars, nor did Clarissa or Mrs. van Dortmund.

"Can't say," Dr. Rhoades shrugged.

"I'm sure it won't," the soldier said gamely, adding, "And if you do get a few, you're pretty enough to bear them. Won't anyone notice, once they see your eyes."

Rachel blushed and was too flustered to pay much attention when the doctor, sighing, cut the soldier's arm with the tip of his scalpel, and the soldier grinned, showing it didn't hurt. The doctor wiped away the blood with a worn cloth and Rachel rolled up her sleeve. The doctor's hand was cold when he slipped it under her arm to hold her steady, and the cut so quick she did not feel it until afterwards, when the skin began to sting and the hot blood welled up. "Just a moment more," the doctor murmured, spreading a thin paste of what Rachel knew with disgust was infected pus on her open wound. The pressure hurt, like a bruise. She caught sight of the soldier staring at her worriedly, and she smiled at him.

"That's it, then," the doctor said, binding up her arm. "Stay in bed and let Mrs. Hendricks take care of you - she knows what to do. Probably it won't be more than a fever, but I'll be back every day to check on you, and if you do get a mild case like Williams over there, it won't be anything to fear."

"But it will keep me in bed longer," Rachel said, trying to tug her sleeve down without letting it touch her wound, which was sore. Dr. Rhoades shrugged and nodded. "Probably," he conceded.

Mrs. Hendricks let Rachel help around the house the rest of the day. "Aren't you going to pretend to be sick and dizzy, so that you have to rest?" Mrs. Hendricks laughed.

"I'm not, in the slightest."

"Yes, I know; the fever needs a while to build in your blood, and you shouldn't feel it tickling at you till tonight or tomorrow. Well, perhaps I shouldn't let you strain yourself this way -"

"I assure you, Mrs. Hendricks, I feel so much better at the thought that I'm not imposing on you more than necessary."

"I'm being paid for my trouble, and it's winter, so I can't tend turnips, I might as well tend soldiers," Mrs. Hendricks replied, but Rachel knew that if she was paid, it was in Continental dollars that wouldn't be good for anything but plastering holes in the wall.

Rachel gave herself a half-bath in the back before going to bed, wetting a rag and sponging down as much of her skin as she dared expose to the night air. She stood beneath a heavy oak tree, twisting around awkwardly and spilling water on her dress, but if Rachel could not see what she was doing, that meant that no one else could see her either, and the house was too crowded for her to be able to attend to her toilette inside. She did not know when she might be strong enough to wash herself again. Still, the sickness had not taken hold yet. She felt no more tired than she usually did at the end of a day, and when she pressed the back of her hand against her cheeks and forehead, they felt cool and dry.

Sleep came unwillingly, even when Rachel soothed herself with the dream of laying her head against Lieutenant Bellew's breast in the woods outside Griffin's Ford. She was too vigilant for signs of approaching fever, and she stared at the moon-grayed ceiling of her little room cataloguing every slight ache or chill, but each of them vanished in turn without growing into something worse.

When morning came, Rachel still showed no sign of disease. She dressed rapidly and presented herself to Mrs. Hendricks to help with breakfast. "Why, you look bright as a new penny!" Mrs. Hendricks remarked, and as the day wore on, Rachel helped with the convalescents and did a little cleaning, although the house did not need it, and chafed at her boredom. She almost prayed for the fever to start, so that she would not mind being trapped inside with too many people who were too agreeable for her to want to offend by seeming stand-offish but who were too busy with their own concerns to provide her much stimulation.

Dr. Rhoades arrived early in the afternoon and seemed surprised to see her up and dressed. He made no comment, grunting to himself and leaving. The next day when he came again, Rachel greeted him at the door, still blooming with health, and he peered at her probingly as he took her pulse and felt her temperature. The third day, when her condition remained unchanged, the doctor lifted his eyebrows and shook his head, smiling. "When should I expect the fever to start, sir?" Rachel asked as he examined her curiously.

"Yesterday at the latest," the doctor replied, peering into her eyes. "Hm." He pulled back and thought a moment. "Have you ever had smallpox before?"

"No, sir. I have never really been sick much. A few colds, I suppose."

"Hm. Have you lived on a farm with cattle, then, by any chance?"

"Well – yes, when I was very young," Rachel answered, puzzled at the sudden change in direction.

"Did you tend to them much?"

"No, sir – I wasn't supposed to. Well, I milked them a few times," Rachel admitted. "My mother was pregnant and my father was busy, and my mother told me to have Christoph, my brother, show me how. But when my father found out, he said I was too small, so I didn't do it any more."

"Were any of the cattle you milked sick or inflamed at the time? Do you recall getting a rash of any sort?"

"I wouldn't know, sir. It was a long time ago," Rachel said, wondering why on earth the doctor could be inquiring about the fate of long-dead cattle.

"Hm. Well, I can't rule out the possibility that you've had cow-pox, although it's hard to say," Dr. Rhoades mused. "If so, you are a very lucky girl."

"I am?"

"Yes – if that's the case, you're quite immune to smallpox already, and the worst you'll get out of this inoculation is the scratch on your arm."

Rachel blinked, and then her heart lifted. "I can go home, then?" she said, her face bright with the realization. "I mean, back to General van Dortmund's house?"

Dr. Rhoades shook his head. "If I were certain you'd had cow-pox, I would say yes, but I am not. I want to keep you here two or three days longer at least. If the fever still shows no sign of appearance, then we'll see, but I think I'll judge you fit for duty." He blinked and grinned, flashing her an amused look. "I've been speaking with soldiers for too long, Miss. I mean of course that I will judge you healthy and able to resume your normal activities and associations."

"Three days?" Rachel said, unable to keep the disappointment from her voice.

Dr. Rhoades looked at her with a faint smile. "Most of my patients are eager to extend their stay as long as possible," he said. "But I suppose they don't have General van Dortmund's hospitality to look forward to."

"It is very nice here," Rachel said hurriedly, hoping she had not cast any doubt on the quality of Mrs. Hendricks's home or care. "It's just that – I do want to get back to my duties, and my, my employer. And I'm not doing much here other than taking a bed and a room that could be put to better use, and – I don't really have anything to do," she admitted at last. "May I go outside, at least?" Mrs. Hendricks had been willing to let Rachel help, as long as she felt up to it, but the widow took her responsibilities too seriously to let Rachel leave the house, and, while grateful for the care given to her well-being, Rachel was so bored she felt her brains liquefying between her ears.

"Of course you can, dear, if you don't stray too far," Dr. Rhoades said. "I must confess I had forgotten that leisure can be something of a burden at times," he laughed. He bent over to snap his bag shut. "Well, perhaps there is some sewing you can do."

"I didn't bring any, and I don't paint, and I didn't bring paint anyway, and I don't know how to play music, and I have only my one book with me, only I've read it so many times," Rachel blurted. "I would gladly trade some of my leisure to you, if I could." The doctor smiled and bowed his head in acknowledgment. He rose to leave to tend to the sick men in the bedroom, when a thought occurred to Rachel. "Doctor – I have been helping Mrs. Hendricks with the convalescents a bit," she began.

"Yes, that's quite safe," the doctor responded, only a little impatiently.

"If it is all right for me to go outside, and it is all right for me to be around the sick men, and you are so pressed – is there anything I could do to aid you?" Rachel asked, looking at him hopefully. "I do not know much about medicine, but I can take direction, and I can certainly hold things when your hands are busy, and – well, maybe talk to the men the way Mr. Williams talked to me and was so kind, and it really was helpful."

Dr. Rhoades paused a moment, considering. "That is a very generous offer, Miss Kolkhorst, leaving me only to wish that you were a medical man. I generally have hands enough to perform the work that is required of me. But I do not mean to reject your assistance," he added quickly, as if worried by the resignation settling on Rachel's shoulders. "The infirm always benefit from more care, even if it is nothing more than a kind word. The townspeople here do what they can, but they have their own lives to lead – well, all right, if you would like, you may come with me on the rest of my rounds today, and I will introduce you, so that you can return as a nurse of sorts later if you feel up to it."

"Oh, I am sure I will!" Rachel said. She stood quickly and smoothed her skirts.

"Not all aspects of nursing are pleasant or delicate. You must remember that some of these men are quite unwell, and that they cannot exhibit the usual control over their physical functions or manner, and that they will be in a state of undress."

"But I've already done a little for the men in the house here. And I have taken care of babies, sir, and I have seen prisoners of war in Philadelphia."

"And farm animals as well," the doctor added with a smile.

"Yes, and farm animals – perhaps that is the best way to put it," Rachel said seriously. "Man is composed of a great deal of mud mixed with a tiny spark of the divine. I do not forget the presence of either, nor their proportions. I assure you that no matter how low these men are laid, I will not shrink from them nor make them feel as though their worth is in any measure diminished in my eyes."

Dr. Rhoades's mouth fell open and then shut again. He looked at her oddly, thick brows knitting together over eyes that were nearly black. "Well, as long as you are not frightened of them, or do not frighten them in turn, I'm sure that will be quite adequate," he said at last, shrugging slightly to himself.

Rachel found Mrs. Hendricks and explained her situation hurriedly, and then she rushed back to the room with the sick men just as Dr. Rhoades was leaving it. Williams had fallen into a doze, but one of the other men teased her, "You won't forget us, will you, Miss Kolkhorst, while you're off hunting for better prospects?"

"You will be my first and last visit and every day," Rachel promised, rather anxious about the flirting that got rather insistent at times, and then she departed with Dr. Rhoades.

The weather was gentle, and Rachel felt her spirits rise as she stepped into the fresh air of day. Dr. Rhoades walked down a beaten dirt path, holding his heavy bag in one hand at his side. They visited several houses very much like Mrs. Hendricks's, and Rachel tried to remember the dozens of new faces and names. She met two girls her own age, and it surprised her to discover how young and unworldly they seemed to her – one was due to be married next month, and that surprised Rachel more, and she felt a sad pang that while she had seen so much more of the world than she had ever expected, she had touched so little of it. What if she did marry one of the convalescents? Would she be happy then, or a better person? But of course she would do no such thing. She would remain with Mrs. Addison forever. She felt it in her bones.

She held Dr. Rhoades's bag for him and soon learned the names of his instruments, and he seemed impressed that she read the labels on the bottles of medicine so quickly. When there was nothing else for her to do, and the sick men too unwell to take even a passing interest in her conversation, she quietly emptied bed-pans, and when she returned, rubbed her hands with a bit of charcoal she took from an uncleaned fire-grate. Dr. Rhoades noticed her doing so, and asked about it afterwards.

"Oh, I know it makes my hands look dirty at first," Rachel said. "But I find it cleans them better if I use charcoal first, and then run water over them. At least, they smell cleaner."

"Does it?" Dr. Rhoades mused, and then, asking her permission, sniffed the palms of her hands. "That does rid the skin of odor remarkably," he said. "I may try that at the end of the day."

He hesitated briefly, took a step, and then stopped again. "Perhaps you would like to go back to your quarters – your hostess now," he said. "You have been a great help already." He reached out his hand for his bag, which Rachel had picked up at the last house and carried for him.

"I'm not tired," Rachel protested. She didn't want to go back to the boredom of Mrs. Hendricks's house and the awkward attention of her roommates, not yet, anyway, and she didn't see any reason for her not to accompany Dr. Rhoades on the rest of his rounds, unless she was doing something wrong or bothering him somehow. But he'd said it was only this once, and she could go on her own later – why would he stop now? "I think I must have had cow-pox – I'm sure of it. I feel no ill effects whatsoever," Rachel persisted, drawing the bag closer to her skirt possessively.

"Yes, but – well, I'll be frank. There is one case in this house that I don't like the looks of," Dr. Rhoades said, "and I am not sure of its outcome. Your energies might be best directed to gentler concerns."

"Then surely this unfortunate requires attention more than all the others put together," Rachel said. She would not have Dr. Rhoades think she was as weak as that – surely she had made a better impression of herself. "Even if he is not well enough to know a friend is near, perhaps there is some slight relief I can offer." She thought of Lieutenant Masterson and the handkerchief. She did not know whether it had meant anything to him, but it seemed to have. "Is he wounded?"

Dr. Rhoades shook his head. "No, I would not inoculate a wounded man. He must have had some prior susceptibility or weakening of the system, I am afraid. No, he is not too bad now, and I have not told him what I fear – that it looks very much as though he will develop full smallpox. I pray I am incorrect, and perhaps I am."

"Then I will pray also," Rachel said. Dr. Rhoades accepted her insistence with a resigned shrug. So she accompanied him into the home, a pleasant wooden house with something of a disused air about it, and met the boy who was watching over the convalescents there while his father worked, and followed Dr. Rhoades into the room where the poor man with full smallpox lay. She knew it was his room because Dr. Rhoades's face took on a somber cast, and he seemed in a hurry to find out whether his suspicions were correct. As she promised, Rachel formed the words of a quick prayer in her mind.

The prayer shattered into a thousand fragments once she looked at the bed and recognized the exhausted form of the man lying beneath crumpled blankets, his face covered in red blotches as if he had been pricked and slapped a thousand times. "Ah, doctor," he said in a tired voice. "It seems I'll be giving you something interesting to look at after all. Why, and you have for me, as well," he added, his eyes lighting on Rachel and crinkling at the corners.

Chapter 31

"Captain O'Malley!" Rachel cried, shoving the bag on a table and rushing forward. She wanted to seize his hands, but stopped herself short – just because he was an invalid did not mean she could take liberties with him and toss him about as if he were a doll. She glanced around the room quickly. It contained no other occupants. "Where is Lieutenant Bellew?"

"*Captain* O'Malley?" Dr. Rhoades inquired.

"It's just plain O'Malley now, Miss Kolkhorst. Did they get our letter?"

"No, they did, I – I forgot, and I'm just used to thinking of you that way," Rachel said, her heart hammering. Mr. O'Malley couldn't develop smallpox – it wouldn't be fair, not with all he'd been through, and his volunteering to remain here, when he might have stayed a Captain. She looked at him closely, trying not to be obtrusive about it. The slenderness of which he had boasted before commencing the ride to Valley Forge had grown wolfishly, so that almost no flesh remained on him to keep his skin from rubbing against his bones. His eyes were wet and dull, like shadows beneath the surface of a muddy pond. His breath came short. The hard, straight lines of bones showed plainly through the inflamed skin of his hands, which lay inert on the bedspread. There was something tenuous about him, like a dewdrop trembling on a blade of grass. She did not need Dr. Rhoades's medical experience to see that O'Malley was terribly ill.

"Well, you can call me anything you like, if it pleases you. Bellew is next door," O'Malley said, moving his head slightly to the side. He winced, as if even the small motion caused discomfort. He managed a smile. "I had such an interesting reaction to the treatment that the good doctor thought I deserved my own room."

Rachel logged the information about Bellew but put it aside. Her heart was cut too deeply to see O'Malley in his condition for her to allow the mention of Bellew to touch her thoughts more than fleetingly. She put a smile on her face, even if it was weaker than O'Malley's effort, and sat beside him, placing her hand gently on his. "When I saw you lying in the prison yard," she said evenly, "I thought it was a pity that you should have nothing but hard masculine company for your recuperation. I may not be

Mrs. Merriwether, but at least I can see to it that fate does not pull the same trick on you twice."

"Perhaps I am getting old," O'Malley replied in a scratchy voice that sounded forced. "I should protest at being seen at anything but my peak by such a lovely girl, but I find it rather agreeable than otherwise to have her attentions, whatever the cause." His hand felt dry and light, except for the painfully swollen blisters. Rachel hoped the pressure of her fingers didn't hurt.

"More likely it means you're still young," the doctor countered. He examined O'Malley, keeping his thoughts to himself, and bled him, and Rachel held the basin to catch the blood. Each metallic ping as a droplet hit the basin felt like grapeshot against her skin. *Out,* she said to herself. *Get all the sickness out.*

"You didn't come all this way to check up on us, did you?" O'Malley asked her, seemingly unfazed by his wounded arm.

"No – I was to be inoculated also. Well, that is, I was inoculated, but it seems I have a prior immunity, and so I asked whether I might make myself useful here until the end of my confinement. I didn't know – it never occurred to me that I might find you here also. Somehow it seemed that everyone had been inoculated already but me."

"I'm glad of that. You're a good girl," O'Malley murmured. Rachel flushed, but his eyes were closed. She thought he had fallen asleep, and perhaps he had, because he remained limp while the doctor bound up the small cuts from the bleeding. Rachel was torn. She wanted to see Bellew badly – how sweet it would be to touch his hand the way she had O'Malley's, and to know he took comfort from it – but she could not bear to leave the side of such a sick man, a man she had always liked. And what would Bellew think, if she scurried away from his dearest friend in his jeopardy, now that his other best friend – the one she had indeed deserted, and in his final moments – was gone.

And now that the prospect was near, she found she was a little afraid of seeing Bellew. Not that his condition would offend or appall, since she knew that Dr. Rhoades felt that O'Malley was his only dangerous patient. Just – did he really want her to visit, or did he even care, and what would she say, and nothing she came up with as an objection was really insuperable, only she felt so shy at confronting him suddenly that it seemed on the whole best if she avoided the issue. Except, she realized, that might seem strange – or cold – and she would regret the missed opportunity so badly, and she knew very well that she would heap reproaches on herself all the black night, and all the gray day that followed, if she could not console herself with the precious image of even a fleeting glance or perhaps having been of some small service to him. Rachel concluded that she simply did not know what she wanted to do.

O'Malley resolved her difficulty. He opened his eyes and moved his wounded arm from Dr. Rhoades's grasp to rest at his side. "If Bellew is awake, be sure and tell him that I was also," he murmured, and Rachel blurted, "I certainly shall, and I'll tell him not to worry." O'Malley's eyelids sank down again, and his face showed no expression.

When they left the room and Dr. Rhoades shut the door gently behind them, Rachel turned to him and began, "Doctor –" but he silenced her with a frown and a quick shake of his head. He walked down the hall and opened the next door. Rachel followed him.

The sole window faced east, so little light filtered through, and shadows hung over the room like cobwebs. Rachel's eyes adjusted slowly to the dark. Four men lay still in their beds.

"Good day, doctor," a voice whispered, and one of the forms shoved itself up to a sitting position by the elbows.

"Now, now, no need to put on a show for the girl, she's here as a nurse," Dr. Rhoades complained, hustling to the man's side and pressing him gently back down. He sat beside the man and took his pulse. The mention of a girl roused the other three, and Rachel recognized Bellew at last. He looked tired, and his skin was flushed, but he seemed mostly unmarked by his ordeal except for two red spots like a snake-bite beneath his left eye. But she knew his face just the same. The same soft, quick eyes, and reddish hair, and the chin that was perhaps a little too pointed, and the straight nose that showed just a small bump before the bridge met his forehead. "Miss Kolkhorst?" he asked, his eyebrows contracting in uncertainty. She smiled at him, her eyes lowered. "Do you have a message for me?"

"Yes, Captain – I mean Mr. O'Malley wanted you particularly to know that he was awake and well when the doctor and I saw him a moment ago," Rachel said, before realizing that of course he'd thought she had come from the van Dortmunds; or rather from Mrs. Addison.

Bellew's face showed a shaky hope. "Is his condition much improved, then?"

"I don't know. It was the first time I saw him since, since the fever, but his spirits are excellent, I can assure you," Rachel said. She could not say what she thought.

"Here – my bag, Miss Kolkhorst," the doctor murmured, and Rachel remembered her duties and stepped quickly to his side. "Yes – you're coming along fine," Dr. Rhoades decided, and moved onto Bellew. He took Bellew's arm, pushing up the sleeve, and pressed his first two fingers against Bellew's wrist. The skin was pale as milk, but Rachel could see the strength of the tendons in his hand and the thicker skin that covered his palm, and she remembered the whispering feel of his hand against her skin from the dance. Bellew watched the doctor's ministrations passively, his eyes occasionally checking Rachel with a slightly worried expression.

The doctor turned his attention to Bellew's face, tilting it to the side so that he could examine the fever marks on Bellew's cheek.

"Mrs. Addison didn't send me." Rachel felt she had to explain this, and it was all right to make noise when the doctor wasn't checking a pulse. "I was sent to be inoculated too, only the fever didn't seem to take hold in me."

This captured Bellew's attention. "Were there cattle on the farm where you grew up?" he inquired. Dr. Rhoades looked at him in surprise.

"Are you a medical man?" he asked.

"No, sir. I had an interest in the topic and hoped to study it once, but my circumstances did not permit me to leave for college. I did do as much reading as I could on my own, in the hopes that some day I might have the opportunity," Bellew said. "But when events changed as they did, I am afraid I gave up the task."

"Perhaps when the war is over."

"Perhaps," Bellew replied slowly, but he did not seem sure of it.

"Well, it is a fine calling, and always a useful one," Dr. Rhoades said. "Now, if you will please lift your shirt."

Bellew hesitated, his eyes returning to Rachel. Dr. Rhoades noticed.

"I assure you, she doesn't faint at the sight of a man's shoulders. She's seen dozens today."

Rachel did blush then. "I could –" But she did not finish speaking, because Bellew nodded in acceptance and pulled his shirt over his head. Rachel lowered her eyes modestly. She heard the soft sounds of shifting bodies as Dr. Rhoades pursued his careful examination. And then, hoping that the darkness of the room would cover the act, she glanced up cautiously through her lashes.

His build was heavier than she had realized, as the width of his shoulders and length of his limbs deceived the eye. The muscles of a man accustomed to exercise or labor defined his chest and stomach, although this definition was a little soft, presumably due to his long captivity. A light patch of fine, dark hair dusted his sternum and trailed in a wispy line down the center of his abdomen. He did not look vulnerable half-naked, unlike so many of the men Rachel had seen today. "That's good," Dr. Rhoades said, and Bellew pulled his shirt on again.

"No other marks," Bellew said.

"No. And if they haven't shown up by now, they're not likely to," the doctor answered. "Just rest, and eat as much as you can."

Bellew eased back down to a lying position. He exhaled softly in relief. "I thought one wasn't supposed to eat much with a fever," he murmured.

"I'm recommending it to everyone. There's plenty of food here, and I'd be happy if all of you put on some weight before I let you go," Dr. Rhoades answered, and Bellew nodded with a grimace.

She followed Dr. Rhoades quietly as he examined the remaining two men, whose condition he seemed to find satisfactory. Before they left, Bellew roused himself again and asked, "Miss Kolkhorst? Are you returning to Briarwood soon?"

"No – well, sooner than I thought. Dr. Rhoades wants to keep me here a few days to be safe." She paused. "Is there a message you'd like me to bring back?"

"No, none," Bellew muttered. "Thank you."

Rachel hesitated again. "Well – if you think of one – I will be back again tomorrow," she said.

That roused him slightly. "Ah – well, I will be very glad to see you, of course, although you always seem to find me at a terrible disadvantage."

"I don't mind," Rachel said, and because that seemed wrong, she quickly added, "I think it is very brave of everyone to endure this illness, and it is surely very clever of General Washington to make sure that we do it when we do not need to fight."

"We?" the man who had tried to sit up prematurely asked, pushing himself up on his elbows again. "Are our lovely maidens taking up arms in defense of our country as well?"

"Don't be so sure you're joking," Bellew replied, smiling a little. "When I first met Miss Kolkhorst, she was traveling by foot towards the fighting and doing so with a definite purpose." His eyes met hers, tired but amused.

"Well, I have - at least I'm doing a little something now," Rachel said guiltily, trying without much success to put the mansions and balls and pretty new clothes that the past few months had given her out of her mind.

When they returned outside, Rachel said, "Doctor - Mr. O'Malley's condition - may I ask candidly your view of it?"

"Because you know the man," Dr. Rhoades said.

"Yes."

He pressed his lips together and looked at his feet. At length, he shrugged. "It is in God's hands more than mine," he said. "It is unquestionably full smallpox. It is possible that he will recover, of course, but even the happiest scenario will take a long time to unfold."

"He just had dysentery," Rachel pleaded, as if the unfairness of it would change Dr. Rhoades's mind - and as if Dr. Rhoades had any say in the matter.

"A prior illness has unpredictable results. Sometimes the recent outrage seems to make the body resist any new illness all the harder, but other times the depletion of energies makes it more susceptible. I fear in this case the latter rule prevailed." He looked at her more closely. "If Mr. O'Malley is a friend of yours, I will give you the same advice I would give to anyone in your position. Cherish the time you have with him, and if God grants more, accept the gift with gratitude and thanks."

The next day, Rachel decided that she would follow the same route as she had with Dr. Rhoades, saving Bellew and O'Malley for last. She wanted to spend as much time as she could with both of them, and she would not be able to do so with a clear conscience if she did not acquit herself of her other responsibilities first. Many of the sick men were dozing or too low to speak much themselves, but she could talk to them anyway, and cool their fevers a little with cloths, and change the bed-pans. She told inconsequential stories about what little she remembered of her life on the farm, mostly, because she found that a great deal of the men here had come from farms themselves and were comforted by the familiar images. It was easy to talk to them, even though they were men and strangers, when no one really expected more from her than the sound of her voice. Only once did she stray into dangerous territory by accident. Her error came from an unexpected direction. One of her patients asked her why she had left her home, and Rachel admitted after a moment that a band of Indians had killed her family.

"You may call 'em the Indians, but it's really the British," the man spat, suddenly animated. "And don't you forget it."

"No – they were Cherokee, I am quite sure," Rachel corrected him, frowning. The man looked as though he were about to grab his knife and march off half-dressed and raving. She wondered if it were an effect of the fever.

"You don't take my meaning. It's the English and their agents going to the dirty savages and riling them up with all sorts of presents and promises if they'll just make trouble, just like the French used to do. We'll never have peace with them breathing down our necks, they can't be trusted –"

"I'm not supposed to let you get excited," Rachel interrupted nervously, and the man, seeing her distress, fortunately complied. She didn't like disturbing her patient, and she liked hearing such vituperation about the Indians even less, even though she had never decided whether she should bear hatred towards them or not. She knew that the English had their agents with the Indians – there was hardly a nation that didn't – but she had never seen any such near her Cherokee family. She almost wished she had seen an Englishman, even a fur trader she might conceivably blame, so that she would not have to bear the wound on her heart knowing, as she did, that she loved both her families, but that the mere existence of the Kolkhorst farm had truly frightened and threatened the Cherokee, and that the Cherokee had truly hurt the Kolkhorsts in return. And it was no outside force that had made them enemies. There was simply no force that could have made them friends, other than separation.

The owner of the cottage where O'Malley and Bellew lay in their recuperation was a widowed soap-maker named Tobias Powell. Neither he nor his son Zachariah were at home when Rachel knocked at the door, so she popped her head into his shop next door, and Mr. Powell told her to let herself in and make herself free of anything she needed, the place was unlocked. She returned to the quiet house and stepped inside cautiously, holding her breath. She looked in on O'Malley first, but he was asleep, so she tiptoed to the other room. Bellew was sleeping too, she saw with a pang of disappointment. A sheen of sweat covered his forehead, but his dreams seemed peaceful, and he lay still beneath his woolen blanket. She could not look at him as long as she would have liked, because two of the other men were awake and acknowledged her happily, glad of the company. She sat beside them and held their hands and spoke to them in whispers for a few minutes. Then she rose to make some weak coffee. The two conscious men drank it happily, so she brought them some bread and cheese as well, mindful of Dr. Rhoades's prescription from yesterday. Bellew still did not awake. She left coffee and a little food at his bedside, and that of the other sleeping man, and then went back to O'Malley's room.

His condition seemed unchanged. No, it seemed worse. Perhaps that was because he was not awake to put on a show for her. The rash still covered his face and hands with inflamed blisters, and the rest of his skin glowed with an unhealthy pallor. His breath came ragged and shallow, as if even that slight effort were a struggle.

She could not bear to leave him. Rachel gently pulled his blanket higher to cover his chest and sat on the wooden stool at the bedside. She hoped he could feel her presence somehow, know that she was thinking of him and near as he dreamed.

Other than his irregular breathing, O'Malley did not move. Rachel watched him for a while, and then she stared out the window at the sky and the neighboring houses, and the slender tips of the evergreens swaying in the wind. She put her hand in her pocket absently and pulled out two of her dollar coins, turning them over in her hand for something to fidget with. It helped pass the time as the shadows lengthened. She felt a little foolish sitting silent beside a sleeping man, but his condition was so poor, and every rasping breath terrified her anew. She did not know how she could bring herself to go even once Mr. Powell returned and there would be someone to wonder at her curious desire to sit in silence by a man who needed nothing from her and did not know she was at hand. Perhaps she would say she was waiting for the doctor, to see what he had to say about O'Malley.

"What's that you've got in your hand?" a thin voice whispered. Rachel startled and almost dropped her coins. O'Malley was awake now, and she had not noticed. He regarded her with the ghost of a smile.

"Oh! Just some dollars. Would you like some coffee, or some food? Mr. Powell said I could prepare anything you needed."

O'Malley shook his head slightly. "No thank you, Miss. You had such a serious look I thought it must be a letter, or a book. I didn't know dollars could inspire much in the way of thought. They never did with me – only their absence, sometimes, but never their presence."

Rachel smiled. "Well, actually I was thinking about them a little." She put the dollars aside and dipped a rag in a bowl of cold water. "Here, I've been watching you sweat, and finally I can do something about it. Are you terribly warm?"

"No, don't trouble yourself over that, I only feel very tired," O'Malley said, but when Rachel laid the cloth on his forehead anyway, he did not object. "Have you been sitting there long?"

"Oh, not very – only a little while. I was hoping you might wake," Rachel said.

"I can't say I don't wonder a little that you would stay with me sleeping, when there are sick men who are awake," O'Malley said.

"I have seen them already, so I had a bit of time and thought I might rest here," Rachel began, and O'Malley lifted his hand in a tired gesture.

"It's all right, lass, I know it's smallpox, even if the doctor won't say so to my face. I knew it when he separated me, and he did too." Rachel turned her face away so that the dark would offer her face a veil. "Ah, now, none of that. There's always a few in every inoculation. It just makes my path a little harder and a little longer. It's all right."

Rachel could not bring herself even to think how often smallpox was fatal. It would not be, in this case. Doctors always used the weakest strain they could find for inoculations – O'Malley would get past it, as he had gotten past the dysentery before. "I know you will, Mr. O'Malley. But it takes months to get over, and you've done so much to be here for the fighting – but when it starts again, you'll still be laid up, and you know Lieutenant – Mr. Bellew won't want to leave you, although he'll be obliged, and – it simply seems unjust."

"But that is simply how the world is," he said. "It is simple enough, even if there is no promise it will be easy. When you are called, you must stand. And when you stand, you must offer everything the situation requires." He smiled. "And not one iota more. You see, my dear, it's the last point that's really the key to the whole thing. I daresay there'll be fighting enough waiting for me. I'll have plenty of hair-raising stories to tell Bellew's children and make a perfect nuisance of myself to his future wife." He lifted a trembling hand and pushed the cloth away from his eye, where some water was leaking into it. Rachel straightened it for him, brushing back his hair. A few sores showed on his scalp, through the thick strands of brown and gray.

"Or your own children. But perhaps you wouldn't want to cross your wife that way. Frighten your grandchildren instead – your daughter-in-law won't dare object, no matter how impossible you've made it for the children to sleep."

"No, I've been married once, and I was too lucky in my Kitty to try my chances again. That foolishness is behind me now."

"You were married?" Rachel said, interested.

O'Malley frowned slightly. "I'd rather not talk about her, if you don't mind," he replied. He smiled again and changed the subject. "You never told me what you were contemplating in those dollars of yours. I must own I'm curious."

"Oh! The dollars." Rachel glanced at them where they lay on the bedside table. She would much rather have heard about O'Malley's wife. "It was nothing but idle foolishness, really."

"Then it will amuse me without taxing me, an ideal combination."

"Well," Rachel said with a diffident shrug, shy about boring him with her inconsequential thoughts, even if that was what he seemed to want, "You see this one here – from '53. It has the coat of arms of Spain on the reverse, of course, and on the front it has such a lovely design – the two sides of the globe, front and back, with the new world eclipsing the old, and they sit between the pillars of Hercules, which proclaim the bold words '*plus ultra*' - 'there is more beyond'."

O'Malley held out his hand, and Rachel gave him the '53 dollar. He tilted it to catch the light. "It is a pretty thing," he murmured. "I never thought to look at one closely."

"And then there is this dollar from four years ago, after the old king had died and the new been crowned. The earth is gone. The pillars of Hercules are gone. The bold words are gone. And what do we have to replace them?" She switched coins with O'Malley, who managed a dry chuckle.

"He's not likely to be hanged for the crime of beauty, is he," O'Malley said. The King of Spain's face with its huge nose, receding chin, sloping forehead, and empty smile was not much improved by the Roman emperor's trappings in which it had been rendered.

"He is not. And yet Charles the Third insists on placing his personal visage, whether anyone feels like seeing it or not, upon every coin. While his predecessor Ferdinand the Sixth was a handsome boy, my father told me, and a sensitive and cultured one as well. My father thought very highly of him."

"Your father traveled in Spain, then?"

Rachel blinked. "I don't know," she admitted. "I was very young - he liked to tell stories about nobles and royalty, and I suppose I never thought to ask how he came by his opinions. Perhaps they were merely stories," she concluded with a shrug, taking back the second dollar.

"Ferdinand was a good fellow, from what I've heard of him," O'Malley said. "I'm sure your father's other judgments were equally just. It is an irony, that the pretty one kept his face a secret and the ugly one wants to push his everywhere."

"It was really the other irony that I was thinking of, though," Rachel said. "Ferdinand the Sixth was sensitive and kind, and Charles the Third is practical and unimaginative, if not positively dull. And yet Charles, people say, is not uninterested in our cause."

"He has his own reasons to dislike England."

Rachel nodded. "I am sure he does. But you would think that it would have been Ferdinand who would have given us a sympathetic ear - and yet

I do not think, somehow, no matter how much poetry he may have held in his heart, that King Ferdinand would have involved himself in any way with our struggle, even if Ferdinand could hear the music of it, and Charles cannot." It felt so natural to think of the rebellion as her own struggle now that *our* slipped out before Rachel realized it.

"And why not?"

"Because he was kind, and because he would not want to flame a war. And because he would not hold spite against England, even if it would serve his purposes."

"You are probably correct," Bellew's voice came from behind her, and Rachel wheeled around on her stool. Bellew's shirt hung loose over the trousers in which he'd slept. He wore no stockings, and his legs and feet were bare. He supported himself against the door frame with one arm, smiling slightly.

"Hullo, Bellew."

"Hullo, O'Malley. Miss Kolkhorst told me your spirits were good, and now I see why. This is the sort of conversation you thrive on."

"It's almost fanciful enough even for you, lad, although a hair cleverer than you deserve."

"Oh, I'm – here, Lieutenant, Mr. Bellew, you must sit down," Rachel said, springing to her feet and freeing up the stool. A pained expression crossed his face. "Please, Mr. Bellew – you're sick, and Dr. Rhoades would never forgive me."

He sketched a quick bow, grimacing in apology as he remembered his disheveled appearance, and took the offered seat. Rachel moved back towards the door to give him room.

The two friends spoke a few moments, and Rachel felt herself increasingly superfluous as the conversation meandered on without her. She wished that Dr. Rhoades would appear, so that she would have an excuse to remain. But Dr. Rhoades remained absent. So Rachel waited a minute, and then she excused herself, curtsying, and returned to Mrs. Hendricks's house.

Shortly after breakfast the next morning, Dr. Rhoades gave Rachel a perfunctory examination and declared that she was now unquestionably out of danger and free to leave quarantine. Before she could decide whether she was happy about this or not, a breathless Zachariah came running from the Powell house. He reported that Mr. Bellew had asked him to please bring back the doctor at once, because Mr. O'Malley was dead.

Chapter 32

"So there was a funeral," Mrs. Addison said, her face serious.

"Yes, ma'am," Rachel reported quietly. "I apologize that I was late getting back, but I could not – I could not deny Mr. O'Malley my final respects." The family sat in the upstairs parlor. General van Dortmund had joined them briefly. For once, his presence did not cast more of a pall on the room than existed already, once Rachel had reported what had delayed her arrival till the evening.

"Of course not, it goes without saying," Mrs. Addison replied with a flick of her hand. "Is Mr. Bellew well?"

"The inoculation has treated him lightly, but he is very broken up about his friend," Rachel said. She could not shake the image of Bellew, hastily dressed, standing at the fresh grave, motionless, one hand covering his face beneath the brim of his hat.

"I am very sorry for him, of course, but I am sure he hardly expected to go to war without losing some comrades," Mrs. van Dortmund put in.

"No, ma'am, he never did. Only his two closest friends have now died without seeing battle, and he takes that pretty hard."

"But since it was not in battle, at least Mr. O'Malley was able to receive a funeral, even if it is not in his home," Clarissa murmured. An expression of melancholy pulled at her features. Her heart was easily touched.

"Yes – that is something," Rachel said quietly. "Dr. Rhoades wanted to keep the matter as small as possible so as not to frighten the other convalescents – but at least twenty of them came nevertheless. The Powell family, and the men who'd been quartered with Mr. O'Malley, and Mrs. Hendricks – that was where I was staying – and the men who were staying there, even one who I really don't think should have roused himself for the effort. And a few others who had met Mr. O'Malley when he first arrived. You couldn't know Mr. O'Malley even a minute, or know someone who did, without loving him." Rachel's eyes darted to Mr. Addison, sitting silent at the other end of the room. Mr. Addison's expression was hardly wounded, but appropriately somber nevertheless. It wasn't Mr. O'Malley against whom Mr. Addison had borne a grudge.

"How I wish that I had known him too!" Clarissa said, placing her hand over Rachel's. Her eyes were bright. "You must tell me everything you know about Mr. O'Malley so that I can help hold onto his memory."

"What a kind thing to say, Miss," Rachel murmured. It pained her how little she knew about the dead man. He had looked after Bellew and been oil on the waters at the Brass Bull; his speech by Griffin's Ford; his illness in Philadelphia; and the final illness in Valley Forge. Rachel wished fervently he had told her about Kitty, but it was his right to take the story to the grave if he so desired. She felt certain now that he had known, the last time he spoke to her, that he was going to die. *When you are called, you must stand. And when you stand, you must offer everything the situation requires. And not one iota more.* She wished she had listened more and talked less, and of all things, foolish prattle about the pillars of Hercules and distant princes.

"Now, you'll stop that and call me Clarissa. I already told you," Clarissa said.

Mr. Addison excused himself shortly afterwards to visit a friend, and General van Dortmund also rose, saying that he had pressing correspondence to attend to, and that he found himself obliged to read his letters carefully before they were sent, because his aide-de-camp was careless.

Mrs. Addison looked up sharply. "But father, I could help you with that," she said.

"Thank you, Margaret, but your spelling leaves something to be desired, and the topics of military communication involve matters not suitable for an outsider, a civilian, nor a woman."

Mrs. Addison shook her head impatiently. "No, not me, father, I know what you think of – You heard the felicity of Mr. Bellew's pen, I am sure, when I read his letter out loud. Now, I had suggested to you before that you find him a place –"

"But he found his own, and quite honorably."

"Yes, but you remember his reasons, father? He and Mr. O'Malley felt they could be of greater service to the main force of the army, and he didn't really have any other options. But wouldn't he be of more service here? Rather than being just one more man in the mud, he could help you manage hundreds – you shouldn't be checking punctuation, papa, there are better things for you to be doing with your time."

Rachel looked at General van Dortmund with sudden hope. She did not know whether Bellew would accept a staff posting, but at least an offer would remind him that he had friends. And if he said yes, he would be living beneath the same roof as Rachel, sharing meals – she could have kissed Mrs. Addison, even if an unworthy part of her was jealous of her mistress for being able to toss about such favors.

"The difference between a comma and a semicolon can mean the difference between living and dead, in our circumstances," General van Dortmund replied coldly.

"Yes, father, that's exactly what I'm talking about – wouldn't it be nice if you didn't have to concern yourself over that any more, because it was in good hands?"

General van Dortmund frowned. "You take a great deal of interest in this young man."

"It all comes of doing favors, Thomas," Mrs. van Dortmund said. "Now Margaret has started it, and she's trapped in the quicksand. Don't you go down the same path."

"Mother –"

"Margaret, hush, I know what I'm about. This Mr. Bellew has been surrounded by nothing but bad luck ever since I first heard of him, and I don't like the thought of bringing that into my house."

"He was there when we got the free potatoes," Rachel offered. Mrs. van Dortmund wheeled around with surprising speed. She tossed her hands in the air before dropping them back into her lap, and she shook her head and frowned at Rachel, as if frustrated beyond all endurance.

"Oh, those potatoes – why on earth does everyone keep harping on those potatoes? Thomas, Clarissa – now you, Rachel, and I thought of you as being so quiet." The reproach in Mrs. van Dortmund's voice was unmistakable. Rachel's ears prickled with heat, and she lowered her eyes in submission. She fingered the fabric of her skirt, determined to be silent now. But she listened with a feverish interest.

General van Dortmund said, "I don't see why you think I should place implicit trust in a man I do not know. My understanding is that he was some sort of sharp-shooter. That may do very well in South Carolina, but it is hardly the expertise I require."

"He isn't just a sharpshooter, father, he's a son of the Baron Bellew of Duleek," Mrs. Addison said.

General van Dortmund looked at her with renewed interest. "Is that so? Did he attend college in Ireland, or in England?"

"I'm not sure," Mrs. Addison shrugged.

"Excuse me," Rachel said. Thus vanished her determination, in fewer than ten seconds. She had not wanted to speak again after Mrs. van Dortmund's retort, but she knew that General van Dortmund was not the man to suffer a misrepresentation, and if Bellew would have any chance of being accepted here, Rachel had to clear up the matter at once. "I happen to know – when he was speaking to Dr. Rhoades – that Mr. Bellew intended to study medicine at college, but there were personal considerations that kept him at home. He tried to study on his own so that he would be prepared when the time came, but he has not – he has not attended college yet. He composes poetry," she added quickly. "Or, that is, I have seen him do it – I don't know whether he does so regularly."

"Oh, father, a poet," Clarissa said longingly. "Wouldn't your letters be elegant?"

"Clarissa, I cannot rescue every wounded bird you and your sister find," General van Dortmund said, but Rachel could tell his resolve was weakening. It astonished her to see. She had viewed General van Dortmund as severe, which he certainly was, but also impregnable – but she had never seen him under concerted attack by both of his daughters before.

"Mr. Bellew is not a wounded bird – he is an undervalued commodity," Mrs. Addison replied firmly, startling Rachel with the use of one of Mr. Addison's phrases. "Yes, of course, our initial favor to him was motivated by his existence rather than his merits, but I have since learned of the latter, and I am simply trying to point out to you that these would be very reasonably available for a service that you seem to require."

"Oh, and father – all his friends dead!" Clarissa exclaimed. "And one of them Mr. O'Malley!" As if O'Malley been one of her dearest friends.

Mrs. Addison shushed her sister crossly. "And as for your aide Captain Browder," Mrs. Addison went on, "I believe he's been asking you for a field command for a long time now. I suspect that his letter-writing is only going to get worse until he gets his way."

"Captain Browder knows very well that poor performance will not recommend him for favor." He breathed out. "Perhaps I will discuss the matter with Captain Browder and General McIntosh. Only perhaps. I must think about it before I broach the matter with either of them, let alone Mr. Bellew. And I will see that note you keep referring to, Margaret – if it is spelled as properly and punctuated correctly as you imply."

"Thomas, if you've made up your mind, why on earth would you want to talk to General McIntosh or Captain Browder about it?" Mrs. van Dortmund said, aghast.

Her husband glanced at her. "I'm sure there would be no trouble over the matter, but it would be only decent to speak to the man Bellew would replace and the officer he currently serves, and sound out their feelings on the matter."

"No trouble! Thomas, kindly remember the example of Abraham."

The room fell silent. Rachel looked at the others to try to untangle this statement. She could not see what Abraham had to do with it.

"Abraham. Abraham," Mrs. van Dortmund insisted, turning around in her chair in her excitement. "Good heavens, have all of you forgotten your Bible? When the Lord commanded Abraham to destroy Sodom and Abraham didn't want to do it, they entered into *negotiations*. Abraham got God to agree that if there were fifty righteous men in Sodom, the city would be spared. And then Abraham talked God down bit by bit all the way to ten righteous men, and things were going awfully well, but then he gave up prematurely, didn't he? Just think what had happened if Abraham had stuck to his guns and gotten it down to one. He would have gotten his way!" Mrs. van Dortmund concluded triumphantly.

"Oh," Clarissa said weakly, trying to be supportive.

"Thank you, my dear. I will bear that in mind, and be firm," General van Dortmund said in a level voice to his wife, bowing. Rachel wondered how these two people had ever seen fit to marry, but she wondered only in passing. She was not sure how much lasting effect Mrs. Addison's and Clarissa's pleas had made on General van Dortmund's opinion, but she was sure that the incomprehensible argument forwarded by Mrs. van Dortmund in opposition made any objections seem less sound by force of association, and she could have kissed that lady as well as both her daughters. She felt certain now that the offer would be made. She did not know what Bellew would think of it - and she did not know whether Mrs. Addison was correct in her assertion that Bellew could do more good as an aide than an infantryman. But she did not really care. She wanted him to come to Briarwood.

Chapter 33

Upon making inquiries, Bellew found a fellow convalescent who had taken a short Brown Bess from a dead redcoat and was eager to sell his plunder. The musket had been well taken care of, Bellew noted with satisfaction, and remained in good working condition. Dr. Rhoades remonstrated with him please to remain in bed, but Bellew felt fine. As long as he was moving and doing things, that is, he felt fine. When he stopped was when he suffered. When he stopped, sometimes Bellew felt as though he were being crushed into the earth, suffocated by hopelessness; and other times he felt as though he were floating in a vast abyss, unconnected to anything by touch or even by sight – simply alone and shunted aside by all creation. So he tried not to stop.

He found a powder-horn and bullets easily enough; they were hardly rare commodities, but he did not trust the army's ability to supply him with anything. Powder was a little more dear than he would have liked, but that was understandable, and he purchased a good stock of it even at the exorbitant price. He bought a knife and a cartridge-box. He ordered two hunting shirts from a local woman who sewed – he would not need to dress well as an enlisted man, and hunting shirts were far more practical than a proper uniform – and he bought cured beef and dried apples and biscuit, as much as he could carry. He was of two minds how much of it he would share with his fellows. He would not be able to afford the provisioning of his entire company, once he was assigned to one, but he knew he could not watch them starve. O'Malley could have seen his way through the thicket, Bellew knew with a dull pain, but he could not. The matter was irresolvable for the moment, so he put it aside.

He had noticed an old Jaeger rifle hanging above Powell's dish-cupboard. A Jaeger was a fussy instrument that required constant nursing, and he missed his old rifle, doubtless in the hands now of some cursed Englishman. But he could not stop looking at the Jaeger every time he passed, and at length he asked Powell whether he might be willing to part with it for any sum.

"Are you a rifleman, Bellew? I thought you were for the infantry," Powell remarked.

"I believe I'm to be assigned to the infantry. But a rifle is my preferred weapon, and I find I don't feel quite at ease without one."

"Then you should have one, of course. But are you sure it's a Jaeger that you want? The fellow that sold this to me can acquire any kind you like. I'll be happy to go see him." Bellew was not allowed to leave quarantine. The marks on his face had burst and crusted over with scabs, but he was still considered infectious until the wounds healed completely.

Bellew's eyes glittered with sudden interest. "I would prefer a long rifle, if that would be possible," he said.

It was indeed possible. Pennsylvania produced plenty of long rifles identical in every detail to the gun Bellew had lost, and by the end of the day, he was the pleased owner of one, along with a supply of rifle-ammunition and greased paper.

Bellew took a drop-cloth outside the cottage and laid it on the ground. He sat Indian-style on the cloth and slowly disassembled his new rifle, checking each part beneath the mellow light of late afternoon and cleaning it carefully. "The rifle's new," Mr. Powell said curiously, emerging to see what Bellew was up to.

"It is. But I require a close knowledge of its ideal condition, so that I can quickly identify any signs of wear." Bellew preferred a rifle to a musket for many reasons. Of course it was better for hunting, due to its superior aim. A rifle's main deficiency in combat was that it was slow to load, although Bellew himself could load a rifle faster than an untrained man could load a musket. An untrained man – not a redcoat. The slowness of the procedure – loading, sighting, aiming – appealed to Bellew philosophically. He knew he was prone to rashness, and the feel of a rifle in his hands was like a charm that placed a spell upon him to think before acting.

Dr. Rhoades walked past. Bellew knew who he was, from the glimpse of the familiar brown coat and black bag in his peripheral vision, but he did not look up. Dr. Rhoades hesitated, and then approached him. The crunch of shoes against dirt. Bellew clenched his jaw and kept his eyes on his work. "Mr. Bellew," Dr. Rhoades began cautiously, "Would it be possible for you to engage in this work inside, where the air is warmer?"

"I'm afraid it would not, doctor. The light is insufficient," Bellew replied. He tried to keep the shortness out of his voice. He had no cause to dislike Dr. Rhoades or bear him a grudge, but he could not wrestle down either feeling completely whenever he saw the man. Dr. Rhoades had done nothing irregular or slipshod in his inoculation, and he had provided O'Malley with all proper care afterwards. His reservations about letting O'Malley's funeral grow too large had been well-founded and judicious. Dr. Rhoades was a patriot risking his livelihood and his future just the same as any Continental infantryman or general, even if he risked his life a little less. The army could not survive without doctors. It was entirely possible that, in the future, Bellew might even owe his continued existence, or the preservation of a limb, to this man.

But right now, Bellew just didn't like seeing him, and he liked hearing his voice even less. Dr. Rhoades nodded and took his leave. Bellew wondered how equably he himself would have been able to bear the silent reproaches of the loved ones of a lost patient, if fate had taken enough turns that he could have followed his first inclination to study medicine. He supposed he would have learned how to endure it, over time. What you must, you do.

Bellew had a grim suspicion how heavy a toll his physical hardships and long absence from practice might have taken on his skill, so he reassembled the rifle, loaded it, and set off into the woods a short distance from town. He probably wasn't supposed to wander quite this far, but he knew that his scabbed-over pox were hardly infectious, if at all, and he could plausibly claim that he wasn't really leaving his ill-defined post. His job now was to recuperate; fine, he was doing that. He was also hunting.

He wanted to test his marksmanship more than his woodcraft, though, so an animal that preferred open spaces would be best. He hoped to take a shot from fifty yards at least. So as he walked beneath the trees, Bellew headed where the brush was less thick, and he might be able to find a flock of turkeys. A slight clearing opened up ahead, naked beneath the sky and its dusting of snow on the ground glittering brilliantly in the low rays of the sun. Bellew tested the fitful wind and circled around the clearing carefully until it would blow his scent in the other direction. He lowered himself onto his belly, his muscles complaining, and wriggled his body until he had a stable base. Between the scrubby twigs of his cover, the rifle pointed into the clearing. He sighted along its barrel. He felt the breeze against his face. Even a whisper of wind could make the difference in a long-range shot. And he waited.

Nothing happened for a long time, except the wind grew sharper and the light faded. Bellew didn't mind either. Bad light and contrary wind would only make a better test. He supposed he could mark targets for himself on some of the far trees, but he resisted the idea. Bellew did not want to spend a bullet on a shot that served nothing other than to gratify his personal vanity, if he even pulled it off. He wanted his bullet to mean something. And since Bellew doubted that the heavens would offer up a lone redcoat for target practice – good God, what a fool he had been in Philadelphia – he would like to be able to produce dinner for the Powells at least.

A rabbit stuck its head out of the ground and sniffed the air. Bellew watched it. The animal popped out of its hole and stood on its hind legs, examining the surroundings. Bellew drew his aim. A rabbit was enough for a thin stew at least.

But the rabbit cocked its head to the side and took off like an arrow. Bellew knew he couldn't have scared the creature himself, not from this distance, so he waited. A moment later two drab, fat turkey-hens emerged from the trees and bobbed their awkward way across the clearing, pecking at the ground and shaking their tiny heads.

Bellew held his fire. He wanted a tom. He knew the hens wouldn't be alone. And, sure enough, a bulky tom strutted along after the hens, his outspread tail-feathers letting no one mistake that he was dominant and pleased about it.

Bellew watched the tom's head. The body made a wider target, but Bellew didn't want a wider target. He wanted both a difficult shot and a clean death. He aimed for the base of the tom's skull. Tracked his movements with the rifle barrel. Pulled two fingers holding the barrel infinitesimally tighter when the wind changed.

Pulled the trigger.

The shot echoed through the trees, and the two hens fled in screaming panic back into the trees. The tom dropped and lay still. Bellew pushed himself up and approached his target.

The tom lay still. His eyes were sightless in his nearly severed head, frozen in blank incomprehension rather than reproach or resignation.

Death had been instantaneous. Bellew was glad of that. He examined the position of the wound. Maybe half an inch lower than he would have liked, severing the turkey's spine through the neck rather than quite at the base of the skull. It was acceptable shooting, but Bellew could do better, and he resolved he'd go hunting every day.

He slit open the carcass and removed the inedible viscera before slinging his prize over his shoulder and heading back to Powell's. He left the stinking mass of organs in a pile, making no effort to conceal them. He saw no danger in attracting carnivores here, and the woods contained plenty of creatures that could use a meal they did not have to fight for.

Night had taken full possession of the sky by the time he returned to the house. Bellew entered the kitchen unseen and hung the tom by a hook in the ceiling. He would pluck it tomorrow and they would have roast turkey with sweet crackling skin for supper.

Powell's son Zachariah, a boy of eight or nine or thereabouts – Bellew had difficulty estimating children's ages – wandered into the room and watched Bellew string up the turkey by its feet with interest. "Did you shoot that turkey yourself, Mr. Bellew?" Zachariah asked shyly when Bellew stepped back from the bird and wiped his hands down his trousers.

Bellew smiled. "Yes. We can have him for supper tomorrow, perhaps."

"Did you shoot him with that rifle?" Zachariah eyed Bellew's rifle, leaning against the wall, with a mixture of reverence and raw desire. Bellew nodded. "Do you think you could show me how to use a rifle properly? I mean, just while you're recuperating." Zachariah stared at Bellew with a pleading, hopeful expression. His eyes kept darting back to the coveted rifle. Bellew smiled again, remembering the near-idolatry he'd felt for guns himself when he was a boy.

"I'll ask your father if he can spare you when I go hunting again," Bellew said and was surprised how happy it made him, and how amused, to see Zachariah stumbling over his thanks and promising he'd be a quick study and no trouble and do everything Mr. Bellew asked him in every particular without question or hesitation. "I am very gratified, Zachariah," Bellew said, holding up his hand and clearing his throat to keep himself from laughing. It was a pleasant feeling. "Believe me, at your enthusiasm. But I hope you'll ask me plenty of questions – I hardly know how to teach you if you won't - and as for hesitation, when you're holding a rifle, hesitation is more often a benefit to your neighbors than otherwise."

"Father says it's annoying when I question him all the time," Zachariah said cautiously.

"Well, it is annoying, he's quite right. But it's necessary sometimes as well, and when you're learning something is one of those times." Then Zachariah promised to question him and hesitate a great deal, and Bellew thanked him.

Bellew's unfortunate example had encouraged the other two convalescents who weren't so badly off to depart from the doctor's orders and return to a few of their usual entertainments, even if they didn't quite feel energetic enough to saunter around town and go shopping and hunting. This evening found them smoking and playing cards next to the fire in the main room. Powell sat by himself at the table, puzzling with an expression of perfect misery over some correspondence that Bellew could see even from this distance was composed more of stains and blots than actual letters. Powell tilted the letter to catch the full light of the candle beside him. He frowned and moved his head closer to the paper, squinting.

"Is that private, or might I be of some service?" Bellew asked.

"Ah, Bellew!" Powell seemed relieved to have an excuse not to look at his letter any more. "Have you been in all this time? I didn't hear you." Bellew explained that he had tested his rifle on a turkey - stepping discreetly around the matter of how far he'd wandered to shoot it - and that he had just returned. Powell expressed his delight at the bird and then got around at last to answering Bellew's question. No, it was nothing private, only a note from his cousin, who was a cabinetmaker in the Jersies and never had anything important to say in the slightest. It was just that Powell had a pressing interest in two points, and only this particular cousin could relieve his mind: one, regarding the fate of a favorite cherry tree whose destruction by Lord Cornwallis had been aborted by the army's need to press on in haste and that had clung to life bravely in its mangled condition for the year following - Powell had high hopes for this cherry tree, the winter being so mild; and two, whether his cousin's wife had delivered the baby yet. Powell was almost certain that the letter said this was the case, and that the unfortunate infant had been hobbled for life by having been assigned the Christian name "Gruenewald". However, neither Powell nor his cousin knew how to form or transcribe the alphabet very well, and this tended to strain their communications.

Bellew took the letter and sat down. He examined it for a few minutes, frowning, sounding out some of the more incomprehensibly spelled words for a clue as to their intent, and then reported to Powell with reasonable confidence that the cherry tree was fine, the child was born, and she was a healthy daughter named Patsy. The cousin's wife was a Gruenewald by birth and proud of it, and so Patsy bore Gruenewald as a middle name, but the cousin concluded jocularly that he did not think she was likely to grow up to encourage people to make free with it.

"Well, that's a relief."

"I am glad to have helped set your mind at ease," Bellew said, folding the letter and sliding it along the table back to Powell. "Powell, is Zachariah at liberty for a few hours tomorrow afternoon? He's expressed an interest in learning the rifle and coming with me to hunt. I could teach him on the Jaeger, if you like," Bellew added quickly, seeing the hesitation in Powell's eyes. "I think a Jaeger is more trouble, in some ways, but it might be a better rifle for a boy. You don't have to ram the bullet in so hard."

"Perhaps – perhaps another time, Bellew," Powell said, his eyes shifting around the shadows on the table.

Bellew nodded briskly. He didn't know why Powell seemed so uncomfortable about the matter. The boy naturally had to attend to his responsibilities first, before refining his ability with a gun; Bellew had hardly expected otherwise. "Of course. I'm planning to hunt every day until my return to duty, so whenever you feel you can spare him –"

"I cannot spare him, Bellew," Powell said, leaning forward suddenly. He still did not raise his eyes. "I cannot spare him."

Bellew frowned, confused. "A boy should know how to shoot a gun," he said.

"A boy who knows how to shoot a gun is a boy who thinks he can shoot a gun, and I won't – I'd already decided, I'll teach him when the war's over," Powell said. "Forgive me for being so blunt. I can't have Zachariah run off to soldier, and I believe he has more than half a mind to. But I can't run the store without him. And even if I could, why should

I? He's my only child. Forgive me, Mr. Bellew. I know others have made greater sacrifices, but please – rebuff Zachariah when he asks you again, but do it gently."

"He's too young to fight anyway," Bellew answered with a shrug. "He could be a fifer, perhaps, or –"

"No he could not. No he could not." Powell's hands were clenched on the table. But his eyes still carried a humble, apologetic look in them, as if he felt ashamed.

Bellew nodded. His brief happiness from the hunt and Zachariah's enthusiasm left a bitter residue as it evaporated. When he spoke, he kept his voice low. "Ah. I stayed home with my mother rather than join the army when she needed me, and I was a great deal older than Zachariah at the time, if you think that will have any sway with him."

Powell met his eyes at last. "You being a soldier, I think it might," he said hopefully.

Bellew nodded and pushed himself back from the table, preparing to leave. He felt defeated and was not quite sure why. The loss of a companion on his hunting was no great thing; he would be able to practice easier alone. And the loss of a potential fifer was too trivial even to consider.

There had been a time when Bellew had desired nothing more than to build a better life for himself and any family he might have. He still hoped to do that, although this practical goal had been superseded by the opportunity for a greater prize: to build a name for himself, which would be his true legacy. If the heavens allowed, he would live to enjoy it and to offer it to his children, and their children, to profit from and burnish with their own contributions. But if the heavens decreed that this name would be no more than a shining tombstone of marble and gold, Bellew knew he could quit the world with satisfaction, if not without regret. He was almost twenty-two years old. The days when England had treated her colonies with benign neglect were already on the wane when he had been a child. The days of bungled impositions and arrogation had grown into the days of open contempt as Bellew had grown into manhood. That contempt had roused his deepest animosity. He knew that he was not a lesser creature for having been raised on these shores, and nothing seemed more manifest to him than that all men, whatever their station, could claim the same. If it had been only his country, Bellew would have fought for her. And yet he felt that by standing now, he linked his fate to the fate of all mankind. There was no prize greater, and to die in its service was to cover one's extinguished life with honor.

But he remembered his first dream, to be a doctor, to move to Charlestown, to build a respectable practice and become a leading citizen over time. And he knew that while this war would not be won without men like himself, who were willing to throw everything into the flames, it would not be won without men like Powell either, who held back so that there would be something standing on that clear day when the flames had burnt themselves out. He did not begrudge Powell his choice. He did not. His heart sank just the same. But what a poor man he would be, he thought – what a partial, imperfect creature he would have seemed to O'Malley, who would have been too kind to say so – if he made Powell feel small for his choice. And, for God's sake, why shouldn't Powell protect his son? Not all men were called to the flames, and not all men should be.

So Bellew did not stand quite yet. He felt he must offer Powell something, some word to show that his respect was unchanged. He made a hesitant noise in his throat, and then he said, "Were you going to reply to your cousin? Perhaps to tender your congratulations, at least."

"Well – ah, well, of course," Powell stammered uncomfortably.

"I only meant to offer my services as amanuensis – a scribe, if you don't mind me knowing the contents of your letter. I performed this function many times for my neighbors who did not trust their own handling of a quill. It occurs to me that perhaps it might be more useful to Zachariah to learn penmanship than – anything else. I won't be able to teach him more than the basics in the few days I have remaining here, but the basics are all that is required, other than consistent and prolonged practice."

Powell's face brightened and he agreed enthusiastically. The peace offering was a success. Zachariah's enthusiasm was less complete when he was summoned to hear the change in topic of his lessons, but he nodded obediently at his father's order. Bellew leaned over and murmured into Zachariah's ear, "I will tell you the 'why' of it later."

Zachariah watched patiently as Bellew transcribed Powell's note onto paper, and then produced under instruction three spotted, scraggling copies of it himself, similar in appearance to the cousin's original note except that the words, as they were copied from Bellew, were spelled correctly. Later that night, when Zachariah retired to his room, Bellew followed him and sat on the bed and explained that there was no point in fighting if there wasn't something worth fighting for and that Zachariah, given his age, was obliged to find himself in the latter category, as well as its future custodian, a task for which he must prepare. The boy seemed disappointed by this. Bellew rested the back of his fingers briefly against the child's soft cheek.

"You don't have to understand yet. Just remember it, keep it close for the day when you will," Bellew said before leaving. The next day he showed Zachariah how to pluck the turkey too, which, being messy and providing a wealth of interesting-looking feathers to play with, proved more popular with the boy.

When Bellew next went hunting, he shot three rabbits with three bullets, no more. Each shot went true. His feel for the rifle had not deserted him, and in a few days, the Powell household had more meat than it could consume and was busily endearing itself to the neighbors with gifts of fresh game.

The next letter that came to the household was addressed to Bellew. He saw who had sent it – General van Dortmund, not Mrs. Addison – and felt a quick stirring of apprehension. He had not informed Briarwood of O'Malley's death, trusting Miss Kolkhorst to relay the sad news. But now he felt that he might have been remiss in his duties to Mrs. Addison, and guilt made him uneasy. He did not feel as pressed as he had before to stay away from her. She had merely slipped from his thoughts, and he supposed with some relief that his dangerous infatuation must have cooled. But she had been a true friend and patron, and neither grief nor distraction nor the ambiguous aftereffects of a dying brushfire passion released him from his responsibility to treat her preferentially, promptly, and candidly.

But he was not sure what to expect from General van Dortmund himself. Surely not a reproach for Bellew's lapses in regard to the General's daughter.

He read the letter. He frowned. He still did not know what to make of it.

"What did he say?" Powell asked eagerly. "Is it orders? Isn't General van Dortmund a Delaware man?"

"He - has offered me a position as his aide-de-camp, the current holder of that position apparently being desirous of a line command," Bellew said. "General McIntosh has agreed to the transfer, on the assumption that it will be agreeable to me. I would be elevated to the rank of captain." He rubbed the letter between his fingers.

"Well, I am just flattered," Williams called out from across the room. "Congratulations, sir!" He saluted with a grin.

"I thought it was only Frenchies that got turned into officers overnight," Williams's card-playing friend put in cheerfully. "That's showing them, Bellew! I mean, Captain Bellew, sir!"

"Thank you," Bellew said quietly.

"It's the letter-writing, isn't it?" Powell said, looking at Bellew with a sort of muted awe. "It's because you can write so well. I knew it was fine, but I didn't know it was good enough for a general!"

"I'm not quite sure how he made that assessment," Bellew admitted. There was the one brief note he had sent to Briarwood, before he and O'Malley had left for their inoculation. It was hardly a literary masterpiece. Competent, he supposed, but not the sort of performance that would vault Bellew to any particular attention, let alone this level of advancement. Mrs. Addison had to be behind this. Did her partiality for him run that deep? And if it did, how dangerous would that be?

Before he knew what he was doing, Bellew flashed to an image of himself married to Mrs. Addison - to Margaret - wealthy, well-placed, well-connected, and joined to a woman of exquisite beauty, a generous heart, and a clever mind. He shoved the image away in horror. She was married, and married she would remain. He knew better than to imagine even for a moment that she would risk the scandal of a divorce - or that he would. That left only the other option - no, he would not let his thoughts wander that far, the only other option that remained was not the unimaginable, but rather a polite friendship and chaste reserve. That was all. Good God, and he didn't even care for her any more. And still his mind ran this way. So his question was answered. How dangerous, if Mrs. Addison favored him a little too much? Extremely.

"And you're showing my Zachariah how to do the same," Powell went on, unaware of Bellew's feverishly turning thoughts. "Maybe someday, when he's grown, some fine gentleman will see Zachariah's letter-writing and take an interest in him, too."

Bellew blinked and smiled absently. "Yes, well – I certainly hope so. You must remind him to practice constantly, and to observe as many good examples as he can."

Powell broke from his happy vision and seemed to notice at last that Bellew did not share the congratulatory mood of the rest of the room. "Surely you must be pleased, as well as honored," he said.

Bellew was not sure he was either. "A – staff position is far from the field," he began hesitantly.

"Aw, you'll get shot at just the same, sir, namely plenty," Williams said.

"But not as much," Bellew replied, feeling that he was being drawn into the quicksand of an argument about precisely how frequently one should desire to be shot at. "I – had hoped to earn a command of my own, not merely a rank," he said.

"Because you can do more good with a command," Powell said, clearly getting at something. "A man of your qualities."

"Whatever ability I have, I would hope to expend to greatest effect."

"You couldn't hope to be a general, though, could you, Captain Bellew?" Powell said. "Not in this war, at any rate."

"No," Bellew admitted.

"Let me show you how I see it," Powell said cheerfully. He walked across the room and took a rough length of wood from the pile where it sat waiting to be placed upon the fire. "Say I want to move that trunk over there. And what I've got to do it with is this bit of timber." He grabbed the wood by one narrow splintered end and jabbed that end at the base of the trunk, a heavy iron-bound thing dark and soft with age. Bellew rather admired the choice of object as a symbol of the enemy and thought fleetingly of Parliament the apple. It had looked like a hard, sour knot of all but indigestible fruit, and Bellew smiled slightly, despite his agitation. Powell glanced back at him and jabbed the chest again for emphasis. "See, now I can't get anywhere like this. All I'm doing is poking at it. But if I get a little farther back, like this." He shifted his grip to the other end of the wood and shoved down hard. The piece of wood, turned into a lever, lifted the edge of the trunk. The now unstable chest wobbled, and Williams moved his chair quickly to scramble out of the way. Powell, sweating a little with effort, released his lever. The trunk landed with a thump that shook the floor. Powell grinned at Bellew, his eyebrows raised.

"Yes, I – understand, and of course I am honored by your opinion –"

"It isn't even my opinion that matters – a gentleman who's sitting right here –" Powell touched the far end of the piece of wood. "–is telling you what he thinks, and, perhaps more importantly, what he thinks he requires. He wants to use you to help push the lever. Now, if you hadn't helped me with that letter from Saul, I don't think I would have made heads or tails of it for a month. I'm sure it's not so bad with General van Dortmund, but what if he's saying it's not too far off? We can't have him wondering what people are sending him, can we, nor worrying about getting his own messages through?"

"Helps a fellow to trust in his orders, when his general knows what's what," Williams added. "We usually sniff out pretty quick when he doesn't."

Bellew thanked the men for their confidence and support and assured them that his hesitation meant only that he wanted to return his answer in the morning, when he could give his full energies to the important task, not of course that he meant to decline it. But in his heart, he still wasn't sure what he meant to do. He had enlisted as a common soldier because he thought his desire for personal advancement and glory had led him into error. Now, were personal considerations leading him astray once more? If he thought about the matter in isolation – if he pretended there were no other concerns – he felt convinced that he would be more than equal to the tasks required of an aide-de-camp. He could write, he could organize, his memory was sharp and clear. What he did not know of more advanced military matters he had no doubt he could learn quickly. And if he broadened the scope of his speculation, he had to admit that of course his personal prospects were far superior as an officer, even a staff officer, than as a foot-soldier down in the mud. Admittedly there was not much glory in letter-writing. But there was also no glory when no one noticed you, and as General van Dortmund's aide, he would have the eye and ear of influential men.

Was he confident enough of himself that he could present himself to these influential men without having earned any laurels in battle? Could he distinguish himself and his responsibility through intelligence and discretion alone, when he did not have a history of physical bravery to defend his intrinsic merit? If he could not, he must not take the post, no matter what.

And then there was the other matter. The one he had just managed to stop thinking of. There was Mrs. Addison. That was a fact that would not go away.

Or, rather, the realization dawned on Bellew, this was a fact that was guaranteed to go away. The Addisons weren't part of the army. They were visiting for a month or two, and then they would be gone – back to the redcoat stronghold of New-York, and from there to London, which was only a hair more inaccessible to a Continental soldier than was New-York.

"Could you check my work, Captain Bellew?" a soft voice said at his side. Bellew startled, coming back to himself. Zachariah held a sheet of paper gingerly, trying not to let the ink that spattered his right hand smirch the page. The boy stood timidly, as if prepared to be chased away, an intrusive and insignificant fly. Bellew wondered how long Zachariah had been standing there, and chagrin filled him. Again, he was thinking too much of himself and too little of the world around.

"I'm sorry, Zachariah, I forgot your lesson. You could have reminded me – have you recopied yesterday's?"

"I made up one of my own, sir. I tried to get all the letters in it." Zachariah presented the sheet shyly.

Bellew placed the paper on the table, where he could see it clearly. Zachariah had written the same sentence eighteen times, in letters of varying size and splotched by spatters and smears of ink. But the words could be made out well enough. Each sentence read: "I bid and enjoyne you Soljers to foller evry comand and requirmint of yer exalent Genrall in all particklers and with do hayste and zeele."

Zachariah looked at him with shining eyes. Bellew swallowed, and then he smiled.

He congratulated Zachariah on the noticeable improvement in his penmanship and gently corrected his spelling. Zachariah took the instruction eagerly. In the morning, Bellew wrote his reply to General van Dortmund, stating that his confinement was expected to last another two weeks, but if that delay was acceptable, he was prepared to accept the general's gracious offer with all humility, gratitude, and a solemn promise of dedicated service. The first copy came out well, but he made a second anyway. The second was perfect.

Chapter 34

Rachel had meant to use the early morning hours, while Mrs. Addison still slept, to help Martha and Hattie a little around the house. Well, Martha particularly. The purpose was not just to make herself useful, although of course she hoped to do that – and how much more, now that *Captain* Bellew (she loved to say the new rank in her mind) would be coming to stay with them so soon. Rachel was also a little afraid of Martha. She had seen the maid give her slighting looks, and Martha seemed to make a point of always serving Rachel last – even though of course that was entirely proper, but it was the way in which Martha did it that worried Rachel that Martha might have thought she was putting on airs and holding herself above her station. At night, she and Martha slept in the same bed, and Martha took the covers to herself even when Rachel was sure she was awake and knew what she was doing; and Martha never spoke to her, except as necessity impelled. There was no doubt that Martha did not like her. Rachel thought she might be able to win her over by helping her with her work, a favor that lazy people rarely rejected, even if they weren't likely to appreciate it much nor to see it for the kindness that it was.

But as it happened, Clarissa was an early riser too, and each morning she managed to make a point of requesting Rachel's company. Of course Rachel could not deny her, and certainly not with the excuse that she wanted to dust and scrub the floors, which she wasn't supposed to be doing anyway. So Martha was left to stew in whatever imagined slights and insults. Rachel wished she could say that she at least wanted to help, but she bore no illusions that Martha would believe her, so she kept her tongue still.

And besides, she liked Clarissa, who was always so sweet and gentle. Rachel was not sure exactly why the girl – Rachel thought of her as a girl, although Clarissa turned out to be two years older than herself – had taken such a shine to her, other than that she was there and that Clarissa, as Mrs. Addison had promised, seemed to like everyone and everything. Their conversations were inconsequential, about clothes and which of General van Dortmund's men seemed unhappy and might do with a kind word and the relative frequency of sparrows in the yard, and Rachel supposed it was all a little dull, really, and relentlessly unimaginative, and never anything other than trivial, only she rarely found herself bored because Clarissa was so good-natured and cheerful herself that it was difficult not to be cheerful in turn in her company. Rachel was glad that Mrs. Addison did not appear to want her to turn her wit on the family, even in private. She would have felt like a dog to have said something cutting about Clarissa, even if the girl's simplicity made her, Rachel had to admit, an easy target.

"Rachel," Clarissa whispered, catching her in the hallway shortly after six in the morning. She wore a simple blue gown and white shawl, and her hair was pulled back in a neat bun, because they were not visiting and a bun was something Clarissa could do herself. She wore no jewelry, except for a locket on a slender golden chain that hung around her neck. Even in this remote camp Mrs. Addison insisted on dressing as elaborately as if she were back in Philadelphia – or perhaps in Paris – and teased her sister sometimes about the plainness of her attire.

Martha stomped past with a perfunctory curtsy and went downstairs. Rachel wondered fleetingly whether the maid would be better-tempered if Mr. Addison were to commit an impropriety with her after all, and was immediately horrified with herself for the thought. If only she could learn to be sweeter! She must learn from her new friend, if she could, and Rachel swore to herself that she would try. The kindness that Rachel wished she had, she knew Clarissa possessed in full.

Clarissa waited until Martha was safely past, and then she bit her lip and said with an air of shy excitement, "Do come to my room a moment, if you would – I have something I would like to show you."

This pricked Rachel's curiosity. She could not imagine any secret Clarissa could have other than a beau, but Rachel, searching her memory quickly, had seen no flashes of understanding between Clarissa and any of the men constantly coming and going in the house. Well, perhaps someone from Delaware had captured Clarissa's heart before this visit to Valley Forge and had just recently sent a particularly tender billet-doux. Rachel wondered what one would look like, if a real love-letter were as hot and damp as a breath in the ear, like the made-up ones she read in novels sometimes. Oh, and that locket Clarissa always wore – perhaps it contained her beloved's miniature. Yes, it must. Rachel determined that she had solved the mystery, but she would pretend to be surprised nevertheless.

A vague ache of jealousy pulled at her as she followed her friend, their skirts whispering down the morning-hushed hallway, and for just a moment, she wondered what it would be like to be someone real, someone with a place in the world, with people who thought of her and remembered her and maybe every now and then longed for her, and not merely as an afterthought. Of course she was happy for Clarissa, to have someone to care for her – and the gentleman, in Rachel's objective opinion, was a lucky man if Clarissa's affection belonged to him in turn. If she were a man, Clarissa was precisely the sort of wife she might have wanted herself. Gentle, meek, and true – any home Clarissa made would always be untroubled and serene, a refuge from the world. When had Rachel ever made a peaceful home? Not even when she was a little girl. When her mother had gotten sick, Rachel had tried, of course, but she had failed, and it only got worse when her mother had died.

So perhaps it wasn't jealousy at all, then, but envy. And while envy ranked as a sin and jealousy as a more minor failing, Rachel felt a little relieved nevertheless. Envy seemed less unkind to Clarissa, less as though Rachel were a would-be thief who would snatch away someone else's treasure, less as if she were – well, less as if she were some kind of Martha, spiteful and full of unthinking selfish resentments. And why, Rachel wondered, was envy a sin after all? It only made her want to better herself.

Oh yes – envy is a fine thing. You might as well say that sloth has the inestimable merit of preserving one's energies, and gluttony is a positive virtue in that it makes you take delight in God's glory of creation, and lust – well, what could be more noble than to propagate the species, and, and to distract people who annoy you by giving them something else to do, Rachel thought severely, pushing all such ruminations firmly out of her mind.

When they reached the room, Clarissa slipped around Rachel and pulled the door shut behind them. Rachel thought that a man must have kept this bedroom before. It was filled with heavy furniture that overwhelmed Clarissa's small form and made her look like a tiny bird taking refuge in a cliff. Clarissa moved past the enormous bed with its silk canopy – a little dusty, Rachel noted critically – and drew back the striped curtains to let in a little watery dawn light. She settled herself in her ladder-back desk chair, resting her hands nervously in her lap and playing with her fingers in a gesture that Rachel recognized with some amusement she shared with both her sister and her mother. Clarissa looked up at Rachel with a wavering smile and seemed unsure how to begin.

"Oh, don't stand there, it makes me feel like I should stand too," Clarissa said, and Rachel perched obediently on a tufted stool. She waited, but Clarissa said nothing more.

"Is it something you wanted to show me, or something to tell me," Rachel prompted gently. She did not need to see the billet-doux itself, if Clarissa was shy about it. She wondered if it contained an open proposal for marriage - yes, that must be it. Nothing else could cause such anxiety. Did General van Dortmund disapprove of the man? That would be interesting - but sad, because Clarissa was hardly a girl who would go against the will of her iron-backed father, and then the romance was doomed, and Rachel felt sorry about it. Or was it merely Clarissa's timidity holding her back? Rachel was desperately curious now. But to be polite, she said, "Or, you don't have to, you know –"

Clarissa shook her head. "No, I want to, it's just I very much want to know your opinion, and – well, maybe I've been foolish, or I've showed a poor hand, and if you say so, I'll know it's honest and true, only – I just wanted to do something. Oh, I'm talking to no purpose, it's no wonder you're looking at me like that, here, this is what I meant." She produced a small leather-bound notebook from the desk. Surprised, Rachel reached out to take it. Clarissa hesitated one last time and then handed it over.

Marriage proposals did not come in notebooks – did they? Rachel ran her thumb down the seam between the marbled-paper band on the cover and the brown leather. She looked to Clarissa for permission to open it.

"It's a book of the dead," Clarissa explained.

Rachel's hand recoiled from the leather. She clutched her hand in a fist to push away the feel of the rough skin.

Clarissa did not seem to notice and continued with a flood of words. "When I asked you about Mr. O'Malley, and you told me those little details about him – what he looked like and sounded like and how brave he was through all his trials – because I said I wanted to help remember him – well, it came to me afterwards that I was a weak vessel, of course I always knew that, but I mean weak even for this task, which is such an honor – and wouldn't it be better if I tried to put down as best I could the things I knew, to preserve Mr. O'Malley, you understand, so that he wouldn't have to rely on just my own silly mind to keep his memory, and then I thought – there are so many others, not just people I've known like my cousin Geoffrey Everett who died of smallpox – he died of smallpox too, Rachel – when he was a little boy, and perhaps we could keep them – in a small way – keep them with us if I just thought to put down what I knew, and so I started this book, and you can put your parents in it if you like, if you don't think – if you think it would be all right – and what about all those men in camp, so many of them have died already, and Rachel, do you think we could go and maybe, perhaps, collect a few remembrances, so that – well, so that they're not forgotten?" She stopped abruptly, wringing her hands all the harder. "But I should let you look at it – do tell me what you think, please. I'll be silent a moment, only – I did want to help, you know."

"Of course you did, and you're the dearest girl in the world," Rachel said. And she did think Clarissa was very dear, and the intention was so tender, but something about the project still unsettled Rachel and struck her as frankly repellant. She opened the book, partly so that she could keep her eyes low and prevent Clarissa from reading their expression.

She flipped past the first two pages, which contained some doodles of flowers and the words "In Loving Rememberance," till she found the proper start, in Clarissa's rounded, fragile hand.

MR. SAMUEL O'MALLEY, aged in his thirties or forties or thereabouts, who died on January 14, in the year of our Lord 1778 whilst undergowing the procedure of innockulation for the smallpox, having taken a case of it and residing in the home of Tobias Powell, soapmaker, outside the Continental Army encampment at Valley Forge.

Mr. O'Malley was a favorite with all who knew him, partickularly of his good friends Mr. Stephen Bellew and Lieutenant Masterson. Mr. O'Malley had previously been a Captain of South Carolina infantry, and Mr. Bellew a Lieutenant of the same, but Mr. O'Malley (as well as Mr. Bellew also for the same reasoning) discerning that the need of the Glorious Cause was greatest at the encampment here at Valley Forge, but that South Carolina had no men here, nobly resigned his commission and signed on with North Carolina. This was a good thing to do and excited much admiration, though Mr. O'Malley never requested this same. Lieutenant Masterson having become deceased before this time, he was unable to have the opportunity to make this manly sacrifise of personal interest.

He was beloved by all, which is a thing that people say, but in Mr. O'Malley's case was a True and Genuine Fact.

He rode to Valley Forge on a brown mare named Acorn that belonged to his friend my sister.

He had been sick of disinterry when he was captured by the redcoats before in Philadelphia but he got through it all right.

He was of below average height and used to be a little fat before he got sick.

He was married once to a woman named Kitty and we think he loved her very much.

One time he was with Mr. Bellew and my sister's maid and companion Rachel when they were coming to Valley Forge, and a Dutch farmer gave them a bag of potatoes for no pay.

When his friend Mr. Bellew almost got into a fight in a tavern, Mr. O'Malley talked him out of it.

He always had a kind word for the aforementioned Rachel.

MASTER GEOFFREY EVERETT, aged seven, who died on June 8 of the year 1773 in his home in Wilmington, having contracted smallpox and succumming to it in his mother's arms as she sang his favorite song "Lavender's Blue"...

Rachel was halfway through the introduction to the unfortunate child Geoffrey Everett before she realized that Mr. O'Malley's section had come to an end. Her lips parted slightly in blank horror. Was that all? Was that really all that was going to be left of Mr. O'Malley – these few empty lines, and nothing more? And she hated to be slighting, but Clarissa hadn't even put in half of what Rachel had told her: the way his eyes crinkled at the corners a moment before he smiled, and his impassioned speech at the recruiting table by Griffin's Ford, or the nearly final words he had spoken to her. The way he had treated Mr. Bellew almost as an adopted son. But surely it was better that something be written of Mr. O'Malley – and yet who would read it, Rachel wondered. Would this book be passed down to Clarissa's children, and their children afterwards, for them to contemplate the minor facts regarding men and children - and women, Rachel saw, flipping forward through the notebook's pages - they had never known in life? Why would they care? And if they did not care, why would they remember? The world bore such a burden of dead souls already, wrapped in its embrace of earth. No mortal could hope to do the same without being crushed by the weight. And yet perhaps it was better to try, and Rachel merely unloving...

Clarissa waited, pushed forward to the edge of her chair in anxiety. Rachel had to say something. "I almost feel as if Mr. O'Malley were standing before me again," she said, looking up with an uncertain smile to meet Clarissa's gaze.

Relief washed over Clarissa's face. "Oh, I'm so glad," she breathed. "Because it's not a eulogy, you know - it's just - the little things that might get lost." She took back the notebook from Rachel's numb hands and held it loosely in her lap. She pressed her lips together and looked at Rachel shyly. "Did - did you want to tell me about your parents?" she asked.

"I -" The single word choked in Rachel's throat. She could not say yes, and yet she did not want to say no either. How could she reduce her parents, whom she had barely known, into a few lines? Her mother at least had a tombstone - her father and Christoph did not. Surely they deserved this slight remembrance in the world. And yet wasn't Rachel herself a remembrance of them? But maybe not as good a one as a few lines in Clarissa's notebook that her father had loved to tell stories, until his sorrows grew too deep and silence overtook him, and that Christoph had been fond of cornbread. "I would have to think about what to say," Rachel continued at last. "I have a particular responsibility to them."

"Of course," Clarissa said, her eyes widening. Rachel did not want her friend to feel as though she was rejecting her kindness.

"I also - my older brother was also - in the same raid where my father - was - killed," she added quickly, forcing out the words although they hardly made sense. "And there were - there were several - other children. I did not know all of them personally. But I do not think, if I - when I - that I could in good conscience omit any of them, so I must - I have to think about it first to gather my recollections properly."

"Why, naturally!" Clarissa exclaimed. "And you must have so much you want to say! Yes, of course, all of them, those dear souls, not just your parents. We'll take care of all of them, Rachel. We will."

"I remember less than I ought," Rachel said. A cold anxiety crept over her at a fresh thought. She could not admit how young she had been when her father and Christoph had been killed, or it would raise the question of how she had spent the intervening years. The Addisons had never seen fit to inquire beyond the assumption that the raiders had chased off the Indians immediately upon the attack on the farm, but Rachel sensed that Clarissa, in her eagerness to be kind, might not so easily be put off the scent. Would Clarissa still like Rachel, if she knew that Rachel had lived with the Cherokee for five years? Oh, of course Clarissa would – it was only everyone else that Rachel had to worry about. Rachel could not have it laid out in plain writing in Clarissa's notebook.

And what of the Cherokee Rachel had known, who were now dead – if Rachel judged her birth family worthy of inclusion, what did it say about her that she would not (for she knew she would not, no matter the moral stain) breathe a whisper about Kamama, who had shown her how to sew and skin animals and cook, and who had died of a bullet in the back of her neck, or little Walosi, who had told her he would marry her when he grew up if no one else did, and who had been burned alive?

But these were only footnotes to an epitaph, after all, so Rachel reasoned perhaps she should not take the matter so much to heart. As in, "Here Lieth John Smith (who stood five foot six inches tall), Beloved Husband (of a red-haired woman named Noreen) and Father (he carved wooden toys for his three boys, of which his carts were pretty good and his horses indifferent), Born 1712 (during a light snowstorm) and Died 1770 (at three o'clock in the afternoon, when he usually liked to dine)." No, no, no, that was terrible of Rachel, she must not even think such wickedly flippant thoughts – she apologized to Mr. O'Malley's spirit, despairing that even his generosity could forgive such disrespect, and she had truly liked him, and was this the best she could repay him, to make his memory the subject of a smart remark? Of course the details of anyone's life were petty; that was their nature. But it was the small things that made them lovable, made them individuals – not the broad facts. No, Clarissa was right. Rachel was wrong, and Rachel's feelings were wrong. The book was a good idea, no matter how distasteful Rachel incorrectly found it. And if Rachel wished it were a little better – well, that was an unkindness to Clarissa.

"Perhaps I shouldn't have brought up your parents – I'm sorry, Rachel," Clarissa said, searching Rachel's face.

Rachel straightened herself and put her expression in order. "Oh, no – I think your book is just lovely, it's such a splendid idea. The problem is – well, it reminded me of something my mother used to say to me."

"What is it?" Clarissa asked eagerly. "I won't write it down yet, if you don't want me to – but I promise I'll remember."

"She told me, when I was very small, that your family is a gift from God that you must spend the rest of your life earning, and I – I know what you're going to say, and please don't, but I don't think I've done very well, I don't think I've earned as much as I should."

"Rachel," Clarissa said severely, straightening in her chair, "I am going to say it, no matter what. She would have been very proud of you, and that's a fact." Rachel smiled and nodded, but felt far from certain of this herself. Her mother had loved her, of course, but as to her opinions about objective merit – Rachel simply had no idea. She did not see where the standards lay, and so she could not guess how far she fell short. The one standard high enough to satisfy any possibility was perfection; but Rachel remained woefully distant from that.

"All our mothers really want from us, anyway, is for us to be proper and to be happy in being proper," Clarissa concluded, her face serene again. Rachel took in an unhappy breath. If this was true, she was even farther away from success than she'd realized. No one had ever found her proper, quite, and as for happy – no, she had to admit, she wasn't happy very often. Even when she enjoyed herself, she lived in terror that her little pleasures trembled so narrowly on a precipice that a breath might knock them over into the abyss – was that happiness, then? She thought her mother would have had little use for it.

Rachel wanted to change the subject. "When you told me you had something to show me, I was sure it was a love-letter," she said.

"Oh!" Clarissa's eyes widened, and one hand flew to her mouth. She laughed nervously, and color rose in her cheeks. "No, no – I don't – no, nothing like that! Rachel! Who did you even think it would *be?*" The speculation seemed to interest her acutely, but Rachel did not think Clarissa had anyone in particular she hoped Rachel would name.

"You will laugh at me when I tell you I had a whole scenario worked out in my mind. He was a man from home, but your father didn't approve of him, and he had just proposed marriage, and you didn't know what to do - you couldn't accept against your father's will, but you couldn't give him up, either."

Clarissa laughed again, her color deepening. She turned her head aside. "Father would never dislike anyone who would make a good -" She stopped abruptly, and then went on. "Well, father would never dislike anyone who was a likely candidate for a good husband, at any rate. But he tends to judge people a little hard sometimes. But I haven't got - any - sort of - you know. When Maggie, before she met Robert, there were always plenty of young men around the house, you can imagine, but none of them - she's so much more dashing than I am, you know, so when she chose Robert and went away, the young men stopped coming, and - really, I'm going to let father arrange something for me. I think that works out best for a certain type of person - a sensible person should have a sensible marriage."

"Did your father not like Mr. Addison at first?" Rachel asked, interested in the hint. She knew she was prying.

Clarissa blinked. She made a small noise in her throat before speaking, and she waved her hands uncomfortably. "He - oh, I don't like talking about unpleasant things, and really, when all is said and done, Maggie has that élan, you know, and father didn't understand that it - it changes the way you look at things." Clarissa pressed her lips together, her eyes turned to the side as if weighing some private thought. Then she looked up at Rachel and leaned forward. Rachel leaned forward too, copying the gesture unconsciously. Their heads almost touched, and the shadows across their faces dropped a veil of secrecy over them, even though no one else was in the room to overhear. Clarissa whispered in a rush: "It's true, though. Father didn't like Mr. Addison, and so Robert and Maggie ran off to get married. They're all fine about it now, of course, and Maggie seems very happy - and all is proper - so everyone is satisfied, but - no, father never gave them his blessing until after the fact." She straightened in her chair again and nodded significantly.

Rachel mulled this over. General van Dortmund's assessment of Mr. Addison had, in Rachel's opinion, probably been correct - Mr. Addison was very rich, and reasonably intelligent, and he certainly gave his wife plenty of leeway to live her life however she saw fit; but he was also stingy with his affection and his regard, and he seemed to have no fixed principles, and was an adulterer. It was not a happy match, not the way it should have been. But he must have loved Mrs. Addison terribly much once, to run away with her like that.

"I think that's very romantic," Rachel said, softening a little to Mr. Addison.

Clarissa's eyes twinkled. "I do too," she confided. "Only I never say so around mama. She would have a fit."

Chapter 35

General van Dortmund caught them playing "Laugh and Lie Down" and made Mrs. van Dortmund throw her deck in the fire. Card-playing was strictly forbidden in camp, by order of General Washington. This came as a heavy blow to Mrs. van Dortmund, although Mr. Addison seemed to take the event with good grace, if not enthusiasm. But Mrs. van Dortmund had fewer amusements open to her. Not many other ladies had joined their husbands in camp yet, and opportunities for entertainment were scarce. Plenty of women lived among the common soldiers, but these were not the sort of women whose acquaintance Mrs. van Dortmund desired. Mr. Addison found some friends among the officers and was very little at home, and so the women had precious little with which to fill their days other than each other's company.

This seemed to suit Mrs. van Dortmund and Clarissa tolerably – even if Mrs. van Dortmund missed her cards – and Rachel didn't really mind, even if she felt a nagging restlessness at the empty days. She didn't object to the pointlessness so much; she enjoyed plenty of things that were perfectly pointless, after all. It was that she suffered a gnawing sense that there were pressing things to be done, while all she was doing with her scarce allotment of time was wasting it. What these things to be done were, Rachel did not exactly know. Other, of course, than the waiting, which was something to be endured, not accomplished. She felt the waiting keenly.

But Mrs. Addison was clearly bored out of her skull, and Rachel feared that she would decide that it was high time they were off to New-York even before Captain Bellew arrived at Briarwood. Rachel wanted to be lively and entertaining for her mistress, but she was not allowed to make sharp remarks, and anyway Mrs. van Dortmund absorbed most of the conversation to herself, limiting Rachel's contributions mostly to smiling and nodding. Mrs. Addison sighed sometimes in private, and complained a little, but so far she had made no noises about actually pulling up stakes. Mostly, Rachel supposed, what kept them here was that it just wasn't proper to make a family visit quite so short, not when years might intervene before the next. Mrs. Addison's annoyance with Mr. Addison's behavior and friends in Philadelphia had forced them to arrive in Valley Forge sooner than they'd intended, so now she simply had to endure a few weeks of dullness before such social life as the camp could provide would debut, and she seemed resigned to this as having been the superior option, if not a good one.

Rachel wondered what business could keep General van Dortmund so occupied every day, with the army at rest, but he seemed to have little time for his family. "Oh, he's always like that," Mrs. Addison said with a shrug. "He cannot bear idleness." And she sighed again, looking out the window and tapping the back of the sofa with her hand. Rachel picked up the tea-pot - they were drinking liberty tea today, a flowery decoction of local roots and leaves - but Mrs. Addison waved it away brusquely. "I've drunk enough to burst my stays."

"Mama, Maggie - I, I have something I would like, I would like -" Clarissa glanced quickly at Rachel for reassurance and produced her leather notebook. Rachel blinked in surprise. Clarissa meant to share her grim project with her mother and sister? Rachel could hardly imagine which of them would like it least. She winced internally.

"Is it a word game? Are we going to play a word game? You know, the one where you think of a word and the rest of us try to guess letters, and - no, wait, we need two notebooks for that, don't we," Mrs. van Dortmund said. "We could play that word game, though."

"No, I - this is -"

"Is it your memory book?" Rachel interposed quickly. She did not want Clarissa to call it a book of the dead again. The morbidity of the name would be as welcome in a drawing-room as an actual corpse, although Clarissa seemed blithely unaware of this, as she was of so much else.

"Yes." And then Clarissa explained her project. Mrs. van Dortmund frowned, and Mrs. Addison looked resigned. "I thought we might - some of father's men surely have friends they would like to add. And perhaps, mama, you could tell me about Donald Lewis again, you remember."

"Donald Lewis? Who on earth is that?"

"He was that stableboy, mother, who got trampled back at home."

"Good heavens, a stableboy was trampled? Where?"

"He was one of ours. I don't know, perhaps ten or fifteen years ago."

"Well, my gracious, I don't know about anything like that. Clarissa, what on earth is the purpose of eulogizing stableboys?"

"Someone gave him gin, I think it was old Mal, to be frank, and he was pestering the horses at night. Honestly, Clarissa, darling, is that the sort of thing you really want to record?" Mrs. Addison said, a faint light of interest showing in her eyes for the first time.

"Well, I – thought there might have been something else to say about him," Clarissa replied weakly, looking down at her lap and fiddling with her notebook. Apparently the news about the gin was novel to her.

Rachel felt she had to come to Clarissa's rescue. "I'm sure the General's men have comrades they've lost who mean something to them," she said.

"Oh la, that's for their families to worry about," Mrs. van Dortmund snapped. "We don't even know these people. Why, if I troubled myself about everyone I didn't know – now my mind has gone completely awhirl, Clarissa, and I don't know how I'll even straighten it out, thank you. Goodness, couldn't you have picked the living instead? There are at least fewer of them."

But Mrs. Addison tilted her head and said, "But we could ask father's men in for tea, if they have the time – surely that wouldn't hurt, mother, and it might provide a diversion – for them, of course, their duties being so very dry."

"Oh well, I don't know that I need soldiers tramping all over my second floor as well." But Mrs. van Dortmund yielded the point eventually, and the invitation was extended, and all the men who came to Briarwood that day either took the time for a brief visit or else promised that they would do so soon.

The soldiers did indeed know men who had died, and many of them. The relentless growth of the list of the dead pressed a suffocating weight against Rachel's chest. Mrs. van Dortmund nodded politely, but did not seem to be able to cross the hurdle of having quite so many common men in her drawing-room. Mrs. Addison took adroit charge of the conversation, allowing the soldiers to add a few lines to Clarissa's book and then quickly turning the conversation to more interesting topics, like their love-affairs and their career prospects. Rachel noted that the soldiers were likelier to bring up fellows they hadn't known well, and that universally they seemed relieved when Mrs. Addison steered them away from Clarissa's topic.

Clarissa did not seem to mind. She wrote as quickly as she could, but not nearly as fast as a man could speak, and she cast grateful glances at her sister when Mrs. Addison changed the subject, presumably believing that Mrs. Addison did so to offer Clarissa's cramped hand a few moments of rest.

The General's aide Captain Browder came up last, having been much occupied by work. He did not look comfortable when he presented himself and declined the liberty tea, but after some initial hemming and hawing about how he didn't like to talk about unpleasant things in front of ladies, he offered up a pair of brothers he had known back in Delaware, both of whom had enlisted at Captain Browder's behest. One had died early on of tetanus from a bayonet wound in the leg, and Captain Browder had felt obliged to look in on the other brother every now and then. This second brother had passed away just last week.

"You mean in camp, or from the inoculation?" Rachel said.

"Oh, nonsense, miss, inoculations don't kill you, that's pure superstition," Captain Browder said sharply, his brows drawing together. "No, he wasn't sick or wounded. I think it was just the hard living that got to him. He'd been pretty low for a while. Hard living, and poor spirits," Captain Browder concluded.

Once the Captain took his leave, Rachel remarked to Clarissa that unless she was mistaken, which she prayed it was, it seemed that a great many soldiers were simply dying in camp of what appeared to be no cause – merely from cold and hunger.

"Yes," Clarissa said quietly, flipping back through her pages. She had blotted them hastily, and the ink remained damp on a few. "It seems so." She looked up. "Mama, do you think perhaps father should inquire about the provisions –"

"Don't be a goose, Clarissa, haven't you heard the shouting?" Mrs. Addison interrupted. Clarissa asserted she had no idea what her sister was talking about. "The shouting the men do – for heaven's sake, on Tuesday it kept me up half the night. 'We need meat'. Over and over again." It had kept Rachel up too, although Martha had slept soundly.

"I heard – I thought they were just doing – military exercises of sorts," Clarissa said, her eyes wide.

"Dearest, you have to listen to the words sometimes. You can make 'em out plain if you half pay attention," Mrs. Addison said. "I very much doubt that the situation has escaped father's notice."

"They really are starving, then," Clarissa said and blinked. She closed her notebook gently, sliding her finger out from the page it held.

"Oh, don't start in on that," Mrs. van Dortmund huffed. "We can't feed six thousand men ourselves, and that's all there is to it."

"Mother, no one is saying that we should –"

"Clarissa will start doing so in just a moment, as you know very well, and that Rachel of yours just might bring up the infernal potatoes again. But I ask you to remember Jesus at the wedding feast, before you go asking me for something I cannot supply."

"Yes, mother," Mrs. Addison said in a flat voice, but Mrs. van Dortmund would not be cheated of an opportunity to triumph in her Biblical knowledge that easily. She caught Rachel's blank expression and pounced upon it. "You – Rachel. You know the story of Jesus at the wedding feast, don't you? From Luke?"

"Why – yes, ma'am," Rachel answered hesitantly.

"And you see what I mean, then, don't you?"

"I – think the Bible provides excellent guidance, and you are quite correct in referring to it," Rachel stalled.

"Well, why don't you explain it to my daughters, then, as they persist as usual in not understanding me."

Rachel had no idea what Mrs. van Dortmund wanted her to say, so she recited the simple story. "Well, one day Jesus attended a wedding feast, and he noticed that as the guests arrived, each took the very best seat he could at the table, so that the places of honor filled up first and only the low places remained. So he addressed the assembly, saying that it was wrong for guests to take the place of highest honor when they came to the table, because each man of course did not know if he were truly worthy of that place, and for all he knew, someone of higher station might come afterwards. And if someone of higher station did subsequently arrive, the host would be obliged to remove the early guest from his good seat and direct him to a lower one proper to his station, which would be an

embarrassment for the guest and host alike. Then Jesus pointed out that
the correct behavior upon arriving at the table was in fact to take the very
lowest seat available. If such was proper to the guest's situation, of course
this would excite no comment or opprobrium; but if a man happened to
take a chair that was below his state, the host would then be obliged to
come forward and move him to a better place, and this would make a
show of both the modesty of the guest and the honor in which he was
held. In short, if you take more than your due, you will be humiliated, but
if you take less, you will be elevated." She looked at Mrs. van Dortmund
uncertainly.

"Yes – so, you see?" Mrs. van Dortmund said, patting her small hands
on her lap. "The point is, people should not take a seat at the table when it
is meant for others. And our table is meant for us, and that's that. No one
else is going to be sitting at it. Clarissa, you will confine your memory book
to your personal acquaintance from here on out, if you please."

Clarissa agreed, but when Mrs. van Dortmund and Mrs. Addison
retired for afternoon naps, and Rachel emerged from helping Mrs.
Addison undress, Clarissa was waiting for her in the hall. "Rachel," she
whispered. "I want you to help me with something."

"Yes, of course."

"I want to go into camp and talk to the soldiers there," Clarissa
confided. "Mama doesn't understand. I have to help them, at least with a
kind word," she said, her voice rising. "It's too awful."

Rachel's heart sank. "It's harder than you think to – to do things
sometimes," she said.

Clarissa shook her head, her shining brown hair swinging against her
shoulders. "It isn't hard for me to write down what people say –"

"Can I tell you something that you must promise never to tell another
living soul?" Rachel said. "This is serious, Clarissa. I know I have no right
– but I cannot speak unless I have your word."

Clarissa paused, surprised. "Of course," she said after a moment.
"Yes, you have my absolute word, upon my honor. I won't tell anyone –
but it isn't anything bad, is it?"

Rachel glanced down the hall. Too close to Mrs. Addison, who might
well not be asleep yet, if at all. So they went to Clarissa's room, and Rachel
revealed at last the secret that had burdened her too long, of her discovery

about Captain Cunningham, and her ill-fated article – leaving out the revelations about General Howe, which Rachel thought might be too direct for Clarissa's well-bred ears – and then the crux of her secret, when she had tried to send a small signal of support to Bellew and O'Malley in the prison, and then what she had done with the rocks afterwards.

"You didn't really," Clarissa breathed, a hand over her mouth.

"I did," Rachel said. "And it was one of the stupidest things I've ever done in my life. I can't tell you the terror I felt running home, and the uselessness of it. Why, it might have been worse than useless – what if I had really hurt someone, and the redcoats had gotten angry, and decided to take measures of some sort?" She felt better for having told someone at last, someone who would listen to her full explanation. Of course she meant to use her experience only as a warning to Clarissa to be careful in her efforts to help the soldiers, because these efforts could have unpredictable and unwelcome results. But Rachel could not deny the purely personal benefit that she breathed more freely for having one less secret of so many pressing against her.

"Oh, Rachel, that was so brave!" Clarissa exclaimed, her eyes shining.

"I – there wasn't any bravery in it, I'm afraid, more like lack of thought. I didn't even realize I'd thrown the rock until after I'd done it," Rachel answered. She frowned slightly. She was glad that Clarissa didn't think worse of her – of course Clarissa wouldn't – but a little concerned that her warning was not coming across the way she had hoped.

Clarissa stood, full of sudden energy, and pressed her notebook to her chest in her excitement. "My book of the dead – excuse me, memory book – is so timid compared to what you've done! Oh, women *can* do something – Rachel, please, let's go now, we still have a little time before everyone wakes. You have to come with me – please. I really haven't the courage to go into camp alone."

Nor could Rachel let Clarissa do so. So she agreed to the trip, despite her misgivings. Would it really help the spirits of the living that much to drag up the shades of the dead? And yet of course the dead deserved that – and there was a sort of comfort to the living in knowing that their departed comrades were not forgotten, and that when they themselves risked their lives, they did not risk complete extirpation from the annals and the hearts of humanity. But it was a grim business nevertheless. "All right, if you think – but we have to make it quick," Rachel said, and Clarissa promised not to keep her out too long, because she surely wanted Mama to know of their errand as little as Rachel wished to be caught missing by Mrs. Addison.

But when they got outside, a heavy bank of clouds had rolled in, dimming the low light of late afternoon to a premature twilight. The ground was almost completely black. Clarissa took a few steps down the hill, and then stopped uncertainly. "Oh," she said, clutching her hands together and looking at Rachel with sad eyes. "Do you think it's going to rain?"

The scent of the woods and of the cold air, clean with the promise of snow, stirred Rachel's blood. Yes, Briarwood was a bit dull compared to Philadelphia – but how she loved to be in the country again!

"I have an idea," Rachel suggested. She knew better than to think that she could talk Clarissa entirely out of her plan, but she thought she might be able to make it seem less morbid and depressing to the troops. In fact, it might turn Clarissa's adventure into something that served some practical use. "It won't take long, and we'll be close enough to Briarwood if the rain comes."

"Try to catch some of father's men as they leave?" Clarissa asked. "Oh, but mama might find out..."

"No, we'll still go into camp, but we'll go tomorrow, or the day afterwards, depending on how it goes. I want to set a trap and catch some game. We'll trade meat for the men's stories – something for the living as well as the dead, you see, and that might – well, you see what I'm saying."

"Oh, what a kind thought," Clarissa replied brightly, not seeming to catch Rachel's full meaning.

"Wait for me just a moment," Rachel said, and she hurried to the stable, where she thought she might be able to find Abraham. She did. He was brushing Thunder's thick winter coat, murmuring in a low voice to the animal as he did so. Thunder whuffled in contentment.

"Abraham," she asked, "Do you have a knife I could borrow? One for cutting sticks."

Abraham's brows knitted together. He kept brushing. "What you cutting sticks for, Miss Rachel?"

"Miss Clarissa and I are going to make a box trap," Rachel said.

Abraham eyed her and scratched the side of his nose. Thunder shivered his hide in reproach when the pleasant currying stopped. "You know how to make a box trap?" Abraham said at last, his voice rising slightly in pitch. For him, it was a sign of great astonishment. "And what you think Miss Clarissa would want to do something like that for?"

"Well – she's just looking for – entertainment," Rachel said, unsure how much she ought to confide in Abraham. "Do you have the knife or not? I promise not to lose it – and I'll sharpen it for you when I get back."

"Now, don't go getting all like that, I'll be the one to sharpen any knives," Abraham sniffed, and he found a large knife with serrations close to the handle for her and gave her a ball of rough twine as well. Rachel had meant to use bark to tie together her sticks, but twine would be faster, and she thanked him hurriedly and rushed back to Clarissa, who stood shivering in the wind in her fine yellow cloak with rabbit-fur trim. Rachel showed her the knife, and Clarissa swallowed.

"Oh, my," she said.

"It's just for cutting sticks, not the actual – we won't catch anything right away," Rachel explained quickly. Clarissa smiled and nodded briskly, apparently summoning all her reserves to do so. Rachel realized that it might be best if she went alone to collect whatever the trap captured later on, if they were even so fortunate. But the woods had seemed full of small game, and Rachel thought that their chances were good.

They gathered sticks as they walked, Rachel flexing each of them slightly to test that it was not rotten and tucking them beneath her arm. Clarissa, watching carefully, copied the gesture, but when one of her sticks snapped with a hollow pop, spitting dust from the break, she squeaked and looked at Rachel with a woebegone expression. "I'm sorry, I ruined it, I must have bent it too hard –"

"No, that's good, that's exactly what we're checking for."

"Oh!" And for the rest of the way, Clarissa tugged at the sticks she found so vigorously that she broke several perfectly good ones. Rachel decided it was best to leave the matter be.

Briarwood had been aptly named, and the surrounding landscape bristled with close underbrush, but Clarissa did not want to tangle her skirts, so they followed a winding path through the clearer spaces. Rachel did not mind. She had forgotten to bring bait for the trap, thinking only of the knife, and she knew she had seen fever bushes in the area and that they thrived best in the emptier areas that got more light. She wondered if there were a proper English name for fever bush, other than her translation from the Cherokee. She did not know one. If she did find some of the berries, she would simply pretend that she was wholly ignorant rather than partly and that she was only guessing that they would be useful.

"Oh! Winterberries," Clarissa said. Rachel had stopped a moment at a tall bush covered in tiny, bright red globes. Its leaves had long since fallen. "Is that how we're going to lure our game into the trap?"

Winterberries. Rachel nodded to herself as she twisted a twig thick with smooth, swollen fruit from its branch. Clarissa must have taken this as an answer to her question, because she did not repeat it. "We've got everything we need, but let's go on a bit farther – no, let's turn around, so we're closer to the house. We just don't want to set ourselves up too near this bush, or I don't think our relatively meager offering will look as appealing as we might hope," Rachel said.

They backtracked a few minutes until Rachel was satisfied with the distance. Then she selected four of the longest sticks and joined them together with twine to make a square roughly two feet long on each side. "If you like, you can sort the other sticks for size," Rachel said, and Clarissa, enchanted by the novelty of the task, set about it capably.

Rachel built up the height of her trap methodically, testing the joints of twine and making each new level slightly narrower than the last so that she would not have too much of an opening to cover at the top. She had to stop several times to trim down her sticks, and Clarissa shot nervous looks at the sky, which was nearly black. Rachel knew the sun had not set, though, because a stripe of bruised purple burned at the horizon about the shaggy low crown of one of the so-called mountains here, Mount Misery or Mount Joy, she wasn't sure. In Rachel's opinion, they weren't much more than hills.

"Is it almost finished?" Clarissa asked in a small voice, shifting on her feet. She pulled her cloak tighter. Rachel glanced up and noticed for the first time that the air had grown damp and cold. It would rain soon.

"I – well, not quite, but I can put the top on now, so we're coming to the end of it," Rachel said. The trap was about two feet high; that would do. So she lashed together a flat line of sticks for a roof and connected it to the frame.

"Is it finished now?" Clarissa said hopefully, throwing a longing glance towards home.

Rachel wondered how on earth Clarissa expected the trap to work – that they would leave an open box on the ground and an animal would obligingly wander into and remain there? But she swallowed down her frustration, cross at herself. She was so ungenerous – so little like Clarissa, as if she'd made no improvement in herself at all over the past few days.

"Well, we do have to set it. That's the last step, and it's a little delicate, but it won't take too long," Rachel replied. She took two sticks she had set aside and notched them with the knife. She wedged the stem of the winterberry twig firmly into one notch and balanced the far end of the stick on the other branch, making an inverted L-shape; and then she held the inverted L in place while she carefully tilted back the box and rested its edge on the trigger. The berries dangled within the shadow of the leaning box.

"That doesn't look very sturdy," Clarissa said. Rachel eyed her work cautiously. It wasn't the best trap she'd ever made, and she felt some chagrin at how clumsy and unskilled she had grown. But the thing was serviceable, she thought.

"It's not supposed to be. It's all supposed to come crashing down when an animal touches the bait."

"Oh, of course, how stupid of me. Rachel – is it finished now?"

"It is. I'm sorry that took so long."

They left, and Clarissa limped as she walked. It turned out that her shoes had been pinching her for some time, because she had not thought to change out of her slippers. Rachel wondered why Clarissa had insisted on standing through the hour it had taken Rachel to construct the trap, but she did not ask. "Well, it's lucky we didn't go into camp after all," she said instead. "Do you want to trade shoes with me?"

"Oh Rachel, you're so kind, but my feet are smaller than yours – just slightly, of course – and I don't think my slippers would fit you."

The wind gusted, and the needles and dead leaves hanging on the trees first whispered and then rattled. "The rain is starting," Rachel said, looking behind them. The sky was quite black now, even at the horizon.

404

"I can't see a thing – you didn't bring a lantern, did you?" Rachel had not, and although she admitted that this had been thoughtless of her, she thought it was a curious thing for Clarissa to ask. Rachel hardly could have hidden anything as large as a lantern in her skirts.

"No, but we aren't far –"

"But I tell you I can't see a thing! We could walk in circles all night – we'll be lost!"

"Truly, Clarissa, don't worry – truly don't," Rachel insisted, frowning. "I remember the way. And if we get lost, your father will send someone to look for us."

"But they'll never find us in the dark! And oh, wouldn't it be awful – everyone so worried, and all the fuss, and they won't even do any good, and if we ever do get home again, how angry they'll be, and with perfect cause, and this was the most terrible thing I've ever done!" Clarissa began to cry as she stumbled along, hanging onto Rachel's arm.

Rachel felt utterly perplexed. She did not even know what to say. They were less than ten minutes from Briarwood, and it was only because of the trees that they could not see the house-lights from here. The shadows hung dark, it was true; but the shadow of trees was denser and thicker than the shadow of air, and so it was not difficult to retrace the path they had taken. But Clarissa seemed lost in despair, and Rachel simply could not discern what the source of it could be.

"It won't be but a few minutes, I promise you," she said after a moment.

"You're just saying that to be nice," she sniffled.

"Honestly," Rachel said, confused, "I'm not." Clarissa tightened her grip on Rachel's arm.

She was silent for a few seconds. Rachel breathed deeply in relief. She was sure this attack of nerves must have been very embarrassing for Clarissa, so Rachel promised herself she'd never mention it. In a moment, Clarissa would surely be herself again.

And then Clarissa spoke, her voice was firm and deep with resolution. "I think we must pray now, Rachel. We must pray with all our earnestness that our souls will meet with mercy."

Rachel's exasperation surged and nearly boiled over. "Clarissa, we're nearly home."

"We're nearly home, I imagine – yes, I expect that we are," Clarissa intoned. "The home that awaits us all."

This was beyond all endurance. "Please, Clarissa, I'm trying to concentrate – of course it is very salutary to pray, and I would never discourage the endeavor, but honestly – even if we were lost all night, we'd hardly perish. It would just be cold and uncomfortable."

"Until we were scalped by Indians or eaten by wolves or caught a pleurisy."

It took all Rachel's control not to stop right there and shake the girl until she came to her senses. How could Clarissa suddenly have turned so silly? She couldn't really believe the nonsense she was spouting, could she? But Clarissa was such a good creature, and she'd even condescended to show Rachel a completely undeserved friendship, and – well, on a practical level, Rachel had a hard time imagining that Mrs. Addison would have too much tolerance for a hireling who had given her sister's brains a rattle. But that remark about Indians, Rachel thought, had been rather unkind. Clarissa knew how Rachel's family had died, of course; had fear made her thoughtless, or had it made her – no, Clarissa could never be cruel.

Just then a fat drop of rain landed on Rachel's nose, cold and heavy as a plumb weight. A scattering of drops followed, peppering their backs and shoulders. Clarissa whimpered, but the brief burst was followed by a wet wind that carried no more rain, for the moment. Either a warning shot or a misfire. Rachel could not be sure; she could not see the clouds in the dark, and she had forgotten how to smell the wind. No matter.

"Clarissa. I was right about the rain. I'm right about Briarwood, too, and we're very nearly there," she said firmly. This, at last, seemed to make an impression. Clarissa's fingers tightened on Rachel's arm.

"Are you sure?"

"I am. But we're going to get wet if we don't hurry."

Clarissa seemed flooded with sudden animation. "Oh, Rachel, I don't care about my shoes – let's run!" And so they did, although it was more of a stumble than a run. Rachel managed to keep them clear of the trees, and in three minutes they were rushing up to the door just as another spit of raindrops hammered down. Clarissa flung the front door open and wheeled around in the foyer, suddenly laughing. Rachel closed the door behind herself and smiled hesitantly at her friend, unsure of this new mood.

"We almost got soaked through!" Clarissa said, clasping her hands together. "Oh, land! What were we thinking! Oh, my feet – you can't imagine how they pinch." She wrinkled her nose and laughed again.

"No, it's not good weather – at least it's not too cold, though," Rachel answered cautiously. Clarissa's hysterics seemed to have vanished as quickly as they had sprung up, but Rachel didn't know how far to trust her friend's new good humor.

"Well, it's plenty cold enough, I think!" Clarissa replied, unfastening her cloak and shaking it before hanging it on a hook. She sat down heavily on a settee and stuck a finger down the heel of a slipper, sliding it off. A gray band of damp sweat marked the outline of her foot through her stocking.

Martha appeared from the direction of the kitchen just as Mrs. van Dortmund came down the stairs. Martha flattened her mouth. She didn't deign to acknowledge either Rachel or Clarissa directly.

"There they are, ma'am," Martha said dryly, bobbed a curtsy, and returned to the kitchen.

Mrs. van Dortmund's face seemed contracted to half its size in annoyance, all except her eyes, which were widened to their full extent. "Clarissa! I must be informed at once what you think you're doing."

"We got caught in the rain – almost got caught in the rain – and my feet hurt," Clarissa answered cheerfully.

"Put your slipper on immediately, miss. Your father still has *soldiers* in here. Rachel? Margaret has been looking for you. Please attend to her."

"Yes, ma'am," Rachel murmured, lowering her eyes and hurrying upstairs. The coldness of Mrs. van Dortmund's voice chilled her a great deal more than the rain. The sound of Clarissa's breathless laughter and Mrs. van Dortmund's remonstrances faded behind her. Rachel found the door, rapped a quick knock, and stepped inside without waiting for an answer.

Mrs. Addison was not just annoyed but actually angry. She sat before her dresser and eyed Rachel coldly.

"I have been awake for thirty minutes and unable to dress. I suppose you think it makes no difference if that slattern comes in to assist me – and perhaps it does not, Rachel, if you are as flighty as that. I know you have cut it precious fine before, and perhaps I should have made myself clear previously. You seem rather clever about some things, so I had not thought it necessary." Her voice was hard as metal.

"You are entirely correct, ma'am," Rachel said, her body like ice and her face a flame. Her hands shook. Mrs. Addison had never spoken like this to her before - never. Nor to anyone else in Rachel's hearing. It had seemed like such a small thing, her absence - but apparently it was not.

Mrs. Addison could dress herself just fine if she wanted to, at least well enough for family, a small voice told Rachel. *She's being unkind. She's being truly unkind.*

Rachel shoved that voice aside. Mrs. Addison wasn't the one who was late - Rachel was. "It won't happen again, not ever," she said. "If it does - if it does I'll just go away immediately." That was the worst punishment Rachel could imagine. She could offer nothing more. Could Mrs. Addison tell that Rachel had been angry for a moment? She was so ashamed. She must never be angry again, never - not at anyone but herself. She did not have so many friends that she could afford to criticize them or drive them off.

Mrs. Addison sounded little mollified. "And I suppose you'd just up and leave me to fend for myself just like that - it's very like you, I'm learning."

"I'm - it's not -" To Rachel's shame, tears poured down her cheeks, even though she wasn't really sad and she wasn't really sorry, she was only frightened and confused. She wiped her face, but her hands were wet from the rain, so it didn't do any good. "I am so sorry. Ma'am, if there's anyone in the world I wouldn't -"

Mrs. Addison remained unmoved. "It isn't the incompetence so much as the disrespect, Rachel."

"I truly -"

"That's all I have to say. If you'll do my hair, please, I'm tired of being in my room."

Rachel wasn't sure how she managed to make her shaking hands function, but she got to work on Mrs. Addison's hair.

"Your skin feels like a fish. What on earth were you doing? There aren't any newspaper offices here," Mrs. Addison said eventually in a level tone, almost sympathetic.

"Clarissa – Miss van Dortmund wanted to go outside."

"Clarissa has a maid of her own if she wants company."

"Yes, ma'am. I just didn't think it was my place to say no to her, she is so very kind – although I do not rightly understand her, but it is not my place to," Rachel added hurriedly. She would not tell Mrs. Addison what they had done outside – she would not betray Clarissa's confidence. But she certainly would not accompany her to the camp tomorrow, or on any other day. She would be firm about that. She would tell Clarissa that it was Mrs. Addison's explicit instruction, and that she would be in terrible difficulty if she disobeyed. And with Captain Bellew arriving in just two days – no, she could and would risk nothing now. Nothing.

"Clarissa is exactly like mother, only younger. It's very simple," Mrs. Addison said. She sighed and continued in a softer tone, "Now, Rachel. I know you like to ingratiate yourself, and perhaps I've simply given you too much time, so that you feel the need to fill it."

"I will so happily assist Martha in the work here – there are dozens of things I could do!" Rachel blurted. "And then I would always be at hand, and I would never be idle –"

"And I don't think you need to ingratiate yourself to that slut Martha, either. Just try to mind yourself a little better – you see how dreadful it can be when you're thoughtless, and I'm sure, you're very sensitive, really, it will make an impression. Now, the other generals' ladies will start arriving soon, I think, and we'll start having our visits again, and it will be just like old times, when you never gave me any grief. It must be the circumstances. Well, it takes breeding, dear, to be able to adapt to different environments – honestly, Rachel, I'm as much at fault as you, but we'll both start off again on a better foot, shall we?"

Rachel was crying again. She didn't want Mrs. Addison to know, so she bumped her shoulder quickly against her eye to soak up some of the tears. "Oh, I couldn't ask you to treat me as your companion again, ma'am," she said in a low voice. Let Mrs. Addison try to come up with her own observations and witticisms.

"Well, you aren't asking me, you're simply following my wishes. You know your place perfectly well in drawing-rooms at least, and you're very entertaining afterwards. See, Rachel? I'm not angry any more. Let's have a look at my hair. I think we're ready to touch up the powder, you're just fussing now, and I want to get to tea. Or whatever that substance is that we're calling liberty tea."

Rachel heard the offer in Mrs. Addison's opening. She swallowed her anger. It was wrong. And she did want to go with Mrs. Addison, she did want to see all the fine people, she did want to hear them laugh at her cleverness. She wanted all of it.

"It is certainly curious that the Continentals were so eager to attach the name of liberty to something that is both a fraud and difficult to swallow," Rachel said.

"There, now you're back in form. That was perfectly feline and would get you shot if you were a man," Mrs. Addison replied with satisfaction.

Rachel did not have to tell Clarissa of her new determination to have no part in any future expeditions. Clarissa came to Rachel herself, taking her arm and pulling her aside later in the evening. "Just imagine if we'd been in the middle of camp, when all that – oh, I can hardly even think of it – all *that* happened," Clarissa said. Rachel was not sure whether Clarissa meant sunset or a few smatterings of rain by this unmentionable horror, but she nodded, glad that their friendship would not be clouded. She truly did care for Clarissa and felt a deep relief that they would be able to avoid a useless risk and an unnecessary venture where, being outside a drawing-room, that affection might be strained. "I was a very foolish girl, Rachel, and you tried to talk sense into me, but I wasn't listening." She shook her head firmly, brown curls swinging. She touched a hand to her locket. "No, Mama was correct, and I should have listened to her too – I should have listened to her first. No, I'll do just what people say, and I'll certainly never try anything like that again, nor even *think* it." Rachel could not help thinking that there was something a little unworthy in that total surrender. And yet had she herself not just sworn the same?

Chapter 36

Although Rachel heartily wished never to leave the house again except when instructed to do so, she could not forget that box trap she had left waiting in the woods. All evening, she could not shake the image of a rabbit, or a young pheasant hen in her first winter, trapped inside the box, tiny heart beating wildly, thrashing against the walls until falling still at last in exhaustion, and then despair, and then, at long, slow last, death. And all for no cause now that Rachel would not be visiting the camp in secret with Clarissa.

When she woke up the next morning, the image remained. Rachel lay still in the bed, cold and blanketless, her face to the darkness of the window and her back turned to Martha. She could have moved closer to her slumbering bedmate to gain a little heat, but she preferred the distance. Perhaps the box trap had not been sprung, and perhaps the rain had knocked it over in the night anyway – although the threatened storm had never quite materialized, and so Rachel doubted this. But if some small creature had been tempted by the berries, with food hard to come by in the depths of winter, it now huddled imprisoned in hopeless misery while Rachel, who wanted for nothing and so did not have to snatch for berries in the night, lay on a soft bed, her stomach full from yesterday's rich meal of mutton pie and baked apples.

Rachel turned her head by careful degrees. Martha seemed to be sleeping soundly. But just as Rachel had convinced herself that it was so, Martha shifted on the mattress, jerking a knee and releasing a soft grunt that smelled of old meat. Rachel's heart hammered and she froze in rigid immobility, as if she had been caught stealing the silverware.

"But I'm not doing anything wrong," she thought. And whenever her heart began to race again, she reminded herself of this as she dressed quietly and tiptoed down the stairs in stocking feet, slipping on her shoes only when she was by the front door. The curious thing, she reflected, is that she knew no one would object to her errand if she could only explain it to them; but it was her ability to explain properly, she supposed, that she doubted. Not that anything in her behavior would arouse suspicion of bad motives. No one would think she was doing anything other than being strange, leaving box traps lying about. But she did not want anyone to think that; she did not want them to consider her strange. Somehow it seemed that this would be an admission of something terrible, something she could not name or describe or identify, but something damning nevertheless.

She slipped outside into the dark. Because she had been so cold in bed, the air did not chill her, although it nipped at her fingers and face. She buried her hands in the warmth of her cloak and hurried through the shadows. A nearly half moon hung in the sky, giving a little light. It was brighter than it had been indoors, at any rate, and she knew the path almost as well as she knew the house, having crossed it so recently. The ground crunched softly beneath her tread, and she realized she was leaving a plain trail in the frost but of so many matters that worried her, this did not. The activity of the day would obscure her footprints soon enough, and it was unlikely that one stray set would excite comment.

She felt invisible and alone as she crept along, feeling like an inconsequential thing next to the bulk of the trees, and the sense of freedom buoyed her spirits. She never felt at ease, not truly, except when there was no one else to see or hear her. The air smelled of ice, and it whispered its strange language to the forest, which answered with its own creaks and rattles. Rachel brushed the palm of her hand against the bristles of a naked bush. The twigs tickled, and she curled her fingers as if to hold the pleasant scratchy sensation so that it could not escape.

The wind picked up and carried what sounded like the ghost of half a recognizable word through its sighs. She smiled at her fancy. The Cherokee for *stink*. Well, she supposed it was too much to hope for that she pleased the air's senses as much as it pleased hers. How agreeable it would be, to sit and listen to the sky and trees all day and night – not to need to eat or drink any more, not to need warmth or comfort or sleep, not to need a single thing, but merely to observe in peace. She pushed back the hood of her cloak so that she could see better. The trap had to lie just ahead.

As she had feared, the box lay flat on the ground. She did not think it had fallen by accident. Rachel ran the last few yards, as if this late burst of speed would make any difference, and as she drew near, she heard frantic scrabbling come from inside the trap. "Don't be afraid," she murmured in what she hoped was a soothing voice and tilted the box open again.

A hiss and a pair of eyes bright with anger greeted her. A tight bundle of dense fur, the stripes on its back glowing in the dim light. It felt like an eternity but must have been less than half a second before she recognized the animal.

"*Dih li!*" she cried, dropping the box and scrambling backwards as fast as she could go. Oh, but the animal – skunk, skunk, why hadn't she used the English word? – had wasted its opportunity for freedom on hissing at her rather than running, and the falling box trapped the creature anew. Rachel could not leave it to starve. But neither could she approach an angry skunk; it would be on its guard now and spray her for certain. Her clothes would be ruined, her presence would be intolerable for days, and she would hardly be able to avoid the question of what she had been doing in the dark predawn. Agitating skunks. No, that would neither recommend nor flatter her much. A surge of resentment surged in her breast. She had only been trying to make Clarissa's foolish plan less humiliating and – through no fault of Clarissa's, of course – cruel, and now the full burden of the stupidity and its concomitant untenability fell square on Rachel's shoulders alone somehow. Clarissa had been able to brush it all off, with no thought for the consequences of anything – and therefore, somehow, no guilt. How on earth would Rachel free this idiotic skunk? If only it were a defenseless thing.

Low laughter sounded behind her. Rachel wheeled around, fear pricking her back. Three forms, tall, men, stepped out of the dark. "*O si yo,*" one of them said, raising his hand. "Hello, little sister."

Indians. Cherokee.

"*O si yo,*" Rachel replied in a small voice, once she decided they were too close for her to be able to run. Not in her heavy dress and cloak and stays. If she were dressed like they were – then she could fly, and she would have been off like a shot. The skunk could wait until she got a stick, or the skunk could hang itself. Clarissa's prattle about dying last night came back to Rachel now, and she cursed herself for three times a fool. She had felt alone in the woods, but she was not. She had merely been blind.

413

"Not what you expected to catch for your meal, little sister?" the Cherokee continued, the grin obvious in his voice even though Rachel could not make out his face. "We saw it as we went by."

"I wanted to free it," Rachel said. The words returned to her easily. It did not feel as though it had been five years since she had spoken them out loud.

"Better food elsewhere? Then you're not from the white men's camp. Don't you know how to prepare a skunk, little sister? Just cut out the smelly part and soak the body in water before you boil it. The meat is sweet."

"I haven't - no, I just wanted to let it go," Rachel said. "I don't need it any more, and leaving it here to die is wicked."

"But what are you doing so far from home, and so close to the white men - ah!" the Cherokee cried, getting closer to her. She could make out his features now, and she supposed he must be able to see her own as well.

"I am staying near the camp, but not in it. Very near. Very near here - with one of their leaders," Rachel said hurriedly, hoping to make it clear that she was not without protection. If it sounded like a boast, so be it - it was not, and it was also preferable to risking injury. "I had thought that I would be able to go into the camp and bring them a present, a little meat, but not - not this, I think. And besides, now I'm not allowed to go to camp at all, and I can't let the skunk die for nothing, with no one even eating it. I - what do you think I should do? If I knock it over with a stick, I'll still be close enough to be in danger. I don't know whether I can throw a rock well enough, or hard enough, from a distance."

The second Cherokee came closer to her and peered directly in her face, close enough that she could smell his skin and feel his warm breath against her. Rachel took a step back, frowning. He smiled and shook his head. "I mean no offense, little sister. I just doubted my eyes that you were a white woman. You speak our language properly and ask our opinion politely. Ha!"

"But she also wants to be polite to the skunk," the third Cherokee put in.

"I -" Rachel stopped, uncertain what she could say that might not come across as offensive.

The Cherokees laughed.

"But perhaps you could take it," Rachel suggested. "If you know how."

"Too much work," the first Cherokee shrugged. "We'll catch what we need as we go."

"You could bring it into the camp, perhaps, before you leave, if you don't need it yourself – just so it doesn't go to waste."

The Cherokee glanced at each other. "We just came from there," the first said. "And we will not be returning. We are tired of it."

Rachel realized they must be deserters. And of course they would leave the army if they were tired of it; and of course they would be hanged if they returned. That explained their presence in this particular place at this dead hour. "Oh, I – I see," she said slowly.

"Don't worry, little sister, we'll help you save your skunk. Here. Come." The first Indian gestured for her to join them. Rachel did so, and they retreated about twenty yards. Then the first Cherokee unslung his bow from his shoulder. He stared into the dark a few moments. Rachel peered in the same direction. The shadowed hump of the box trap seemed awfully small. But if he shot the skunk by accident through the trap, at least it would not suffer. And she would do something with the meat and hide even if they did not. She felt so terribly responsible for this skunk. She knew it was ridiculous.

The Cherokee nocked an arrow, paused the barest of moments, and then let it fly. A sharp crack as sticks shattered. "Hi!" the Cherokee cried, laughing. "Off with you, little skunk! And stay far away, if you appreciate anything we have done! Don't blame the white woman – they like to keep things in cages!"

"Ha! What woman doesn't," the third Cherokee replied cheerfully.

The arrow had hit the very top of the trap cleanly, and the skunk was obligingly nowhere to be seen when they returned to the site to retrieve the arrow, which seemed unharmed and came free with only a little gentle wiggling. Rachel thanked them profusely.

"It was nothing," the first Cherokee replied. "Sometimes we cannot correct our mistakes alone."

The Cherokees' heads lifted in unison then, and in a moment Rachel heard it too. Hoofbeats – one horse trotting, she thought, although she wasn't sure. Her senses had grown so dull. She wished she could train her mind again to know these things without thinking about them. "Oh, you should leave," she whispered. They could not be caught.

The Indians nodded silently and touched her on the shoulder, and they melted into the night, their soft boots crunching against the frost until even that sound vanished. The sky had taken on a hesitant gray. It must have been half past six or so, and the sun would be rising soon. Rachel had to get back. This horseback rider – he must be from camp, probably heading for Briarwood, though this was a little off the path. She hoped he was not looking for the deserting Indians; if he asked, she would say that she had seen and heard nothing. The law of the army was not her law.

So she started back, and it did not surprise her to see the rider very soon, as there were few enough trails through the woods that had little enough brush and space enough between the trees for a horse's easy passage. The man was a soldier, she had been correct, wearing a sharp new uniform beneath his open cloak but riding a large horse that had a great deal of agricultural stolidity about it more than warlike fire. She raised her hand in greeting and stepped to the side so that he would see her and not be startled.

He looked up at her movement, and the scant light sketched out the bare lines of his face. Her heart stopped.

"Captain Bellew!" she exclaimed. And brought a chapped hand to clutch the fabric of her cloak at her throat.

Chapter 37

He had already seen her, and at the sound of her voice, he raised one hand, which she saw held a pistol. "Are you all right?" he snapped, bringing the horse to a quick stop.

"Yes, of course," Rachel said.

"I heard Indians." His face had a hard set that both frightened and thrilled her. "Men – and a woman. Did you see them?"

She reconfigured her intentions quickly. "Yes, but they were only passing by, they weren't unfriendly, they even helped me – it's me, Captain Bellew, Rachel Kolkhorst, I'm sorry, it's dark."

"Yes, I recognized you. My apologies, Miss Kolkhorst, for not greeting you first. I was simply concerned," Bellew replied with a tight voice, his eyes still searching the forest. "Where are they now?"

"They left – they really were just helping me, but when we heard your horse – they thought it was more prudent to leave."

"It d– ...certainly was," Bellew said, swallowing the oath. "Let's get you away from here. What on earth are you doing out alone like this?" He swung his leg around and dismounted, the pistol still in his hand.

"It is going to sound very foolish," Rachel said. "I hardly know where to begin. But I assure you that the Indians were nothing but amiable, and in fact they extracted me from a difficulty." He frowned and watched the woods rather than her face as she told him a partial truth, that she and Clarissa had meant to visit the men in camp to cheer them up, only Rachel had thought that it would be better if they brought a practical gift as well – and thus the box trap, with its captive left to starve once the planned trip to the camp had fallen through, until its rescue by the Indians.

"They didn't take the prey for themselves," Bellew said, his face softening.

"No, of course not, they viewed it as mine to dispose of as I pleased, though they offered to help me with it – if I wanted to cook skunk."

His eyebrows shot up, and a smile quirked his mouth. "Ah," he said. He released the half-cock on his pistol and holstered it.

"That was what they were talking about so much, you see. We retreated a distance and one of them shot the trap with an arrow. The adventure seemed to amuse them."

"Fair enough. Although I don't like their being so near."

"Well, the Indians come and go as they please," Rachel said.

"Yes, or as we or the English pay them. If they're ours, I doubt they should be here at this hour. And if they're theirs, I don't like their spying business one bit."

"I did not get the impression they held any such allegiance," Rachel said cautiously. Technically, this was true. "They didn't ask me anything, although they could have."

"Well, if they're traveling with a woman, they're probably neither spies nor soldiers," Bellew answered. "I did not mean to suggest any disservice to people who have been kind. I should not have done so. I was simply - I heard their voices, and I was suspicious. Then when I saw you, I was angry." Rachel fidgeted, and his eyes widened. "Not at you, Miss Kolkhorst, heavens - not at you, of all people. You satisfied my curiosity at your presence here, although I think you meant it as an explanation, which was not required. I was angry they might have done you some harm - you assure me they did not?"

A pleasant warmth spread over Rachel's face. "No, of course not - only the box trap took a little damage," she murmured happily. "You were - you were going to present yourself to General van Dortmund?"

He blinked at the change of topic. "Yes; a day earlier than I had planned, but I found Dr. Rhoades last evening and convinced him that a day one way or the other could do me nor others any harm. He remarked that I seemed to have quite enough spirit to indicate good health, if I was arguing so much. I think what turned the matter in my favor is that he knew I would be eating well at Briarwood. I should have sent a messenger, only it was late when I won the point, and I figured I could bear the news as well myself. If I am premature, I return to town for a day with no harm. At least it lets me move around a little," he concluded with a rueful shrug. "I have been still far too long."

"I have been feeing much the same," Rachel said, and he looked at her with amusement.

"Have you? And thus your adventures with box traps and such, I suppose," he said quietly.

"They told Martha to get your room ready yesterday, but I don't think she's done it yet, she's – a little slow about things sometimes," Rachel said. "The house won't rise for another half an hour, but I can let you in, of course, and get you anything you need."

Bellew smiled. "I am glad I was delayed, then. You meant to slip out and in with no one the wiser."

"I thought – "

He shook his head. "More good deeds should be done that way," he said. "Then we'd know they were honest."

"You do me too much credit," Rachel said.

"I will beg your indulgence that I always think I know best."

"Yes, but –" She had not told him so many things that she knew she could hardly claim honesty. She wished she could tell him everything, though. It would make her life so much easier, her heart so much lighter; now that he was being kind to her, and interested, and somehow it terrified her a thousand times more than any silence or indifference, because he might like a little part of her, but discover he did not much care for the whole, and then she knew her heart would break forever. "I am so much happier that you know what I meant to do, even though it was a terribly small good deed, if such at all, that I can take no credit for disinterestedness."

"So you were going to regale the Addisons and the van Dortmunds with your rescue of the endangered skunk after all," Bellew said with a grin.

"No, they don't matter, only you!" Rachel blurted.

Bellew froze a moment, his face going blank and all signs of teasing gone. He looked at her curiously. She lowered her eyes, cursing every fiber of her heedless, tactless, presumptuous soul, a soul that could not allow her to have even one sweet unsullied memory of affection without grasping for more with muddy hands and laying everything to waste. She felt the cold suddenly, and her body trembled. Bellew said nothing. She did not dare look up.

His hand cupped her shoulder gently. "You're shaking, Miss Kolkhorst," he whispered. Her skin tingled beneath her dress.

Perhaps she could use the cold as an excuse for her words – the cold, and the tiredness of this early hour. She raised her face and opened her mouth to apologize, but he stood close, much closer than she had known, and his lips were on hers before she could step back. His mouth was cold, and so was hers, but he pressed her closer, and they grew warm. She could not feel the ground beneath her feet, and she placed her hand on his breast between his shoulder and neck to steady herself. Her palm was damp with sweat, and a metal button of his jacket felt slick as melting ice under her skin.

When she touched him, Bellew pulled back slightly. He might have stepped farther, but Rachel's fingers pressed into his shoulder, and he kept his hand upon her. They regarded each other.

"You are well within your rights to rebuke me," he said after a moment, his eyes uncertain.

Rachel shook her head, hoping he would understand her – she could not speak. He smiled and cocked his head a fraction to the right, and she thought he meant to kiss her again, and he did. Her eyes sank closed so she could drink in the feel of him. And then she opened them again so she could see his face. His eyes were open only a fraction, unseeing, intent. She slipped her other arm around him – she did not want him to let her go. His shoulders were strong and heavy, and she could feel the muscles shift when he tightened his hold. She did not know why he had kissed her; she felt she knew him, because she had thought of him so often, but she knew that he had not done so of her, or she would have sensed it. And yet there was something that he liked, perhaps – unless he desired nothing but a quick intrigue. She did not know what she would do if that were the case. She felt that she would die if their bodies separated now, if she could not feel the buttons of his uniform pressing into her sides through her dress and the force of his hands upon her shoulders. His breath against her cheek. She wished she could feel the roughness of his hands as well as their strength. Her body ached.

He swallowed and pushed her back slightly, just enough to separate them. Rachel felt dizzy, and the air cold against the ghost of wetness on her lips. She closed her mouth and tasted the slight bitterness his lips had left there, both foreign and familiar and gone all too soon. "I should not –"

he began hesitantly, and then he closed his mouth too, and Rachel saw him taste his own lips.

* * *

Bellew did not know why he kissed her at first, other than she was so terribly pretty and had always been sweet – and that her heedless words revealed perhaps she bore him some partiality as well. When a pretty girl favors a man, it is only a blasted fool who turns away. And it had been much too long since he had held a girl in his arms. Not since his mother's final illness, when he had withdrawn from company and sport to tend her.

Before then, he had held plenty. He knew he was not bad-looking, even if hardly the picture of ideal male beauty, and the interest of his name and family history had dealt him far too easy a hand with the local girls of his youth, and far too easy an excuse for not taking his little adventures with them seriously. Probably a few of those girls had hoped he might; but no one expected it as a matter of course. Everyone assumed he would probably marry better than a simple farm-girl, and Bellew himself too had some vague notions of more elevated company in his future. He knew very well the equation he would have to balance to rise in the world. He would bring his name and his accomplishments – once he had any to claim. The girl would bring money and local connections. Anything before then was merely a delightful pastime and physical release.

And yet here he was with one of those farm-girls, poor and unconnected, without even a shred of family, but an obviously chaste and tender-hearted creature whom he could not put in difficulties. And the daughter of his new patron was jealous of both Bellew and her little maid, as he well knew. He had made a ridiculous and unnecessary complexity out of everything, and yet he felt nothing but delight. Delight, and an extremely awkward physical arousal, as if his body meant to overrule his every objection to the match.

Perhaps, he mused as he held this darling little creature in his arms, his accomplishments would be enough; perhaps the girl need bring nothing more than herself. War held so many opportunities. But he must not throw them away. If anything would happen with this girl – and he realized he wished that it would, and badly, although God knows he did not know her well nor she him, and he had no reason for suddenly wanting her so much – he must make matters clear.

"Miss -" he began again and then stopped. He must not take a distant tone with her; better a perhaps too familiar one, so that she did not misconstrue his words. "Rachel," he said in a low voice, and she smiled. Her right hand remained on his shoulder, and he covered it with his own fingers. "Ah, you should say my name, dear."

"Stephen," she whispered. A smile came unbidden to his own lips. She was half shyer than a deer and half bolder than a Bengal tiger; she needed the prompt, but only one. O'Malley had been right, as always - Bellew had underestimated her. And O'Malley had tried to turn his attention to her before, Bellew remembered now. God, what a stubborn fool he was. If he'd noticed her in Philadelphia, they could have been married by now. He would have kissed her and asked her, and they would have settled the matter one way or the other then and there. Although perhaps she wouldn't leave her place - it would be asking a great deal. But if, if, if. He could have set her up in a room with Mrs. Merriwether. Or sent her back to the farm, if he hadn't sold it. He might have borrowed more money from O'Malley. And there wouldn't have been all this complexity. If. Now everything was going to be like picking a path over ice in the mountains.

"There, now I have heard you do it." He squeezed her hand. "I hope you will not consider me - well, more precipitate than I have already shown myself to be, and I promise you that I am not presuming upon the course of - any courtship that you should see fit to allow. But - perhaps I should ask your thoughts first." She tilted her head and dropped her eyes, fidgeting with a button that lay beside her thumb. Bellew repressed a grin and wiggled her shoulder playfully. "Now, if you're too shy to tell me your thoughts, you'll make me afraid of you," he said, suddenly curious. He knew that girls struggled more often than not to admit that they liked a man, and it wasn't that she hadn't made it clear enough, but more that he wanted to hear her say it. For the moment, this enchanting obstacle drove other concerns from his mind. And if she liked him only a little, or was too meek after all, it was better to cut it off now.

"My thoughts are odd, and not to the point - you wouldn't want to hear them, it is just the way I think," she murmured, turning her head away and contracting in on herself.

"But I have said I do, dear. Rachel." He pressed her hand.

"Well, I - well. It isn't a thought so much perhaps as a feeling," she said, her brows contracting slightly. Ah, here it was. He felt the triumph and kissed her lightly on the little bump of skin that formed above her nose, and he brushed his cheek against her hair. His heart beat light and steady. She continued in a wondering murmur, "It is as though I had been living in a sort of cellar for a long time, and I had long since grown resigned to it - four walls that I knew like the back of my hand, a dirt floor, a close ceiling. And then I suddenly came upon a cupboard-door. And the door frightened me, because I did not know whether it had always been there and I had never searched properly, even though I thought I knew everything about the place I was trapped. And I feared that if I opened it there might be some danger behind it, or some duty that I was meant to have seen long ago. But I hoped that there might be some food, or perhaps a pocket-watch so I could measure the passage of time. And yet what I found, when I opened the door - was freedom. The door opens to the outside, where the whole world lies before me in the glory of creation, forests and oceans and mountains, and the silvery light of the moon mixing with the pink glow of dawn shining over the waters. I feel as though I have just discovered the entire world." She lowered her head again. "That is - it is just the sort of thing that fills my mind, I know it is foolish."

"It is anything but," Bellew answered thoughtfully. She was partial to him all right. It was what he had hoped for, and yet the strangeness and fervency and elaboration of her views unsettled him a little, just as he found them entrancing. "I could never have said such a thing, but when you do, I see it, and understand it - my thoughts are, I am afraid, much more prosaic, but I hope you will understand the motivation behind them." The more he thought, the better he liked what she had said. She did want him, and he was glad. But more than that - she felt he offered her the world, somehow, and yet she knew his circumstances; knew that he'd been living on borrowed money only a month ago and was by rights a common enlisted man. Her certainty that he could do this for her elated him - almost as if he too had found a door that opened the world. He would prove her right.

He stroked the back of his fingers against her cheek. "There are some difficulties, Rachel. I will be frank with you. I am in no position to marry now. I have sold my home even and now lack even that, although I have some ready cash – not very much." Her face grew serious, searching him for meaning. A niggle of frustration vexed him. He was simply trying to explain the situation. "Please – your mistress is a splendid woman, of course, but jealous of her friends, Rachel, I think you must know that, and I am not only beholden to her good offices but dependent upon her father's patronage. It is a little – no, forgive me, it is extraordinarily premature of me to claim the right of a lover, or to expect that – I didn't think things through, you see, I just –"

Rachel nodded and smiled slightly, her eyes slipping away, and she drew back. He caught her hand and kept it upon his breast.

"No, Rachel, I am not – I like you very well, if you still like me – I hope you do. I meant only that we would have to be discreet, very much so, at least until the Addisons leave for New-York, and then – if you have not grown tired of me by then, we will have a terribly awkward choice, but if you stay – matters should be simpler." This was as delicate as he could be. If he meant to have this girl, a dear creature rather than a rich one, they would have to be careful, and if she could not be an ally, it would not come off. And he did mean to have this girl. He had such a strange feeling of – peace, almost, beneath the agitation of desire. He had always felt comfortable in her presence, but he realized it only now. It was such an easy thing to overlook but having seen it, he could not get it out of his mind.

He found he very much wanted to know her opinion, and immediately, although that was not fair.

"They travel to London after New-York," she said.

"I know. And I doubt they will remain in New-York long. From what I have heard from my fellows, the fire was fairly comprehensive. The city offers few enjoyments. It is not what it was, and it is certainly not Philadelphia." The conversation's turn to practical details aggravated him, but it was his own fault.

"But are you sure this is what you want?" Rachel said in a small voice, her hand as light as a sheet of paper against his breast. Bellew burst into a smile. This was what he wanted to hear. She returned the smile a little uncertainly. "I don't mind waiting – I won't mind waiting for you at all," she said, starting slow and finishing quick, and he kissed her again. Then he kissed her once more because he realized it was getting late, and soon they must be at the house, and no matter what she said, he knew it would weigh heavy on her heart to spend so many hours and days near her lover but without any sign of love from him.

Chapter 38

Rachel needed to hurry, and Bellew needed to wait. But when she said that she ought to walk back alone ahead, it thrilled her to see his slate-blue eyes widen and then narrow in frustration. "Rachel – darling, I can't imagine what you're thinking. And this time I don't want you to tell me," he said, and he lifted her onto the back of the horse and mounted before her. When she circled her arms around his waist, he felt her cold hands and pulled them inside his cloak, and she had no choice but to lean her body fully against him. She pressed her cheek against his cloak, and Bellew set the horse to a gentle walk. When they came within sight of Briarwood, he hopped to the ground and handed her down. He paused a moment with his hands on her sides but did not kiss her again.

"I suppose – I'll see you in an hour or so," Rachel said at last in a small voice. Bellew nodded and pulled back his hands.

"Should I wait that long?"

"General van Dortmund is at his most amiable after his breakfast coffee and right before the day's work has begun," Rachel said, and the shadow of a smile crossed Bellew's lips. He produced an aged pocket-watch from beneath his cloak and checked it.

"Seven-thirty, then."

It was easier to separate now that he was not touching her, but not easy, and she spoke quickly to keep him from leaving – just not quite yet. "I think he'll be pleased you came a day early. He holds a high opinion of the moral content of work. As well as the moral content of good health, so your early release will speak in your favor."

"Do any of the General's judgments not involve moral content?"

"I don't believe so. Oh! And I should tell you," Rachel added hurriedly, placing her hand on his shoulder again so that he would not go, although he'd made no movement to do so. "Mrs. van Dortmund is somewhat idiosyncratic in her perceptions. If you can manage to agree with her on as much as possible, or at least correct her in nothing, you'll make yourself a favorite in no time. Even the General does so."

"Well," Bellew laughed, "I certainly won't second-guess my superior's tactics."

"Clarissa – Miss van Dortmund – is a perfect angel, but a little – a little timid. She'll love you straight away; she already does. She helped Mrs. Addison convince their father of your merits."

"Then I had better demonstrate some. And you had better hurry, or you'll end up having to explain your skunk after all." He glanced at the dark windows of the house and lifted her hand from his shoulder, kissing her palm briefly, and then he was on his horse and riding back into the woods to fill the hour.

The force of his absence fell like a physical blow. Rachel blinked, disoriented. The world shifted around her, and when it settled, she found it was not the place she had known before. The difference puzzled her. She ached with separation; not to be able to lift her hand and touch Bellew, now that she had the right to do so, a little, was a cruel pain that choked her. And yet she was so happy. And the world so beautiful. She had always thought it beautiful before, something she could look at but not touch. And now it was as though everything touched her, was a part of her. She stroked the rough side of an oak, feeling its scratchy bark as though discovering it for the first time. Tingles shot through her skin. That every sensation should suddenly be so acute – a strange panic took hold of her. It was like strychnine poisoning, where every nervous symptom became so exaggerated that at last the body collapsed beneath the weight of sheer excitement. Could she die of being too happy?

She laughed out loud at her foolishness. The sound of her voice in the cold morning air startled her, and she fell quickly silent. But she remained amused, and happy. Perhaps she could tell Bellew how love felt like strychnine – no, he might not find it as droll as she did, and perhaps would not relish being compared to a poisoner. Ah, but the next time one of Mrs. Addison's acquaintance suffered an infatuation and burbled about everything in view – Rachel could make the point then, and Mrs. Addison would be pleased.

Mrs. Addison. The thought brought her up short. Rachel would not be going to New-York now, nor to London – perhaps someday, but not as an employee. Rachel would lose the closest thing she had to a friend, and it brought a pang of remorse. She did want to see New-York and London, and she did enjoy being privy to the conversation of – ah, she had forgotten to tell Clarissa that line of O'Malley's for her book, *what happens when rich people get inbred.* Society. But Clarissa would not have cared for the observation much.

When I see New-York and London, it will be with my husband at my side – and we will be about our own business – and the friends I make will be my own friends, Rachel told herself. The way she pretended sometimes to be a poor younger sister of Mrs. Addison's – well, perhaps now there could be some truth to it, someday, and they could meet on more equal footing, and then Mrs. Addison would see at last that Rachel truly did love her, that affection and regard remained even in the absence of necessity and obligation. But nothing would ever be quite the same, and Rachel felt the sting, even though it had not yet come to pass.

And yet nothing was more important than her dear Bellew. Nothing. She did not know why. She had never known. But her happiness was proof of it. Her soul had lacked something; and now she had touched it, and she knew what it was, and understood that she depended upon him utterly.

She felt as though she were hovering, unable to push herself free of the spot where Bellew had left her. She did not want to return inside. But Bellew would be there soon; and these last few weeks or months of intimacy with Mrs. Addison were precious. Rachel felt a sudden urgency about seeing her mistress again. The bitter showed the sweet to its finest advantage, the way jewelers used a cloth as dark as night and soft as dust to bring out the bright fire and clean lines of gems on display. Even if she had not felt so tender about everything, she could never have loved Mrs. Addison as well as she did now. And overcome at last by the awareness of how long she had dawdled with her airy thoughts, Rachel hurried to the house.

She unlocked the door swiftly and closed it behind her with a gentle push, so that the latch would not be loud when it caught. But before Rachel gained the stairs, she saw Clarissa at their head, looking down with wide eyes. "I thought I heard something," Clarissa whispered. "Rachel, what have you been doing?"

Rachel came up the stairs, and Clarissa pressed her cold hands, tutting. "Why don't I make the coffee," Rachel suggested. But when they got to the kitchen, they discovered that Hattie had already put it on to boil, and the older maid shooed them out. When Rachel accompanied

Clarissa, Hattie treated her as some sort of school-friend or neighbor, although when she accompanied Mrs. Addison, Hattie acted more as though Rachel were – well, what she really was, a dependent companion. But she was with Clarissa now, so Hattie insisted that she'd bring them coffee in the sitting-room and make a fresh pot for the General's breakfast. It was too much fuss, and she hardly needed coffee, but Rachel felt unable to object.

"It was the trap," Rachel confided when they had settled. "I couldn't leave it lying there." Her thoughts were too addled to come up with a lie – or a complete lie, at least.

Clarissa's eyes widened in astonishment, and a hand fluttered to her cheek. "Oh, of course! Oh, the poor little animals. It had gone clean out of my head! You should have waited for me, though – I would have helped. But you look so happy; it must have been a success."

"Yes," Rachel said with a smile. "No, I was – well, I wouldn't have liked you there. It was better I went alone."

"I don't see why!" Clarissa almost looked hurt.

"But Clarissa – there was a skunk inside. And I wouldn't have liked to put you at risk of that," Rachel laughed, making up a story about how she had thrown rocks at the trap until it tumbled, because she thought it would not do well to bring Indians into the matter. "And you weren't responsible, anyway. The trap was my foolishness. I simply made things too complicated, and it was up to me to fix it." And how glad Rachel was of everything. If she had not set that trap – even if the Indians had not chanced by – she would not have stumbled across Bellew, and he would not have seen her alone, nor worried about her, nor – the rest of it. And this time she knew it was fate that had brought them together, and not Mrs. Addison. At last there was a reason that she had lived through everything that should have killed her or sent her into the gutter to be trampled with the other things that nature and man throw away. The sitting-room faded from her consciousness as she felt the whisper of his breath against her lips and the warmth of his hands around her back again. The smell of his skin seemed to have worked into her clothes. It amazed her Clarissa hadn't noticed it.

Clarissa's voice snapped her back to the present.

"A skunk!" she exclaimed, shaking her head and frowning. "Oh, you can't take chances like that, Rachel! We could have gotten one of father's men to take care of it."

Rachel shrugged and waved a hand absently. "That reminds me. I don't think Martha has gotten Captain Bellew's room ready yet. Why don't you let me take care of it? She has enough to do." Her heart tripped faster when she said his name, but she managed not to stumble on it. She wanted to be inside his room. She knew she was being foolish; there was nothing of him in there, not yet – he'd never even seen it.

"What? Oh. No no no, Hattie won't mind, I'll ask her when she brings the coffee, you have to tell me about this *skunk*," Clarissa said, snatching the prize from Rachel's grasp. Rachel had so wanted to smooth her hands over the sheets where his body would lie and clean the floor so that the air he breathed would be sweet. But it was nothing but skunks for Rachel, and she made as much of the story as she could, given that all the interesting elements had to be deleted in deference to Clarissa's sensibilities, as well as discretion.

When they heard the General's tread upon the stairs, they rose automatically and headed for the dining room. It was the signal for breakfast. The household regulated itself by the General's habits rather than a timepiece, the General being more consistent. He acknowledged them with a grunt and a nod, already busy reading through some correspondence left over from the previous day. Rachel knew he wouldn't need to trouble himself about that any more, once Bellew had taken the uninspired Captain Browder's place.

"Did you still want some more?" Hattie asked with the coffee-pot in her hand, hesitating before returning to the kitchen after filling the General's cup.

"I feel very awake myself, Hattie. But Rachel looks like she's lost in a cloud, doesn't she? Are you sure you've shaken off your dreams yet, sweet?" Clarissa patted Rachel's hand and winked at her.

The General glanced from his work. "Up early then, you two?" Hattie took this as a suggestion that more coffee would do very well, and she refilled both Clarissa's and Rachel's cups.

"Oh, papa, you know I can't sleep through sunlight."

"The other women in this household seem to find it little enough impediment. Except," he added as an afterthought, indicating Rachel.

Rachel merely smiled, but the General held his gaze on her a moment curiously before returning to his letter.

A sharp rap at the door felt like it came from inside Rachel's chest. She startled, rattling her cup against the saucer. The General looked at her again, frowning this time. Rachel hardly noticed.

"Too much coffee after all, miss, better put some of that toast beneath it to give you ballast," Hattie said blandly and went to open the door. Rachel fiddled with her toast, but her mouth was too dry to swallow. She heard voices, Bellew's low and Hattie's high and inquisitive, and in a moment Hattie returned to announce, "General, Captain Bellew's here; he says the doctor let him go a day early and he hoped he might be able to make use of the time productively, if you've got anything for him to do today – or Captain Browder could show him his duties."

The General grunted a noncommittal acknowledgment, but a tiny spark of approval lit his eyes. "Did you inquire whether he's had his breakfast?"

Hattie bristled visibly at the implication she might not have but kept it out of her voice. She was no Martha. "I did, sir – he had a bit in town before he set off. Says he wasn't sure what hours you kept but wanted to be sure he didn't get in after you started in on everything and be a disruption."

The General grunted again and pushed his chair back from the table. He tapped his letter against the wood and refolded it. "I'll show him to the office myself. We'll take another pot of coffee there. When Captain Browder comes to breakfast, tell him we've already begun, and he can join us at his leisure. Assure him it will be no disruption." He hesitated. "Is Captain Bellew's room ready yet?"

"It's funny, papa, Rachel was reminding me of that just this morning," Clarissa said.

"If it is not done, please see to it that it is," the General replied, and he strode briskly into the other room. Rachel strained to make out the conversation. Only a few words drifted through clearly: *sir*, and *hope*, and *if I could*. But she could make out their tones plainly. Bellew was firm, decisive, polite. And the General was pleased. Perhaps she should not have worried; there was a kind of similarity between the two men, as Mrs. Addison had pointed out before. But Rachel knew there was a difference, too. Something inside Bellew was hot, and it tempered him; whereas something inside the General was cold, and it hardened him. She wondered if she should tell Bellew, or if it was another one of those thoughts best kept to herself like love reminding her of strychnine. If she were strange too often too soon, she felt that surely he must start to feel uncertain, and if he were uncertain, perhaps he would doubt, and if he doubted, he might come not to trust her. And if he did not trust her, he would never love her. No, she would keep her own counsel.

Two sets of booted footsteps retreated into the house, and a door shut quietly. Rachel felt a pang of loss. Clarissa must have noticed something, because she said, "Oh, you know how father is with work – I'm sure he'll introduce Captain Bellew later. I mean, bring him in – well, introduce him to me. Although I feel I know him already! But he sounded so decisive, when I am used to thinking of him as sad somehow."

Rachel turned in surprise. "Sad?" she said.

"Well, yes – with his friends dying, and giving up his commission because there wasn't a place for him here – although now he's got a much better one, thank heavens."

"You are probably correct," Rachel admitted. "When I have seen him hurt, he has always looked more angry than sad. But he must have been." The thought did not settle easily with her, and that Clarissa had made the observation and Rachel had not gave her a twinge of uncomfortable jealousy.

Mrs. Addison did not rise until ten. Rachel told her straight away, upon responding to the bell and helping her dress, that Captain Bellew had arrived earlier that morning.

"Oh did he? No, put away that drab woolen thing – la, Rachel, are you trying to put me in mourning? Where's my orange silk?"

"But the gray is better for morning – oh, I'm sorry, I see what you meant."

Rachel put back the gray wool and smoothed her hands down the cool silk, as she always did when Mrs. Addison wore this dress, her favorite. The color brought out Mrs. Addison's complexion, and she prided herself on that; not everyone, as she had pointed out several times, could wear orange.

"You're a little slow today, dear – did you not have coffee?" Mrs. Addison said cheerfully. "Is Mr. Addison up yet?"

"I'm not sure; he may have gone out."

"What time did Captain Bellew arrive?"

"Oh, quite early – about seven-thirty. Your father had just finished breakfast."

"He must have left at five or thereabouts then. Father will like that." Mrs. Addison laughed. "Well, I'm sure Robert is about somewhere. And I rather imagine we'll find he won't be going out today. No, what are you bringing out the powder for – not with this dress."

"I'm sorry."

"Gracious, it's like you've forgotten the last few months all of a sudden," Mrs. Addison said, tilting her head to the side and fastening a garnet earring. "Did you sleep poorly?"

"Martha is rather prone to take the blankets." It was true. Rachel wasn't lying.

Mrs. Addison laughed again. "And if you're awake and she's not, why don't you just snatch them back? Ah well, I suppose you wouldn't."

Mrs. van Dortmund possessed a near-infinite knowledge of frivolous parlor games, including plenty that did not involve cards. One of her favorites involved everyone picking a seven-letter word and then taking turns either guessing at someone else's secret or else asking whether it possessed a certain letter and so gaining a clue. Rachel had won the first time they played, on the merits of the word *anodyne*, but the victory proved hollow when Mrs. van Dortmund announced that there was no point in trying to play a game of wits if someone insisted upon being clever. Rachel apologized for not having understood the rules, and subsequent matches proved more satisfactory. Clarissa did not mind losing, and Rachel pretended not to, so both of them frequently did, and the game would settle into a cool, drawn-out engagement between Mrs. Addison and her mother. Mrs. Addison frequently came out the worse for the battle, because her mother could not spell.

So Rachel was pleased when Mrs. van Dortmund announced her determination that they should spend what remained of the morning in this occupation. She would be knocked out of contention early and be left to her own thoughts, letting their softness settle about her and comfort her rather than have to be swatting them away all the time. Her body's every nerve trembled at each little thump and creak in the house - how many of them might be caused by *him*, moving his chair, taking a step, leaning against a wall.

Rachel was glad, now that she'd had time to consider the matter, that their attachment must remain secret. The idea that he was her lover would bind Bellew, she knew him that well; and her faithfulness to him through the intervening months, her dependency upon him once she gave up her place with Mrs. Addison, would make it unthinkable to him that he would not marry her. And then she never need fear losing him ever again. He was like her in that way - fate had placed him in the eye of the storm. He was never free of the winds that rent the earth, but neither did they destroy him. She belonged with him.

"Ha ha, dear, I think I've got you," Mrs. Addison said. "Your word is *martial.*"

Rachel blinked and shook her head, smiling. Mrs. Addison's mouth popped open slightly. "But your letters are a, i, l, m, r, and t. That's all that's left."

"Yes, but that isn't my word."

"Rachel! Don't confirm your letters - Margaret's supposed to figure that out for herself," Mrs. van Dortmund said, stiffening her back. "Honestly. Margaret, you're cheating."

"Oh, dock me a turn, then," Mrs. Addison said. "La, mother."

"I believe I shall. Now, Clarissa - does your word contain the letter d?"

"No, mama."

"You asked that already," Mrs. Addison said.

"Oh, I forgot to mark it. Well, then, I get to go again. Clarissa, does your word contain the letter y?"

"It does not."

"Really? Oh, this *is* getting exciting. I shall have to think about *this* one, I can tell."

"Clarissa is supposed to go after me, mother."

"Yes, all right, of course."

Clarissa ventured a half-hearted and unsuccessful foray at her mother's word, and everyone's attention turned to Clarissa's puzzle. Rachel was fairly certain that Clarissa's word was *pickles* - Clarissa frequently used plurals - but she did not want to knock her friend out of the game yet.

When it came round to Mrs. Addison again, she frowned and said, "All right, Rachel - is it *rattail?*"

"I'm afraid not."

"Really," Mrs. Addison frowned.

"There you go, Margaret, we're hot on Clarissa's heels and all you can do is worry about Rachel. We'll get her in a moment."

"I thought you said there was an m in it," Clarissa said. "Didn't she?"

"Is that a guess?" Rachel teased.

"Oh, all right," Clarissa laughed. "Is there an m? I just don't remember."

"Well, there is."

"Will everyone stop going on about this? Rachel - your word is *marital,* as is perfectly obvious, thank you."

"Yes, ma'am - now you've got me," Rachel answered, putting down her paper and pencil. Mrs. Addison leaned forward and frowned at the paper for confirmation.

"Ah," she said. "So it is."

Chapter 39

She did not see Bellew until dinner at three. The household save for the General and his staff was seated already and had started on the soup when Mr. Addison - who had indeed remained close to home - pushed himself back from the table abruptly and stood. Rachel placed her spoon on the saucer, her hand trembling with a sudden weakness. The clink of metal against china felt like a physical blow, and she quickly drew her cold, damp hands into her lap. She did not turn her head; she felt she would fall off the chair if she tried.

"General," Mr. Addison said with a nod, and then sat again before the General had finished introducing Bellew.

Rachel might have been seeing him for the first time. A strange note of cool appraisal inserted itself into her observation of him, and calm replaced her agitation. His nose was a little crooked, his eyes a little too quick and sharp to appear wholly amiable, his height not a jot above average.

And then his gaze flicked to her briefly, and he smiled and murmured, "Miss Kolkhorst" as he took the chair beside hers, and love swept over her again, and her body was flame encased in ice, melting. Each imperfection made him all the more dear - like a tiny cut that she would kiss to make better.

"I trust you traveled well," she replied, realizing she had no idea what the others had been saying for the past minute and hoping she was not repeating something inanely.

"Quite well, thank you. I prefer the early morning hours," he said and glanced up at Martha behind him. "Ah, yes, thank you." Martha ladled broth into his bowl, and Rachel remembered her own unfinished soup.

Bellew made certain that the General had begun his meal, and then he started in on his broth. Part of her wanted to watch the fascinating process of Bellew swallowing for an eternity, and part of her hated that broth with savage envy because he was paying attention to it, and seemed to have no mind of her, while all she could think about was him.

A light tap knocked against her foot beneath the table. Before she had time to wonder whether it was an accident, the conspiratorial tap came again.

"Miss Kolkhorst, you're going to lose your soup if you leave your spoon hanging much longer," Captain Browder laughed. Rachel jumped slightly and brought the spoon to her lips with most of its contents intact.

"She's been mazy all day and quite lost in it."

"I always suspected it was a pretty complicated business being female," Captain Browder replied. "I'm sure I'd find myself wholly baffled by it. Mastering spoons would be a step too far most days." He winked at Rachel and grinned. He'd been in good spirits ever since the promise of a field command, and Bellew's early arrival left him almost giddy.

Bellew left his foot next to hers, a slight pressure through the fabric of her shoe. Rachel smiled at Captain Browder and did not look at Bellew. She did not need to now; he remembered her. She held her foot very still.

"I don't think it's terribly complicated." Mrs. van Dortmund looked pleased. "It's all quite natural."

"Ah, madam, that is a height of art to which I do not and cannot aspire. But you've trained your daughters well in it - Mrs. Addison, you are always remarkable, but today you're quite breathtaking. That dress makes you glorious as the sun."

Bellew glanced up and smiled. "It is uncommonly fine."

"La, to hear you two talk you'd think you'd seen nothing but soldiers in uniform all your life. It's just the same old thing I've had for ages, Captain Bellew, I'm sure you remember."

"Do I? I've got no head for clothes, I'm afraid; I must cast my lot with Captain Browder and own it all far too complicated for me," Bellew said cheerfully, returning to his food. He looked up quickly again at Mrs. Addison's silence and added, "But I admire it in no measure less for my incomprehension - in fact a good deal more. I can see the thing is well done but will never for the life of me know exactly how."

"I doubt Maggie could tell you herself. She used to try to dress me up, but it never looked the same on me somehow," Clarissa said.

"A dove wears different plumage than an eagle, Miss van Dortmund, but no less lovely," Bellew replied, nudging Rachel's foot. Clarissa blushed happily.

After dinner, the ladies retired to their rooms for a nap. "While I'm sleeping, dear, see that you clean the orange silk," Mrs. Addison said as Rachel brushed out her hair.

"You want to wear it again?"

"Of course I want to wear it again," Mrs. Addison snapped. "Oh, you mean I want to wear it again *soon.* Yes, probably – Mrs. Washington arrived this morning, that was that note mother got –"

"Did she?" Rachel cried. "Oh, how lovely."

"Yes, if you'll let me finish. So we've been invited, or rather mother and Clarissa and I have been invited, and of course I want you along, darling, Thursday, and I think we'll be starting to go out more regularly now, so I can't have my clothes just sitting and waiting with wrinkles in them."

"Have I gotten behind?" Rachel said. "I'm sorry, I hadn't realized – I thought everything was clean –"

"Oh, I hadn't checked, I just assumed you'd been too busy. Well, if it's just the orange silk that needs tending, that's fine, but I still want it done today."

"Yes, ma'am," Rachel murmured. Mrs. Addison's mood was sour enough that she did not want to risk saying more than that. Rachel brushed in silence, tugging the bristles gently through the residue of pomade.

"Or would you rather stay behind?" Mrs. Addison added abruptly.

"I – wherever you'd like me to be, of course, ma'am, but – if I'm not doing any chores, I ought to be your companion, oughtn't I, or – perhaps you have more than enough company now?" Rachel said. She felt nervous, but her heart did not fall out of her chest the way it had before at any hint her position might be impermanent. Rachel knew it was impermanent. She would not be leaving for New-York or London; she would remain here as long as Bellew did, and then when he moved on with the army, she supposed she would start a household somewhere – why, probably back in South Carolina, since that was home to both of them – and not see him again until the next pause in military operations.

It would sadden her if Mrs. Addison released her now, but it would also, she had to admit, come as a relief. It would spare her words she did not know how she would find later on: that Rachel was leaving Mrs. Addison behind. No, much better if it were Mrs. Addison's doing.

"Don't be silly, I was teasing you. I can't wait to hear what you think of everyone. And I'll want you to keep your ears sharp. There now, don't brush the hair off my head, that'll be fine, I think."

Rachel pulled the loose strands from the brush and placed it on the dressing-table. She twirled the hair into a ball in her fingers. "What do you want me to listen for?" she asked curiously.

"If any of the ladies seem to be short-staffed and might do with a couple of Negroes," Mrs. Addison replied.

"You don't mean Abraham and Jacob," Rachel realized after a moment. "Not to sell them?"

"Of course I do. We never meant to bring them to England," Mrs. Addison said, lifting her eyebrows.

"Why not? I'm sure they're as eager to see London as anyone would be."

"Yes, but there's the difficulty in England, where you can bring them in, you see, but you can't necessarily take them back out again, if they don't want to go. And we can *have* them there but we can't *sell* them - it's some endless picky business with the technicalities of the law. So we might find ourselves lumbered with a very expensive investment that we can neither dispose of nor retain. Oh, Rachel, don't look that way - I'm sure they'd much rather stay in more familiar surroundings where there isn't quite so much to learn."

"But they're terribly devoted to you, ma'am, and to Mr. Addison as well - I'm sure they'd never try to bolt," Rachel said. She could not bear the thought of either of them bound to a master who might treat them cruelly or use them hard. It had never occurred to her before that Abraham and Jacob would not be with the Addisons forever. "Ma'am, a stranger might ask anything of them - they're so happy with you, and Jacob is so loyal, and no one could ever be better with horses and animals than Abraham, he almost got General Lee's hounds under control, even."

"Well, while you're listening about, Rachel, perhaps you can find a purchaser that meets your standards."

"But how will you travel without them?"

"O la, Rachel, please. We can either borrow them for the trip or send them back once we get to New-York. Or we can hire a man. But we won't be able to sell them in New-York, not from what I hear of the condition of things there. In fact, I'm not even sure we'll be heading to New-York at all. We might leave from Philadelphia, and Robert can drive the carriage that far. It will be much easier to get rid of the carriage in Philadelphia. Yes, I think that's a much better plan – everything I hear makes New-York sound worse. It's not what it was before the fire. And we'll have you to tend to the little things along the way, won't we. Have you ever been on a ship, Rachel? No, of course not. Well, it's a thousand times worse than a carriage-ride. I get terribly sea-sick. Robert, of course, is immune."

Rachel had difficulty napping at any time, and certainly sleep was impossible today. After pulling the curtains to in Mrs. Addison's room, she took the orange silk with her for cleaning. The task required little time or attention, and her mind turned over the problem of Jacob and Abraham. She could not let them be sold to someone who might treat them poorly. The Addisons should keep them. They would never bolt, Rachel felt sure of it. Or was there work for them somehow in England – would they be able to find a place there, if they seized their freedom? She wondered what she would do in Abraham's position. Perhaps she would try to save up a little money from odd jobs – surely the Addisons would permit this – and then, upon refusing to travel further with her owners, present them with the full sum of her own purchase. She decided that would make a fine gesture. And, she had to admit, not too plausible a scenario. If she were a slave, she would need that money herself quite badly after her liberty was effected.

Perhaps she would bolt, she realized. But it did not matter. It was more important that Jacob and Abraham not risk maltreatment than that the Addisons should risk a few hundred dollars, or a thousand, or whatever it was.

She would simply tell Mrs. Addison that she could not find a purchaser – no, Mrs. Addison would not be deterred, and would ask around herself. Rachel decided on a new plan. She would tell Mr. Addison that she'd heard whoever Mrs. Addison settled upon gloat that the slaves were worth twice what they were paying, and then he'd surely prevent the deal from going through. Although perhaps he would be all the more nervous then about losing his money altogether by risking the slaves on English soil – it was a puzzle, but she had to solve it, and Rachel was still turning it over in her mind when she wandered downstairs to the sitting-room with some vague notion of being closer to Bellew while he worked.

She saw him fastening his cloak by the door as she descended the stairs. Bellew turned at the sound of her footfalls, and his face shone with a sudden light that made her heart stop in her chest. He raised a finger to his lips and tilted his head at the door. Rachel hurried down the last of the steps and slipped outside through the door he left open behind him.

He walked ahead of her as if he'd forgotten her existence until they were a distance from the house, and then he wheeled around suddenly and caught her in his arms.

"My poor cold little thing," he said, kissing her nose. His hat knocked itself askew against her head, and he laughed, straightening it. "But I'll keep you only a moment. I have a message for General Washington – a response – to deliver."

"You're meeting him already," Rachel said.

Bellew looked pleased. "I don't think he'll take much notice of who hands his aide the letter."

"Yes, but he'll remember you."

"Perhaps, eventually. More likely General Lee will remember me, hopefully well." He brushed his lips against her mouth, but Rachel stiffened. She had thought that General Lee was safely in the past.

"The English won't let General Lee go."

"Oh, I think they may – it turns out we've got a fair number of their officers waiting for a trade. I believe we've been saving them up for the chance. We may not have a general to offer, but we'll get him back, dear, don't worry."

This was not welcome news.

"Are we going to try? Are we doing that?"

He laughed. "Well, naturally; General van Dortmund says they've been working on it for ages – you're terribly interested. Do I need to be jealous?"

"Capt - Stephen. We mustn't do this," Rachel said with sudden urgency. "I tried to tell Mrs. Addison before, but she didn't believe me."

"Ah, now you're a partisan of General Washington's." He kissed her ear.

"No, Stephen - I saw something in Philadelphia. Please, you have to believe me." And then she told him what she had read in General Lee's room.

Bellew's face grew more somber as she spoke, and he pulled back slightly, though his arms remained around her. He frowned when she finished, and then shook his head. "Darling," he said at last, squeezing her shoulder, "you must have misunderstood."

"It was perfectly plain. He wants recognition, and he isn't partial where it comes from."

"It may have been a trick."

"But he said - I read only part of it, but he said the same sorts of things in the plan that he did when talking strategy for our side - that we cannot fight in the field. He tells us we need to harry the English to pieces. Well, he told General Howe to force a straight set-piece battle and annihilate us at one blow."

"And if it was such clever advice, why didn't General Howe take it - or come up with it himself?" Before she could answer, he kissed her again. "Don't worry, sweetheart. Today wasn't so hard on you, was it?"

Frustration mounted in her breast. "General Howe has his own reasons - Stephen, don't let them trade for General Lee. We'll do fine without him."

"I have not the slightest effect on any such decision - even General van Dortmund doesn't, and I am only his letter-writer," Bellew said.

"Then promise me you won't trust General Lee if he comes back - and tell General Washington not to do so."

"I am hardly in such a position as you think. I would not be believed, and then I would not be trusted. I'll be careful, dear, I promise you that, I do. But I have to go, or I won't be considered a capable messenger, let alone a strategist. You'll go straight inside, won't you? Ah, I wish I could give you my cloak -" He kissed her once more and headed for the stable, and Rachel had to content herself with his promise to be on his guard, even if she was fiercely dissatisfied with his dismissal of her thoughts. Perhaps the trade would not go through. It had not done so yet, after all.

And yet she could not help fearing that if she were General Howe, she would be more than happy to place a rotten plank in the heart of the resistance, to eat away at it from the inside and make sure it never grew strong. She could not help fearing that General Howe was only biding his time on the trade, because he had to seem unwilling. She could not help fearing that this delicate balance General Howe hoped to preserve would mean not a hard-won victory for Bellew, but a slow death by strangulation. Or a quick one. If Bellew were a common soldier, he might be permitted to return home after a failed rebellion. But as an officer, the aide to a general, he would likely hang.

Chapter 40

The more he thought about Rachel, the happier Bellew felt about his decision. He always trusted more to his feelings after the fact; matters that seemed quite simple in advance had a habit of becoming more complicated later on, and his gut usually warned him of it before his head did. Quick enough to correct a mistake, usually, if unfortunately not to prevent the initial error. But he felt nothing but peace and satisfaction about Rachel, and he knew he'd done the right thing somehow when he'd kissed her.

He would have to know more about her, of course, before he married her, but the thought gave him little concern. She was too young and had been forced to work too hard to have much in the way of secrets – he felt certain she'd had no lovers before him, the main risk with girls on their own, and especially such pretty ones. Her naïveté was too obvious, all the more so for her manifest ignorance of it. Bellew brushed his hand against the soft needles of a passing tree as he rode in the dappled light, smiling at the memory of her kisses. The first kiss, her mouth had remained still; the second, her lips had moved only a hesitant fraction; and the third, she had kissed him back properly. She learned quickly, but clearly she was learning for the first time. He snapped a twig free, twirling it. He wanted to kiss her again, immediately.

He wondered why he'd taken so little note of Rachel's beauty before. He'd seen that she was pretty, of course, but somehow it had never taken root in his mind, and his image of her had always been a bit drab. Then it had been dark when he kissed her, and it was only at Briarwood that he'd taken a good look at her at last and found her so much lovelier than he had imagined that he'd been torn between the desire to stand stock-still in shock and to hit himself on the head for stupidity. Her face was a perfect oval; her eyes the startling blue of a fine day; her mouth full and with a delightful curl to her lips. When she lost the childishness that clothed her cheeks in darling plumpness, her proportions would suit a Greek statue, but more slender. That someone had not snatched the prize before him was astounding; that she loved him, more so. But love him she clearly did.

She took such obvious pride and delight in his advancement. And she worried about him.

Her concerns about General Lee concerned him a little in turn in that she might let her feelings show on her innocent face at an inopportune moment, but he would talk to her more later and calm that storm. If she would simply be her quiet self, Bellew felt sure that she could win General Lee over, or at least not antagonize him – General Lee not being too easy to befriend. That had been a clever trick, sending a false offer of help to General Howe; Bellew supposed that Howe was far too practiced and wily to fall for the scheme, however subtle the carefully crafted flaws in the plan, but at least Lee had been doing something productive with his ambiguous situation in Philadelphia, unlike Bellew.

"You're a good beast," he said, flinging the twig aside and patting his even-tempered new horse's neck. "And a lovely one, and sweet-tempered. I'd call you Lady Dove if I could – well, perhaps I will, if I can find a stallion and don't have to take you into battle." He had already named Rachel Lady Dove in his mind, although he had not told her. The horse accepted his caresses mutely.

When he cleared the trees, he nudged the horse faster, and the steady drum of her hooves cleared his mind. The Potts house where General Washington kept his headquarters came into view, a tidy structure built of brown stone joined with thick mortar, much smaller than Briarwood, and Bellew would have thought he'd gotten his directions wrong if he hadn't seen soldiers milling in the yard – two colonels and a general among them. Bellew straightened in his saddle and tugged his jacket beneath his cloak.

There was too much activity for anyone to take much notice of him. Bellew tied Lady Dove loosely and announced himself to a lieutenant hurrying out the door. The lieutenant saluted perfunctorily and pointed him towards the main room.

Bellew picked out General Washington at once; the man was a giant a full head taller than anyone else, his body thick with muscle born from long years of exercise. His face seemed chiseled roughly from stone as if from a broad pattern of handsomeness that had not been fully executed. General Washington sat on a chair leaning his enormous head against a hand the size of a frying-pan as he dictated instructions to a slender colonel who wrote nothing down but nodded his head sharply at intervals.

A young French general spoke animatedly to two other officers in his own tongue. Bellew felt very out of place.

General Washington paused and raised his eyes. Bellew snapped to attention and saluted. "Your Excellency. General van Dortmund sends his reply."

General Washington nodded, and the little colonel turned around briskly, sizing Bellew up in an instant. "Routine correspondence on the upper left corner of the desk, captain," the colonel said, and turned around again without waiting for a reply.

"Yes, sir." Bellew scanned the room and found three desks in it. The one by the French general was less fine and contained the most paper, so Bellew placed the letter there on the existing upper-left pile. He glanced up briefly for confirmation that he had chosen the correct desk and position. The colonel and General Washington remained deep in their one-sided conversation, but the French general, noticing Bellew's uncertainty, smiled and nodded. Bellew saluted, relieved for the confirmation but embarrassed that he had been caught seeking it, and took his leave.

For all its triviality, the success of his errand renewed his confidence. When he returned, Bellew, having pondered General Washington's aide-de-camp's organizational techniques on the ride back, asked Captain Browder to go through the files with him so that he could sort the documents by, in reverse order, date, correspondent, and broader category: routine communications (including general news and copies of letters between other parties), urgent requests, civilian queries, and governmental instructions. Bellew discovered that Captain Browder had followed no organizational scheme of his own, having cheerfully assumed that whatever was in the front of the file was the most recent and leaving it at that, but he took to the task with good humor enough. Reading the old letters gave Bellew a better grasp of the broader situation and the names of the people involved, and soon he was using Captain Browder only to double-check his judgments. General van Dortmund sat across the room, re-reading a very long letter himself but mostly listening. Although Bellew directed no comments to his superior, he spoke loudly enough to be heard by him.

"I think you've got your feet under you now, Captain Bellew," Captain Browder concluded at last, but Bellew took little satisfaction in it until General van Dortmund added, "Yes, I believe you've got it well in hand. Captain Browder – report to your regiment first thing tomorrow."

"Yes, *sir*," Captain Browder answered with a grin he did not try to conceal, and he wiped the ink-stains from his hands as if he could not be rid of them soon enough. Bellew suffered a quick pang of jealousy. He hoped he would not make himself too indispensable here. Everything he saw in General van Dortmund's letters emphasized his belief that what they needed to do was not to spout more words or squabble over their definitions and denotative or connotative content but to fight, and fight consistently, and he yearned to be a part of it.

They had taken a little cold beef and bread while they worked, and Bellew discovered upon Captain Browder's dismissal that deep night had fallen, and he suddenly felt weary to the bone. But he kept at the sorting even when General van Dortmund rose, until the older man said, "Leave it for tomorrow, Captain."

"Sir, only two drawers remain –"

"If you put in a day tomorrow like you've done today, you'll have it straightened out. It's waited a good while anyway. I don't want you slow in the morning; I postponed the bulk of the new correspondence and a review when you turned up."

"Yes, sir. And my apologies again, sir – I only thought that it served no purpose to send a boy with the message that I was available, and lose half the day, when I could come myself –"

"And I quite agree. Good night."

"Good night, sir." Bellew straightened the papers on the desk – his desk, now – so that everything would be in readiness for the new day, and he heard the General's voice from the next room saying, "Margaret, are you still up?"

And her high, musical voice answered, "Well, I've been reading a book – I just couldn't sleep. I can't get used to army hours. But you're up late too, aren't you?"

"Trying to keep up with my new aide. Good night."

Bellew wondered quickly if there were another route to his room, and realized with a curse that he did not even know where in the house his room lay – he had forgotten to ask earlier, and now everyone was in bed except for Mrs. Addison. Of course she was only reading a book, and he would ask her for directions, and that would be the end of it – no, he wasn't that much of a fool. She'd been waiting for him, and foreboding filled his heart. Surely she did not want to continue their flirtation here; even if he'd felt the same about Mrs. Addison, and even if Rachel had not intervened – and he didn't and she had – the stupidity of carrying on under the same roof as her husband and under the eye of a censorious father who held Bellew's entire career in his power staggered him. It was well and good for her to be careless with herself, if she chose, but to have so little consideration for him while pretending only to hold him dear was damnably light, and even cruel. Even if it was partly his own fault that the situation existed – which he admitted freely.

The spark of anger in his gut stiffened his movements and hardened his face, and he entered the sitting room with an air of impregnable reserve. Mrs. Addison lounged on a settee, half-propped on one elbow with her book held rather too close to her face. Near-sighted, apparently. It did not surprise him, and it surprised him less that she didn't wear glasses even when she needed them. A dying fire bathed the room in a faint red glow, and a single candle on the table beside Mrs. Addison gave her light to read. She was terribly beautiful, he noted coldly.

"Oh, Captain Bellew, you're still working as well," she said with a smile, closing her book without marking her place and sitting up straight. She ran a hand down her skirt to straighten it.

Bellew bowed. He kept his face neutral. "I have a great deal to learn. I have received a great opportunity here, and cannot but believe that it is due to your good offices. It would be a stain upon my honor and a poor return to your kindness if I were to fail in it. But tomorrow will begin the real test, so I had better get as much sleep as I can – could you tell me which room is meant for me?"

Mrs. Addison laughed. "It would hardly do to go about opening doors at random, would it? Although it might get you in some interesting situations."

"All the more reason to avoid it; I have no time for interests or situations, I am afraid."

"You sound just like father. I'm sure you'll get along famously – I always knew it. Well, la, I'm glad you've found a proper place at last, Captain Bellew, although I regret that I won't be able to renew our acquaintance for long."

Bellew blinked in surprise. Mrs. Addison could have done nothing less expected if she'd come at him with a knife. "I – beg your pardon?" he stammered.

A small smile played on her lips. "Well, we won't be staying as long as I thought – which is a pity, what with the officers' wives just starting to arrive. But Robert really does need to get back to London."

"I – how long do you remain?" Bellew asked, his mind spinning. To be free of the risk of Mrs. Addison was an enormous relief – but it brought the Rachel issue to the fore.

"About a week, I think." A week! Well, then, a week – he would marry her in a week. Yes, there was no reason why not – she could take lodgings in the village, perhaps with that woman who'd kept her before – no, that wouldn't do, not if Rachel were pregnant, as Bellew hoped she would be in short order, not with all the smallpox about; well, at another house nearby, one that was not used for convalescents.

"I will regret your absence keenly, of course," Bellew answered. "But I suppose it is not a comfortable environment for Mr. Addison – irrespective of his love and regard for your family."

"Oh la, everyone knows Robert's not exactly keen for rebellion, but he gets along with everyone anyway." Bellew had some personal reservations to that statement that he kept to himself. "No one says anything sensitive around him, and it's all very social. No, that's easily handled, and it makes no difference, other than I think he might be a little bored and put out by mother. But to tell you the truth, although it had no bearing on things, I've realized that I'm a little uncomfortable having Rachel in the house here."

"Rachel?" Bellew asked blankly.

"Miss Kolkhorst. My companion," Mrs. Addison said. "She's such a dyed-in-the-wool Tory, you know, and I didn't think it really mattered – of course she'd keep her views to herself, she's pretty far from a fool – but it occurred to me afterwards that the thought of her being around father's confidential communications seems like asking a bit too much of her discretion. You know, what might she say when she writes to Captain André - even if just by accident."

He had forgotten about the English captain.

"Is she in communication with him?"

"Well, I can't say I know all her friends. But I've kept her from performing any duties in the house; I'm hoping that keeps sensitive information from passing under her eyes. Really, it's for her own peace of mind more than anything; I'm sure she wouldn't want to have to make any awkward choices. Anyway, I won't have to worry about it any more once we get back to Philadelphia, and of course in London they'll be delighted with her, so that will be a weight off my mind."

"I'm sure you're mistaken about her opinions."

"I don't see how I could be," Mrs. Addison laughed.

"I have heard myself what she has said -"

"Well, la, you can decide for yourself," Mrs. Addison answered abruptly, rising and lifting the candle, making the shadows in the room lurch. "She laid out her views quite clearly in an article for the *Sentinel-Observer* - she was terribly pleased with herself at the time. And of course she should have been; it's very clever for a girl to get a piece in the newspaper. I kept a copy for her, but I'll let you borrow it. Here, accompany me, it's on the way to your room."

Chapter 41

Rachel's mind brimmed with too many thoughts for her to be able to sleep except in brief, unsatisfying snatches. There were her worries about Mrs. Addison and Jacob and Abraham, to be sure, and she was not able to lay her concerns about General Lee wholly aside, but all of it paled before the blazing sun of the fact of Bellew's love. She could not stop thinking about him - the feel of his hands and his lips, his gentle teasing, his sudden tenderness towards her, as if she had somehow turned from a lump of clay into wrought crystal. She did not feel the time pass. So when the first light of dawn tickled the curtains, Rachel shot out of bed with a start; if she had slept, she would have been up before now. She hoped tiredness had not put off her looks. But she did not feel weary in the slightest.

"Martha - Martha, it's morning," she said cheerfully as she stood in her bare feet on the cold wooden floor, earning herself a grunt and a cross stare. Martha should have been up long ago too, but she never was. A pity she didn't get along with Mrs. Addison - they kept the same hours.

"I am suitably amazed," Martha replied at last with a yawn.

Rachel dressed quickly and hurried down the stairs to find Bellew, the General, and Clarissa already at the table. "Good morning," she murmured, dropping her head and smiling. She looked up through her lashes to catch a peek of Bellew. He had spent a restless night too, she could tell. Shadows marked his face, and his skin had an unusual pallor. And such a hard day he would have ahead of him; she wished she could make it better.

He did not meet her eyes, inclining his head slightly. Rachel took the seat beside him, smiling at Hattie.

"Rachel - I was just telling Captain Bellew. I had the oddest dream last night," Clarissa said. "I am sure it must mean something." Pink health glowed on her cheeks; Clarissa at least had slept well. But she always did.

"Why, I hope it was something good, then," Rachel answered.

Bellew finished the last of his coffee in a quick swallow. "If you will excuse me, sir - I would like to work on the files." Rachel glanced up, but he still did not look at her.

"Certainly. I'll be along in a moment."

Rachel tried to keep the forlorn expression from her face as Bellew's footsteps faded behind her. She should not be jealous of his work; she would not be much of a helpmeet to him if she did. And she knew they had to be careful. But she would have given her eyeteeth for a little nudge of his foot like he'd offered her yesterday.

"I dreamt I had the prettiest bouquet of flowers."

"Did you," Rachel said absently.

"I did - no, don't be silly, that isn't the strange part. Then I was carrying my bouquet everywhere because I was so proud of it, and suddenly I found myself in a field full of flowers, and I thought oh no, how terrible, flowers should grow in the earth, not be cut and fade."

"Excuse me, Clarissa - I should get to work also." The General took his coffee with him and left.

"Yes, of course, father - he gets bored with dreams," Clarissa confided, wrinkling her nose. "Well, so there I was with my bouquet, and now it made me feel just awful."

Rachel found it easier now to pay attention to Clarissa's dream. "But flowers don't last forever anyway - even in the soil, they fade and die at last."

"I know, but - well, I started planting them right and left hoping that they would take root, and I was trying to think, but you know how it is in dreams, trying to remember if a flower would grow roots ever again once it had been cut. And I just couldn't figure it out. And then I remembered potatoes."

"Potatoes?"

"Yes, if you put them in water, they'll sprout. Haven't you ever seen that?"

"I have not," Rachel said.

"Well, they do. And then I thought I should bring a bucket of water and hang my flowers in it and see if that made them grow roots. And then I was so flustered trying to figure out where I could get a bucket of water that I woke right up. Isn't that strange?"

"I - yes. Cut flowers don't do that at all," Rachel said. "But it would be nice if they did, wouldn't it? You could have them in a vase and then plant them in the yard, and start all over again."

"It would, but I hadn't even thought of that. Just imagine trying to compare a flower to a potato!"

"Well, there is no accounting for dreams." But Rachel found it all a little less fascinating than Clarissa did, and her mind wandered back to its single irresistible topic. Since she could not speak of it, her conversation was limited.

At ten, Rachel returned upstairs and knocked lightly on Mrs. Addison's door before opening it. The room was dark and silent, and Rachel pulled back the curtains. When she turned around, she discovered the bed empty and untouched, which surprised her.

Voices came from the adjoining room, followed by laughter. The connecting door opened, and Mrs. Addison appeared in her nightgown. Rachel caught a flash of Mr. Addison's bare torso, fat and hairy, in his bed, a sight as unexpected as it was unfamiliar. She turned her head aside, blushing. Apparently there had transpired a thaw in the Addisons' marriage, which pleased her. Mrs. Addison should feel love, and loved, as well - everyone should.

"I apologize, Rachel, I'd lost track of the time," Mrs. Addison said, pulling the door to behind her.

"Oh, I'm sure I'm too early -"

"You never are, dear. No, don't worry about that. Sit down, Rachel. I want to talk to you for a moment. No, wait, bring me my dressing robe first. It's chilly. Ah, there - thank you."

Rachel sat as instructed, curious. Was there some other piece of gossip she wanted Rachel to discover from Mrs. Washington's house?

"Well, Rachel, I don't know quite how to begin this - but I believe congratulations are in order first." Mrs. Addison smiled at Rachel's expression. "Now, don't be coy, sweet - it's as plain as the nose on your face that there's something up between you and our Captain."

"I - did he say something?" Rachel squeaked, thunderstruck.

"It was as unnecessary for him to do so as it was for you. Now, dear, I rather hoped to put off this business longer, but let me put it to you straight - you don't want to go to London, do you?"

Rachel's body went numb. She took in a breath and steeled herself. "Mrs. Addison - I believe - I believe that I will not be able to do so, despite my love and gratitude, which will always remain – so much more than I can tell you!" There – it was out.

Mrs. Addison showed no change in expression, however deep Rachel searched her face. She merely nodded, the faint smile still on her lips. "Particularly given that Mr. Addison and I are leaving sooner than anticipated. We'll be gone at the end of the week."

"A week – what happened?" Rachel grabbed the side of her chair. Events were moving much too quickly for her comfort.

Mrs. Addison shrugged. "Mr. Addison's affairs require attention. Don't worry, Rachel, I'll see whether I can pick up a maid in Philadelphia; and if I can't, it won't be a tragedy, there's no point in dressing well on a ship, especially given that I'm not likely to leave the cabin too blessed often. Here – bring me my purse. There, that's your wages through the end of the week, and it's settled. You're at liberty."

Rachel held the money in her hand like a dead thing. Her body felt loose and light, as if she were tumbling through the air. "I – feel quite bereft, ma'am," she whispered. She had not expected the crisis to come so soon; in a way, she had not expected it all. Despite her plans, there had been some vague, irrational hope lurking in the corner of her thoughts that somehow she might be able to remain with Mrs. Addison even as she became Mrs. Bellew.

"Nonsense; girls fall in love. It happens. My next maid will be an atrocious old hag, upon my life. Now help me get dressed, and let's not talk about it any more. We really haven't been together very long, you know. It's not worth agonizing over."

"I would like – would it be all right if I wrote to you sometimes?" Rachel said in a small voice.

Mrs. Addison shrugged. "If you find you wish to do so," she replied.

The die was cast. Rachel spent the remainder of the morning in a daze, stunned by too many blows. She had to see Bellew at once and explain her changed circumstances – he had not asked her to marry him outright, after all, only that he might court her, and if necessary, which it probably was, she would find work somewhere else in the interim, somewhere nearby. Or perhaps she would not. She had some money saved; she could remain at liberty for a little while. That would make a sweet life, to spend her days reading and walking through the trees, interspersed with tender visits from Bellew. But no – the winter pause was too brief. These moments were precious; he would be gone wherever the army took him in the springtime. They should be married now. She hoped he would think the same. She did not want to wait another year until they could be truly joined, all the long months in constant fear for his life and safety and with nothing to soothe the ache of love but letter-writing and dreams.

She had to see him. It could not wait.

"Rachel, where is your head today? You've confirmed nine letters – nine. Now, I demand you tell me which of them are superfluous. And look at your paper this time."

Rachel blinked. She had chosen a nine-letter word. "I think I must default on this round, ma'am. I'm not quite sure how to regroup from this error."

Mrs. van Dortmund sighed theatrically, but Mrs. Addison interposed, "Now, mother, everyone makes mistakes, and Rachel seems to have a great deal on her mind." Her eyes sparkled with hidden meaning. Warm relief mixed with gratitude surged through Rachel, and she smiled quickly in return. Mrs. Addison had joined in on her secret –they were truly friends at last. She would miss her so terribly.

"A companion is supposed to supply company, Maggie, not to be some sort of balky horse that demands constant attention and still won't go straight because it has *things on its mind*. I've wasted six turns on her word."

Rachel promised to do better the next round, and she did, losing with agreeable dispatch. She could not wait for dinner, and she despaired of its ever arriving. Time had never been such a sullen, inert thing before. Her hands were too cold and her face was too hot. Her clothes itched. She felt as light-headed as if she were hungry, but the thought of food turned her stomach. Rachel couldn't talk sense into herself; or rather she could, but her heart would not listen. She was in a blind panic, which was stupid. If Bellew was not ready to marry her yet, that mattered nothing – she had already dispensed with that difficulty in her mind. She could keep herself comfortably for months even without finding new work. No threat of cold or starvation hung over her – nothing she could not deal with in plenty of time. And yet her heart cried *run, run* as if a bayonet pricked her throat.

Run from what? No, *to* what – to him. Bellew would comfort her – whatever he said, she knew it would be a balm. And he could not fail to be moved that she would not press the marriage or protest his obligation to her. Even if she were starving that very moment, she would do no such thing. But she would not tell him that.

She could not stand it any longer. Rachel excused herself after her next loss, but instead of returning to her room, she crept down the stairs, wincing at every creak of the floorboards, and slipped into the sitting-room so that she would see Bellew the moment he emerged. Surely he would understand that she needed a word with him – just a brief one – even if he did not yet know its urgency.

When she arrived in the room, Rachel realized how bald a gesture it would be if she merely sat there, waiting, watching the door, although that was all she felt fit to do. Fortunately, a knock came from the entrance, giving her a task. Rachel opened it and found a corporal she did not recognize.

"For the General," he said, holding up a folded and sealed letter. He did not offer to hand it to her.

"Yes, of course," Rachel said and brought him inside, but he knew the way already and strode past her, rapping sharply on the office door and disappearing beyond it. Rachel saw no more of Bellew than a flash of leg; she did not catch his eye. Nor should she distract him while he was in the middle of things.

She stood uncertainly for a moment and then decided to lay a fire. That would give her a reason to be in the room for a few minutes longer, and of course Martha hadn't tended to it yet, and of course the room was cold enough that it couldn't fail to bleed a chill into the office. She pulled the grate aside and set two large, resinous logs in the hearth with a neat pile of kindling beneath. She found the tinder-box after only a brief search, but after three tries, she still could not bring a spark from it. She wondered if the dampness of her hands were suffocating the flame.

The door opened behind her. Rachel spun around, but it had shut again by the time she faced it. The corporal glanced at her and smiled. "Having trouble?" he asked.

"A bit."

"Here, I'll get that." He took the tinder-box from her hand and failed twice. "Ah, I see the problem now," he laughed.

"What is it?" Rachel peered over his shoulder.

"That this is a terrible tinder-box." But the third strike took, and the kindling lit up nicely. The corporal straightened and brushed his hands down his trousers.

The door opened and shut again. "The General's reply," Bellew said briskly, addressing the corporal. Rachel smiled at him, but he still ignored her, as if she had turned into air.

"Very good, sir." The corporal accepted the letter – it couldn't have been more than a note, really – saluted, and left.

Bellew turned. She should not interrupt him, truly, but it would take only a moment – no more than that. "Captain Bellew?" she whispered.

He stopped as if struck by a hammer-blow but did not turn around at once. "Miss Kolkhorst," he replied coolly.

She hurried next to him and kept her voice low, so that the General would not hear. "I'm sorry – there's just been a change in circumstances, and I thought I should let you know at once," she said. Suddenly it did not seem so very urgent any more, and her pressing the matter seemed foolish. What difference would it make whether he knew about the Addisons' departure now, or an hour from now, or a day?

He nodded to himself and pressed his lips together. His face was grim. He turned to her at last. "Yes," he replied. "The Addisons are leaving, and I am undeceived."

"You know?" she said, astonished and relieved – almost. But he was so cold in manner. And then the rest of his words unraveled in her mind, and she frowned. "Undeceived about what?"

"Undeceived about your interest, Miss Kolkhorst – your interest and your interests," he said in a voice as hard as stone. Before Rachel could ask him what he meant, he brought a hand to his pocket – it shook, she noticed – and withdrew a folded newspaper-copy. "This is yours, I am given to understand."

Rachel reached for it, but she had already recognized the *Sentinel-Observer*. Bile rose in her throat. "You have to let me explain."

"What could be clearer? You never said which side you meant to join – I thought of it a great deal, Miss Kolkhorst, and I found I remembered your words precisely. You have an exceeding fondness for General Howe, a close friendship with Captain André, you possess curiously specific knowledge of Lieutenant Masterson's fate, you try to turn my mind against General Lee and to insert poisonous insinuations about him to general command, and Christ Almighty only knows what you meant to learn from your connection with me. But that connection is severed, miss. And I feel the sooner you are quit of these premises, the better; although I assure you I have informed General van Dortmund of your sympathies, and he will take all precautions as long as you remain."

He did not love her any more.

He held her in such contempt that he swore in front of her. He had shamed her in front of General van Dortmund – but all of it was untrue, he simply did not understand, she had to make him listen, if only her throat were not so tight she could barely speak, her heart so fast she could hardly stand, her mind so scattered by the whirlwind she could not form a single thought.

"With that article – you must listen to me, I was trying to protect the Continentals, please, Stephen – Captain," she said. "I'd heard General Howe say that he did not want to eliminate the extremists –"

"We are not extremists, miss. You show your hand again."

"Please listen to me," she begged. "Please, Stephen – just a moment. It was his word, not mind. When I heard General Howe say that he hoped to avoid destroying the Continental Army as long as –"

"And how exactly did you come by this incomprehensible conclusion?"

"I heard him – the Addisons were friendly with him, you know that. And you don't hold it against *her*," Rachel said with a sudden flare of white rage. The newspaper article could have come from only one source.

"Neither Mr. nor Mrs. Addison ever represented themselves otherwise. Mr. Addison holds his tongue while he is with his wife's family; his wife is a social creature, not a political one. Neither of them," he said distinctly, "is a spy."

"Stephen –"

"Good day, Miss Kolkhorst," Bellew said, his jaw knotted. She touched his shoulder, but he brushed off her hand like a fleck of dirt, and then he was gone.

The world ended soundlessly: an explosion of silence. In its aftermath, Rachel noted in numb amazement, nothing remained. Not a single shard. She would have clutched at it gladly, however sharp it cut her. But she could not clutch at a void.

Run, run.

Chapter 42

She could not face them again, not any of them, not ever. She made her way blindly to her room and threw her belongings in a bag as if in a dream, coming to her senses only a little when she had filled one bag and started upon a second. Her possessions made a bulky pile on the bed, far more than she'd already packed. She simply could not bring it all.

She would not need the formal dresses that Mrs. Addison had given her as cast-offs. Rachel, on her own, would not be attending any society teas or balls. The high-heeled slippers were useless to her. Rachel set them aside slowly. She had thought so little of her small store of finery just a day before – and now she was unlikely ever to wear such a beautiful dress ever again, or even to see one except at a distance. That world was closed to her. She touched a scratchy ribbon of lace, willing her fingers to remember the feel of it.

But she could not part from the dress she had worn to Mrs. Loring's ball. Without the high-heeled slippers, and the petticoats, and the mask, and the jewelry she had borrowed, Rachel could never make the same appearance she had that night, but she had been happy then, and she wanted always to be able to remind herself that she had been so once. Or perhaps she simply felt sorry for herself; she could not decide, and did not care. She could not bear to leave it; she rolled the dress up neatly and wrapped it in a shawl, and she stuffed it in her bag. Two work-dresses; a few papers; her Alexander Pope. An almanac would have been more use, she supposed, but she did not have one. The Indian's bag. She blessed that poor dead Indian in her mind. His knife meant that she would not starve, even if she had to remain in the wilderness for part of her journey. Because she meant to travel far from here – far west – away from everyone who had known her before and found her worthless. Perhaps she would build a tent for herself and live off the land; perhaps she would find a small town on the frontier and start her modest shop. She had money enough for that, she thought, if she did not mind a shop that was very small and very humble.

The bell announcing dinner tinkled below. Rachel froze. She heard the house stir, and feet upon the stairs.

The money. She had been paid through the end of the week. She could not keep those wages and be taken for a thief, though if Mrs. Addison had offered her a thousand times more, it would have been nothing against her cruel trick.

Dear Clarissa:

These wages have been paid to me for work I did not do; please return them to your sister, with all...

Rachel's pencil froze.

...with all due regard. And know that while it is not in my power to love you as much as you deserve, I love you with all the strength I possess.

R. Kolkhorst

She could not say more.

She left the extra dresses and other unwanted sundries upon the bed, but she took the note with the money with her and slipped them into Clarissa's room, and then she stole down the back stairs, holding her breath so that she would not make a sound. She could hear low voices and the tinkle of cutlery against plates.

Her disappearance out the back meant she would be unable to collect her cloak, and she regretted it; her jacket would suffice for walking if the weather held but would make a poor blanket at night. But she could not risk being stopped or questioned; she refused to be seen. She could bear any privation; she could not bear shame.

She opened the rear door quietly and pushed it softly so that the latch barely caught. The day was bright and cheerful, one more cruel reminder of how little she mattered in the world. She shouldered her bag higher and cut across the back yard, meaning to circle around the front through the trees before she headed east, along the same general path the Indians had taken a few days ago.

"Hi, Miss Rachel? What you doin' runnin' off like that?" Abraham stood outside the stable, wiping his hands against his shirt.

Rachel contemplated making a run for it. But that would only excite Abraham's curiosity. He could catch her easily, and he might shout. She shook her head for silence and walked up to him. "Abraham – I'm sorry, I'm leaving, I would have said good-bye, but – please don't tell them you saw me, don't mention that I'm gone, I'd like to be well quit before anyone – well, they won't come looking, but if they did – I don't want them to, and..." She tapered off in confusion. She just wanted to be gone.

Abraham regarded her stoically. "You boltin'?" he asked.

"Mrs. Addison is aware – she terminated my employment earlier, and it will not come as a surprise to her, I think, that I have left early. I didn't take the money," she added hastily.

"What money?" Abraham scowled.

"My last week's wages. I didn't – you don't think I'm a thief, Abraham, do you?" Rachel answered. Tears pricked her eyes. It seemed that everyone held her in contempt. "I'm not. I just want to go – please don't mention you saw me."

"You ain't dressed for it," Abraham said after a moment. "Seems like a fool rush to me." Rachel opened her mouth but no words came out. "And I suppose I can figure out why without you tellin' me. It's that captain, ain't it? I told you, Miss Rachel."

Rachel's forehead wrinkled. Had Abraham warned her about Bellew? She remembered no such thing. And how had he known?

Abraham sighed. "Never you mind – it's too late now anyhow. I saw you two out the front, and I hoped you'd have some sense, but then if you was passin' time with him so close to the house, I suppose sense was already thrown out the window."

"But I love him," Rachel said.

Abraham grimaced. "You promise me this, Miss Rachel. The next time you thinks the words 'but I love him' about anyone at any time under any circumstances, you remember this day right now, cause I heard a few women talk in my time, and nothin' ever comes of it but what you feelin' right now. Here." He removed his battered slouch hat and placed it on her head. "Your head gonna make you feel cold in two minutes. Now git. My dinner's gettin' cold in the kitchen, and Jacob's gonna eat it all up."

"Thank you," Rachel whispered, and then she added quickly, "Please give my fondest regards to Jacob – I will miss both of you terribly."

"Can't do that without sayin' I seen you, Miss Rachel."

"Yes, of course – Abraham!" He had started to go, but her voice stopped him. Rachel swallowed. "I believe – my understanding is, if you go to London, you and Jacob, that – it is possible for you to be considered free men there."

"Now, don't you go tryin' to get back at Missus Addison like that."

"I'm not -" Rachel said, but Abraham shook his head and made his way to the kitchen.

It occurred to her later, as she had plenty of time to think during her walk, that Abraham had not asked why Bellew had not come to her aid in her difficulty, and that perhaps he possessed a fuller understanding even than she'd given him credit for. Yes, he had warned her, she realized now - he had warned her about Mrs. Addison's pride. But she had not listened.

The sun took on a reddish hue as it sank towards the horizon before her. She caught only glimpses of it between the branches of the trees. The land was thick with undergrowth and hilly, and she made slow progress. Brambles caught at her skirt. She would be all night picking them out, she supposed, if she even bothered. But she should. She had to present a good appearance, if she meant to pass unnoticed, unrejected.

She did not try to find a road. Not until she had put more distance between herself and Valley Forge. Even if she had left the wages behind, what else might Mrs. Addison claim about her? Rachel had taken the ball-dress, after all - it had been a gift, but Mrs. Addison could say otherwise if she chose, and everyone would believe her, and no one would believe Rachel. She should have left it behind, but it was too late now.

She did not grieve. She felt shame, and anger, and confusion, but when she reached for the sadness she knew must lie in her heart, she found only cold resignation, as if failure had been inevitable. Her only desire was to travel away - west.

West is always the direction of going away, she mused. *It is the natural direction of both day and night. And because they tread the same path at the same pace, they never meet, but only follow each other eternally.* She was not quite sure of the point of this observation, but it pleased her somehow.

When the light faded to the bare hint of a glow, she began for the first time to feel a little lost and concerned. It would be foolish in the extreme to spend the night in the open; she must make a shelter or find one, and she cursed herself belatedly for having chosen to keep off the road. No one would come looking for her; they'd wanted her only to be gone, and she had obliged. When Rachel put it to the point, she realized quite plainly that Mrs. Addison wouldn't prosecute her revenge past poisoning Bellew's mind. Any imaginings that they would be looking for her were nothing but self-aggrandizement, if not self-destruction, because her fear of the road had kept her from finding an inn. And now it was too late for Rachel to do anything but make the best with what she could find in nature.

She could still see a bit, and she found a hollow between the roots of an ancient tree that was wide and deep enough to provide a little shelter from the wind. Rachel dropped her bag on the ground and gathered twigs to weave a rough mat, and she placed it in the hollow so that the dampness would not seep through her clothes and freeze her. Hunger pinched her stomach, and thirst gummed her mouth. She had brought no provisions, not so much as a biscuit. But a day's fast would not kill her. She would sleep through the worst of it, and in the morning, she would find provisions. If she did not come upon a tavern or inn, she would simply catch food for herself. There was no hurry now; she could stay anywhere as long as she liked. There was nothing to do, nowhere to be except as her immediate needs dictated. She was completely free.

She thought that sleep would come quickly, despite the early hour, because her muscles ached with the unfamiliar exertion, and she had slept so little the night before, and the day's events had exhausted her. But when she laid herself upon her rough mat, with a work-dress spread over her as a blanket and her bag for a pillow, her mind spun with thoughts she could not catch, and she found no peace. And yet none of the thoughts had any content, nothing she could hold onto and resolve or put away – fragments and glimpses of faces and feelings that whirled in a storm. She found it terribly unfair. She wanted only to escape into unconsciousness. She had nothing to do now but to eat, drink, and sleep for the rest of her life. The cares that worried other people – duty, love, recognition, friendship, honor – none of them had any bearing upon her any longer. She had become a beast, and beasts never worried themselves from sleeping when they had a place to lay their heads.

You know how to soothe your mind, a stray thought reminded her.

"Not any more," Rachel told herself. But the thought wouldn't go away. And, to her shame, she let the familiar fantasy unfold. The woods by

Griffin's Ford – Bellew finding her lost – and she closed her eyes and imagined resting her cheek upon his breast, his arm around her shoulders, his cloak covering them both as they lay side by side. And sleep came at last.

She rose before first light, stiff and cold and unsure for a moment where she was or even how old. Then she remembered herself, and a dull weight settled upon her. She looked into the sky and saw by the stars that morning would come soon. Today she would find the road.

But it seemed to her, as she sat waiting for enough light to travel, that she had been far more foolish, and far more lucky, than she had realized when traveling alone a few months before. An unprotected girl was not safe, especially not with so many soldiers crawling through the land, tired, bored, hungry, armed to the teeth.

But an Indian – an Indian was feared. Even a boy.

The idea seemed so daring that she sat motionless even once she'd made up her mind, as if she didn't really expect herself to follow through. But why not? Rachel Kolkhorst had vanished, unmourned and unregretted. Rachel gained nothing by clinging to an identity that no one wanted, and whose skirts put her at constant risk of disparagement and injury.

But perhaps the Indian's clothes would not fit.

Rachel dug through her bag quickly and extracted the dead Indian's satchel. She shook out the trousers, stiff with cold, and pulled them over her legs. She did not have to remove her boots.

The waist was a little wide, and the inseam a little long, but when Rachel used a spare stocking for a belt, the fit wasn't too bad.

Rachel tucked her shift into the trousers, and that helped too, and then she loosened her stays and brought them a bit higher. She fiddled with the lacing until it was tight at the top and loose down below, giving her more of a straight up-and-down shape, and then she shrugged on the dead man's jacket, fastening it up to the neck.

She wished she could see herself, to know whether she looked an utter fool. But there was no dressing-glass here. She simply had to hope for the best or else give it up entirely. She braided her hair in a single plait that hung down her back, and then she jammed Abraham's hat low over her eyes. The shoes were wrong, but she did not expect anyone would be examining her that closely. No one would take her for a born Indian; she was too pale, and her hair dove-brown, far from black. But that she was a white boy who had been raised by the Indians – that they would believe easily enough. And that would make her an Indian in their view.

Which she supposed perhaps she was. If it mattered; which it did not. Did a horse ponder what it was, or a cat, or a bear?

She set off walking.

Her body soon warmed with exercise. She expected the road must lie to the north, because she had not crossed it yesterday, but it must have twisted and turned a great deal because she walked a solid hour without any sign of it. She did spy a farmhouse, though. She knew it was not abandoned, because a thin breath of smoke blew over its thatched roof from a hidden chimney, and Rachel picked up her step. She might be able to buy a drink of milk; her mouth filled with the taste of rich, sweet cream in anticipation.

A little girl outside scattered grain for a swarm of bobbing brown chickens that fussed and crowded her, knocking against her legs. Rachel smiled, remembering her childhood. The girl flung the grain farther away, chiding the creatures, and then she looked up and saw Rachel. Rachel raised her hand. The girl remained still for a moment, and then she rushed back inside.

Rachel had forgotten her new appearance already. She still wanted the milk, but thought she might not be able to buy it. But she needed directions too, and she approached the rough wooden fence nervously, keeping her hands in plain view. If she meant not to be taken for a girl, she realized, she had to stop acting like one. Of course she was frightening now; that had been her intention in changing clothes.

A thick-bodied man in shirt-sleeves emerged moments later holding a musket. "Morning," he shouted.

Rachel held her hands before her. "I'm just looking for the road," she called back, speaking at the lower timber of her voice.

"Track that leads you to it is about half a mile that way," he answered, not warming to her in the slightest. He gestured with his musket to show the direction.

"Thank you, sir," Rachel replied. "And do you know if there is an inn anywhere nearby?"

"How many you lookin' for room for?"

"Just one."

The man relaxed a little. "Which way you headed?"

"West."

"Then keep on the road about three miles. You'll come to the Speckled Axe. They're all right. After that – depends on the way you go, I guess." He squinted at her, frowning. "You Indian or white?"

"Indian, sir," she answered after a moment's hesitation. "But I've lived with both."

"You tradin'?"

"No, sir. Just moving on," she replied. She did not ask about the milk.

She found the track, which seemed to be a cow-path, and followed it to the road. Although it was early, a few other travelers were about. A boy walked with a placid goat on a rope. A man clicked impatiently at his horse. Two women gossiped with hands flying as they walked, a basket on one woman's arm swinging so hard it threatened to spill its burden of eggs. Rachel quickly learned not to look up when she passed any of them, because they would not meet her eyes in return. It felt strange to be invisible; she had always merited a smile and a nod from strangers at least. But the isolation brought a kind of relief.

Her hunger had sunk to a dull ache below the level of her consciousness when the sight of the Spotted Axe brought it roaring back with a vengeance. It was a sprawling, rattletrap wooden building three stories tall – it was a hard ride's length from Philadelphia and must have capitalized, in better days, on a steady flow of travelers to and from that great city – with a large stable. A painted sign of a grinning woodcutter hefting a tankard with his axe, presumably a spotted one, slung forgotten upon his back showed her the door to the tavern, and Rachel quickened her step.

She pushed the door open and was greeted by the smell of bacon and a fog of warmth that stung her hands and face. A few men sat at their breakfast. They glanced at her quickly and then looked away, uninterested.

Rachel hesitated. She had never given thought to how a man would enter a tavern differently than a woman, but she cast her mind back to the

Brass Bull and, straightening herself, walked with a firm step to an unoccupied table, slung her bag to her feet, and rapped the table with the side of a half-crown. Before the serving-woman had even reached her, Rachel called out in a sharp voice, "A full breakfast, with plenty of that bacon. And coffee. And cider." And then she leaned back in her chair and draped her bent arm over the back of it. Thinking a moment longer, she jiggled one leg. She had seen men of the rougher sort do that often; they got fidgety. Well, now, so would she.

The serving-woman glanced at the coin, nodded, and returned a moment later with everything Rachel had asked. "Will there be anything else, child?" she asked politely.

Rachel kept her head tilted forward so that the brim of her hat shadowed her face. "Let me eat first," she replied. She had not decided yet if she should spend the day here and get a night's sleep in a bed before moving on. She would inquire discreetly how full they were; if she could get a room alone, perhaps she would stay. She did not trust last night's sleep and was not sure how long it would last her. She wondered if she should try to purchase a horse. Dressed as a boy, she would have no difficulty with riding, and it would make her travel easier. But then she would have to concern herself about the beast's needs as well as her own, and she was not sure she wanted the trouble.

"...damned fools just sitting there staring at each other. We'll have another year of this idiocy at least."

Rachel pricked up her ears to the conversation at the nearest table, three men who looked as though they might have been sitting there since the night before.

"They took five of my cows last week. Conscription, they said. So I guess that means they're turnin' 'em into soldiers."

The men snorted. "Which side?"

"Redcoats."

"Continentals took three of mine. I wish it'd been the redcoats. Worst thing was when the sergeant said he'd pay me for it - here." The man took out a piece of elaborately printed paper. "Can't even spell right - look, it says Philadepkia. Where in blazes is Philadelpkia?"

"I guess they figure they can't write Philadelphia if they don't hold it."

"Can't spell, can't fight, can't do nothing but make trouble for everyone else."

"Excuse me, sir." Rachel had spoken before she even realized she meant to. Three pairs of eyes turned to her. She cleared her throat – no, a man would not do that. She tightened her jaw. "The Continentals have placed their own lives and property in jeopardy first, before yours, and completely."

"Aye," the man with the paper said, "And if they'd limit to that, they'd be no less fools, but a good deal less disagreeable."

Rachel frowned. "But surely – but surely, sir, you understand the grievances they cannot bear."

"What?" the man exclaimed. "Taxes on Boston? After Boston run riot? What's that to do with me?"

"We got a little Indian rebel here."

"Boys get notions in their heads."

"Shame he don't have a father to whip 'em outta him. Indians don't get notions, though, except what they're paid for – and this boy got money."

"Guess the Continentals pay their Indians with the good money."

"I am a trader, sir, in furs," Rachel said stiffly, having decided upon that story. "The Continentals have not and cannot pay for my opinions."

"Damned fancy Indian."

"But surely you see," Rachel persisted, "that the issue is not taxes – it is contempt."

The man with the paper laughed. "Millie Shaw holds me in contempt – she told me so straight out – and I don't go to war with her, nor steal anyone's cattle cause of it."

"But you don't love her any more, do you?" Rachel said.

"Course not. Never did – that little chit. Get a few years on you, boy, and you'll understand why you try to kiss a girl you don't love." The man chuckled. Rachel ignored it, despite the sting.

"Contempt is a knife that severs all bonds. What if Millie said she despised you and that you were obliged to do her chores for her and give her a dollar a week besides, nevertheless?"

"I'd tell her to ask the Devil for it," the man replied pleasantly.

"Indians don't have to marry a girl to have their way with her," one of his companions put in, his face alight with interest.

"Well, maybe I'll turn Indian myself one of these days!"

"Course then you're stuck with Indian girls."

"A girl's much the same. You don't have to take her out in public, you know." The conversation drifted away from Rachel, and she let it do so, finishing her meal. She should not have involved herself, but the heat of her reaction had left her no choice.

That heat puzzled her. The fight was nothing to her; she had been attracted to it from fatalism, perhaps, or curiosity, and the expectation that something valuable might churn out of the mud for her benefit. And it had. She was in a far better condition than she had been three months before. She had money enough to start a business. She had clothes to cover her. She had health and liberty. She had everything she had always desired: just enough for perfect independence.

And yet she had felt so cold and so tired until that stranger's words had fired her in defense of a fight that she knew very well was imperfect in both justification and execution. But she had never felt more clearly than she did now, with all her connections to it cut, that the cause was right.

Her opinion on that, however, did not matter. Her future was west, a little store in a village where no one knew her, where she could eat and drink and sleep in an uninterrupted rhythm until God collected her to His bosom. Her heart cooled, and she felt her tiredness again, and chewed her food slowly. A fur trader – yes, that was a good idea, even if it had been an impulsive lie. She could catch animals on her own, and if she could find any Indians who spoke Cherokee, she could parlay with them as well. It was a profitable business. And her mixed heritage would finally be some use, rather than a burdensome secret. Secrets did not matter any more; her entire appearance was a lie, and she did not care.

She paid for her meal and left, one of the men offering a parting shot that she would kindly keep her rebel hands to herself and off his cattle, although she was welcome to Millie.

She paused when she reached the road. West, or should she cut south? She was likelier to find Cherokee south, if she truly meant to trade with the Indians, which increasingly seemed the most profitable plan. But west would take her farther away and faster from the close settlements that she wished to avoid.

West or south? A simple matter. Both options had merit.

She stood several minutes in reflection, until she almost pinched herself in frustration. Why couldn't she make up her mind? None of it really mattered; west or south, it was all the same, she should just pick one and be done with it.

She suddenly realized how much she wished she cared. But she simply did not. There was no fire in her heart for the eating and drinking and sleeping that waited for her equally to the west or the south. The little routines of life meant nothing, except as means to an end. And she was trying to make of them an end in themselves. She could not.

She had to care about something.

And she knew very well that she did.

The sun hung low in the eastern sky, still early in its course.

Rachel turned and walked towards it.

The End, Book 1

www.ingramcontent.com/pod-product-compliance
Lightning Source LLC
Chambersburg PA
CBHW020629020726
47494CB00001B/113